THE STARLIGHT TRILOGY

THE WISHING STAR
STAR LIGHT, STAR BRIGHT
MORNING STAR

THREE BESTSELLING NOVELS COMPLETE IN ONE VOLUME

MARIAN WELLS

INSPIRATIONAL PRESS
NEW YORK

First Inspirational Press edition published in 1999.

Inspirational Press
A division of BBS Publishing Corporation
386 Park Avenue South
New York, NY 10016

Inspirational Press is a registered trademark of
BBS Publishing Corporation.

Published by arrangement with Bethany House Publishers,
a division of Bethany Fellowship, Inc.

Library of Congress Catalog Card Number: 98-75434

ISBN: 0-88486-238-0

Printed in the United States of America.

CONTENTS

THE
WISHING
STAR

THE STARLIGHT TRILOGY

THE WAR OF 1812 was America's second war for independence, as if this young country must stamp its foot and remind the world once more that it had to be totally free. America would not, after all her struggles, endure fetters of any kind. When the first European foot touched American soil, it stepped forward in an enormous stride toward freedom. And freedom was the banner flung over all, forever.

But people can be trusted with freedom only when truth is coupled with liberty. Truth can best be discovered in freedom, but sometimes people unwittingly allow themselves to be enslaved in their search for truth.

After this second war, as America stirred and stretched, rumbles of freedom began in the churches. From 1814 to 1830, many of America's old mainline churches were split apart, each intent upon establishing its own freedom—and its own view of truth. And during this time, just before the outbreak of genuine revival, large numbers of new religions emerged.

America began to see herself possessing a unique position in God's sight, providing a pattern of freedom and holiness for all people, becoming a leader for the world. Just as people reached out for land during the westward expansion, they also reached for new experiences and new ideas. Rapt attention was given to the second coming of Christ, and nowhere did this doctrine stimulate more anticipation and frenzied excitement than in the new religions.

The new religions bore strangely similar traits which have been broken down into common dominators: a compelling leader, direct communication from God to that leader, a belief that here was *the* truth, and a twisted chunk of Christianity which was to color the whole, lending credibility to the institution.

This mixture of religious confusion becomes the setting for our story. *The Starlight Trilogy* pictures the emergence of one of these new religions, The Church of Jesus Christ of Latter-day Saints as founded by Joseph

Smith. As one of today's few survivors of the new religions of that period, it must become a symbol to Christians of the danger of truth colored by divergent, seemingly innocuous beliefs.

The Joseph Smith story is a difficult one to write and impossible to handle lightly—there is too much of a dark, brooding aura about it all. For the uninitiated this has been projected as the mysterious; for the Christian there are intimations of another voice which must not be either ignored or feared.

Joseph Smith's story begins here with his late teen years, and is marked by an early thrust into the supernatural. Toward the end of his life, the picture is of a poor boy making good, at least by the standards of this world. From farm boy he rose to become rich, influential, loved, and revered. At the same time he was hated and scorned.

While Joseph shoulders, dances and coerces his way through life with the words, "Thus saith the Lord," he is throwing a net of mysticism around his people. To them and to the world he paints his own image with the white color of holiness and teaches his people to do likewise.

Histories have been written on the life of Joseph Smith, but there is more to be considered. Beyond his personal story are the people of his kingdom, the hangers-on, the bewitched and the seekers after truth. And the story can best be told through the seekers.

Our story is set in the framework of a historical novel as seen through the life of one of the seekers, Jenny Timmons. It is historical in the sense that main events, locations and many characters actually appear in records of the period; and fictional in development and style. Jenny herself is representative of young women of that time who were caught up in the tide of interest in the supernatural and the new religions.

To read Jenny's story means suffering along with her, through the excitement of the mysterious, the fears of the unknown, and the emptiness of being merely human with only human powers. Along with Jenny, the reader will see the struggle of the people as they accept, not without heartache, the claims of the prophet and try to assume their roles as Children of Israel, seeking their Zion.

The daughter of a poor family living in the eastern states, Jenny Timmons' earliest years were shaped by poverty and superstition. Her mother held an unformed but earnest awareness of God. Most often these beliefs puzzled and frightened Jenny, perhaps because even in her formative years she was allowing herself to be manipulated by another force.

Just as Jenny was nearing her twelfth birthday in South Bainbridge, New York, she met a young man who held an uncanny fascination for her. Thus began her early dabblings in the occult and, eventually, her wanderings into Mormonism. The emphasis on the occult continues throughout

Jenny's story because the same thread of belief is woven through the Mormon church.

The Starlight Trilogy picks up shortly before the Mormon church is established to explore the spiritual roots of Joseph Smith and those who followed him. The main thrust of its message is that the occult and "magic" are much more than something indulged in for the fun of it. There is a deep, satanic influence that wraps itself around people's lives once they allow themselves to be involved in the rituals, the charms, the books, and the people who promote it. We see this happening in Jenny's life, as well as in Joseph Smith's.

To understand how Jenny and others like her are pulled further and further into the occult from seemingly innocent activities, her thoughts and feelings—as well as events—are described in some detail, but not in complete enough form to be "copied" if someone should want to try. Finally, the occult is shown not to be something beautiful and intriguing and providing power but as something thoroughly satanic with no common thread in Christianity.

True biblical Christianity alone can satisfy the spiritual needs of people. And only God's power can break the bondages and devastating influences of the occult in a person's life. No darkness, however oppressive it may be, is greater than the light of the "Morning Star," Jesus Christ himself.

1

SCREAMING WITH PAIN, Jenny dodged the razor strap that snapped at her legs. As her father reeled toward her, she dashed across the splintery floor, leaped through the open door, and with a cry of terror fled for the woods.

Still sobbing, heedless of danger, she ran between the broken plow and jagged pieces of firewood. Finally the searing pain in her side slowed her. Gasping, Jenny cast a fearful look behind her. The sagging gray shack across the field blurred before her eyes. She wiped away her tears and peered again.

The doorway was dark. If Pa were there, she would see the red of his dirty old shirt. If Ma were standing in that spot, there would be the light square of her apron. Jenny leaned against the maple that marked the edge of the Timmons' field. Nearly twelve years old, small and thin, she snuggled against the rough bark of the tree. She knew her size, the dark tumble of hair, and her eyes colored like the woodland creatures made her nearly invisible to those in the house.

When her ragged breathing had calmed, she looked around. The patch of broken ground lying between her and the littered farmyard was filled with rustling brown cornstalks and decaying pumpkins. She felt all brown and withery, too.

Her mother's sad face rose in her mind. Jenny's hands curled; she pressed them against her bony chest to keep the aching sobs from coming past her throat. How badly she wanted to throw herself into her mother's arms, to feel the warmth and the love that must be there. *I'll be good, Ma. I promise I'll be good!* The ache subsided, but nothing was changed, either inside or out.

She squared her shoulders and focused on the door where her father soon would be standing. Rubbing her tattered sleeve across her nose and then sniffing sharply, she jutted her lower lip out in a way she wouldn't dare if she were facing him. "Pa," she muttered, even now not daring to say the words above a whisper, "you're nothin' but a drunken old sot. If it weren't for Ma's naggin' and fetchin' in the ladies' babies, we'd all starve.

And you doin' little 'sides tippin' the bottle and yellin' at Tom for not gettin' at the plowing."

She shivered as the October afternoon poked chilly fingers through her thin dress. Wrapping her skinny arms around herself, she shook back her heavy dark hair and shifted from one bare foot to the other. Her eyes moved constantly, checking the house, the door, wondering how long it would take Pa to leave and weave his way down the road to the tavern in town. "If he don't go pretty soon, I'm gonna freeze.—But better that than the strap again."

She spied a shadow approaching the house from down the road—her brother Tom. Jenny watched him leave the path and head for the door.

Conscious now of the welts on her legs, she hopped from one foot to the other. A gasping sigh ended in a hiccup. "Poor Tom, you'll get it now," she muttered. Tom was seventeen—old enough to be called a man. But the droop of his shoulders said it all: he would never be a man as long as Pa was there to swing that razor strap.

She shivered and looked down at her legs. The white welts had turned red and begun to bleed. Miserably she watched as Tom crossed the yard and leaped the high step into the shack. She could guess what would happen next.

With a sob, Jenny turned and limped into the darkening woods. "He'll be coming," she whispered. "Pa'll send him after me. Like as not, Tom'll regret fetchin' me as much as I'll regret goin'. Next thing, Pa'll be jawin' me again for takin' the book; after that I'll get strapped 'cause I run out on him. I'll get twice beat for nothin'."

Weariness seeped through every part of Jenny's body, but she forced herself into a spiritless stride, winding her way into the forest toward that quiet, shadowed glen known only to Tom and herself. As she walked her thoughts dulled. She knew only the moss underfoot and the occasional sharp prick of twigs and dried leaves against her bare feet.

At last she stopped on the rim of a bowl-shaped depression in the forest floor. She trembled, listening for footsteps. But the quietness satisfied her.

She stood peering into the shadows beneath her. Some said such holes were Indian diggings, but now it was moss-carpeted, crowded with young hickory and elm. It was a place to hide and, sometimes, to dream.

She wiped her damp face, but her breath still caught at her aching throat in ragged sobs. Somewhere a twig snapped. With a quick jump, Jenny launched herself into the middle of the hollow and burrowed into a pile of wind-tumbled leaves.

She held her breath, listening. Finally, cradled by the quietness and growing shadows, she dared relax against her pillow of acrid leaves. She knew those gray-brown leaves were nearly the shade of her eyes, and somehow that knowledge made her feel secure, like a creature of the forest.

Overhead one crack of dusky sky was visible through the arch of trees. It wasn't dark enough for stars yet, but no matter—it was worth a try. Jenny whispered, "Star light, star bright, first star I see tonight, wish I may, wish I might, have the wish I wish tonight." For a moment she waited wistfully. If only, just once, that distant star would wink in response, telling her she was heard. She needed to believe there were good things ahead. Since the day she had learned to read, the world of books had opened the door of hope, but sometimes the hope grew dim.

Jenny sighed, but before she had time to escape into a distant world of castles and thrones, bowing servants and halls filled with unending tables of food, she heard the crunch of Tom's boots. Only half hoping he wouldn't guess her here, she pushed leaves about her shoulders and waited.

"Jen," he called. His boots crunched to the rim of her hiding place. "I know you're there, so say so."

"So," she muttered and waited for him to slide down to her. "Pa sent you?"

He nodded. "Whatcha been up to now?" His voice was harsh and impatient, but the hand that reached for her hair was gentle. His calloused hand under her chin forced it upward.

While the aching misery seeped back into Jenny, she studied her brother's face. Beneath the rough cap of tow hair, his pale gray eyes shone like bright marbles in his rough-hewn, wind-burned face. She saw the gentleness in his eyes, and knew that part of that gentleness for her was because of Pa. Tom accepted their lot, at least on the outside, but she couldn't. She muttered, "You're not like Pa, never."

He sighed, "Ya poor little urchin, you're scrawny black and white like a baby skunk. Times I wish you were, then Pa'd leave you alone." He ran his hand across her shoulders and arms while he studied her face. "Pa's drunk. You're too little to remember him when he was different." His face brightened. "But, Jen, it's all gonna change. Not having money and a chance to get ahead has been makin' him this way."

"Tom, you're tetched," Jenny retorted. "Every penny he's had has gone to the tavern in South Bainbridge. You know every cent Ma's earned for fetchin' the babies into the world has gone there too. Now he's stormin' like it's her fault a real doctor's moved into town and does all the fetchin'."

She paused and studied his face suspiciously. His grin made her uneasy; he'd been involved in shenanigans in the past. Slowly she said, "I don't mind you fetchin' a stray chicken home, but I mind you gettin' caught and feeling the strap like I did." Her hand crept down to her bare leg and Tom pulled her up onto his knees.

His voice crooned comfort as he gently examined the welts. Jenny fought tears and squared her shoulders. "There weren't no call, either; I was just lookin' at his old book."

"The green one, the witching one. Jenny, you know he's smacked you for that before! Why do ya get into it? I can't even read it, and neither can you." His eyes were mildly curious. She moved impatiently. How could you explain it to one like Tom? She knew how he was prone to take whatever life pushed at him.

"I can so read, Tom. You quit treatin' me like a little baby. I'm nearly twelve, or will be come January. There's even littler ones pushin' me out of my place."

"Just two," he replied. Tom was cuddling her close in his warm, rough arms.

With a sigh of contentment she snuggled in. "Tell me about the Indians makin' these holes. About the treasure buried deep down. Tom, what does it take to get down to the money and such?"

Tom got to his feet, sliding Jenny to the ground. "I don't know, but I sure aim to find out. That's one of the good things I have in mind. Come along, or we'll both feel the strap."

"You didn't say what you're up to." Jenny stood up. Her legs were stinging; oozing blood had clotted on the welts. After taking one painful step she sat down again.

Tom studied her for a moment. "I'll have to carry you then," he warned. She shook her head and got up. When she was standing, Tom started to speak, then cocked his head to listen. "I hear something, and I'm guessin' it's Pa comin' after the two of us. Let's head down the trail and come out on the other side of town. 'Twill give him time to forget, or get drunk. Quick!" Grasping her hand, he hurried her deeper into the woods.

Jenny trotted after Tom, trying to ignore the pain in her legs. When the trail rounded a hill, Tom suddenly stopped. Jenny stumbled into him and gasped with alarm. In front of them a shadowy figure, crowned in white, crouched in the middle of the trail. "Ghost!" she gasped, reaching for Tom.

"Hallo," Tom called. "Fancy seein' you here." Jenny scooted closer to Tom as the large figure moved. A face emerged as he rose to his feet. He shook himself and came toward them.

Jenny tilted her head backward and studied the figure. "Why, you're just a young'un, but 'bout the biggest thing I've ever seen."

He blinked slowly as if just awakening, then courteously removed his white hat. His bright blonde hair seemed full of sunshine, and his blue eyes sparkled as he grinned at both of them.

"A prince," she murmured. "But where's your steed? And what's that?" She jabbed at the tattered white object. The hat flew out of his hand, and when it struck the ground a stone rolled out from the crown.

Jenny poked at it with her bare foot. "I'd expect a toad or an elf, but an old rock—"

In a flash he grabbed the rock and shoved it into his pocket. He still smiled, but now his eyes were cold as he bent down to her level. "Little girl, you're as ugly as something found under a rock."

"She's my sister," Tom explained. The fellow turned at the recognition of Tom's voice, and Jenny watched the careless, happy grin again claim his face. "My friend!" he exclaimed. "Have you settled your mind to join us?"

Tom cast a quick look at Jenny and nodded. "I'd be a fool to do otherwise."

The stranger turned toward Jenny, warning, "Now, keep it quiet; there's no profit if we're including the whole village in the scheme." Jenny stopped studying the length and breadth of him and focused her attention on his face.

Eyeing the bright hair and sharply arching nose that dominated his pale face, she demanded, "Tom, who is he?"

Tom touched her shoulder, "I told you. Remember the silver? We're gonna be rich, then Pa—" She moved her shoulders impatiently. Tom turned back to the youth, saying carelessly over his shoulder, "This is Joe. That rock—he sees things and he knows where there's buried treasure that the Spaniards got tired of totin' and hid in these hills."

Jenny studied Joe curiously a moment more, and then looked at the ground. Stubbing her bare toes in the soft black soil, she thought about it all. Their dream of buried treasure didn't seem much different than the thoughts and pictures that filled her head when she was alone in the glen.

She tilted her head and looked up into the blue eyes watching her. "It's like havin' pictures in your mind and makin' them come true, isn't it?" She paused a moment. "Does sayin' it all out loud *make* it come true?"

Caution crept into Joe's expression. "Like putting a curse or a blessing on something? That's so, little girl. But you're far too smart for the size of you." He turned abruptly to Tom and said from the corner of his mouth, "I'll be talking to you later when there's no threat of the news spreading." He ducked his head and without so much as a glance at Jenny strode rapidly out of sight.

"What was he doin' down there on the ground?"

"I'll be switched if I know." Tom's voice was perplexed. "But I'm guessin' it has something to do with our huntin' for the silver. Somehow that fella makes me believe he can find it."

"Just sayin' so makes it come true," Jenny mused thoughtfully. "Well, that bein' the case, I'm goin' to marry that Joe when I grow up."

Tom threw his head back and laughed in astonishment. She watched him silently and resentfully until he wiped his eyes. "Now, why did you say that?" Tom was sober now, staring down at his sister.

"It's just in my bones. And if sayin' makes it so, why, then this'll be the way to find out."

"Jen, you're just a tyke—you've no idea what you're sayin'." His voice was the grown-up one, the one that signaled the five years between them, and she hated it. Giving voice to her thoughts had cut him off from her. Her shoulders sagged.

Turning, she started down the trail. His long steps brought him even with her, and in silence they trudged through the woods to the far side of South Bainbridge. Avoiding the saloon on the town's main street, they hurried on. As they neared home from the opposite side, their steps became slow and cautious. Tom took Jenny's hand, and they walked down the lane leading to the ramshackle farm.

As they crossed the yard the sun dropped behind the wooded hills, and Jenny shivered. Her dreamy thoughts about the afternoon were gone; now she was conscious only of her thin dress and throbbing legs. After a quick glance at her, Tom stepped through the door of the cabin.

Jenny held her breath until she heard the relief in his voice. "Pa's gone." She heard her mother's rocking chair creak, and Jenny leaped through the door.

"Ma!" Jenny crowded as near as she dared without touching her. Ma didn't much like being touched. "I didn't mean no harm." Deepening lines creased her mother's face and darkness shrouded her eyes. Jenny's own throat was aching. She shifted her feet, still hesitating, wanting desperately to say and hear the things she needed.

But she swallowed the painful tears and studied her mother, the weary droop to her thin shoulders, the streaks of gray in her hair.

Ma turned from Jenny to Tom, peering through the shadows of the room to fasten on him as if grasping a sturdy oak. Tom moved uneasily. "Pa?" he questioned.

"Followed you a piece and then headed for town." She sighed and lifted the lamp to the center of the table. "Come on, young'uns. There's bread and milk for supper. I want you bedded afore . . ." Her voice trailed away, but knowing her meaning, Tom and Jenny watched silently as she moved heavily about the room, placing the dishes and lifting the jug of milk.

Suddenly her face brightened. Jenny saw the change—as if Ma had returned from a far country. It was the signal Jenny wanted. She flung herself at her mother, clasping her waist and pressing her face against the warmth. "I'm sorry." Jenny felt the rough hand on her hair and the quick gentle tug and heard the heavy sigh.

"I don't know what to do with you, child. You and him always at logger-heads." She shook her head and turned to raise her voice. "You up there, come."

Overhead scuffled feet, and Jenny looked at the ladder leading to the loft. Her sister Nancy was peering down, her face a pale oval in the dusk.

Jenny didn't need light to remind her of Nancy's blonde prettiness and dainty ways which made Jenny feel grubby and awkward. More scuffles overhead, and two more tiny pale ovals appeared beside Nancy.

Jenny watched thirteen-year-old Nancy lift Matt and push at Dorcas. Jenny's throat tightened again and she scrubbed at her eyes with her fists, quickly, before Nancy saw her. That afternoon those terrified faces had watched as the strap lifted and snapped.

"I'm the one, ain't I? It's my fault Pa's the way he is!" Jenny demanded, her voice shaky.

Ma straightened from her task of dividing the bread and stared. "Child, what's got into you?"

"Tom said I don't remember how it was before, because I was too little."

Ma looked at Tom before answering. Then, her voice dreamy, she mur-mured, "It was different." She sighed and shook her head. "But, no, it isn't you." For a long time she was silent, and Jenny thought she had forgotten her. Then reluctantly she said, "Could be hard times just bring out some-thing that was there the whole time, but hid."

Finally Jenny sat down to her bowl of bread and milk, but she was watching Dorcas and Matty. Nearly two years separated them, but by their sober round faces, they could have been twins.

As she lifted the spoon, her heart was still heavy. Her mother was watching. Gently she said, "You could leave his things alone."

"I only want to read and learn."

"There's school for that. I don't read well enough to know the book. But I've heard him talk about the magic and such. I wasn't raised that way—to believe in those things. They make—" She stopped and shifted her shoul-ders uneasily. There was a troubled frown on her face as she slowly started again. "Maybe he's better'n you credit him. Could be he wants you to grow up knowin' the important things, and findin' a man who'll give you a good life."

She sighed and looked around the dimly lighted room. "Seems if a body looks for the good, he's bound to find it." Her fingers picked listlessly at a frayed spot on her apron. Abruptly she raised her head. "If you're bent on readin', there's my Bible. I don't know enough to read it for myself. But I know it says things that we're supposed to honor."

Jenny frowned over her mother's words, then slipped from her stool and pressed her cheek against Ma's shoulder. " 'Night, Ma. And I'll try to remember that and be lookin' for the good. Maybe just thinkin' hard and sayin' it out loud will make it be."

With one foot on the ladder, Jenny paused, wondering about all her mother had said. Why did it do any good to honor a book instead of reading it? She turned her face to the figure slumped in the circle of pale light. The question rose to her lips, but Jenny remembered that most often her asking things left Ma frowning, with questions in her eyes. Slowly she climbed the ladder.

2

THE SOUTH BAINBRIDGE school was set on the edge of town in a lonesome place. Sometimes it made Jenny feel as if she were in another world. Just enough timber had been hacked out of the woods to clear a spot for the school and to pile fuel high enough for the winter.

Jenny loved the fresh wood scent of the log building; in fact, she loved nearly everything about the school—the sharp clamor of the school bell, even the musty smell of old books and damp woolen mufflers. But at times the high-spirited students made her pull in against the side of the building. There, like a stray field mouse, she watched them vent their boundless energy, twenty pairs of restless feet wearing the grasses of the field to a nub.

This October afternoon was one of the days Jenny clung to the side of the school. Dust hung like a curtain over the playground, while a gust of wind swished through the trees, tearing at the tortured soil. The wind moaning in the trees caught Jenny's attention, lifting her away from the school and the playground and filling her with a sense of utter isolation.

That wind meant winter was drawing near. Listening and watching, Jenny clenched her fists, wishing she could spread sunshine and wild roses across the field.

The shouting of the students broke through her thoughts and brought her back to the playground. Shoving away from the warm logs, she crept close to the group.

"Go, go!" rooted the students in the circle. "Amos, are ye callin' it quits? Scaredy cat!" The dust settled to reveal the victor—the new student, Joe. Jenny saw the grin on his battered lips as he flexed his arms and shoved at his sleeves.

"Come on, who's next?" he shouted. The ring of fellows eyed him cautiously as he tossed his bright hair, but no one would accept the challenge.

Jenny chuckled silently. Joe didn't seem to be much of a student, but he sure could fight.

Since that autumn day when she and Tom had discovered the twenty-year-old lad hunkered beside the trail with his face buried in his battered white hat, she had been paying sharp attention to him.

Granted, he was an on-again, off-again student. Since the day Jenny had first seen his bulk crammed between six-year-old Emily and ten-year-old Nat, with that wild beak of a nose humbled two inches from his slate, she had watched him. At first he could barely push the pencil over his sums, and her awe of him changed to scorn, particularly when she listened to him read.

But later the scorn was salted with respect when she saw him lick every youth in town. And later still her feelings were spiced with a nameless fascination as she watched Nancy bat her eyes at him and Prudence follow him about the school yard like an absolute ninny.

At this moment, the thought of those silly girls carrying extra cookies to him and offering to do his sums for him made Jenny snort with impatience. As if Mrs. Stowell wasn't feeding him right and his head didn't need to learn his own sums.

Jenny applied her scorn to Prudence, the lass who had tossed her long blonde curls, batted her eyelashes, smoothed her flowered apron, and said, "Jennifer Timmons, you are jealous!" Her eyes shrewdly surveyed Jenny and she added spitefully, *"You've* plenty of call to be. Scrawny as a scarecrow and brown as a gypsy, you are." She flounced away, swinging her skirts until her petticoats showed.

It wouldn't have been so bad, Jenny decided, thinking about it later, but the fellow who was filling in for Mr. Searles, the regular teacher, had taken it upon himself to smooth her ruffled feathers.

Just remembering had Jenny muttering to herself. "Didn't hurt, her bein' so uppity and proud, 'til he had to come and fuss over me."

At the end of this October day, Jenny was still busy thinking as she and Tom walked toward home. She found herself stripping away the pretty pictures her mind had built and facing things as they really were.

It hurt to admit that Prudence was right. Even Joe had said she was ugly. Life was bad. And Tom—she looked up at her brother and tried to see him clearly.

Tom was one of those on-again and off-again students, too. Jenny suspected he was more on-again recently because of the new fellow. "That Joe," she muttered. "Seems both of you go because of the other. Either that or it's better'n diggin' stumps in Mr. Stowell's field all day."

She turned on him. "You'd better be listenin' to Ma about forgettin' the ideas circulating. She says there's no way on this earth a man's goin' to get rich except by workin' hard at life. Tom, you know she's tryin' her best for us, not wantin' us to turn out like Pa."

"Dreamin' on rainbows," Tom said shortly as he hunched his shoulders and shuffled his feet in the leaves along the path.

"Is that it?" For a moment Jenny stopped, kicking at the leaves thoughtfully. When she looked up at Tom, she was searching his face for confirmation. "There's some who believe they can change things just by thinkin' hard and willing it so, and by makin' charms and chantin'.'"

"They are the ones who think they have power."

"Do they?"

"Some do, some don't." He stopped to grasp her arm. But his eyes were looking beyond her, shining as if he knew secrets. "Jenny," he whispered, "there's power out there to be had by the ones who know how to get it. Joe knows some of those things, and I intend to find out."

"Ma says there's secret things, but they're bad. Tom, Ma shivered when she said that, and I could tell she was mighty scared."

Tom turned to look at Jenny, and his eyes were very serious. "If that's so, why doesn't she make you stay away from that green book of Pa's? She says if you must read, read that black one. But then she turns her back when you get Pa's book. I say she's scared, but she knows where the power is." His eyes were big again, staring past her.

"Tom, you best be listenin' to Ma." But he wasn't listening, and she tugged at his shirt. "Ma says everybody thinks diggin' will get him rich if he can just find a mine or treasure, but she says people dig and dig and never find a thing. She says a body needs to quit foolin' himself and settle down to pluggin' away for a living." By the time Jenny had delivered her speech they had reached home, and Tom went grinning on his way.

Jenny suspected he was proud of himself because he'd let her run on like a scolding mother. Suddenly the weight of her heavy thoughts slid away, and she was filled with a bubbling-up, running-over affection for Tom. Sometimes he was more like a friend than a brother.

When Jenny entered the cabin her father was asleep, sprawled across the bed with his mouth open. This was real life. Sometimes she needed to be reminded that make-believe wasn't real. She turned her face away to hide the fearful feelings that churned inside her.

Ma was at the table, bending over a pile of bright, new cloth. She lifted her face. "I've a dress finished for Mrs. Harper. I want you to carry it to her; we're needin' the money." She snipped at the thread. "Mighty uppity she's gettin', needin' somebody to do her sewin' for her. Last summer she was just a peddler's wife, common like the rest of us. Now she's puttin' on airs.—But never mind, we're reapin' well from her folly."

"Folly?" Jenny repeated, wondering what the word meant and why Ma used it on Mrs. Harper.

"Just hush and take it. Wrap that torn sheet over it, so you don't soil it." As Jenny reached for the heap of flowered material, Ma turned and peered at her. "Just look at you," she scolded. "Hair a mess and grubby clear to the elbows. Why can't you be like Nancy? Seems I never have to fuss about her washin' her face."

Listening to her mother scold, Jenny thought of her sister sitting at home with a bit of sewing while she hoed in the field or hired out to the Moores when they needed a hand to pitch fodder to the hogs. In the honesty of the afternoon she still had a clear picture in her mind: Prudence with blonde curls and fair skin standing beside Jenny, weather-chapped and browned.

"I'm of a mind to grow plump and be delicate like Nancy and Prudence," she stated, "but I can't clean Mr. Moore's hog pen and come out looking like a lady."

Ma nodded her head. "And kind he is to find ways to help you earn a few pennies," she said with a sigh, touching Jenny lightly on the cheek. "You earn your keep; like as not Nancy will too with her needle. And like as not one of these days, you'll cease chasing after chickens and boys and take up the needle." She turned back to her sewing. "Now, brush your hair afore you go. Don't forget to fetch the money home safe."

Jenny brushed her hair, wrapped the dress in a scrap of clean sheeting, and pulled her mother's shawl across her shoulders.

The day had been sharp with the hint of the winter to come, and now— all too soon, it seemed—the evening shadows were tagging the heels of late afternoon.

Jenny hurried down the lane. Any excuse to go into town was a treat. If she scooted about her task, there'd be time to mosey home, to stare in the shop windows and watch the people.

For the time being she hastened her steps, passing the saloon, the dry-goods store, the sheriff's office, and the tiny little log building they called the lawyer's office.

Just as she was passing that office, studying it curiously in her usual fashion, the door flew open. She sidestepped to avoid running into the young man who rushed out in front of her.

"Oh, beg your pardon, ma'am." He spun around, then with a laugh he corrected himself. "You're not ma'am, you're Jenny, aren't you? Remember me? I taught school one day for Lemuel."

Jenny nodded, "Mr. Cartwright. 'Twas the day Joe Smith wrestled all the big boys and you wouldn't take him on."

"That'd make the newspaper. 'Substitute teacher wrestles student!' Seemed wisest not. You think I couldn't handle him?" The man grinned down at Jenny, and she realized he wasn't much older than Tom.

Silently she shook her head. "What does that mean?" he demanded. "Could or couldn't?" But Jenny just shrugged. She saw only his shiny shoes and the white shirt knotted with a silk tie. Overcome with shyness, she dropped her head, hugged the bundle close, and quickened her steps.

He kept pace with her. After a moment of silence, he said, "Jenny, you have a good mind. The best reader in the bunch. I hope you get to stay in school."

She stopped in the middle of the path, "Oh, yes; but why ever wouldn't I? Is teacher leaving?"

"No—" The word was drawn out, hesitant, and Jenny watched his face. He frowned as he studied her. "Do you have books at home to read?"

"Only one. It's Pa's, and he ain't too keen on me readin' it. Sometimes when he's gone, I snitch it. Ma pretends she doesn't see; otherwise she'd be in trouble with me."

"If you're careful with it, he wouldn't object."

She was shaking her head. "You don't know Pa. I even wash first. Just as long as he doesn't smack Ma, I'm willin' to risk the strap."

They walked on in silence until finally he asked, "Where are you going?"

She raised the bundle. "Ma's been sewin' for Mrs. Harper. She says it's about like one hog scratchin' another's back, but she doesn't mind. It brings in money."

"What do you mean?"

"He's nothin' but a peddler. Mrs. Harper should be doin' her own duds, not wastin' money like a fancy lady gettin' someone else to do her sewin' for her—"

"Mark, you heading for the Harpers', too?" They both turned and watched the young man approach.

"Yes. Michael saw the sheriff leave in a hurry, so he sent me to snoop around. Trust an attorney to have a nose for news." Jenny hesitated shyly and then walked ahead of the two as they began to talk. Their voices dropped and Jenny quickened her steps.

"Jenny," Mr. Cartwright called. She turned and he stepped forward, saying, "Ah—couldn't you deliver that dress tomorrow?"

She shook her head. "Ma'll skin me. I'm to get the money tonight."

He hesitated and shrugged. With an apologetic glance at his companion, he muttered. "Could be just gossip."

"Like as not."

The three of them had just turned up the lane leading to the Harpers' when a horse cantered toward them. The rider sawed on the reins and said in a low voice, "Go on up, she'll need all the help she can get, poor soul." They watched him dig his heels in the horse.

Cartwright looked after the man. Soberly he said, "My friend, I think your information is correct." He turned to Jenny, and as he paused a wail came from the vine-covered cottage in front of them.

Jenny hugged herself and shivered, but before the men could move, the door burst open and Mrs. Harper rushed out. Screaming, she ran toward them and threw herself into Cartwright's arms.

Jenny gulped and watched, while Cartwright was patting and murmuring. He was also looking uncomfortably from her to the youth at his side.

Stepping forward, Jenny thrust the bundle at Mrs. Harper. "Ma'am, Ma's finished your flowered dress. Here 'tis."

The woman raised her head from Cartwright's shoulder and stared at Jenny. "My husband is dead! You're bringin' me a flowered dress and my husband is dead!—they're totin' him in here, butchered like a hog . . ."

"Butchered like a hog." Through the days and weeks that followed, the words stayed with Jenny, often goaded into her mind by the memory of that long, shrouded bundle being carried up the path. She still shivered over the horror she felt as Jake Evans nearly dropped his end when he first glimpsed Mrs. Harper and tried to snatch his cap off his head.

Later more details came out, and the words Jenny heard continued to be passed around town. Peddler Harper, God rest his soul, had been found deep in the woods with his throat slashed from ear to ear.

For weeks the tiny village of South Bainbridge, New York, vibrated with fear. Doors that had never had a lock were barricaded with the heaviest pieces of furniture in the house. Children were scurried indoors before sunset.

Scarcely had the nerves begun to steady when the murderer was apprehended. Word was passed through the streets by clusters of neighbors who met to discuss the news. The question was, Why? Who could imagine a man like that Jason Treadwell murdering a poor old peddler? Even Jenny recalled his sad, pale face.

In a town as small as South Bainbridge, there were only two places people could congregate to discuss the local news: the general store and the tavern. In each place the slant of the news differed.

The tavern version came out at the Timmons' table. Jenny sat between her mother and father, while her head turned from one to the other. Her father's dark brooding eyes moved across Tom, then shifted to her. "Where's a man to be safe? When a no-'count like Harper is done in, who'll be next?"

While he lifted his spoon and the others waited, Jenny looked around the group. Little Matty and Dorcas were too young to be touched by it all, but their eyes were round as they silently watched.

Pa scowled, shoved his bowl back, and took up his conversation. "There's things out there. Spirits. I've had enough experience in my life to know ya can't mess around with 'em if'n you don't know how to handle 'em. Harper for sure didn't. He shouldn't have been diggin' in the first place, messin' around in their territory." From beneath the scowling shelf of his bushy eyebrows he watched Tom. Jenny saw her brother squirm uncomfortably. Pa had that expression on his face—the one he used when he whipped her for taking his green book.

Jenny studied Tom; was it possible he had been reading the book?

"There's nothin' wrong with a little diggin'," said Tom, interrupting Pa's silent stare.

" 'Tis a waste if'n you don't have the power," he said heavily. "You're not even willing to study it out. I'm sayin' you best leave it all alone. If you don't you'll get in a fix. Them spirits are stronger than you. Messin' in their territory will getcha trouble, and nothin' more." His hooded eyes stared at Jenny, and she knew he was warning her, too.

Jenny's thoughts were full of the questions she was aching to ask. Ma said them for her. Gently her voice chided, "Now, Pa, be careful or the young'uns will think you're encouraging them in the craft. Has it ever got you a thing?"

Jenny watched the anger twist his face. The muscles on his neck knotted into ropes. But quickly before he could speak, Ma continued, "You know we weren't raised that way. Good, God-fearing families we both came from. They say the Bible teaches against spells and such, against believin' in the power."

Jenny's jaw dropped. Never before had she heard Ma talk like that to her pa. Caught in astonishment, Jenny nearly lost Pa's reply.

Now he roared, "Woman, you don't know what you're a-sayin'! The craft's been around longer than your black Book. If I haven't succeeded, it's 'cause you're never willin' to take chances, run a risk. This town's too goody-goody. I tell you, I'm sick of it, and I intend to quit it!"

Ma dropped her spoon and raised a troubled face. "Where'd we go?"

He shrugged while she looked around the room lighted only by the glow of the fire. The trouble faded from her face and Jenny watched hope brighten her eyes. "If we moved to the city you'd get a job. Like in a factory. And there'd be good churches." For a moment there was a question in her eyes. "If we could just get back in where there's proper church, everything would be different. I hear tell of camp meetings, and I pine for . . ." her voice trailed to silence and she sighed.

"I'm thinkin' of west," he muttered. "Farther west there's a heap o' land nearly for the takin'. And there ain't no churches." Jenny studied his face, wondering at the satisfaction in his voice.

Jenny watched Nancy gracefully gather the dishes and stack them in the dishpan. Ma was speaking now, and Jenny knew it was talk from the store.

"Mrs. Taylor says Harper's widder is recoverin' right well. I guess I'd better get those dresses to her. Judgin' from the looks of her, she's gonna be a merry widder. Don't know what's goin' on, but there's talk she's signed an agreement with some fellas and is in line to make a heap of money. Don't sound moral to me."

Tom sputtered and choked. "Ma, 'tis business. She's just a-carryin' on a business deal her old man started."

Pa turned on Tom. "How come you know?"

Tom opened his mouth, closed it, and shrugged. Ma was staring at him and Jenny watched the frown grow on her face, "There's talk at the store about that new lad in town. If I heard right his name's Joe. They say he's bringin' trouble," Ma stated.

Tom protested, "That's no fair. 'Tis a busybody linkin' him with Harper's death."

" 'Tweren't that, even though everybody knows they were in on the business deal together," Ma answered. "It's the talk about the diggin' goin' on. They're sayin' Stowell brung that young fella out here on some crazy notion he has about findin' money by diggin'."

Tom jumped to his feet, knocking his stool aside. "He's just a young'un. I can't understand why people don't accept him like they'd do another's relation."

"He's nobody's relation," Nancy put in. "Besides, a fella that good-looking either has people pulling or pushing." She dried a plate and put it on the table. Leaning across, she faced Tom. "Just like you," she quipped. "How come you're so hot for defending him?"

There was no answer from Tom. Jenny watched him stare at his bowl. When she looked at her sister, Jenny saw the changing expression on her face. The saucy questioning air disappeared and a slight frown creased her forehead.

"Seems," Nancy said slowly, "the fella affects a person. There's something about him that makes a body hate or love him."

Caught by the statement, Jenny stood watching Nancy turn aside with a sigh. She heard her mother say, "Nancy, you're not fourteen yet. You're not even supposed to know there's fellas like that." An anxious note in her voice made Jenny wonder what she meant.

Jenny was still thinking about that statement the next afternoon when she and Tom met Joe on their way home from school. Jenny had suggested cutting through the edge of the forest, and there was Joe sitting beside the trail. It was cold and crisp, and snow rimmed the rocks and bushes, but he was sitting there as relaxed as if it were a day in June.

When Tom hailed him, he got to his feet and waited for them to reach him. Speaking in a whisper, he said, "You know, when there's been a death like old man Harper, there's a surge of energy released in the spirit world. I was feeling it. Sitting here I was wondering how best to take advantage of the power."

Jenny shivered and jumped around on the trail. She too spoke in a whisper. "Are you goin' to be diggin' for treasure? Will you teach me how to use the rod? Tom said you knew all about it. What are charms? Are you afraid of the spirits? Have you ever seen one?"

He hunkered down beside her and grinned unexpectedly. "Hey, are you that uppity little kid from school? How come you aren't asking these questions during recess?"

She studied him for a minute, still dancing on her toes with excitement. "Because Ma says this diggin' for treasure is all wrong. Nancy would tell on me. Will you show me how to draw circles so the demons won't get me?"

He got to his feet, laughing. Jenny was disappointed to see the mood of mystery had faded from him. Hands on hips, she stood in the path staring up at him. "No one will take me serious. I'm tryin' to learn. If you and Tom won't teach me, where's a body to learn?"

Still chuckling, he said, "Too bad my pa isn't here. He's the one I learned from." And Jenny had to be content with that. She and Tom dallied a moment longer before leaving. When they turned toward home, Tom was whistling happily.

3

ONE OCTOBER AFTERNOON, Jenny lingered behind the rest of the students, reluctant to go home. The waning afternoon was still warm, and the bright autumn trees surrounding the schoolhouse enticed Jenny. Turning her back to the raucous group headed down the trail, she watched the wind flick the red maple leaves like brilliant flags.

While she hesitated, staring at the trail cutting into the trees, a movement in the deeper shadows of pine caught her attention. A pale patch flashed, and she caught a brief glimpse of bright hair before the dark shadows swallowed the tall figure.

Quickly Jenny turned and trotted down the path. Without a doubt it was Joe. But just before she reached the trees, she hesitated. She was disobeying Ma. How many times had she been scolded for tarrying after school, and for tagging after the fellows instead of staying close to Nancy?

Jenny's feet began to drag, but all of the questions she had been wanting to ask Joe tumbled into her mind. If she hurried, he might show her how to use the rod.

As Jenny moved down the trail, she began to hear the clink of shovel against stone.

He was in a clearing, standing on a mound of dirt, digging. Suddenly shy, she hung back in the trees, watching. When he threw down his shovel and pulled the stone out of his pocket, she forgot everything except her curiosity. As she ran toward him, he jumped to his feet and turned. The quick smile on his face changed to a frown when he saw her. "What are you doing here?"

"I saw you comin' this way. I want to help. What are you seein' with the stone? Would I be able to see, too?"

"Jen, go home," he muttered. "Better yet, go tell Tom I need him to help me. There's something down there, for certain."

"Tom's helpin' on the Goodman farm today. They're diggin' potatoes and he's gonna get some."

"Just my luck," Joe muttered. "There's spirits down there protecting the treasure, and I sure can't get it without some help."

"I'll help. I know enough about diggin' to draw a circle for you." He was still frowning. "Tom could come tomorrow. I'll tell him tonight. Joe—" her voice dropped to a whisper, "are there really spirits guarding it?"

He studied her for a moment. "On your life there are. Come here and I'll tell you what I'm seeing. This is where the Spaniards buried a heap of silver. There were two of them, but one killed the other. It's the murdered one who's doing the guarding. I can see his slit throat." Jenny shivered and moved closer. "You want to look in my stone? We'll see if you have the gift."

Jenny eyed the dark stone he held out. After a moment she slowly shook her head. "I'm afraid," she whispered. "What would I do if I saw a spirit or something? Joe, I'm afraid." She backed away from him.

"You're a silly little baby," he teased.

"I'm not. It's just—" She hesitated, then crept closer. Climbing on the log beside the diggings, she peered down into the hole and then turned to look Joseph in the eye. He was close, and his head was nearly on a level with hers. "You just don't understand young'uns," she said. "Or girls. Some people get scared easier."

The teasing disappeared. "We have a house full of 'em." He put the shovel down and sat beside her on the log. "It isn't fun being poor, is it? 'Specially when no one takes you serious because your pa's—well . . ."

"My pa drinks and then uses the strap on us. Tom and me. Nancy and the little ones don't get it."

He was nodding, talking slowly like he had forgotten she was around. "Seems we were moving all the time. People pushing for money and pushing just because they thought they could get by with it. Always moving. Poor, too many kids around. Ma running a ginger beer and cake shop, painting old oilcloth just to keep us eating. No matter where we go, seems luck has run off and left us."

Now he straightened and grinned at her. "But it won't be like that forever. I'm going to *be* somebody. I'm going to make people sit up and take notice. No more will they be saying, 'There goes that Smith kid looking for trouble again.' " Abruptly he turned and grasped Jenny's shoulder. "Tyke, I'll tell you something, and don't you forget it. There's power out there. If you learn to tap the forces, you can have anything you want out of life."

"How do you know?" Jenny whispered.

His voice lowered, and his eyes glittered. "There's spirits out there to do my bidding. If you learn how to control the forces of the spirit world and use the rod and the stone properly, there's riches and treasure for the taking. Jenny, it's the rich man, the one who's learned all these things, who's respected. And it's for the taking.

"Back home, there's this fella. He's a magician and he knows all about these things and he's teaching me. Now my pa knows a little bit about it, but he doesn't have the power. He's worked with the rod and the digging for years, and he knows there's evil spirits guarding the treasures, but he doesn't have the power to break through them. But I have confidence in this fella Walters. He'll show me how to get the money and treasures."

As Jenny headed for home, she thought of what Joe had said; more important than the words was the feeling that now they were friends. Now Joe would tell her the things she needed to know, things that were in the green book. What would he think if she were to tell him how much she wanted the same things he wanted? But even as the thoughts came into her mind, she knew he wouldn't listen. He thought she was too young—but someday she wouldn't be.

Later that week, Jenny came home from school to find her father at home. Gratefully she took the egg basket Ma offered and scurried out to the barn. When Pa was drinking this early, she knew better than to tarry.

In the barn she found Tom bridling his horse.

"Where ya goin'?" Jenny asked. Pulling her shawl close, she leaned against the horse's flanks.

Startled, Tom jerked his head and looked down at Jenny. "Didn't know you were around. What difference does it make? Your nose is red," he added. "Did you just get home from school?" She nodded and watched him adjust the bridle over the horse's ears. "Better get in the house," he urged, " 'tis close to snowing."

"Been in. Pa's home." He turned to look at her, and she supplied the information with a nod. "I'm stayin' out of there. Lemme go with you."

He shook his head. "No. It'll be dark and cold before I'm back."

Jenny tightened the shawl about her and sniffed. "I can't go in 'til he's asleep. You and Joe weren't in school today; where were you?"

Still watching her, he shrugged and asked, "You been readin' his book again?" Jenny chewed her thumb and considered the question. How badly she wanted to tell him about the book, about all the secrets in it! She'd tell how at night the pictures and the strange words rolled around in her mind. Just now, thinking about the book made her ache to know what it all meant.

But Ma had said the book was evil. And Tom had been there listening, nodding his head, agreeing with Ma. If Jenny were to admit reading the book again, Tom could get her into real trouble. She shook her head.

"Honest, Tom, I haven't had it since—I never said a word, he just started in on me, and Ma said to look for eggs. She knows those hens haven't laid any for a month now."

The temptation was too great to resist. "Tom, do you really believe all those things Ma said about the book? How magic and money diggin' and usin' charms is of the devil? Do you really think the devil's out there just waitin' to get children who don't mind their parents and go to church and leave the witchin' things alone, do you?"

He gave her a quick glance before replying, "I haven't ever seen a devil. It would be hard to convince me to be scared of something I haven't met. Now take this stuff we're doin'; it's not a hard and fast way to make money, but it's interesting and a little exciting, just hoping."

Jenny saw the softening on his face and pleaded, "Please, Tom. Let me hang on behind you; I won't be a bit of trouble."

He tightened the cinch and sat down on the log. "Wouldn't set so good if I bring my little sister."

"Are you going to dig at the mine the fellas found? I heard you and Joe talkin' about it. I'd be quiet and nice. I want to see the mine."

"For one thing, it's miles from here. For another, that's not where I'm headed. We gotta wait on that."

"Where do I go 'til Pa's asleep?" Tom's hands made a helpless, questioning arc and Jenny pressed, "I'd hide in the bushes and just wait for you." With a sigh, Tom reached for her, and she grinned with relief.

The horse was old and stiff and her gait threw Jenny from side to side, but she clung to Tom and gritted her teeth.

They left South Bainbridge and when they had nearly reached Colesville, Tom cut south. Here the trees were thick and the underbrush almost covered the trail.

When the horse slowed to a walk, Jenny ventured, "No timber's been pulled across this road recently."

"That's fine, just fine," Tom muttered. The excitement in his voice brought Jenny leaning far over to see his face. He turned his head and warned. "Now you remember, you hide. Don't let on you're there while we have our meeting."

"With Joe?"

"And some of the others who'll be a-workin' with us."

"Mrs. Harper be there?"

"She's not workin' the mine; she's just a partner," replied Tom.

"I thought partners worked too."

"Well—" Tom sounded like he was scratching his head and Jenny tried to see his face. "Not if they're, well, silent partners. Harper was the workin' partner; now he's gone, she's his inheritor." Tom paused and slowed the horse. "I think this is the place. That hill. Joe says there's money buried in the mound."

"How'd he know?"

"He's been lookin' with his stone. We were out here last week, but the enchantment was bad. Joe says we're goin' to have to break it if we have a hope of reachin' the money."

Jenny peered at Tom. "Honest! How'd he find out?"

"I'm not right sure, but he's been doin' this long enough to have a pretty good idea how to go about it. He and his pa's been diggin' for years now."

"They must be rich."

"Naw," Tom paused. "Seems to be a pretty tricky thing, this gettin' the money. Joe says things have to go just right or the spirits whisk the whole treasure away."

Jenny shivered and hugged Tom close. "If it's so, it's a mighty risky gamble. Seems a waste of time."

"On the other hand," Tom added, "one good find makes all the failures worth the trouble.—Okay, off the horse and into the bushes."

Jenny slid off the horse and ran across the clearing. The bushes Tom pointed out were growing above the spot where the men had dug. By hanging on to the branches and leaning forward she could peer into the hole. After a minute Tom rode back to her and tossed his heavy canvas bags to her, saying, "Might as well sit on these until we need them."

By the time Tom's shadowy figure rode into the clearing, it had started to snow. Jenny huddled deep into her shawl and pulled one of the bags over her head and shoulders. The sound of horses and distant voices carried clearly on the cold air. She knelt on a bag and leaned forward to part the bushes.

A rider was calling out orders as he came into the clearing. "Now get this brush cleaned out of here. Every bit of litter has to go." She could see the speaker and guessed from the size of him that it was Joe. She heard him say, "No wonder you couldn't fetch up the chest before. All this mess is begging for trouble."

"Joe, if you'd come with us instead of staying at Stowell's peering in that stone, we'd known to clear the brush."

Jenny heard his heavy voice turn to the fellow talking. "And if I'd been here, we'd never have known all those spirits were guarding the treasure. Doubtless, even then it was needing more than digging to fetch that chest up."

"Did you get something for a sacrifice?"

"Stowell's bringing it."

When Jenny heard the word *sacrifice,* her heart began to pound. She leaned forward and eagerly studied the group clustered on the edge of the hole. "Aw, shucks," she muttered when she saw the men. Tom and Joe were the only ones she recognized, but the rest were very ordinary. They looked like farmers from the area.

Jen, you got your hopes up, didn't ya? she thought in disgust, even as common sense reminded her that the vision of satin capes and plumed velvet hats didn't have a place in this snowy forest. They were found only in books—and in Jenny's dreams. But she couldn't help her disappointed sigh.

For just a moment she dared to hope all those secret and glorious things in her father's book were about to take place before her very eyes. Then pictures of demons, especially of the one with a head like a goat, rose in her mind, and she shuddered involuntarily. If the book weren't evil, as Pa had said, why did she become fearful thinking about the mysterious dark words?

But fascination overcame her fear. Almost immediately Jenny heard the bleat of a lamb. Then a voice, "All right, Smith, here 'tis." Surely that voice belonged to Mr. Stowell.

She parted the bushes and eased herself forward just far enough to see the clearing. The group worked in silence. Several of the men shoveled debris, while others chopped dead branches out of the way.

Joe was showing Tom how to cut long stakes. Someone handed Joe a shiny sword, which he used to mark a wide circle around the diggings. Jenny's breath came faster as he marked a second circle. It was just like Pa's book!

"Why ya doin' two of 'em?" asked the man beside him.

"Instructions," Joe said tersely. "Now, lemme have the stakes. They're to keep off the evil spirits while we do the digging. See, we weren't careful enough last time. The enchantment is more powerful than we thought. Must mean there's more money down there than we'd guessed." Jenny felt the excitement run through the group.

Joe stood back to watch the last stake being placed, then he turned and disappeared. While Jenny stirred restlessly on the canvas bags, she again heard the bleat of the lamb. Suddenly there was an anguished squeal, and Joe appeared carrying the lamb. She watched with mingled pity and horror as he moved into the inner circle and marched slowly around carrying the struggling, bleeding lamb.

The men were waiting silently. The only sound was the low murmuring Joe was doing as he finished marching around, dripping the blood. When the lamb was quiet and limp, he nodded his head.

Now the men jumped for their tools and moved to the center of the circle. The group was still silent; only the sound of shovels against the earth broke the quiet of the night. When one grated against stone, Jenny rubbed her face and licked her lips. Edging nearer, she leaned breathlessly over the incline.

A shovel clunked woodenly, and a voice cried, "There's somethin' there!"

"Oh!" Jenny's cry of alarm rose to a scream as the branch she had grabbed snapped and she flew down the slope.

Sliding to a stop, she cautiously opened her eyes. A ring of muddy boots surrounded her. A man loomed above her, arm uplifted. Jenny gasped. *The sword!* She stared in horror, not daring to move, but deep inside she knew Pa's book was coming alive before her eyes.

The group about her was silent, motionless. Now she heard a sigh of resignation close to her ear and felt Tom's arms lifting her. "You all right, Jen?" She nodded mutely, looking from Tom's sober face to Joe's scowling one.

"Well, I guess that just about fixed it but good; we'll never be able to get the thing now." He looked around the group. "Fellas, let's go home," he said shortly.

From the shelter of Tom's arms, Jenny watched the silent group gather their tools in disgust and disappear behind the curtain of falling snow. It seemed like a dream. Nearly. At that moment she caught another glimpse of the crumpled, blood-smeared lamb beside the line of stakes.

4

NOVEMBER PASSED. WITH Christmas came winter. In addition, as heavy as the clouds and as chilling as the rain and snow, came uneasy talk that moved through South Bainbridge, New York.

Jenny knew it first at school when she approached Mr. Searles, asking, "Joe Smith ain't been to school for weeks. Why?"

He peered at her. "Don't say 'ain't,' say 'hasn't.' Jenny, you're getting to be a young lady, and ladies don't talk like farmers. If you've a desire to make people sit up and listen to you, then learn to talk like a lady."

She twisted her face, thinking about what he had said, and he added, "Don't twist your mouth like that either."

"Why do you care how I talk?" She couldn't keep the wistful note out of her voice.

"I don't rightly know," he said slowly as he studied her curiously. "Guess it mostly has to do with Cartwright's saying you've got potential. He ought to know, he's had more teaching than most of us. He's heading east to read law at some attorney friend's office. When he comes back here, he'll be a lawyer. Maybe a justice of the peace like that fellow, Albert Neely. South Bainbridge is growing up, and we need all the learning we can get around here."

Jenny let the words swirl about her while she stared up at Lemuel Searles. Her mind was filled with the vision of Prudence with her blonde curls and crisply starched petticoats. "Even Prue doesn't speak all that good."

For a moment he looked like he did when he'd lost his place in the midst of reading the big book. "Jenny, it's you we're discussing."

"Joe Smith," she reminded. Confusion slid over his face. "Mr. Searles," Jenny insisted, "it's Joe I'm a-askin' after." He took a deep breath, and while she watched his chest swell, Arnold Thompson scooted up and stopped beside Jenny.

"You know something new about Joe?" he asked. "The town's a-buzzin'. Pa said he heard things, weird-like."

Mr. Searles picked up the school bell and handed it to Arnold. "It's time for class, Arnold. You may ring the bell."

Curiosity nipped at Jenny like a playful pup. It wasn't the first time gossip about Joe had come up; but always, like the autumn leaves in a swirling wind, it had scattered and spun away. This time, she vowed, the talk would not slip past her.

During the rest of the day Jenny kept watching Arnold, sometimes meeting his teasing eyes. Once when she mouthed the message to him, "Tell me after school," he only grinned.

When the final bell rang, Jenny fought her way through the crowded room. Arnold was already out the door and with one teasing shout thrown to the wind, he was off across the fields.

When she caught up with him, he was waiting to torment her, saying, "If you was as pretty as Prue, I'd make you give me a kiss for tellin'."

She glared at him, "Just as I thought, you got no news, you're just joshin'." She started to turn away.

He caught her arm, saying, "I do so. If you'll buy me a licorice, I'll tell ya."

"I haven't a penny."

"Then you snitch it while I keep Miz Lewis busy." She shook her head. "Ma'll have a fit if I do and get caught." Arnold was hopping backward down the lane, still grinning. She ran to catch up with him. "All right— anything to know." They turned and ran toward town.

The store was crowded. Jenny paused to sniff deeply of the mingled odors. The smell of sweet spices floated above the mouth-watering scents of smoked ham and pickled herring. Arnold poked her and they squirmed their way between the Mortons and old Mrs. Johnson.

After a few well-placed jabs, the line in front of the candy jars parted. Arnold muttered and pointed out his choice.

"Can't," Jenny whispered. "There's too many lookin'."

"Just wait," he muttered; "they'll all clear out soon."

They drifted back and forth through the store, examining everything at nose level.

Jenny was conscious of the eyes watching them. Jake Lewis's were suspicious and alert; the others were curious. As she waited she listened to the conversation passing back and forth among those who lingered around the potbellied stove.

"Uncommonly coincidental." The white-haired man leaned on his walking stick and puffed at his pipe. Jenny studied him. His hair curled neatly against his stiff white collar. His walking stick was of dark wood, carved and polished, and capped with shiny brass. The man's gaze flitted across Jenny and Arnold and fastened on the portly man beside him.

"Oliver Harper's death was strange enough, coming on the heels of the gossip about the diggings, but coupled with this new development, it is indeed strange."

Jenny's mind screamed, *What new development*? She studied the floor and edged nearer the stove.

The portly man asked the question. "Meaning?"

"The agreement those fellas have signed. Seems Mrs. Harper will be getting a sizable chunk of money from that mine, providing those Spaniards really deposited a pile of silver in that cave."

The other chuckled, "Conscience money?"

"There's too much belief in the miraculous connected to it. Joe's made no bones about using a seer stone to hunt for treasure. Anybody will tell you there's plenty of conjuring taking place. Anybody who'll talk, that is. Seems the town is uncommonly quiet right now except for the rumblings behind the scene. And the rumblings are growing louder." He puffed on his pipe before saying, "If nothing else, I'd be happy to have the fear of God put into the sorcerers. It bothers me mightily to see the country accepting witchcraft as a good thing. Granted, not all think that way, but there's enough accepting it." When he stopped talking, he raised his head and Jenny watched his eyes sweep the length and breadth of the store. Turning, she saw the cluster of people caught motionless, listening.

In the silence that seemed to cloak them all, Jake Lewis moved. His voice was suddenly loud in the quiet store. "Here you, Arnold and Jenny, there's a piece of licorice for you to split. You've been waitin' an hour for a piece to hop out at you. So take it and be gone. My patience and my eyes are wearing out." He broke the stick of candy and offered it to them. Jenny and Arnold reached and scooted out the door.

Over her mouthful, Jenny said, "You got your candy. Are you going to tell?"

He shook his head. "If you'd given me yours I mighta told you. This way I'll hold on to the news until I get hungry for another piece."

Jenny shrugged. "You couldn't top what that important-looking fella said, and I'll not be riskin' my neck to hear more of your stories."

When Jenny reached home Pa sat silent, glowering beside the fireplace. Tom was hunkered down on a log on the other side of the fire, his face sullen. Jenny watched him whittle a stick with quick, impatient jabs of his knife.

Ma was moving about the room, the carpet slippers she had made out of Pa's old felt hat, patched together with odd bits of cloth, slapping softly against the uneven board floor.

Jenny sat down at the table. "When I get growed, I'm gonna learn to talk like a lady so's people will listen to me. I'm gonna get Ma some shoes, and we'll all be rich. I'm right tired of livin' like this."

"You could start your reforming by learning to keep your face clean and your hair combed," Nancy retorted. "Nobody in this town talks good, but even that dumb Prue keeps her face clean. What's on your face, anyway?"

"Licorice," Jenny said, applying her tongue to the remains of the candy.

"How'd you come by licorice?" Dorcas asked, pressing wistfully against Jenny. The look stabbed remorse through Jenny, and she added *candy for Dorcas* to her mental list.

"Arnold and me were in the store. For no account, Mr. Lewis gave us a stick to share. I reckon if you'd be sweet like an angel the next time Ma takes you with her, he just might give you one."

"Not with the bill we owe," Ma said sharply. Pa heaved himself to his feet. Abruptly he kicked at Tom's muddy boot.

"If'n you'd be tryin' to bring home an honest buck instead of hangin' around that lazy Joe, we'd be gettin' caught up on the bills."

In January Jason Treadwell was executed for the murder of Oliver Harper, peddler and money digger.

For a time the rumbles in South Bainbridge subsided as if in honor of the dead. But feelings and words, like a mole tunneling through a field, must surface. As February rolled around and the weather softened enough for conversation but not enough for work in the fields, clusters of people juggled words and sifted gossip.

In the log cabin that served as a meeting place for the Presbyterian congregation, the people were warned against the devices of the evil one. And the devices named were hunting treasures in the earth and dabbling with the ancient arts of witchcraft.

Ma was nodding her head vigorously. While Jenny listened, she noticed that the leader, Josiah Stowell, who had stood right up front in the past, calling the worship and leading the songs, was absent. She wondered why. Mostly she wanted to see his face and hear what he would say when they talked about the digging and the dead lamb.

Jenny was silent as she walked homeward. Just ahead of her, Nancy and Ma were talking. Jenny studied Ma's faded dress with the tear in the hem. She was thinking of the bright flowered dresses her mother had made for Mrs. Harper. Abruptly she said, "Money diggin' and the like can't be too bad if a body is able to earn a livin' from it."

Nancy and Ma stopped suddenly and Jenny bumped into them. Ma stared down at Jenny. "Child, what's got into you? Sure, I know that money diggin' is going on and that instead of fearin' it as the device of the devil, people are a-scornin' it as an idiot's folly, but you've been raised better."

"Have I?" Jenny was staring up at the two of them. She noticed that Ma was dark like she was, while Nancy was fair like Tom. Bewildered by their expressions, she realized she didn't feel related to either of them.

Nancy was demanding, "Didn't you hear what the parson said? Jenny, I fear for your soul."

"Nancy, you've no call to be uppity. There's too many good folks around usin' the rod and diggin'." Jenny flounced past her sister and scooted down the path.

It wasn't long after, that another stranger came to town. Jenny had been passing down the street on her way to school when she first saw Peter Bridgman standing in front of the lawyer's office with Mark Cartwright. She lingered on the corner watching them. She loved seeing and hearing new things. She felt like the world was flooded with sunlight and every detail of the street was bright with it, though the sun wasn't even shining.

Later she learned the stranger, Peter Bridgman, was nephew to Miriam Stowell, and he was asking hard questions. With Peter Bridgman around, the town heaved a collective sigh of relief. Now someone would *do* something. Poor Mrs. Stowell. Her husband, good man that he was, was being led astray.

Josiah Stowell, they said, had been the one who had gotten the notion all on his own to go to Palmyra and fetch the young seer here to help him decide where to dig for treasure. He'd heard that young Joe had a talent for finding things in the earth.

So Josiah's silver lined the pockets of that tall, young, blonde fella. It was strange enough for a man like Stowell, a good, solid, hard-working farmer, to decide in his old age to listen to those stories about hidden treasure; but he was risking the inheritance of his wife and children on his foolishness, as well. So Peter Bridgman was in town asking his questions. What Stowell's wife, sons, and daughters dared not say, Peter must, if the family fortune were to be saved.

One day Jenny followed Tom out to the barn. While he milked the cow, Jenny hung over the gate and whispered her questions. "Why does that Mr. Bridgman care about what Mr. Stowell's doin'? Seems if there's money to be made, it won't make no difference how he's doin' it."

Tom leaned his head against the cow's flank and studied Jenny's face. His Adam's apple slid up and down his neck; finally he replied, "Jen, can't you understand people frown on treasure huntin'?"

"Why?" He shrugged and Jenny persisted, "Seems a body's entitled to work in his own way." She paused to lick her lip. " 'Sides, all that money's goin' be found by someone, so might as well be the one that wants to do the diggin'."

"If there's really money to be found," Tom said shortly as he returned to his milking.

"You think there isn't?" Jenny asked, astonished.

"There's stories. People always are diggin' and diggin' and never findin' a thing." Tom's voice dragged out the words slowly as he studied the pail between his knees.

Jenny settled back to think of the book, of those promises it made—if a person just did it right. Slowly the old excitement burned through her, excitement mingled with fear. She opened her mouth to tell Tom about all she was feeling, about what Joe said.

The eerie pictures she had seen in Pa's book crowded into her mind, and she stopped. How could she ever put them into words and make them as real to Tom as they were becoming to her? Tom looked like he had quit hoping in anything as he leaned against the side of the cow, squirting milk into the pail. She turned away. "Ma'll get me if I don't find the eggs before dark."

Suddenly winter was finished with New York State. The ice broke on the Susquehanna. March softened the air with gentle winds, and green fringes appeared on all the snowbanks. Life seemed to stir afresh even in the streets of South Bainbridge.

Jenny was walking to school alone, thinking restless springtime thoughts, when Arnold caught up with her.

"How about some more licorice?"

She eyed him suspiciously. "That means you have news to trade. Well, I'm not about to snitch anything for the likes of you."

"Aw, Jenny," he tormented, "you're a poor sport!"

"Go do your kissin' on Prue; then I'll get the information for nothin'. She can't keep a secret."

"Would it make a difference if ya knew it was about Joe Smith?"

Jenny stood still. Of course it would, but she wasn't going to let Arnold know that. She eyed him, seeing the way his eyes sparkled with excitement. Then she ducked her head and continued to walk slowly.

Tim Morgan caught up with them. "Say, Jenny, I suppose Arnold here has told ya all about it, huh?" He elbowed his way between them. "I'd never have guessed old Bridgman was that serious. Arrested! Ya goin' to the trial? Pa says we can. Everybody's goin'."

"She don't know!" Arnold howled. "You're spoilin' it all!"

"Of course I'm goin'," Jenny trilled while staring defiantly at Arnold. "Only problem, I don't know when it is."

"Tomorrow. Wouldn't surprise me if Teach lets school. Since it's Joe, he'll be wantin' to go too."

Jenny clenched her teeth and tossed her head. Her stomach was churning with the agony of unasked questions, but she smiled sweetly at Arnold and hurried her feet along the path. "There's the bell. Gotta run!"

The school buzzed with the news. She listened, but saved her questions for Tom. A wrenching inside advised her that silence was best.

After school she flew across the yard, leaving the talk behind, and ran to find Tom. Halfway home she caught up with him. "There's talk," her shortened breath ended with a sob. "They're sayin' Joe's been arrested, and that there'll be a trial. Why?"

Tom lifted his head. "You're takin' on like it's the end of the world. Bridgman's claimin' Joe's up to no good with his lookin' for the mine. Stowells are puttin' it all on to him. They're not wantin' to risk a thing." He shook his head mournfully. "Only way you can make a buck is by a-riskin' something."

Now he turned to look at her. "Say," he said slowly, "you're actin' like Joe's kin. Don't be worryin' your head about the menfolks, Jen. We can take care of ourselves. 'Tweren't all that bad. Old Joe'll have his day in court and then we'll be back to diggin'. Wanna go hear it all? It's tomorrow."

She nodded, rubbing at the dampness in her eyes. "You make it sound like funnin'—nothin' serious."

"Aw, Joe's a good guy. With that smooth tongue he'll be able to talk himself outta anything."

5

JENNY'S MOOD LIGHTENED with dawn. She skipped beside Tom as they headed for town. "There's Mrs. Harper wearing her new dress," Jennie hissed. Others were in holiday garb, too. The two joined the crowd walking toward the only building in town large enough for the trial.

"Hurry!" Tom warned. "The seats'll be goin' fast. I hear they're gettin' in two justices of the peace besides Neely. They're callin' it a Court of Special Sessions."

"How come you know so much about it?" Jenny asked, quickening her steps.

"I was down here when he got examined by Neely to see if he had to have a trial. They even had him in jail overnight. That's because he didn't have bail money."

"Will the Stowells be here?"

"My guess, he'll be testifyin'," Tom answered shortly.

Tom and Jenny had just wedged themselves into place on one of the narrow benches when the court was brought to order. The judge pounded his gavel on the desk, and Jenny leaned forward, craning her neck to see.

Jenny watched the serious faces of the men clustered at the front of the room. She recognized the man with the white hair and the walking stick. The portly gentleman was there too, and the doctor, taking notes.

On the right side of the justices, the witnesses formed a straggly line on the bench. She recognized Mr. Stowell, but most of the others were strangers to her. She did see Mr. McMaster, and Thompson, who worked for Stowell. He had been one of the men in the group the night Tom had taken her to the diggings.

As she settled back to wait, Jenny recalled that night. Even now she shuddered at the memory of opening her eyes to find that man standing over her with the sword.

The clerk called Joe forward, and Jenny slid out to the end of the bench to study the bright-haired youth as he took his place. The men grouped together, their voices low. Jenny asked Tom, "What are they doin' now?"

"Swearin' in Joe." Behind Tom came a hiss for silence.

They had asked him a question, and he was telling them about his stone: "Back home there's a girl who had a stone. She could look into it and see things nobody else could see. I went to visit her and she let me take a look in hers." Joe's voice had lost its waver and it rose, filling the room with confidence.

"All I could see was a stone, far away but coming close to me. Turned out it was *my* stone. It shone like a light." Again Jenny caught a glimpse of the same strange gleam in his eye she had first seen when she was with Joe in the woods. He paused to take a breath and his voice deepened and dropped. "I could not rest until I found it. I got myself a grub bag and set out. I worked my way, following what I knew to be the direction to the exact location. I knew I would find it, and I did. 'Twas buried under a tree. I dug it up, carried it down to the crick and washed it."

Joe paused, and with his voice deepening again, he said, "I put it in my hat, and lo, I discovered I possessed one of the attributes of deity, an all-seeing eye."

A murmur rose and swept the room. Jenny looked around at the people and then turned back to Joe. Justice Neely was asking him something. With an eloquent sweep of his hand, Joe held up the small chocolate-colored stone, by now familiar to Jenny. Silence settled on the room as the people studied the object.

Close to Jenny came a whisper, "There's those who really do see things in a peep stone. Reckon he's one of them?"

"He'll have to prove the power."

Another whisper asked, "What's he being charged with?"

The reply came, "Being a vagrant, a disorderly person and an imposter."

" 'Tis a shame; he's nothing but a tad. Let him have a little fun."

"Must be something to it, if he's come to trial."

Then Jenny heard Joe speaking again. "Josiah Stowell came to Manchester after me, and I've been working for him, looking for a silver mine and working around the farm. In between times, I've been going to school."

There was a question and the answer came. "He came lookin' for me because he heard I had the gift of seership."

And then the question. "Did you find the mine?"

"No. I persuaded him to give up looking."

Joe Smith sat down, and Josiah Stowell took his place. In the murmur of questions, the voice rose. Justice Neely was speaking. His voice was solemn, but the room was filled with his thundering question. "Josiah Stowell, do you swear before God that you actually believe the defendant is able, with the use of his peep stone, to see objects buried in the ground just as clearly as you can see the objects on this table?"

The old man straightened and, with a determination that set his double chin to wagging, declared, "Your Honor, it isn't only a matter of belief; I positively know that Joseph Smith can see these marvelous things!"

In the uproar, the gavel smote the table and the next witness, Mr. Thompson, was called. "This here fella says to Mr. Stowell that many years ago a band of robbers buried a treasure. They placed a charm over it all by having a sacrifice done, so it couldn't be got at less'n he had what he called a talismanic influence. So they decided to go after it. Joe called for some praying and fasting, and then they set out and commenced to dig." He paused to swallow hard, then continued.

"They found the treasure all right; we heard the shovel hit the box. But the harder they dug, the more it slipped away from them. One fella even managed to get his hand on it before it slid clear away from him. Finally Joe called a council of war against this foe of darkness—spirit, he said it was. We knew it was a lack of faith or something wrong with our thinking, so Joe devised a plan."

There was a gulp and Thompson's voice rose with excitement. "We got a lamb. Stowell knelt down and prayed while Joe slit the lamb's throat and spread the blood around the hole. This was a propitiation to the spirit. But we never did get the money."

A sigh swept the room and Jenny squirmed and looked at Tom. " 'Tweren't the time you was there," he muttered.

As the day warmed, the crowded room grew stuffy. More witnesses were called, and Jenny moved restlessly on the bench. When the last witness had taken his seat, the heads of the justices tilted together.

Justice Neely then slowly got to his feet. His voice droned in the heavy air of the room. Although Jenny strained to understand, his words were meaningless to her until she heard, "We the court find the defendant— guilty as charged."

There was a second of silence, and in the breathless pause Jenny saw Joe leap to his feet and dash through the crowded room. But Jenny's eyes were riveted on the men at the front of the room.

Justice Neely was still standing, hands calm at his side. The other justices hunched over the table just as quietly, watching Joe run. He passed the constable who was sitting beside the door with his chair tilted back against the wall, his hat shading his eyes.

"He's gone," Tom breathed softly. "He's taken leg bail, and I've a notion they don't care a snitch. Reckon we'll never see the likes of him again." There was a twinge of regret in his voice.

Over the sudden babble of voices, Justice Neely shouted, "Court is closed for this session!"

The only sounds in the stifling room were the rustle of skirts and the clatter of heavy boots. Slowly Tom and Jenny got to their feet to follow the crowd out the door. Jenny peered around Tom and saw the justices clustered by the table talking. She measured the distance and studied their broad, black backs. With a quick movement, she turned and dashed to the front of the room. The man with the white hair and the walking stick was saying, "I just can't see crippling the chances of this young fellow. He looks like, given a proper chance, he'll make good. I hope my hunch isn't wrong. Otherwise I'll be regretting this the rest of my life."

"I hope so, too. He was pretty eager to take leg bail once it was suggested. Must have had a few fears—at least he sure could run." The black-coated men moved restlessly and Jenny scooted for the door.

When she caught up with Tom, the crowd was standing in the street, somber-faced and questioning. Tom and Jenny joined the others and watched as the building was locked. They were still waiting as the line of dark coats moved quietly down the street with the constable following along behind. Now his hat was squared on his head and his hunch-shouldered gait made him look like a gnarled guardian angel, a protective shield between the justices and the questioning citizens of South Bainbridge.

When the last man had disappeared from sight, the crowd stirred. "Why do you suppose they went to all that trouble and then just set there and let him run?"

"He weren't much more'n a tad," a sympathetic voice answered. "Those gentlemen are right fatherly. I hear they're feelin' he's a deprived youth who needs a good warnin' to straighten him up."

"I wonder if that's really the case," came a voice from the depths of the crowd. "Is that all he is? There's been a heap of riling up since he's been around. I'll not forget the way those fellas toted Peddler Harper down off the hill, stone-cold."

Jenny squirmed her way through the crowd to see the speaker's face, and the square-shouldered man standing beside him turned to look at her. It was Mark Cartwright. For a moment, Jenny's eyes caught his and she saw the questioning frown.

Now another spoke reluctantly, "I heard a fella say, and I'm not mentioning names, that he asked young Joe if he really could see money and all these wonderful treasures. He said Joe hesitated a bit and then said, 'Between the two of us, I can't see 'em any more than you or anybody else, but a body's gotta make a living.' "

Tom tugged at Jenny. "Let's get along for home." He turned down the street, Jenny trotting to keep up with his long strides. When they had left the town behind, Tom slowed and Jenny caught up with him.

"Did you see that Mark Cartwright?" she asked breathlessly. "He was listenin' to it all, and I don't think he was agreein'."

"You mean about Joe takin' leg bail?" She nodded, and Tom said, " 'Tis always that way. The rich can't be sympathetic about the poor."

Jenny was pondering Tom's words when they turned up the lane toward the Timmons' shack. She looked at the yard, the litter, and the straggle of hens, and her impatience boiled over. Flying at the chickens roosting on the porch and plow and scattered firewood, she whipped her shawl from her shoulders and shouted, "Out, you silly things! You belong in the barn!"

When she returned to Tom, he was watching her with a puckered frown on his face. "What's got into you, girl? Take life as you find it, Jen. You're a woman. That means you make no fuss. Remember your place in life. If you're born to be poor, well then, be content with it."

"And be abidin' this for the rest of my life? Tom, when I see people such as those fellas were, the justices and that Mark Cartwright, it makes me boil up inside—'specially when you talk like they're way up high, beyond the reach of us common folk."

As March slipped into April, the mellowing of springtime moved through the southern part of New York State. Blossoms on the wild plum and apple, dandelions and tiny buttons of meadow flowers added their scent to the newness of grass in the pungent pastureland.

Calves, black and white miniatures, took their places beside their placid mothers. Winter-stained flocks of sheep budded out with new white lambs. Spring rains blackened the woody branches of the trees along the pasture wall, and their halo of green seemed to bind everything together.

Fingers of green moss outlined the northerly edges of the stone walls as if spring had an abundance of green to spare. When Jenny closed her eyes like two tiny slits, it seemed that the green, like paint, was dabbed everywhere.

One by one the older boys had dropped out of school to take their places in the fields. Now the girls went to school with only the very young children. And during recess, Jenny had Mr. Searle all to herself. The request was always the same.

Most often he would nod and point to the line of books on the shelf behind his desk, saying, "If you can't sound them out, ask." Jenny would choose a book and carry it back to her bench.

By late afternoon Jenny would walk slowly homeward, her mind full of the words and pictures. For a short time the books had helped her forget the other troubles that nagged at her thoughts.

Spring had brought a dark threat closer, one the Timmons family had felt all winter—Pa's spring stirring, the yearly urge to move west. But the urge was stronger this year. And over all was the troubling knowledge that Ma would soon be birthing again.

On the homeward walk Nancy talked about the West and Jenny thought with regret of all the books she hadn't been able to read.

"I hear it all," she replied grudgingly to Nancy's excitement. "But you forget the West is full of wild Injuns, with no stores or schools or books." She stopped to slant a look at her older sister's neat hair and patched dress.

"I doubt you'll ever have your dream of gettin' rich and having new frocks."

Nancy stopped in the middle of the path. The expression on her face, Jenny thought, was like being hungry with nothing to fill the hunger. Slowly she turned. Jenny needn't look to know she was seeing the peaceful pasture filled with black and white cows, and the rows of newly turned soil beyond. For just a moment, Jenny felt her spirit soar unfettered. "Maybe it won't be so bad."

Then Nancy turned to her. "Jen, what do you want most of all?"

Jenny answered quickly, and her reply caught even her by surprise. "To learn." Her toes dug down into the loamy, rich soil. "Like this, I want to dig into everything just to see what makes it go. I want to know about all the 'whys.'"

"Is that why you won't leave Pa's book alone?" Jenny's head snapped up and, startled, she nodded. Nancy looked thoughtful for a moment, "You're growing up, Jen. Last year you'd have gone for a stick of candy."

Silently they walked home. Candy. The last time Jenny had thought of candy, Arnold had promised information about Joe. And she had told Tom that she would marry Joe. Her lips curled at her silly, childish proclamation. She still recalled the way Tom had looked at her. He thought she had suddenly gone wild.

"One thing's certain," Jenny spoke out of the silence, "we've seen the last of Joe. When he hightailed out of the courtroom, I doubt he stopped 'til he got back to his ma's."

Nancy turned her green eyes on Jenny. "That happened over three months ago. You're still thinking about him—why?"

Jenny shrugged, but as they walked slowly up the lane toward home, she thought again about Joe and about the green book, wondering if all the promises it made could come true.

She'd told Nancy she wanted to learn. She'd told Tom she didn't want to live like this for the rest of her life. She'd told Joe she wanted to find the secrets of Pa's book. Maybe all those desires were somehow connected—maybe they would all come true together someday. Maybe wishing hard enough and saying it out loud would make it happen.

"I'm still scared," she whispered to herself, "of that glitter in Joe's eye when he talks about the spirits, and of the pictures in Pa's green witchin' book. But—" she paused, taking a deep breath, "I'm not goin' to be a baby about it anymore. If there's power to be had, spirit power to change the way things are, then I'll find it—no matter what!"

6

SUMMER LEAVES WERE turning yellow and drying around the edges when the Timmons' covered wagon creaked down the main street of Manchester, New York.

From the eldest to the youngest, they were silent and slack-jawed as the marvels of the town unfolded before them. When the wagon had nearly reached the end of the main street, Nancy recovered enough to say, "Jen, I don't know where you got your information about the West, but this town is *bonny*; I could stay here forever!"

" 'Tain't the West," Pa muttered, gawking about with the rest of them, "but it's gonna have to do for now. I'm 'bout tuckered out."

Jenny's attention snapped back to the wagon, and she looked from her bleary-eyed father to her mother leaning against the wagon seat. The sight of her drawn face and swollen stomach tightened the fearful knot in Jenny's throat. Just for a moment, as she glanced at her father, anger surged through her. Quickly she turned her face before he could see the feelings that were becoming harder to hide.

Nancy touched her mother's shoulder. "It's far enough for now. Ma's not feeling up to another mile."

Jenny spoke slowly, trying to control the hope in her voice. "There's a school, and that's some kind of a big mill ahead. Pa, if we were to stay here, we could all go to school—even Matty's old enough now. Maybe—" She couldn't say *job* and *work* and *money,* but the thoughts were there. He frowned, glancing at her mother, and hauled back on the reins.

Tom finally tipped the balance in favor of staying on in Manchester. Pa had stopped the wagon beside the livery stable to wait for him—herding the milk cow kept Tom lagging far behind the wagon.

When he finally caught up, the pleased smile on his face slowly turned into a frown of concern as he looked at his mother, but his words were for his father. "The fella down the street asked me if we were stayin'. He says there's a place over two streets for let. Man at the livery stable owns it. He's lookin' for a hand. Name's Harris. I'm of a mind to see what he'll offer."

Before nightfall, the Timmons were moved into the small log cabin on a shady street. The cow and the crate of chickens were settled in the make-shift barn. While Tom and Jenny unloaded the wagon, Nancy swept a season's litter of dead leaves and dust out the door.

Later Tom straightened the sagging stovepipe and started a fire in the little stove. Now Jenny watched Pa. He was hesitating in the doorway and she wondered what excuse he would find. He finally said, "I'm of a mind to mosey on down the street and see if I can find a piece of glass for that broken window." Ma bit her lip and turned away.

Before she could stop them, Jenny said the words Ma had given up on: "We can get along without glass for right now. Why don't you just get some bread at that baker's shop and stay clear of the tavern."

His mouth gaped with astonishment, and Jenny brushed past him. Her impulsive words had startled her beyond fear. Maybe they had startled him beyond response. Jenny, stiff with remembered pain, waited for the blow that didn't come.

When Pa disappeared down the street, Tom turned to Jenny. "Your smart talk ain't usin' good sense."

Ma added, "Jen, don't be rilin' him. It just makes it worse." Jenny stared up at her mother, still unable to admit ownership of the words that had burst from her lips. Nancy clutched the broom, and Tom frowned.

Slowly Ma sat down on the chair Tom placed for her, saying, "Jenny, your sass ain't makin' life easier for any of us. What's got into you, child?"

Very soon, while the golden days of autumn were still warm and before the crystal ice began lining the streams, Ma felt stronger and was out getting acquainted. Jenny and Nancy took turns going with her. Wrapped in her old black shawl to hide her bulging abdomen, though it was some-times warm enough to bead perspiration on her lip, Ma slowly strolled down the streets and investigated every shop.

One day when it was Jenny's turn to walk with Ma, she noted her flushed face and said, "Ma, I'll carry the shawl."

Ma's face flushed even brighter. "Lands no, child. With a family this size, I don't want to be pitied afore I even know my neighbors."

Jenny remained quiet, thinking new thoughts about being poor and having a pa like they had. She looked curiously at Ma, trying to see her as the neighbors would see her, but she couldn't get past the rusty old shawl and the faded calico squeezed tight over her body. Tired eyes were always ready to beg the pardon of the nearest person. Today she wore a timid smile, half in hiding until called upon.

When they stopped at the first gate, Ma hesitated, waiting for the woman sweeping her steps to look up. She was studying the neat house, and the frock the woman wore. Jenny knew Ma was calculating her chances of finding sewing. She also knew Ma was getting ready to pick at the woman's thoughts. Jenny remembered from the past that Ma would come home with a pocketful of facts. Like Matt collecting his marbles, she examined each one and carefully guarded it.

While Ma leaned over the fence and talked, Jenny noted how the apple tree bent under the load of shiny red apples. Her quick eyes took in the row of marigolds along the garden path. With another part of her mind, Jenny was admiring the way Ma was picking her store of facts from the woman, neat and quick—*like apples off that tree,* Jenny noted.

The woman said, "Camp meeting? My, but we've had them. There's one scheduled before the end of the month." She turned to wave her hand. "Over yonder there's a clearing, just the other side of the meetinghouse. Already they're fixing up a brush arbor. Don't know the fella's name who's coming. Don't matter much. People will either come to hear them all or they won't come to hear a one."

She turned back, leaning on her broom. "Me, I like them all. Gives a body something to do. My family's grown so's there's not much to keep me busy." Jenny saw her eyes move over the bulging black shawl.

Jenny pushed closer to the fence and said, "I'm goin' to school this fall; they're talkin' at recess time about some of the goings-on. A bunch went to Sodus Bay to see the Shakers. It sounded like a fun time, watchin' the dancin' around and such. The big girls were whisperin' and laughin', but they wouldn't tell me why."

Ma's face flushed as they walked toward the shops. "Jen," she remonstrated as they hurried on, "you don't go makin' fun of religion when you don't know how a body believes."

"Does it matter how a body believes?" Jenny asked. " 'Sides, I didn't know I was makin' fun. It was just strange. Lettie was talkin' about some of the other goings-on. She says that last year the schoolteacher, his name's John Samuel Thompson, had a vision. He told folks he saw Christ and he talked to Him. Another fella said there's a man over in Amsterdam, New York, who'd talked with God and was told every denomination of Christians is corrupt, and two-thirds of all the people livin' on the earth are about to be destroyed."

Ma shivered, then said firmly, "One thing's certain. Now that we're livin' in a town where there's a sizable church and the circuit riders get around regular like, we're goin' to be gettin' ourselves into church." Her voice dropped nearly to a whisper as she said, "Your pa don't cotton to gettin' salvation, but he was raised to know better."

Jenny was still wondering about "getting salvation" two weeks later as the evening of the first revival meeting approached. It seemed everyone in town was going. They talked about it at school and even Pa and Tom had promised Ma they would go.

That first evening, the sun was dropping behind the trees when the people started across town to the clearing behind the church. The Timmons joined the crowd, carrying shawls and quilts to pad the rough benches.

As they took their places, Jenny saw a black-coated man wearing a somber expression. Another man carried a shiny horn. When the man began to play the horn and the people began to sing, Jenny poked her mother and asked, pointing, "What's that?"

"The mourners' bench; now hush and don't ask questions. You'll see all soon enough."

After the singing, Jenny watched the somber-faced man open the black book, brace his feet, and lean toward the audience. When quietness stretched to the edges of the clearing and the only sound was raspy breathing and the chirping of crickets, the man began to speak.

He was holding the book high, but he didn't look at it. The words rolled from his tongue like music. " 'For God so loved the world, that he gave his only begotten Son, that whosoever believeth in him should not perish, but have everlasting life.' 'For the wages of sin is death; but the gift of God is eternal life through Jesus Christ our Lord.' 'For by grace are ye saved through faith; and that not of yourselves: it is the gift of God: not of works, lest any man should boast.' "

Jenny leaned across her mother, "*Grace,* that's pretty, isn't it? If you get a little girl, please name her Grace."

"Shush!" Ma's hand covered Jenny's mouth and her eyes were stern. Jenny was soon lost in contemplation as her mind drifted from one unfamiliar word to another.

The images these new words evoked were ethereal and meaningless, but she noticed their impact on those around her.

When Ma first began to tremble and Pa shuffled restlessly, Jenny sensed the mood of the crowd and the mounting tension. Often enough she had heard Pa say "hell," but now the man up front was wrapping the word in smoke and fire while the audience stirred uneasily.

Day after day the camp meetings went on and the tension in the town continued to build. Emotions were unleashed that varied from fear to joy, sorrow to happiness. And while the man with the book built pictures in Jenny's mind and poured the word-music over her, she saw Pa tremble and eventually refuse to accompany them to the meetings. She saw Nancy walk down the path to the mourners' bench and watched the tight sullen expression on Tom's face.

Suddenly the meetings were over, the leaves dropped from the trees, and ice skimmed the water pail. Warm emotions disappeared like autumn, and life returned to being ice-rimmed and cold.

And while Jenny was still frowning over it and trying to understand all she had seen and heard, there was now a settling back into the same old patterns.

The neighbor down the way, Mrs. Barfield, explained it all. Her marigolds were now black nubs, and both apples and leaves had disappeared from the tree. She said, with a touch of discontent in her voice. "Just like always. Expectation greater than the goods delivered. Them men talk with a great deal of steam, like kneeling there in the sawdust is the greatest thing ever happened to a body. Seems those kneeling think so too—for about a week or so. Then life's back to normal except for a few who try to go around convertin' the rest of us, just like we didn't really get converted in the first place.

"It's too bad the excitement don't last. That's what we're wanting. Oh, well, long as we escape hell, I guess that's all that matters. The preachers come around often enough to take care of the seekers. Seems it would be nicer, though, if the excitement would just last the winter." She shivered. Hesitating before she turned back to her house, she added, "Now, take them Shakers and some of those strange religions springing up all over the country. I don't cotton to them. There's too much in the name of religion that isn't. But, somehow, they end up makin' the rest of us decent folks wish we could share some of what enthuses them . . . people. I guess we're never happy."

The little rented house behind the livery stable now had the new baby; then Pa landed a job.

In the evenings after school, Jenny rocked the cradle and reflected that it was just as well little James was fretful. It kept her busy and seemed to ease her own restlessness a little, besides allowing her to read from time to time. Life at home was easier, now that Pa was working at the blast furnace. He seemed to be more content with himself and didn't take his frustration out on her.

Jenny, Nancy, Dorcas, and Matt were going to school. Tom was working at the livery stable, and Ma was sewing for some of the ladies they had met at church.

As Nancy had said, Manchester was a goodly town. It boasted pleasant homes on tree-lined streets, shops, a school, and—to Jenny the most important thing of all—there was a library. The town also had a woolen mill, a flour mill, and a paper mill, as well as the blast furnace where Pa worked.

On Sundays, the people donned their best clothes and paraded through the village on their way to the Presbyterian church. That is, most did. Tom didn't, and Pa didn't. And Jenny rebelled. "Jenny," Tom asked, "what's got into you?"

She felt the same kind of discontent that Mrs. Barfield had talked about, but Jenny saw it differently than Ma did. "It's not fair," she protested. "The one day I have to read, Ma makes me go to church."

She could have said it was boring, but she kept her silence while Ma talked about reading the Bible and Pa nodded his head in agreement. Jenny was separated, standing apart in her mind, knowing they would never understand. Even Nancy and Dorcas were lined up with serious faces and puckered frowns. To Jenny, the glance Ma threw at them seemed like a pat of approval.

Later, Tom repeated his question with a furrowed brow. He was milking the cow, and Jenny was pitching straw down to the pigpen. "Jen, what's got into you?" Jenny turned to look at him. The thoughts from Pa's green book stirred in her, and his question made the words burst from her. "Tom, aren't you hankerin' for more than this?"

He lifted his head from the cow's flank, and Jenny met his startled expression with a bravely lifted chin. She watched his eyes change, admitting the secrets they shared, and she went on in a whisper, "It's like you get a taste and then this isn't enough."

"Then I'm not the only one," he said slowly. After a moment he continued reluctantly, "Jen, you're such a young'un. How do you come to have such thoughts?" She could only shake her head, not quite daring to put it into words. The feelings the book aroused in her were frightening, but she was fascinated and attracted nevertheless.

"Are you thinkin' of what we were doin' last year?" He studied her intently. "With Joe, diggin' for money?" She nodded.

"You got a likin' for that in a hurry." Tom spoke thoughtfully. "It ain't usual for the womenfolk to be that interested. Leastwise, the only one I know of is Lucy Smith."

"The only Lucy Smith I know is that little old lady at church."

He nodded. "Joe's ma."

"Joe Smith's? You mean she goes diggin'?"

He shrugged, "Naw, just interested."

"I didn't know Joe came from around here," she said slowly as she plucked the straw from her hair. "Smith is a pretty common name."

Tom nodded. "He's from here. You probably go to school with most of the young'uns in the family. Best get acquainted."

The next afternoon, walking home from school by herself, Jenny mulled over the restlessness she recognized in Tom. Her feelings were colored by a special kinship to him. She knew he was feeling the tug, too. She yearned to talk to him about Pa's book, but there was always the chance he would let it slip to Pa.

Jenny trembled, recalling the last time she had dared sneak the book from the rafters. Pa had nearly caught her. *Seems a body'd share it,* she reflected, even as she puzzled over the strange excitement that ran through her when she read the book. The feelings were akin to the ones she felt when she and Tom had gone to the diggings.

Abruptly Jenny realized she was already in front of the dry-goods store. Even as she stood there, she knew where her half-formed thoughts were going to take her. Quickly she turned away from her home and ran down the country lane. Earlier, Tom had pointed the way to the Smiths' cottage.

Though it was late and nearly time for chores, Jenny cut across the plowed field and headed into the trees beyond. She ran as fast as she could. Every minute saved meant more time with the woman named Lucy Smith.

Rounding a curve in the dim corridor of trees, Jenny caught her toe on a root and plunged headlong into the bushes. As she struck the ground, the bushes erupted with a flurry of movement. Gasping for breath, she stared upward at the unexpected flash of light. Heavy boots landed in front of her face. Shoving at the earth, she managed to push herself upright. She stopped, terror-stricken: a sheath of metal gleamed just inches from her nose.

"You're Tom Timmons' sister, ain't you?" the man barked. Then settling back on his heels and putting the sword on the ground, he continued. "Why you nosin' around?"

Gasping for breath, she shook her head. The hard expression on his face softened. "Scared the livin' daylights out o' you, didn't I?" Jenny examined her torn stocking and bleeding knee and didn't dare answer. "I'm Hyrum Smith. Come on, I'll have Ma fix up that knee. What you doin' out in the middle of the woods, anyhow?" He grasped her hand and pulled her to her feet.

Jenny tried moving her leg as she looked around. Just beyond Hyrum's shoulder she saw freshly turned earth. Glancing at the sword he held, she asked, "Been diggin'?"

He shook his head. "Them's old diggin's. Come along to the house." He added, "There's lots more diggin's around here."

"Did you find any treasure in them?" He shook his head. Shoving the sword into the sheath strapped to his waist, he explained, "Since we first moved here, we've been diggin' in the vicinity. The whole place is covered with holes."

When they reached the cabin and she was settled beside the table, she looked at the ring of curious eyes that surrounded her, and Jenny realized her problem was solved. Running through the woods, she had been wondering how she would explain her visit. It wasn't necessary now.

Lucy Smith talked constantly as she swabbed the blood from Jenny's leg. By the time the soothing ointment was applied, Jenny felt she knew everything there was to know about the Smiths.

The room was full of Joe Smith's relations, his sisters and brothers. Beside the fire stood a tall, gaunt man watching her. Their eyes met, and Jenny realized she had seen him in South Bainbridge.

The man with the sword was Joseph's older brother. She eyed the sword, trying to hide her intrigue. Hyrum must have guessed her curiosity. He pulled up a chair and held out the sword for her to see. Jenny hugged herself with excitement as he began to explain the markings. It was just as the book had described. Soon Lucy Smith was adding her comments, telling Jenny about the markings on the sheath.

"See this?" she pointed. "It's all to do with breakin' the charms the spirits have placed. You really need the sword to drive away the demon spirits. There's lots out there to be learned before a body can hope to be successful."

"Successful," Jenny repeated slowly. "You mean gettin' power?"

Lucy turned to peer at Jenny. "Lands, child, you set me back! I didn't expect such a young one with the knowledge. Yes, power. There's lots of hard work involved in gettin' it. Right now we're feelin' the lack and wonderin' if it's worth our time to study out Masonry to get the faculty of Abrac."

Lucy Smith leaned close to Jenny. "We're not wantin' anyone to think we spend all our time at this. But 'tis hard work to get everything to come out right. I keep tellin' them they gotta concentrate on the faculty of Abrac."

Jenny leaned forward and whispered, "What's that?"

"Abrac is a magic word. Some folks call it a formula, a way to release power. Better and more powerful than a charm. You put it on an amulet in order to work magic. See, you must learn what's necessary to make the word work for you. I'm guessin' that's why it's so hard to come by. I been hearin' that the Masons know how to conceal the way to get the power, so we're goin' to have to get on the good side of them if we want the power. When we get it, there's no stoppin' us. Too bad the Masons won't let womenfolk into their secret society. Guess we'll just have to let the men handle the problem."

"Abrac, is that—" Jenny gulped, but she must ask the question. "Is that why Joe couldn't get the money the Spaniards hid up?"

Lucy was nodding and murmuring, "Very likely. See, the word is from others, from Abracadabra and Abraxis. There's a lot more we need to know if we're to have success."

As Jenny got to her feet to leave, Joe's father addressed her. "So you're from South Bainbridge, huh?" She nodded. "Did ya go to the trial?" Again she nodded. He studied her for a moment, then continued, "Then you heard him tell everybody about how he got his seer stone. When he told me, I wasn't right thrilled about it all. The whole thing left a bad taste in people's mouths. They got the wrong idea. See, it mortifies us that people don't get the right picture. What he has is a mighty gift from God. It's terrible to think that the only outlet for it right now is in the findin' of filthy lucre, or earthly treasures. I'm prayin' constantly that the heavenly Father'll show His will concerning the use of this gift. He needs to illuminate Joe's heart, make the boy see what He has in store for him."

He stopped and turned his piercing gaze on Jenny again. "Now, I don't know why I'm a-wastin' my time tellin' a slip of a girl like you all these things big people needs to be worryin' about. But there it is, and you be a-doin' as you see fit.—Kinda like the fella, huh?"

One of Joe's sisters snickered, "Aw, Pa. She's just a babe, and you'll be a-tellin' her that all the gals like Joe."

" 'Tis true." Mrs. Smith got to her feet. "Even if he's my son, I admit he's a good-lookin' boy and all the girls know it. Now, Jen, please come back to visit."

At the end of January, Tom came home from the livery stable with his news. "Jen, you'll never guess what." He slid into his place at the table. "Joe Smith's back in town, goin' to be workin' with his pa."

Tom paused to take a bite of bread and Jenny's heart leaped. He added, "He's come with a wife. Married Isaac Hale's daughter, Emma. You remember Hale from the trial? He's the one from Harmony that's known for his huntin'."

"I remember," Jenny answered slowly, stunned by the news. "Only, I didn't think he liked Joe very much."

"Married!" Nancy exclaimed.

"Aw, come on," Tom retorted, "don't be tellin' me you're soft on him too!" He turned to his father, "I've never seen the like. Every girl in the place fancies herself in love with Joe Smith. You'd think he was the only good-lookin' fella in town."

"What's he goin' to be doin' with his pa?" Ma asked.

"I have an idea they'll be gettin' back into the money-diggin' business," Tom answered. " 'Tis the only business I've heard tell them doin'."

"He been doin' good at it?" Pa asked, leaning across the table to look at Tom.

Tom shrugged, "I don't know. Old man Smith says he's been doin' it for thirty years."

"Is that so," Pa said, chewing. " 'Spect he's knowledgeable. The readin' I've been doin' of late leads me to believe there's profit to be had along that line. Might be a good idea for me to get acquainted with the old man."

Ma's spoon clattered to the table. "Now, you know better than that." She was chiding again. "Have you ever in your life heard of a body gettin' anything except trouble from that kind of business?"

The following Sunday Jenny went to church, but she spent most of the service trying to see whether Joe and his new bride were sitting in the pew beside Mrs. Smith, Hyrum and Samuel. Nancy noticed her peeking and whispered, "If you're looking for the newlyweds, well, they're not here." She poked Jenny and leaned closer. "Little ones like you don't get soft on big strapping fellas like Joe."

" 'Soft' like you and Prudence and the rest at school in South Bainbridge? I've never seen a bunch of girls as silly as you were last year," Jenny whispered back scornfully.

"You're just jealous you weren't big enough for a fella to notice you."

"I'm just too smart to line up behind the barn and play silly kissin' games with those slobby boys just to get kissed by Joe," Jenny hissed back, and was mollified when Nancy blushed.

7

WITH THE COMING of January 9, 1827, her thirteenth birthday, Jenny experienced a growing consciousness of newness in her life. Trying hard to understand the feeling, she labeled it happiness and hugged it to herself.

The feeling was especially intense one day as she walked home from school. Winter was still hard upon the country, bringing bone-chilling dampness and vicious ice storms. But this day, the weather couldn't diminish the bliss that enfolded her.

She lifted her head high and allowed her mother's old shawl to slip back on her shoulders. Looking around as she walked homeward, seeing the stores, the library, even the blast furnace where Pa worked, Jenny felt for a moment what it was like to have everything she wanted. She gloried in the feeling. The best part of her life was school and the library. But there was another element. Her family was happy. She knew it by looking into their faces, listening to Tom whistle. Even Pa seemed at peace with himself.

During the remainder of the winter, the birthday feeling stayed with Jenny. She was content with her world of school, library, and home.

About springtime, when Jenny put down the latest library book long enough to notice, she saw changes in her family. Nancy was as tall as Ma. She walked and talked like a lady. When Jenny compared her own grubbiness with Nancy's new appearance, she was conscious only that she no longer knew this Nancy.

Ma and Nancy were often seen with their heads together. The new scholars, Dorcas and Matty, were becoming happy companions. And the picture of Jenny rocking James's cradle with one hand while the other held a book was also very familiar.

Just before winter gave way to spring, Jenny saw, for the first time, the maple trees in the valley being tapped for their precious sap. Soon the aromatic woodsmoke flavored with maple wrapped like a scarf of sweetness around the town.

When the snow slipped back to reveal the meadows carpeted in gentle greens, Pa began to show his yearly urge to move on. As usual, his unrest riled the family. But this year, Jenny, still wrapped in winter's peace, apart and separated, did not respond to the unrest. She held her silence as she watched her mother's uneasy frown and Tom's eternal pacing. Even James, who had grown into a plump, placid baby, responded fretfully.

"Teethin'," Ma declared. Matty and Dorcas just stayed in their corner and Nancy kept herself busy with stitching.

When it was time for plowing, all Pa could talk about was the West with its promise of virgin soil. Over and over they heard the arguments, and knew they were true. "Look at old man Smith," he said. "He told me hisself that when he came here in 1816 he paid near 'bout six dollars for an acre. If he'd gone to Ohio he could have had land just as good for a dollar and a quarter an acre. 'Sides, you know yourselves, the whole East is in depression." Desire for those fertile fields lay heavy upon him, so heavy that this year there would be no turning him back.

From her sanctuary behind the dishpan, Jenny listened, and finally she awakened again to reality, and her heart began to ache. It was impossible to believe there would be another town like Manchester. Just closing her eyes made her see the long line of library books she had not yet read.

At night she would kneel beside the loft window and whisper, "Star light, star bright—" Then she would pause, unable to put that nameless wish into words.

Then one cool, breezy evening, Tom spoke, his voice wavering only slightly. "I'm not goin'. I'm growed, and it's time I found my own way. I'd rather work at the livery for a year or so, then I'll . . ."

Studying his face, Jenny could only guess at the things he dared not say. But secretly she was applauding him. For the first time, Tom had stood up to Pa. As she stared at him, he straightened his shoulders, and a hint of a smile gleamed in his eye. Jenny didn't need to grin at him; he knew how she felt. She turned away, sad for herself but glad for him.

Pa watched them all for a moment. Jenny felt his eyes upon her. He broke the silence. "So be it. I can't be a-hangin' on to you if you've made up your mind. The rest of us will be goin'." Thoughtfully he studied Tom and then added, "It'll be lonesome for you. You'll be needin' to find a place to board, and that'll cut into your wages." But Tom's jaw was set, and Pa said no more.

On the warmest day of the spring, with the door open wide to catch any passing breeze, Jenny worked in the stifling cabin. She was fretfully begrudging the errand which had taken Nancy to the store. As she wiped perspiration from her face, she was even begrudging her mother's tasks outdoors as she washed and hung laundry on the bushes.

But while Jenny was lifting pans from the high shelf, she found the book.

"Oh, there it is!" she exclaimed with satisfaction. Hugging the book like an old, dear friend, she settled down on a bench and stroked the dusty cover. "For sure I thought he'd chucked you for good."

She studied the cover. It wasn't like the dark, somber book that belonged to her mother; this one was bright green with the figure of a woman on it, outlined in gold. Jenny traced her finger over the shiny illustration, again wondering about it. She ached with longing to open it, to read those enticing passages. Jenny ran her fingers over the gold letters of the title, *The Greater Key of Solomon.*

She peeked once, then was immediately lost to her surroundings. "Raphael," she murmured to herself. "I wonder who he is?" Her finger followed the words down the page, fumbled and turned the next page, and the next. The title of one chapter caught her attention, and excitement coursed through her as she continued, "This chapter is about how to render yourself master of a treasure possessed by a spirit. That's what Joe was tryin' to do. I wonder if he's read this book."

As she continued to stare at the page before her, she recalled her father talking about reading the book. For a moment her heart contracted as a picture arose in her mind: Jenny and her father, miraculously changed, working together as friends with the book between them. Jenny and her father, together with Joe Smith, digging up treasure—gold, silver, more than her mind could conceive. Her eager eyes again sought the words.

When the page before her dimmed, she realized the afternoon was gone. Then to her horror she discovered that the darker shadow was Pa! By his silence she knew he had been watching for some time.

"Why you lick your lips like that when you read the words?" he asked. He had lifted the razor strap down from the wall beside the washbasin. Jenny's vision exploded like a bubble. She tried to focus on the battered tin bucket. "Answer me! Why can't you leave my book alone?" he shouted.

His first blow knocked the book across the room. It spun out of sight under the edge of the bed quilt. She tried to see it even as she willed it to stay hidden.

When the blows had ceased and the scent of his alcohol-laden breath filled the room, when the blood was warm and wet on her legs, Jenny knew she would be staying in Manchester when Pa and the others moved on.

When Tom saw Jenny's bleeding legs and listened to her, he turned and without a word left. When he returned, he had a promise of a position for Jenny with the Martin Harris family. Harris owned the livery stable where

Tom worked. She took comfort in that. *It's a link to Tom,* she thought as he told her Mrs. Harris needed a girl.

June found Jenny settled in her new home. Some days she regretted her position as hired girl in the household, especially when she stirred the wrath of Martin Harris. While his stern words condemned the dust in the corner and the weeds in the garden, his wife patted Jenny's shoulder, saying, "Never mind a word he says. He knows we couldn't be gettin' along without you."

It was true. Mrs. Harris was lame this spring, and limped slowly about her house and garden. They expected Jenny to fill the gap.

When her family had left, Jenny had watched the wagon lurch away from the little house behind the livery stable, carrying them away from her. As she thought about that scene, even now, the tears blurred that final picture. If it hadn't been for the pain in her bruised body and Tom's restraining hand on her shoulder, she would have run after the wagon, begging for her old place beside Nancy. If the tears hadn't filled her eyes, would she have been able to find in Ma's face the tenderness she longed for?

She recalled the day Pa had used the razor strap on her. She could still see how Ma had turned away when she saw the blood. Tom had washed her legs and rubbed in the ointment. Not Ma, not Nancy. Had her sin been too much? She didn't need to be told they thought she deserved the hurts.

Nowadays it helped to have Tom and the hard tasks at her new home. They wiped out the miserable, lonesome thoughts.

Tom had been given a spot in the loft at the Harris home, and he took his board with them. During the evening hours, he split logs and stacked them under the eaves to pay for his keep.

As the summer passed, Jenny continued to nurse the one secret she hadn't dared share with even Tom. She promised herself that she would. But as time drifted by, she forgot how Ma had turned away and how Nancy had scorned her. The guilty secret didn't seem as frightening nor as important now.

Come evenings, Jenny took out Pa's green book and looked at it, no longer trembling with guilt for stealing it. She still promised herself once in a while that she would share her secret with Tom.

As autumn approached, the Sabbath day became a high spot in Jenny's week. After the breakfast dishes were done and the dinner roast shoved into the oven, Jenny was free to change her dress and go with Mrs. Harris to the Presbyterian church.

Not that church had become important—however, for this one day Jenny would be beyond the disapproving eye of Mr. Harris.

On that first Sabbath, Mrs. Harris had seen Jenny's perplexed frown as Martin Harris settled down on the porch, still wearing his carpet slippers. In the wagon Lucy Harris snapped the reins along the backs of the team and tried to explain her husband's newest beliefs. Jenny's eyes grew round with wonder.

"Why does he keep joinin' so many churches?" she asked. "I've heard of the Quakers, but what's a Restorationist and a Universalist?"

Mrs. Harris shrugged and forced a weak smile, but Jenny could see the pain behind her eyes. "Child," she said, "some people just never seem to be satisfied with settlin' for the truth. My husband Martin, he's a good man, been raised with true religion. But he's so restless, he's never made a commitment of himself to the truth. So he keeps lookin' for something new—and he always seems to find it."

Jenny stared at her new mistress, dumbfounded. Her own mother had taught her to honor the Bible and to read it instead of Pa's green book. But no one had ever talked about truth in this way.

"You mean," she stammered, "there's just one truth, one power?"

They had reached the church, and Mrs. Harris turned and looked Jenny square in the eye. "Lots of powers, child—some good, some bad. Only one truth." Her eyes softened. "Maybe someday you'll understand." She turned and limped ahead to find her friends.

In church, Jenny was becoming conscious of the people around her. She heard the pastor read the black book, using words she still couldn't understand. But her neighbors and school friends, the grocer and the man who had worked with Pa at the foundry were all changed. On the Sabbath day laughing faces were sober, thoughtful. School-yard folly was forgotten. Dirty shirts were exchanged for clean, and tousled hair was neatly braided.

Somehow there was a tie between this place, the words that man was reading, the serious faces under smoothed hair, and the truth of which Mrs. Harris spoke. She saw responses from the parson's listeners, and the quiet atmosphere of the church became shivery with intense feeling. Although Jenny didn't quite recognize it, the feeling awed, even frightened her.

Sometimes she was nudged into thinking thoughts about sin, about evil, about her soul, about heaven and hell.

She pushed aside that sense of foreboding and thought of her desire for spirit power. There were lots of powers, Lucy Harris had said. Which power, she wondered, was the one she wanted?

For some reason she couldn't understand the parson's words about sin and evil. But it made Jenny think of the stolen green book, the pictures of spirits, and the words of power. Again she felt the mingled fear and fascination and remembered the strange glitter in Joe Smith's eyes. *He knows,* she thought, *of the gold of the treasures guarded by the power of the spirits.*

Often at night, when Jenny was in her room under the eaves, seeing the moonlight, listening to the crickets and feeling alone, she found she couldn't sleep. Wide-eyed she would lie in the drift of moonlight, missing the sounds of her family's soft breathing in the room, lonesome for the warmth of Dorcas beside her.

One night, when the moon was high and the Harrises had set the rafters to trembling with their snoring, Jenny heard the creak of the barn door. She crept to the window, heard the distant clank of shovel against stone, and saw dim shadows slip through the yard.

The next day she followed Tom to the barn. "Tom, you're diggin' nights. Why can't I go with you?"

He looked astonished, then glanced quickly around. "Hush. I don't want Mrs. Harris to know. Look, Jen, I gotta get it across to you; this isn't fun, it's serious business. We can't risk a young'un messin' it up again."

"You're still blamin' me for not findin' the treasure over at South Bainbridge, aren't you?"

"Well, let's put it this way," he said shortly. "There's enough chance you did it that none of us will risk it again."

She studied him curiously for a moment before she said, "Look, I'm older now. Trust me. From the way you said that, there must be some in the bunch knowin' about last time. There's no one else around except the Smiths."

He nodded, "You're right." He closed his lips tightly and turned to lift a forkful of hay to the cows. Jenny studied his expression. Tom wasn't going to say more.

She tried to find a way to break past the barrier. "Tom, you're shuttin' me out on purpose. We're all the family there is now." She let the lonesome feelings tremble through her voice.

He rumpled her hair. "Aw, Jen. You're the best sis I could have, but you can't be out followin' the fellas."

"Do you really think you'll be findin' something this time?"

He said nothing. In frustration she turned away.

The matter would probably have ended with Tom's stubborn silence if it hadn't been for the trip to Palmyra. It stirred afresh her desire to be in on the digging.

The Harris farm lay tucked between the two villages of Manchester and Palmyra, New York. Jenny knew Manchester well—it was a wonderful place with its shops and mills. But she had never been to Palmyra.

The day Martin Harris declared he was going to Palmyra, Lucy Harris elected to go with him. Mr. Harris sighed in resignation. "Might as well take Jenny. I'll not have the time to tote you around, so ye better have company."

Martin Harris was unusually talkative on the ride. Watching his face as he described the building of the Erie Canal, Jenny was surprised to see his dreamy, contented expression. It was unlike the employer she had come to fear.

When the wagon reached the Palmyra side of the bridge, he said, "This is a great country, this United States of America. Just watch. The nation will be great because our democracy is based on the laws of nature. We'll steadily become more perfect and our people will be purified. One day the whole world will come running after us to follow our example." He waved his whip at the canal. "This Erie Canal is part of the dream. Sure, it costs, but it makes progress possible on a grand scale. It costs in lives and money for us to be moving westward. It's brave men doing it. There's not a power on earth can stop the progress once the Lord wills it. Manifest Destiny, they are calling it. This canal's been open less'n two years, but look at the boats."

When they reached Palmyra Jenny gaped at the crowds, whispering, "It's so big! Bet it's bigger'n New York City."

Harris laughed. "Less'n four thousand people." But sobering, he said, "That's a goodly lot though, and it's a fair town. You ladies be at your shoppin' and get back to the stables. I wanna be outta here before mid-afternoon."

As they climbed out of the wagon, Jenny spotted one of the stores and exclaimed, "Look! That shop has just books!"

Mrs. Harris glanced around and said, "Oh my, it does. Funny I never noticed it before." She studied Jenny curiously and added, "I don't claim to be all that interested in reading. If there's time later, I'll let you have a look."

With her mind filled with that one thought, Jenny trailed around the shops with Mrs. Harris, trying to be patient.

Finally, Jenny's arms loaded with parcels and Mrs. Harris's bag bulging, the woman announced her shopping completed and they turned toward the stables. Halfway back, Mrs. Harris stopped to talk to a friend. When Jenny shifted from foot to foot, the woman said, "Be off to the book shop, and then go on to the wagon."

When Jenny stopped, breathless and flustered, in the doorway of the bookstore, she could only fidget and sniff deeply of the dust and leather and ink.

"Yes, young lady, what would you like to see?" Jenny looked past a very white shirt and black string tie to a round face as friendly as the parson's. She smiled at him.

"Oh, everything," Jenny whispered. "Do you mind if I look? I'll be careful." She rubbed her sweaty palms on her dress.

He chuckled. "You're not the usual kind. Help yourself," he pointed to the double rows of bookcases, and Jenny eased herself between them, wondering where to begin. There were leather books and cloth-bound ones, dark covers and bright. Some wore strange titles she didn't understand. She also saw familiar books, ones she had read at school and at the library in Manchester, the ones the librarian had called classics.

As Jenny moved slowly down the aisle, touching books with a cautious finger, yet not daring to pull them from the shelf, a bright green cover caught her eye. Hardly believing what she saw, she tipped it out of the shelf. It was the same from green cover to the gold outlines on the front.

The shopkeeper was at her elbow now. "You wouldn't want the likes of that book," he said gently. "It's not for fine young ladies."

She turned. "Why not?" she asked, surprised. Her hand still held the book. "It's a bonny book, all green with the gold lady."

He cleared his throat and continued to smile kindly at her. Leaning closer, he whispered, "It's a book about magic, witchcraft, and the like. Now, if I were to have my say, such a book wouldn't even be in town, but there's some who set great store by such things. Nowadays we don't hear much said against such teachings, but frankly I believe it is wrong, terribly so. I think this treasure-digging and using seer stones to hunt for lost articles or for telling fortunes is of the devil. But the owner, Mr. Anderson, insists we must provide what the people want."

"The book's bad?" Jenny asked, still fingering it.

His smile was gentle, his eyes full of concern. "It's of the devil. Satan is behind the likes of such stuff."

"Satan," Jenny stated flatly. She pulled the book down and turned the pages. "It's talkin' about power, knowledge, how to get things you want. Isn't that good?"

He looked astonished. "Child," he said, "there's power, and there's power. Not all power is good." His sensitive eyes took her in, and he was about to continue when the door opened. He turned and moved toward the front of the shop.

Jenny slowly replaced the book. She frowned, thinking about the strange manner of the little man, hearing the echo of Mrs. Harris's words. The booming voice from the front of the store caught her attention. As she looked up she heard the man ask, "You have some Masonic books?"

"Right this way." Beneath the clomp of boots, Jenny heard the shopkeeper ask, "Why would you be needing them?"

After a pause the man said, "I'm joining the lodge."

Suddenly Jenny recognized the voice. She popped around the corner of the bookcase. "Hyrum!"

They left the shop together. Jenny was chattering, running to keep up with Hyrum, when they met Mrs. Smith and the Harrises talking together on the street corner.

Martin Harris looked up at Hyrum and said, "Your mother's tellin' me you're about to join the Masonic lodge."

Mrs. Smith reached for the package Hyrum carried. "You found a book?" Her fingers picked nervously at the paper before she tucked it into her bag. She met Jenny's gaze. "Hyrum's been tellin' me about how this Masonic book might be helpin' a mite. He says we'll understand more of how to get the faculty of Abrac."

When the Smiths had gone their way, Jenny and Lucy Harris trailed far behind Martin Harris as he headed for the livery stable. Mrs. Harris shook her head. "That Smith bunch! I've never seen the likes of them, always wantin' something they don't have. First they used the seer stone to tell fortunes, and now this. But I suppose I'd be worryin' myself too if I were ridin' as close to losin' my place as they are."

Jenny turned to look after the little woman and her tall son hurrying down the street. "That's sad," she said, painfully aware of want. "The faculty of Abrac; I wonder—"

Mrs. Harris interrupted with a snort, "Hogwash to them! You should hear the latest story the mister is puttin' out. I heard him myself. He was talkin' to that man Chase. Says several years ago his son, Joe, had an appearance. 'Twas a spirit come to Joseph, informing him there was gold plates hidden near his home. Young Joe tried to get them, he says, but there was a toad guardin' them. Well, this toad changed into a man and hit him a wallop on the side of the head.

"Old man Smith's sayin' that in September Joe's to be let have the plates—genuine gold, he says, and need some translatin'. There's supposed to be a story about the ancient people on this continent.—I'm thinkin' if Lucy gets hold of them, she'll be translatin' them into cold, hard cash."

They were nearly to the livery stable. Jenny saw Lucy's quick glance toward Martin Harris's sturdy back. She also saw the tear in the corner of her eye and the impatient hand that flicked it away. Straightening her shoulders, Lucy Harris marched toward her husband, Jenny tagging slowly along behind.

8

LUCY HARRIS TURNED from the stove. "Jenny, run out to the barn and fetch me some eggs."

With a quick nod, Jenny dropped her dish towel and headed for the back door. As she crossed the yard, she saw Tom lean over the railing of the pigpen, tilting a pail. The air was filled with the shrill squealing of hungry pigs. Jenny paused to watch Mr. Harris poke at the pig sow.

"Get out o' there and let the little 'uns have a chance!" he roared, flailing at her shoulders.

Jenny went into the barn and climbed to the loft to search through the straw for eggs. The squealing in the pigpen subsided, and Mr. Harris's voice rose. "Well, I'll be a-goin' out with you tonight. Joe said Walters will be there. I can't miss that. 'Sides, the other members of the Gold Bible Company will be there." Jenny heard the low rumble of Tom's voice answering him. She folded the eggs into her apron and slipped back down the ladder.

As she walked toward the door of the barn, Harris spoke again. His voice was low and deliberate. "The boy's got a talent. There's something there, and I believe he's learnin' how to get it. It'll help a lot if Hyrum will learn how to get the extra power from the faculty of Abrac." His earnest voice stopped Jenny just inside the door. "He's pretty convinced that joinin' the Masons will do it.

"You know, I was out to his pa's place once. Joe was a talkin' and I was standin' there pickin' my teeth with a pin. I dropped the thing in some straw and couldn't find it. Well, old Joseph and Northrop Sweet were there and they couldn't find it either. Just jokin' I said, 'Joe, use your stone and find it.' I didn't even know he had it with him. He pulled it outta his pocket, and stuck his face in his hat. Pretty soon he was feelin' around on the ground—without lookin', mind you. Then he moved a stick and there was my pin. That boy has a talent, and I'll be waitin' around to see what he does with it."

Slowly Jenny walked to the pen. "You believe it too? Do you 'spect he'll be findin' a treasure?"

She watched the excitement light his eyes and felt her own heart thump. "Something big," he said. "There's things buried out there. And there's forces fightin' against you. A fella over Palmyra way said they were diggin' by the old schoolhouse and the whole place lit up. Scared them so the bunch of them took out o' there. Later they were diggin' again, close to a barn. They looked up and a fella was sittin' on top of the barn. They say he was eight or nine feet tall. He motioned them to get outta there. They kept on workin', but finally they got so scared they took off."

Tom leaned on his pitchfork. "Do you know anything about using the rods?"

"Naw, but old man Smith can tell you about them if you want to know. He's been usin' them for years."

"Findin' treasure?" Jenny asked eagerly.

He shrugged. "Maybe. Depends on who you talk to."

"Jenny!" Mrs. Harris called and Jenny scooted for the house.

Martin Harris watched her go and said, "For a little 'un, your sister's sure interested in diggin', isn't she?"

Tom nodded soberly and went back to pitching straw. "Yeah. She's so little it's hard to take her serious. Is it possible for young'uns to get caught up in the craft?"

"Willard Chase's sister did. She has a green glass seer stone she uses all the time." Harris paused and then added, "I wouldn't be a-discouragin' it. Never know, she might really get the power."

That evening after Jenny had finished the dishes, she went upstairs and dug the green book out of the cubbyhole where she had hidden it. Studying the cover, she stroked it thoughtfully. She pondered about the strange uneasiness she had been sensing in church. She needed something, and she must reach for it, but the reaching couldn't be done with her bare hands.

As she thumbed through the book, she began to wonder—could it have anything to do with the power Hyrum had talked about it? She recalled Martin Harris's excitement, talking about the Gold Bible Company. Surely that didn't have anything to do with the black Bible the solemn-faced man at church read before he started to talk.

She sighed deeply and rubbed her eyes. Questions—the world was full of unanswered ones. Did Pa's book hold the answers for any? Could this green book give her the mysterious power it seemed to promise?

Mrs. Harris was still downstairs by the fire—maybe she would know.

Jenny crept down the stairs cautiously, Pa's stolen green book in her hand. As she reached the landing, the last stair creaked, and Mrs. Harris's head, bent over her worn leather Bible, snapped up with a start.

"Jenny, child!" she laughed. "You nearly did this old heart in! I thought you'd been asleep by now."

"I—I knew you were still up," Jenny stammered. "And—well, there's something I want to ask you."

"Come, sit, child." Mrs. Harris patted the footstool near her rocker and motioned Jenny nearer the fire. "What you got there?" She reached for the book, and Jenny pulled back.

"It's—was—my pa's." Jenny faltered, then her desperate curiosity overcame her. "I been readin' in it some, and I don't understand it all, but it talks about gettin' power—like Mr. Harris and Joe Smith are tryin' to do—" She gasped for a breath, then went on before Mrs. Harris could interject a word. "An' like the parson talks about on Sundays, and—" Jenny stopped, astonished at her own boldness. "Mrs. Harris," she plunged, "this black Bible of yours and this book—do they say the same, about gettin' the power, I mean?"

Mrs. Harris reached for the green book and gently pried Jenny's fingers from the spine. She winced slightly as she looked at the cover, then fingered the gold design thoughtfully.

"Jenny," she began, "I ain't much of a reader, and I'll confess I ain't read this book, but I know what's in it—least, I know what it's about." She handed the book back to Jenny. "An' I know something of that Joe Smith."

She paused. "Child," she sighed, "remember me tellin' you that there's only one truth, but there's lots of powers?"

Jenny nodded slowly.

"This here," she raised the black book that lay in her lap, "holds both—the truth and the power. That 'un," she pointed to the green book crushed against Jenny's chest, "that book may tell you about some power, but it won't tell you the truth."

Jenny pondered this before she spoke. "Mrs. Harris," she drew out her words slowly, deliberately, "what is the truth?"

Mrs. Harris smiled faintly. "Somebody else asked that same question, child, a long time ago. An' the answer he got is the same one you'll come to someday. Truth ain't an idea, or even a way to get power. It's a person—Jesus, who died on the cross to save us all."

"From sin?" Jenny interjected anxiously, remembering the parson's sermons, seeing the strange wild glint in Joe Smith's eyes, feeling the stolen book burning against her arms and chest.

"From sin," Mrs. Harris agreed, "and from yourself. From greed and the burnin' for wealth and power like Joe Smith's got; from the stubbornness of doin' things your own way like my Martin's got . . ."

"Power," whispered Jenny. She turned her full attention to the firelit face of the mistress. "Mrs. Harris, my ma said this book is evil, but she didn't say why. The little man at the book shop said the power in it is from the devil. Is power evil? Is it?"

Lucy Harris's eyes were hidden in the shadows as her hands fingered the worn pages of the Bible. When she looked again at Jenny, a single tear had left a trail down her cheek, glistening in the light of the dying fire.

"Jenny," she began, "the only lastin' power lies in the truth. There may be power in the spells told about in your pa's book, or in Joe's seer stone and divinin' rods. But the real power to be had don't come through such tricks. It comes through faith, through God."

Jenny went to bed restless, disturbed by her conversation with Mrs. Harris. Faith seemed an awfully slow, awfully uncertain way of getting the power. And it didn't seem to offer much in the way of benefit for the here and now. Pa's book and Joe's stone promised a more immediate fulfill-ment—and it was easier to come by, too. The right words, a sword, some blood from a goat or a lamb, and a person could have riches *and* power, served up by the spirits like the rich folks' Christmas goose!

But what if Mrs. Harris is right? Jenny shivered at the thought. *If it really does matter where the power comes from—*

Jenny's thoughts were interrupted by the creak of the stairs.

She sat up in bed, straining to hear. Only one familiar snore was coming from down the hall. When the creaking stopped, she slipped from her bed and knelt beside the window.

Twin shadows left the barn and moved down the road. Bright moonlight clearly revealed the progress of the two until they disappeared over the hill. Jenny continued to kneel at the window, thinking of the section in the book about moonlit nights. There was unusual power on these nights.

She fidgeted, rubbed at her tumbled hair, then jumped to her feet. Shoving aside the scary nighttime feelings and the echoes of her discussion with Mrs. Harris, she pulled on her clothes and crept down the stairs.

At the door she paused, but not long enough to heed her fears, then flew down the road after the men.

In the darkness of the woods, the road disappeared and the moonlight vanished. Groping with her hands before her, Jenny crept forward. Now excitement had her heart pounding. She moved from tree to tree, stopping to listen at each one.

When she heard the clank of metal and saw the bobbing light, she moved off the trail and slipped behind the group.

The lantern revealed Tom, Mr. Harris, and a dark man wrapped in a long black cloak. There were others, but she had eyes only for the cloaked figure.

Spellbound, she watched, certain this must be the man they called Walters the Magician. He was reading from a book. She strained to hear, but his words were an indistinct rumble of sound. As she watched his black-draped arms arching through the air, punctuating his words, she shivered, and a strange thrill moved over her.

The lantern light flashed off a sword, and Jenny crept closer. It was Hyrum. Joseph stood by holding a flapping rooster.

Carefully easing into the bushes, Jenny watched. Hyrum drew the circle, making the familiar marks. Restlessly she rubbed her hands together. *If only, just once, they'd let me be part of the group.*

After Joe spread the blood from the rooster, they all began to dig. The chill of the late night made Jenny shiver, and she hugged herself. Would the rooster turn the trick this time?

Silently, through the long night, they dug, while Jenny watched with growing frustration. Finally Martin Harris threw down his shovel in disgust.

They turned and walked back the way they had come, and only then did Jenny realize the east was brightening. She forced her numb legs to carry her down the trail. Dazed and disappointed, she didn't need to remind herself there had been no shouts of triumph to interrupt the black night. As she ran, tears of frustration welled up in her eyes. "Joe," she whispered, "you taught me all this. Why don't you fellas let me try?"

I am certain of one thing, she thought. *I am going to read that book and find the power.*

But Jenny's feet slowed as she remembered Mrs. Harris and the words the parson had read at church. Suddenly she was filled with a certainty that she should not read the book anymore.

As Jenny hesitated in the path, the sun burst through the trees. She lifted her chin and shrugged. *It's just a book. And if it teaches me the power, what harm can there be?*

When she opened the door to the kitchen, she discovered Martin Harris shouting for his breakfast, his anger breaking through every word his wife uttered. One quick glance at the gloomy faces sealed Jenny's silence, and she crept unnoticed about the room.

In September the rumors started flying. For several days there had been whispers at school. But Jenny had heard whispers before. This time she ignored them.

At lunchtime one day, she carried her pail down to the creek to join the students under the trees. As she reached them, the conversation stopped. Jenny saw the shared looks and was ready to turn away when one of the older girls called, "Jenny, wait!"

The girl's apologetic look swept through the group and she said, "She's living at the Harrises and he's been friendly with the Smiths; maybe she can tell us about it." Turning back to Jenny she asked, "Have you seen the gold plates?"

Jenny settled to the ground and crossed her legs. "Gold plates," she said with a frown. She flipped her braids over her shoulders and pushed hair out of her eyes. "I don't know what you're talkin' about."

"I guess everybody thought you were in on it because of Harris. People know he's friendly with Joe."

Jenny recalled what Mrs. Harris had told them, and thought briefly of Lucy's response. "What about gold plates?" she asked slowly as she concentrated on prying the lid off her lunch pail.

Mary Beth, the oldest girl at school, settled down beside Jenny. "They're saying the Smiths have circulated a story about Joe finding a bunch of genuine gold plates with writing all over them."

"Well, why don't you ask one of Joe's sisters instead of me?" Jenny questioned with a frown.

"There hasn't been a one of the Smith bunch in school since the story started making the rounds."

Now Cindy, Mary Beth's best friend, scooted close to Jenny and added, "Joe is saying he found them in a stone box along with a sword and a breastplate and some spectacles to translate the writing on the plates. He's calling the spectacles the magic 'Urim and Thummin.' I guess like in the Bible. Least the parson talked about such."

"They say Joe's getting set to translate the plates. There's trouble brewing 'cause he won't let a soul see them. He's claiming folks'll die if they do," Elizabeth said.

"Some of the fellas are mad because he promised to share the money with them, and now they're saying he won't even let them see what he has. But he's sure got something," Cindy continued. "Even his family owns they've seen something all done up tight in a piece of cloth."

After school that afternoon, Jenny walked slowly home. There were chores waiting, but she was thinking hard. Not since she had heard about Joe getting married had she returned to the Smiths. A sore spot still twinged in her heart whenever she thought of him. Now she clenched her fists and muttered, "Joe, I hate you for marryin' that gal. Didn't you guess you were mine? And I hate you, prissy missy, for daring to run off with him."

Jenny's hands relaxed. Her curiosity was bigger than her hate. Quickly she turned and ran down the trail that ended at the Smith farm.

Despite her bravery, she was relieved to discover only Lucy Smith at home that afternoon. Once settled in the gloomy cabin, across the table from Lucy Smith, she studied the woman. From her knot of graying hair to her button-bright eyes and curving shoulders, excitement possessed her. Jenny said, "I hear Joe's found a gold book."

Lucy leaned close to Jenny. "Oh my, he has! We've known for a time that it was to be. Joe's been workin' the stone and the charms, tryin' to get past the spirits a-guardin' the whole lot. It's been hard work and he's suffered much in order to get them."

"Did you see them?"

"Oh, no. Joe said he was instructed that no man could see the plates with his naked eyes and live. That's part of the reason he was given these funny spectacles. They're diamonds set in glass held together with bows, like regular ones. They're to be used to translate words on the plates."

"Is it a story written on them?"

"No. Joe says it's a history of the ancient people who lived here many years ago." Now she chuckled and patted Jenny's knee. "Just be patient and wait. Sooner or later you'll all be seein' them. I aim to exhibit them when Joe's all through translatin'. I'll be chargin' a price to see them, but after all the work, that's only fair."

One afternoon in late autumn, Jenny came in from school to find Martin Harris pacing the kitchen floor. She stood just inside the door, looking from his excited face to Mrs. Harris at the table. Her hands lay idle in the apple peelings, as she studied the knife she held.

Jenny glanced at Mr. Harris as he said, "Here I was just a-walkin' down the street when he came up to me. Proud, kinglike he was. He says, 'Martin, the Lord told me to ask the first honest man I met for money to get me to Harmony to get along with the translatin' of the gold plates.'"

Lucy Harris looked up at him in dismay, and he circled back to her in his pacing. "Quit thinkin' about the fifty dollars! Wife, I fear for your soul if you can't trust when a man says the Lord's directin' him. You know I've been searchin' for the truth all my life."

Jenny watched Mrs. Harris open her mouth as if to speak. Then she got to her feet, slowly, as if she had been hoeing in the garden all day.

When Martin turned to Jenny, she found the courage to say, "At school they're talkin'. Said Joe Smith found a book."

"The gold plates," Mr. Harris said reverently. "All that diggin' paid off. Yonder up the hill he found 'em."

On Sunday at church, Lucy Smith was the center of attention. Jenny elbowed her way through the crowd and listened as someone asked, "Mrs. Smith, what do the plates look like?"

"Well, Joe's not showin' them yet, but he did let me see the things that came with 'em. There's magic spectacles like diamonds. They are just like three-cornered diamonds set in glass and the glass set in silver bows.

They're for readin' the plates. With them was a breastplate, big enough to fit a good-sized man. The whole thing was worth at least five hundred dollars."

Amid appreciative murmurs, Lucy continued, "The plates, they're gold. Like leaves of a regular Bible they are, only gold. I 'spect we'll be a-makin' a pile of money off this find. Joe's goin' to translate the plates and then I'll be a-showin' them. Figure I can charge twenty-five cents for a peek."

Later when Jenny started home, she passed a group talking on the street corner. Peter Ingersoll was speaking, and she waited to hear him.

"Well, judge for yourself," he was saying. "I met Joe walkin' toward home one day, carryin' something all wrapped up in his jacket. Didn't think too much about it all until a couple of days later; then he told me he had carried home some pretty white sand. His folks were all a-sittin' round the dinner table, he said, and they were a-wantin' to know what he had. Said he happened to think about a story he'd heard of a fella in Canada who claimed he found a book containing the history of the original settlers. He called it a gold Bible. So Joe says when they asked him, the words jest popped out, 'gold Bible.' He was just funnin', but they took him serious.

"So when they wanted to see the thing, he said they could go ahead and look, but he'd had a commandment sayin' that no man could look at it with the naked eye and live. Not a one of them would look at it. Then Joe slapped his knee and told me he had them all fixed and he intended to be havin' some fun with them."

Peter paused and Jenny stared up into his face. He frowned and slowly said, "This whole affair might be going too far. Chase here had dealin's with him, too."

"Right," the man beside Peter spoke up. "Joe come to me and asked me to make a carryin' case for his plates. I told him I didn't have time. I heard later that he told one of the neighbors he didn't have any book of gold plates and that he never did have, but he was just tryin' to trick me into makin' him a chest."

When Jenny was back in the Harris's kitchen, Mr. Harris was saying, "I've never seen such jealousy. Every man in the place is wishin' he'd been the one to find the plates. Now they're all a-tryin' to make off with them. Seems some fellas are claimin' Joe made promises and that he owes them shares in the plates. He's been sweatin' it out tryin' to keep a step ahead of them."

"What do you mean?" Jenny stepped up to the table.

"Well, Willard Chase's sister used her little green stone to divine up where Joe had hid the plates. 'Twas across the street from the Smiths' in the cobbler's shop. During the night a bunch got in the place and tore it up lookin' for the plates. They found the chest and split it open, but there weren't nothin' in it. That Joe's a cool one. While the others were all hot about the plates being stole, he admitted he got up durin' the night and moved the plates. You'd better believe no one will outwit that fella!"

A week later Jenny came home from school to find Mrs. Harris sitting at the table, her eyes red from weeping.

Jenny hesitated just inside the door. As she studied the face of the one who had befriended her, she wanted to throw her arms around the woman and comfort her. But shadowy things lurked in Jenny's mind. She was not quite fourteen and just a hireling—that alone was a difficult position to be in.

And how could she admit she knew about those sounds in the night? The angry voices, the bumping, and the smack of flesh against flesh. Could she admit hearing those cries from Mrs. Harris and at the same time admit that she had crouched, fearful and trembling, not daring to go to the rescue? Just thinking about those sounds plunged her back into the memory of last year—the picture of her father's face looming over her, twisted with anger.

A fly filled the silence with its buzzing. Jenny's gaze, riveted on the flushed face of the woman, was caught by the noise. She dashed for a newspaper, attacked the offender, and then walked to the pail of water beside the door. Still mute, she filled the dipper and carried it to Mrs. Harris.

With a nod, Lucy Harris drained the dipper, wiped her mouth and spoke. "He's gone. Flew in here, grabbed up a few things and left. I'm certain he's followed that Joe Smith and his wife to Pennsylvania. Seems there was too much persecution goin' on around here for Joe to settle down and get his translatin' done." Bitterly she added, "Martin's got more money than anyone else in this town, and is more gullible. Give him a flight of fancy, and he's off. God only knows what will happen. The Smiths all have glib tongues. If it's like in the past, it wouldn't surprise me a bit to see Martin separated from his money. He's lookin' for truth, and truth for Martin is always what tickles his fancy at the time."

Jenny searched for words of comfort. Finally she straightened up and said, "Mrs. Harris, if this is from the Lord, we can't be hinderin' it."

"You're soundin' like that Smith woman," she returned. "Truth is, Martin's always gone huntin' after any new idea for makin' money. Dear Lord, if only he could see!"

9

MARTIN DIDN'T STAY long in Pennsylvania. However, Jenny's curiosity about the whole affair scarcely had time to be satisfied before a visitor provided some distraction.

Just after Jenny's fourteenth birthday, January 1828, Abigail Harris, Martin's sister-in-law, stopped by. She was there when Jenny came back from school; Jenny studied her with awe.

From her regal tower of graying hair to her bright, all-seeing eyes and her rustling black taffeta frock, she seemed the embodiment of authority. Whether it were skeletons or spiders hidden in the closet, Abigail Harris would be the one to find them.

Just after dinner, Lucy Smith and her husband Joseph also paid a visit to the Harris farm. As Mrs. Harris opened the door to the Smiths, Jenny had finished washing the dishes, and she crept into the parlor. Watching and listening, she winced. Lucy Smith was talking freely and eagerly, her little sparrow head bobbing about. "We're calling it the Gold Bible Business."

She scarcely gave Abigail time to ask a question before the details were spun out. Jenny squirmed with chagrin as she watched the sharp-eyed woman measure Lucy Smith's flow of words. The astonishment and surprise that swept across Abigail's face made Jenny cringe. When that expression changed to speculation and Abigail leaned back in her chair with her arms folded across her bony front, Jenny began to listen to Lucy's words.

". . . It was a spirit of one of those saints already living on the continent back before Columbus discovered it. He revealed to Joe all about the plates and told him where to find them."

Abigail leaned forward, her eyes narrowed. "I haven't seen a spirit. What did he look like?"

"Well," Lucy said, wrinkling her brow, "I'm thinking he must have been a Quaker." Without even noticing the trap, she hurried on, "He was dressed very plain. At that time, he told Joe the plates he was to have first off were only an introduction to the gold Bible. All of the plates on which the Bible was written up were so heavy, it would take at least four stout men just to load them into the cart to haul them home."

She continued, "It's interesting that Joseph was able to discover through looking in the stone the exact vessel the gold was melted in. He also saw the machine that rolled out the plates. At the bottom of the vessel there were three balls of gold left over, each the size of his fist."

Abigail's skepticism was lost on Lucy in her enthusiastic recounting of the tale.

Early the next morning, Jenny was at work in the kitchen, mulling over the conversation which had kept them all up so late that the Smiths too had decided to stay overnight. Abigail soon joined her. As Jenny prepared breakfast, Lucy Smith entered the room.

Lucy closed the door quietly behind her and, standing close to Abigail, spoke in a low voice. "Have you four or five dollars you could spare until our business is producing?" She added, "The spirit has promised you'll receive fourfold."

Abigail clattered the cutlery to the table. "And why do you need it?"

"Joe is in Pennsylvania, and he wants to return to see how things are going with us all."

Abigail continued to set the table, her face expressionless. "If Joe needs to know, I would think he'd look in his stone and save his time and money."

Jenny watched a perplexed frown creep across Lucy's face. Without a word, she turned and left the room.

During the following days, Jenny was glad to escape to school. At best, life on the Harris farm had settled into monotony as the snows outside deepened.

In the evenings, Mrs. Harris and Jenny sewed and knitted, while Martin and Tom talked constantly. Struggling with the knitting needles and tangled yarn, Jenny's attention wandered toward their conversation. She noticed it always seemed to circle back to the mystery of Joe Smith.

As she listened to Martin talk, Jenny decided that just like the winds of winter, first calm, then swirling in indecisive fury, the winds of Martin's passions swept him freely about. She guessed his restless feet would soon carry him east and south to Harmony.

Eventually his reasoning surfaced. "I've put a whole lot of money into this so far, and I aim to protect my investment."

Mrs. Harris's reply was similarly predictable. "It's chasin' the wind, nothin' but a dream. You'd best forget the fifty dollars before it costs you more."

But he left in midwinter, and a month went by before he returned. Coming in from school, Jenny discovered him pacing excitedly around the kitchen table and immediately noticed a new undercurrent in his voice. He was telling his Lucy how wife Emma was acting as Joe's scribe, taking down the words as he gave them to her. Word by word, the plates were being translated.

"What did they say? Did you see the papers?"

While he described it all, Harris's eyes danced. Finally Mrs. Harris demanded, "I know there's something more you haven't said—what is it?"

"Well, all your doubtin' and fussin' made me struggle with my faith, and I finally decided to do something about it. Joe gave me a copy of some of the characters, and I took them to New York to see a Mr. Mitchell. I was thinkin' he could decipher some of this for me and tell me more about the characters. He didn't know nothin'. But he sent me on to a Professor Anthon. This fella was a mighty smart man, but he sure is an infidel. First he was real excited about it all until he found out where I got the information. Even if he wouldn't give me a written statement, he did admit lots, and it's all stored right up here." He chuckled and tapped his head.

Tom leaned forward and asked eagerly, "And what did he say? Did he think there was something to it?"

Martin chuckled contentedly, "Yes, sir! He said the characters were ancient, shorthand Egyptian. So Joe was right all along. He also admitted they were Chaldaic, Assyriac, and Arabic."

By April, Martin Harris could endure the suspense no longer. He announced his intentions after breakfast. "You, Tom, you can handle the plowin' and plantin' evenings. There's Jake and Amos to help, too. I'm goin' to Harmony."

And Lucy Harris announced hers. "If you're going down there for months, I'll be goin' with you. Jenny is able to keep up the little that needs to be done around here and see that her brother is fed." Martin looked dubious, but realizing there was no sense to arguing he shrugged, and they departed.

At school, since the brothers and sisters of Joe Smith were seldom present, it seemed to be Jenny's lot to endure alone the curious stares and questions.

But Jenny was as confused as the other students as she faced their speculations: "I hear tell it was a spirit giving out the place of the plates." "I hear they are saying a divine one handed out the plates." "Jenny, does Martin get to see the plates?" Jenny could only shake her head. One thing she did know: they assumed she knew secret things. Deeply conscious of the tide of feeling, Jenny recognized a chasm widening between herself and the other students. Their questions made clear that she was seen as part of the inner circle, along with Martin Harris and the Smiths. They expected her to *know*.

It troubled her, not because she was suddenly marked as belonging to the money-digging group, but because of the barrier caused by the questions. She sensed from those glances and the whispers that the line was impossible to cross. Jenny was very lonely.

She had only begun to relax into the dream of being mistress of the house for a few weeks when Lucy Harris returned. "Rode in on the stage," Lucy announced as she moved about the house putting her possessions in order. She eyed Jenny sharply. "He'll never get away with it."

"No, ma'am," Jenny replied meekly, wondering what she meant.

"I searched the place over and didn't find a thing to indicate to me there were gold plates or even copper ones around. Tore through every cupboard, looked under the beds, and even scratched around in the woods lookin' for a place where they might be hid." Mrs. Harris concluded wearily, "Martin's been duped again. How that man can fall for such a line . . ." She settled down in her rocker, and Jenny brought her a cup of tea from the boiling kettle.

As the woman sipped she studied Jenny thoughtfully. "My, a few weeks away from home, and I see the change in you. I've neglected my duty to your mother long enough. She was right insistent that I make a lady out of you. She hadn't the opportunities I've had of education, and I aim to see you learn a little more'n her."

Jenny nodded. Mrs. Harris was beginning to sound like Lemuel Searles, saying she should be talking right and learning. She didn't voice her next thought. Lucy, after all, didn't talk much better than anyone else in Manchester.

She looked around the room, eyeing the books, the fancywork, the china. Jenny sighed wistfully. Yes, there *was* much more to learn, but she wasn't sure Mrs. Harris was the one to teach her.

Later Lucy had more to tell. She talked about Emma, and Jenny was aware of strange stirrings inside as she listened. "Pregnant she is, and Joe's sayin' that the plates couldn't be opened under penalty of death by anyone except by his firstborn, and that his child will be a boy. Some say this little fella will be the one to translate the plates when he's two or three years old."

"When is Mr. Harris coming home?" Jenny asked.

"I don't know," she replied slowly. "He's takin' over the transcribin' from Emma. Mighty important he's feelin', writin' down the Lord's words as Joseph is seein' them in the stone, one by one. I don't know . . ." she repeated slowly, "I just don't know."

As she stared at Jenny, her eyes darkened. She looked around the room, sighing. "He's taken so, I'm wonderin' if he'll ever be back."

But he was. In June Martin returned in triumph. He wore his air of excitement and mystery well, but his secrets were only for his household.

Jenny was there when he took out the papers and spread them on the table. Mrs. Harris leaned over to read them, mouthing the words slowly. She lifted her head. "What is this?"

"You wouldn't believe me, so I talked Joe into lettin' me bring all we'd translated so's you could see and read for yourself."

She jerked her head. "You mean this is the translation from the gold plates?"

He nodded, "The words that Emma and I've been takin' down while Joe translated."

Slowly she sat down to the table and pulled the sheaf of papers toward her. Martin got to his feet. "I'll do the chores, and we'll talk about it later." He was chuckling to himself as he took up his hat and left the house. Jenny watched him walk to the barn. His shoulders were squared, and he strode along as if he owned the earth.

Turning back to the table, Jenny settled down across from Mrs. Harris and watched her read. The paper rustled and Mrs. Harris sighed with exasperation. Now her brow furrowed and her finger traced down the page. "It's all so—"

"Can I see?" Jenny asked. Mrs. Harris lifted her face, her eyes snapping. She stared at Jenny without seeing her. And then suddenly she jumped to her feet. With quick movements she rustled the papers together and dashed to the stove. Another quick movement and she had shoved the papers inside. Immediately the flames shot up, engulfing the pages.

At Jenny's horrified gasp, Mrs. Harris responded. "Jenny, false teachin' like this must be destroyed. If I'm wrong, if this is truly all divine, then it won't be a bit of trouble to get another copy. Now, let's you and me finish cleaning the kitchen and go to bed before he comes in. I'd rather he asked me about this in the mornin' when he's better tempered."

Eager to win his wife over and supposing Joe's translations were safe with her sewing supplies, Martin held off discussing the translation with her.

Now the July heat lay heavy upon Manchester, though not as heavy as the tension Jenny felt waiting for Martin to discover what his wife had done. In the garden it was especially hot. Jenny straightened her back and leaned against the hoe. Even on the willows bordering the stream that cut through Martin Harris's farm, the leaves hung limp and dusty.

Her gleanings—carrots, beets, and onions—were also beginning to wilt. Glad for the excuse to return to the house, she dropped the hoe and gathered up the vegetables.

Jenny saw a strange horse tethered under the trees. Jenny had just reached the porch steps when she heard Martin. The agony in his voice stopped her and she caught her breath at the cry, "I have lost my soul!"

Overlapping it came another voice, familiar even though wrung with anguish. "Oh, my God, all is lost! What shall I do?" Heavy boots struck the floor, marking Jenny shiver with dread. "Are you certain? Go search once more."

Martin's voice came through again, "I've ripped pillows and beds. I've torn the place apart lookin'. If they was hidden, I'd have found them."

A chill swept through Jenny, for the visitor could be only one person. She hugged her arms to herself. It had been so long. Not since South Bainbridge and the trial had she been near him.

Curiosity overcame her dread of certain confrontation, and Jenny entered the house. Both men turned as she stopped in the doorway of the parlor, her apron sagging under the load of wilting vegetables. She realized she was gawking, but she must see if his hair was still bright as sunlight. Even as she studied his long arrogant nose and glowing blue eyes, she was reduced to shy trembling. With only the slightest nod to acknowledge her presence, Joe demanded, "Where is your mistress?"

Jenny shook her head numbly. "I don't know," she whispered, not having the voice to admit more. She glanced quickly at Mr. Harris and saw that his face was white. The roll of flesh under his chin trembled. Jenny ducked her head and backed toward the door. "Excuse me. These must go in water."

In the kitchen Jenny moved quickly about her tasks, but she was straining to hear. The voices in the parlor continued their uneasy, troubled rumbling. Jenny's fingers trembled in the biscuit dough as she thought about the evening before them. If it were only possible to send thoughts warning Lucy Harris to stay away!

But when the back door opened and Lucy came in, Jenny watched in astonishment. Flying about the kitchen, frying the fresh pork, poking at the boiling greens, Lucy held them all spellbound as her words kept pace with her busy hands. She was totally in command.

The men had moved to the kitchen at the sound of Lucy's voice. As the conversation continued, Joseph was reduced to being an awkward boy once again. He told of the birth and death of his baby son. With his heart in his eyes, with sorrowful words, he was weaving a picture of familial devotion that left Jenny awed and envious.

She crept closer to listen even as she wondered at the emotion that dug into her like tearing hands. But throughout the story of Emma's confinement and near death, Lucy Harris remained in command.

Her words soothed and then reduced him. He admitted, "I'll confess; I'm not a worthy husband or father." His face brightened. "But I will be."

"How?" Lucy's voice was suspicious.

"Well," he paused and then lifted his face. "I'm reforming my ways. I'm seeing how all the little things add up in my wife's eyes. I'm aiming to please her." He noticed Lucy's suspicious expression and added, "I really mean it. Knowing the importance, 'specially to her, I joined the Methodist church there in Harmony."

"You did!" Even Lucy was surprised and a pleased look crossed her face. "Well, there's hopes for the likes of you yet. After gettin' acquainted with your wife while I was there, I'm guessin' she was terribly pleased."

A shadow crossed his face. Heavily he said, "I gotta admit, it didn't take."

"Your gettin' religion?"

He shook his head. "They brought up that old story about money digging and using the stone, and they rejected me. I couldn't join, even after they'd already accepted me.—But I tried," he added ruefully. "I was a member for three days."

During the meal, Jenny lost interest in the conversation. After they had finished eating, she cleared the dishes from the table, while the others went into the parlor. Having finished her kitchen duties, she returned to the parlor to listen.

Settling herself in the corner, she watched Joe as he talked to Martin. Something about him puzzled her. She felt as if she knew him, yet she didn't. The youth she had known in South Bainbridge had been fun, careless—even thoughtless. Now he spoke deliberately as if weighing his words. His eyes constantly sought the others in the room. This wasn't the student, the young lad who had stood trial in South Bainbridge two years ago. With a shock, she accepted the truth. Young Joe had become a man.

Jenny looked down at her stained hands and wondered if she had changed. If she had, Joe Smith didn't know it. She might have been a stick of furniture, for all the attention she was catching.

Her thoughts continued to drift, moving with unseen currents as the conversation moved about her unheeded. She felt a growing need to do something, to say something. She closed her eyes. Could she will herself to become a different Jenny?

As if thought made her free, her mind rose to wander the airy heights of imagination. Jenny, tall and poised, and Joe Smith really seeing her, bending his bright head to kiss her hand.

"Jenny!" The back door banged shut. The vision vanished. Tom was back from the fields, wanting his supper.

Jenny stared at her stained hands. But now there was a difference. She remembered the book, and a fresh desire was born.

10

JENNY CAME INTO the kitchen just as Mrs. Harris said, "All he has to do is get a 'word from the Lord' and he can get himself out of any problem he wants. Martin Harris, how can you fail to see through it all?"

Lucy Harris was swishing about the kitchen packing bread and meat into a pail. Jenny guessed that Harris was leaving. As she continued to listen, Mrs. Harris's talk made it clear he was headed for Harmony again.

Jenny shrugged slightly as she sat down. These days she found it hard to sympathize with either one. In the back of her mind she felt the fuss over Joe would soon quiet down and everyone would forget him, just as they had at South Bainbridge.

Martin was very quiet, but Jenny noticed the excitement burning in his eyes. "Thin as paper it is," Lucy was declaring. "He can't come up with what he's already dictated, so he solves it with a 'word from the Lord,' sayin' Satan will try to confuse the work by givin' out different words. Then what does he do? He gets the plates of Nephi with a little different version of the same stuff." She shook her head. "Clever man; Martin, is there nothin' I can say to keep you from bein' his slave and dupe? I'm at my wits' end." Jenny was absolutely amazed at the woman's presence in the face of what she had done. She seemed to give not a snap of the finger to the fact that Jenny had seen her burn the manuscript.

Martin got to his feet and Jenny watched him pace the floor. His quick, hard strides across the room and back caught Jenny's attention and she began to feel his excitement. Lucy Harris continued to chide him, but neither her nor Jenny was listening to her.

When he passed Jenny again and saw she was watching, he stopped and said in a low voice, "She's makin' it all sound crazy, but don't you heed it. The fella's humble spirit testifies to the holiness of the callin'."

"What do you mean?" Jenny asked, moving closer to Martin. Lucy stopped her muttering to listen.

With his palms flat on the table, Martin leaned toward them and whispered, "This book is the Lord talkin'. Joe's been mighty reluctant to divulge it all at once, but bit by bit it's all comin' out. This last visit I had with him kinda loosened him up when he come to see that I believe in him and have confidence in what he has to say. Now he knows I'll not be blabbin' it all over the country."

Lucy retorted, "Like this?"

Ignoring her, he continued, "It's all comin' out. This book Joe has is holy. There's the divine behind the translatin' and the writin' of it."

Lucy demanded, "How do you expect to prove that?"

"It's been proven. But even more than that, the Lord is beginnin' to reveal himself to Joseph in a much deeper way. He's communicatin' through what Joe calls revelations."

"What does He have to say?" Lucy's voice was suspicious.

Martin pulled a crumpled letter out of his pocket and spread it on the table. "He's given me a copy of the revelation." Jenny watched his hands reverently pressing the creases out before he held it up. "Mind you now, this is the Lord talkin'. Otherwise, I'd not pass along the words. First off, the Lord's tellin' Joe that His plans can't be frustrated." He paused to slant a sharp glance at his wife.

"I'd have read you this before, but you were so busy fussin' over the little bit I did tell you, I decided to wait. Now listen. He also tells Joe that he's been called to do the work of the Lord. He's sayin' there's just no way to shy away from the callin'. He must be faithful or he'll end up bein' just like other men, without gifts or calling. He made it pretty clear to Joe that He has appointed him to get the message of the gold Bible out to the Lamanites."

"The Indians." Lucy's words broke the spell surrounding Jenny, bumping her back to earth. Now *gold Bible, Lamanites,* and *revelations* were just words, not corridors of mystery.

Jenny turned to look out the window. The nighttime wind had blown the last of the leaves off the trees, and dark clouds made it look near to snowing. She shivered as she realized, *It's almost Halloween.*

When Lucy spoke now the strident note was gone from her voice and Jenny thought she sounded worried. "It'll be a hard trip to Harmony. Don't you want to take Tom with you? Amos can handle the livestock by himself."

Martin shook his head. "No, I need Tom here. I've no way of knowin' how long I'll be gone. There's much translatin' to be done."

"Well, be holdin' your tongue." Lucy added wifely advice. "Your boastin' about it all before the fact isn't winnin' you friends around Manchester. Pretty soon you'll have a reputation for braggin' that rivals the Smiths'."

"Now, just what are you referrin' to?" Martin asked, turning reddened cheeks toward his wife. "I'm not braggin', and you know it."

Lucy Harris stepped in front of her husband. With fists planted on her hips, she looked him in the eyes. "It's around town and well nigh the gossip of the church folks how you're sayin' you've had revelations given out by the Lord."

"I've said they're from the Lord, and they are." His defensive tone belied the statement.

"That you saw Jesus Christ in the form of a deer and that the devil appeared a jackass with hair like a mouse?" She shook her head. "My, what details! And they're saying you've prophesied that Palmyra would be destroyed in 1836, and by the year 1838, Joe Smith's church would be so large there wouldn't be any need for a president of the United States. You might as well have gone the whole way and said you'd be second in command over all these United States!"

Martin Harris rubbed at his jaw and scratched his ear. He had just opened his mouth to speak when the door slammed.

Jenny forced her fascinated gaze from Mr. Harris to Tom entering. He said, "I hear tell the new schoolmaster is boarding with the Smiths." Washing his hands at the basin beside the door, he continued. "I also hear he's from back Vermont way and that his folks are known by the Smiths. I'll need to be getting acquainted with the fella."

His voice revealed so much satisfaction that Jenny couldn't help saying, "I don't think you'll like him. He's like a towel that's been overwashed."

"You're talkin' about your schoolteacher!" Mrs. Harris's eyebrows rose halfway up her forehead as she turned to Jenny.

"They say he's good with the rod," Jenny said quickly. No need to explain she meant "divining rod," not the rod of correction. Lucy Harris would not approve of the first, and she *would* approve of the second, especially the fact that Jenny was pointing it out. "He's tryin' to help out the Smiths. They sure do need the money." Tom gave her a quick nod of agreement.

They sat down around the table and Mrs. Harris began ladling the stew onto plates. Martin Harris reached for the bread. "Tom, too bad I can't spare you around here. You'd enjoy the going's on in Harmony. But then I 'spect in another year we'll be seein' that young rascal Joe Smith paradin' around the streets of Manchester, a-wearin' his gold breastplate and carryin' a sword, with the gold Bible tucked under his arm."

"Mrs. Smith says," Jenny volunteered, gulping and wiping her hands on her apron, "that they are going to be makin' a heap of money off the gold plates. Joe's pa is tellin' people they're gonna use the money to pay for their money-digging business."

After supper was over, while Jenny cleared the dishes from the table, Martin Harris came into the room buttoning a clean shirt. Pulling on his coat and taking up his hat, he muttered, "I'll be out most of the evenin'. Don't wait up for me."

Jenny saw the troubled expression on Mrs. Harris's face as she turned to pick up her knitting. But as Jenny poured hot water into the dishpan, she was thinking not of Lucy Harris's expression but of Martin Harris's prophecies.

Swishing the dishcloth through the suds, watching the bubbles burst, Jenny began to sense the bubbles bursting in her heart. The sadness surprised her. Why had it suddenly become important to believe like Martin did?

Speaking through the silence from her rocking chair beside the fire, Lucy said, as if reading Jenny's thoughts, "It's no good placin' confidence in the religion Martin Harris promotes."

Tom got to his feet. "I'd not worry much. I hear Pa Smith is callin' the whole thing about the gold Bible a 'speculation.' That don't sound too serious to me. At least, it don't seem like it'll be a hellfire and damnation kind of religion." Chuckling, he left the house.

Martin Harris left for Harmony, Pennsylvania, without a promise of his return. As he packed his saddlebags, he said, "I'm just lucky the Lord will allow me to translate for Joseph again. This time I don't intend to let any trick of the evil one keep me from gettin' the task done." He threw a scowl at his wife and shouldered the bag. "I'll be back when the work's finished. The fellas here can tend to the plantin' if'n I'm not back before then."

Not withstanding the dismay Lucy Harris felt over her husband's departure, life without Martin Harris quickly slipped into an easy routine. Amos and Tom continued to handle the chores about the farm, leaving Mrs. Harris free to visit her friends or nod beside the fire with her knitting in her hands.

Jenny moved between farm and school in a bemused state, happy with the crisp autumn and her circumstances. She was keenly aware of bare fields and wind-lashed elm and birch shedding leaves in preparation for their ritual of rest. The backdrop of the dark fir forest seemed to cover the rolling hills of Manchester with mystery and solitude.

Each day Jenny followed a path to school which skirted the hills and the woods bordering the farm. Her walk was long, but Jenny didn't mind. Other students often slipped onto the path with her. First the Anderson twins joined her—Timothy and Angela were ten. At times, when Mr. Cowdery was busy with the little ones, Jenny had been called upon to help the twins with their sums and reading lesson.

Farther down the path Mary Beth and Cindy joined them. But this school year, the two girls whispered just between themselves, and they seldom made a place for her. Jenny had noticed, but only Timothy dared explain it to her. "It's cause of Martin Harris being credulous."

"What do you mean?" She had kept her voice low, as the girls in front of them began to hurry. "It's all this about Joe Smith and the plates. Pa says people aren't taken in by it at all, leastwise no one much except Martin Harris."

"I suppose so," Jenny answered slowly, "but why does it make Mary Beth and Cindy shun me?"

"They think you are credulous too." Jenny had forgotten about the conversation with Timothy until late in October. Halloween was next week and the students were trying to outdo each other with stories of mystery and terror. Equally fantastic stories of bravery and daring surfaced. At noon Jenny joined the groups around the story-tellers and blended her screams of terror with others.

When there were no more stories to be told, Jeff Naylor began questioning Jenny. "I hear old Harris believes all those stories the Smiths have been circulating."

Jenny looked about the group, searching vainly for one of Joseph's brothers or sisters. Finally she straightened her back and met the curious eyes. "You'll have to be askin' him that. If you're tryin' to pin me with believing ghost stories told by the big people, I can't help you. I've never seen a ghost."

"And what would you do if you did?"

"Not believe it until I could walk right through him," she replied saucily.

Now Cindy, with her eyes wide, said, "I heard Samuel Smith say they were out digging over by the old schoolhouse one night and it all lit up. He said there was a fella at least nine feet tall sitting on the roof, yelling at them to clear out."

The group groaned their awe and dismay; Jenny thought about the story she'd heard Martin telling. Mary Beth was studying her intently. Jenny forced a smile and said, "Credulous they are. Now I don't believe—"

Nicholas interrupted, "Everybody that isn't credulous stick up your hand." And when all hands were quickly raised, he continued. "Okay, tomorrow's Halloween. I say you all be here at the schoolhouse just as soon as it's dark, and we'll all go over to the old school and prove there's no such thing as spooks." His eyes were on Jenny as he said, "And if you can get some doughnuts and apples, all the better; we'll make it a party. But you better all be here or we'll come after you."

The next evening Lucy Harris said, "I don't have any doughnuts, and that's the silliest thing I've heard of, going out there just to scare yourselves. You can take some apples."

As soon as the supper dishes were washed, Jenny wrapped Tom's old jacket around herself and stuffed the pockets with apples. Her excitement was almost as high as the time she had followed Tom and Martin to their meeting with Walters. But now as she scurried down the dark path, she felt her emotions flattening. "Silly baby stuff," she muttered, "pretendin' there's ghosts and goblins just to get scared."

Norton and Jeff and Nicholas had lanterns. Cindy and Mary Beth came with their pockets loaded with doughnuts. Norton was licking his lips with anticipation as he said, "Leave the goodies here. After we go and investigate the spooks, we'll all meet back here and eat the doughnuts. You fellas douse the lights when we get to the edge of the cornfield. We don't want anyone to see us and have a hysteria."

There were giggles, and a long line formed behind the lantern-bearers. "Quiet back there. Not a sound, now!"

A lonesome voice from the back of the line squeaked, "If the sheriff finds out, will he put us all in jail?" Hoots of laughter drowned the young boy's fears.

Only a sliver of moon hung in the sky, and even that disappeared as the path dipped into the trees. The group walked in silence except for an occasional gasp of dismay as someone bumped into his neighbor or a tree.

When they could hear the rustle of dry cornstalks, the warning hiss came to darken the lanterns. The wind was rising; Jenny could hear it keening through the fir trees. The sliver of moonlight appeared and disappeared as clouds blew by, and from behind Jenny came nervous whispers.

When they reached the far side of the cornfield, they could see the shadowy bulk of the old schoolhouse. The rising wind slapped loose shutters, and the sudden banging brought out a nervous whimper. Quietly the group formed a semicircle on the edge of the deserted school yard.

The creaking old building was dark. Norton said bravely, "There's not even a ghost on the roof." They waited and the quietness of the night seemed to grow, broadcasting whispers of sound. The soft sighs of the students became eerie, and chattering teeth seemed to pound in Jenny's ears. When the clouds drifted away from the moon, Nicholas whispered, "Everybody satisfied?"

"We haven't even looked inside," voiced someone.

There was another whimper. "My ma said to hurry home."

Then out of the silence, "Seems a brave body oughta go inside and investigate."

"Without a light?"

After a pause, "There a volunteer?" Only the shuffle of feet in the dry grass broke the silence.

"Seems the one accused of being credulous would be the most eager."

The cornstalks rustled, the wind rose. Finally Jenny moved and swallowed hard. "You're meanin' me. So, we can't go have doughnuts 'til I do." She tried to make her voice brave, but it was thin, and the only response was silence.

Again feet shuffled and teeth chattered. The group melted back and Jenny faced the sagging door. "Oh, you babies," she hissed, moving quickly toward the door. In the sliver of moonlight, she could see the broken floor slanting inward. "How far do I go?" she whispered.

"To the far wall," a voice breathed in her ear. She shivered and stepped toward the slanting floor.

There was a hand on her back. She opened her mouth to protest, but her feet were on the slanting boards, and the boards were moving with a life of their own. Behind her the door crashed shut, and sealed Jenny in oppressive darkness.

When she slammed into the far wall, Jenny sat for a moment, stunned and trembling. Close to her head a rhythmic tapping began and a ghostly laugh rose. "Let me out!" she screamed. The laugh was drifting away.

Jenny jumped to her feet but the boards tilted, dumping her. She scrambled, scratching and clawing her way up the ruined floor. Now sobbing with terror, she discovered she was surrounded by boards that had a will of their own. They slanted and dumped her, pricked and stabbed. Some boards bound her feet and others slapped her face. In the deep darkness only silence answered her cries.

When she was nearly voiceless from screaming, she heard a sound. Rats. Rustles, scratching, a noise that must be gnawing; she gave one last feeble scream of terror.

A voice answered her. The schoolhouse door creaked outward and a dark shadow filled the doorway. Jenny flew toward it. Warm flesh, a beard and musty wool were against her face. It was a strange beard, but at least it wasn't rats.

"What happened?" The voice was strangely melodious, strangely familiar. He led her away from the building while she gasped out her story.

In the dim lantern light she could see the beard, the black cloak, and a shiny disk. The last time she had seen that disk it had been circling and glowing in the light of a lantern beside the diggings. She studied the man's face. "Are you Walters the Magician?"

"Of course. Who else would I be?" The remembered melody of his voice returned to her. Forgetting her terror and exhaustion, Jenny wanted only to hear him reading those singing words out of his book again.

11

DID HER ENCOUNTER with Walters the Magician radically change Jenny, or was it the final disappointment of her friends' betrayal? Whatever the answer, Halloween night irreparably separated Jenny from her schoolmates. She felt the division strongly. Jenny stood alone, the one against the many.

Fortunately for Jenny, the Smith youngsters returned to school. They were immediately pushed to her side of the chasm. Now Jenny had friends, just as she also had a label she didn't understand.

She continued to skirt the hills going to and from school, lonely now in her solitary walk. As autumn passed, she began to experience the deepening calm of the trees—or so she thought it.

One afternoon as she stood beneath a fir tree, watching the wind lash its top branches, she felt as if her mind were unfurling and becoming one with the surging forces of nature. The sensation of sharpened awareness left her feeling as if she were mentally standing on tiptoe.

The silence surrounded her, sharpened and real. What was happening? Was this sensation rising only from the wellspring of loneliness in her life?

Waiting, wondering if it was all just chance, she reached out, wanting to touch that appealing sense of aliveness. She sat motionless, unmindful of the cold, searching for words that would link her with that sensation of mystery. Finally a scrap of rhyme popped into her mind.

"Luna, every woman's friend,
To me thy goodness condescend,
Let this night in visions see
Emblems of my destiny."

Jenny had started reading the green book again, and lately a strangeness surrounded her reading. She had been reaching out to the unknown and now the unknown was reaching out to her.

The penetrating cold through Jenny's thin shawl brought her back to reality. Shivering, she hurried down the path toward the farm. She thought of Lucy Harris nodding by the fire in the evening, while Jenny carried the green book downstairs to read. Although Lucy had made clear to Jenny her feelings about the book with the golden lady on the front, she had never forbidden Jenny to read it. For the first time since she had discovered Pa's strange book and been captivated by it, Jenny felt completely free of the fear of punishment.

As Jenny passed the wind-lashed firs each day, her thoughts always seemed to circle back to the book as if drawn into focus by the forest.

The forest attracted more than Jenny's thoughts. One evening, a sudden impulse sent her scurrying from the familiar path into the trees. Once she entered the shadowed depths, a new quietness surrounded her. She wandered deeper into the woods, and her mind wandered as well. Without willing it, pictures from the book leaped into her thoughts—some intriguing, some frightening. Immediately her mind was filled with alarm, as if a thousand warning bells hammered in her soul.

Shivering with fear, Jenny turned and ran back to the path, back to daylight and away from the eerie calmness. Did she fancy she heard her name called as she left the forest? She ran the rest of the way home. Not until she stood panting on the stoop outside Harris's kitchen did she dare to admit, "If I didn't believe in spooks before, I'm beginnin' to now."

The next time Jenny passed along the path, while the wind moaned and the trees lashed, she found herself hesitating, reaching out, wanting to know. Again, quickly before she could debate, she turned off the path and the lashing trees for the calm forest.

The mysterious stillness had begun to encircle her with a reality that tightened her throat and made her heart pound, when just ahead of her she saw a dark-clad figure moving slowly through the woods, poking at drifts of leaves with a long stick.

With relief Jenny ran toward the figure. "Hello there!" she called.

The woman turned and waited for her. "Are you lost?" she called. As she hurried toward the woman, Jenny studied her face, trying to identify the stranger. Surprisingly, the dark-cloaked woman was young and beautiful. In the shadows her face seemed a pale oval, but her eyes were large and dark. Her dark hair was swept back from her brow, and the widow's peak made her face heart-shaped.

Jenny was still studying the woman, wishing she could be just like her. Slowly Jenny said, "I don't reckon I know you. I'm Jenny Timmons, the Harris's hired girl."

The woman nodded as if she knew. "You're very young to be working for your living." Without warning, tears stung Jenny's eyes. She rubbed at them, wondering why she was feeling the kindness so keenly. "Your parents have left you here. Do you miss them greatly?" Jenny shook her head, wondering how to answer such a question.

Slowly they walked together through the woods. Jenny responded to the gentle, probing questions as she still tried to identify the woman. Her face seemed familiar, but Jenny couldn't make her fit anywhere.

Suddenly the woman stopped. She pointed, saying, "There's Martin Harris's cornfield; you can cut through here."

"Oh my!" Jenny exclaimed. "We've circled the whole farm. I didn't mean for you to take me home." The woman was smiling, stepping backward down the trail. Jenny watched her curiously. "What's your name?"

She hesitated. "You may call me Adela."

"That's pretty. It sounds like bells." Now shy, Jenny dropped her head and scuffed her toe in the pine needles, wondering when she had ever before chattered on like this to a perfect stranger. She raised her head to speak, but the woman was gone.

Several times during the winter months, Jenny saw Adela when she ventured into the forest on her way home from school. Always she seemed to be poking, prodding with her stick, always alone. Jenny never felt free to ask about her activities nor to learn more about her.

One evening as Jenny left the forest after an encounter with the woman, she mused aloud, "Methinks, Adela the bella, you're as mysterious as—as a sylph." Her tongue slid over the unfamiliar word. Hadn't that word been in the book? She began to wonder why Adela made her think of the book. And more and more she realized that she didn't know the mysterious woman at all.

Finally, shyly, she described Adela to Lucy Harris and found her description as vaporous as her understanding of the woman. Lucy looked at her in confusion and Jenny ended her questions with a shrug.

So for a time, and for reasons Jenny couldn't explain, she avoided the forest path and the mysterious encounters.

As the winter waned, Mrs. Harris became an enthusiastic housekeeper, waging war against winter's accumulated dirt. She also took up the task of making a young lady out of Jenny, much to the distress of both.

As often as she dared, Jenny dallied in the afternoons instead of hurrying homeward. Still hesitant to go back into the forest, she frequently followed the Smith children home. Jenny enjoyed the chatter and laughter, the teasing and playful pranks. Aware of her loneliness, she was irresistibly drawn to the large family, despite Lucy Harris's disapproval.

Often the young schoolmaster, Oliver Cowdery, walked with them. In the past Jenny had found him morose and withdrawn, but on these walks he regaled the group with exciting stories of Vermont. Along with the stories he had to tell, he would demonstrate the art of using the rod.

The rod, delicately balanced on Oliver's fingers, would tilt as Oliver walked slowly down the path. "There!" he exclaimed. "That's signifying water's to be found here."

He was unabashed when Jenny exclaimed, "Who wants to dig a well in the middle of the woods?"

One afternoon in April Jenny followed the Smiths and their youthful schoolmaster home. It had been a beautiful day, full of the joy of spring and the excitement of a school term drawing to a close. But they met gloom as they stepped into the cabin crowded with people and piles of household belongings.

Lucy was talking rapidly, darting about the cabin gathering up bedding. Hyrum sat at the table watching his mother. His expression silenced the chattering brood.

Mrs. Smith clattered a load of kettles onto the middle of the table and turned to survey the silent group. "Well, 'tis the worst," she advised them. "We've lost the place. Get your things together; we're goin' home with Hyrum." The outcry began, but her raised hand cut through. "No fussin'. Don't give them the satisfaction of knowin'. 'Sides, we'll be back as soon as Joe starts a-sellin' the gold Bible and makin' a heap of money." She turned to Cowdery. "I 'spect the best you could do is go to Harmony and be helpin' with the translatin' to hurry things along a speck."

When Jenny carried the news home, Lucy Harris paused in her house-cleaning long enough to think. She finally spoke, as if she were pulling out the thoughts like yarn from her knitting. "That'll mean Martin will be back soon." She eyed Jenny and sighed, "What's goin' to become of us all?"

"What are you meaning?" Jenny asked slowly.

"I expect more turmoil." She paused, then spoke briskly. "First things first," she instructed. She stepped down from the chair she was standing on and dusted her hands together. "Before I get the cleanin' done, there's something more important."

"What?" Jenny asked, mystified, as she looked at the litter of dishes and pans Lucy Harris had pulled from the shelf.

"I'm goin' to take the team and go into Palmyra and see the preacher at the church."

"Whatever for?"

"First off, I'm goin' to do something I promised I'd do long ago. I'm goin' to set up your baptism."

"What baptism?"

"Jenny"—Lucy leaned her face close to Jenny's—"we've talked before about the truth, remember? That real power, spiritual power, has the truth as its source. That truth—the only truth—is in Jesus, in His death and resurrection."

Jenny nodded, "But—"

"I know you've seen and heard—and read—a lot about other kinds of power. Even my husband Martin has shown you the other. And I let you go on and read your pa's book even though I didn't like it, and I let you run off to the Smiths and hear that Lucy's wild tales of gold plates and—"

Mrs. Harris paused, looking squarely at Jenny. "I don't claim to know all there is to know about the Bible," she sighed. "That's why I want to take you into Palmyra to talk to the parson. Everybody's got to make a choice, Jenny. If you don't make one—well, you make one anyway. And now's the time for you to think about yours."

Jenny thought about the church in Palmyra.

Every Sabbath day in that sanctuary, she had sat in cold, hard pews and listened to the organ draw threads of sound around her that amazed and awed her. She had looked at the small circle window of stained glass, showering arrows of brilliant color over the shoulders of worshipers, and had dreamed of them as mystical fingers bestowing blessing and fortune. Sometimes the parson's words dropped on Jenny with raw-nerve intensity, creating a moment of awareness. But for the most part, Jenny's Sabbaths were empty of the meaning of worship.

On this day, with Mrs. Harris, she reluctantly entered the cold building with solitary and lonely thoughts. In the gloom the round window was a beacon, throwing colorful shadows throughout the sanctuary and tipping the heavy wooden cross behind the pulpit with shades of light. Did it happen by chance that afternoon shadows funneled one beam of rich light into a pinpoint finger precisely at the center of that wooden cross?

Jenny's mind amplified the results. As she sat facing that cross, listening to that somber man spread heavy words she didn't understand, she felt the weight of light and form.

She watched him turn and lift the silver chalice from the sanctuary table. At the moment he poured the wine, purple light from the window caught the chalice, spinning webs of brilliance for Jenny's eyes. That moment of awe fell against her with greater weight than the words he spoke. The wonder of the total experience robbed words of meaning for her.

Jenny's mind reeled with the possibilities. In the cold church building, she had felt a sensation akin to what she had felt in the woods—with one exception. She was moved, but not frightened as she had been among the trees. The image of the chalice and the cross rose again and again to the surface of her thinking, until finally her question overcame her hesitancy, and she sought out Mrs. Harris.

"The cross?" Lucy Harris replied. "Why, Jesus died on the cross for our salvation. The silver cup holds the wine—representing His blood—that we drink at communion."

As Lucy tried patiently to answer the questions, Jenny's confusion grew. *Was the blood of Jesus in the chalice like the blood of the rooster sprinkled around the circle where Tom and Joe were digging? Was the cross like the sword Hyrum Smith carried—did it have power to break through the spells of spirits? Is this act of baptism the one event that will launch me into the world of true power?*

The next Sabbath day, in the shadow of the same cross, Jenny Timmons was duly baptized at Palmyra Presbyterian Church. But the finger of light at the center of the cross was gone; the web of color that haloed the chalice was gone. And Jenny wondered if this way of faith really was the way of power.

Just before she slipped under the water, her eyes met the eyes of that somber parson. For a moment his face brightened until he almost looked glad. She heard his words. "Jennifer Timmons, I baptize you in the name of our Lord Jesus Christ, the great God and Savior, who gave himself to redeem and to purify you. And just as He was buried to be lifted up, you shall be baptized to be lifted up for everlasting life."

"Child," said Lucy Harris at breakfast the next morning, "don't you just feel wonderful, now that you've chosen for the Lord?"

Jenny murmured a halfhearted agreement and went about her chores, while Lucy watched and waited for the significance of Jenny's decision to take effect. Jenny waited, too. She waited for the power to come, for the feelings she had known in the woods and in the church to return, for her mind to understand, for the vague thoughts that had haunted her to crystallize.

She was still waiting when Martin Harris returned to Manchester the following Wednesday. Subdued and tired, he was nevertheless full of talk of getting the gold Bible printed.

They were visiting Martin's brother Peter and his wife Abigail when Lucy Harris finally had heard enough about the gold Bible. "Martin!" she cried, exasperated. "This gold Bible business is no religious crusade! It's just a bunch of wild stories conjured up by those who'd take a gullible man for what he's worth. Like every other project you've been duped into—when you get a new idea into your head, you get shaken loose from your money. Please, Martin, can't you see—"

"Woman!" he roared, jumping to his feet and flinging his chair aside. "Will you leave me alone? What if it *is* a lie? If you'll just mind your business, I'll stand to make a pile of money out of it yet!" He stomped out of the house, leaving Jenny and Mrs. Harris to gather their belongings and follow.

During these turbulent days, Jenny noticed how often Lucy Harris bore bruises. Many mornings Jenny observed the woman's tear-reddened eyes and sensed her troubled spirit. As the summer drew to a close, Jenny's own tension mounted; then, abruptly, there was release.

Martin Harris turned jovial, kind—at least the few times he was at home. Most conspicuous was his absence.

One late summer evening Jenny watched the man don a clean shirt and leave the house. She turned to Mrs. Harris and said, "He's happy now. Where's he going?"

The woman's lips quivered. "He's happy because he's off chasin' after a woman." Jenny's fingers crept over her errant mouth, and Lucy Harris said, "You needn't be embarrassed. Everybody in town knows Martin's shenanigans. I can't change him—but I wish the Lord would."

Autumn crept up and Jenny was getting acquainted with another new schoolmaster. Rumor had it that her previous teacher, Oliver Cowdery, had finished the translating of Joseph's golden Bible—but not in Harmony, Pennsylvania. The whispers said that because Mr. Hale, Emma's father, had vowed to see the plates, a fellow by the name of David Whitmer had moved Joseph Smith, his wife, and the whole translation business to Fayette, New York. Now there was serious talk about having the manuscript printed.

One day, after Mrs. Harris had left to visit her sister for a week, Jenny discovered some additional information quite by accident. As she hurried about the kitchen preparing the noon meal, Martin strode into the kitchen ahead of Tom and Amos. He paced the floor with quick, excited steps.

"Mr. Harris," she apologized, "I'm hurrying. I just didn't figure on you coming so soon."

Unexpectedly he turned a sudden smile on her. "Jenny, lass," he chuckled, "don't give me no mind. I'm a-thinkin' about all that's goin' on with the gold Bible business and it excites me, my it does!" Tom came into the kitchen and began to wash up. With a note of apology in his voice, Martin said, "Tom, I'm about to run out on you again. I can't stand not knowin' what's goin' on in Fayette."

Tom slowly straightened from the washbasin and reached for the towel. "The writin' is all done; what's comin' up next?"

"I couldn't tell the old lady all this; she can only ridicule." He paused and shook his head piously. "I'm fearin' for her soul, makin' fun of the Lord's anointed like that. You see, Joe's had orders to be startin' a new church. All this translatin' is for a purpose. The Lord's given him a mission of goin' to the Lamanites with the story of their brothers and the early settlement of this country. He's appointed to take the news of the restored gospel to them, and we're all to help him."

"Where did you hear all this?" Tom asked as he took his place at the table.

"That's what the book is all about. The history of the lost tribes of Israel and how they settled in this country. Joe's responsible to get the story of Jesus Christ out to them. He's been gettin' revelations from the Lord right along, tellin' him what he's to be doin' for the Lord."

"Such as—" Tom said slowly.

"Well," Martin answered just as slowly, but with an edge of enthusiasm, "Joe had a revelation that there was a man in Toronto, Canada, eager to buy the history and be printin' it. Cowdery and Hiram Page went up there."

"So they sold it?" Tom asked, and Jenny was surprised to hear the regret in his voice.

"Naw," Martin paced the room again. "They never could find the man."

"Why, that's surprising!" Tom exclaimed. "If the Lord sent them, you'd think—"

But Martin began to pace again. When he came back to the table, Jenny saw he was having a hard time controlling his excitement. "I'll tell you something else, if'n you can keep it under your hat. Me'n Oliver Cowdery and David Whitmer got the privilege of being witnesses to the book." His smile faded as he studied their blank faces. "You're not understandin' what that means, are you?" Slowly he sat down at the table and pulled his plate toward him.

"I don't rightly know how to explain it all so you'll see how important it was. See, Joe had a promise that some were to see the gold plates in order to bear witness. We went out prayin'. Now, I'll admit I don't convert easy—it took a lot of prayin' for me to get enough faith to see them, but when I did, I was convinced. Nobody can take that away from me. This angel from the Lord appeared. He was so bright it about put my eyes out to look at him, but he made himself known and then held out the plates so I could see them."

Tom and Jenny stared at him for a moment before Tom asked, "You really did, huh? How'd the angel look?"

Jenny heard the clatter of Amos's boots, and Martin whispered, "Hush about it. Joe doesn't want it nosed about for now."

During the winter of 1829 and into 1830, Martin Harris made several more trips to Fayette, New York, to see Joseph Smith. Just after he had returned in the early spring, Jenny came from school one day and accidentally interrupted something. She stepped inside the door and was halted by the sight of her mistress' flushed face. Although she knew she should leave, curiosity held her fast.

Lucy was standing in front of the rocking chair where Martin sat. "Martin! How could you promise to get that book printed even if you must sell your farm! Martin Harris, come to your senses! Because of that book, would you give up all we've struggled hard for? Has he *bewitched* you?"

He surged out of his chair, roaring, "You'll not be a-talkin' that way about the Lord's anointed!" Jenny scooted out the door. She dashed back down the trail, remembering her father's rage and desperately wishing for Tom.

As she ran, Mrs. Harris's words sank into her heart with undeniable impact. She slowed to a walk. "Jen, you could be without a home right soon," she murmured aloud. Thinking of Mrs. Harris, she winced, hearing again the dreadful sound of that whip snapping against her back. She fled into the sanctuary of the woods.

Jenny nearly tumbled over Adela before she saw her. Panting, she leaned against the nearest tree and watched the dark-cloaked woman on the fallen log. Snugly wrapped in the cloak, motionless, she could have been taken for a rock. Now her dark eyes glowed, blinked.

"You are a very disturbed young lady." The cadence in the woman's voice made Jenny think of music.

Jenny saw the stick beside her, took a deep breath, and asked, "Lookin' for treasure?"

Adela opened her eyes very wide and straightened up. "Oh," she murmured, "I've been sitting here for so long."

"You're waiting for someone?" Adela shook her head and smiled. "Someone to go digging with you? I'll go."

She laughed merrily, "Oh, Jenny, you are a funny child. You are thinking I'm like these silly little-boy treasure diggers. Who have you been talking to?"

Jenny felt her shame and was grateful for the deep shadows. "I'm sorry," she muttered. "But you were talking about the ancient religion, and how you are a nature worshiper."

"Now, Jenny," her voice was sharp, "that wasn't what I said. If you want to quote me, please get it right."

"Then please say it again so I'll understand."

"You're referring to what I said about my religion. Jenny, there's only one god; no matter how, or where, or when you choose to worship him, it's all right. I choose to worship him through nature. When I understand him and cooperate with him, I understand the mysteries of life and I am strong." Her voice dropped to a whisper. "He gives knowledge of the eternal, to know how god thinks. God-knowledge. Isn't that what mankind wants to know more than anything else?"

Jenny hesitated, thinking. Gnawing in the back of her mind was the half-formed belief that what Adela was saying was not quite right. Something was wrong—but what? Jenny grappled with the question for a moment or two; when she finally looked up, Adela was gazing at her with a strange, distant expression.

Although she was silent, her dark eyes shone, and Jenny felt as if Adela were peering deep into her, knowing all that Jenny felt and feared. But there was more. Even though Jenny didn't understand the strange woman, the words she uttered wrapped about the two of them, binding them together.

12

SPRING CAME TO Manchester, New York, surging with life. The whole countryside seemed to move and stretch and come alive at the same moment. But feelings Jenny had experienced all winter—that discontent, the vague yearnings, the desire to split the narrow seams of her life— moved over her with an intensity she couldn't deny.

As if propelled by unseen forces, Jenny went into the forest nearly every afternoon carrying the green book. Part of her resolve this spring had been to question Adela about the book, but initially she was disappointed. Now that she had decided on action, she expected Adela to be there waiting, but it was many days before she saw the woman in black.

At the beginning of her wait for Adela she was filled with impatience. Forced into patience, she discovered the world about her and found that it all reminded her of Adela.

Often the still air of the fir forest seemed to blanket her away from thought and sound, releasing her to experience the quiet. On occasion, a lone shaft of sunlight would penetrate the darkness. That single ray reminded her of the light in the church, and she tried to reconcile that experience with what Adela had said about worship.

Under the intensity of that arrow of light, she discovered flowers blooming in miniature, with an extra wash of color. She found the herbs and mushrooms Adela had gathered so eagerly with her long stick. Jenny tried to recall the ways Adela had used them, and she remembered one occasion when Adela had dipped a jug full of the fetid swamp water, guarding it as if it were a treasure.

When Jenny's thoughts were spun out, when she was tired of sighing with loneliness, she opened the green book and studied the strange words and promises.

In April, before she had seen Adela again, Smith came back to Manchester. Coming in from school one day, Jenny heard his voice, and at the same time, she heard Martin. Every word the man uttered sounded like a prayer. Jenny crept through the hallway to the parlor, and peered through the draperies. She saw the difference; this Joseph stood tall and square-shouldered before the cold fireplace. His presence commanded attention, and Martin was most certainly giving it to him.

Joseph's arm rested on the mantle, nearly against Lucy's best lamp. Jenny was heedless of his words; she had eyes only for the arm that pushed against the lamp. Remembering Lucy's last encounter with Joe in her kitchen, Jenny was mesmerized by the lamp. If he were to knock it to the floor, would Lucy dare chastise him?

But then the words and Joe's solemn expression caught her attention. "Martin," he was saying, "I've long delayed coming, but the Lord reminds me I have a grave obligation. He's given me a message and a mission that I must not ignore—on pain of death."

Again Jenny marveled at the difference between this powerful presence and the bright-haired boy with the peepstone. "Bet Emma has been working on his talking," she muttered to herself. "He sounds like a gentleman."

Smith dropped his arms from the mantle and folded them across his chest. There was regret in his voice as he spoke slowly and softly. "Martin, are you man enough to hear what the Lord has commanded me to say to you?" Martin hesitated a moment, then nodded his head.

"He let me know that you were wicked when you wearied me for the manuscript. It is only because of his purposes which must stand that I'm forgiven and restored for letting you have the papers. But I told you this last year. I'm only reminding you now so you'll remember how fearful it is to neglect any word of the Lord."

Jenny watched him pace the room and then stop in front of Martin. "Now, Martin, here is a new message from the Lord. You are to repent. I have written out the revelation and I will let you read it for yourself, but I am to warn you to your face and then let you dwell upon it.

"Do you remember how in the revelation to Oliver, the Lord said that when man has truth given to him, he is to study it in his mind? If it is correct and from the Lord, he will have a burning in his bosom. This will let you know what is right. Don't forget, Martin, it's the burning in the bosom."

Joe paced the room again, and Martin pleaded, "Please tell me. I know it's bad, but I'd rather just hear it."

"For one thing," Joe's voice was gentle, kind, "He's said that if you don't repent, you must suffer. Martin, He's said you are not to covet your neighbor's wife, nor to seek the life of your neighbor. You are not to covet your own property, but to impart it freely for the publishing of the Book of Mormon, the word of God. He has commanded you to pay up the printer's debt and release yourself from bondage. Leave your house and home, except when you want to be here."

The import of the words struck Jenny and she shoved her knuckles against her teeth. She was trembling, but she willed herself to silence. There was a tumble of words from Martin and in the confusion, Jenny slipped from her hiding place and rushed through the kitchen and up to her room in the loft.

"What is *sabbat*?" Jenny sat on the log beside Adela. She clutched the green book tight and waited.

Slowly Adela moved, stirring as if just awakening. She looked at Jenny. "Where did you get the book?"

"It belonged to my pa."

"And he let you have it?"

Jenny hesitated only a second. Somehow she knew that Adela wouldn't disapprove. "I stole it from him. When they left for the West without me, I just took it."

Adela smiled gently, her voice dreamy and soft. "You really want the knowledge, don't you? I think that back in the past there was someone in your family, someone who—"

She didn't finish her statement, but Jenny saw her eyes shine their approval. Adela stood, moving as if she were drifting to her feet. "Jenny, you are very young. There's much to learn. This is a start, reading the book, but now you must let me lead you step by step." As she spoke her hands moved as if drawing an arc in the air.

She whispered, "If you will learn the mysteries truly, if you allow them to sink into your mind, they will shape you into a person of power." Her hands reached toward Jenny and then abruptly she pulled back. She whispered, "It must be done in the right way." She pulled the cloak about her and started down the trail. "Come now, there are many things for you to see."

Jenny trotted to keep up, but her stomach knotted with an unknown apprehension. She watched Adela using the long-forked stick as a walking stick. Eyeing the stick she said, "Martin said Joe had a revelation from the Lord for Oliver Cowdery, and the Lord told Oliver that using the rod was a gift from the Lord and that he was to use the rod to hear messages from God."

"It's true. He has it right. There's only one god, just many different ways to know him." She turned to face Jenny again and said, "I am anxious to teach you this way. Jenny, you'll have power to help people, to heal them, to do good—or evil—in their lives. It is for you to decide how you'll use the power."

That night, long after the supper dishes had been cleared away and Jenny lay in her room under the eaves, Adela's words continued to ring through Jenny's thoughts.

Restlessly she tossed and turned, excited, troubled, questioning, uncertain. Images from the past danced through her mind. She could see Tom laughing, throwing back his head and shouting with glee when she had informed him that someday she would marry Joseph Smith.

Funny, the thought was still there—cold and lifeless, but still there. *Power.* Jenny was filled with uneasy desire. Adela had said, "There's just one god, and how you worship doesn't matter. But I can show you how to have power, power for all the things you desire. Jenny, what do you desire more than anything else in this world?"

Jenny hadn't answered. Adela's words hadn't seemed real at the time, but now with the full moon streaming its silver light into her room, Jenny realized that her old desire had not diminished but gained new strength.

She sat up in bed and hugged her knees against her chest. She could feel her breasts against her legs, and the soft fullness reminded her that her life was changing, moving forward.

"Jenny," she whispered to herself, "just like Adela said, you've lots to learn. If Joe Smith can change, so can you. If the moon is what you want, Adela can tell you how to get it. They say Joe's wife is sickly and can't give him young'uns. I'll be the second Mrs. Smith, and I won't share him with another woman on earth."

The next day Jenny eagerly sought out Adela. Once again she sat on the log beside her with the green book hugged tightly in her arms. Adela was talking but Jenny was only vaguely conscious of the rhythm of her words; instead, she was studying Adela, from her flawless ivory skin to the red chiffon that showed through the heavy folds of her cape. She murmured yes to questions that slid over her head. But mostly she wondered how she could become like Adela.

Abruptly she asked, "Where did you get your pretty red dress?"

Adela pulled away from her and for a moment her lips tightened with displeasure. "You have not been listening to me! Jenny, how do you expect to learn? You wouldn't treat your schoolteacher that way, would you?" Suddenly her face softened, "Jenny, I didn't mean to scold. You're young. I forget. At your age it is hard to take life seriously. Never you mind. I'll be patient till you see."

Abruptly she jumped to her feet and dropped the dark cloak. Before Jenny had time to blink her startled eyes, Adela spun away from her in a dance. Her red dress rose and fell like a flame as she danced through the trees, dipping, swirling. She retreated through the firs, then came flying back to Jenny.

When she finally stopped Jenny watched the flame red dress slowly float downward, quiet again. Adela pulled the shrouding cape around her shoulders and dropped to the ground in front of Jenny.

"I feel part of the god of light when I dance," she murmured. "Only then do I transcend this place and reach the eternal and become one with him."

Jenny frowned trying to understand the concepts, and Adela patted her knee. "You need to read more. Here, I'll mark portions for you to read, just like your teacher at school!"

Jenny spoke slowly. "You asked what I desired in life, and I couldn't answer. Now I know. How do I get the power to have my desires?"

Adela studied Jenny and her pretty lips pulled down into a mocking pout. "You make a light thing of it all; what do you want, a new dress like mine?"

Jenny shook her head. "No, it's—well it's personal and I just can't talk about it. But I want it very much."

Jenny saw Adela look down at her clenched hands as she said dryly, "I don't think you yet realize we are not trading for little favors. Serving the god of the universe for a new dress isn't done. Jenny, I've tried to tell you that this is serious business. True, there is great satisfaction and power, but more—there is great responsibility. You don't enter lightly into searching out the eternals. You don't learn the secrets and mysteries of life itself without a great deal of—of soul searching. This is a pathway; once you start there is no turning back. You yourself will become in tune with nature itself. Like a harp plucked by the hand of the master, you must respond.

"If you will use, you must be used. Taking vows is serious, embarking on the tunnel toward that light is a glorious journey, freeing the spirit to soar with others of our kind." Now she leaned close to Jenny and peered into her eyes. Jenny could only shiver, transfixed; she felt she had already started down the path.

But later, on another day, Jenny opened the book in Adela's presence and ran her fingers under horrifying words. "Adela, they don't mean this, do they, about drinking blood?"

Adela nodded in affirmation, and her face hardened in response to Jenny's whispered, "No!" But as soon as Jenny said it, she knew she had to decide. The thought of losing Adela—and Joe—was unbearable.

When the woman's face softened and she knelt before Jenny with that beautiful smile, Jenny knew she couldn't say no. Finally, when they both stood, Adela smiled gently, "Before the power begins, you must go to the sabbat with me and prove you are ready to start down the path of power."

Jenny started to ask her again about the word *sabbat,* but decided against it. If she went to one, she would learn what it was.

The time came, the eve of May Day. For weeks Jenny had trembled between wanting what Adela had promised, and fearing the coming unknown in a way she could neither identify nor understand.

Even now, on this chosen night, Jenny hesitated, filled with doubt. She slipped from the silent, sleeping house just before midnight. For a moment she was filled with a voiceless plea for Tom. Then she straightened her shoulders. Adela would be there; that was all she needed.

At the end of the path, at the edge of the dark forest, Adela met her. Without a word they moved swiftly through the woods toward a pale light shining through the trees. Jenny realized they stood on a moonlit path at the edge of town. She gave a gasp of relief as Adela motioned her on.

When they stopped in front of the church, Jenny's words burst out in astonishment. "I didn't know we were goin' to church! You said—"

"Where else would one go to worship the beautiful god of light?"

Jenny shrugged. Trying vainly to express her tumbled thoughts, she said, "I—I guess when you explained about renouncing all other covenants and talked about the new communion, I guess I just—" Other shadowy figures were joining them, and Jenny said no more.

The church was lighted only by a tiny cluster of candles. For a moment Jenny thought back to the afternoon she had come here with Lucy Harris. How brilliant the beautiful light had been! Now the dark-robed group moved slowly and silently toward the candles.

A sudden chill swept over Jenny. The cross which had hung on the wall was being lifted down. They dropped it in front of the candles, and one dark figure kicked it into position.

A black-robed man with a goat's head tied around his neck began to sing. And after a few minutes the singing gave way to chanting, a strange rhythmic chanting which surged and pulsed through Jenny's body. Their chant was strange and disturbing.

Abruptly the chanting ceased, and Jenny felt the strange, heavy silence settle over her spirit. A man moved slowly toward the priest. She watched him take a deep breath and lift his head. Clearly his voice rang out, "I beg you, honorable one, that you add my name to the Book of Death. It is only by moving beyond this life and into the next that I will enter the eternal progression."

For a moment Jenny lost the thread of thought as the man continued with his vows. She was frowning, trying to understand what he was saying. Suddenly new words grabbed her attention, spreading meaning over her with a chilling blast.

The priest was saying, "Do you deny the Christian faith, the creator of heaven and earth? Do you renounce your baptism and promise to give your allegiance only to the god of light?"

The words were still underlining themselves in her mind, spreading confusion and a fear that she didn't understand, but she pushed them away as the man squared his shoulders. She heard the first initiate echo a dark-sounding oath, and she felt an urge to run. She cringed as he stomped on the cross. Then they removed the chalice from the altar and poured a dark substance into it. This chalice she had drunk from on that day of glory and light, they were desecrating with animal's blood!

Clasping her hands against her throat, Jenny backed away, shuddering as horror coursed through her. Jenny felt hands pushing her forward, cold and insistent, for she was the next initiate. Adela's sharp voice reminded her, "You said you would do anything for power. Have you changed your mind?"

As Jenny hesitated, a clear picture of Joe's intense face framed with bright hair rose in her mind. Still she pulled back as Adela's cold hand pushed. As she took a step, the group parted to accept her. The cross lay at her feet.

Suddenly she whirled and ran down the long aisle, past Adela and the motionless dark figures. Through the darkened streets Jenny ran, her mind filled with remembered glory—brilliant color broken by the window and thrown against the cross and the chalice.

All that night horror held her motionless, wide-eyed in the darkness of her room. As morning broke she watched for the sun with hungry eyes, wishing she could get enough of it to last her through the coming night and then the next.

But within the week a new horror came. Life with Martin Harris had been rising to a climax for a long time. Jenny had felt this, but even she was surprised that evening.

He came in for his supper, saying in a matter-of-fact tone of voice, "I've sold part of the farm."

Lucy was very quiet for a moment. Then she sighed and moved. "How much did you get?"

"Three thousand—and there's not a penny for you," he said stoutly. "It's all for the Lord's work. Joe's had a revelation sayin' I'm to pay the printer's debt."

He settled himself at the table and pulled the plate of bread toward him. "The printer's debt," Lucy repeated slowly. "You mean you're paying for printing Joe's gold Bible with the money from our farm?" She walked slowly toward him. "Martin, I can't hold my peace any longer. You've always been restless, seekin' after new religions, never satisfied with the truth. But to sell the farm for this heresy—"

"That's enough, woman!" Martin roared. "I'm leavin' you. You're rebelling against the Lord and I'll have nothin' more to do with you! You'll have this house, but you'll have to feed and clothe yourself. Maybe that Lord of yours will take care of you!" He jumped to his feet and headed for the door.

Lucy ran toward him, reaching for his arm. Jenny stood horrified, unable to move as the quick sweep of his arm threw off Lucy's clinging hands. Without thinking, Jenny rushed toward her as Lucy spun off balance.

"You leave her be!" Martin roared, and swung at Jenny. Again and again he struck her, then turned on Lucy. When Jenny returned to consciousness and looked around for Lucy, Martin was long gone.

They surveyed each other's wounds; then their eyes met. Heavily Lucy said, "You can't fight a revelation. He thinks it's God speakin' to him—but God don't make people mean."

During the following week, Jenny and Lucy did little more than nurse their battered bodies. But the memory of the terror returned when Tom came home and saw the results of Martin's fury. Anger and despair swept his face; he hugged Jenny and she cried with pain. During that week, he scarcely let Lucy and Jenny out of his sight.

One evening as Jenny limped into the kitchen, she heard Tom talking to Lucy. "Ma'am, there's no work here, and you don't need the worry of extra mouths to feed. Amos and the others have found a spot for themselves, and I mean to be off myself. A buddy's in town and he's talkin' me into movin' east with him. I—"

Jenny's cry broke through his words, and the two turned to her. "Oh, Tom, you can't leave me! Not now!" The arm she stretched toward him was still badly bruised and she saw him wince. "Take me with you, please."

While Tom hesitated, Lucy sighed, "Much as I hate to lose her, Tom, she's right to ask. You're her blood relation and that means much to a young'un. Take her away from this place and find her a position wherever you go."

Jenny's poor battered body robbed her of the sense to ask about their destination and with whom they would travel. When the day came and she stood in front of Mark Cartwright with her bundles of belongings at her feet, she realized that Tom hadn't mentioned her to Mark, either.

Tom stumbled over his explanations and Mark's frown changed to pity. While his eyes measured the bruises on her bare arms, Jenny realized that her ordeal had become an asset. It was winning her release from this place.

13

THE STAGECOACH WAS just beginning to roll, pulling out of Manchester for eastern New York. Mark Cartwright and Tom sat facing Jenny. At the crack of the driver's whip and his shout, "Move it out!" the horses responded with a surge of speed and the stage rocked around the corner. Jenny's knuckles were white as she gripped the handrail.

"Your first time on a stagecoach?" Mark observed and was given a tense nod. Cautiously she leaned against the doorframe to watch Manchester disappear from sight.

Tom lowered his voice. "We've just traveled in Pa's wagon. Mark, we're greenhorns, and mighty grateful we could travel with you. You've got kin in Cobleskill? I've never heard of Cobleskill."

Jenny leaned forward. "Your ma and pa there?"

Mark shook his head. He was studying Jenny, marveling at the difference four years had made. "My mother lives in Ohio, just inland from Cleveland. My father died three years ago. I'm headed for Albany, New York. An uncle on my mother's side has offered this fledgling attorney a spot in his law office until I get some experience." He watched curiosity flit across Jenny's face. "My mother has a sister in Cobleskill," he added. As Jenny's large gray eyes watched him intently, he lapsed into silence, remembering South Bainbridge. What a pathetic little tyke she had been in those days! Only her eyes still seemed the same—curious gray flecked with amber, just as steadfast and serious now as when they had caught his attention in the schoolroom at South Bainbridge.

Mark continued to watch Jenny as she shifted her attention to Tom. He found himself speaking just to recapture that play of expression on her face, to see the changing light in her eyes. When Tom was voicing his fears of the future again, the shadows in Jenny's eyes had Mark leaning forward, raising his voice against the clatter of the coach and the shout of the driver.

"Tom, I'll help you find a position. There are friends enough around Cobleskill who'll know of jobs for the two of you. You needn't settle for just anything; you've both worked, and you'll find good positions. Don't worry about a thing."

When they reached Cobleskill Mark was true to his word. He soon found work for Jenny, but things just weren't working out for Tom. Tom was figuring how to explain this to Jenny as he sat in the kitchen of the Hamilton Barton home. Watching his sister working in the kitchen, he couldn't help admire her easy manner.

"You're fittin' in well," he observed, nodding his head toward the hall. "I was sure flabbergasted when I saw the place. Mark did well for you."

"It was actually Mrs. Weber, his aunt Mabel. She knew the Bartons were needing a girl." She paused in her task of mixing bread and lifted doughy hands. "I've Lucy Harris to thank for showing me the way around a lady's kitchen. But I'm also thinking Mrs. Barton's mighty generous to take on such a raw one and train me up; no doubt Mark and his aunt had something to do with it all. Leastwise, the Bartons seems to think well of Mark." She covered the bread pans and turned to Tom. "You didn't come just for a chat, did you?"

Tom shrugged and then admitted, "Jen, I'm for goin' back."

"Back!" she echoed, whirling around. "You don't mean Manchester."

"I'm not sure where," he admitted miserably. He knew he was failing her. "I can't get myself settled to anything, and I thought if I were to just wander back for a time, it might settle my feelings."

She continued to watch him and he resisted the urge to squirm. Her eyes were too much like Ma's, guessing his thoughts. Slowly she said, "I think what you're feeling has something to do with Joe Smith. He was sure getting lots of sympathy from you."

"Jen, he's my friend. It hurts to remember how the people back there ain't givin' him a chance to prove himself. A crowd is followin' him now, and listenin' to him, everywhere except Palmyra and Manchester. There they wouldn't even let him have the town hall to have his say."

Jenny rubbed her chin with a floury hand, and Tom chuckled at the childish gesture. Gently he said, "Rub the flour off your chin. Jen, I'm not tryin' to lay my burdens on you; I only want you to understand why I'm leavin' now."

"Tom, I'll not hold you. I've this position here and I'll make it. Only—" her voice caught and she took a breath, "just come see me once in a while. You're all I have. Sometimes I pine for Ma and I think to look for her. I wish they'd be writing, so I'd know where to find them."

"You know Ma can't hardly put a pen to paper," Tom responded, getting to his feet. She only nodded as she followed him to the door.

Jenny's words and the memory of the one tear that had escaped down her cheek stayed with Tom as he packed his gear and headed back. As he trudged the roads and trails, passing through small towns and walking the country roads past prospering farms, he pondered and chided himself. "Tom, here you are, twenty-one years old and roamin' the country like a tad with nothin' to do. Seems you ought to be settlin' down."

But then he admitted it—he had unrest inside, and this was the only thing he knew to do to get rid of it. Abruptly his feet veered off the west-bound road and sought the southward cut toward Pennsylvania. Later, when he wondered why he had chosen that path just then, he concluded it must have been the Lord giving him one more chance to pay attention.

It was a late summer afternoon when he reached the main street of South Bainbridge, weary and foot-sore. Trudging into town, he could see the school through the trees; just ahead was the tavern, to his right the general store. Absorbed by memories, Tom nearly stumbled into a group of men standing on the corner.

"Tom Timmons, can I be dreamin'?" Tom stopped abruptly and his startled eyes met those of Martin Harris. Behind him stood Joe Smith and Oliver Cowdery. Joe grinned with delight as he clapped Tom on the shoulder.

"The Lord is good!" Joe exclaimed. "David Whitmer, this is Tom Timmons from up Manchester way." He turned his attention to Tom. With a broad grin he said, "You've come just in time to celebrate with us. How did the news travel so fast?"

"News?" Tom blinked, still not believing his eyes. "I'm just travelin' through—what news?"

For a moment Joe looked startled; then he threw back his head. "The Lord sent you! That's even better!"

Tom looked slowly around the group of sober men. "What's goin' on?"

Joe stepped closer and clapped Tom on the shoulder again, "Let me tell you. We've been bringing the gospel to the people of South Bainbridge and Colesville, and the Lord's blessing mightily. Everybody's buying the *Book of Mormon* and they're falling over themselves to join the church."

"So you really have started a church," Tom said slowly.

Joe nodded. "April 6, 1830, at Fayette, New York, the Church of Christ was organized with six people. Now there's so many converts we can hardly keep up with the baptizing. This will go down in history, mark my word. The Lord has revealed His restored gospel in these latter days, just before the end of all things as we know them. Tom, my lad, there's a new day dawning. The Lord's going to be returning to claim His own and set up His kingdom. It is our task to carry the news to everyone. Will you be joining us?"

"Joe," Tom said slowly, studying his face, "you're so changed I can't hardly believe it's you. I was wantin' to find you, to see if we could get the diggin' bunch together again. I'd heard you was serious about this church business, but I didn't reckon it had gone this far. Join, huh?" He scratched his forehead. "Mind if I hang around a while and see what's goin' on?"

"I'll bring you up-to-date," Martin said eagerly, not noticing how Tom pulled away from him. "Soon as we started havin' a little success convertin' folks here, the soreheads began makin' things hot. They brung up that old charge against Joe here."

He paused to snort his disgust. Tom thought incredulously, *This man beat up his wife and my sister, and he stands here talking to me like nothing's wrong!*

"Chawin' it like a dog with a bone," Martin continued. "I don't see the sense of it. They made a big fuss over Joe usin' the seer stone, like it was the worst thing that could happen. I set them straight. Leastwise, they shut up when I told them that Joe used the stone to find the gold plates. I think that pretty well convinced them the business couldn't be bad."

Tom recalled the battered faces of Jenny and Lucy Harris. Finally, he shook his head as if to clear it as Martin's excited words and joyful face pushed through that ugly picture. It was impossible to understand, to fit the two views of Martin together.

"It was the churches," Cowdery added. "They didn't like seeing their people so happy, seeing them pull out of the old dead places and go to the true church. That's why they brought up those old charges against Joe. Lo and behold, the statute of limitations had passed, so they had to let him off scot-free!"

David added enthusiastically, "Practically as soon as he stepped out of court, the law from Colesville slapped him with another warrant. But they couldn't stick him with anything there, either."

Martin Harris chuckled, "Court spent twenty-three hours listenin' to everybody in the country complain about the man. But they weren't able to make a thing stick. The feelin' is that Judge Noble wasn't a bit happy with his decision. He was sayin', aside like, that you cain't do much with a fella who's practicin' his religion, even if you don't like the way he's a-doin' it."

"Joe's lucky." Tom turned to see the stern-faced older man speaking. "The laws against digging for money and treasures been on the books since 1788, and I don't expect them to be dropped soon. I'm advising him to keep his nose clean."

Joe threw his head back and laughed joyously. "Ah, Thompson, the Lord's a step ahead of you. An angel's come and told me to give up the digging business." Tom began to chuckle and Joe linked his arm through Tom's. "Why don't you come along with us?" Tom nodded, and immediately Joe sobered. "Tom, this may just seem jolly, but it's a burden, and don't you ever forget it. The Lord's laid a mighty responsibility on me, and I need all the help I can get from my true friends."

Looking back on it all later, Tom continued to marvel at the tilting of events that had so quickly tumbled him back into Joe Smith's life again.

The easy camaraderie among these men made the whole situation nearly unbelievable to Tom. But life seemed to fluctuate incessantly. The group shifted from gaiety to desperate prayer and fasting until Joseph sent them two by two into the surrounding area with their bundles of books and the tale of the new church.

All the while, Tom stood by as a spectator, watching the events surrounding Joe. New converts continued to flock forward for baptism, and opposition continued, too. Just as quickly as Joe erected dams for his baptismal pools, townspeople tore them out.

Tom watched Joe struggle with the tension between his new converts and the need to support his wife. Joe finally went back to farming. On a day that Oliver Cowdery paid his visit, Tom was pitching hay while Joe drove the team of horses.

When Tom rammed his pitchfork into the ground and walked up to the wagon, he heard Oliver Cowdery chiding Joe about neglecting the church. Even Tom breathed a sigh of relief when Joe recited a new revelation from the Lord, telling him that the new church was to support him and his wife. But the hard words at the end of the revelation, stating the Lord would send curses instead of blessings if His people didn't follow this command, left Tom feeling uneasy.

The first leaves had donned autumn colors before Tom gave serious consideration to the winter ahead. He chewed a straw and pondered the end of the carefree summer. "Tom," he addressed himself, "it's time for funnin' to end. The winter will be hard and hungry if'n you don't get yourself a real job and snug in for the season."

He was still muttering to himself when Joe came out to lean on the fence rail beside him. "Tom," he said, facing him with that penetrating gaze which still made Tom squirm, "I've been meaning to have a talk with you. Seems you're still on the fence about your beliefs. Now, Tom, you know I'm not pushing a single person to accept what his mind refuses to entertain. But, my friend, I must caution you to not delay. If you are convinced that all this is from the Lord, then choose ye whom ye will serve."

"Joe, it isn't that. You're my good friend, and I'm happy bein' around you, but this is all like a box canyon. I gotta get out and be gettin' on with life. I've a livin' to earn, body and soul to keep together."

His lips twisted at his attempted humor, but Joe's steady gaze tore the grin away. "You're not facing the seriousness of it at all. Tom, if this is from the Lord, there's no way you can turn your back on it without losing your soul."

Tom chewed his straw and thought. Finally Joe said softly, "I'm not of a mind to persuade anybody. Tom, you must decide for yourself, but I can give you some help. The Lord gave some good advice to Oliver and I'm prone to use it to help you. He said to him that a body is to be studying out truth in his mind. Then he should ask the Lord if it is right. The Lord will cause his bosom to burn within as a testimony if it is."

"Joe, it isn't that I doubt. It's just that I don't care for religion. Seems to me there's enough trouble in life without gettin' connected with more. And I see you headed for opposition."

"So, other things are more important than following the Lord's commandments? You need to open your heart to what He's revealing. I'll be praying that the Lord will convince you otherwise." Joe paused for a moment and then added, "You're footloose now. How about coming to Fayette with us for the general conference of the church? Might help you to see how the Lord's operating now."

At the church conference Tom listened as Hiram Page stood to his feet and humbly confessed the sin of having used a seer stone. With a voice full of contrition, he admitted, "I was a-tryin' to elevate myself. I promise to give it up. I know now it is only the Prophet who has the gifts. I'll never use the stone again."

Tom met Newel Knight at the conference and heard his story. "The Prophet cast a devil out of me," he said soberly. His tiny wife nodded at his elbow, as he added, "If it hadn't happened, I'd be dead now. Satan had me by the throat squeezing the life outta me, and I was even unconscious for a time. When you have a testimony like this, you know this has gotta be the right church."

In October, Tom left Fayette with a group going on the first missionary journey to the Lamanites. When he returned, there was a new face among the converts—Sidney Rigdon. Rigdon was a preacher, formerly a member of the Campbellites.

It didn't take Tom long to see this new convert's impact on the scraggly bunch of farmers who comprised the new church. This dignified man had the voice and demeanor of a professional orator.

Standing in the shadows watching the two men together, Tom saw Joseph stumble in his youthful inexperience. He also saw the attention the new convert was attracting and began to wonder if Joe was losing out to the newcomer. But while pity was stirring in Tom's breast, the Lord spoke to Joseph again.

When Tom heard the revelation read, he breathed a sigh of relief for Joe. "That's right good," he muttered to Martin Harris standing beside him. "Now we all know for certain that the Lord sent Rigdon to Joseph just as He sent John the Baptist to Jesus. Rigdon's to be Joe's helper. It's good to know that the Lord approves of Joe just the way he is, and He isn't faultin' him 'cause he's not the smooth talker Rigdon is."

14

"I TELL YOU, these are the last days!" Tom was watching as Joe Smith leaned forward to rest his hand on Rigdon's knee. Joe's earnest gaze was fastened on the older man as he repeated, "The last days. It wouldn't surprise me none to see Jesus Christ return during my lifetime. Sidney, we've much to do before His return!"

It was the end of October 1830. Joe, his family, and some of his followers had taken up residence in Fayette, New York. They were on the Whitmer farm where the new church had been started the previous summer.

Tom looked around the tiny room where that event had taken place. Rigdon's voice was taut with excitement as he answered Joe, and Tom felt a shiver run up his back. "I know, I know. The whole country is feeling it, talking about it, and doing nothing at all." He paced the room, saying, "Every other soapbox has a prophet on it nowadays, proclaiming the return. But they will all fail."

Joe's voice overlapped Rigdon's, "We've a big mission for these few short years. With the Lord on our side, nothing on this earth will stand in our way. Priestcraft has corrupted the church Jesus started; no wonder He swept truth from the earth! But now the true church of Jesus Christ has been restored in these latter days." He stressed his next words, "In this dispensation God has prepared men's hearts to accept the truth."

Rigdon's eager hand reached out, but Joe shook it off. "That guarantees success," he continued. "But it isn't only telling about the true, restored church and bringing the lost tribes into the fold." His voice deepened. "There's something else that must be done."

Rigdon shifted forward on his chair and waited. Tom's attention was caught by the older man's excitement before he heard Joe's words.

"*Zion,*" he said. "We have been given the task of building Zion on this continent. Jesus Christ is going to return to this continent, not to Jerusalem. How do I know? He's told me so. Let me read to you from the latest revelation."

The sun of the late October day streamed through the window. Joe wiped perspiration from his face and picked up a sheaf of papers. Clearing his throat, Joe began, "Now this is just part of it: 'And Enoch and all his people walked with God, and he dwelt in the midst of Zion; and it came to pass that Zion was not, for God received it up into His own bosom; and from thence went forth the saying, *Zion is fled.*'

"Enoch built such a perfect city God removed it from earth." In the quiet Tom heard a fly buzz against the window. Joe sighed and leaned forward. "Sidney, my friend, we have been given the task of building the New Jerusalem. When Christ returns, the city of Enoch will descend out of heaven to that very spot."

Sidney Rigdon jumped to his feet and paced the room in quick, hard strides. He stopped in front of Joe, his eyes burning with excitement. Surprisingly his voice was low and controlled. "Smith, we've got a whole bunch of converts just sitting out there waiting for us."

Joe looked startled, and Sidney explained. "Kirtland, Ohio. These people are ready for the message right now, and we mustn't delay." He paused and then added, "You know, converting them will be easier if we're all there."

Astonished, Tom cut into the conversation. "We're to uproot the whole lot and move to Ohio? Get the people from Manchester and Palmyra, Colesville and Bainbridge all to move? Rigdon, that's asking too much." Tom looked at the man's square jaw and hastily added, "I guess I'd better get busy with my chores."

During the following weeks Tom held his tongue while the members of the new church argued with Joseph. Through it all ran Joseph's quiet persuasion as he reminded the people of the Lord's instruction. "Kirtland is the eastern boundary of the promised land. We must claim our inheritance."

When the next general conference of the church convened, winter was well upon New York State. Outside the crowded building snow was falling steadily. When Joe Smith arrived, the sixty members met him with worried gazes.

Moving purposefully, he turned the pages of the newest revelation he had received from the Lord. "My friends and fellow laborers together, I beg your attention while I instruct you with the Lord's wisdom." Tom was sitting where he could see the faces as Joe read the words. There were smiles of satisfaction at the description of Zion. ". . . a land flowing with milk and honey." But Tom saw their despair at the words, "And they that have farms that cannot be sold, let them be left or rented as seemeth good."

Later as the people pushed their way out of the hall, Tom listened to the comments. "Lucky for us he's appointed someone to take care of the poor; I'm feeling we're all going to fall in that category." "At least we know the riches of the earth are the Lord's to give; maybe we'll get some of that by and by." "Do we have to wait fer the Second Comin' to get 'em?"

One terse remark that reached Tom's ears troubled him for weeks. He had nearly reached the door when he heard, "I think Joe himself invented that revelation just so he can get a spot of cash from all these farms."

During January and February, the first line of wagons and carts headed for Ohio. Joseph Smith and his pregnant wife left by sleigh. Some of the more fortunate had shipped down Lake Erie to Cleveland, but Tom bartered a ride in a sleigh traveling along behind Joseph.

Nearly as quickly as the first body of believers descended on Kirtland, the eager and the curious began to pour into town to see this new prophet.

The story of the golden Bible attracted them, but they stayed when they saw the miracles and heard Joe's sermons, which kept the listeners in gales of laughter, or suddenly reduced them to tears.

While the growing community of New Yorkers settled in the town of Thompson, Joe Smith took up residence in the Whitney home and began his translation of the New Testament. Tom had found a position working in the livery stable. From there he watched and marveled.

The weather had just begun to soften with a hint of spring when Emma's second pregnancy ended in the loss of twins. Tom had known nothing of the event on the day he rode out to visit the Prophet. He had nearly reached the Smith farm when he spotted the lonely figure trudging toward him.

"Hello, Joe, my friend!" he hailed. As Joe drew near, Tom slipped from his horse. "What's wrong, Joe?" The Prophet's face was white and drawn, and his eyes were troubled.

"Why is it," he asked Tom, as if continuing a conversation, "I've the power to heal everyone except my wife? I can bless others with health, but I can't call down the power to deliver my wife of a live child."

Tom shook his head, startled.

"Twins this time; they both died. I was powerless. It was only the gift from heaven that kept Emma from following them."

"What do you mean?"

"God gave us twin girls. Their mother died in the birthing. Another man's loss, my gain." Joe seemed to brighten, to toss aside the dark questions. As they rode toward his farm, and Joe talked about the translating and the newest revelation, Tom remembered his mission.

He interrupted, "Joe, my friend, I feel I should report the gossip."

Joseph grinned wryly. "Let me guess. It's the revelation on the United Order, isn't it?"

"Well, every other religion's pullin' the same thing. Rigdon's fellow Campbellites had been practicin' communal living, sharin' everything. They said a body could expect to see his shirt goin' down the street on someone else's back. It's not settin' too good with people who've been right particular about their belongings. I'm reluctant, too, about sharing my money and horse."

"Don't fault me," Joe said defensively. "You know this isn't my idea; it's a revelation from the Lord. My only responsibility is to teach it."

"Part of the bad feelings have to do with Rigdon's flock bein' caught up in this before we came."

"Don't forget we got a church full of people along with Rigdon," Joe cautioned. "Count it wisdom of the Lord to show us how to live together."

Tom still hesitated. "Well, revelation about the Order was a mighty long one, and it just hit wrong."

"What was hitting wrong? The part about murder and there being no forgiveness, or was it about loving your wife with all your heart and not cleaving to anyone, not committing adultery? The people of God ought to be able to live with that instruction."

"No, 'twasn't that; it was the money thing. The part about writin' a deed, which can't be broken, givin' all a man's belongings to the church. That's pretty hard. What's a man to do if he decides he don't want to be a part of the church anymore?"

Impatiently Joe said, "Tom, are you suggesting that I change the revelation? Do you realize what you're saying? This is the Lord's command! Not a word is to be altered. Changing's saying God doesn't give perfect revelations."

Tom stuck his hands in his pockets and muttered, "Sorry, Joe. That wasn't what I had in mind. If you could just find a way to make it a little easier to swallow."

"Well, we've found it! You know the people from New York have all settled in Thompson. Thanks to their obeying the Lord, Leman Copley and Ezra Thayer have given generously of a big chunk of land to provide for the people."

"You don't say!" Tom exclaimed, slapping the reins of his horse across his hand. "That's Jim Dandy. Just the verification that everybody's been lookin' for."

"Verification?" Joseph stopped and turned a sorrowful look on Tom. "I'm surprised you even admitted it. Tom, that isn't faith!" He continued to study Tom with sad eyes.

In the silence Tom remembered another reason for his visit. "Joe, I wanted you to know I'm plannin' a trip to see my sister for a bit. She's hanging on me, since we're family, but I'll be back." But Joe Smith was lost in thought and he merely nodded.

In May, Tom once again sat in the Bartons' kitchen. He watched Jenny moving about her work, marveling at the stroke of luck that had provided this work for her. He also measured her size and the changes in her body.

"Jen, this place agrees with ya. I left a little 'un; now you're taller and fillin' out like a young lady should." Surprised to see her blush, he exclaimed, "Aw, Jen, I'm your brother."

She detoured from dashing about the kitchen, and pressed a kiss against his beard. "I'm not faulting you. It's just unexpected, having family. Do I look better?"

He studied the coil of dark hair on her neck and admired the way the smooth sweep of her hair emphasized the heart shape of her face. "That widow's peak, I guess they call it, makes your gray eyes twice the size they oughta be. I 'spect next time I see you, the fellas will be a-sparkin' ya." She threw him a startled glance, and he hooted, "So! They're startin' already."

"No—" She drew out the reply slowly, then quickly looked at him. "It's just Mark. He don't count, though."

Mrs. Barton swished through the door and said, "Jennifer, the word should be *doesn't*. Mark is coming to tea. I'm sure he'd like to see your brother." With a quick nod in Tom's direction, she left the kitchen.

At tea, sitting stiffly in the Bartons' sitting room while Jenny served them, Tom juggled his new images of his sister. *Which picture is the true Jenny?* he wondered. And when he saw Mark's attention wholly devoted to her, he added another picture of her, one colored with respect.

Curiously he studied the young man in the well-tailored suit, admiring the silk string tie and the polished boots. As Mark talked, Tom became sharply aware of the contrast between Mark and the fellows Tom had been listening to lately. *You just automatically hang a "gentleman" tag on him,* Tom mused.

Returning his attention to Jenny, Tom noticed the new neatness, the polish that hadn't been there a year ago. Jenny was becoming a lady. Glancing quickly back to Mark, he decided that anything was possible.

During the days Tom spent with Jenny, he followed her about the Barton household, talking about all that had happened to him since he had last seen her. He held the basket of laundry while she fastened the sheets to the lines. "I'd no intention of going Bainbridge way," he admitted, "but once there, it was like old times. There were new faces in the crowd, the Whitmers and an odd fellow named Thompson, but with Joe around, everybody was easy-like."

Jenny frowned and jerked the clothespin from her mouth. "I suppose you were all off digging."

Tom shook his head, "No, there wasn't time. The new church seems to keep him hoppin'. People are at him all the time. Seems he's preachin', or prayin', or doin' his paperwork constant like."

"Paperwork, what's that?"

"Well, he's getting plenty of revelations, and he's makin' a translation of the New Testament—you know, the Bible. The Lord's let him know that the present translation's been corrupted. But there's more. The Lord's revealed much about the Second Coming. He's tellin' Joe to get ready to build the city of Zion—but then He told Joe that He won't give him any further information about all this until he gets the New Testament translated."

"You don't say." Jenny turned to study Tom with those curious gray eyes, and he was caught by the play of expression in them. The questioning frown between her eyes smoothed out, but she still chewed at her lip.

"What is it, Jen?" he asked. "I'm your brother, remember?"

"I'm thinking about it all. The things you said about Joe. Tom, he used to be a friend; now you act like you really do believe he's a prophet from God."

Tom cleared his throat nervously. "Jen, I know this seems strange to you, that I could change and suddenly start believin'. But I'm findin' if you stick your neck out, lookin' for answers, you have to take them when they come."

"Meaning?"

"He said I was obligated to myself to investigate, that my hereafter depended on it. He said to study out the truth and then ask God, and He'll make you have a burnin' in your bosom if it's right. Well, I asked about Joe and I had the burnin'. Even if it sometimes goes against my grain to say it, I gotta admit, I've had the witness."

He saw dark questions of disbelief appear in Jenny's face. "Jen," he went on slowly, "another revelation Joe had I think is for people like you. It says some are given by the Holy Ghost to know and have all these gifts from God, and others believe on their words. I think that means believe on their belief." There was a faraway expression in her eyes. He asked, "What ya thinkin'?"

"I was remembering South Bainbridge. He was tryin' to teach me some of the things he knew. There's not that much difference in it all—his beliefs before and after the book." After a moment she asked, "Did you join Joe's new church?"

"Well, not yet, but I figure I will."

A strange expression veiled her eyes now. "So Emma's lost twins. A man sets a store by a family, so I guess Joe's pretty unhappy. Is she well now?"

Tom nodded. "Adopting the little girl twins took care of their wanting a family. Least, Joe hasn't said more."

When it was time for Tom to return to Ohio, he sensed Jenny's restless spirit. "I've got to go," he apologized. "I promised Joe." Then he brightened, "Maybe you could come to Ohio for a visit, see it for yourself. From the sound of it all, it's goin' to be the new Zion. Joe's talkin' some about puttin' up a big meetin'house. I think he called it a temple, like in Jerusalem."

After Tom left, Jenny surveyed her domain, filled with a new discontent. "This was nearly heaven itself," she muttered gloomily as she surveyed the littered kitchen and piles of dirty dishes. "I'd thought everything in the past was gone, even that—" She sighed deeply, unable to speak of those past desires she had entertained for bright-haired Joseph.

During the following weeks, only half of Jenny's mind worked on the tasks in which she had once taken delight. One day while she slowly pushed a scrub brush across the floor, Mrs. Barton spoke from the doorway. "Jenny, what's wrong? I've been watching you drag about this house for weeks. Are you ill?"

Jenny rolled back on her heels and surveyed the messy puddle under her brush. "Ma'am, I don't know. The heart's gone from me. I miss Tom." She lifted her eyes to give the lie.

"Oh, Jenny!" Mrs. Barton knelt and squeezed Jenny against her. "I'm thoughtless, taking for granted that everyone on this earth has had a life as pleasant as mine.—I came to bring you a letter. Here, go to your room and rest while I finish. It's senseless to work hard in this heat, anyway."

Tucked in her room under the eaves, the fresh scent of growing things wafting through the window on the afternoon breeze, Jenny leaned against her pillows and studied the envelope. The return address indicated it was from Lucy Harris.

Slowly she pried open the envelope and pushed aside newspaper clippings to find the letter. There were two. Jenny sat up and stared in disbelief. The first was a letter from Nancy!

Dear Jenny, she read, *I've just moved back to Manchester and Lucy Harris has guilted me terribly for not having written to you. We did make an attempt to write, but the letter was returned. I have married and now am expecting a child.* Jenny stopped to check the name on the paper: Alexander MacAdams. It was unfamiliar and Jenny returned to the letter. *Ma and Pa have moved on west. Of course you would expect that. Even I have lost track of them. Mostly I wanted to write and tell you that Ma and the rest never ceased grieving about leaving you behind. Mostly because of your tender age. Please, if you can, come visit me in Manchester and meet your new brother-in-law and the little niece or nephew you will soon have. I would like to contact Tom, too. Mostly, Jenny, I am heavy over the way we left you. We all suffered thinking that Satan had his iron grip on your life. Mrs. Harris seems to think all things have worked out well for you. I am your affectionate sister, Nancy.*

Jenny frowned as she studied the brief letter. The words had stripped away the rosy glow around her memories of home and family. Jenny leaned against the pillows and whispered, "Satan."

How often, during those final months, Ma and Nancy had aligned against her with puzzled frowns. Search as she might, Jenny couldn't recall a reason for the frowns.

With a sigh, Jenny dug into the envelope. She fingered the newspaper clippings, then rejected them in favor of the other letter.

Jenny read rapidly. Lucy seemed contented. She hadn't seen Martin since he had left Manchester for Fayette. Her life was narrowed by money worries, but pleasant. She recounted the events since Jenny and Tom had left, then said: *I've been nagged into writing to you since last February when these articles came out in the Palmyra* Reflector. *I'd intended writing before, but didn't. Jenny, I've done much thinking and praying since you've left. I'm still uneasy about your time here and thinking that I didn't do my duty by you. Somehow, despite the church meetings and the baptism, I don't think you understand all I wanted badly to teach you about being a Christian. In a short letter, there's little space to make up the lack. For most of us it takes a lifetime of living to come to an understanding that bears weight. But there must be a beginning. For some of us, going to church, being baptized and partaking of the elements is enough to want to love God. But I'm beginning to think that for some it isn't enough. It's like breaking a horse. For some it's easy, others it's nigh on a death struggle. Now, Jenny, I don't want you to think I'm calling you a rebel, for I'm not. You are a very dear girl. But your spirit runs deep and high. Most of us have gentle streams of a spirit, content with the low, easy path. My girl, I sense you may have to fight your spirit, maybe much harder than most, in order to hear what God is trying to say to you.*

Down at the end of the letter was a postscript. It said, *What I meant to say all along was, I think you should read your Bible.*

Jenny folded the letter and pushed it back into the envelope, still trying to understand why Lucy Harris cared enough to fuss over her.

Pulling the newspaper clippings out, Jenny saw immediately that they dealt with Joseph Smith. An amused smile touched her lips as she straightened the paper on her knees. Why would these clippings finally force Lucy to write her letter? Maybe the unsaid things in Lucy's letter were that she needed to be in church learning about God. No matter what church, any was better than none.

Lucy had underlined parts of the article and Jenny's amusement grew as she read. The first article, dated February 14, 1831, pointed out that prior to the discovery of the gold plates, a spirit in the form of a little old man had appeared to Joseph. He had promised great treasure and a book about ancient inhabitants. The article concluded by saying that at the time the event was said to have happened, no divine activity was claimed, although citizens of the area well recollected the incident. Jenny was genuinely puzzled as she thought back over the events of that time. There was that bunch of men calling themselves the Gold Bible Company. There was also the talk of spirits and that little old man. Was the article meaning the two views didn't add up to the divine? She frowned and shook her head, remembering those things Adela had said about worship.

The next article, dated February 28, 1831, started out by saying that Joe had never claimed communion with angels until a long time after the advent of the book. The article also mentioned his peep stone and Joseph's accounts of seeing wonders in it, as well as his interviews with the spirit who had custody of the hidden treasures. For a moment Jenny thought about the time Joe had offered to let her look in his stone. Now she was filled with regret for her timidity.

Reading on, she murmured, "So it was Cicero's *Orations* I heard Walters reading! Whatever he was reading, it was beautiful." She finished the article, amused by the report of the digging she had witnessed from the bushes on the night she had followed Tom and Martin Harris into the forest. "Little did I know that there was someone else hiding out in the bushes!" she chuckled. Slipping the articles back into the envelope, Jenny leaned against her pillows and stared out the window.

She let the words of the letters and the articles tumble through her thoughts in a haphazard manner. Slowly an uneasiness began to grow, and a few of the words kept circling back: *Satan, baptism, rebel.*

She turned away from the window and looked at the green book wedged in the shelf between her sewing basket and her hat. Deliberately she forced out of her mind all thoughts generated by the letters and articles and began thinking back to those long-ago days. Foremost was her childhood resolution regarding Joe which had fastened itself on her mind; then she recalled Tom's words. "So Emma is well and Joseph is happy," she murmured.

Like wings whisking her away, her thoughts transported her in time and place. The dark, mysterious forest of Manchester surrounded her, and out of the blackness danced a figure in red. "Ah—Adela," Jenny murmured with a smile. "I wish you were as easy to come by as thoughts. I'd like to

talk to you. What would you have to say about my feelings? I know; I've
listened to you often enough to know you'd ask what I really wanted from
life, and then you'd tell me that I could have anything as long as I wanted
it bad enough to—" Jenny stopped, shuddering at the memory of the last
time she had seen Adela.

She recoiled from the memory of the horrible scene in the church. But
in spite of herself she was murmuring, "Adela, I ruined forever my
chances of truly being your friend, didn't I? I wish I could have another
chance."

Jenny fell to musing about it all, weighing the significance of the step
Adela had urged her to take. Once again she shivered; then, as if returning
from a far country, quickly she sat up and smoothed her hair. Adela's
suggestion was impossible, but there must be another way. Maybe Joseph
and his new church held the answers.

Although the hot sunlight streamed in her bedroom window, Jenny
smoothed her tumbled hair and murmured:

"Luna, every woman's friend
To me thy goodness condescend.
Let this night in visions see
Emblems of my destiny."

Jenny felt better after her rest and went downstairs to her tasks with a
lighter heart.

As summer gained momentum, life pressed hard against her. Mrs. Barton wasn't a difficult person to please, but it was a busy household.

One day Mrs. Barton looked at Jenny's tired face and said, "I must find
another girl. You're doing the work of two right now, and there's school
soon."

So at harvest time Clara joined the household. Clara was short and
plump, with a frizzle of light hair. Her blue eyes, Jenny immediately noticed, were prone to disappear completely when she laughed, and that was
often. *Too often,* Jenny thought as she moved behind Clara, catching broken pieces, and rescuing abandoned tasks.

Soon Jenny was as frayed as Clara's hair. If it hadn't been for the book,
Jenny realized later, her nerves would have been as fragmented as Mrs.
Barton's berry bowl when Clara tried to wash it.

During the hot, heavy days of August, Mark came calling. Mrs. Barton
called it "courting," and she said it with a gentle smile. But whatever it
was, Jenny was glad to see him.

They sat on the side porch, shaded by vines that wandered up the lattice
to the second story, and Mark filled her full of his tales of the law office.

Later as she slowly climbed the stairs to her room, she mulled over the meaning of his visit, and frowned over the memory of the look in his eyes and the way he had pressed her hand.

She lingered on the stairs trying to understand her emotions. Were the mingled memories of the past responsible for the discontent she felt around him? Fleetingly, she wondered what he would think about the green book and the growing need she was feeling in her life.

The moment before she touched her door, she saw the slit of light. "Clara!" she exclaimed, then saw the book she held. "Oh!"

Closing the book, Clara laughed merrily. "Your face! Jenny, don't look so frightened. I won't tell our good Presbyterian lady, and I won't be corrupted. You see, I know all about it." Her voice dropped to a whisper. "Perhaps I'm sent to help you understand even better."

15

WHEN TOM RETURNED to Kirtland after visiting Jenny, he had the sense of being dropped back to earth with a jolt. Going about his duties at the livery stable, he mulled over the feeling. Had he painted a rosy picture for Jenny that didn't exist? Did the complaints and gossip he had been hearing since his return reveal the true facts?

Just this morning, Knight had stepped into the stable. His usual good humor had been masked behind a perplexed frown. "What's your trouble?" Tom asked his employer as he stabled Knight's horse and tossed in hay.

"Just chewin' over events," he muttered, picking up the account books and heading for the office.

"Like what? You forget I've been gone."

He turned in the doorway. "I did forget you've not been hearing the rumbling. Right now seems everyone's out to prove he's special with the Lord. Joseph started it with his promise of blessings. My idea is that Rigdon's glory halo rankles Joe. He ought not feel that way. 'Tis obvious Joseph's the Lord's favorite."

He stopped to glance at Tom. "Then a new thing happened to shake people's faith. The Mortinsens over Thompson way had a sick baby. They were all set to take him to the doctor, and one of the brethren told them not to. Said the Lord had promised the child would be healed."

"So, isn't that the way we are supposed to be livin'?"

He looked at Tom. "So they say. The Mortinsens are having a hard time believing that. Their baby died. Now a faction's saying only false prophets have their prophecies fail. No matter. I experienced the Lord's healing at Joseph's hand." He turned and left the room.

The next day was the first day of the June church conference. Slicked up and wearing a new shirt, Tom walked toward the meetinghouse with Lyman Wight. The older man was bringing him up-to-date, detailing all that had happened while Tom had been in New York. "You should've heard Joe," Wight said, shaking his head. "There's sure been a high tide of feeling that the Lord's about to be blessin' us in an unusual way."

"What did he say?" Tom questioned as he followed Lyman to his seat in the assembly hall.

For a moment Lyman looked startled. "Oh, he said that not three days would pass before someone would see the Savior face to face." He continued, "This is like it was last year when we first came, the excitement."

While Tom looked around, greeting friends who had come to hear the Prophet, Joseph Smith got to his feet. From the podium his eyes swept the room as he spoke. "I've much to reveal to you of the Lord's wisdom and plans for these final days before the Second Coming. Now I want to give you the story of just what happened to the ten lost tribes of Israel. I will also be revealing to you God's plan for the priesthood in these latter days.

"In the past only Jesus Christ and Melchizedek held this priesthood, but now it is ours. We have been given the power to become high priests before Him. Now is the time to confer this order of priesthood on the righteous."

With beckoning hands, Joseph Smith called out names and began to ordain his men to the priesthood. Joseph's gaze swept toward Tom, hesitated, and moved on. Tom's pounding heart attested to the tension in the room, but he reminded himself, "Fella, there's no call to get excited. You had your chance when Joe pressed you to join up with him, and you put it off. Now stand back and watch the others get the blessin'." His disappointment was tempered as he began to realize the responsibility these men were taking upon themselves. "The true church," he whispered. " 'Tis a big task to take out the message to the world."

Beside him, Lyman Wight suddenly surged to his feet. With outstretched arms held rigid, he shouted, "You want to see a sign? Look at me. I see the heavens open and the Son of Man!"

In the confusion there came another cry, "Brother Joseph, Ben here's been struck deaf and dumb. Come heal him." While the Prophet crossed the room, Tom was wondering if the others remembered how Joseph's prayers for healing had failed in the past. The man sitting beside Tom whispered, "Just yesterday Joe said that now was the time for great miracles to break out upon the church."

As Joseph reached out to touch the man, Tom found he was holding his breath. Joseph turned to the congregation and said, "Remember, now's the time for the Lord to break out upon us. Pray, my friends, pray!" His voice was rising in intensity, and a surge of excitement filled the room. As people jumped to their feet, Tom could no longer see. He heard a sigh of relief, and then, "He's healed!" Tom saw the beaming face of the man.

With new confidence, Joseph whirled about and crossed the room. He stopped before a man with a crippled hand. Grasping the bent and tortured limb, he cried, "Brother, in the name of Jesus Christ I command you, straighten this hand." Grasping the crumpled hand he pulled it straight. But once released it returned to its tortured position.

The crowd waited and the silence stretched uneasily. Suddenly the door opened and a man and woman entered. Tom saw the bundle they carried, and with a sinking heart he recognized the Mortinsens.

"Prophet Smith," the man said, speaking softly and rapidly, "our baby is dead, and I bring him here to you. Restore him to life." The man's voice broke. Together, he and his wife, clasping the gray form of their infant, dropped to their knees before Joseph.

Quietness held the room like a vise. Tom studied the patch of sunlight spreading across the floor. Feeling his unbelief poison the very air, he dared not lift his eyes to the group, although he could hear Joseph's prayer.

At last Joseph stepped back. With a face nearly as gray as the dead infant's, he whispered, "I cannot."

In the waiting moment, Tom was aware of the buzz of flies, the uneasy creak of chairs. When Mortinsen arose, still clutching the limp form, he turned to a bowed and sobbing man seated nearby. "Brother," he whispered, "you advised me that the Lord would heal, and that there was no need to go to the doctor." His voice was heavy. "In the name of God, I hold you responsible for destroying the life of my son."

A troubled Tom made his way back to his room over the livery stable. As he did his evening chores around the stable, Newel Knight entered.

"Tom," he asked soberly, "are you hearing rumbles about what happened today?"

"Yeah, there's a whole tide of bad feelin's adrift, what with Joe pullin' these healings and nothin' comin' of it."

"I urged caution, but a little success goes a long way."

"It's worse than just the failure," Tom said as he pitched hay to the horses. "It's what it's doin' to these here folks."

Knight sighed and nodded. He cinched the saddle tight and led his horse out the gate. "Well, tomorrow's another day; maybe Joseph will receive the words to undo the harm."

The second day of the conference the Sabbath services had only begun when Rigdon slowly got to his feet, lifted his hands, and pronounced the benediction. Tom sat in stunned disbelief.

On the way out Tom heard a man beside him mutter, "The spirit was tellin' me we needed a sermon; how come the spirit told him different?" Tom had reached the door, but on impulse he turned. Joseph and Sidney Rigdon were still facing each other at the front of the room.

A stranger, too, hesitated for one last look, and the eyes he turned toward Tom were scornful. Dryly he said, "I'm waitin' to hear how he explains this." Tom watched him walk away before he made his way toward Joseph.

"You realize what this can do to the church, don't you?" A sober Joseph nodded in reply to Rigdon and turned as Tom stopped beside him.

"You may as well hear it now," he said heavily to Tom. "Williams just brought word from the town of Thompson that Copley and Thayer have yanked their gift of land to the church."

"That isn't all," Rigdon said as he took quick, nervous steps across the room and back. "They're using the law to dump themselves of what they're calling New York trespassers. That means we've a bunch of people without a home."

Jenny and Clara were sitting in the middle of Jenny's bed, the green book open between them. Jenny ran her fingers under the words and lifted her face. "Clara, what can you tell me about charms?"

"How come you have the book and have been learnin' under Adela and yet you know so little?"

"If she told me about them, I've forgotten. Maybe I wasn't needing them."

"Charms. A love potion? I'm thinkin' you'll not need it for that young man."

"Mark? Oh, no—and not a *love* potion. Oh, dear," she murmured, suddenly visualizing how Mark's face would look if he were listening to the conversation.

Her horror must have shown on her face, because Clara laughed and said, "Don't give it a worry. I don't go spreading tales."

But the memory of Mark's face and his clear, steady eyes wouldn't leave Jenny. Quickly she led Clara away from the subject. "Tell me, Clara, how did you come to get into—this."

"You can't say it, can you? You needn't think it's all so awful. I'm a white witch."

"What's that?"

"That means that I don't do evil things to people. Except for callin' up storms, I try to do only good things for others."

"Some don't count the difference; to them a witch is a witch."

"That's 'cause they don't understand the craft. 'Tis the oldest, the most ancient religion. 'Tis nature's religion. All we do is worship the way we were intended to worship from the very beginning of time. I know you've been fed a different story. See, it's all twisted. The lie's been twisted and given as truth and the real truth is being lied about. You know how to tell the real truth, don't you?"

"Well, I'm beginning to wonder," Jenny faltered, remembering Lucy Harris's words about truth and power.

"It's the power. If you get power, then you know it's the truth."

"Do you?" Jenny whispered.

Clara nodded and patted the book. "I've never seen the book before, but I've been taught by my mother and grandma. What the book says is just what they say."

"Have you—" Jenny's voice dropped to a whisper, but she felt compelled to say it. "Do you go to sabbats?"

"Of course. It seems you've had a bad time. Granted, it takes some gettin' use to. But there's lots in life that takes bein' brave." Jenny saw the sly look creep across her face.

Hastily Jenny asked, "What power do you have?"

"I told you about the storms. That's the one that's most easy to see. Want me to demonstrate?" Jenny nodded and Clara continued, "I'm doing charms too, to keep off the bad spirits and to bring good luck, things like that."

"Tell me a charm to use."

"Well, you have one yourself—didn't you recognize it as such? You're prayin' to the moon goddess when you recite that Luna verse asking for emblems of destiny."

"It is!" Jenny exclaimed in surprise. "Then why don't I find out about my destiny?"

"You're just sayin' it; you're not bringing down the power. See, if you want to get the knowledge, you put a prayerbook under your pillow and place on it a key, a ring, flowers, a sprig of willow . . ." and Clara's voice continued the list of common enough items.

In silence Jenny pondered Clara's instructions, and deep within she found her spirit sinking. How could she possibly believe in Clara's charm? Finally she sighed and asked, "What did you have to promise to get the power?"

Clara looked at her quizzically. "Nothing. Just use the charms and follow the rituals."

"You didn't have to—to make a pact with the devil?"

Clara laughed merrily, "Oh, Jenny, your face! Your eyes are as big as saucers. It's hard to take you serious-like when you're so scared. Jenny, don't fuss so; relax and enjoy yourself. That's the whole meanin' behind life."

Her voice dropped to a gentle note as she studied Jenny's face. "If something big comes up and nothing else works, you may have to make a pact; it all depends how important it is to you. Some things mean more'n life."

After Clara left her room, Jenny picked up the book and slowly thumbed through it until she reached the section that talked about making a pact with Lucifer, god of light, god of good.

She closed her eyes, willing the memory of Joe's face to come before her. She studied the remembered features, that beak of a nose, those laughing eyes. How her hands ached to move through that shining bright hair! "Too bad just thinking isn't enough to put you here," she murmured.

As Jenny thought about what Clara said, she hesitated, shivering. What about that unknown cost? Was Joseph really worth it? The thought grew in her mind. But also there grew the feeling she must be certain before she took that step.

Jenny had just finished the noon dishes. Summer heat simmered in the air, sucking out moisture and giving dust in exchange. She trailed her finger across the dusty table just as Clara walked in.

The girl was grinning and beckoning, excitement sparkling in her eyes. Today was the day Clara had chosen. Clara's face wore a funny half-smile, like the Bartons' cat, just in from the pasture full of mice. "It's a good time to go. Let's be off." Her eyes narrowed to slits of ecstasy. "Perfect. Not a cloud in the sky, and hasn't been for days. And the hay's in, so we'll do no harm."

As soon as they stepped into the woods, Jenny was aware of the change coming over her companion. No longer playfully happy and carefree, she began to walk with slow, deliberate steps. The deeper they moved into the woods, the more oppressive her spirit became. Glancing at her face, Jenny was surprised to see the heavy frown.

For a moment she thought to tease Clara about looking like the clouds of storm she hoped to conjure, but then she saw Clara's eyes. It would be impossible to get her attention.

When they reached the deepest gloom of the forest, Clara waved Jenny aside while she moved about her task. Now Jenny was aware of the low, guttural murmuring that Clara was making as she moved methodically, marking a circle, inscribing strange figures in the soil, and stacking sticks with crumbled dry herb over all.

When she finished, she sat down in the circle. Jenny settled down on a fallen log and fought the sleepiness that seemed to be washing over her in waves. She lost track of time and had nearly forgotten where she was. Abruptly Clara jumped to her feet. "We must hurry!" she gasped, and she turned and ran back down the trail.

When they reached the edge of the forest, Jenny understood why. The sky was a mass of dark, boiling clouds. As they ran across the pasture, the thunder grew louder and the lightning flashed. They reached the kitchen door just after the rain began.

Mrs. Barton was standing by the stove, and she turned to them with a worried frown. "Oh my, you're wet. But then, who would have guessed we'd have a storm like this!"

On the third day of the church conference, Tom sat on his bench and looked at Joseph Smith and Sidney Rigdon. They were on the platform, quietly facing the congregation. Rigdon's face was pale, and Joseph seemed subdued. Tom moved uneasily on his bench and wished that he'd had the gumption to stay home this meeting. Nat Johnson was sitting beside him. His smooth, expressionless face did nothing to calm Tom's churning insides.

When Joseph stood to talk, Tom breathed a sigh of relief. At least Joe was his usual jovial self. "My friends and fellow believers—" He paused, and his gaze swept about the room until every rustle stilled and all were hanging on his words. "I deeply regret all that happened on the first day of conference, and I've been rebuked by the Lord for failing to understand and accept. I have a revelation from the Lord which I will read to you, and then you will comprehend what the Lord is trying to do for us."

He lifted the paper and cleared his throat. "I the Lord will make known to you . . . the next conference, which shall be held in Missouri, on the land which I will consecrate unto my people." The revelation was long, and only a few words hit Tom with meaning. He heard that the land of Missouri was the inheritance, but it was also the land of their enemies.

There was a low growl beside Tom, and Johnson said, "Zion, Missouri. The Lord is givin' us a hard assignment. That means we'll be a-fightin' for it."

When Joe folded the papers and tucked them away, he said, "The Lord has very plainly told me there will be no miracles until we are settled in Zion. There we will erect a glorious temple. Now you men who have been commanded by the Lord, be part of this first group. Spy out the land and prepare a home for those who will be moving from Thompson to Missouri. I say, obey the Lord, and prepare to go."

16

IN JUNE 1831, Joseph Smith and Sidney Rigdon, along with thirty others chosen by the Lord, left for Missouri. The men were instructed to go two by two, making their way to Missouri, preaching the gospel as they went. Joseph and Rigdon were to travel as far as St. Louis by steamship.

Though Tom was disappointed in not being included, he busied himself around the livery stable, while the men were gone. One day, soon after Joe's return, Tom was shoeing Knight's saddle horse when Joe came into the shop. "Looks like Knight's bound to make a smithy out of you."

Tom grunted and drove the last nail into the horse's hoof. "I'm hired jack-of-all-trades," he said shortly, "and I'm glad to be learnin' this. If I had stayed in Manchester, I *might* have worked up to this in another year." He released the horse and stood up. "I hear you've moved your family to Hiram."

"That's right. The Lord's been impressing me with the need to get at the translation of the New Testament." Tom wrapped the reins around his hand and Joseph fell in step with him. "You're heavy-hearted; what's troubling you? Is it the reports of the trip that have you down?"

Astonished and curious, Tom turned to look at Joseph. "I've not heard a thing. I'm heavy because I was thinkin' about losin' my job when Knight and the rest move to Zion."

"Well, you needn't be worrying yet," Joe said abruptly. "The Lord's instructed Knight and Whitney both to keep their businesses here until the last of the church has moved to Zion. From the looks of things, it'll be a while."

"Well, I'm glad," Tom answered. "But from the slant of the revelations, I figured we'd all be a-pullin' up stakes right away."

With a rueful sigh, Joe said, "Some of the Lord's anointed in Missouri would like to see that happen, but the Lord's revealed most of the elders are to return here and support their families while they get busy with spreading the gospel in the eastern part of the country. Anyone who wants to settle in Zion right now will do it only after his prayers assault heaven for the privilege."

"Why's that?" Tom asked.

" 'Tis a fair land," Joseph said slowly, "but it's costly. The price of moving to Missouri will only be met when every man here gives liberally to the Lord. But that isn't all. The Lord doesn't want His people complacent and mingling with the Gentiles. His revelation says God's people'll push the Gentiles off the ends of the earth."

They stopped at the hitching post in front of Whitney's general store. Tom looped the reins of the horse around it and turned to wave at Knight who was standing in the doorway. "Your filly's the proud owner of new shoes," he called.

"Well, maybe Missouri was a disappointment to some," Joe continued, "but at least things are moving in the right direction here."

"You sound satisfied," Tom said. "What's happened?"

"The United Order has received a loan of $10,000 from Charles Holmes. I've appointed Whitney bishop, and his store'll be the storehouse and commissary."

Tom pondered the information in silence, and then added, "So the translation business is back in full swing."

"Tom, the Lord's blessing us in these last days!" Joe exclaimed. "He's given me a special blessing. Translating in Genesis, I've discovered a prophecy concerning my coming."

"No foolin'!" Tom turned to look at his friend in awe. "Are you sure?"

"Well, what would you think if you read that the Lord will raise up a seer in the last days and give him the power to bring forth the word of the Lord? And his name will be Joseph just as his father's name is Joseph."

"Huh!" Tom grunted. "You sure can't argue that."

" 'Twas a great comfort to find He promised safety," Joseph added seriously. "I needed the assurance that the Lord was on my side."

"What did He say?"

" 'Those who seek to destroy the seer, Joseph, will be confounded.' "

At the livery stable the two of them perched on the fence rail while Joe continued. "Another thing, the Lord's made known the degrees of glory. There's three kingdoms in the eternities. All men will be assigned to one of them. The highest is celestial for the members of the true church, the terrestrial is the dwelling place of those who've never heard the gospel, and the third degree is called telestial, for those who've refused the law of the Lord. Liars, sorcerers, adulterers will be going there."

"You mean there's a heaven for everybody?" Tom said slowly. "Well, that takes a big load off my chest; I guess I just won't worry no more."

Joseph threw back his head and laughed. "Then you're not wanting to be part of Zion. You're throwing away the privilege of being with the people building the city of God. Tom, my lad, you're a gambler at heart.

But I know you won't pass up that glory. When are you going to join up? I saw your face during conference. You were wanting to go to Zion so bad it hurt."

"You're right," Tom admitted, recalling that day. He raised his head and slapped Joe's leg. "Oh, all right. What do I need to do?"

Jenny pushed open the Bartons' kitchen door and a wintry blast followed her. She tumbled her books inside and turned out to the entry to shake her snow-laden shawl. Popping back into the kitchen, she shook her hair, exclaiming, "What a storm! It makes a body glad to be home and warm and dry." She tossed her hair back from her face, then stopped. Mark and Mrs. Barton were sitting at the kitchen table.

"Mark!" she exclaimed, as astonished at her glad rush of surprise as she was by his unexpected presence. "It's been so long!" She hurried forward. "Oh, you're already having tea," her voice flattened with disappointment.

Mrs. Barton laughed. "We couldn't wait; it *is* cold out. You might offer him some of the cookies you baked yesterday."

Mark was pulling a chair forward and grinning down at Jenny. "I've never before seen you with such rosy cheeks. That's nice. Shall I bring tea for you? From the looks of you, you intend to let snowflakes melt into your cup."

Mrs. Barton handed her a towel. "You'd better let me get the cookies." She disappeared into the pantry and Jenny dared look at Mark. Wordlessly he beamed at her until the cookies were placed between them.

Later Jenny wondered what Mrs. Barton had been saying before she came. But for now she watched Mark eating her spicy raisin cookies as if he were starved.

"I came intending to entice you into ice skating, but I *may* be snowed in for a week." He grinned happily.

"Ice skating?" Jenny whispered in panic. "I've never even touched a pair of ice skates."

"Well, you shall now, and I promise I won't let you fall."

Mark *was* snowed in, as was everyone else in town. Clara had gone visiting early in the day, and it was three days before she returned. Mark volunteered to fill in for her.

During the three days, as Mark carried in wood and dried dishes, Jenny's surprise grew. She was discovering a Mark totally different from her picture of the nice young schoolmaster with his spotless white shirt and shiny boots.

As she watched him roll up his sleeves and scrub pans, she listened to him talk. First law, then books; next he described a hunting trip into the mountains with his father.

Blue-misted mountains, crimson trees, and the mingled scent of wood-smoke and frying bacon lingered in his memories. What he described in detail wasn't the deer he shot, but the leggy fawn, faltering timid and curious on the edge of the clearing.

They discovered there were books they had both read, and they discussed them eagerly. They shared the poetry he could quote, and the plays he wanted her to see.

When the sky cleared, a dozen eager boys pushed snow from the lake and Mark and Jenny tried out the ice skates.

At first Jenny was shy with this new Mark, but she gradually thawed beneath his genuine warmth. Before the week was over, she knew that she was privy to a secret side of him. She sensed it first when he quoted poetry to her; even more clearly she recognized the difference when Clara walked into the kitchen, and the contained shell of the old Mark settled around him like a protective armor.

As Jenny said good-bye, Mark lifted her warm hand to his cheek and then he was gone.

Jenny watched through the kitchen window as his horse loped down the lane. Secret whispers moved through her heart, reminding her that rich young men married proper girls from proper families. The real Mark, those whispers nagged at her, was the one she watched as he joked around and teased Clara. The casual shell was real, the tenderness inside was a dream.

In Kirtland the new year slipped in on snowy feet, nearly unheralded. At Hiram, Joseph Smith and Sidney Ridgon continued to work at the task of writing. But unsettling things were going on. Often the rumbles started at the livery stable in Kirtland, where winter-bound men gathered to talk. But there were winter discontents in Hiram, too.

Ezra Booth, formerly a Methodist minister, then Mormon convert, had turned apostate after the first trip to Zion. Now he was exciting curiosity. Copies of letters written by him and printed in *The Ohio Star* were read and passed around the stable. The first comment was, "Joe shouldn't have taken him in to begin with. A preacher in the Methodist church is bound to be a mighty poor follower. Has too many ideas of his own." Another said, "Some of his complaints were right, like Partridge's quarrel with Smith."

A few nodded, and a voice spoke from the back of the group. "Partridge didn't make no bones. Told Joseph he didn't like the land and Joseph told him heaven chose it. So then Partridge told him he wished he wouldn't say he knew things by the spirit when he didn't, such as that Oliver had raised up a big church when it was plain to see he hadn't. Joe said if he said it, then it would be."

"What about Ridgon telling him the vision of Zion was a bad thing?"

There was silence when Tom replied, "Seems it falls in a category of faultin' the Lord." He went back to his workbench.

While Tom mended harnesses in front of the sheet iron stove at the rear of the stables, he listened to the talk going on around him. *Malcontents,* he decided. But some of the men had been on that journey to Missouri. They supported Ezra's statements in the newspaper.

One thing was certain, a storm of unrest was brewing among the men of the church. Later, when news from Missouri indicated that Zion was suffering the same kind of unrest, Tom decided it was time to visit his friend in Hiram.

It was late that March evening before Tom could leave the livery stable to go to Hiram. Even in the small town of Kirtland, Saturday night revelry added to the chores that must be done before the Sabbath.

Tom rode his horse toward Joseph's home, grateful for March's softening wind. He was nearly to the outskirts of Hiram when he met a group of riders coming toward him.

Thinking that he recognized one of them, he called, "Hello, is that you, Williams?" No answer came, but the riders veered away. Slowly he rode on, pondering the strange event.

As he reached the Johnson farm where Joseph Smith was living, Tom noticed light spilling out the open door; but until he stood in Joseph's parlor staring at the spectacle, he didn't understand. Slowly he walked across the room.

Emma was already digging at the mess of tar and feathers which covered her husband. "What happened?"

Joseph could only mutter, while Emma answered shortly, "Busted in here, the whole lot of them, and dragged him out into the night. This is the way he came back."

Throughout the night, Tom and Emma dug at the mess that covered Joseph's body. It was nearly morning when Joseph picked up a quilt and handed it to Tom. "Here, my friend and bodyguard, stretch out in front of the fire. You'll need a little sleep to stay awake during my sermon this morning."

"Joseph!" Emma exclaimed in horror. "Surely you don't intend to stand before the church and preach!"

But he did, and Tom was there to watch and listen and gain new admiration for his friend. The sermon, delivered in quiet dignity, made no reference to the incident of the previous evening. And if the culprits were in the crowd, they were wearing the robes of righteousness this Sabbath.

The Monday morning crowd at the livery stable seemed to know the details of Saturday night.

"They say he had it coming . . . Word's going round that Eli Johnson got the mob together . . . Said it was 'cause Joseph has been too intimate with his sister, Nancy Marinda . . . Eli wanted to castrate Joe, but the doc chickened out."

Five days after the tarring and feathering, one of the twins adopted by Joe and Emma died. Tom was there afterward to help move Emma back to Kirtland to live while Joseph and Rigdon journeyed to Missouri.

Mrs. Barton came into the kitchen as Jenny was finishing the dishes. She picked up the dish towel and a handful of spoons. Jenny shook off her dreamy mood and reached for another pot. When Mrs. Barton reached for the forks, she said, "Jenny, you've had your eighteenth birthday. Have you given any thought to your future? Young ladies your age have married. And as for school, you're educated enough to teach. I'm afraid there's little more they can offer you."

"Oh," Jenny sighed, abruptly realizing she hadn't given a thought to life as Mrs. Barton was seeing it. She shivered, thinking how horrified that good woman would be if she were to tell her what she had in mind for the future.

"Jenny, don't misunderstand," Mrs. Barton continued. "I'm not at all anxious to have you leave us; you'll have a position here as long as you wish."

"Thank you, ma'am," Jenny replied meekly, still wondering what she could say.

"Also," Mrs. Barton continued, wiping more slowly now, "I'm concerned about Clara. Not that I think you're easily led astray, but there's strange goings-on in her life." She hung the towel on its rack. "If you're troubled and need to talk about it, please—"

Jenny widened her eyes. "Clara *is* strange, Mrs. Barton, but she doesn't trouble me."

"That's good. Now, Mark is coming tonight, isn't he?"

"Yes." Jenny looked at Mrs. Barton, wondering if she could sense the churning inside her.

"He's a fine young man. I've met his mother and think well of her."

Without planning, the words burst from Jenny, "Fine young men don't marry kitchen maids!"

"I have a feeling that young man is looking beyond the kitchen," Mrs. Barton responded gently. She watched Jenny carefully empty the dishwater into the pail beside the door, and just as carefully Jenny avoided Mrs.

Barton's eyes. She didn't want to talk about Mark; she didn't even want to think about the confusion of her emotions every time he came to visit.

Jenny looked at the floor, fearful her eyes would reveal her thoughts, thoughts about what she and Clara had been studying together. They just didn't fit into the picture with Mark.

By the time Mark arrived, the evening was cooling and the primroses were slowly unfolding their tight buds. Jenny was sitting on the side porch, thinking of nothing except the evening calm spreading itself across the land.

Then Mark was there, offering her a yellow primrose. "Jenny," he whispered with a teasing grin, "tell me your secret. Does it take the mysterious night to bring you into full bloom? Most times I find you a tight little bud like an evening primrose at high noon."

"I think it takes the moonlight to bring me to life," she whispered back. "I need to follow the creek until it disappears into the moon. I need to walk the pasture fence until it falls off the earth."

"Walk the pasture fence!" he exclaimed, dropping down beside her. "That is a very different thing to do."

"See there—" She pointed to the line of fence that rose and fell with the contours of the earth. She knew that at the point of disappearance, it followed the slip of the hill.

"It does fall off the earth," he whispered. "But maybe it tunnels under the haystack; then where would you be?"

"Why, I'd be obligated to tunnel, too."

"Then let's go!" He took her hand and pulled her to her feet, toward the pasture. When they reached the fence, he lifted her to the top rung. Gathering her skirt in a tight wad that threatened her knees with exposure, Jenny ran lightly along the rail, slowing only to step gingerly across the posts before she ran on again.

At the end of it, when the fence plunged down the hill, Jenny jumped lightly to the ground. With a thud, Mark landed beside her. "You did it, too!" she exclaimed in delight. "Mark, the lawyer! You must be good to me, or I will tell all your clients that you are addlepated. That I know, because you walk fence rails in the moonlight!"

"Oh, my dear Jenny!" In mock horror he threw himself to his knees beside her. "I implore you, marry me, marry me so that I can keep you silenced forever. With trinkets and baubles and all of my gold, I pledge my heart as long as I may have your vow of silence." And they both laughed in joyful merriment.

Much later Jenny ran lightly up the backstairs to her room, still chuckling her enjoyment over Mark's foolishness. Clara was sitting on Jenny's bed, in the center of the patch of bright moonlight. "I needed to do my thinking, and there wasn't moonlight in my room."

Silently Jenny took her place beside Clara. Crossing her legs, she folded her arms and waited. She heard the faint sound of a horse trotting down the lane—Mark's. In the renewed silence the crickets took up their chirping and from the creek the frogs answered. The heavy night air wrapped scent and sound about the two.

Finally, Jenny asked, "What are you thinking?"

"You were very joyful and happy, laughing your way up the stairs."

Jenny thought back and then whispered, "I was. I hadn't thought of it that way. It was the night, the moon, and—"

"Mark?" Clara whispered. "Jenny, where does he fit into all this?" Her gesture swept only the room, but Jenny knew what she was thinking.

"He doesn't." Slowly pulling the pins from her hair, Jenny began to put into words all that she had avoided thinking about before. "Mark wouldn't approve; I'm sure of that. He is my good friend, but he wouldn't be if he were to know. He mustn't find out."

Out of a long, dreamy silence, Clara finally spoke. "Jenny it's gettin' near the solstice. If you are serious about learning more, you'll need to go to the sabbat."

For a moment Jenny closed her eyes against the bright moonlight; almost against her will she whispered, "Power! If only I could have it all."

Clara was whispering too, "Mark or the craft, Jenny? You must choose. I'm feelin' there's much you are unwilling to tell me. So be it; decide alone then what's important. I'm feelin' he won't allow Mark in your life."

Although the night air was heavy and warm, Jenny shivered as if a winter wind had chilled her. Clara had just said "he," but the unnamed one struck terror in Jenny. How much longer could she avoid facing that *he*?

17

IN MAY OF 1832 Kirtland seethed with excitement. Not for more than a moment could the young church forget these were the days of gathering. Very soon Jesus Christ would be returning to claim His own, and the Mormon people had been chosen to prepare Zion for His dwelling place.

Tom was well aware of the excitement as he walked into the assembly hall on that first Sabbath day following Joseph's return from Missouri. Beside him was his friend Aaron Seamond.

Aaron had been one of Sidney Rigdon's followers when Kirtland's people had belonged to the Campbellite group. At times Tom had been prone to charge Aaron with cynicism, but today his fervor was as high as Tom's as they listened eagerly. Joseph was giving the details of his trip.

"Brothers and sisters, I know the Lord has chosen you to bear the gospel in this generation. The Lord has blessed us mightily; He has let us know by revelation all He commands us to do. Brethren, we must be about the Lord's business.

"On every hand we see these are the last days. Very soon the Lord will be walking the earth, His footstool. This whole continent is sacred ground!

"Now, I will tell you what transpired on my journey. By the Lord's direction we have combined the United Order under one governing body. Presently we are negotiating for a $15,000 loan. This has been a glorious year in Jackson County, Missouri! The church has grown; we have a membership of three hundred. Many more will be coming.

"Now, let me tell you about the remnant of Jacob. Bless the Lord! The federal government is cooperating with the Lord. Thousands of these people are being moved through Independence. Shawnees, Kickapoos, and Pattawattamies—all are being moved from lands in Ohio, Kentucky, and Illinois.

"Old Andrew Jackson doesn't know it, but he's a tool in the hands of the Almighty, helping Him prepare for the gathering of Israel!" Joseph leaned forward, his voice dropping nearly to a whisper. "I'm predicting the Second Coming is less than nine years away!"

The high tide of excitement which greeted Joseph Smith's prediction that Sabbath morning lingered with the people of Kirtland and colored their lives.

Tom didn't see much of Joe Smith that summer, but then, that was to be expected. Both arms of the church, as well as the heavy writing schedule, demanded most of his time. Tom was aware of the new mood of confidence in the people. In Kirtland the unrest of the winter was given a passing salute of apology by the church members as they began working doubly hard. With renewed enthusiasm they scurried about the country with the message of the church and the *Book of Mormon.*

It was nearly October when the Prophet came into the livery stable. "Let me guess!" Tom exclaimed. "You want shoes on that filly right this minute."

"Wrong. I'm taking the stage to New York City. I intend to negotiate loans in the name of the Kirtland United Order."

Tom thought he detected a slight swagger as Joe paced the room, saying, "The way we're growing, this church will stand with the best of them, and we might as well put ourselves on the map by growing as fast in our business dealings as the Lord indicates we should."

"We'll be anxious to hear what's goin' on."

Joseph's brilliant smile lighted his face. "You shall, my friend and bodyguard. When I get back, I'll take time to sit down with you and tell it all. I'm not forgetting your faithfulness to me, and the next trip I make to Missouri, you will be going too."

On November 6, 1832, Emma gave birth to a son, and to the relief of all, the child survived and was named Joseph after his father. The whole community rejoiced at the news, and Tom felt much like a proud uncle.

The child was two weeks old when Tom rode out to the farm for his first peek at little Joseph. He had his brief glimpse and heaped his awkward congratulations on Joe and Emma. Taking his arm, Joseph said, "I don't think we're wanted in here. I'm headed for the woods to split a couple of logs; want to give a hand?"

"You've grown pretty soft pushing that pen; guess I'd better," Tom joshed, following the Prophet out the door.

They worked most of the afternoon. When Tom paused to wipe the sweat from his face, he said, "My, the smell of that pine puts me in mind of splitting logs in Manchester. I like the feel of an axe in my hands."

"Hello there! Is Joseph with you?" The hail came faintly through the trees.

"Right here!" Joseph bellowed back, saying to Tom, "From the sound of the horses, it's a battalion. Did you bring your gun?" Tom looked at him in astonishment and Joe threw back his head and laughed.

The men burst through the trees and John Whitmer threw himself off his horse. "Have a fella here who wants to meet you. This here is Brigham Young."

Tom watched the stocky older man slowly dismount. There was an air about him that caught Tom's attention. Without a doubt, this was a man of action and authority. Joseph must have felt it, too. Tom watched the two men, now deep in conversation. Young was talking about reading the *Book of Mormon* as he and Joseph wandered toward the edge of the clearing.

Suddenly Joseph stopped and turned. "I clean forgot what I was doing. Tom, you're right about my being soft. Could you and John finish up the cutting and then come on back to the house for a bite of supper?"

That evening after they had eaten, the men continued to talk, and finally they prayed together. Tom wondered if the excitement he was feeling was evident to the others. He knelt beside his bench and listened. When it was Brigham's turn, Tom found himself straining his ears to understand the words. Suddenly it dawned on Tom that this new fellow was praying in tongues.

"Well, Brig," Tom muttered into his sleeve, "you just cooked your goose. Someone should a-warned you how Joe's dealt with this kind of thing in the past."

Tom felt the tension creeping over him. The others must have sensed it too; abruptly the prayer meeting was over. As the men got awkwardly to their feet, Joseph spoke. He was shaking Brigham Young's hand. "Fellas, I want you to remember this night. Our friend here has been speaking in the true Adamic language."

Later, as Tom prepared to leave, he bent over the cradle for another look at the baby and Joseph asked, "Tom, just when are you going to take up the yoke of matrimony?" Tom ruefully rubbed his jaw, and Joseph burst into laughter. "That expression! What's the problem? It wouldn't hurt to do something besides shoeing horses."

Indeed, Tom took up letter writing—to Jenny. Spurred by his guilty conscience, knowing he had neglected his sister, and driven by his memory of how hard she worked at the Bartons', he wrote. "Jen, I miss you sore. Why don't you take the stage and come visit me. I've already talked to old Mrs. Knight and she will be glad to put you up at her house." He paused to reflect on the implications, and a slow grin came across his face.

Although he did not say so in his letter, he realized having Jenny here would settle a problem he had been ignoring. Joe was always urging the missionary work on him. And he was convinced, too, that Jenny needed to do something about her salvation. Jenny's coming would take care of his brotherly responsibility and possibly also convert her.

"Wonderful!" he muttered; then he wrote, "I miss you, Jen. Since I can't come see you, well, it looks like you could see your duty clear to visit here." As a postcript, he added, "Emma Smith has finally gone and done it. She produced a little boy for them. His name is Joseph, after his father."

And Jenny received the letter. Sitting in the rocking chair in the Bartons' kitchen, she rocked lazily and read the letter with a gentle smile. Dear Tom! She chuckled over the scrawly words and wondered what could have spurred him to such an enormous endeavor. Shaking her head, she murmured, "Tom, knowing your love of the written word, I'd expect a journey to see me would have involved less pain and time."

Mrs. Barton came into the kitchen, saying, "That lazy Clara! It takes her twice as long to run an errand as it would the average person.—A letter?"

Jenny nodded. "From my brother. Oh, there's a postscript." She caught her breath and when her voice broke in mid-sentence, Mrs. Barton turned in surprise. "Joseph Smith and his wife have a little baby boy, named Joseph."

Mrs. Barton was frowning. "And that saddens you."

"Oh, it doesn't," Jenny gasped. "It's just unexpected." After a moment, she added, "Tom's wanting me to come visit."

Mrs. Barton, still studying her face, said slowly, "You could take the stage."

"I would like to see Tom," Jenny said wistfully, "and," she rushed on, "I've never been as far west as Ohio. Everyone's talking about going west; I'd like to at least see Ohio."

Jenny realized later that her reply to Mrs. Barton had been simply words—the kind of words she was prone to pick up and toss around, just because words were expected.

But those words had consequence, and almost before she knew it, she was on her way to Kirtland, Ohio.

Leaning out the window of the stagecoach as it swayed slowly through the streets of Kirtland, Jenny finally accepted it. This was Joseph's town. Seeing it was like tying two ends of a dream together, making reality.

Tom was there to lift her down from the stagecoach; his rough hug and whiskery kiss filled her eyes with tears. "Oh, Tom, I didn't realize I missed you so much!"

"Tom!" the booming voice came from just behind her. "I see you've taken my advice, but I meant for you to choose from among our own."

Tom squeezed Jenny again and whispered, "See, I told you that you're all grown up. Even Joe didn't recognize you."

"Oh." Slowly Jenny stepped out of Tom's arms, and just as slowly she turned. Blinking, she stared up at the man. Twice as tall and broad as she remembered, he was clad in dignified black, and for a moment she wished for the farmboy's shirt. She stepped backward to see his face. It was the same cheerful grin beneath the bright hair. The grin became puzzled and now Jenny could laugh. "You really don't remember me, do you? I'll give you a hint. The first time you saw me, you said I was the ugliest thing you'd ever seen."

"Ma'am, I'm humbly begging your pardon, but no lady as fair as you would merit such talk from me."

"Joe, you're puttin' on," Tom protested. "This is my sister, Jenny." And by his grin, she knew he did remember.

Jenny stayed three weeks in Kirtland, Ohio. As she rode the stage back to Cobleskill, her mind was a patchwork quilt of pictures and words, woven together with emotions as brittle as old thread.

Tom was heavier than she remembered, with bundles of knotted muscles from his work at the forge. She had watched him pounding the glowing iron against the anvil until she expected the two to merge. She walked to church on his arm, and quietly listened to his constant stream of talk.

He obviously felt compelled to convert her to the new church. And while her eyes were busy about the town, sorting and storing impressions, seeing faces that she would remember, she was amused by Tom's earnestness.

In three weeks' time, the shape of her thoughts and feelings were influenced not by the commitment of these people nor by the thrust of their creed, although they saw to it that she was bombarded with fearsome words about her fate; the real attraction of Kirtland was one dark-coated figure. All others became peripheral images, colored only to supply contrast to him.

She had witnessed a painful scene, too. From a distance she had seen Joe and the woman beside him bending over a bundle in her arms. At Jenny's whispered words, "Why, Emma is dark, too!" Tom looked at her in surprise.

"Too?" Tom questioned. Jenny bit her tongue.

Jenny had been astonished by another scene also. From the window at the Knights' home she had spotted a cloud of dust and heard cries. One of Newel's sisters joined Jenny in her dash from the house. They found the crowd and wormed their way toward the center.

Betsy backed off in disgust. "It's nothing but a bunch of grown men going at it again. One of these days the Prophet'll have someone catch him at these shenanigans, and he'll wish they didn't."

Beside her a man turned, saying, "Prophet! You mean that's the Prophet in there wrestlin' like a commoner? Lady, we've come from Pennsylvania hearin' about how this is God's people preparin' for the end times, with His word writ out on leaves of gold, and you're tellin' me this is the man who did it all?" He turned and grasped the arm of the dusty woman beside him. "Mattie, I can't follow a man who spends his time wrestlin' in a dust pile."

Jenny watched the couple leave and shrugged. A victory shout cut the air and the dust settled. Joseph Smith sat astraddle a panting young giant with a torn shirt.

She was smiling as she followed Betsy back to the house. Later she saw Joseph, properly free of dust and impropriety, standing behind the pulpit. His solemnity nearly dulled her resolve, but in the middle of his sermon a smile crossed his face, and he delivered an illustration wrapped in the homey scent of the farm.

On the way back to the Knights' home, Tom had anxiously asked, " 'Twas a good sermon, wasn't it?" She looked at him in amusement and nodded. She needn't tell him only one illustration lingered in her thoughts.

Once again in Cobleskill, Jenny discovered discontentment dogging her heels and coloring her days. When Clara confronted Jenny in her room under the eaves, Jenny was forced to admit all that she had been thrusting to the back of her mind. And yet she couldn't tell it all.

"There's a man there," Jenny admitted.

Clara's eyes were shrewd. "Being a good looker like you, you shouldn't have no problem." Jenny shrugged and Clara said, "Oh, one of those situations, huh? Well, get ye some dandelion root and some river water. I've the other charms. Want me to come while you make a circle and cast your spell?"

"Isn't that too easy? Is it fair?"

"It isn't easy. Fair? All's fair in love and war."

Clara went with Jenny, giving her instructions. Later, at home, Jenny was emotionally drained, despairing of success.

In the kitchen she said, "I'll write to Tom; he can keep me posted."

Once again Clara's shrewd eyes pierced her pretense. "If it's that bad, you can have some beeswax for a voodoo doll of the woman in your way." Jenny's heart chilled. "If that don't work, you may have to make a pact." Slowly Jenny turned and looked at her friend. For just a moment Jenny closed her eyes and saw that page in the book over which she had trembled in the past. She could only shake her head, and Clara's smile shamed her. "You don't want to admit you don't understand how it works, do you?"

"I've read a little bit about it," she answered in a low voice. "But if you were to tell me, it might help."

Later Jenny tossed on her bed and tried to forget what Clara had suggested. The questions tumbled through her mind, and finally she slipped from her bed, lighted a candle, and opened the book.

Carefully she avoided that section. Thumbing through the book, she muttered, "There's got to be another way."

The next morning, while she and Clara were preparing breakfast, Jenny asked, "Clara, do you know anything about talismans?"

"Of course—I have one. Wanna see it?" Jenny's hands trembled as she nodded.

It was late afternoon before the two of them could slip away to Clara's room. Kneeling beside her bed, Clara pulled out her satchel. "You're supposed to wear or carry this all the time for it to have the most good, but I paid a good sum for it, and I can't afford to lose it. 'Tisn't as important I carry it right now as it will be in the future when I really plan to use it."

"When are you going to use it?" Jenny watched the sly expression creep into Clara's eyes as she placed the strange object in Jenny's hands.

After a moment she replied, "When I find a man I really want. See, there's power here and I don't want it attractin' just anybody."

"Tell me what it means." Jenny turned the round object over in her hand. The heavy gray metal was marked with curious designs and unfamiliar letters.

"Well, in the first place, it's a table. The markings add up to meanin's that are related to the energy of the stars. The writin's different names for God, and blessings."

"What'll it do?"

"Well, for instance, see these little marks? They mean you can call upon the celestial powers that's been assigned to you. They can be invoked. That's where I get my power to make charms and cause storms."

"Is that all?"

"No, there's lots more. You can use it to get rich, have power and love, peace—oh, just lots of good things. But for some of them, it takes a bit of practice."

"How's that?"

"Well, I'm good at storms, but so far, I guess I haven't tried love too hard."

"Clara, will you sell this to me?" Clara drew back, and Jenny pressed. "You said you didn't even carry it yet. You can get another one. I need one now."

"These are hard to come by. A special man makes 'em, and he's got to do it at a special time and in a special frame of mind. Serene like, or there won't be the proper magnetism in it." She studied Jenny's face. "Why don't you tell me what's goin' on? If there's a person on this earth who can help you, it's me. I figured out that you were settin' your cap for Mark. But you've come back from your trip all like a thundercloud."

Jenny took a deep breath and slowly lifted her face. She was still clutching the talisman in her damp hand, desperately knowing she must have it. "If I do, will you promise to sell the talisman to me now?"

After studying her face for a moment, Clara nodded.

"It's Joseph Smith. I want him."

"The Mormon prophet," Clara said slowly. "I can't see any person in their right mind wantin' to be stuck with a preacher. And he's already married."

Jenny slowly shook her head. Miserably she whispered, "I don't know why either, but ever since I was a little tyke I've loved him. He's never paid any attention to me. It hurt when he got married, but then she was sickly and losing her babies. I thought sure the heavens had willed me to have him. Now I see I need help."

"Maybe so, maybe so." Clara pursed her lips. "You're wantin' her to die, aren't you?" Jenny hid her face in her hands and nodded. "Well, I guess you've come to the right place, 'cause there's no way on this earth you'll get what you want except through the craft."

Clara watched Jenny make a tiny pouch of cotton to hold the talisman which she pinned inside her dress, just over her heart. Clara chuckled and said, "You're wantin' him bad, aren't you?" She nodded. "Well, I have a feelin' it's gonna take a lot of power. Better think about what else you're willin' to do to get him. Have you figgered out yet how you'll know when the talisman's workin'?"

Jenny caught her breath and for a moment stood very still, lost in thought. "This is real, isn't it? Well, I guess when I hear from Tom that— that she's dead."

18

THE SOUND OF sawing and hammering was music in the streets of Kirtland. The Mormons were building a temple. On the construction site workmen swarmed, thick as ants. But twice as thick were the crowds who constantly walked the streets, keeping track of every nail and board and the scores of quarried stones piled high beside the excavation.

The spectators saw Joseph Smith working beside his men, cheerfully heaving the foundation stones into place. They also saw Sidney Rigdon, well known for his emotionalism, walking the masonry at night with tears raining down his cheeks as he petitioned heaven for the blessings of God upon the new temple.

When Tom joined the spectators, he frowned at it all. Sweating and panting, Joseph came to him, grinning.

"Joe, how can you call this a temple?" Tom challenged. "I recollect your sayin' this isn't consecrated ground and that we're to be a-movin' to Zion."

"Call it what you wish," Joe said shortly, his grin replaced with a frown. "Until we do move to Zion, we need a house of worship, and a place for learning. Remember, we are still waiting for the Lord to instruct us when to move." His brilliant smile again in place, he said, "I'll tell you another thing. The Lord himself has set the timing of all this. Now He has commanded that the building of the temple in Zion be commenced. There needs be a tithing collected from the people immediately. For now, how about giving us a hand on this job?"

Several days later, while Tom was on the construction site working beside Joseph, Oliver Cowdery appeared. He was striding through the piles of lumber when Tom spotted him. His face was lined with fatigue and his clothes still bore Missouri dust.

"Joe, look," Tom said slowly. Together they waited in silence as the man walked toward them.

With a terse nod, Oliver handed a folded paper to Joseph and then sat down on a quarry-stone to wait. It was a Missouri newspaper, *Western Monitor,* dated August 2, 1833. Slowly Joseph read aloud, "Number one says no Mormons are to settle in Jackson County in the future. Two, those settled are to sell out and leave." His startled eyes turned to Cowdery and then returned to the article. "Number three, the Mormon press, the storehouse, and the shops are to close immediately. Four, the leaders are to stop emigration from Ohio. Five, the brethren, referred to as those with the gift of divination, are to be informed of the fate that awaits if they fail to comply." Joe snorted and crumpled the paper.

"Cowdery, what happened?" Tom asked.

"They've smashed the press. Everything's gone. Took all the copies of the *Book of Commandments*; Partridge and Allen got tarred and feathered. Later the Gentiles threatened to burn the crops and houses if we didn't promise to clear out."

Tom turned to pace the construction site as Joseph continued to talk to Oliver. Miserably he studied the jumble in front of him and thought about the revelation which Joseph had just sent to Missouri, commanding them to gather tithes in order to start the temple in Zion. "Temple," he muttered. "Bet they wish they'd never heard of the place."

Oliver left and Tom went back to Joseph. "I've letters to write to send back with Oliver," Joseph said abruptly. "I'll walk down the street with you."

"What ya gonna say?" Tom asked.

"The Spirit tells me to instruct them to renounce war, work for peace, and put up with the fussing," After a moment he added, "I'll instruct the brethren there to petition the governor for justice. He will not fail to give ear to them."

Tom stopped by Joseph's office the next day. A still weary Oliver Cowdery was waiting for a final letter before starting his return journey.

Joseph finished writing, then lifted the paper. "You might as well hear the letter I've written. I'm not the least surprised at what's happened. I can't help thinking that Zion's brought the trouble on herself. Notwithstanding the articles written by Phelps in the *Western Monitor*, there's a deeper reason for the problems. It all goes back to men not being willing to obey counsel and take instruction from those the Lord puts over them." Silently he folded the letter and handed it to Oliver. With a sigh and shake of his head, Joe added, "All I can do is allow the Lord's wrath to be poured upon His people until they will confess their sins."

It was well into September 1833 before another communication was received from Jackson County, Missouri.

The day it came, Joseph stopped at the livery stable and waited until Tom finished shoeing Hyrum's horse before he showed the letter to him. "My friend," he said, "much of this matter with Zion can't be discussed with just anyone on the street. Bear with me while I tell you about this letter and air the problems. It relieves me to see they're handling the situation in a worthy manner, but still—" He unfolded the letter.

"Phelps, the writer of those articles, explains the explosion down there. Seems it started with his article in the *Western Monitor*; he was just trying to handle a sticky problem. Since Missouri is a slave state, they're mighty edgy over the issue, more so than ever since they know we prophesied that slavery will be abolished."

Tom added, "Cowdery admitted to me that part of the problem is our own people bein' too free with the prophecy that Jackson County is goin' to be cleared of the Gentiles and become the inheritance of the people of God."

Joseph moved his shoulders impatiently and continued, "They got wind that some free Negroes had converted to the church and were trying to emigrate to Independence. Phelps discovered a Missouri law that decreed they must have citizenship papers from another state before they could enter Missouri. After that came the article stating that the church had no policy regarding colored people. That blew the powder keg! Phelps says he tried to right things by admitting he wasn't only trying to stop them from coming, but to prevent them from joining the church."

"Doesn't seem enough to start those problems!"

"The Gentiles said it was an open invitation for the Negro to emigrate, and that it would stir up problems with the slaves in the state," Joseph sighed.

"Phelps said they've petitioned the governor for troops to keep order until their suit for damages is settled. Since that's under control now, Sidney and I can make our trip to Canada with an easy conscience."

"And since you're leavin', I think I'll be makin' my own missionary trip," Tom stated. Joe turned to look at him, and Tom added, "To see my sister Jenny."

"You bringing her back with you?"

Tom shook his head. "I've no ideas on that line. I just feel the Spirit's urge to talk to her about her salvation."

Tom didn't bother to write to Jenny that he was coming. Reflecting on her teasing about his letter writing, he decided he could beat the letter there.

When he walked into the Bartons' kitchen that October evening, Jenny's surprise held her motionless, and then she threw herself into his arms, crying, "Tom! I am so glad to see you!"

As she continued to cling to him, hugging and patting, he said, "Well, Joe thinks I should bring you back with me."

She tipped her head and slowly said, "Whatever for?"

"He thinks you'd make a good Mormon." In a moment she began to laugh. "That surprises you?" he asked. "Well, Joe doesn't think of much else."

Later Tom met Clara, and then Mark Cartwright made an unexpected appearance. As Tom shook his hand, he said, "Jen didn't tell me she was expecting company."

"I'm not really company," Mark said with a glance at Jenny. "I'm over this way frequently since my Uncle Thomas is ailing. I offer only moral support, but Auntie seems to need it."

Clara was unable to take her eyes off Tom, saying, "So you're the Mormon." Jenny wished desperately that she hadn't shared her secrets with Clara.

During the following week Mark stayed in Cobleskill because of his uncle's health, and Tom lingered on at the Bartons'. In the evenings, after the Bartons and Clara had gone off to their bedrooms, Mark, Jenny, and Tom sat by the fire with apples and corn to pop.

Mark asked a flood of questions about Joseph and his new church. Jenny listened and watched his keen eyes probing her brother's as Tom talked.

Mark's voice was low. "I've not forgotten the things that happened in South Bainbridge. Tom, you and I both know that an awful lot of shady things came out at that trial, and there were many unanswered questions. Wouldn't the Lord demand a higher level of integrity in choosing a prophet?"

Tom's gaze was just as earnest. "Mark, Joseph was just a happy-go-lucky youngster back in those days. You have to know Joseph the Prophet. The mantle of authority and righteousness clearly rests upon him."

On subsequent evenings Mark asked about the *Book of Mormon,* and Tom could admit to knowing only what he had heard read aloud. Mark persisted, "Then what do some of these other men have to say about the book? What about Sidney Rigdon? I'm hearing he's a Campbellite preacher and well-educated. Has he investigated it all?"

"Well, in the beginnin' he wasn't sold on the idea, but after he took the occasion to ask the Lord for a sign, he could believe. He said that if we aren't familiar enough with our God to ask for a sign from Him, and if He weren't willin' to give us one, well—I think he said God was no better than a Juggernaut, whatever that is."

Mark slowly chewed his apple, swallowed, and said, "*Juggernaut* is the American title for the Hindu Vishnu; it means *lord of the world.* So Rigdon thinks a God that doesn't do what is demanded of Him is really no God at all!"

And when Mark ceased asking his questions, Tom turned his earnest argument on Jenny. "You've heard Joseph and the others preach. You know yourself that we ought not neglect our salvation. Jen, I'm wantin' to see you join up. Joseph said that to turn our backs on the revealed truth in these last days means we won't make it. That's eternal damnation."

Jenny shivered and Mark laughed. "Tom, you take life and other men's thoughts too seriously." There was a touch of scorn in his voice as he leaned forward and added, "The plain, good, old-fashioned religion has been around long enough to convince me that the tried and true way can be depended on. But right now, religion doesn't interest me. I intend to leave it all until I'm so old I have nothing more important to think about."

His eyes danced toward Jenny, "And now I do have more important things to think about. I'd like to squeeze your pretty little hand before I say good night, and I'd also like to extract a promise that you'll accompany me to the Christmas festival the first week in December."

And so Mark departed and Tom prepared, rather gloomily, to leave Cobleskill for Kirtland in the morning. Jenny was left to muse over their conversations; her only reaction had been a hearty laugh over Mark's silly conclusion to the matter.

That night as she prepared for bed, she chanced to see a corner of the green book protruding from under a stack of schoolbooks; her heart grew heavy with its old burdens. *One thing is certain,* she decided as she pulled pins from her thick dark hair, *at times Mark nearly tears me away from that resolve.* She frowned. *I wonder,* she thought briefly, *whether that is good or bad.*

By the time Tom reached Kirtland, Joseph Smith and Sidney Rigdon had returned from their preaching mission in Canada. Within two days of his return, Tom heard rumbles in the community against Joseph for his lack of action in defense of Zion. But things settled down with time.

Soon Oliver Cowdery returned from New York with his new printing press. Joseph had promised him the position as editor of the *Star* if he would set up the press in Kirtland.

One crisp morning in early December when Tom walked into Whitney's store, he found Joseph Smith clutching a letter and Whitney stoking the potbellied stove.

Tom glanced at Joseph's sober face and then at the letter. "Soon as I think things are runnin' smooth around here," Tom said, "you get another letter."

Joe lifted it. "It's from Missouri. On October 31, fifty men attacked us just west of the Big Blue River. They ruined ten cabins and whipped our people into the forest. Later they got into the storehouse and were caught

redhanded. For the trouble of catching the culprits, our men were jailed."
His voice dropped to a rumble as he studied the letter. "Next, David
Whitmer banded together a bunch to protect their places. They tangled
with the Gentiles, and in the scuffle two Gentiles and one of our men were
killed.

"Whitmer says here the story got blown twice its size, and soon the
Gentiles were threatening to kill those in jail. Well, the militia was sent out
to meet our men, and old Boggs sweet-talked our men into laying down
their arms."

"Who's Boggs?"

"The lieutenant governor of Missouri." Joseph continued, "That night
every Mormon community was attacked, and by morning all twelve hundred of our people were driven out of their homes. A few of them went to
Clay County, he says, but the rest of them are shivering in the cottonwoods
along the river. Everything's gone."

He continued reading. The Mormons' lawyers had won support from
Governor Dunklin. Dunklin quickly gave the Mormons the promise of
military escort to return to their homes. Dunklin also instructed them to
raise a militia and granted them public arms.

On a happier note, the letter ended with the tale of a miraculous display
of meteor showers. To the exiles, it was a glorious sign of the end of the
world.

As soon as the news of the letter was out, the city of Kirtland rocked
with confusion. These were kinfolk and neighbors; these were the children
of Israel, and this was their Zion! Joseph sent a quick dispatch to the
leaders in Missouri, ordering them to remain as near Jackson County as
possible. He also ordered them to retain their lands.

The following Sabbath when Joseph stood before his people and relayed
the information to them, a mighty cheer went up. When he raised his hand
for silence, he added, "I believe in law and justice. The Lord inspired
noble men to write the Constitution of the United States. Justice will
prevail."

As the crowd voiced their hearty approval again, Tom sat back and
beamed with pride. Lately, Joseph had disappointed him; he had thought
there should have been action and encouragement, and that Joe had a
blind spot.

Now Joseph lifted another sheet of paper. "Brethren," he called, and
there was instant silence. "I instructed Phelps to petition Washington for
help. I have also prepared a letter to President Andrew Jackson, which I
mailed along with a copy of the latest revelation given by the Lord. I will
read to you only snatches of this December 16 revelation, because it is

very long and I don't want any of you to go to sleep on me and fall off your benches, as Michael Williams did last week." The levity caught everyone by surprise, and Joseph waited for silence. Even Tom grinned, remembering the youth's embarrassment.

Joseph rattled the paper. "Oliver Cowdery has our new press set up, and he will be glad to sell you copies of the revelation for one dollar apiece.—Now, referring to the people in Kirtland: 'Verily . . . I the Lord have allowed the afflictions in consequence of their transgressions. . . .' " A sigh and murmur swept the room. " 'Zion shall not be moved; there is none other place appointed for the gathering of my saints. A commandment I give to all the churches: purchase all the land around Zion which can be had. There is already an abundance of money to redeem Zion.' "

Above the murmur sweeping the room, Joseph's voice rose: "Now regarding their present trouble: 'Let them importune the judge . . . the governor . . . the president. If he will not heed, I the Lord will arise . . . and vex the nation.' "

In April the Kirtland council dissolved the United Order. Tom heard about it at the livery stable, and he crossed the street to Whitney's store to confront Joseph.

"I hear the Order's finished," he said. "And I also am hearin' funny things about the revelation dealin' with it."

Joseph got to his feet and stared down at Tom. "They're saying it's funny, huh? Well, the revelation isn't to be given out just yet. It's dealing with the distribution of property and it's the business of the council."

Tom returned his stare, unwavering. "Joseph, they are also sayin' you've had a letter from Phelps in Missouri, that the people are in desperate condition. Is it right that the innocent must suffer with the guilty? Surely all of those people there aren't sinnin'."

"You're suggesting that I step in and do something about it? Any such action before the Lord gives the command puts my soul in jeopardy. Let the Lord handle it. I understand most of the people have settled in Clay County. I've instructed them to hang on to their land." He paused a moment, then added, "About the revelation, the council is mindful of who's involved. No one else need know." Joe's level gaze quickly reminded Tom he had no business probing into the Prophet's affairs.

The silence stretched between them until suddenly Joe smiled. "Tom, looks like you might just get your wish to visit Missouri. Pratt and Wight are back in town and they have some pretty good ideas. They also brought the news that Governor Dunklin is working for us; among other things he's urging the church to apply for public arms, and go to work defending themselves. But, as the fellows pointed out, even with all our men holding guns, the old settlers still have us outnumbered."

"Now, who was it preachin' that in Bible times the children of Israel were outnumbered mighty often, and the Lord was pleased to do their fightin' for them?" Tom murmured.

Joseph ignored Tom and continued, "Well, here's the plan they proposed, and the revelation the Lord gave. They suggest we get us an army together, a well-trained one, but move into the area like a bunch of settlers. The army would just hang around until the church can buy up all the land of those Gentiles opposing us. The Lord's affirmed that we're to redeem Zion by power, and that He's already raised up a man to lead the army of the Lord, like Moses led his people. I've already got fellows out recruiting from all the churches. Tom, you can join up if you have five dollars and a good shooting iron."

Joseph's army didn't grow as quickly as Tom expected, but he swallowed his disappointment and continued to work at settling his affairs.

Writing to Jenny, he informed her of his plans. "Right now, it looks like we'll be leaving this spring and won't be back until Zion is well-established and prospering. Hopefully, by then there won't be a Gentile in the state. You know the revelation from the Lord about the settling of Zion; He has said we are to inherit their land and their riches. I don't feel too sorry for them; they've been warned they'll either have to join us or forfeit it all. I'm led to believe that this very revelation has caused some hard feelings in Missouri. I suppose, if I were one of that bunch, I might have a hard time swallowin' it, too."

On May 4, 1834, the day before they were to leave for Missouri, the army gathered in Kirtland to hear an address by Sidney Rigdon. Looking about the packed hall, Tom whispered to James Taylor, "The church could use this kind of enthusiasm every Sunday!"

"Yeah," James returned, "but it would take a new army every week to see it done."

During the course of his address, he urged the church to change their name from Church of Christ to Church of Latter-day Saints. The crowd rustled with excitement, and James whispered, "I like the sound of that; it has a good ring to it."

Tom nodded. "Maybe he's got somethin' there. We'd be sheddin' the tag of Mormonites; nobody's heard of Latter-day Saints. That could be a real advantage when we run into any opposition."

The following day, as the army started marching across Ohio, Tom could see that more than just good sense dictated the name change. Looking around at the motley crew called Zion's Camp, Tom saw old muskets, ancient pistols, and rusty swords. Some of the men were armed with butcher knives. No wonder Joseph Smith wanted as little commotion possible as the army marched westward! It made good sense to divide the army into small groups and take different routes through larger communities along the way.

Joseph was at ease, even content, in his new role. During a three-day rest period at Salt Creek, Illinois, he took over the instruction and drilling practice the men sorely needed. Under his direction, within a short time the men mastered the simple maneuvers.

But not many days passed before Tom began to be puzzled about his colorful leader.

James brought up the subject. He and Tom sat together on the far side of the campfire, polishing their rifles. In a low voice James asked, "Does it strike you odd that the Prophet spends so much time hiding who he is? I heard him tellin' Wight to pass his name off as Captain Cook to strangers."

Tom drawled, "Well, it might just keep us all safe if there's questions asked."

James nodded and added, "But he keeps changin' his position in the company, even to ridin' in the supply wagons. And that dog—the nasty tempered thing—oughta be better'n the twenty men he's askin' for as bodyguards."

Tom tried to shrug off the questions, but in the following days he became aware of his own doubts. The feeling guilted him until he saw the measuring look Brigham Young turned on Joseph the day his anger lashed out at Sylvester over the bulldog.

Tom heard the tirade of abuse spilling from Sylvester and came running. He arrived just as the man screamed, "If that dog bites me, I'll kill him!"

And Joe roared back, "I'll whip you in the name of the Lord. If you don't repent, that dog will eat the flesh from your bones."

After a moment of stunned silence, Thompson exclaimed, "Aw, Joe, that dog is a blamed nuisance all around. There's not a fella here who can tolerate 'im."

Tucker, a quiet, serious-minded man, spoke thoughtfully, "Joseph, you ought not go around talking of whipping in the name of the Lord. It's unseemly for a prophet."

Joe took a quick step backward, and his words drew that look from Brigham. "You're seeing how this all looks. I did it on purpose to show you how base your attitudes are! Like animals. Men ought not to place themselves that low."

As Tom and his tentmate had bedded down a couple nights later, Matt commented on the large white dog, curled up in front of Joseph's tent. "Seems strange," he muttered, pulling off his boots. "The Prophet being on such good terms with the Almighty, getting revelations that the Lord will fight our battles for us, and yet he gets an old dog to stand guard."

During the second watch of the night, a single gunshot brought the men running from their tents. Joseph was kneeling in the dust before his tent, and the white bulldog was making his last convulsive movements. The apologetic guard stood hat in hand. "Forgot about the dog," he muttered. "Just saw a movement and shot quick."

When Tom and Matt crawled back into their tent, Matt yawned and said, "Well, guess now Joseph's going to *have* to rely on men and angels."

19

THE CONFRONTATION BETWEEN Joseph and Sylvester soon was pushed into the background, forgotten in the light of a more compelling issue.

Orson Hyde and Parley Pratt rode into camp after their conference with Governor Dunklin. They had barely dismounted when the entire army surrounded to hear the news. Taking their cue from the men's grim faces, the foot soldiers waited quietly as Joseph and Lyman Wight joined them.

"It's not good news," Pratt said shortly. He wiped his hands wearily across his face before continuing. "Unbeknownst to us, Governor Dunklin has been working for our cause. He's been dickering with the War Office to secure a federal arsenal, with plans to build it in Jackson County." He paused and added, "Right in our own backyard, along with the federal army as a guard."

"Glory be!" Wight exclaimed. "There's not much chance of the Gentiles fightin' us under those circumstances."

"But wait," Pratt interrupted, "on top of that, Dunklin was considering dividing Jackson County so our people and the Gentiles would have equal shares. Later in our meeting he dropped the information that on May 2, he dispatched orders to Colonel Lucas to restore the arms they took from us. But before Lucas got the order, news of the coming of Zion's Camp leaked." He looked slowly around the assembled men. Deliberately he added, "Dunklin said the Missourians stormed the jail where our arms were stored and took every one of them."

With a muttered curse, Wight flung his battered old hat to the ground and stalked away. Joseph watched him go, then turned back to Pratt. "Before any action could be taken they ravaged the rest of our property. Every last one of the hundred and fifty houses was destroyed."

Groans of dismay erupted in angry words, and finally Joseph lifted his hand. His face white and rigid, he said, "Let's hear the rest of it."

"Well, that cooked our goose with Dunklin. He was pretty frosty. Said the comin' of Zion's Camp plus the fact that all our houses were destroyed made it impossible at this time to restore our property to us." He paced the trampled ground in front of Joe.

Watching Pratt, Hyde added, "News about the army has traveled fast. We're findin' out it ran like wildfire ahead of us. Militias from four different counties have moved out to meet us. They had our number right off. They knew we were an army, not a bunch of farmers with a sack of grain to plant. The word was passin' ahead of us, with people yellin', 'The Mormons are comin'; they'll murder our women and children!' "

The group turned to Joseph and waited in stunned silence as he paced back and forth, head bowed, hands clasped behind him. Wight had crept back to the edge of the crowd, and Joseph stopped in front of him. "I tell you, it's best we don't make a wrong move; we're sitting ducks!"

Wight bristled, looking at the men clustered around them. "We can't go back, not after comin' this far!" A rumble of assent rose from the men, and Tom remembered the confident assertion that angels would fight for them.

Finally the army moved out, advancing cautiously, disheartened and confused. The men needn't be told that Joseph was as deeply disturbed as they. On the second day further bad news drifted back. An armed band was waiting across the Missouri with plans to attack.

Immediately Joseph Smith ordered the men to move out to the prairie.

"Smith!" Lyman Wight roared. "These men'll have neither decent water or wood for fire. I say let 'em all spend the night in the woods."

Joe turned back to argue the matter, and then impatiently wheeled about. Raising his voice, he shouted, "Thus saith the Lord God, march on!"

In disgust, Wight silently turned aside and waved his men to camp in the woods. Sylvester turned to shout at Joseph's men, "Who are you following? Wight's in charge of this army!"

That night, just as Wight predicted, Tom and the group who had followed Joseph were forced to drink bad water and eat raw pork.

The following day, Tom was surprised to hear Joseph defending his position before the men. Stepping close to Joseph, Tom growled from the side of his mouth, "Forget it, 'tis all come to naught."

But Joseph pressed his case. "By the Spirit of God I know when to sing, to pray, to talk, even to laugh."

Wight and some of the other men became apologetic, but Sylvester raged. "You want a man in bondage, without the freedom to speak! These prophecies, they're lies in the name of the Lord. You're as corrupt as the devil himself in your heart."

Joseph seized the horn used to call the men to prayer and threw it at Sylvester. Tom caught his breath, then gasped with relief as the horn missed the man and smashed into pieces.

Three days later, the Camp of Zion moved up the bank of Fishing River, just on the border of Clay County. But before Joseph could advance his troops, cholera struck.

One by one the ranks of Zion's Camp fell victim to the dread disease. Within two weeks sixty-eight of the army had succumbed.

Thus far Tom had been spared, but each day he counted his chances with a sinking heart as more of his comrades took to their pallets. Carrying water and the common remedy of whiskey mixed with flour, Tom made his rounds among the sick. At the same time, Joseph moved among his men, praying and laying hands upon the stricken.

Early one morning, Joseph approached as Tom filled his jugs. "You're looking mighty worried this morning," Tom said as he mixed the whiskey and flour together.

"Leave that mess for someone else," Joseph ordered in a low voice. "I've another task for you." He led Tom away from the men. "I understand today's the day of the confab across the river in Clay County. You know we've promised to stay put until the business is settled, so I can't stick my nose over there. I hear a Judge Ryland is meeting with the Gentiles and the Mormons to read them all the governor wants done to settle this problem."

Tom looked at him for a moment and said slowly, "You want me to slip over easy-like, huh?"

Joseph nodded, "I want a quick report from someone I can trust to give me the truth."

"Still scratchin' for a fight?"

"Not me," Joseph said bitterly. "I want a peaceful settlement of all this. It's Wight who's itching to use that cannon."

Tom nodded slowly. "You're bein' cautious, but I heard the fellas talkin'; from something you've said, they're believin' that once they strike a sword, there's gonna be angels right there fightin' for them."

Joseph turned away. "Just get over there and find out what's going on. Keep your mouth shut as to who you are."

Tom cut downstream and found a youth idly fishing from the security of his crudely made raft. Pulling a packet of fishhooks from his pocket, Tom hailed the boy. "You headin' across the river?"

The boy poled closer to shore and blurted, "Them's hooks? I wasn't, but I would for hooks."

It was nearly noon when Tom sauntered into the clearing where the two groups belligerently faced each other. Another group of men approached, and Tom silently merged with them, resisting the urge to pull his hat down to his ears.

He was eyed suspiciously, but was momentarily forgotten as a gentleman entered the clearing. The drift of conversation about him stopped as he surveyed the two groups. "Come close, men; I've no intention of straining my voice. The original settlers of Jackson County have drawn up a list of proposals to present to the group of Mormon settlers. With no further ado, I intend to read them to you, and then, gentlemen, the mode of settlement is upon your shoulders.

"Be advised that Governor Dunklin insists that a settlement be agreed upon. Adherence to the settlement will be enforced by law. There are a number of points that need to be made before we read the proposals, points made by legal counsel which must be taken into advisement before a satisfactory solution to the problem can be reached. First of all, Governor Dunklin points out that the Constitution of the United States guarantees that the citizens of any state shall be entitled to privileges and considerations in all states; the state boundary is no license for discrimination regarding emigration. The constitution of this state allows men the right to bear arms in defense of themselves. Also, the Constitution of these United States guarantees freedom to worship according to the dictates of a man's conscience.

"I wish to point out that whereas the state allows arms for defense, it is strictly illegal for any group to promote the use of cannon. That is considered aggressive action, not defensive. It is rumored that both sides of this faction are preparing to use cannon." An angry growl swept through the crowd, and Tom noticed hostile looks turned his direction. He held his breath and returned the glances with a level stare.

"Now," continued the judge, "the proposals set out by the residents of Jackson County are as follows. With due appraisal by disinterested parties, the residents of Jackson County are prepared to buy the property of the resident Mormons of Jackson County at double the appraised value, to be paid within thirty days. If this proposal is not met with agreement by the Mormons, then the counter-proposal, the sale of the Missourians' land under the same agreement, is also made."

Silence held both groups. Tom was busy thinking of all the implications. The foremost memory he had was that revelation from the Lord. Briefly he closed his eyes and could clearly hear those words: "Zion shall not be moved out of her place. . . . There is no other place appointed."

When Tom opened his eyes, Phelps was walking toward the judge. His voice rang with confidence and conviction. "Sir, we cannot accept your proposals at this time, but I do promise you that until a settlement is reached, Zion's Camp will remain in their position on Fishing River."

Tom straightened his shoulders, and his heart soared. Phelp's statement brought to mind all those other revelations concerning Zion—surely not one of them would fail!

The Gentiles didn't look as if they were planning to give up any of their positions, either. So the two groups parted with the understanding that the governor would look further into the matter.

As he made his way back across the river, Tom thought about the revelation the Lord had given Joseph in 1831. Of all the promises, this one was the most vivid, telling Joseph that Satan was stirring the Missourians to anger, to the shedding of blood, and that the land of Zion couldn't be obtained except by purchase or the shedding of blood. Well, it didn't look like there would be a purchase.

In Zion's Camp, the cholera continued to claim its victims. Besides the army deaths, fourteen more in the camp died before the disease abated.

Just two days after Tom's foray as spy, Gilliam, Clay County's sheriff, visited the camp. Handing Joseph Smith a copy of a letter written by the chairman of the Jackson County committee, he settled back and waited for him to read it.

When Joe folded the letter, he said, "I understand you want me to pay particular attention to the section underlined, in which it is noted that our communication is signed by persons not directly owning land in Jackson County, in other words, the heads of the church; and therefore we have no right to our claims. It's correct that we don't directly own land there, but we are spokesmen for the church."

The man spoke dryly, "We understand your church has given all the property into the hands of the leaders, but around here I don't think that'll work. It's each man for himself."

Joe chewed his lip. "You are also using a revelation from the Lord to prove we have come with the intent of shedding blood. The Lord was only alerting us to the character of the inhabitants of this county. You're trying to prove we have no intention to come by the land honorably. Seems you're using this means to force us to buy out the Gentiles. I refuse to be threatened."

The man pressed, "Dunklin's directive has also stated that militia from outside the counties is unlawful. You've no legal right to enter the county with weapons unless you have permission from him. It is obvious you have come to Missouri with only one intention—to show force."

"That is not the truth." Joseph paced back and forth before the man. "We've come in peace!"

Tom listened as the men continued to argue; finally Joseph drew himself erect. "Gilliam, I have a plan to offer you." An expression of surprise and relief crossed the sheriff's face. While Joseph explained his plan, Tom watched Gilliam's jaw drop. Then he jumped to his feet as Joseph said, "We will purchase all the property of the settlers who've been the warmongers. Have twelve men set the price, to be paid in one year. Then from that price we shall deduct the amount of damages sustained by our people."

"Only if you throw in the moon to boot!" Gilliam exploded as he stomped out of the camp.

Tom watched Joseph turn away. Without another word, he entered his tent. Late in the afternoon, Joseph reappeared and called his men together to hear the latest revelation from the Lord.

Sitting on the edge of the crowd, Tom studied the men's faces. Some of them were recovering from cholera, others had watched their friends die. All of them, from the beginning, had fretted over the whole sad situation. All were listening intently. For the first time in days, Tom watched relief and hope flicker on their weary faces.

Tom turned his attention to the words Joseph was reading. "Wait for the redemption of Zion. I will fight your battles for you. I will send the destroyer in my time to lay waste mine enemies . . ."

Tom's relief and satisfaction were total—almost, until he heard the final words. As he walked back to his tent, the man in front of him limped along slowly, quoting the words bitterly. " 'It is expedient that they should be brought thus far for a trial of their faith.' " He turned and saw Tom. "I can't see a blessing in the temple helping out those lads who died. That was a sore trial for the Lord to put on us." He continued on his way, sadly shaking his head. At the sound of an angry voice rising beyond the circle of tents, Tom stopped and listened. With a sigh he turned back.

It was Wight. Standing in front of the Prophet's tent, he shouted, "If you choose to back out now, all right, but I'm going to fight! The Lord has promised to help, and I'll hold Him to it!"

As Tom reached the tent, Joe Smith stepped through the doorway, revelation in hand. Thrusting the papers at Wight, he spoke quietly, "Here, read it for yourself. I know you're disappointed, but thus saith the Lord. It may help you to know that in three years' time, we'll march against Jackson County, and there won't be a dog to open his mouth against us. The Lord revealed the date unto me. The day for the redemption of Zion has been set—September 11, 1836."

That night Tom accompanied the Prophet across the river to visit the Mormons in Clay County. Joe comforted the little band of discouraged settlers with his promise to return to Ohio and raise money to buy all of Jackson County.

Finally, Joe ordered the leaders of Zion to return with him to Kirtland, Ohio, to receive their special endowments in the temple. Before they left Missouri, Joe instructed the people remaining behind to hold no public meetings and to stay away from the upcoming elections. "Don't give them opportunity to quarrel with you," he concluded.

Zion's Camp tarried just long enough to hear that their settlement proposal had been rejected.

Phelps rode into camp with a copy of the *Liberty Enquirer*. There was a wry twist to Joseph's grin as he read the paper. Tossing it aside, he said, "The educated opinion of the editor is that the Mormons have scattered and that the war is over. Little do they know the Lord has promised to sweep away their pollution from the land."

20

IN MAY OF 1834, Jenny received a letter from Tom which disrupted the peaceful procession of ordinary days on the farm. Suddenly her mind was filled with the romantic picture of Joe, astride his steed, commanding Zion's Camp as they marched into Missouri to claim their sacred possession.

Together with Clara in the kitchen, Jenny was preparing to feed haying crews. Caught up in her thoughts of Joseph and Missouri, Jenny stood at the kitchen window. The sun-baked fields of ripening grain and the mounding hay stacks retreated into a haze of sun-shot gold. Opening her eyes wide, she sighed and blinked.

"Jenny!" Clara waved a butcher knife at her. "You're goin' to blind yourself starin' into the sun. Give that chicken a turn and go to shuckin' that corn. Those fellas are going to be in here for their dinner. Mrs. Barton won't be a bit happy if we make 'em wait for it." She continued to study Jenny. "You haven't said much lately. What's the problem?"

Jenny walked to the stove and picked up the meat fork. "I've Tom on my mind a bit. He's gone out Missouri way with Joseph Smith's army to rescue their settlers there. I've been feeling lonesome, thinking how it would be if he were killed. Clara, you don't know what it's like, when you've got ten brothers and sisters. Tom's all I have."

"If you were being sensible, you could have Mark." Clara sighed, shook her head, and began to slice bread to stack on the platter. "Shall I do three loaves? There's all that corn and 'taters. I hope the rhubarb pie is sweet enough." She threw a quick glance toward the door. "With a fella as promisin' as Mark, with all that money he's bound to inherit from his mother, and bein' an attorney, I'll never understand how you got your stars crossed and ended up wantin' that preacher Smith."

Jenny was forking the sizzling chicken onto platters. As she lifted the first platter to carry out to the tables under the trees, she glared at Clara.

"All right," Clara muttered, "so you don't like hearin' about it. I guess I'll be settin' *my* cap for him."

She looked at Clara and then laughed. "I give you my permission. But you can't have your talisman back."

Mrs. Barton came into the kitchen and threw a startled glance at Jenny. Then she asked, "Where's the tomatoes and cukes?"

"Settin' under a damp cloth on the table," Clara said hastily, heading for the door with the bread. Jenny scooted for the backyard. "Are you fetchin' the milk?" Clara called.

Later, when Jenny was washing dishes, her thoughts returned to the subject that never released its grip on her restless heart. It was true that she had been thinking about that march to Missouri, feeling the sun smite her eyes just as it would those soldiers, but it hadn't been Tom who occupied her thoughts. As she moved the dishcloth slowly over the plates, she dreamed about the sun turning Joseph's hair as bright as his golden plates.

When Clara carried in the last dish, she whispered to Jenny, "In that letter, did Tom say anythin' about—about her?" Jenny shook her head without looking up. "Do you wanna try that other?"

Scratching at the crusty skillet, Jenny said slowly, "Clara, I can't even think that way."

"You don't even understand *why,* do you?" Clara whispered. "Can't you see we have the *right* to order the events of the universe? Life and death's all part of it. Because you don't like to see someone die, you think death is bad, but that is because you're lookin' at it from down here. People only progress to a better life by passin' through death."

Mrs. Barton spoke from the doorway. "Clara, it's mighty hard to convince people of that when they've just seen someone die. Mark's Uncle Thomas has just passed away today. I don't recommend your philosophy for him."

Jenny turned quickly, "Oh, I'm sorry. Mark was very close to him. I suppose they will need help."

"Yes," Mrs. Barton said. "I was thinking of food, but with folks coming in from as far away as Albany, it will be good household help they'll need. Jenny, the menfolk won't be harvesting again until next week. Why don't you help me wrap up this ham and some preserves and we'll take them over. Take your bag. If need be, I'll leave you there for several days."

Mrs. Barton's offer of Jenny was gladly accepted by the Webers, and she was immediately settled in the garret with Phoebe, Weber's hired girl.

In the kitchen with Phoebe, listening to the sound of carriages arriving and the tide of voices rising in the parlor, Jenny soon discovered why Mark's Aunt Mabel had welcomed her with gratitude. Phoebe was frozen into mindlessness by the crisis. Jenny sorted the jumbled pantry, planned meals, and shoved teacups into Phoebe's limp hands. Late that night, with the windows open to catch the slightest breeze, Jenny stood at the kitchen table rolling out sugar cookies and sand tarts. A lone horse moved past the house, and the back door creaked, but she didn't look up from her task until the hesitant steps stopped.

"Jenny, is that really you?"

"Mark!" Jenny bit her lip, recalling the last time she had seen him. What a silly quarrel it had been! His last visit had come close on the heels of Tom's letter, and her mind had been filled with the vision of Joseph.

Now looking at his wretched face, her heart squeezed tight with pity. He was still wearing his dark suit. She watched him dab at the perspiration on his forehead and tug impatiently at his tight collar.

"I suppose they've all retired for the night."

She nodded. "I think so. Take off your coat and I'll bring you some cold buttermilk." He was staring down at the table when she returned from the springhouse.

"Do you always bake at midnight! And what are you doing here?"

"It's cooler at midnight, and I've just come today. Mark, have you had supper?"

He shook his head. "I'd be happy with a cookie to go with the milk."

He reached for a sand tart and Jenny said, "There's cold ham; wouldn't you like some?"

She was caught by the sadness in his eyes, the tired lines around his mouth. "Mark, I'm sorry."

Quickly he asked, "Then you'll forgive me?"

"What? Oh, that silly quarrel. I've forgotten why we even argued."

"It wasn't the argument," he said thoughtfully. "It was my pigheaded need to be right. Jenny, you've a fine mind, which shouldn't be put down. Be patient with me as I learn to deserve you."

He bit into the cookie and turned away. Jenny stared at him while all he had just said rolled around through her thoughts. How could a man like Mark talk to Jenny, the hired hand, like this?

He turned abruptly. "Are your cookies burning?"

In the days that followed, Jenny saw Mark infrequently as he took charge of the Weber family. Up until the funeral the stream of carriages seemed unending, and Jenny was always ready with tall glasses of lemonade and cups of tea.

Phoebe continued to move only as pushed—all thought had slipped from her mind except for the task before her.

When the day of the funeral finally came, the sound of carriage wheels and horses suddenly ceased. Phoebe signaled the change by collapsing. Mark took her home and returned to beg Jenny to stay on a few days longer. Aunt Mabel came to the kitchen to add her plea; then both she and Mark settled down at the table as if it were the most pleasant spot on earth.

The kitchen table conferences grew into midnight trysts for the three-some, with sandwiches and cookies served by pale lamplight. Jenny felt herself prodded and probed by Mark and Mabel, but she also knew their friendly jabs were without rancor.

One night after Mark had left the room, Mabel turned back to Jenny and said, "You know he loves you, don't you?" Jenny felt her back stiffen, and Mabel continued, "I'm not trying to give you that speech about how you are as good as any of us; I believe you know that. But I sense you're not taking him seriously, and I can't understand that. You see, Mark means a great deal to me. You seem so sensitive to our every need and emotion, yet—" She leaned forward to study Jenny's face. "Why do I feel you're set apart and divided from us? You know I welcome you with open arms. If you're worried about his mother, you can rest assured my sister will love you just as I do."

Jenny watched Mrs. Weber walk from the room. She was thinking about the talisman pinned inside her dress, and about the green book. Could those other thoughts make all this difference?

The following evening Jenny was a spectator as Mark and Mabel carried on a lively argument. She was thinking about Mark, and wondering for the first time how he really felt about her. There had been those times when she had felt as if unseen bonds were drawing them together in a way she neither understood nor really wanted.

She studied his face; he was the same Mark she remembered from the Bainbridge days; his youthful face was open, honest. His sandy hair and freckles, the square jaw and eyes—not quite green and not quite blue—seemed very ordinary. Yet—she frowned, wondering why there was that memory from the Bainbridge days. She recalled the day she had first seen Mark and that other young man. For a moment they had seemed wrapped in a splendor more brilliant than any dream she had known. Then unbid-den, the vision of Joseph Smith appeared, and Jenny moved her shoulders uneasily.

Mark reached for Jenny's hand and lifted it. "I don't know anything about reading palms, but just guessing your past, I'd say, young lady, that one day you'll drop in your tracks if you don't start taking more rest." He turned to his aunt. "If Jenny's to be returned day after tomorrow when Phoebe comes back, please, Aunt Mabel, may I take this fair lady to the city tomorrow?" Mabel nodded with a pleased smile.

While Jenny waited for Mark the next morning, she contemplated their day in the city and wondered at her mounting excitement.

He had his aunt's carriage, and Aunt Mabel had lent Jenny her straw bonnet covered with silk blossoms. Mark was wearing a straw hat that made him look suddenly mature even as it heightened the effect of his boyish grim.

She settled herself primly, asking, "What goes on in the city on a common old workday?"

"The fair, with booths and displays and fireworks and a band in the park. When it gets dark I shall sneak you behind the bushes and teach you to dance."

"Oh, horrors!" The impulsive words leaped out before she could think to harness them. "I understand that Joseph Smith excommunicated members of his church for dancing. Do you think—"

He looked at her strangely. "I didn't know you were keeping score for the Mormons."

After a long moment, she could say, "But Tom—"

At the fair he held her hand while they petted little black lambs. They ate ice cream and watched fireworks. They sat in the park and listened to the band. There was dancing on a proper floor, and with a teasing grin, Mark led her through the steps.

And when the moon was cresting the trees, he put her in the buggy and held her hand. Beside Mabel Weber's barn, he lifted her down, even though she could have hopped from the carriage just as she had on other days. When he cupped her chin in his hands, Jenny couldn't remember why she shouldn't rest her hands on his shoulders and lift her face. But when he whispered, "Jenny, I'm falling in love with you," she shook her head. "Don't, Mark."

Phoebe came back the next day, and Mark returned Jenny to the Bartons. They rode in the same buggy, but now Jenny wore her faded calico bonnet, and there were unspoken questions in Mark's eyes.

When she stood in the Bartons' kitchen and watched Mark's square shoulders disappearing down the lane in a cloud of dust rising from the buggy wheels, Jenny touched the hard metal disk fastened in the folds of her dress.

Months rolled by, and although she heard of Mark's frequent visits with his aunt, he hadn't called. Jenny thought she had nearly forgotten him; certainly, he had forgotten her.

The autumn leaves were crisping underfoot and the aroma of the apples Jenny was picking filled her senses with an earthy impulse to dance through the orchard, hugging all its glory to herself. She had her eyes closed as she sat in the comfortable cradle of tree branches. Holding the apple against her nose, she breathed deeply and gloried in the gentle warmth of the sun and the touch of wind.

"Hello!" Her eyes popped open, and she saw Mark's eyes nearly on a level with her knee. "I see you've picked lots of apples today." He was peering into the basket which held three apples.

Jenny smiled, pulled off an apple bobbing at her elbow, scrubbed it against her sleeve, and offered it to Mark. She watched him sink his teeth into it; all the while her emotions skithered skyward and then settled down like milkweed.

"How's lawyering?" she began.

"Pretty fair." He was watching her from the corner of his eyes as he pitched the apple core through the trees. "I would ask you if you're still enjoying doing dishes, but I'm afraid you'll say no, and I've nothing better to offer."

In silence she sorted through his words, grabbing and then discarding meaning. In the open neck of his white shirt, she could see the heavy beat of his pulse, and her fingers wanted desperately to touch the pulse, to steady its throb.

"Jenny—" he paused, then with more control said, "I've missed you terribly. I've come to ask you to marry me."

Jenny bowed her head against the roughness of the tree and slowly shook her head. Her mind filled, not with Mark, but with that bright, arrogant head. The talisman cut into her shoulder as she pressed against the tree, but she kept her eyes shut to hide what she knew she would see in Mark's face. "Mark, please go."

The sun had ceased to warm her skin when she raised her head. Mark was gone. Quickly now, she stripped the apples from the branches, shivering in the hostile tree.

21

TOM CHEWED THE end of his pencil and stared at the blank sheet of paper in front of him. It was a cold January, and the stove in the tack-room of the livery stable glowed red-hot. The door behind him creaked open and slammed shut before he stirred himself enough to turn.

The Prophet was shaking snow from his coat and slapping his old hat against the horse collars lining the wall. "You're studying that paper like you expect it to bite." He sat down and lifted his icy boots toward the glow of the stove.

"Since gettin' back from Missouri last summer, I've been meanin' to write a letter to Jenny," Tom muttered, shoving the pencil into his pocket with a sigh of relief. "I left her with the information we'd be stayin' in Missouri a spell."

Joseph pondered Tom's statement in silence. With a rueful grimace he said, "Tom, maybe the sadness of the trip doesn't warrant writing about."

"I wasn't thinkin' to air grievances," he said shortly. "I just had in mind lettin' her know I'm still in the land of the living. In addition, I'm lonesome for family."

"If you're serious about her soul and getting her into the only means of salvation, why aren't you urging her to move to Kirtland?"

"I'd not given it much thought," Tom answered slowly. "She's happy where she is."

"I could ask around and find a position for her," Joseph said thoughtfully. "If this had come up sooner, Emma could have used her help. The little ones had her about worn down. We've relief now, with hiring Fannie Alger."

"I've seen Fannie at meetings, a right comely gal," Tom observed. "The fellas around are wishin' Emma didn't keep her so busy. They'd all like to try their hand at sparkin'."

Joseph laughed. "My idea is that she's not interested in the ones presenting themselves at the door." He lowered his feet and leaned forward,

"Seriously, why don't you speak to Jenny about coming? She's a comely lass, too. If we can't find a position for her, we'll be marrying her off shortly."

"Marryin'—" Tom hesitated. "I guess she's old enough. I still forget she's not a tyke. Matter of fact, she's had her twenty-first birthday this month."

Joseph stood up and reached for his coat. "I'm headed for the temple. We've good news. A fellow by the name of John Tanner heard about the money troubles and met the foreclosure notice on the temple mortgage. He'd sold his farms and timber acreage, getting set to move to Missouri, so once again the Lord's provided for us."

"And the temple will be finished on time and things will be movin' just like the Lord promised in the revelation," Tom said softly.

"That's right," Joseph agreed. "First the temple is to be completed, and then the elders will be endowed with power from on high. Brother Tom, this will be a time of the outpouring of the Lord on the whole church, but especially on the leaders. I'm expecting a manifestation of the Lord's blessing at the time the temple is dedicated, and then we will be released from this place to possess Zion.

"Soon 'twill be time for the gathering up of money to purchase Zion," Joseph continued. "The Lord has promised that He will fight our battles for us. He has also said the destroyer has been sent forth to destroy, and it will not be many years hence until the Gentiles won't be left to pollute and blaspheme the promised land of Zion."

"How will we know when that time will be?" Tom asked.

"When the other promise is fulfilled, when the army of Israel becomes very great." While Tom remembered the poor army which had marched into Missouri last May, Joseph's words cut through his thoughts again. "At that time, the Lord will not hold us guiltless if we don't possess the land and avenge Him of His enemies."

Jenny was bending over the pile of calico in her lap when Clara came into her room. "Ugh," she declared. "I've not seen the likes. Every time I look, you're sewin' another fancy dress for yourself. I 'spect every cent of your pay has gone that way. How many does this make?"

Jenny raised her head, "Counting the winter frocks and the cape, 'tis five. I've a new bonnet too, see?" she nodded toward the shelf.

Clara looked and said softly, "Jenny, we'll be missin' you. Does Mrs. Barton know?"

"No, I've not set a date in my mind yet and she's not asked, though she's seen the frocks."

"I'm not certain you're ready," Clara said slowly. "You're claimin' power, what with the talisman, but you've not heard from your brother. I can't get you to a sabbat, and another solstice has passed. I've told you about the wax, but ya won't do a thing except wear the talisman and work with the herbs and charms." She shook her head sadly.

"But I *feel* ready," Jenny insisted. "I've read; I'm gaining power. For nearly a year now, I've been practicing up, learning to use the herbs and charms for healing. Mrs. Barton doesn't know it, but I healed her of the ague. She thought the herbs I mixed and gave to her did the trick, but you and I know it was the charms. Where I'm going there'll be a need, and I want to use the power to heal."

Clara was shaking her head. "I'm still thinkin' you've no idea of the real power needed if you're goin' to be more'n a white witch. You're play actin', Jenny. When you're ready to make a pact, then the *real* power will be yours."

Jenny studied Clara's serious face. "But *you* haven't made a pact; why must I?"

"Our power is limited, but do you want to be a white witch all your life? That's all I intend for myself. Bein' a good witch, helpin' people. I've the idea you had something else in mind."

Jenny was silent, staring at the sewing in her lap. Finally she shrugged and stood up. "Anyway," she said lightly, "I'll have a chance to practice my power on Mark this evening. He's coming to take me to a concert at the town hall. I'm tempted to wear my new cape even though it's nearly too warm for a wrap."

Clara went to the window. "I can't believe winter's gone and spring is here." Abruptly she turned from the window and asked, "Are you certain you don't care if I use a talisman on Mark?"

Startled, Jenny raised her head to meet Clara's worried eyes. She visualized Clara's frizz of hair and pudgy figure in soiled calico alongside Mark in his dark suit and shiny boots. She kept her face averted as she said, "You were the one who told me everything was fair in love and war. Besides, there's still Joe Smith; and didn't you say that where there's life, there's hope?"

When Clara's eyes began to shine and she opened her mouth to speak, Jenny added hastily, "But tonight is mine; sometime I must tell him my intentions."

In the end it turned out to be easier than Jenny expected. Mr. Barton had carried in Tom's letter just minutes before Mark arrived. Jenny, wearing the new dark challis print, was still holding the unopened letter when she heard Mark's footsteps on the porch.

When she went to greet him she waved the letter and asked, "Do you mind?"

They sat together on the bench under the kitchen window and she pried open the envelope. "It's the first I've heard from him since the army went to Missouri. They were to stay until Zion's problems were solved, but—" She had the letter open and was scanning it. She sighed and frowned.

"It doesn't seem things worked out as they had expected," she said slowly, puzzling over Tom's fragmented letter that nearly ignored the Missouri trip. She slowly refolded the letter, saying, "Tom's urging me to join him. He says Joseph Smith has promised to find a position for me."

"Do you want to go?" Mark's voice was low, and Jenny was tensely aware of that distance between them. She studied his face half hidden by evening shadows, knowing again the misery she felt every time they were together. Since apple-picking time last autumn, the times they had been together could be counted on one hand; even then he had stayed away until nearly Christmastime.

As she studied him, she was aware of his restraint. The old happy, easy days were gone. This new Mark was serious, cordial, persistent. And Jenny felt uneasily helpless in the face of his determination. Each time she had seen him, she had vowed it would be the last, yet the resolve wasn't kept and the reason she had for not keeping it grew more troublingly vague each time.

She sighed and got to her feet. "Isn't it time to go?"

He stood. "It is. I've taken the liberty of promising us to Auntie Mabel for a reception after the concert. You must have at least a shawl; it will be cool later." When she handed him the new cape, she saw the approval in his eyes. "Is it new?" he inquired. At her nod, he said, "That's a becoming dress, too."

It was late when they departed from Mabel Weber's home, and Jenny left reluctantly. Walking out to the carriage with Mark, she admitted, "Those people made me forget I'm the Bartons' hired girl."

He turned to her with a puzzled frown. "Jenny, what difference does it make? You're well-read and intelligent; those are the qualities that endear you to others. I wish you would stop being sensitive about your position." He helped her into the carriage and took the seat beside her.

"Mark, I don't fit in, and I'll never forget my poor beginnings. I wish you would find company more suitable to—you are going to be an attorney!" She knew her voice was stilted; she gulped and added, "Besides—"

"Jenny!" Mark interrupted. He was dragging on the horses' reins, guiding them off the main road onto a bumpy trail. Under the trees, he pulled the team to a halt and wrapped the reins around the hand rail.

He took her hand and turned her toward him. "Jenny," he said again in a voice so firm, almost stern, that she moved away from him. "I'm trying patiently to get across to you that I love you for yourself. I want to marry you, and I'll not take no for an answer."

She shook her head slowly, studying his determined face and shrinking further back into the shadows. Now his voice was gentle and low. "I've tried to talk myself out of feeling this way, but I'm convinced that you love me despite your attempts to push me away—which, by the way, seem rather feeble. If you mean no, I'd expect a little greater force behind the word." He had clasped her shoulders in his two hands and was gently pulling her closer. The hands Jenny lifted were leaden, but she must plant them against his chest and push.

"Why?" he asked gently. "Don't I deserve knowing why?"

She turned away and after a moment found that she could answer in an emotionless, even manner. "Mark, I count you the dearest friend I have. Never will I forget you, and never do I expect you to understand, but I can't marry you. I'm leaving the Bartons very soon; I'll be joining Tom in Ohio."

At last he stirred and spoke. "I think I'm beginning to understand. It's the pull of Joseph's new religion, isn't it? It would be easier to let you go if you assure me that you don't love me."

Jenny was silent for a long time; when at last she answered him, she knew her confusion echoed through every word. "Mark, I—I honestly wonder what love is."

On the trip to Kirtland, as the stagecoach bounced through rutty roads and the mud clutched at the wheels and flew from the hoofs of the team, Jenny had plenty of time to think about that last conversation with Mark. Only her fellow passengers were aware of her sighs, but she did finish the trip with a conviction. If she loved Mark, then she loved two men. If the intense desire she felt for Joseph was love, then denial was surely impossible.

Partly out of curiosity and partly out of obligation, Jenny stayed over in Manchester a few days. Stepping into Lucy Harris's open arms was almost like sitting on her own mother's lap again. Nancy was thrilled to see her, and Nancy's lanky husband, Alexander, just about crushed her hand with his long, bony fingers. Baby Andrew, named after President Jackson, added a life to their home which Jenny had forgotten was possible.

Still, Jenny was glad to be back on the bumpy coach three days later. She was weary with Nancy's religious prying. And Tom and Joseph waited at the end of her journey.

Her previous visit with Tom had taught Jenny her way around Kirtland. She stepped from the stagecoach and headed for the livery stable. Tom was at the forge. Standing behind him, she said, "I'm here."

Tom turned, dropped the horseshoe back into the fire, and rubbed his arms across his sweaty face. "Jen!" he exclaimed, "I didn't know you were comin'."

"You invited me." She moved restlessly. "I had a little trouble making up my mind, but when I did, it seemed best to come immediately."

He studied her face for a moment. "Mark?" She nodded and turned away. "Well," he sighed, "Joseph has found you a place at Andy Morgan's home. He's married now and his wife needs help with the young'un she's just given him."

Tom loaded Jenny's trunk into a wagon and drove her across town to the Morgan home. As they rode, he announced, "That's the temple," and pointed his whip toward the quarried stone edifice on the hill. "There's three stories. The top one's to be the school for the prophets. The auditoriums aren't finished yet, but they'll be grand. Joseph's fixin' them up with pulpits for the apostles."

"What's an apostle?"

"Joe's had a revelation about the structure of the church—the governing body, I mean. Right tonight there's to be a council meeting with blessings on us all."

She studied his face. "Then you'll be part of it?"

"The governing body? Yes, many of the army will be members of the Seventy."

She nodded toward the building. "You'll meet here?"

"No, the temple isn't finished. Dedication's still a year off. 'Twill be a grand event." Suddenly he turned to her with a happy grin. "Jen, I'm right glad you're here. There's big things in store for the church, and you're gettin' in on it just at the right time. Things are lookin' up for us. The Lord's supplied the money for the temple, and soon as it's finished and the elders get their endowments, we'll be about buildin' Zion in Missouri."

"A temple here and then Zion?" Jenny questioned slowly. "Sounds like there'll be parts of Joe's church scattered all across the United States."

"Eventually. He's plannin' to keep headquarters here for a time until we're really settled in Missouri."

That evening Tom went to the assembly hall, knowing this was the final council meeting before the twelve apostles were to be sent on their missions around the country.

When he walked in, Joseph and Rigdon were standing at the entrance. As Tom approached, Joseph hailed him. "Well, my brother, the grapevine has it that you've had a blessed surprise this afternoon."

Tom nodded. "Jen finally made the break and moved out. She'll probably be comin' to see you shortly."

"She's settled at the Morgans'?" Tom nodded, and Joseph turned to follow Rigdon to the podium.

After the twelve had been called forward for the laying on of hands, prayer was offered for power and blessing. Joseph returned to the podium to speak to the men.

The rustle and rumbles in the room subsided and Joseph spread his papers before him. "You men have been chosen by the Lord to be the governing body of the restored church of Jesus Christ. Tonight I want to instruct you about the Lord's revelation on the orders of the priesthood. In Old Testament times, this priesthood was passed down from father to son. But we lost knowledge; through sinning it passed from us.

"There are two divisions in the priesthood, the Melchizedek and the Aaronic. The Melchizedek is the highest order and holds the right of presidency. In other words, the church president will be taken from this priesthood. No one will be able to hold the office of the Aaronic priesthood unless he is a direct descendant of Aaron."

There was an uneasy flutter of movement throughout the room, and Joseph lifted his hand. "Now, don't you fret. The Lord has revealed to me just how many of you are in that lineage. Also, there is a provision through the power of the Lord, whereby those men becoming members of the church will literally have their blood replaced with new through the power of the Holy Ghost. Thus you will become the seed of Abraham.

"Now, three years before the death of Adam, he gathered together all who were high priests from his posterity, taking them to the valley of Adam-ondi-Ahman for a final blessing."

Joseph paused a moment. "Most of you had the privilege of being with me when we discovered the valley of Adam-ondi-Ahman in the promised land of Zion."

An excited rustle rose and subsided, then Joseph continued. "At this time of blessing, the Lord appeared to them, and they rose up to bless Adam, calling him Michael, the prince, the archangel. The Lord comforted Adam, telling him at that time that a multitude was to come from him and that he was to be a prince over them forever. He told him that he would sit on a throne of fiery flame, just as the prophet Daniel predicted. All of these things are written in the book of Enoch, and they will be given to you in due time."

Later Tom, thinking over what the Prophet had said, joined the hushed group of men making their way toward the door. From the quietness of the men surrounding him, Tom guessed the others felt the weight of blessing and the burden of responsibility just as he did.

When he stepped out into the starlit night, he lifted his face to the cool breeze and his heart responded with gladness. "Jen," he whispered, "oh, Jen, how good that you've come now before the fullness of time!"

22

THE MORGAN HOME was a pleasant one, built of log like many others in Kirtland. Situated on the far edge of town, it provided ample room for a vegetable garden and corrals for the livestock.

Jenny gloried in the fresh, clear air and the view of the young town encircled by the forest of oak, hickory, ash, and maple. Trees towering beyond the town placed a hedge of solitude and separation around the Mormon community, separation which to Jenny seemed symbolic. The isolation of Kirtland made it hard for her to realize that Lake Erie, with its busy ports, lay just north.

Living with the Morgans was a new experience for Jenny. A young couple not much older than she, they were obviously deeply in love. Jenny blamed her uneasiness in the situation on her role as the outsider. She was needed, certainly; the new mother had her hands full caring for her baby. In truth, Sally Morgan didn't know her way around her own kitchen.

During her first weeks, Jenny aired her uneasiness about being the extra person in the household. Sally, sitting in the rocking chair holding her infant daughter, looked up at Jenny with blue eyes as wide and innocent as the baby Tamara's, and exclaimed, "Oh, Jenny, how can you possibly feel that? Haven't you noticed how many of the homes in Kirtland have boarders in them? Most aren't nearly as valuable as you. You know we need you terribly. We Mormons are getting accustomed to sharing our homes. Otherwise there just isn't enough room for everyone."

"I've heard even the Smiths have a girl living with them," Jenny said in a low voice.

"Yes, Emma's had her there quite some time. She calls her an adopted daughter, and right fond they are of each other. Poor soul, with the Prophet gone so much and the trouble she's had with babies, Fannie is a great help."

Although Sally's reassurance helped, Jenny could see there was scarcely enough work to occupy the two of them. She was glad to busy herself in the vegetable garden, but her free time increased as the summer wore on.

As Jenny became acquainted with Kirtland and her neighbors, she readily observed the truth in Sally's statement about the Prophet. He was gone much of the time. She heard he was busy with missionary journeys about the country.

She also discovered that Kirtland had grown into a bustling town. Since Jenny's last visit new buildings had been erected everywhere, and daily more structures were being planned. The early homes had been of log, garnered from the citizens' front yards. The newer ones were of planed lumber, stone, and brick.

When Tom was there to listen, she commented about the expansion. "Joseph's much aware of the need to expand and build up the Lord's country," he answered. "While we're here, Kirtland's the Lord's country and our responsibility."

It didn't take Jenny long to discover that what she had heard about Kirtland was true. Joseph and his people had one object in mind: to prepare for the second coming of Christ. All life was bent in that direction.

"See," Sally said, "Joseph's received it from the Lord that we're to build up a city for the Lord to come back to. That's why it's so important we possess Zion in Missouri. Much depends on us. It helps to know the Lord is going before us; He will conquer His enemies through us in order that His purposes will prevail. Nothing must stand in the way of doing what He's instructed through Joseph."

Jenny was silent as she thought about Sally's speech. It sounded memorized, rehearsed.

Sally's voice broke through Jenny's reverie. "First off, Joseph started excommunicating those who were insisting on dancing. He's right determined to keep us serious and holy." She slanted her blue eyes at Jenny. "There's a few jolly parties, but you'd best be happiest with going to church. Joseph's strict about keeping the church pure. It could be a bore, but we can take it since Christ is returning very soon. You know, Jenny," she shivered fearfully, "it will be terrible for those not ready, for those who've rejected the Prophet's teaching."

"Tom told me there was a school started for adults," Jenny said. "I guess that's to help prepare people. He called it a school for prophets."

"Oh, that's just for the menfolk." Sally lifted the baby to her shoulder. "Only the men can have the priesthood. Besides, they just study the revelations Joseph's had from the Lord."

"Well, do the women do anything?"

"Yes. Joseph's urging them to busy themselves. He's of the opinion that the best way to be content is to work. There's quilting bees and such all the time."

"After Tamara is older and you don't need me so much, I'm of a mind to find a way to occupy myself." Jenny said. "I understand there's a newspaper here now. Do you suppose they'd let a woman work there?"

"It's Cowdery's pet; I suppose the best he'd allow is for you to sweep the floor."

"Oh, Oliver—I know him!" Jenny exclaimed. "But he was in Missouri the last time I was here."

"The newspaper was destroyed there. Joseph promised Cowdery he could be editor here."

Kirtland was a town populated only by Mormons, and slowly Jenny came to see just what that meant. Everywhere she heard, *Joseph says . . . The Prophet tells us . . . The revelations say this is the way we are to live. We must sacrifice for Zion.*

Just as Jenny began to chafe against the restricted life, discontented and frustrated by a prophet who was either away or writing scripture, summer burst upon Kirtland. Roses spilled over fences and crowded ditch banks; daisies and bluebells filled every nook; and Jenny discovered life in Kirtland was as unexpected as the bounty of nature.

She had been busy with her own thoughts, feeling the weight of summer on her restless soul. She imagined the horror on Sally's sweet, gentle face if she were to reveal her secret thoughts. While Sally trembled over being holy enough for Joseph's church, Jenny was studying, planning, plotting— but not how to possess a spot in the kingdom; Jenny's designs were for Joseph himself.

Guilt surged through her as she compared her seething spirit with Sally's sweet serenity.

And then Joseph Smith was striding toward her. His large figure was clad in his customary black broadcloth. She had barely seen him when he gave a curt nod and continued down the street. She hesitated on the sidewalk, stunned. Turning, she dashed across the street to the livery stable.

The tack-room was empty, but the blast of heat and the clang of metal led her on. "Tom!" she gasped, circling the anvil and facing him. "I've just seen Joseph Smith, and he's had a terrible accident. His face is all battered and swollen until I hardly recognized him."

Tom paused. "Well, did you ask him why?"

"He plowed on past me like he didn't know me."

Tom struck the cooling metal with his hammer. "He tangled with his brother William." Dropping the hammer and turning away from the fire, he said, "It's no wonder he didn't do no extra talkin'; the whole church is ashamed of the Prophet bein' whipped by his own brother. William accused him of bein' a false prophet. The fightin' is not something the lot of us can take easy-like."

Jenny was thinking aloud. "When I last visited, he was scrapping in the street. Then the people cheered him on."

"But now he's been whipped good. There's a difference. Then he was winnin'. You can overlook 'bout anythin' when a fella is winnin'. If he's losin', you question."

Jenny recalled Tom's words next when Joseph's excitement surfaced again. This time, when she joined the spectators and listened to him lecture, she realized he was on the winning side. The incident with William seemed forgiven and forgotten.

The new excitement that buzzed in Kirtland was about mummies from Egypt. Jenny joined the crowd outside the office building which had been hastily renovated to hold the pine cases. When she joined the group, Joseph had just opened them and pointed to the withered human figures.

"What are those things?" Jenny asked.

Someone hissed for silence, but the woman beside Jenny whispered, "They're Egyptian mummies. 'Tis the finger of God sending that fella into Kirtland with those mummies. Joseph's found out there's important writings with them."

Standing on tiptoe, Jenny watched Joseph hold strange, stiff documents so everyone could see the markings, "This one," he pointed, "has the writings of Abraham, and another bears the writings of Joseph of Egypt. I will be formulating the Egyptian alphabet and grammar in order to complete the translation of these writings."

When he finished speaking, Joseph stepped aside and allowed the people of Kirtland to file past the pine cases.

During the remainder of the summer, all of Kirtland waited eagerly while Joseph struggled with the Egyptian writings. Even Jenny's discontent was swallowed up in the curiosity of the event. Some voiced their impatience as he painstakingly labored with the Egyptian alphabet and grammar. They suggested he return to writing by inspiration instead of trying to learn Egyptian. After all, inspiration had given them the *Book of Mormon*.

Some satisfaction did come, however. Joseph discovered enough about the papyrus containing the writings of Abraham to be able to reveal important teachings to the church.

One hot August afternoon, Jenny and Sally had been sharing the latest gossip about the mummies when Sally suddenly asked, "Jenny, are you for joining the church?"

Jenny hesitated for a moment. She recalled the many times she had intimated to others that she intended to join the church. She had even led Tom to believe she was seriously considering the step. She stared at Sally.

How can I say yes? But yes, if that's what it takes to get Joseph. You can't tell people you intend to run off with their prophet because you find him a very attractive man. How do you admit that your designs on a holy man are not holy at all?

Jenny lifted innocent eyes. "Why do you think I left my job and moved to Ohio?"

Sally leaned forward and clasped Jenny's hands. "I know the feeling. It's an irresistible pulling of the Almighty. Jenny, do you know that some women here in town have left husbands and children to follow this man of God?"

"I haven't joined yet," Jenny said hastily, "but I'm considering."

"Well then, you need to be learning about the laws and ordinances of the gospel. Jenny, the church conference is in a couple of weeks. I believe this is important for you. I'm so convinced, I want you to take time off. Do nothing that week except attend the meetings."

Jenny was ready to protest. She wanted to do almost anything rather than sit in a boring meeting, listening to silly old farmers. Sally lifted her hand. "I know you don't want to be beholden, but your soul's welfare is more important."

So on August 17, 1835, Jenny found herself adorned in her most modest dress walking beside Sally's neighbor, old Mrs. Applewaite. The woman was heavy and walked slowly, but her mind and tongue were quick; she showered Jenny with a fine sprinkling of town talk that bordered on gossip.

"When you get to be my age, there's not much left to life except sittin' on your own front stoop and watchin' the world go by. But that's interestin'. Doesn't take long to begin puttin' two and two together. Like, do you know what's goin' to happen in the Baily-Knight situation? And who's goin' to win out with the Fannie Alger gal? Me, I'm a-keepin' my thoughts to myself on that one, but I don't see any of the young men scorin'."

Jenny slanted a glance at the perspiring, red-faced woman and said, " 'Tis such an effort for you to get to meeting, they'll be thinking you've earned those jewels for your crown, most certainly."

She chuckled, "It's worth the effort to hear what those stuffy men will find to talk about today. Some days it's right ear-ticklin'. Won't be so good today; the Prophet's out of town and Rigdon's inclined to be a straight-laced one."

"Oh, my," Jenny sighed and her disappointment was genuine. Any further inclination to attend the meeting vanished, replaced by mounting frustration. She had failed again. The dream which had brought her to Kirtland contained only two people—Jenny and Joseph. It was up to Jenny to make the dream come true—but how could that happen?

They slid into their row and Mrs. Applewaite began fanning herself vigorously. "Whew, 'tis hot! I'm glad we didn't come this morning, too." A dark-suited man headed for the front. "That's Levi Hancock. I guess we'll be singing. There's some good hymns they're a-gettin' up."

When Oliver Cowdery got to his feet, Jenny recalled the Manchester school days and stifled her yawn. He was saying, "I'm before you this afternoon to introduce to you the *Book of Doctrine and Covenants.* Pursuant to this morning's activities, our task will be the endorsement of the book this afternoon."

Rigdon followed him to the podium and began to introduce those chosen to endorse the book. Mrs. Applewaite whispered the names of the men, as if Jenny hadn't already identified most of them on the platform. "That's Phelps. He's the one who got us into a peck of trouble in Missouri by what he wrote in the newspaper there."

Jenny nearly lost track of the day between the woman's whispers and the sameness of the dark-coated men who took their places and advised the congregation that they knew the revelations in the book were true, and that they had been given by the inspiration of the Lord.

In the midst of Mrs. Applewaite's whispered commentary, an idea took shape in Jenny's mind. It had come as Mrs. Applewaite said, "I'm of a mind that most of the people don't have an idea of what's in the revelations. Sure, we've heard snatches and we remember the scary parts, but other than that, we take our beliefs spoon-fed. Ten years from now, we'll have no idea what we believe, betcha. But I reckon it doesn't make much difference; we're followin' the man and a-trustin' him to give it to us straight."

Although Jenny seemed composed and attentive, her fluttering hands twisted the handkerchief into knots, her thoughts as busy as her fingers. In the months since arriving in Kirtland, she had not managed more than a word with Joseph Smith. Certainly not once had there been a chance to be alone with him. She hadn't even a hint of how to bring that about. Now Mrs. Applewaite had given her the solution, gift-wrapped in a clumsy book.

During the rest of the afternoon, Jenny's attention surfaced occasionally as she grasped at straws of information coming from the pulpit; then she succumbed to her private thoughts again. Near the end of the day, the entire congregation was given the opportunity to endorse the *Book of Doctrine and Covenants.* As Jenny's attention lagged, Phelps approached the podium to read an article on marriage. Immediately Jenny's mind was captured, and she strained to catch every word.

Phelps, in his sonorous voice, declared, "Inasmuch as this church has been accused of the crime of fornication and polygamy, we wish to advise the world that we believe one man should have one wife and one woman should have but one husband, except in the case of death, when either is at liberty to marry again. It is not lawful to influence a wife to leave her husband; it is not lawful to influence a child to embrace a religion other than the religion of his parents. It is not right to prevent members of the church from marrying outside of the church, and we believe marriage performed by other authorities than this church is valid. All marriages made before a person becomes a member of this church are to be held sacred." Jenny sat back, lost in thought . . . *except in the case of death, when either is at liberty to marry again.* Unbidden, the picture of the waxen figure came into her mind.

When Oliver Cowdery stood at the podium and opened his paper, Jenny's thoughts were still in turmoil, first attracted by the possibilities, then repelled.

When she finally pushed those dark thoughts aside and straightened, she heard Cowdery saying, "We believe it is right to preach the gospel to all of the earth, for this is the means of salvation. The righteous must be warned to save themselves from corruption. But we do not believe it is right to interfere with bondservants, and this means preaching the gospel to them and baptizing them contrary to the desires of their masters."

When Cowdery finished reading, the article was accepted and ordered to be printed into the *Book of Doctrine and Covenants* by a unanimous vote.

Jenny followed Mrs. Applewaite out of the meeting hall and they turned down the winding lane that led to the far edge of town. Mrs. Applewaite, uncharacteristically silent, was walking rapidly. Jenny studied her face as she trotted to keep up.

Finally Jenny asked, "What did you think of it all?"

"I'm still wonderin' about that last article," she puffed. "I can't decide whether it's sayin' the bondservant's soul isn't all that important or if it's sayin' you keep peace with his masters regardless. Right now, I'm guessin' the writin' came at a pretty important time, considerin' the trouble Joseph and his men had in Missouri. Missouri is a slave state, you know."

When Jenny's path separated from Mrs. Applewaite's, she dropped the good woman's argument just as quickly. As she walked slowly back to the Morgan home, she wondered what polygamy was and why William Phelps was called upon to denounce it.

23

"I'M STARTING TO feel like a library book!" Jenny exclaimed. Sally laughed as she held the soft blue shawl against her face before folding it. Jenny commented, "That blue matches your eyes—nearly makes me think it's Tamara peeking over at me."

"Oh, do you think we look alike?" Sally asked, pleased. "Her papa thinks so, but I believe he's partial."

"To what?" They turned as Andy Morgan entered the kitchen and Sally crossed the room to her husband. Jenny watched her smile up at him while she stroked his arm. Picking up the laundry, Jenny started up the stairs to her room. As she glanced back, Andy was pulling Sally close.

Unbidden, Mark's face interrupted her thoughts. Jenny recalled the curious blue-green of his eyes, the glint of red the sun coaxed into his sandy hair.

Now Sally was climbing the stairs behind her. "And why do you feel like a library book?"

"Because I keep being checked out."

"Oh, you mean the nursing, the way we pass you around. 'Tis your fault; you proved capable when we had the ague. I still don't know whether it was the nursing or those funny things you mixed together and burned while you were mumbling to yourself. Or perhaps it was the little packet of herbs you made us wear in our clothes." Her eyes reflected curiosity as she studied Jenny. "At times I think I don't know you at all—but, whatever, we need you, Jenny—all of us."

"So you check me out and pass me around."

"Well, you're the most popular book in Kirtland. But you'd better come back to this library when you've served your purpose."

Jenny finished packing her bag. "I hope I'm as good at the lying-in as I was at the ague. I've never been at a birthing, though my mother often was." Jenny sighed, and for a moment was silent, missing her mother and remembering the hard times.

"No matter, you've a knack. Did you learn from your mother how to use the charms and herbs?" Jenny winced and shook her head. How horrified her mother would have been to hear Sally's question! But for a moment she was caught up, seeing a similarity she hadn't considered before. As far back as she remembered, Ma had been busy nursing the sick back to health and sitting with new mothers.

Jenny turned to Sally. "You've made me think about my mother, and I'm seeing ways we are alike. I'd never thought of it before. Seems when I was at home, I considered Ma's nursing people just a way to earn a penny, but now I see it different."

She noticed the curiosity in Sally's eyes and hastily answered the unspoken question. "I've been living out as a hired girl in Manchester and Cobleskill since my folks moved west."

"Why did they go west?"

Jenny shrugged. "Same as everyone. Hard times and expensive land. They were saying the good land was all west; eastern land was worked out. Must've been true; folks all around us were moving west."

Both women were silent, busy with their thoughts until Jenny recalled her unfinished story. "Anyway, now I'm remembering how Ma would act about her nursing. She had an excitement we young'uns couldn't understand. All we knew was we were being left again. Now I see that the nursing made her feel important, as if she had found a place where she was terribly needed. That's sort of the way I feel. They need me and I feel good when I see people on the mend. I guess Ma and I aren't so different after all."

After Sally walked down the stairs, Jenny amended her statement, but she didn't say the words aloud. They would have shocked gentle Sally. *One difference between Ma and me,* Jenny thought. *Ma was just being a good Christian lady; I'm working with the power. They call me a white witch. And Christian ladies don't like white witches because they can never get past the word* witch. *They haven't discovered there's no difference in the work we're all doing, but there is a difference in the power to do it. Poor Ma, she could have been a really successful nurse. See, Ma, it isn't the herbs, it's the words you say over them and the power that you bring down that does the healing.*

Two weeks later, Jenny was walking through the streets of Kirtland, headed for a meeting with Joseph Smith—in his office, alone. Tom had passed the information on, and there had been a speculative glint in his eyes. Jenny asked, "Why does he want to see me?"

"Joseph's been hearin' about your nursin' duties and wants to ask a few questions."

While crossing Kirtland, Jenny resolved to question Joseph Smith about his book, the *Doctrine and Covenants.* With the press of nursing duties this autumn, she had been forced to abandon her attempt to confront Joseph.

Now she rehearsed the questions she would ask. Surely he would find time to instruct a convert!

"Perhaps, Joseph," she murmured, "we will have many of these meetings." She pressed her hand against that sudden heavy pulse in her throat.

Jenny stopped in front of the print shop. Lingering on the stoop she wiped her sweaty palms with her handkerchief and tried to quiet her racing heart. The door stood open, and she could hear the clatter and thump of the press coming from behind closed doors inside. The aroma of printer's ink was heavy in the air. She sniffed and tried to recapture the excitement and curiosity print shops had inspired in her in the past. But today only one thought occupied her mind, and it had nothing to do with printing.

She bit her trembling lip and took a deep breath. "You silly baby!" she muttered. Over the rumble of the press, she heard the clatter of footsteps and raised her head. Joseph was lumbering down the stairs, two at a time. Abruptly that emotion-charged vision of Joseph and Jenny vanished and she was grinning up at her remembered friend.

Leading the way up the stairs, he opened the door of the room over the print shop, apologizing, "I'm sorry for the poor office, but I seem to be having a time settling down to one spot for more than a season. Next year, when the temple is completed, Rigdon and I will have offices there. Did they tell you the top floor is to be the School of the Prophets?"

She nodded and looked around the shabby room. The whole building was vibrating with the thump of the press at the foot of the stairs. Was it only fancy that the wooden floor moved beneath her feet as she walked? The plain room disappointed her. It was sparsely furnished with a row of narrow wooden chairs facing a table covered with books and papers. Across the room was a couch. And the single window was heavily curtained.

As she sat on one of the chairs, she murmured, "My, it's close in here. Can't we have that window open, Joseph? 'Tis only September; cherish the warm air later."

He laughed. "To tell the truth, that window's been nailed shut. It kept falling out of its casing."

She leaned forward to study the papers littering the table. "Is that part of your translation?" He nodded. "The New Testament? I heard the men talking at the store last week, they were wondering if you'll have to go back and rewrite the *Book of Mormon* now that you've done the translating on the Bible. They're saying the Bible parts in it are all the old—now how do you say it?" She paused, and when he didn't help, she struggled on, "Well, there's not been a Christian church on earth for 1400 years, so the King James Bible was not done by the power of God. This means the

Book of Mormon needs to be changed where it's quoting the King James Bible, doesn't it?"

Joseph studied her for a long time before he answered. His voice was gentle when he spoke. "Jenny, I didn't bring you here to discuss my translating work. I'm afraid you'll have to leave those things to the presidency for their handling.—I understand that you've been passed around the town as a healer. Is that so?"

Jenny gasped. "Healer! That's the way they see my herbs and such?" She thought about it for a time. Slowly but with growing excitement, she said, "They really believe I can heal them. That's important. They don't think it's just chance. Maybe the power really is starting up!" She sighed a gusty sigh of relief and leaned back in the chair.

Joseph was pacing the room in slow, thoughtful steps. When he stopped he spoke again, "Jenny, you are a beautiful woman, but don't believe your beauty will win you favors."

"What do you mean?" she asked, searching his face and eyes for the kind of gentle charm she had seen at church. "I'm afraid I don't understand."

"You really don't?" He pulled one of the wooden chairs close and sat down facing her. His bright blue eyes seemed curiously light, and in an effort to steady herself, she forced her gaze down to the splintered wooden floor. "Jenny," he commanded her attention again. "You haven't been listening to the right gossip. Haven't they told you about the power struggle? Haven't they talked about Hiram Page using the seer stone, about the others faking the gifts of the Lord? Haven't they told you how the Lord dealt with them severely 'til they admitted they were trying to steal power and gifts that weren't rightly theirs?"

Jenny stared at him. She had heard the stories, but never once did she dream Joseph would see *her* in this light. She chewed at the corner of her mouth, ashamed and contrite. He was saying she was no better than the others. Now she straightened in her chair, realizing the implication of his words. Joseph was angry and jealous because she had power! He was saying she was a threat.

She looked up into that cold, troubled face and an idea surfaced in her thoughts. "I'm sorry," she whispered. "Tell me what I should do."

A smile swept his face with relief, and she closed her eyes against the sight, not knowing why she must, but feeling for a moment as if everything were out of control. He had taken her hands and was tugging her closer. "Jenny, my dear, does that mean that you are ready to let the Lord instruct you? Does that mean you are determined to become one of His chosen?"

She fought a dizzy sensation, like a whirlpool sweeping over her.

Now she remembered why she was here. Pulling her hands free, she opened her eyes, saying, "Joseph, if you've had your say, then I'll have mine. I think you need all the help you can get with these people, and I intend to continue using the power I have to help them."

He was still studying her warily. "Jenny, I've renounced the old ways."

"You mean you've given up using the seer stone and hunting for treasure? Joseph, why?"

"The Lord is helping me see there is a better way. The taint of the seer stone and all the rest will harm the church. I intend to stamp out the credulous and teach these people to rely on the Lord."

She looked at him curiously. "You're acting like you think the stone is bad."

"It's fakery."

The words burst from her before she could measure them. "All those other things, do you really believe them? That the Lord will fight your battles, give you Zion and the wealth of the land? Do you really believe that those who reject your new word from the Lord and the church you have started will be damned to hell?"

Again he captured her hands. "Does that last statement make any difference to you?" Unexpectedly she shivered. Leaning forward he forced her eyes to meet his, saying, "Jenny, I do believe it. All this is truth, and I will prevail as the Lord's chosen until His return to this earth."

With a gasp, Jenny pulled her hands free and jumped to her feet. "Joseph, I—I just can't think anymore today." She turned toward the door, and his hand was on her shoulder.

"Already I sense you are an unusual one. Little Jenny, who would have guessed you would grow into a beautiful—and powerful—woman." His fingers slipped under her chin and forced her to meet his eyes again. "I have a strong feeling that you can help me in the Lord's work." She closed her eyes against the intensity of that expression, but his hands drew her still closer.

For a moment the dizziness touched her again. "Joseph!" she gasped, stepping backward.

"Don't, sister," he warned, holding her firmly. "Jenny, my dear sister in the Lord. You have no idea of the great things that are in store for this church. The Lord himself is just now beginning to tell me His will concerning us."

"Us?" she echoed. "You mean me?" As he nodded and turned back to the table, her thoughts tumbled ahead. Was there a message behind his words? Power, a position close to Joseph, eventually Emma's place. The waxen figure loomed in her mind again—but he didn't know that part. She hesitated before turning back to the table.

Joseph was sitting quietly, barricaded by his books and papers. She rested her palms lightly in the litter and leaned forward. "You asked if I was ready to become one of the chosen—you call them the children of Israel, don't you? And the Indians—are they the lost tribes of Israel? Joseph, there is much I don't know about your church. You've already credited me with intelligence; I demand the satisfaction of knowing what I'm getting into before I join anything."

His lips twisted with amusement. "That's an unusual conversion. Aren't you afraid to risk hellfire and damnation while you are doing your questioning? Methinks you've decided on a better way than faith."

"I've never heard of being asked to believe something I know nothing about."

"Then ask your questions. I prefer that to having you charge out of here saying Joseph Smith demands blind obedience."

She stared at him for a moment, then leaned closer. "Joseph, you are a powerful man; I feel it. But you aren't so powerful that you can elicit cowlike devotion from me."

"And you are so proud that you can't imagine being humbled! Jenny, my dear, that is a challenge."

Now she sat down and smiled, confident that he didn't know how she trembled inside. Folding her hands in her lap, she met his gaze. "Joseph, I attended your church conference meetings. It was nothing more than a bunch of addlepated men who stood up, saying they believe the *Doctrine and Covenants* book is true and from God. I would like to read it for myself and decide whether or not I agree."

"How do you, a credulous child, expect to decide this? I suggest you take their testimony and start believing."

"And I don't get to read it? I haven't read the *Book of Mormon* either. Is that the way you treat all of your converts?"

"On your way out, stop in the print shop and Cowdery will sell you a copy."

She studied his hard jaw and couldn't resist spilling the gossip. "They say you are soft over women, and that Emma only needs to shake her finger to keep you in line. I may cry in order to get my book for nothing."

He bowed. "Go ahead, if you desire to be seen walking down the street with red eyes and the *Book of Mormon*. You may win more converts for me."

Laughing, she jumped to her feet. "Oh, Joseph, I think I shall enjoy taking religious instruction from you! Please sign me up for your classes."

His face froze. "You don't understand. There are no women in any classes I teach. If you need to learn, go to any of the godly women in the church, and they'll teach you."

"Their teaching falls in the category of sewing a quilt or diapering an infant."

His face admitted the truth. "You are right, Jenny. I'll give you books and you bring me your questions."

She got to her feet and leaned across the table. "Thank you, sir; I value your proposal. Now, I'll take the *Book of Mormon,* the *Doctrine and Covenants* and—" She spied the tattered book just under his elbow. "What is that? It looks interesting."

"You can't have that. It's called *Sacred Geography.*"

"They say you're still struggling with the Book of Abraham." Instantly she saw the change in him and pressed, "Have you finished it?"

"No, but I've discovered many important things. How good the Lord was to use this method of bringing the books to us! He's given me understanding of the mathematics of heaven. I've learned more now about the star Kolob and how God measures time. He's revealed that the stars are inhabited by eternal spirits.

"—But back to more earthly things. The papyrus of Abraham reveals how the Negro came into being. When Noah cursed his son Canaan, his posterity was marked by black skin, signifying the continuing curse. Old Pharaoh of Egypt was the son of Ham's daughter. Through her line all the Egyptians inherit dark skin."

Jenny interrupted, "And the Negro slaves are part of the cursed ones? What is that supposed to mean to us? At the meetings I heard they weren't to be given the gospel if their owners object."

"That's right. Furthermore, because of their curse, no Negro will ever reach the exalted state. It is impossible to offer the priesthood to a man who wears the curse of Canaan." He sighed heavily but as he stood up, his smile washed over Jenny, lifting the dismal mood of his words.

Touching her shoulder, he said, "But don't let that trouble your pretty head. Just go home and read your books and pass it all around Kirtland that you bested the Prophet and seer by obtaining books for nothing. But be advised, I may have you scrub my floors yet."

Jenny went on her way laughing, but before the books were opened there was yet another call for nursing. It was old granny Lewis filling Jenny's time with the last of her tyrannical demands.

When autumn's browns rimmed with frost, the church took a new step forward. Since Tom's boss, Newel Knight, was involved, Jenny heard about it nearly as soon as the word was released.

For some time Jenny had known that Sarah, young Knight's wife, had died. In fact, until the arrival of Lydia Baily, Tom had tried to push Newel and Jenny together.

One November day Jenny went into the livery stable and found Tom looking as if he had adopted a permanent grin. "Give," she demanded and waited until he put down the harness he held.

"Well, it's this way, my sister, you've forfeited your chance, and Newel has won out doubly."

"Aw, Lydia's husband has consented to divorce."

For a moment his smile wavered. "No." He frowned, hesitated and said, "I'm supposing the world will fuss, but right now I'm too glad. I'll give it no thought."

"Well, what has happened?"

"You know already that Joseph doesn't have a legal state right to perform a marriage ceremony, because he isn't a regular ordained minister like Rigdon. Even a ninny knows that's ridiculous. Seein' he's subject to a higher power and with all the authority of the heavens behind him, well, he took it upon himself to do the marriage anyway."

Slowly Jenny said, "You mean she didn't get divorced, and Joseph married them without having the authority to do so?"

Tom scratched his head as if her words shed new light on the situation. "Jen, I can't understand it all, but I do have faith in Joseph's judgment. You know he has been given the keys of the kingdom. What he binds on earth will be bound in heaven; what he loosens on earth will be loosened in heaven. Matter of fact, Newel said Joseph implied that the church has been given other revelations to the ancient order of marriage that are yet to be dispersed."

Jennie frowned at Tom, watching his face. His smile was uneasy now, and she guessed it was the time to ask the question. "Tom, I heard whispers that Joseph had instructed some of the men going to Missouri to take Indian wives. I also heard Joseph promised that a man would be blessed of the Lord if he were to do so."

Tom moved uneasily. "Yeah, I heard likewise. It hasn't been put to me personally, so I conclude it's rumor." He turned to pick up another harness and Jenny went on her way, puzzling over it all. In the end she shrugged off the questions, laughing at the strange twist of events. She also reminded herself that it was time to forget about all the church structure and rules she had known in the past. This new dispensation had rules of its own, and they must be her rules if she hoped to gain her heart's desire.

24

"JEN, YOU'RE LOOKIN' mighty puny these days," Tom said as he stopped on the snowy streets of Kirtland and waited for Jenny to catch up with him. He took the valise she carried and asked, "Where you headed?"

"Back to the Morgans. Mrs. Lewis finally died," she said with a sigh. "Poor soul, I can't wish her dead, but she was a trial to us all. Angela and Cassy helped me, but she kept us all hoppin'. No doubt she was in pain, but the pain her tongue gave out balanced it all."

"And your herbs and amulets did no good?"

"Nor the charms," she said shortly. "This is likely to ruin my nursing."

"Oh, I don't doubt that you'll have the business."

" 'Tisn't the business!" she snapped. "I'm worried about believing when everything works against the power."

"You think there's a greater power to be had?"

"Could be. It is a lack in me, most certain." Abruptly Jenny lifted her head to look at Tom. "Why the questions? Have you been hearing things?"

"There's talk. People admire the things they can't understand. Where there's indications of the mysterious at work, they're right there lookin'." Tom continued to study the thin little figure at his side. Her shoulders drooped wearily and her head was bowed against the icy pricking of snow filling the air. "Why don't you come to the stable for some hot tea?"

She nodded and silently followed him across the street, through the building, and up the stairs to his room.

The heat of the forge provided warmth for the shabby room Tom called home. Gratefully Jenny sat down on his one straight chair and watched as he stirred up the embers in his stove and pulled the kettle of water over the heat.

After he put the mugs on the table, Tom placed a stool close to the stove and said, "You're pulled a mite too thin. Do you good to get off that horse you're ridin' and walk a spell."

"Meaning?" Jenny pulled the mittens from her hands and unwound her muffler. When Tom didn't answer, she continued, "I've a notion to look for something to do besides nursing. It gets me down at times. Especially when you're expecting results and there's nothing." Abruptly she shivered.

"What's wrong, Jen?"

She looked up. "Oh, I'm remembering the way Mrs. Lewis died. It was like all the spirits on earth congregated. Tom, I don't understand, but she died screaming and pointing. She had been muttering something for days that none of us could understand, talking about turning back. A foul old woman, no doubt, but she frightened us all to the bottom of our shoes." Jenny shivered again and was silent.

At last she roused herself. "I'm pricked with a desire to know the workings of the printing office. Tom, is there a chance Oliver Cowdery would have a little work for me in there? I know women don't normally do such things unless they are married to the fellow running the place, and that's out of the question, since Cowdery's married.—I wouldn't have him anyway. But I would like to look into the business."

"There's little chance. I 'spect the Missus would have your neck if you even went into the place. There's been some talk around about him not minding his manners around the females." Tom got up from his stool to pour the boiling water into his teapot. He was mulling over the problems that had been filling him with unrest for the past month. He glanced at Jenny, studied her innocent, girlish face, and felt again the stab of remorse. *What if she were to become another Fannie Alger?*

He watched her sip tea and then lift her face to smile at him. "Ah, Tom, you were right. I am pressing life too close, and I've a mind to take it easy for a few weeks. Could be I'll feel different about the healing then." The tender, nearly childish smile made him decide.

Taking a deep breath, Tom hunched his stool closer to Jenny and quickly, before he could change his mind, he said, "Jen, there's a few things I need to say to you. First off, Joseph sent a message. I don't know why you've come up with this thing about the healing with the charms and herbs, but for some reason Joe's bothered by it all. Could be it's related to the trouble we had in the beginning.

"See, Rigdon's followers, those that were in Kirtland when we arrived, were into some funny things. Come meeting times, they would work themselves into a real frenzy a-talkin' in a queer language and a-rollin' around on the ground and pretendin' to be convertin' the Indians, such stuff. Anyways, Joe cracked down on it and said it was all from Satan and that people had better be a-drawin' up tight and listenin' to him, since he was the prophet, seer, and revelator.

"Now, your healin's making him a bit uneasy. So I don't blame him. He called me in with a message. He didn't say 'thus saith the Lord,' like he does sometimes, but from the way he said it, I felt it anyway. Jen, he said if you're goin' to be actin' so saintly and do the healin' and all, that you'd better be bringin' forth the fruits of repentance."

Jenny frowned, "Now what on earth does he mean by that?"

"Simple. Joinin' the church and gettin' to services regular. You know Joseph won't abide people a-claimin' a religion they don't follow right."

"I've heard that," Jenny said dryly. "The Morgans let me know right off that I was expected to shun evil, such as dancing and fancy frocks and too much fun instead of work." She waved her mug, "But this latest about not drinking tea and such, I don't understand, especially in the cold of winter. What difference does it make whether we eat meat all year round or just in the winter?"

Tom didn't answer; he was busy thinking about the other things and wondering how he could warn Jenny. He took a deep breath. "First off, I want to remind you that I believe Joseph is called of God. I believe his book is from God, and that's because I asked God and He gave me the burnin' in the bosom to verify the truth of it all. This keeps me faithful and trustin', even when I don't understand. Jen, I know I'm not too smart and book learnin' just didn't take with me. You'll never know how much I appreciate havin' a prophet and knowin' that I can trust him."

He was silent, staring into the growing dusk. "You were at the last church meeting when President Phelps read the article on marriage. What did you think of it?"

"Think?" Jenny echoed. "Why, nothing. Seems it's not a bit different than what we've always been told."

"Well," Tom said slowly, "I mostly wondered if you'd been hearin' rumors about some of the men misbehavin'. There's rumors circulatin' 'bout the Mormons practicing polygamy." At her blank look, he added, "Havin' more'n one wife. Jen, don't you believe it, and don't you let any fella persuade you different."

Jen laughed. "Oh, Tom," she said, "I'm not newborn. I know there's fellows who'll pass off any story, and I'm not swayed by their talk." She got to her feet and pressed her face against his for a moment. "You are the dearest brother a person could have. I love you for caring for your silly little sister. Now I'll be going before the snow's too heavy for walking."

Tom watched her walk down the street, relieved that he had said part of it, but still troubled by the serious-faced men he had confronted that morning.

"Our prophet," he addressed the line of harnesses hanging in the deserted tack-room, "is too good-lookin' for his own welfare. I hope his good looks don't do him in." He sighed heavily.

The words Warren Parrish and Oliver Cowdery had said followed Tom as he went about his work. *We know for a fact that Joseph has Fannie as wife; we've spied on them and found them together.*

As he sorted harnesses he muttered, "Joe, you told me those fellas were lyin'. I've got to believe you, no matter what. There's nothin' else I know, and there's Jenny; I'm responsible for her."

Jenny went home to Sally and Andy Morgan and baby Tamara. Her dismal failure at the Lewis home was soon forgotten, and January slipped into February.

Sally had assured Jenny that anyone would have failed with old Mrs. Lewis. But Jenny's thoughts whispered back, *Not a white witch. And not someone who's looking for even more power.*

On the days Sally and Jenny weren't busy, Jenny slipped away to her room to read deeply in the green book. After one frustrating session, she closed it, saying, "Oh, how I long to see Clara; if only Adela were here!" Even as she whispered the words, she admitted that the reason for her unhappiness was not her failure with Mrs. Lewis, but the feeling of power-lessness. Staring at the book, she whispered, "If I couldn't succeed with her, how do I get what I want?"

Crossing the room, she pulled out the hunk of wax Clara had given her. "Emma," she whispered. But immediately she pushed it away, shivering at the horrible images it conjured.

Later she pulled out the *Book of Mormon* and the *Doctrine and Covenants* and tried to read them, but within minutes she yawned and exclaimed, "Brother Joseph, we must have a conference!"

When she started down the street that February day, with blessings and admonition from Sally, she whispered to herself, "I've never seen a bunch of people so eager to convert me to the church as these Mormons. Even Lucy Harris wasn't this eager about her church. I can wrap anything up as a desire to know more about Mormonism, and I shall immediately have what I want."

But Jenny changed her mind as soon as she stepped into the print shop. The press was clanging and clattering and the building was vibrating. First she needed to find Cowdery to make her presence known.

When she stepped into the press room, she saw a strange look cross his face. Clasping the book tight, she bravely marched toward him, pushed on by her desire to learn printing. Oliver shut down the press. Giving a quick glance toward the stairs leading to Joseph's office, he closed the door to the street. "Jenny, he doesn't like young ladies in the print shop."

"Even those who would like to learn a little about the business?" she pleaded. "I'd sweep the floor for you if you'd only let me look on, Oliver Cowdery."

His inky hand tugged at his shirt collar and he tried to smile, but she was aware of his uneasiness. "Jenny, you were a good scholar back in the Manchester days, but a good scholar doesn't necessarily make a printer, especially a female."

"I've really come to see Joseph today," she admitted.

He hesitated, glancing upward. As he turned and marched across the press room, he spoke over his shoulder. "He's busy right this minute. This bundle of papers goes down to Whitney. If you'll deliver them for me, so's they can get in the afternoon mail, I'll put you next in line to see the Prophet."

When Jenny returned from Whitney's store, she was licking a peppermint stick. She was nearly to the print shop when the door opened and a young woman stepped out. Glancing at Jenny with a pleasant smile, she murmured, "Good afternoon. We haven't met, but I know you are Jenny. I'm Fannie." She glanced down at the candy.

On impulse Jenny broke the stick and handed Fannie a piece. "Fannie Alger. Sally's mentioned you, said you're the Smiths' adopted daughter." A shadow crossed Fannie's face as she accepted the candy and licked it.

"Oh, thank you, Jenny. It makes today a holiday!" With another pleasant smile she continued down the street, and Jenny entered the shop.

Oliver, now free of printer's ink, was standing at the foot of the stairs. Quickly he said, "Miss Jenny, do go up."

Jenny licked the peppermint and noted his nervousness. "I'd stay here with you if you'd let me help," she bargained, then nearly dropped her candy as a red flush washed across Oliver's face. Muttering, he turned and entered the press room, firmly closing the door.

Jenny was still shaking her head in bewilderment as she climbed the stairs and reached for the door. With her hand on the knob, she saw the sign on the door: *Positively No Admittance.* She was still hesitating when the door was snatched open. "Jenny, come in."

"That sign," she murmured. "I nearly left."

"You've a book." He walked to his chair and sat down. Indicating the chair across from him, he said, "I take it you've read it."

She shook her head. "No. As a matter of fact, I found it boring, and I decided to come ask questions instead."

"I told you it was too much for women to handle. Are you now willing to let the men wrestle with the doctrine and just be a good little lady like the others?"

She grinned up at him. "How do you expect me to be a good little lady when I haven't been told *how?*"

"That is another challenge," he replied softly.

In the silence of the room, she was becoming very aware of Joseph. Slumped and at ease across from her, he smiled and waited. She studied his fair hair and light blue eyes, wondering why sitting in the same room with him caused all her carefully prepared questions to flee her mind.

Not one question concerning the doctrine of his church presented itself, but other thoughts arose, the gossip. She wanted to ask him if it were true that he and Emma were having problems. What had Tom meant when he referred to the whisper of polygamy?

Jenny's mind floundered. Under the steady eyes, she struggled and brought up the only thing she could remember. "Your mother went to the Manchester church we attended. She was saying in front of us all that when the translating of the gold plates was done, she intended to show them. Now I'm hearing rumbles because you didn't. Why?"

Slowly Joseph sat up and leaned forward. He had discarded his jacket and loosened his tie. Watching him pick up a slender letter opener and flex the blade, she studied him. The muscles in his shoulders rippled as he played with the letter opener. For a time he bent the shiny blade back and forth. When he looked up the serenity was gone; a restlessness in his eyes caught her attention. The troubled frown darkened his face, making her forget her vision of the bright young giant.

"There's too many of these rumbles. Sometimes I hear about them. Sometimes I don't." He paused to pass his hand across his face in a weary gesture. Jenny was filled with an overwhelming desire to go to him, to touch away the weariness. She recoiled in horror when she realized the direction her thoughts were taking her.

As he got up and paced the room, Jenny bit her lip and clasped her hands together. One thing was certain: if just once she gave into those strange impulses, all hope of winning Joseph would be gone. She would be only a woman of the street. "Easy come, easy go," she whispered, grateful that somehow her mother had impressed her with that message.

He turned, "What did you say?"

"Nothing." She nearly stuttered the word. He crossed the room and sat beside her.

"Jenny—" His forced smile was twisted and miserable, his eyes troubled. "This being a prophet isn't easy street. It's a mighty lonely business. No matter how straight I walk the line, there's those who gossip and pick fault. My own close followers undermine me and try to ruin me. They don't understand. I didn't dream up the teachings and the revelations. I'm following God. Jenny, do you see? I need a friend. I need someone who will keep me informed of the whispers. I need to know how to answer these people. Will you be that person, to stand by me and be willing to tell me my faults, to help me in this business?"

"But I thought Rigdon was supposed to be that person. In the revelations the Lord said Sidney was to be your John the Baptist. I read that far."

Joseph shook his head. "He's too close. I suppose he has stars in his eyes. But I sense in you a willingness to tell me the worst and demand an answer. Help me, Jenny." For a moment he dropped his head and that bright hair was only inches from her face. She caught her breath and pushed back against the chair. When he raised his head his eyes searched her face.

"Of course, Joseph," she whispered. "You know I would do anything to help you."

And when she was at the door, ready to walk downstairs, she turned. There was a question in his eyes as he waited. She said, "You didn't answer me." She saw he didn't remember, and prodded. "I asked why you didn't show the plates like Lucy said you would."

He came and bent close so she could see the torment in his eyes. Slowly he said, "Jenny, I was deceived. Do you hear me, do you understand? Ask no more."

As she walked back to the Morgans', her thoughts were full of Joseph; particularly she was thinking of that last statement. *Who had deceived Joseph? Did this have something to do with his failure with the seer stone and his reluctance to use it now?*

The next Sabbath Jenny came down to breakfast wearing her dark challis print. Sally's eyes widened and Jenny nodded. "Your guess is right. I'm going to church with you today." The questions still filled Sally's eyes as Jenny sliced bread and carried dishes to the table.

"See, I've decided, just like Tom told me, that if I intend to join the church I'd better be finding out what's being preached on the Sabbath. Also, I've shunned church so I scarcely know my neighbors. Do you know, I met Fannie Alger coming out of Joseph's office the other day, and I didn't know who she was until—" Jenny stopped and watched Andy Morgan sputtering over his breakfast. Sally was thumping him on the back. "Whatever is wrong?" Jenny asked.

"I don't know." Sally's face tilted toward Jenny. "Get some water. Oh my, I hope it isn't his heart."

He pushed back from her restraining hands. "I'm all right, wife." His voice still sounded strangled as he said, "You are right, Jenny. It is proper that you go to church. What were you doing at the printing office?"

"Why, Joseph gave me books to read."

Walking to church, Jenny wondered about that strange expression on Andy's face. But she shed her thoughts at the door, uncomfortably aware that since last August's church meeting, she had filled every Sabbath with activity rather than face the restraint of the weekly meetings.

"Jenny Timmons—I do declare." The voice gasped close to Jenny's elbow, and she turned to see Lucy Smith, the Prophet's mother.

"Oh, Mrs. Smith!" she gave the little woman a quick hug. "And Mr. Smith," she added as she saw the tall, lanky man beside Lucy.

"It's been so long," Lucy continued, "since the Manchester days. I wouldn't have known you except that Tom told me you are livin' here now. You must come and visit."

When the couple sat down on the bench in front of her, Jenny realized, with a pang of regret, that she had missed them. The sermon droned around her head, but Jenny's thoughts were full of memories of the Smith home, and she quickly grew eager to take up the friendship again.

On Tuesday of the same week with directions from Sally, Jenny went to call on the Smiths.

Jenny had Lucy all to herself. With cups of the forbidden tea, the two spent the morning talking about all they remembered of Manchester.

At noon Mr. Smith returned with Oliver Cowdery in tow. Jenny was surprised at Oliver's discomfort. Excusing herself, she went to help Lucy prepare a meal for the men.

When she carried the bowl of stew to the table, she found the men reminiscing. They were crowded together on the bench, and Mr. Smith reached for her arm, saying, "We were a-talkin' about the things that transpired when Joe found the gold Bible. My, those were the days!"

"Fearful, wonderful days," Lucy said comfortably as she took her place at the table. "I was just thinkin' the other day of the findin' of it."

Oliver helped himself to the stew. "Willard Chase was telling me what you'd related to him, about dressing Joe up in his black suit of clothes and finding a black horse for him to ride. He also told me how when Joe got out the book of gold, he made the mistake of placing it back, and it disappeared. He explained that Joe found the book back in the box where it had been in the first place. He tried to take it out and was hindered by something in the box that looked like a toad; then, before his eyes the toad changed into the appearance of a man and struck him." Shaking his head, Oliver paused in his story and picked up his spoon.

Mr. Smith wiped his mouth and said, "Well, I'll tell you, those devils sure made a commotion."

"Devils!" Jenny exclaimed. "I didn't know about them."

"Yessir," he nodded. "Joe took a pillowcase to put the plates in and a bunch of devils followed him. See, they were trying to keep him from gettin' the plates. One kicked him a good one. Joe had black and blue marks for days."

Oliver nodded, saying, "Joe himself told me that when he first went to the Hill Cumorah, he saw the prince of darkness surrounded by his cohorts."

It was late when Jenny left the Smith home, much later than she had intended. As she walked through the shadowy streets of Kirtland, she realized she was the only person out.

The evening mists were drifting through the empty streets. The soft glow of lamplight filled the windows of the small log houses, streaking the street with pale light. She quickened her steps and heard the echo rebounding from the brick of the printing office and Whitney's store.

Now she caught the sound of footsteps ahead. With her mind full of the tales she had heard at the Smith home, she began to hurry, running to catch up with those other lonesome feet. Rounding a corner, she saw the dark-cloaked figure ahead. Jenny called, "Hello!"

Jenny saw a brief flash of red as the woman turned and the light from a supper lamp momentarily illuminated her. Jenny ran toward her, but the woman disappeared around the corner.

25

HALFWAY THROUGH FEBRUARY, Jenny stood at the kitchen window in the Morgans' snug log house. Behind her the sun had painted bright strips across the whitewashed walls and the teakettle was shooting steam into the air. But Jenny was heedless of the pleasant picture Sally's kitchen presented; she was studying the landscape still painted in snowy outlines. A rustle behind her, followed by a coo and a gurgle announced Sally and Tamara's presence.

"I'm trying to list the changes in the neighborhood that indicate spring's on the way," she explained without turning. "Just moments ago I saw a cardinal—but that doesn't mean spring. The snow is starting to shrink in upon itself like old Mrs. Lewis did before she died."

Sally's skirts rustled again and Jenny turned. "You want gruel for Tamara?" As she passed the pair she fingered the baby's soft curls. "Oh, that's a pretty baby today." Tamara rewarded her with a gurgle while Sally nodded and smiled. Jenny poured the boiling water over cornmeal and stirred it as the thin mixture bubbled on the stove.

Sally sat down and tucked a bib under Tamara's chin. "Andy tells me that Joseph's talking hard about sending him to Missouri with the others in two weeks' time. I hope you won't be called to nursing. I'm so lonesome when he's gone I nearly perish."

Andy Morgan walked into the room in time to hear her lament. He bent over his wife and daughter and kissed them both. "I'm flattered," he murmured; "also relieved that you prefer Jenny's company."

Sally tipped her head back and looked at her husband. "Andy, what can you possibly mean by that?"

"Only that you are a beautiful woman and I don't want to share you."

Sally's voice was dry as she answered, "I'm also married." The silence in the room was broken only by Tamara's contented sounds and the clink of the spoon against the dish. Sally lifted her head again and watched her husband struggling with the buttons on his collar. "You are a very dignified attorney, and I am proud of you."

"I only wish there were a few more dignified attorneys in town; then I'd spend some time at home." His voice was grim, and Jenny turned from her spot at the window to study his face. He saw her and smiled, but she still noticed the tired lines on his face.

As Jenny checked the biscuits in the oven and turned the bacon in the skillet, she pondered the troubled air that had followed Andy into the room.

Breakfast ended and the outer door had closed behind Andy. Jenny, her hands moving among the dishes, gently asked, "Why is Andy going to Missouri, and why is he so disturbed?" When there was no answer, she turned to look at Sally. The blonde head was bent close to Tamara's as she wiped at the baby's face, but Jenny could see she was chewing her lip. Jenny waited until Sally lifted her head.

"You might as well know." Her voice was throaty with tears. "There's gossip among some of the apostles and the Seventy that Joseph's been making indecent proposals to some of the married women in Kirtland. Every good-looking woman in town is suspect, particularly by her husband." She gasped and continued, "Oh, Jenny, don't look at me in that manner! I'm not making this up. I didn't know about it at all until Andy began questioning me as if I were on trial in court."

Sally's tears won out, and Jenny went to take the baby. As she cuddled the soft, milk-scented body against her face, she watched Sally struggle for control. Finally she knelt beside Sally and said, "Andy can't believe those things about you."

"You don't know. He was so jealous before we were married that I dared not smile at anything in trousers."

"I'll have to go see Joseph today," Jenny declared. "I'll see that he reassures Andy."

Sally mopped tears from her eyes and soberly studied Jenny. "I wish that, but I wonder how much effect it will have. I understand the men are trying to quiet the rumors before they reach the church's enemies."

As Jenny walked toward the print shop, she was thinking of her first visit. Abruptly she realized she was giving Joseph the assistance he requested.

But at the office, Oliver's sweating face came between her and the stairs that led up to the little room. "Miss Jenny, I've told you before you must have an appointment. The Prophet is a busy man."

"Then announce me; I know he'll see me." Oliver's face flushed and the look he turned on her was perplexing. She frowned and waited.

His face cleared abruptly and he said, "You've been wanting to see the workings of the press—come ahead. I was just starting it up."

As they were bending over the neat rows of lead type and Jenny was trying to read the reversed words, a whisper of sound and creaking boards made her look up. Joseph was closing the street door after a dark-cloaked woman. Jenny's pounding heart gave weight to her guesses.

"Who was that woman?" Her voice came in a whisper as she moved toward Joseph, and the Prophet studied her with a frown before he answered. "She is Mrs. Martindale; her first name is Adela and her husband is William."

Now her voice squeaked, "They live in Kirtland?"

"Yes. They've just converted to the church and I expect we will benefit greatly. Martindale is an exporter worth a great deal of money."

Jenny followed him up the stairs. After his enigmatic look at her question, she dared not ask where the couple lived. He settled behind the desk and waited with a quizzical expression in his eyes. Jenny still hesitated over her mission; she was fighting the impact of his presence.

He broke the silence, "Did you read the books?"

She shook her head. "I haven't had time. Since last autumn I've had one round of nursing care after another."

"I've heard," he answered shortly. "And what is your rate of cure?"

"All of them." But she had to admit, "Likely they'd all have recovered without the charms and amulets."

"But you did a great deal of chanting and fussing and everybody treated you like God Himself."

She sat on her hands to keep from squirming and retorted, "But isn't that the way they treat *you*?"

"Yes, but I am the Prophet and I deserve the recognition."

"Because you hear from God. More than I? Joseph, why is—" Abruptly and impatiently he got to his feet and stomped around the desk to her.

"Jenny Timmons, I will broach no sass from the baby sister of one of my men. Neither will you draw people to yourself. The Lord has commanded against such as this. If you had been reading the *Book of Commandments* you would know this." He pointed toward the door. "Now go and don't return until you've read them all."

"I didn't come to—"

"Go." His jaw tightened, and the color fled from his face. Jenny bit her lip and turned away.

"Joseph," she whispered, freely allowing the disappointment to well up in her voice. Her frustration was augmented by the memory of what she had heard—they said tears melted Joseph. "You've asked me to—to tell you, and now you won't listen." She touched her eyes and moved toward the door.

"Wait!" As she heard the command, she also heard the clink of metal striking the floor. She turned and saw a silvery disk spinning on the floor between them.

While Joseph fumbled with his handkerchief, she snatched up the talisman and held it in her hand. The strange markings were familiar, but where her own talisman had a woman's figure, his carried only strange letters inscribed within squares.

She was still busy comparing it with her own when the import of it all struck her. She raised her face to meet his eyes. "What does it all mean?"

"The letters? Jenny, it isn't important to you." He held out his hand for the talisman, and she quickly stepped away. He was perspiring.

"Not important? Then I'd like to keep it. I'll show it to my grandchildren to prove I've known the man from God, the Prophet Joseph Smith."

"Jenny!" he spoke sharply, moving toward her. She slipped the shiny metal down the front of her dress and hurried around the table.

"Joseph," she said, "what about Abbah and El Ob and Josiphiel?"

"Why, they are the names of God. How did you know?"

She patted the front of the frock. "And what are the powers at your disposal?"

He hesitated a moment before answering, but when he spoke, the words lay lightly on his tongue. "The celestial intelligences assigned to this metal will help me in all my endeavors."

She repeated slowly, "Abbah, El Ob, and Josiphiel—I know the last means Jehovah speaks for God. But the other two I don't understand."

Leaning forward he whispered earnestly, excitement mounting in his voice, "When these intelligences are invoked properly with all of the power of ancient magic, I am guaranteed riches, power, honor. Do you know, Jenny, when I control these forces properly, no one can resist my love, neither friend nor foe, man nor woman." He still held her with that penetrating gaze, and she felt the pulse in her throat mount in tempo.

She whispered, "But now the talisman is in my hands. Does that mean all the powers are for me?"

"You will give it back right now, or I will take it!" Turning, Jenny fled to the door. She had nearly reached it when she stumbled, and he was there with his arms tightening around her. He turned her, holding her motionless. "This is what you wanted all along. Yes, Jenny, the power is mine." He bent over her and his lips were hard and then gentle against hers. When he raised his head, he said simply, "It does work, doesn't it?"

She was trembling, and she took a moment to be certain her voice was firm before saying, "Yes, it works, but are you certain it is working for you? Remember, I hold it now." She laughed merrily at the startled expression on his face.

Now out of his arms, she moved to the door just as a pounding began on the other side. "Joseph!" came the low urgent voice, "Michael says Emma is coming to the print shop."

Joseph stared at her in dismay. "Quick, give it to me." She shook her head. "I will shake it out."

"Then you will be shaking it out when Emma comes."

Disbelief and distaste swept his face. He yanked at the door. "Jenny, you are a witch. I'll have you yet."

As he shoved her through the door, she hissed, "Andy Morgan will have your hide if you don't explain the gossip before nightfall. How is that for seeing the future?" She flew down the stairs.

The talisman bit into Jenny's flesh, but she hugged her shawl tight, put on a sweet smile, and walked serenely down the street.

A few weeks later Tom had left the stable and was turning his horse toward Thompson. Now, full of troubled thoughts about Jenny, he felt a compulsion. Abruptly he turned his horse off Kirtland's well-traveled main street and headed down the lane that led to the Morgans'.

The early March day had been balmy and sweet, and the evening sky was filled with color. Tom noted with pleasure that the few clouds visible were puffy and pale like mounds of whipped cream. Jenny was crossing the Morgans' yard.

"Sis, hold it!" When he reached her side, he said, "I'm thinkin' the Lord's promptin' me to go to Hyrum tonight. How would you like to ride with me? Joseph told me he would be leadin' a cottage meeting there this evenin'." While she hesitated, he added, "You made a good start with your church attendance until lately. Maybe the Lord's wantin' me to prod you on by takin' you to meetin' with me."

Jenny stood on the step with the warm eggs clasped in her apron and cocked her head to study Tom's earnest face. "I wouldn't mind going, but horseback doesn't appeal."

Sally stuck her head out the door. "I heard you, Tom. If your horse is willing, the horsecart's in the barn; you're welcome to it."

So Tom and Jenny set off for Hyrum in the Morgans' cart, with Jenny asking, "Why is Joseph in Hyrum?"

"I don't know his exact business, but I do know he was goin' to the Johnson farm where he lived some time back. He told me earlier he intends stoppin' by the Rollins farm, too. Sometime back they'd extracted a promise from him to hold a meetin' there."

"Cottage meeting," Jenny mused. "I've never heard of such a thing."

"Some mighty good meetin's we've had, when the Prophet's right down among us. You'll see."

By the time Jenny and Tom reached Hyrum, dusk had brought a chill with the drifting mists. Jenny snuggled gratefully into her shawl. "There's several wagons and carts here. How did the word pass so quickly?"

Tom shrugged. "I don't know. These folks work hard to get the Prophet to themselves for an evenin'."

Inside the tiny cottage Jenny and Tom found seats on the planks supported by boxes. The room was crowded, and the kerosene lamps were turned nearly to the smoking point. Jenny folded her shawl away from her shoulders and tried to make herself inconspicuous. She hadn't seen Joe since that day, two weeks past, when she had confronted him in his office. Now his talisman was pinned next to her own, and her lips tingled again with the remembered pressure of his kiss. She glanced about, wondering whether Emma Smith was in the room. Jenny was still darting quick glances about when Joseph entered. In the dimness his white collar above the dark coat framed his face with light, and Jenny felt her pulse quicken.

Even after the meeting started, people continued to arrive. Jenny and Tom squeezed close together along with everyone else. During prayer and singing, Jenny stumbled over the unfamiliar words. Finally Joseph stood to speak, but she was oblivious to his message as she studied his face.

Suddenly he stopped mid-sentence and stared out over the heads of his rapt audience. The moment of silence stretched, and Jenny felt tension mount; not a whisper of sound stirred the air. She watched Joseph's face pale and his eyes glow; their brilliance seemed to spread and infuse every pore of his face with light.

The silence held, but now Jenny was aware of a strange movement through her body, as if unseen forces were propelling her closer to the Prophet. His whole being filled her vision, and nothing else existed.

When his voice broke through, Jenny sighed deeply, hearing him say, "My brothers and sisters in the Lord, do you know who has been in our midst tonight?"

A breathy sigh echoed the answer, "An angel of the Lord."

Suddenly a man sitting on a box facing the Prophet dropped to his knees and wrapped his arms around Joseph's legs. Jenny watched his head tilt backward in adoration and the murmur of his voice held the room. "It was our Lord and Savior, Jesus Christ."

With a gentle smile, Joseph looked down at the man. As he placed his hand upon his head, he said, "Martin Harris, God revealed this to you. My brothers and sisters, I want you always to remember this. The Savior has been in your midst.

"Because you are weak in the Lord, He must cast a veil over you. You cannot endure the splendor of His presence. I want you to remember this.

He has given you to me, commanding me to seal you up for everlasting life."

As Jenny and Tom rode back to Kirtland, he said, "Jen, you're awfully quiet. Did it affect you that way too?"

She stirred and sighed, trying to sort through the jumble of feelings, especially that most troubling one. "Martin Harris. I didn't realize he was in Kirtland." She shuddered, remembering the horror of the day in Manchester when he had beaten her and his wife.

Tom's arm wrapped about Jenny, and she knew he felt the trembling. He cleared his throat. "Tyke, Martin Harris is no angel, but if gettin' religion changes a man, you better believe Martin'll never be beatin' another woman."

26

THE TEMPLE WAS complete. The last stone and shingle had been placed, the final brush of paint had dried, and the last canvas veil had been hung. Only a few days remained before the dedication, and excitement in Kirtland was mounting.

The temple was situated on a slight rise, away from the congestion of the main section of town. Already the three-story stone building with its square steeple had attracted people from miles around.

These days Tom often found himself standing in the doorway of the blacksmith shop watching the people on the street. Like an indulgent uncle, he listened to their comments and noted their obvious pride as they detoured from their accustomed routes in order to pass by the temple.

"It's sure been a grand undertakin'," Tom said to Newel. "From the hole in the ground to the pile of stone and wood shapin' up, it belongs to everybody in town."

Newel matter-of-factly said, "It is. It's our money and sweat and even a little blood that's built it."

"Make you wonder what's goin' to happen at the dedication?"

Newel nodded, flipping away the twig he had been chewing. "Particularly after Zion's Camp." They fell silent, both remembering the pain and failure of that time in Missouri. Then Newel roused himself. "Prophet Joseph said the Lord promised a great blessing to the elders when the temple was completed."

"Even if it doesn't live up to what we're hopin' for," Tom continued soberly, "there's still the promise that just gettin' it built and dedicated releases us to go and redeem Zion."

"Thus saith the Lord," Newel said softly, turning away.

Later that day, while Tom was sweating at the forge, Newel came in. "The Prophet has called a special meeting in the temple."

Tom shoved the sheet metal back into the forge to heat. "What's goin' on?"

"The apostles and the Seventy as well as the councils are going to be given the rites for the temple ceremonials." He touched his forehead. "See you tonight. I've got to spread the word."

That evening when Tom walked into the temple with the other men, he was struck by the quiet dignity of the place. The group assembled in the lower auditorium. Tom knew from his work on the building that the floor above them held another auditorium with the same unusual feature— twelve pulpits to accommodate the twelve apostles.

Walking to the front of the auditorium, Tom stood looking up at the window arching behind the pulpits constructed for the members of the Melchizedek priesthood. Above the window, stretching like a banner, were the words, *HOLINESS UNTO THE LORD.* Soberly Tom took his place. The words ushered him into a solemn mood that made it easy to enter into the service.

When Joseph walked into the auditorium carrying the bottle of oil, the men were hushed and waiting. The lanky, graying father of the Prophet was called forward, placed on a stool, and surrounded by elders. Joseph raised his right hand and bade the men do likewise.

After Joseph had blessed the oil and poured some upon the head of his father, he motioned his men to come together. Gathering as close as they could, the men in the center placed their hands upon the gray hair of the man before them.

In the candlelight Joseph's face became transfixed and pale. Looking upward, he softly intoned, "The heavens are open before me. I am seeing the celestial kingdom of God with all attending glory. Whether in the body or out, I do not know. I see glorious beauty . . ." His words moved on, sweeping around Tom. "The gate, like circling flames of fire, the blazing throne of God, and seated thereon, the Father and the Son."

Each of the elders in turn took his place to receive his blessing. With a shout, one lifted his arms and exclaimed, "I see the heavens opening before me!" Later another acknowledged, "The angels are ministering to us."

On successive nights the rest of the elders received their blessings. In culmination, Joseph sealed all of the blessings, instructing the men in this final ceremony that all which had transpired had been sealed in heaven.

At home Andy Morgan talked about these events. "He called this the patriarchal blessings," Andy said. "These days have yielded wonderful visions and promises given to the men called out to do the work of the Lord. Some of the patriarchal blessings were particularly noteworthy." He was silent for a moment and Jenny continued her work about the kitchen.

While Morgan talked about the meeting, a troubled frown kept appearing on his face. Now, as if suddenly recalling that he had stopped mid-tale, he raised his head and continued. "When James Brewster was receiving his blessing, it was revealed that he was to be a prophet, seer, revelator and translator. Power is to be given from God to enable him to discover and obtain treasures that are hidden in the earth." Jenny dropped the pan she was wiping and Andy jerked upright in his chair. "What's—"

"Oh, nothing," she broke in hastily. Biting her lip, she added, "But I understood that treasure digging was all in the past, that it was to be forgotten now."

Andy shook his head slowly. "I'd heard that too," Andy agreed. "I can't understand. But then, who knows the mind of the Lord except the Prophet?" He sighed and continued. "There was another one that was truly amazing. Joseph's father gave this blessing. He told a youth that before he reaches the age of twenty-one, he will preach the gospel to the inhabitants of the islands of the sea and even to the inhabitants of the moon."

Finally, hands on hips, Jenny demanded, "You're telling of the most wonderful things. Yet at the same time I see you frowning over it all. Why?"

He stared at her in astonishment. Slowly he said, "I can't forget the beginning days of the Mormons in Kirtland. You see, Jenny, I was one of Rigdon's original followers. At the time it rubbed us wrong to have this young man, Joseph Smith, claiming to be a prophet from the Lord, spouting the language of an uncouth farm boy while he was telling our silver-tongued Rigdon what to do. One of the first things he undertook was to call all the Spirit outpouring the devil's work and demand that we forget it all." He stopped suddenly and flushed.

Jenny nodded, "And now the same thing is going on in the temple. The town's rocking with it. No wonder you frown."

His face cleared, and with a relieved smile he said, "I don't mean to complain; it's just a hard thing to swallow. Jenny, I do believe he's a prophet from the Lord; don't doubt my loyalty. Any common plowboy who can convince this lawyer he's from God, well—it's truth."

Sally had been nodding her head at every word her husband spoke. But Jenny was surprised at the wistful note in her voice as she added, "It is true, he is a prophet from God, and we must believe everything he says or we'll be damned for all eternity. It is impossible to reject truth and still make it to heaven."

The dedication took place on March 27, 1836. As Jenny walked through the streets of Kirtland to the temple, she was still mulling over Sally Morgan's statement. There had been something strange about her declaration, something that had tugged at Jenny and left her feeling uneasy. How deeply Sally feared for her soul's salvation!

Although Jenny had purposely left the Morgan home early in order to have a choice seat, the streets were already filled with people heading toward the temple. As she quickened her steps, the air of excitement engulfing the people grabbed her, too.

A reverent hush touched all who entered the auditorium. She recognized it as she took her seat beside her fellow worshipers.

Later, Joseph Smith, with the presidency and the twelve, filed into the building. How solemn their faces were! Their expressions reflected the awe she was feeling. The songs they sang, the music they heard seemed to echo about as if wafted on angels' wings. Later in the muted silence, even the smallest infant was quiet.

When the Prophet stood to speak, Jenny studied his broad, tall figure suitably clothed in black. The black heightened the pallor of his face as he shook back his bright hair and lifted his face heavenward. The words of his prayer fell like jewels on his eager followers.

Jenny forgot to bow her head. Caught by the mysterious air that filled the temple, she was momentarily transfixed. But suddenly her mood was shattered by a clear memory of the last time she had been with Joseph. He had been in shirtsleeves, with his collar loosened, kissing her freely, even passionately.

Jenny's eyes drifted toward the corner where she knew Emma was sitting with her children. The dark head was modestly bent. Jenny wondered at the astonishment and uneasiness that suddenly possessed her. Restlessly she moved, gripped by emotion. Was it because she was in the temple and under the mysterious influence called God? She studied the solemn face of the prophet and suddenly laughter formed deep within her. *If I am uneasy,* she thought, *what must HE feel?*

When Jenny walked home, the conversation around her reflected the grandeur and awe. A thousand believers had crowded the temple auditorium, and another thousand had lingered outside. But there was one note of disappointment. As old Mrs. Bolton said, "We didn't hear none of those grand things like those who got their patriarchal blessings saw and heard. I'm right disappointed about that. And seems on this day they'd let the womenfolk worship in there with the men come evening."

She paused for a moment and then added, "Those that got their blessings said that in the midst of the Prophet's praying, he stopped death-still and the men saw a white dove fly through the window and light on the Prophet's shoulder. He told them later it was the Holy Spirit."

That dedication evening the men began two days and two nights of worshiping and fasting in the temple. The women grumbled, but their curiosity remained unsatisfied except for occasional reports drifting out to them. The first report told of the Savior appearing to some, while others said angels ministered to them.

According to Tom, the Prophet had urged the men to prophesy, saying that the first to open his mouth would receive the gift of prophecy, and that whatsoever he prophesied would come to pass. At one point a sound like a rushing mighty wind filled the temple, and men jumped to their feet, speaking in tongues and seeing visions. As the stories spread, townspeople rushed to the temple to stand outside and stare in awe at the bright light coming from within. Angels had filled the temple, Joseph reported.

The final hours were recounted by Andy Morgan. Joseph and Oliver Cowdery climbed into their pulpits and lowered the canvas veils around them. He and his friends, Morgan said, had sat in the audience, hardly daring to breathe in the silence.

When the curtains were rolled back, the watching men gasped. Deathly pale, Oliver sat looking heavenward. Joseph stood to his feet and, lifting his arm heavenward, declared softly, "We have seen the Lord. He stood on the breastwork of the pulpit before us. Underneath His feet lay a path of pure gold, and His entire countenance gleamed. His message was that our sins are forgiven us. We are to lift up our heads and rejoice because the Lord has accepted this house and His name shall be here. Then Moses appeared and he committed to us the keys for the gathering up of the children of Israel from the farthest parts of the earth, beginning with the tribes in the northernmost regions of the world, the Eskimos.

"Then Elias and Elijah told us that we have the keys for this dispensation committed to us. By this we are to know that the Great Day of the Lord is close at hand."

"Oh my!" Sally gasped on hearing the report. Relief flooded her face with color and brightness, and she touched a finger to the corner of her eye. Reports continued to circulate and magnify. Jenny was aware that she was not untouched by it all, but Sally's later question made her face the issue squarely.

Jenny and Sally were working in the spring-warmed garden, and Jenny was particularly aware of the texture and odor of the soil. Sally broke the calm. "Jen, not once have you commented on the dedication of the temple. I know you have a seeking mind. What did you think of it all? Do you believe it was a manifestation of God?"

In the moment of waiting, Jenny realized that this was the question that had burdened her since the event. Examining the evidence, she realized there was only one answer. Rocking back on her heels, she looked up at Sally. "Of course. How could I possibly think otherwise?" But the answer left her feeling empty.

During the following two months, Jenny was surprised to find that no one in Kirtland needed her services as a nurse. Sally advised her to not fret about it; possibly the Lord realized she needed a rest and was keeping the Saints well. Then with a stern eye lifted from her sewing she said, "I'd spend the time reading up in those books you told the Prophet you must read before joining the church. Jenny, I must warn you; the Lord won't be patient forever—especially since you have the witness."

Thus on a bright day in May, Jenny tucked the *Book of Mormon* and the *Book of Commandments* under her arm and set out for the woods. She carried several small muslin bags in the pocket of her apron, knowing she would spend most of the time enjoying the sunshine and searching for those special plants to dry and grind into powder for potions.

With her nose bent earthward, muttering the names of the plants she should seek, Jenny was mostly oblivious to the day and the beauty that surrounded her.

Her restless feet roamed back and forth across the trail which cut through the woods. The various paths joined the settled areas around Kirtland.

"Salsify, cinquefoil, bluebonnet, vitch," she was murmuring when a voice broke in upon her reverie.

"It's Jenny. I do declare." Jenny heard the melodious voice and raised her head to blink into the shadows, searching for the speaker. "From the looks of things I do believe you are searching for the secret ingredients. That means only one thing."

Jenny gasped. "Adela! It has been years since I've seen you, but I'd know you anywhere. You haven't changed."

"You've grown," the silky voice continued. Jenny sat down on the log beside the woman and studied her carefully. From the glossy hair streaming down her back to the smooth ivory of her skin, she was indeed, the same. But there was one difference: Adela was now wearing the modest dress and apron of a common housewife.

"You aren't wearing your beautiful red chiffon!" Jenny exclaimed. "What a disappointment!"

"You nearly surprised me once in my red chiffon."

Jenny studied the woman, "So that *was* you. I dared not hope. I tried to hail you." Jenny was silent a moment thinking of the cloaked woman coming out of Joseph's office.

Adela folded her arms. "So you weren't ready for the sabbat. You ran like a silly baby, leaving us all to think you a waste. You nearly ruined the whole evening. Only after a great deal of effort were we able to salvage the ceremony. We had to coax before the spirits would come back."

Speaking as if in a dream, Jenny murmured, "The townsmen were angry the next day when they found what you had done to the church."

"But you didn't tell." Adela was whispering, leaning close to scrutinize Jenny's face. Jenny was certain she read her inmost secrets, but perhaps Adela had known them all along.

"For a while I was afraid we had lost you to Mark. Jenny, you will be successful, and you can have anything or anyone except Mark. If you are determined to follow through now, determined to work for the power, I will help you. This time you must not fail. They will not take lightly any more of your broken promises. Do you have any idea what angry spirits do to faithless followers?"

She settled back on her log and waited for Jenny to speak. The horror of the sabbat was still vivid in Jenny's mind. Now her thoughts were flitting back and forth between the memory of that night and Adela's words. Despair filled Jenny, and only then did she realize she was still fighting that final step.

As if guessing, Adela spoke again. "We have been very patient. You know we have the right to demand your cooperation. You used us to your purposes, tampered with our power. Now you think you can claim power with Joseph's talisman as well as your own. Jenny, have all of your lessons been for nothing? You know the spirits respond only as you approach them in the proper way. You cannot demand power; you are a weakling.

"Only those who have worked hard will be granted the powers of the universe to command as they wish. Jenny, even I have not earned that right yet. You are only a poor little sorcerer, not even a real witch. We have been patient with your silly charms and pallid potions. Jenny, it's the sabbat or nothing."

Adela stood and paced with impatient quick steps before saying, "You began all this when you chose to read your father's book. Jenny, the next step is a pact with his Highness. When the new moon comes, I will see you right here."

Jenny covered her face with her hands. *Only two weeks are left before the new moon,* she thought. Jenny was flooded with the memories—wishing for another chance with Adela. Then she saw a picture of the silver chalice, surrounded by the heavy scent of fresh blood. Jenny slipped from the log. Only when her face felt the freshness of forest fern did she realize she had fainted.

The afternoon was far spent now, but Jenny continued to sit numbly until the cool breeze and the musty dampness forced her to her feet. With a sigh she stooped to pick up the Mormon books she had brought to read. Then suddenly caught by a new thought, she stared at them.

Both Tom and Andy had been filling her with glorious reports of power and mystery. Even before the dedication, there had been stories of visions and prophecies. Maybe the church was the way to gain the power she needed without going through the sabbat! Maybe Joseph knew the secrets, after all!

Carefully she knelt beside the log and tipped open the first book. Before she began to read, she recalled her past amusement and disbelief. But that was in the past. Trembling, eager now, her eyes skimmed the pages, searching for the secret of power, the kind of power Joseph had. And Adela. Surely that had been Adela in the office. She must be searching for power in the church, too.

When it was dark and she could no longer see the page before her, she sighed, stood up, and gathered her books.

Sally met her at the Morgans' back door. "Where have you been?" she cried. "We've been frantic."

Strangely detached, as if she no longer lived in her own body, Jenny eyed Sally's perturbed face. "Why do you carry on so? You act as fearful as if ghosts and goblins inhabited the woods." Sally's concern faded and questions grew in her eyes.

Feeling as dry and lifeless as Joseph's mummies, she prepared for bed. Only briefly did she wonder how Adela knew about everything, including Mark.

A week passed and a second was rapidly drawing to a close. One night Jenny stood at her window, looking down over the pale gleam of Kirtland, deeply conscious of the energy forces moving toward that time of the new moon. All nature seemed astir with the power. Night creatures rustled in the grasses. Far in the distance a wolf lifted his voice in a howl of desperation.

A brooding melancholy wrapped about Jenny. In one clear moment of illumination she saw her world's true state—without hope or comfort. "Powerless," she murmured into the night.

The moon was rising, and its heavy form seemed liquid and full of energy. Her eyes widened as she watched it; pulsing energy seemed to emanate from it. With a shiver she moved restlessly, but found herself unable to leave the window. Was moon energy surrounding her, holding her fast, striking off the minutes that remained? Had it staked a claim on her that she couldn't deny?

"Luna," she whispered, "every woman's friend—" Suddenly Adela's dark face and penetrating eyes seemed to sweep between Jenny and the moon.

The horror of the sabbat rose to overwhelm her. She pressed her hands over her eyes. "I can't, I just can't face that again." Even as she murmured the words, she shivered and wrapped her arms about herself, pressing Joseph's talisman between her breasts.

Slowly she dropped her arms and stared out into the night, now silent, cold, and powerless, as clouds slid over the moon. "It's an omen," she whispered. Her fingers reached to touch the metal disk, warm with the heat of her body. "It is an omen. God is telling me to escape Adela's terrible plan to force me to sell myself to Satan. Only with Joseph is there hope. Just like those men in the temple, I will have power. But there's another confirmation—Adela's secret. She's searching for more power, too, and she's doing it through joining Joseph's church."

27

THE DOOR TO Joseph's office stood open. Jenny, standing at the foot of the stairs, cocked her head and listened. The press was still and Oliver didn't seem to be around. Quickly and lightly she ran up the stairs.

Joseph's chair was tipped against the wall, his feet cushioned on the books and papers spread across his desk. His eyes were closed, and a wide grin covered his face. For a moment Jenny froze, unable to move. Unexpectedly her heart was pounding painfully hard, and it wasn't from the run up the stairs.

Dismayed, she recognized herself a captive of her own emotions. She trembled with the need to rush into his arms, to press her lips against that silly grin and bright hair.

Chewing her lip, she waited for her heart to slow. Once again she must face the questions that had been tearing her apart. Was there power to be had in the church, or was the idea a trick to force her to surrender that dearest dream?

She studied the face that was becoming as familiar as her own. For a fleeting moment, she wondered if the desire she possessed in reality possessed her. But she shrugged off the idea and clenched her fists. Power—it must be hers! Still she hesitated, poised to fly away from the resolution which had brought her here.

Could she trust this new promise of power through the church? The echo of Tom's entreaty to join the church thrust her into the room. She took one step, determining that if he did not hear her, it was to be an omen against joining the church.

Joseph's eyes popped open while chair and feet struck the floor. He recovered his composure, but papers and books slid to the floor at Jenny's feet.

She dropped to her knees to pick them up and he was beside her, his face nearly touching hers. His blue eyes were teasing, tempting. She rocked back on her heels and picked up a black leather book. "Holy Bible," she read, and looking up said, "My mother had one of these."

"Did you read it?"

"No. I was too busy sneaking my father's grimoire." She saw instantly that she needn't explain that a grimoire was a book of magic. He was grinning and shaking his head.

"And now you have so much power you are bringing my talisman back?"

"No, I've come to join the church." She watched the grin disappear. "You don't act too eager to have me."

He stood and walked back to his chair. "Tell me, Jenny, why do you wish to join?"

"Does it matter?" His eyes seemed to bore into hers, measuring, weighing. She knew hers were answering, but she didn't know what their promise was. Now his expression brightened, and she guessed he was pleased about something.

He chuckled. "So Jenny wants to be part of Zion's children. Tell me, was it the promises and the glory of the temple, or is it the enticement of some young man?"

"Of course it was the temple dedication," she answered lightly. From his expression she decided that he was encouraged. But she also knew there was an element in his expression that she couldn't fathom.

"Very well," he said, getting to his feet. "I'll put you on the roll right away."

"What do I have to do?" she asked in a playfully mocking tone. She saw the Bible. "Do you expect me to read that since I've not yet made it through the *Book of Mormon?*"

"No, that won't be necessary. You've only to be baptized at the first suitable time."

"Oh, don't trouble yourself," she said hastily. "I was baptized when I joined the Presbyterian church."

He shook his head, still slightly smiling. "Jenny, you don't understand. If you had bothered to read the *Book of Commandments,* you would have discovered the Lord's instruction."

"What do you mean?"

Picking up a book he began reading to her. "Revelation number twenty-three. The Lord has caused all past covenants to be done away, and even though you've been baptized a hundred times, it's worthless in this dispensation. Because of man's dead works, God needed to perform this new work. There's no other way, Jenny. This is the new and everlasting covenant. You must be baptized in the Church of the Latter-day Saints."

"Oh, all right; I suppose I'll survive another dipping." She turned impatiently toward the door.

"That isn't all, Jenny—" She turned back and saw his outstretched hand. "The talisman, Jenny. Give me the talisman."

She nearly walked out, but at that dark moment, the horror of the sabbat swept over her again and she felt those cold fingers clutching, demanding satisfaction. Still, she hesitated a long moment.

Slowly the rigid expression on Joseph's face gave way to a smile of satisfaction. With a sigh of resignation she said, "You must turn your back."

When she handed him the talisman, still warm from her body, he smiled. "Warm and sweet, like Jenny. That is a promise, isn't it?"

"I don't know what you mean," she said coolly. "I intend to be a good church member. I want all the—" She caught herself before she said *power.*

"My dear, I promise you, the women in my church will reap all the benefits of eternity, providing they are willing to follow the ordinances of the gospel."

Jenny walked slowly home, full of misgivings. She had gone expecting to come away victor, triumphant with the step which would release her into the realm of new power. Now she was feeling very much like the loser. The expression on Joseph's face stayed with her.

Briefly she thought of Emma and wondered how she was going to fit this new situation into her resolve to be the only Mrs. Smith. Would that most desperate measure, the waxen image, have to be utilized?

Jenny went out to tell her friends that she had joined the church. With the handshakes, hugs, and kisses, she was immediately drawn into an inner circle she didn't dream existed. Within a few weeks she discovered another benefit: once again she was being deluged with requests for her nursing services.

After one such week spent taking care of a newborn and his mother, Jenny returned to the Morgans' to find Andy at the kitchen table poring over his account ledgers.

"Jenny," he said. "I'm just sitting here seeing in these figures the picture of all that lies ahead of us. I can't get over it. The Lord is preparing to bless the Saints just as He has promised. Look, last year, just over here in Buffalo, people were spending $500 for an acre of land. This year the same acre is worth $10,000."

Jenny dropped her valise on the floor and gasped. "That much! How can people possibly buy?"

"They aren't. Right here in Kirtland the price of a lot has risen from $50 to $2,000. Even the farms next to us have gone from $10 or $15 an acre to $150. Joseph thinks it behooves us to hang on to the land with all our strength. Right now, if there's buying and selling, it's done in shares and with securities or notes."

She frowned at him. "Then we actually don't have money to buy and sell."

"No, we don't. That's why I say the Lord is *preparing* to bless us. This is just the leading edge of the blessings. We must be very wise and cautious right now."

He was silent and Jenny could see his agitation. "What is it, Andy?"

Andy looked up from the ledger. "Jenny, you are one of us now. Also, you are a very intelligent woman." For a moment Jenny nearly lost his words as she considered his description of her; then she heard, "It is no secret; our Prophet doesn't manage money well. He is impulsive and good-hearted. That kind of handling the finances will get us in a fix sooner or later. So I've been trying to get council to suggest we put Brigham Young in charge of the financial affairs, but not a man is willing to push the idea." He sighed heavily and stroked his beard. "We need to get a financial advisor or an attorney to come in and work with him."

He moved restlessly. "Trouble is, Joseph doesn't take kindly to the men under him lifting reins of responsibility. I guess I'll continue to search for a lawyer to come give me advice and work himself into Joseph's good graces."

A vision of Mark burst into Jenny's thoughts. Even as she recognized his suitability, she was recalling those last painful scenes with him. She winced and Andy saw it. "You don't agree?"

"I was thinking of a young man who seems ideal, but I was also wondering how I could avoid being involved in the situation."

Andy studied her thoughtfully, saying, "I wondered why an attractive young woman like you ignored the local swains. I understand. I'd be willing to give him a chance just for your sake, Jenny." She stared back at him, realizing explanations would only complicate matters.

He pulled a blank sheet of paper and picked up his pen. Lifting his head, he said, "Now, name and address, please."

Once alerted to the changing financial picture, Jenny began to see the events taking place in Kirtland with new eyes. Obviously the Saints were astir with the same money excitement that infused all the western United States.

Even Joseph Smith reacted to the excitement. He took to the auctioneer's block, and the Saints responded with enthusiasm. Under his hand, town lots were going from a hundred dollars to three and four thousand.

Some days Jenny joined the crowd just to feel the excitement and hear people's comments.

Emotions were riding high, and cautious ones said, "Doesn't seem proper for the Prophet to be buying and selling." The answer came back:

"The prosperity of the Lord is His blessing for being a good Mormon and keeping the ordinances of the Lord. What's more fittin' than for Joseph to help the Lord dish it out."

Jenny spent June with the Walker family. Matilda Walker had been ill with the summer fever, and it had taken all Jenny's skill with the charms and potions to nurse her back to health.

She left the Walkers with their praises ringing in her ears, but she also left exhausted, feeling as if life had been abandoned for the month's time.

As she often did after a nursing job, she stopped on her way through town to see Tom at the stables. She found him agitated and angry. "What's upsetting you?" she asked, settling herself beside the cold forge to watch him sort and clean his tools. When he raised his head she saw the tight, white line of anger around his mouth.

He continued to rattle his tools before replying. When he lifted his head again, he caught her gaze and held it. "How would you like an Indian for a sister-in-law?" She gasped and he added, "That's right. A plain old uncivilized squaw who can't even speak English."

"Tom, you're trying to shock me. If you choose to love an Indian, why, I'll accept her."

His face softened and he managed a crooked grin. "Sorry. I suppose the Lord is just trying my patience and willingness to obey the Prophet. Joseph's goin' to be sending me to Missouri right soon. And he's told me, since I'm not married, that I'm to marry an Indian when I get there. The Lord commanded that this be done. It's pleasin' to Him."

"I can't believe he intends you to just marry the first Indian you meet," Jenny soothed.

Tom snorted and flung a file to the trash heap. Looking at Jenny with a sheepish grin, Tom apologized, "I didn't mean to unload on you. It's just that some of these revelations try body and soul together. Jen, things are goin' bad in Missouri. I know Joseph is waitin' for direction before we all head west, but we can't go there until some of these troubles get solved."

"What's going on?" Jenny asked slowly.

"When the Saints were run out of Jackson County, most of them settled in Clay County, with the blessing of the residents. But now the same tide of feelin' is sweepin' Clay County; in short, we're not welcome there anymore.

"Joseph is aware of this. Just in March, he sent men to Missouri with fourteen hundred and fifty dollars to buy land up in the northern part.

"They say the land isn't as fair as the southern part of the state, but it must do, and it's cheaper. Jenny, the people are sufferin' for want of food and clothin' as well as freedom. I fear that any day now we're goin' to hear that the Missourians have run our people out of Clay."

Jenny listened and studied Tom's face. Puzzled by his rambling explanation, she began to realize he was talking over the whole situation in an effort to understand why Joseph was pressuring him.

Tom paused in his work. "There's that revelation sayin' the Indians will be white and delightsome when they accept the gospel. Joseph's obviously tryin' to hurry things along by havin' his men marry the natives."

"But you said the Lord promised blessing if you were to do so." Jenny watched his face twist. As she pondered that expression, she realized that for the first time, Tom's whole manner revealed a skepticism he wouldn't yet admit.

When she arrived home, Sally met her. "Oh my, does Andy ever have a surprise for you!"

Jenny frowned. "I can't even begin to guess."

"Is there anyone on earth you are terribly lonesome for?"

Jenny's mind immediately flooded with thoughts of Mark Cartwright, but she restrained herself. "I wasn't aware of being lonesome, but you've made me think. Does it have to do with the name I gave Andy?"

"Oh, shy one you are! Just for that, you'll wait." She gave Jenny a quick squeeze and went to rescue her crying child.

Jenny carried her valise upstairs to her room. After settling her clothes in their proper place, she opened the window and leaned far out. Soft breezes wafted woody perfume from the trees pressing the fringes of the Morgans' property. The late June air bore the scent of every growing thing imaginable, and Jenny was overwhelmed with the need to be out of the house and among the trees.

For one moment, as she started for the stairs, she hesitated. Not since her last encounter with Adela, just before she joined the church, had she walked in the woods, nor had she again met Adela. Jenny shivered. Despite her best resolve, the memory of that one sabbat still invaded her dreams.

But the call of the woods won out and Jenny fled toward their serenity, wandering carefree and nearly happy. As the afternoon wore on, Jenny gathered mint and wildflowers as an excuse to barter time alone.

Jenny relaxed, forgetting her initial reluctance to enter the woods and the afternoon passed. In a dreamy mood she circled deeper into the trees. The sun-warmed air softened and sweetened with new smells as she walked around the moist swamplands.

Jenny didn't realize she was lost until she spied the little log cabin just beyond the marshy meadow. Stopping to study the building, she tried to guess where she was. As she peered at the cabin, the outline of a tall man was visible in the doorway. "Well, at least it is inhabited," she murmured, looking around to get her bearings.

Jenny tried to retrace her steps, but discovered the lush undergrowth hid the trail and familiar landmarks.

When frogs began their evening chorus, she turned and fled toward the cabin. She was muttering to herself, "Be grateful that Adela can't see you now. Fine witch you are! You can't even find your way home, let alone call down the powers."

The cabin was just across a marshy section, and she had to plunge through ankle-deep water to reach it. When she was nearly to the door, Joseph stepped out onto the stoop. He was pulling on his coat, and he stiffened when he saw her.

"Jenny Timmons, what are you doing here?" For a moment Jenny was surprised and distracted by the hard expression in his eyes. As she searched for words, the conviction that he suspected her of spying swept across her.

"I—I—" she shuttered and then laughed, "Oh, Joseph. I'm not trying to discover all those secret things you men are supposed to talk about when the women aren't around. I'm lost." She pointed to muddy boots. He studied her for a moment, then swung the door open.

"Come in. You'll find nothing more interesting than a quiet spot where we men have our prayer meetings." The one room was plainly furnished with a cot, a table, and a scattering of chairs. "I would offer you tea, but I have none," he said. "There's not even a fire, but you could rest for a moment before I send you on your way.

"Jenny, I have meant to talk to you. It has been a month since you joined the church. We need to have you baptized, and I haven't seen you in meeting."

"I've been nursing again," she explained, and saw his quick frown.

"That also merits some discussion," he added with a nod. "I've been hearing more about your charms and amulets and all the potions you use."

Jenny sat down on the chair Joseph indicated, accepted the towel he offered, and wiped her feet.

"It smacks a little of witchcraft," he said slowly as he continued to watch her. "But anything that keeps down the fever will be demanded by the people. I can't complain unless you go into competition with me."

She stared at him hard, trying to understand what he meant. He was beginning to relax, and the grin on his face became friendly. Abruptly he crossed the room to her chair and squatted close to her. "Jenny, tell me the real reason you wanted to join the church."

Shaking her head and looking away from him, all those visions of the sabbat filled her mind. She put the towel aside and looked up. The expression on his face was changing and his eyes glowed with a sweetness she didn't understand.

"Dear Jenny," he said. He took her hands and lifted her up. With his hands on her shoulders, he held her only inches away from him. The unexpected touch left her nearly swooning, unable to think of anything except his closeness.

Now he was saying, "You don't have to explain. I know. Jenny, I want you to realize that I understand you better than you do yourself. Do you trust me enough to follow all the directions from the Lord without question? During the next few years, the Lord will reveal many marvelous things to us." His voice dropped to a whisper as he said, "Trust me. I'll have you yet."

She was wondering whether she had heard correctly. But just as her foolish heart began its hurried, hopeful beat, his words snapped her to attention. "Jenny, one of the first responsibilities you have in your new church is to get married."

The room spun; she couldn't believe her ears. Woodenly she said, "Married? I don't want to marry, I—" She shut her hasty lips before they betrayed her. Disappointment flooded through her. His new command made her realize that his past caresses meant nothing. Her back stiffened and her chin lifted. Plainly, he was saying that those kisses had been an impulsive liberty; this was his signal that they had best be forgotten. "Joseph, church is one thing and a person's love life is another," she said frostily.

"You don't understand, Jenny. All the revelations haven't yet been written down and presented to the people, but God is making it very clear to me that it is His will for marriage to be the basis for a new and everlasting covenant in the hereafter. You see, we are not to be just human. Through His provision of exaltation, we shall become as He is right now. With kingdoms and powers, we shall possess more earths than you've ever dreamed about."

His voice deepened. "There are spirits already waiting in the spirit world. We need to provide bodies for them. That's part of our mission here and now. Together with them, we'll inhabit new worlds. Later, one of the most important teachings in the church will be about marriage. For now, the only thing you need know is that God wills you to be married."

Jenny was filled with the shock of Joseph's proclamation as he guided her to the right path and walked through the woods with her. Only when Jenny saw the lights of the Morgans' kitchen was she able to salvage her composure.

As she hurried toward the house, one word Joseph had said rang through her mind. *Power*—that word made all the difference in the world.

She forced a cheerful smile and opened the back door into the house. Mark was there. Slowly the events of the afternoon receded, like a dark stormcloud pushed by the wind. Against that backdrop, Mark was an oasis. She found herself clinging to his hand as she studied every familiar feature of his face.

It was easy to say, "Mark, it is good to see you. I'd not realized just how good it possibly could be." When she saw the flush of pleasure on his face, the wounds inflicted by the afternoon began to heal.

28

DURING JULY, SALLY determined to further the courtship of Mark and Jenny. At the same time Andy set out to make Mark into a financial advisor acceptable to Joseph and the first presidency. Jenny watched with amusement as the tug-of-war for Mark's attention lurched back and forth.

But Jenny had to admit, even secretly, that she had expected Mark to press his suit immediately, since it was obvious she was responsible for his being in Kirtland. To Jenny's confusion and even dismay, Mark was seldom at the Morgan residence except to consult with Andy. Even Sally's frequent dinner invitations didn't cause him to linger long in the soft summer evenings.

While Jenny was secretly troubled, Sally's annoyance boiled over one evening. After Mark and Andy escaped the house immediately after dinner, Sally shook the butcher knife she had been drying and exclaimed, "Do you have any idea of what you are getting yourself into? That Mark is not good husband material. Why I picked someone like Andy, who loves work more than wife, I'll never know. Haven't you taken lessons from the Morgan household?"

Suddenly she burst into tears, and Jenny's indulgent chuckle died away. "Oh, Sally! I'm sorry to take your problem so lightly. I didn't realize you felt this way about Andy being gone so much."

Sally blew her nose and wiped at her eyes. "It's all right," she muttered, shamefaced. "I'm angry because he carried off Mark right after dinner again."

Try as she might to forget the problem, Sally's words had an effect. As the days passed, Jenny's irritation over Mark's neglect developed into full-blown hurt. Jenny knew of no way around the problem, and the matter might have hung there in limbo if it hadn't been for another meeting with Joseph.

The day Tom was to leave for Missouri, Jenny had gone to the stables to bid him good-bye. Watching his gloomy face as he tightened the last pack on his horse, she said, "You know, you don't have to go. You are free to do as you wish about this whole affair, including marrying an Indian woman."

He looked at her, and she noticed the thinness of his features. "You are mistaken," he said shortly. "Joseph holds the keys of the kingdom. He is to be as God to us. Not one of us will reach heaven in the hereafter without his approval."

"Maybe heaven isn't that important," Jenny said slowly.

His hands stilled on the straps, and he looked at her in surprise. "Jenny, I don't think you have any understanding of hell. It's—"

With a half-laugh, she interrupted him, "I only fear things that go bump in the night. Besides, a good God wouldn't send people to hell."

Soberly he said, "I heard someone say God doesn't send us to hell; we send ourselves."

Later Jenny walked down the street, thinking about Tom's statement. Old Mr. Lewis was sitting in front of Whitney's store, whittling, and she stopped to watch. After more strokes with the knife, a whistle emerged from the wood. He brushed the last shaving of wood from it, put it to his lips and blew. The sound was surprisingly shrill. She watched him hand the toy to the little boy at his elbow.

Jenny thought, *It would be nice to whittle like that on my mind. I've a feeling that after stripping away the wood there'd be something completely different than I guessed.*

She continued on her way, her thoughts drifting to Mark and how she had responded to his presence in Kirtland. How strange, after months of being aware only of Joseph, she felt pulled asunder by Mark's neglect!

Suddenly Joseph was in front of her and he took her arm. "*Miss* Jenny Timmons, still, I presume. I will have a word with you in my office." She followed him meekly and stood beside his desk as he took his place.

"I understand that you knew Mark Cartwright before he came to Kirtland. Is that true?" She nodded. "I like the man; he's honest and I think he'll make a good Mormon."

"Mark has a mind of his own; he will be hard to win to your church. You've forgotten that he was in South Bainbridge."

He ignored her statement and promptly continued. "Jenny, since you seem unable to settle on any of the lads in Kirtland, I suggest you marry young Cartwright and bring him into the church. It will be a good union, and we'll be pleased to have him as a member."

"Just like that," she snapped bitterly. "Joseph Smith, you can't order people around in this fashion!"

He was still smiling pleasantly. "Oh yes, I can. You are forgetting who you are talking to." He paused and then, holding her eyes with his own, he added slowly and deliberately, "Jenny, I am the greatest prophet ever arisen. I am as good as Jesus Christ. Don't ever forget that again. When I speak, I speak by the power of the Holy Ghost. Your place is to obey." He got to his feet.

"Remember, Jenny, joining the church was your idea, not mine. Now you are expected to obey—unless you have apostasy in mind." He remained silent for a moment, waiting for her response.

Apostasy. The ultimate sin. She looked up at him, stunned by his statement. Images and word fragments piled up in her mind: the sun throwing blinding purple spears against the silver chalice filled with wine. *Jesus, the light of the world. He who has the Son has life. Baptized in death, raised to life.* But those words out of the past didn't spark her to life, not the way Joseph did. Now caught, looking deep into his eyes, she was conscious that she must please this man if she were to have faith. Faith, not power? Faith was the route to power that Lucy Harris offered her so long ago. Now Joseph, too, was speaking of faith, but the word seemed dry and dusty. Must power always give way to faith?

Now his voice was gentle. "I don't think Mark will refuse you. How could any man?" She started to leave. "Remember, urge him to join the church."

That word *apostasy* still vibrated through Jenny, and she found herself wondering why suddenly she was filled with the same dread she had seen in others at the mention of the word.

Within twenty-four hours, Mark appeared for dinner again. This time Sally waved the butcher knife at her husband, and with a laugh he tucked her hand under his arm, saying, "I shall lose my scalp if I fail to walk Sally and Tamara to the river."

When the door closed, Mark was silent. Jenny stood watching him, aware of the gulf that separated them. Now he was only a quiet, distant friend. How could she admit to him the strange yearnings she was having? How could she have taken the sweet things that had budded between them, stifle the life out of them, and then hope for a word to change it all?

Jenny moved, putting the kitchen back into order while she searched for words. Each time she passed Mark, she dropped pleasant words and received back his monosyllables.

Suddenly she circled the table and sat across from Mark. Smiling at him, she said, "Do you remember what it was like when we were snowed in?" He looked squarely at her and for just a moment, she saw the pain in his eyes before he readied the smile and opened his mouth to give a teasing reply.

Shaking her head she put out her hand to stop him. "Don't, Mark." He waited and she sighed, hunting for words. Her impatience broke through and she leaned toward him. "Mark, will you marry me?" The slender wooden spoon he held snapped and he looked at it in amazement.

She couldn't leave false impressions. "I've become a member of the church and Joseph Smith says I must marry. He says the new dispensation requires marriage to be an important part of the church."

"And you can find no other to marry you?"

She shook her head vigorously. "I *want* no other."

"What must I do?"

Of course Mark would ask that. His attorney's mind was always searching for facts. "Join the church."

"Joseph must want my services badly if he's reduced to bribing me. But I find it nearly impossible to resist the bribe."

"Nearly?" Jenny's hands were trembling and she didn't know whether she felt anger or some other emotion. She got to her feet and turned away from the table. "Sally won't be happy about the broken spoon. It was her favorite."

"Jenny, come here." When she turned he was standing and all that teasing laughter had disappeared from his eyes. She came, shyly. His strong warm hand lifted her chin and caressed it as he looked into her eyes. Gently his lips touched hers, he waited for her response before wrapping his arms about her.

When he raised his head, he clasped her face between his two warm hands. "I knew it; I was so sure," he murmured, kissing her again. She was reaching too, straining toward his lips, his arms.

Finally she remembered to ask. Loathe to leave his arms, she leaned back to see his face. "What did you know?"

"That you love me." His fingers explored the contour of her face. Just before he kissed her eyelids, she saw the expression in his eyes.

She was trembling as she pressed her face against his shoulder. *This was Mark revealed, not minding that she saw the tears. This was her Mark, that splendid gentleman acting as if she had just crowned him king.*

His voice was husky. "I'd join every church in America if it would bring me you."

He held her close. In the moment of silence Jenny began to feel the impact of her hasty proposal. He raised his face and said, "There's one thing. My mother lives only a day's journey from here, but she is unable to travel. I want her to meet you now and witness our marriage. Will you come home with me to the family farm to be married? And soon?"

Startled, Jenny leaned back to study his face. Was he fearful even now? There was a shadow in his eyes, dark but quickly fleeing. Was he remembering her long-ago statement, the time just before she left Cobleskill when she had told Mark she didn't know what love was?

He stirred uncomfortably and quickly Jenny replied, "Yes, of course I'll come." The dark shadow was gone as tenderness and joy lighted his face.

Hot tears burned Jenny's eyes. Even as his hand touched hers again and she was filled with the desire to run into his arms, she began to tremble over the irrevocable step she had taken.

Jenny was painfully conscious that the old dream still existed, the one that had sent her fleeing from Mark. "Mark," she whispered, "what am I doing to you? You are the best friend I've ever had. You deserve so much more than—than *Jenny, the kit*—"

His hand covered her mouth. "You'll not say that again." She could see his command was delivered with love, and fresh guilt swept over her. She sighed, recalling the conclusion she had reached as the stagecoach had sped down the road toward Kirtland, Ohio: If she loved Mark, then she loved two men.

Briefly she closed her eyes against the pain, and then she remembered Joseph's statement. She was marrying Mark because Joseph commanded it. The cold facts surrounding that final scene in the cabin with Joseph had stripped away any possibility of that old dream coming true. That dream was in ashes. Once again she was filled with the sure knowledge that she must do as Joseph commanded.

Jenny felt Mark's hand against her face, and once again she opened her eyes to see the love in his eyes. She reminded herself of how much this was meaning to Mark. She was *his* dream come true.

She brushed away the guilty knowledge that she was cheating him, offering only a fragmented love. As she hesitated before lifting her face for his kisses, once again she wondered why his touch left her trembling and yearning.

In the short week before Jenny and Mark left for Cleveland to be married, they searched for a house for the two of them and made arrangements to have furniture delivered.

Jenny was there on the day the wagons arrived with the load of new furniture. While she was watching the little house become a home, Jenny suddenly realized their whispered plans were taking on the shape of reality. This was the house in which *she* would be mistress.

She washed the new flower-sprigged china and smoothed the linens on their shelves. As she shifted Mark's new chair nearer the kitchen stove, she was reminding herself that soon she would be this man's wife.

Slowly she sat down in the chair to think about it. *A marriage means a husband, children.* Caught up in the issue of obeying the Prophet, she hadn't really considered what all was involved in this marriage.

Now she was seeing Mark's clear, steady eyes and feeling the weight of responsibility. Didn't she now owe more to Mark than she did the Prophet? *God.* Where did God count in all of this? Jenny's thoughts drifted back to her mother, seeing her with that black Book she had duti-fully carried to meetings in Manchester. *Grace.* Jenny smiled.

Mark came into the kitchen. "Why are you smiling?"

"I was thinking about home. Ma took me to camp meetings services when we first moved to Manchester. The preacher was talking about grace, and I said I'd like Ma to name the baby Grace. She had another boy."

Mark said, as he looked approvingly around the room, "Grace, that's the religion the other churches preach. You're saved by grace, not works. I guess I'm glad you're Mormon."

"Why?"

"You have a reason for marrying me."

"Mark!" She stopped abruptly and then added, "Will that ruin every-thing?"

"No. I'll take any excuse for marriage, but I intend for us to have a *good* marriage."

Mark paid the lorry driver and watched him leave before picking up the conversation again. Jenny watched Mark walk around the house, looking at it all. His eyes reflected the thoughts she was having. Jenny was consid-ering all those things marriage meant as Mark pressed her hand against his face and kissed the palm.

Jenny felt something nearly like a prayer of gratitude. Those dark, shad-owy dreams of Joseph had not become reality, and suddenly that was very important.

In a moment she spoke hesitantly, "I'm beginning to get the shivers. Mark, we're going to be a family. That's important to me." She studied his face, wondering about the real feelings buried in the usually light-hearted Mark.

She took a deep breath, saying, "You've talked about your family, and I find that scary. How will I ever live up to it all? The expectations of your mother . . ."

Mark was very sober as he took her hand and led her to the bench beside the kitchen window. "I guess I haven't been thinking that far in advance either. Just the now." Slowly he added, "Perhaps its best for us to forget our families and concentrate on building our own life together."

She had to say it: "You know how important this new church is to me." Jenny looked out the window as she added, "Will it mean that much to you?"

Mark hesitated before answering, "I've never given church much thought. But I've always assumed it would have its place. Right now I'm thinking any church is as good as the next." Back in character, he gave a quick grin.

Jenny was bringing back fragments of thought, needing to put words to them for the first time as she brooded over the troubling thoughts of God. Almost, she could hear and see that camp meeting: *the wages of sin, the gift of God.* "Always it seems there's been this big hole in my life," she said in a low voice. Mark sobered again as he saw how serious she was. "For a time I thought it was because we were poor and Pa didn't have much time for us young 'uns. But lately, since I've been grown, I wonder if it isn't a deep-down need to line myself up with religion just so I can know about God."

Mark's face was thoughtful as he leaned over to kiss her cheek. "You make me ashamed of taking this too lightly. I wasn't raised that way."

"What do you mean?"

"The search for God. Without a doubt man knows there's a quest. Jenny, I promise you, I'll join you." He pulled her to her feet, saying, "Right now I'm just grateful we'll have the rest of our lives—together."

Both hope and unrest stirred deep within her as she stared into Mark's eyes. *Can anyone really know God?* she wondered. *Can I?* She leaned her head briefly on Mark's shoulder. Where would her search take her? Take them?

Mark hugged Jenny. "We'll find God—I'm sure we will."

STAR
LIGHT,
STAR
BRIGHT

INTRODUCTION

IN THE FIRST book of this trilogy, *The Wishing Star,* Jenny Timmons, "nearly twelve—come January," is living in South Bainbridge, New York. Her family is poor, and except for the green book, life holds little excitement or interest.

Then Jenny's best friend, her brother Tom, introduces Jenny to his new friend, Joe Smith, a fascinating youth whose ideas about life seem to parallel the discoveries she has made through reading the forbidden green book. Intrigued by the mystery surrounding Joe and Tom, Jenny is determined to insert herself in the middle of their fascinating enterprises. While Jenny struggles with her world, Joseph Smith provides South Bainbridge with a new touch of excitement. Even from those early years, people either loved or hated Joseph.

Within the year, Jenny's father gives in to his yearning to go west. The family moves to Manchester, New York, the first leg of the westward trek.

That year, Tom becomes a stable-hand, working for a man named Martin Harris. After one happy year, Pa's feet begin to itch again, and in the process of packing the wagon to move, Pa finds Jenny reading his forbidden book. When the wagon leaves, Tom and Jenny remain behind, both working for Martin Harris—Tom in the stables and Jenny as the hired girl. And Pa's green book stays behind as well—stolen by Jenny and hidden away for safekeeping.

Manchester is a small town, nestled close to Palmyra, New York. At school, and at the Presbyterian church on Sunday, Jenny becomes acquainted with the Smith youngsters and their parents. She develops a fondness for Lucy Smith. Once again the threads of life stretch between Jenny and Joseph Smith.

But one of those threads has been snapped. When Jenny had first met Joseph Smith, she had vowed to marry him. Now her girlish dreams of romance are terminated when Joseph Smith takes Emma Hale as his wife.

For a short period of time, Joseph and Emma live in Palmyra, New York. During this time, Martin Harris becomes involved with Joseph, and the rumors grow. Talk of the Gold Bible Company and other mysterious events surround the lives of the Smith family.

Jenny's life in Manchester becomes filled with excitement and trauma. Martin Harris' strange beliefs and uncontrolled anger rise to a climax. When he sells his farm in order to finance the printing of the gold Bible, his wife Lucy resists him, and he responds in rage, beating both her and Jenny.

Thus Jenny and Tom Timmons find themselves without employment.

Befriended by Mark Cartwright, a young man Jenny and Tom first met in South Bainbridge, New York, at the time of Joseph's first trial, the brother and sister go to eastern New York State. But soon Tom's restless feet lead him after his friend, Joseph Smith.

Jenny stays behind as a hired girl, and finds security and the promise of power in the forbidden green book she took from Pa.

Her fascination and curiosity with the book send her delving into the occult. Jenny still believes herself in control of her life, but desires born back in South Bainbridge days begin manifesting themselves in strange ways.

As Jenny matures, the choices she makes include a search for secret power, leading her to Kirtland, Ohio, to a prophet, her old friend, Joseph Smith.

Jenny becomes a follower of this new church. In time she learns that Joseph's control over his people extends even into their personal lives. Joseph instructs her to ask Mark Cartwright to marry her. And she obeys.

1

THE BUGGY WAS finally moving along rapidly. Since Mark and Jenny had left Kirtland early in the morning, every buggy and wagon in the Cleveland area seemed to conspire to bog them in traffic forever. Each mile that brought them closer to Cleveland had added more vehicles to the road.

Now they both breathed a sigh of relief as their path turned away from the wharf and meandered down country lanes. Overhead trees sheltered their way with shade. With the absence of shouting men, clanging bells and snorting horses, they began to relax. Bawling peddlers and angry wagoneers behind them, Mark sighed with relief and settled back to allow the horses to pick their own pace.

Now Jenny felt his warm glances, and saw the pleased grin. But the high tide of emotion she was feeling kept her silent. It had been early dawn when they self-consciously faced each other. There had been a moment of panic as Mark helped her into the buggy; just knowing this was *the* day made Jenny pause, fighting the impulse to run and hide. How badly she wanted once again to hear Mark's assurance that his mother would *really* be pleased that they were marrying! Still trying to hide the tumble of strange new emotions, Jenny was only shy, while Mark was proud, rightfully possessive.

Through the silence Jenny was doubly aware of the rhythm of the horses' hooves clicking against the hard-packed earth; it was the only sound on this quiet road. At the start of the day, Jenny had been full of chatter and laughter. She guessed Mark knew that her mood was designed to hide her real thoughts. Not all of those thoughts were to be shared, though, and eventually they had lapsed into the present silence.

Jenny studied Mark out of the corner of her eye. The sun picked out copper glints in his hair and illuminated the broad shoulders of the well-tailored suit. A gentleman. Jenny looked down at her dress, one she had made herself. *Kitchenmaid.* She winced painfully, suddenly wondering if she shouldn't be back where she belonged. Surely that was anywhere but here!

Abruptly, scenes from the South Bainbridge days filled her thoughts: the shabby shack, Pa and Ma, all the young'uns, and not enough milk to go around. She thought of Jenny and Nancy, of their faded dresses lined against Prue's daffodil yellow. And she remembered Joe Smith, the diggings, and the green book of Pa's. How could she have dared involve Mark Cartwright in all this?

She chewed at her lip, trying desperately, even now, to find an excuse to run away from it all. But even as she thought that perhaps Mrs. Cartwright would take one look and send her packing, Jenny realized how badly she wanted to marry this man.

She was taking a deep, shaky breath when Mark reached for her hand and gave it a gentle tug. "I'm glad I don't have to meet *your* mother today. She'd probably say I'm not good enough for her daughter."

"Oh, Mark!" Was he guessing how she felt? Suddenly she could face him, and the expression in his eyes was reassuring.

He teased, "There's not another person on this road; please prove you are real, not a pretty dream to vanish when I blink my eyes."

"Mark, you are silly, not the least like a dignified attorney at all."

"It's taken this long for you to discover the fact?" Now she saw his eyes were serious, but he was still tugging at her hand. "Since we left Kirtland this morning, you've been as wide-eyed as little Jenny with her nose pressed to the window of the candy shop."

Jenny winced. How it hurt to be reminded of those South Bainbridge days. Looking up at him she said slowly, "Mark, I am. I'm even fearful. What am I doing to you?"

"What will your mother think of me?" It was a whisper.

"You'll find that out in less than an hour." His voice was confident, "I don't think she'll be disappointed." Mark studied her for another moment before he turned to point the whip to the north. "You'd never guess, but just beyond that line of trees is the biggest body of water you've ever seen."

But Jenny would not be distracted. Her voice was brooding as she said, "There are disadvantages to marrying a man who has known you since you were a little tyke. Mark, you needn't remind me there will be no surprises in our marriage. You know me too well."

For a moment his face was still, and then she saw a hint of shadow in his eyes. "I only wish I did. Jenny, I sense I'll never be certain of knowing you completely. Life will always be full of surprises with you, I'm guessing. I hope I prove nimble enough to keep up with you." He was teasing again, and his smile was warm. With a quick grin his mood changed, "Little owl eyes, look yonder—that is the beginning of the Cartwright acres."

"All of this?" Jenny turned wondering eyes back to Mark. He saw again that expression, the little-kitchenmaid one.

"Jenny, don't forget, you are now a part of the Cartwright family—at least you will be just as soon as we can get that preacher to come listen to us promise to love and honor each other for the rest of our lives."

He brushed his lips across her cheek, and she blinked tears out of her eyes as she smiled up at him. "Mark, I will love belonging to you, but not because your family has more acres than I've ever ridden across." Her voice was wistful as she touched his face. "It's all like a dream. And I didn't really think I'd ever be in the middle of the dream."

Later, Mark's mother held her face and kissed her. When she felt Mrs. Cartwright's tears, Jenny, with a shock, saw herself unworthy and guilty; and the emotion had nothing to do with Mark's wealth.

With his mother's words, in one bewildered moment, Jenny discovered herself to be sailing under a false banner. *Strange,* she thought as the woman talked, *never before have I seen myself in just this light.* With difficulty she forced herself to smile as Mrs. Cartwright held her away to study her face. Would she guess her averted eyes were more than shyness?

The woman continued, "Jenny, you'll never know how I've prayed for this day." The fragile white-haired woman whispered, "My son is twenty-seven years old, and I had begun to think I wouldn't live to know his wife and children."

Later, over tea in the parlor, Jenny tried to act calm and relaxed. Mark and his mother, pointing to an alcove lined with windows, talked about candles and flowers and music, while Jenny's thoughts churned on. Mrs. Cartwright had *prayed* for a wife for Mark. She, Jenny, was that answer.

He had called her, with a bit of awe in his voice, a fine Christian lady. Right now Jenny was having difficulty swallowing the tea; her thoughts were on the green book of magic, the charms, the talisman she wore hidden in the folds of her dress. She nearly choked on the tea as she visualized the horror on Mrs. Cartwright's face were she to hear Clara advising Jenny to build the waxen figure of Emma Smith and insert the pins.

Mark and his mother returned to the tea table. Sentiment was forgotten now as Mrs. Cartwright, her eyes bright with curiosity, surveyed Jenny over the top of her teacup and asked, "Your parents?"

Jenny was shaking her head and explaining. For a moment she was caught by the picture of her mother in these surroundings. The mental image left her with an aching heart.

But Mrs. Cartwright was moving on. "Tell me about your home. Do you have brothers and sisters? I assume you attended church." While Jenny struggled over the necessary answers, Mrs. Cartwright continued talking, her brow furrowed as if her own problem of explanation was too great. "When Mark was tiny, I gave him to God. See, Jenny, I had a dream of having my son measure up to the best that God expected of him."

Something in her eyes sought confirmation; Jenny was left wondering how she could hope to be that best. Looking into the candid eyes of Mrs. Cartwright, she desperately wanted to reassure her. Jenny searched for words, but the only words she could find were the ones she had already decided mustn't be said around Mark: *power, talisman, charms, grimoire.*

The contrast startled Jenny. She looked at Mark, suddenly realizing the width of the gulf between them. Was she sentencing herself to a lifetime of constantly guarding her tongue? As she studied the face that had become dear and familiar, Adela's words echoed through her: *Anything except Mark.* Jenny's fingers tightened around the handle of the teacup and then relaxed. *Remember, Jenny,* she advised herself, *you've chosen Joseph's way, not Adela's.*

Mrs. Cartwright was still talking about God, and with amusement Jenny decided she was trying to cover life with one cozy blanket. Jenny needn't tell her that she didn't like the blanket, and besides, she had discovered long ago that the blanket of faith had holes in it.

Jenny settled herself to listen to the story. Mark's grandfather and even his great-grandfather were Methodist preachers. "We've always been a Bible-believing and practicing people. I want to see it carried down into your generation." She gave a gentle shiver. "There's so much abroad today that is anti-God. It seems as if in these past ten years people have turned restless, searching for something more than old-time religion. I pray that the spirit of revival will sweep this nation. There is the potential; we're seeing a new breed of men coming into the pulpit."

Abruptly Mark took notice. "Is that so? To whom are you referring?"

She was nodding with enthusiasm as she replied. "I was specifically referring to young Charles Finney. He's advocating a deeper life, deriding the trend toward religion that's all show. He's asking for a heart-changing experience with God. If it will happen, this nation can be changed in every area, from the social to the governmental." She stopped abruptly and Jenny saw the touch of sadness in her eyes as she watched her son stir impatiently.

Before Jenny could leave the room, she had to ask, "You believe God changes hearts? How people think and feel, and even act?" Mrs. Cartwright nodded, but Jenny could ask no more.

The next day Jenny stood at her bedroom window and decided that the Cartwright home was mellow like Mrs. Barton's fruitcake: perfect, opulent. Her troubled eyes swept over the scene, and she remembered her own corn bread beginnings.

Thinking back to yesterday, she breathed a sigh of relief. She might have been forced to give detailed explanations, but Mrs. Cartwright had kindly accepted her fumbling answers without further questions.

The Cartwright home was quiet and green, away from the noisy waterfront and the bustle of town. The estate, from the stately old oak trees to the stone-and-timber home, looked settled and peaceful, as if it had always been part of the landscape.

With a sigh Jenny shook her head and moved away from the window. She still wondered why a man like Mark noticed her, why he had allowed himself to be talked into marrying her.

Briefly she touched the talisman pinned securely into the waistband of her dress. Could that metal be responsible, or was Mark simply too much of a gentleman to say no? She was still pondering her dark thoughts when she heard a tap at the door.

Mrs. Cartwright came into the room followed by a wide-eyed young girl carrying a dress in its dust cover. Jenny found herself studying the awkward, poorly dressed girl, seeing the awe on her face and the expression of defeat. For a moment Jenny pressed her fingers to her eyes. It was like looking at the young Jenny, and the picture was painful.

"Jenny," Mrs. Cartwright said softly, "I know you've had little opportunity to shop for a wedding gown. When I wore this dress I dreamed of the daughter I would have and who would someday wear it. Mark's baby sister died before her first birthday. I don't insist that you wear the dress, but if you would like to wear it, it is yours. If you were to wear it, I would be completely happy on your wedding day." Touching her fingertips to her eyes, she turned and left the room.

Completely? The hard, sore spot around Jenny's heart softened.

The following Sunday Jenny again stood at her bedroom window, marveling at the scene before her. How could this great assembly of people and those tremendous quantities of food have been summoned within a week's time?

Walking gracefully down the curving staircase, wearing Mrs. Cartwright's lace gown, squeezing the cascading bouquet of yellow roses against her pounding heart, Jenny paused on the stairs. The hallway below was a sea of strange but friendly faces tipped upward, smiling and nodding. They clustered after her as she went into the parlor where Mark waited to take her hand.

She faced the solemn, graying man with piercing eyes who would seal her fate with Mark's. For a moment she trembled. Mark's hand, steady and warm, linked her with life and response and reality.

The minister declared, "It is before this group as witness, in the presence of the great eternal God, that we meet together to join this man and woman together in holy matrimony. Marriage, holy, ordained by God, is to be maintained as a sacred trust between these two people."

The vows she pledged under Mark's serious gaze became weighted with meaning that grew, doubling and tripling in strength until she felt the vows amplified to the very heavens. Her whispered promises were, to her, shouts of eternal declaration, binding Jenny with cords of integrity when she didn't know the meaning of the word. Caught up, knowing only that she was partner in a holy act, she faced Mark and murmured, "I pledge you my love, my honor."

Astonished, she watched and listened to Mark. With tears in his eyes, he promised to love and care for her as long as she lived. For one swift second her father's face seemed to rise up between the two of them. Trembling, she knew herself to be at the terrible mercy of this man.

At the reception, she lifted a fragment of wedding cake to his lips, and the glow of the golden wedding ring flashed between their eyes. His eyes were sparkling with joy, and she carefully smeared icing on the end of his nose. Amid the laughter, Attorney Cartwright transferred the icing to her cheek, and the specter of Jenny's father disappeared forever.

"A hurried wedding I will tolerate gladly, lest you change your mind," Mark had said, "but a leisurely wedding trip I will not forego." He had promptly booked passage on a lake steamer for a two-week trip around Lake Erie.

When Mark and Jenny returned home to Kirtland, Ohio, still basking in the glow of their honeymoon, they were amazed to find their previous world unchanged. And while Jenny dreamed about her house and cooked meals for her husband, Mark faced the world to which he had been innocently summoned.

Because Mark was Mark, firmly believing with his lawyer's mind that black was black and white only white, Jenny was called upon to share his feelings and be a sounding board for his questions as he explored the thought and structure of this new world—the Mormons.

During one of those early dinners, after he had remarked on the fine roast, he said, "Just today I found the Prophet has gone to Salem, Massachusetts."

"Whatever for? Salem is a strange place for him to be."

"There seems to be a bit of secrecy involved. Some say it's a missionary trip and that he's taken men with him. Andy is disturbed."

"Oh, you've seen Sally?"

"No, just her husband. Jenny, you smell better than the apple pie."

"Must you go out tonight?"

"No, of course not." Jenny touched his face. *Sally was mistaken,* she thought, *when she said Mark was not good husband material.* But she wistfully admitted that this perfect moment wouldn't last forever.

As the days of September gradually became more golden, their marriage mellowed and became more precious.

Though her happiness seemed a steady and constant thing, at times she felt the frightening edge of uncertainty. Jenny had erected barriers in her life because of the nameless dread. The barrier she was least willing to explain was her reluctance to walk in the woods.

The small stone cottage Mark had purchased for them was separated from the Morgan home by an uncleared strip of timber. Although the forest was warm and friendly, with a rich golden light, Jenny chose walking the extra distance through the center of Kirtland to reach Sally's home.

One day in the middle of September, Jenny piled a basket with apples and started through town to visit Sally. When she passed the printing office, she met Sidney Rigdon just leaving Joseph at the door. Sidney bowed and passed on without a word, and impulsively Jenny turned in at the door.

Oliver disappeared into the press room, but not before she saw the disgruntled expression on his face. She looked up at Joseph. "Of the lot, you're the only one who hasn't been into the sour apples."

He laughed and took her arm. "Then come to my office and tell me all that's transpired in Kirtland the past month."

She followed and took a chair before saying, "I can tell you nothing except that the Thomas family has a new baby. Will that suffice? Tell me about your trip. It was very mysterious. We returned from our wedding to find you gone. Both Andy and Mark are upset. I don't know why they can't juggle funds without your presence."

Joseph shot her a quick look and then concentrated on removing his tie. "Perhaps because there are so few to juggle." He met her eyes and she was caught by the sharp, questioning expression in them. "Jenny, you know that the church is in dire circumstances financially." He got to his feet and restlessly paced the room. "Missouri has great needs right now. You've heard of the specie circular, I'm sure, since you're married to an attorney."

"Pray, sir," she said primly, "I've been on my honeymoon. We haven't discussed finances."

He grinned now, holding her eyes with his own in a way that brought the blood to her face. In another moment he was saying, "The specie circular issued by Jackson forbids the acceptance of anything except gold and silver for the purchase of public lands. Of course this makes the situation in Missouri impossible."

Still watching her, his voice softened as he explained, "It is imperative that we have gold to buy land in Missouri. The Lord has promised; He will provide."

Jenny frowned and said slowly, "I am trying to understand it all, but there's a missing link. Did concern for money relate to your trip to Salem?"

Now he was startled. After studying her face, he said slowly, "I'd thought the gossip had come home before I did. Jenny, I suppose I shall tell you since you've asked, and since the word will be around Kirtland before long." He paused to shuffle through the papers spread across the table.

"Before I left for Salem, I knew what I was doing and where I was going. Suffice it to say that the enemy was working with all his powers to prevent me. Fortunately, the Lord gave me this revelation while I was there; otherwise my companions would have been greatly discouraged. You may read it."

As Jenny read she muttered the key words, *treasure.* Why did He say *folly? You have power over Salem, with the wealth of silver and gold belonging to you.* She dropped the paper into her lap and leaned forward, "Joseph," she whispered, "what does this mean? What have you been doing?"

Despite her resolve, she knew that her eyes were sparkling with excitement; she knew it by the answer from his own. Leaning close he said, "Jenny, a fellow came to me and told me about a house in Salem where there's gold and silver buried in the basement. I knew the Lord was giving it to me to pay the debts and to purchase land in Missouri."

"The folly?"

"I went back to the rod and the stone in order to find—"

Like a scolding mother, reacting before thinking, Jenny cut him off, "Joseph, you told me the Lord had forbidden you to use the stone, forbidden you to search for hidden treasures!"

"I know, but this was such a sure thing, and the need was so great. Besides, you've seen the revelation. He's said it's all right."

Jenny was shaking her head in bewilderment. "I don't understand God at all. But since He's told you the treasure was for you, I suppose it was okay to keep it."

There was a strangled noise from Joseph and she looked up. "Jenny, we didn't find any." But when he saw her face he quickly added, "We've retained the house and will go back next spring to try again."

Jenny walked home, still shaking her head in disbelief. When Mark returned home that evening, she was unable to tell him of her conversation with the Prophet. As she hurried about her kitchen, setting the table with the pretty new china and taking reassuring sniffs of the stew, she was miserably aware that she was keeping a secret from Mark, deliberately hiding the conversation with Joseph. During the short walk home, the facts weighing on her mind had become warped and ugly.

The next day Mark brought her a letter from Tom. After dinner she eagerly tore it open, saying to Mark, "I'm so anxious to hear his reaction to our marriage. Shall I read it aloud?"

"Only if you are certain he won't be angry with me for taking his sister," he said with a chuckle.

"Oh, Mark, you know he won't." She spread the sheets and began to read. "It's addressed to both of us. He says:

Having you married to Mark makes me the happiest man alive. I am grateful, too, that he has joined the church. If I'm called upon to shed blood in Missouri, I'll die happy knowing my dearest kin are part of God's Zion.

She paused and looked up, "Oh, Mark, he sounds so dreary and formal." Looking back to the letter, she brushed at her eyes.

Yes, things are as bad as you've been hearing. Late June the Missourians in Clay County requested the Saints to move elsewhere, and as you know, the appeal to Governor Dunklin for help was denied. He had received the same complaint given last time, but amplified. They're accusing us of wrong motives in our relations with the Indians. They refuse to consider the red men as Lamanites, or to believe that we, as God's people, have an obligation to bring them into the fold. For the time being, this response makes it impossible to follow Joseph's injunction to marry a Lamanite, and I can't say that makes me unhappy.

When she paused to turn the page, she glanced at Mark.

He nodded, "I'd heard about Joseph's revelation."

She waited, but he didn't add to his comment. Returning to the letter, she continued:

Our spirits were kept high, despite having the people of Clay County turn against us. We remembered the prophecy given by Joseph, appointing September 11, 1836, as the day for the redemption of Zion.

Needless to say, some of us spent the day in prayer and fasting, looking for a miraculous sign that this would take place. Our disappointment when nothing happened was exceedingly hard to bear, and we were forced to prepare for our trek to the northern part of Missouri before more pressure was brought to bear.

The prairie land is bleak, with water and timber in short supply. But we must keep our hopes high, remembering this is our promised Zion. God, true to His word, will in time deliver into our hands, not only the land but also the riches of the Gentiles. For brass we will receive gold; for iron, silver. All the Saints here in Zion are looking forward to the day when Joseph Smith will be able to surrender the reins in Kirtland and move to the Lord's Zion.

For now, nearly all the Saints in Missouri have moved to the new county named Caldwell. We are working hastily to settle ourselves and will be proud to show what we have done when the Kirtland Saints move here. This, despite the fact that we have been short of the needed and promised funds to buy more land. We call our goodly town by the name of Far West. Already our cultivated fields show our industry, and we are proud of them. Until you and my new brother-in-law, Mark, move to Zion, I remain faithfully,

Thomas Timmons

Jenny slowly folded the letter. Tom must have spent days on the writing. It helped explain Joseph's trip to Salem. She wished she dared question Mark about the financial problems being rumored around. But as she studied his somber face, she was uneasily aware that she couldn't endure hearing criticism of Joseph.

2

As THE WINTER snows began to pile up around Kirtland, covering the landscape and chilling the bones, so did events that most intimately concerned the citizens of the little community. But the new year was well under way before Jenny was aware of the further unrest throwing the town into upheaval.

In the months since her marriage, Jenny had been content in her role as housewife, comfortable with Mark's love. But her isolation had its drawbacks. Jenny knew little of the forces digging at the roots of the community. Her contentment had lulled her into avoiding the gossip and rumors.

As autumn slipped into winter, Jenny enjoyed not only the esteem she and Mark had as a newly married couple, but also the respect Mark's position was earning for him as a financial advisor in the church. She was also becoming aware of the increased demands upon his time.

Early in January, on a glowering day that made her loneliness more acute, Jenny trudged through the snow to visit Sally. As she slowly unwound her shawl and sat down at the kitchen table, Sally's first words pressed her into facing life. As she listened, Sally's worried face and dire news seemed to pick the cotton padding away from her, letting in the unpleasant realities Jenny had shunned. Sally was enumerating the grave financial woes besetting Kirtland.

Jenny listened and watched as Sally paced the room, holding her fussing daughter against her shoulder. "Did you know that Joseph made a trip to New York to borrow money, and has started a bank?"

"That doesn't seem wise." Jenny shook the last of the snow from her frock. "Did he use the borrowed money?"

Sally shook her head, "No, that was to pay off creditors. Andy says the bank intends to print notes, with the purpose of exchanging them for hard money."

Jenny frowned. "I can't understand how that would put them ahead in the game. Sounds like it's closer to—"

"Illegal? Did Mark tell you how worried he and Andy are about the whole situation?"

"He didn't say worried," Jenny said slowly, "and he didn't talk about borrowed money. He did tell me that Sidney Rigdon is president and Joseph is cashier of the new bank. He sounded concerned when he said there's a whole flock of banks springing up around the country, all doing the same thing. He said they were printing notes and exchanging them for anything of value as well as gold and silver."

"The bank was established by a revelation," Sally continued, "and the Prophet has predicted that like Aaron's rod, it will swallow up all the other banks around it. He also said it will grow and flourish to the ends of the earth, surviving when others are in ruins."

"Then I guess we needn't worry," Jenny remarked without looking at her.

"Oh, Jenny, be sensible. Our money is in that bank!"

Jenny stared at her friend. She was thinking not of Sally, but of the money Mark had given her. Back in November she had deposited it in the bank. How proud she had been to make her first transaction as "Mrs. Cartwright"! She winced as she recalled plunking down one thousand dollars in silver and gold, and the way Sidney Rigdon's eyes had brightened.

Now Sally demanded, "Why do you look so concerned? What have you done?"

Jenny straightened and lifted her chin. "Just what any other housewife would have done. Mark gave me a thousand dollars and I deposited it in the bank."

Slowly Sally sat down and shifted Tamara to her lap. "Then you haven't read the newspaper. The Ohio legislature refused to incorporate the bank. Jenny, the bank is operating illegally."

"Oh!"

Sally looked up at Jenny's exclamation and frowned. Jenny explained, "Now it makes sense. Mark said they changed the name of the bank to the Kirtland Safety Society Anti-Banking Company. Mark mentioned it one day as he flew out the door, but he hasn't talked about it again."

"Does he know you've put your money there?" Jenny shook her head. "Then you'd be wise to hightail it right down there and quick draw it out while they are still above the waves."

"What do you mean?"

"Andy says everybody in town's running around with his pockets full of notes. Joseph's paid off all the debts around and even sent bills back east to clear the mercantile businesses in town."

"But why are you so worried about the bank?"

Sally's lips were tightly pressed together, and if the shake of her head didn't convince Jenny her silence was sealed, the expression in her eyes did. Jenny couldn't resist guessing, "You don't think the church has the funds they're advertising they have." Sally didn't answer.

Jenny was nearly home when she stopped and turned back toward the bank. Since leaving the Morgans' house, she had been mulling over the events Sally had discussed.

Jenny began to hurry toward the red-brick building on the corner. A newly painted sign stretched across the face of the building. She stopped just long enough to read, *Kirtland Safety Society Anti-Banking Company*. Inside the door Warren Parrish hurried to meet her. "Well, Jenny—I mean, Mrs. Cartwright—what may I do for you?"

She took a deep breath. "Mr. Parrish, I've come to withdraw my money from the bank."

"And how much?"

"One thousand dollars."

She saw him pale and quickly turn aside. "Jenny, that is rather un-usual—at least, such a large sum is."

"You didn't say that when I deposited it in November."

He leaned close and whispered, "If you are doing this because of the rumors, I assure you that they are unfounded."

She whispered back, "How do I know?"

He hesitated and glanced around the empty room. "This is unusual, but since it is you, come with me and I'll prove it to you." She followed his rapid steps through dark corridors and heavy doors. When the last door creaked open, he struck a match and carefully lighted a row of candles. "There!" He waved toward the shelves lining the narrow room.

Stepping forward, Jenny saw each shelf held numerous wooden boxes, each clearly marked as holding one thousand dollars. "Oh!" she ex-claimed, "shall I take one?"

"No, no," he interrupted. "I merely wanted to reassure you. I—" He stopped and cocked his head. "Someone has come in. I'll return in a moment."

She watched him disappear and then went to stand on tiptoe beside the shelves. A box just at nose level was heaped with shiny silver fifty-cent pieces. So were all the other boxes she could see. She paced the floor, waiting for Warren to return, amused at being left in a bank vault filled with money. After another trip around the room, she paused beside the nearest box, cast a quick glance over her shoulder and dug her fingers into the box of coins.

"Ouch!" She pulled her hand away and looked at her bleeding finger. Again on tiptoe, she carefully lifted aside the top layer of coins and cau-tiously probed. Once again there was the sharpness against her finger.

Quickly she pulled the box down and peered inside. Beneath the silver coins she saw iron nails and jagged chunks of metal.

Shoving the box into its place, she moved quickly down the length of the shelves inserting her fingers into each box. Some boxes contained sand, others held chunks of lead and the rest were filled with old nails. "Joseph," she murmured, "you rascal!" She almost began to chuckle.

Breathlessly, Warren popped back into the room. "Oh my, sorry to keep you waiting. I'm glad to see you in such good humor. Dark rooms aren't to my liking."

"You are a brave man to leave me with so much money. But maybe not. There's not too much I could carry, since it's all in fifty-cent pieces."

Back in the brightly lighted room, Jenny looked up at the worried, gray face and said, "I suppose for now, I'll just leave the money."

On her way home, she alternately chuckled and shook her head, then abruptly faced the implications of her discovery.

By the time Jenny had prepared Mark's dinner and set her table with the best china, she had decided that as soon as the meal was finished she would share her discoveries with him.

Dinner was a silent affair. Jenny was still busy planning her speech. Just when she thought of a way to broach the subject, she became aware of Mark's preoccupation. Studying his face and his unfinished dinner, she asked, "Mark, don't you feel well?"

He stared at her for a moment. "Oh, my dear, I've neglected you. Sorry. I've been miles away with business problems." He reached out to touch her cheek. "No need to trouble you with them. I do wish I needn't go out again this evening."

"Oh, Mark," she said in dismay, then saw his distress. "I'm sorry. But I'll miss you terribly. It is so cold and I was hoping—"

"I know." He rose to kiss her and reached for his coat. "Don't wait up for me. I must see Brewster about his will. I've promised for weeks, and now I'll need to track him down."

Outside, Mark hesitated beside the barn and then muttered, "I'll be warmer with the walk, and the mare won't have to wait in the cold." He set off down the street, striding rapidly as he headed for the Brewster home.

He was breathing the sweet, winter air, spiced only lightly with the scent of burning wood, thinking what a relief it would be if the fresh exchange of air in his lungs could cleanse his troubled thoughts. He sighed heavily, thinking of Jenny, wishing he could press his head against her softness and unburden all the turmoil he was feeling.

Mark had spent the day arguing with Joseph and trying to juggle impossible figures. Even after facing the hard reality of facts, the Prophet's

avowal of faith and confidence had left Mark feeling as if he were bat-
tering against an impregnable wall.

As he hurried through the snow to meet Brewster, Mark lashed himself
for failure to exercise his newfound faith, at least to the degree of believing in the Prophet. He was also trying to push aside the gossip he had
heard and the doubts that assailed him.

Suddenly he threw his shoulders back and breathed deeply of the fresh
air. "In new, out old," he called out toward the moon. His usual good
humor made him shrug off the binding thoughts, and he found himself
free to contemplate his lot. Joseph had gotten himself another church
member, and he had his wife. Mark chuckled with delight, seeing himself
as the winner after all. For just a moment he shook his head in disbelief
over Joseph's suggestion that he would win favor with both man and God
were he to invest all of his worldly goods in the betterment of the church.

He was still shaking his head when he reached the small log house
where the Brewsters lived. Perhaps old man Brewster had been approached with the same suggestion, and that had promoted the idea of a
will.

Mark had barely freed himself of snow and settled beside the fire when
a tap was heard at the Brewster door. He recognized the bent, white-
haired man coming in the door as the Prophet's father, Joseph Smith,
Senior.

When the old man settled himself beside the fire and rubbed his hands,
he said, "On a night like this a good nip would help." He twisted his
rheumatic body to face the elder Brewster. "But I didn't come to be socia-
ble. There's a task before us." His voice dropped to a low rumble as he
pointed his finger at Brewster's son, James. "I've told you before, there's
money hid in the earth and it's our duty to obtain it." His voice was slow
and shaky as he added, "My friend, to fail to do so will cause the curse of
God to fall upon us."

Mark saw the look of distaste cross the elder Brewster's face. In a
playful manner Mark said, "Brother Smith, money digging is an old, old
scheme of the wicked one to get us to dissipate our energies in running
after a dream."

Unexpectedly Smith turned on him and shook his finger. "Now, young
man, don't you be disputin' your elders. I know more about money diggin'
than any man in this generation, seein' I've been in the business for more
than thirty years."

Mark had only a moment for surprise before the man turned to James,
saying, "Must I remind you again of your patriarchal blessing? You know
the Lord promised power for you to discover and obtain treasures hidden
in the earth."

Facing Mark again, he went on, "I know how you fancy young'uns don't hold with usin' the rod and such, but I know the Lord approves. Why, we've even taken the rods and the seein' stones into the temple, anointed them with consecrated oil and prayed over them so that the devil wouldn't be deceivin' the menfolk as they sought the treasures."

"Have they found any?" Mark asked curiously.

With a snort of disgust, the elder Brewster answered, "Nope, no treasure found yet."

Smith got to his feet. "Now come along, James. The rest of the fellows are waitin' at the temple. Beaman and I will stay there and pray while you youngsters get out there and do your lookin'." He paused to glare at old Mr. Brewster. "The Lord rebuke you for your unbelief. You best stay home, lest that unbelief taint the others."

For a moment he fastened Mark with an eagle eye, then turned toward the door without another word.

Mark was whistling as he started for home. For once he had found reason to be glad his faith was very feeble. But as he looked beyond the evening with Jenny, he sobered. Tomorrow, juggling the church's figures would take more faith than even old Joseph Smith possessed.

The following evening when he returned home, Mark found Jenny sitting at the kitchen table, surrounded by newspapers.

She lowered the paper she held and explained before he could ask. "We haven't been getting the papers, so I borrowed them from Sally. Mark, do you realize I've scarcely been aware of what has been going on for months now?"

"And why is that, my dear wife?" He came to nuzzle her neck. "I know, it is because you have been busy keeping house and cooking for me."

"I suspect my husband thinks he is protecting me from uncomfortable news." Jenny's gaze was very serious now. Yesterday's humor over Joseph's money boxes had disappeared and dismay had taken its place. "Since I assume you haven't read the papers either, let me read to you."

He interrupted. "I have read them. I could nearly quote them. Jenny, don't be angry. I know how much you believe in Joseph and his new church, and I couldn't bear to have you hurt. You also know how little I believe. You know why I joined the church." Lightly he added, "I would have walked the nearest gangplank in order to have you. Let's not pretend I believe in religion."

And Jenny looked up at him, sensing the love that was visible more often than spoken. Searching his face, seeing things that had escaped her attention before, she was filled with dismay. Those tired lines on his face—was she beginning to see the consequences of following her flighty heart? Where would it lead her next?

Lifting the paper she stated solemnly, "Well, I don't know the words by heart, and right now I need very much to know what is taking place out there. Please, dear husband," she begged, "don't keep these things from me."

Mark sat quietly beside the fire until she had finished and folded the last paper. "Is there a suggestion that the Prophet isn't entirely honest?" Jenny asked. "Yesterday's *Painesville Republican* sounds cynical. The advice to circulate the specie in order to benefit the community seems sound, however."

"Wife, do I get my dinner now?" Jenny jumped to her feet, but as she folded the papers and hurried to rescue her meal, she tried to hide the irritation she felt. At times Mark seemed to view her as only a child.

Still feeling that irritation days later, she stood at her window one evening and watched the snow fall. It was late and Mark should have been home. She looked down at the newspaper she clutched and read again the words that made her think of a house of cards, stacked and swaying until the last placed card sent them all tumbling. Which word was that final card?

The newspaper was old. It was now February and she knew the events that were rocking the town. This paper, the *Painesville Telegraph,* informed her that the Prophet had closed up shop. His bank wouldn't redeem another dollar except for land. Jenny tried to feel sorry for Joseph; an amused grin twisted her lips. Like a cat, he would land on his feet and once again triumph.

Joseph was plainly running just one step ahead of them all. He had closed the bank just as the newspaper stories nudged loose a stream of people, running with their bills, suddenly frantic for their money. She also knew that by the first of February the bank notes had been worth only twelve and a half cents on the dollar. Mark had told her that Joseph Smith and Sidney Rigdon had both resigned their positions in the bank.

As Jenny continued to stand at the window and watch the snow, her thoughts were not of the stories in the paper, or even of the loss of her money. She was thinking of Mark's tired, worn face, wondering why he must suffer so deeply over affairs that were not really his concern. She frowned over the contrasting pictures her mind cast: Mark, serious and plodding; Joseph, laughing, running through life a step ahead of everyone else.

In the quiet of the house, Jenny heard the fire pop and the clock chime. A timber creaked and Jenny's heart began to thump slowly and heavily. With that sense she had lately refused to exercise, she was being made aware of the hidden movements in the room. Was it possible that just thinking forbidden thoughts had unleashed the spirit forces?

In her acquiescence to life, was she gaining power that had been denied her before? Her eyes were busily searching the room; she felt herself pushed and twisted by thoughts of Joseph. Were they trying to get her away from home, from Mark? Momentarily, her mind fastened on the warning given by Adela: *Anything except Mark.*

Jenny frowned, and her restless eyes probed the dark corners, searching out reasons for the nameless sounds in the room. Now her thoughts flew to the green book safely hidden in the attic. "Do I no longer control me?" she whispered.

She closed her eyes and immediately saw her fingers turning the pages of the book, underlining those words, tracing those pictures. Now she knew, without a doubt, there was a presence in the room. Not daring to open her eyes, she waited breathlessly for the manifestation.

Her body seemed to lighten, barely aware of substance under and around her. There was a touch against her face, fingers lifting her chin. She tried to move and was powerless; behind her closed lids she saw Joseph's laughing face, felt his hands.

"No!" The scream came from her own lips, and suddenly she was across the room, staring at the spot beside the windows. Empty now, moments before it had been filled with moving, surging spirit life.

Now her voice was low and guttural. "No, never!" Even as she saw Adela's face, her mind was filled with white lace and yellow roses. On that day Mark and their special vows had been carved forever into her heart. But now, even as she stood trembling at her own fireside, she sensed there was a battle going on again, one that had begun in her mind years ago on a wooded trail near South Bainbridge. Her marriage to Mark had caused the conflict to recede to the background, but it was far from over. She thought of the talisman Joseph once again possessed, and her heart sank.

Jenny clasped her hands, lifting her face ceilingward. She prayed like they did in church: "Kind heavenly Father, I beseech You—"

She stopped. Adela's words rolled through her mind. Jenny saw the woman, heard again her musical voice: "There is only one god, and many different ways to worship him."

Slowly Jenny settled in the rocking chair and compared all the pictures of God that were in her mind. In her quest for power through Adela's teaching, the resulting picture of God was frightening. Joseph's image of God was diffused, unclear. Only one clear impression captured her mind, created the moment she and Mark had stood before that pastor and pledged those vows.

She closed her eyes. She recalled a sense of presence on that day, commanding and strong. But there was another element to it, and she didn't know how to define it, except to admit it left her feeling an emptiness in her life. It reminded her of the church, bathed in violet light from afternoon sunbeams through the windows; of Lucy Harris's attempts to help her understand God; of Mark's mother's insistent questions about her own faith.

Jenny sighed over the picture. Then she heard Mark's step at the kitchen door and flew to welcome him. As he held her quietly in his arms, Jenny didn't see the lost expression on his face.

3

LATER THAT SPRING Jenny faced Mark across the kitchen table. "No!" she exclaimed, then fell silent, caught by the defeat on his face. How long had she been seeing those sad, tired eyes? And how often had she turned away, feeling only her own helplessness and defeat? Now she wanted badly to go to him, but more than the table lay between them.

Unable to endure his expression, she looked out the window at the newness of May. As the snow had melted and the flowers bloomed, their marriage had seemed to frost and wither. She watched the wild roses pressing across the picket fence and wished she had forced Mark earlier to share the burdens that had been weighing him down.

Now it was obviously too late. When she turned he was shaking his head. "I'm just as caught as you are, Jenny. How can I prove my loyalty to Joseph by less than obedience? Besides, I won't be gone forever. And right now maybe we need a time apart." He paused, and she saw the painful twist to his lips.

"It has been bad, hasn't it, Mark? How miserably I've failed you!" She watched him turn away and nearly ran to him. But she had asked him to marry, and Mark was too much of a gentleman to ignore all that had come before that proposal. Jenny, the kitchenmaid, proposing to Attorney Cartwright! Now her bitter smile mirrored his. How blind she had been!

But she must pretend. She turned from the window with a bright smile and a bustle of energy. "So Joseph Smith has tapped my husband with his reward, the opportunity to go to merry old England to convert the land to Mormonism."

"And the irony is in your voice, not mine." Mark came around the table to face her.

She forced herself to look at him, to search those weary lines. "It has been bad. All these problems heaped on the church simply because of that foolish banking idea." He ignored the hand she stretched toward him, but she continued. "Knowing you, I can guess how you cautioned against the venture in the first place. No doubt it's been difficult charging Joseph with operating the bank illegally when he knew by law it should have been shut down months ago. But you see, Mark, Joseph fails to see himself bound by the laws of this land, and—"

Mark interrupted, "The only thing that has kept him from looking like a complete scoundrel has been all the other banks tumbling down." He looked away for a moment.

"Despite the rightness of the court's decision, it was very unfortunate Joseph had to lose his suit for operating the bank illegally. Some poor Saint's thousand dollars paid his fine," Mark added bitterly, and Jenny searched his face, wondering if he had guessed it was likely her money— their money.

Desperately she sought for something to say. "I'm surprised that Joseph chose you to go now. With all these suits pending against him, I'd think he would need you here more than ever."

"Let's say I spoke my feelings one time too many. He's testing my loyalty. I must obey or I'll lose everything I've worked so desperately to gain." Jenny turned quickly, hoping to see some sign that Mark's words referred to her. But he was fumbling through the papers in his cubbyhole of a desk in the corner of the kitchen.

Jenny's shoulders sagged in defeat. "When must you leave?"

"There's a bunch going in June. He wants us to encourage converts to come with their money and settle among us." When he paused, Jenny reviewed his words, searching for scorn, but there was none. Again she felt his heavy spirit and regretted the past months of emotional strain.

Now Mark was quoting Joseph. "He promised that this place will be built up and that every brother who helps discharge these contracts will be rich."

Since their marriage, Jenny had never inquired into Mark's financial affairs. Timidly she asked, "Did you—"

With an amused smile he said, "Fortunately, even were I so inclined, I couldn't. My father's estate is completely in the hands of trustees as long as my mother lives." Jenny couldn't hide her small expression of relief.

With a grin, backed by an expression so dark she couldn't understand it, Mark added, "Just the other day, Heber C. Kimball stated that he thinks there's not twenty people on earth right now who believe Joseph is truly a prophet of God. But cheer up, my dear, things will smooth out, and you will all get your faith back."

Trying to read the expression in his eyes, Jenny wondered whether Mark blamed Joseph's church for the widening gulf between the two of them. Her heart was heavy with the sense of failure. In the beginning, only love was necessary, she had thought. Now she knew that as deeply as she had learned to love Mark, she still sensed a barrier. One look into his hurt eyes convinced Jenny that Mark was as much aware of the lack as she. Jenny turned away with a sigh.

June came, and Mark and the other chosen ones departed on the first missionary assignment to a foreign land. Jenny was left wondering how one as bitter and disheartened as Mark could hope to baptize converts for Zion.

Despite her loneliness and despair during the weeks immediately following Mark's departure, Jenny found reason to be glad: he was not there to see the turmoil. For a time, it looked as if the entire church structure would crumble. Six of the twelve apostles were in open rebellion against Joseph, and even Parley Pratt threatened to bring suit against the Prophet.

Soon Sally carried another tale to her. Warren Parrish, who had earlier resigned as cashier, had now left the church and was openly describing the Prophet's banking methods.

She added that Parrish was now being accused of absconding with $25,000. Even Jenny was surprised when Sally bit her lip and then let the bitter words burst out. "What rot! If the church has that much money, it's all in bank notes." Her agitated pacing around Jenny's kitchen was her final comment on the state of affairs. Again, Jenny was grateful Mark had escaped this.

On the day after her conversation with Sally, Jenny was pulling weeds and sighing over the sad state of her garden. When she heard the gate squeak, she gladly dropped her hoe and went to sit in the shade with Nettie.

"Seems the Prophet's just having more trouble than goes with the job," Nettie said. "Even Jesus Christ had to contend with trouble, but only one skipped out on Him."

"You're comparing Joseph with Jesus?" Jenny asked curiously.

"Of course; he's the Christ for this time in history."

Jenny thought about that for a moment before saying, "Well, I don't have the grounds to argue the case. It would be nice if the Prophet had a school for the women so we could be learning just like the men are doing."

Nettie sighed. "Most of us are just too busy. Maybe when we move to Zion there will be time for such. I hear some women are a mite uneasy with some of the teaching they hear. Might be our duty to help them along by studying together. What about the Prophet's wife, Emma? She's strong-minded and needs something to do other than tend babies. Might be she'd consent to teach us."

As Jenny searched for words, she remembered the chunk of wax and Clara's advice to get rid of Emma once and for all. Now Nettie leaned close to Jenny. "That reminds me of the real reason I came. I just heard it this morning, and I had to rush to tell someone. The Prophet's neighbor, Alma, said she heard a great commotion during the night and got up to peek out. All the lights were a-blazing at the Smiths', so she put on a shawl, thinking they needed help. When she went out, there stood Emma on the front steps in her nightgown, waving a broom. She had chased Fannie Alger clear outside—in her nightclothes, too. Alma said as she came on the scene, Joseph was trying to quiet Emma down, and she was waving her broom and yelling about getting Fannie out of there because she was in the family way. Joseph was sure nervous, but he took Fannie and headed toward Oliver Cowdery's place.

"This morning I walked past the Smiths'. The Prophet is getting ready for a missionary trip to Canada. I saw the two of them out in front, and Emma was just as nice as pie. Poor girl, I'm not surprised about it all. There's sure been the talk lately. I wonder what's lackin' over there? Oh, well men will be men, you know." In a few minutes she left to carry her news down the street, and Jenny tarried in her garden, pulling weeds and wondering at the strange churnings inside of her.

Later that week while Jenny and Sally carried their shopping baskets down Kirtland's main street, Jenny said, "It's easy to guess the Prophet's out of town. The whole town feels different, doesn't it?"

Sally's eyes widened as she looked from Jenny to the nearly deserted street. "It is strange, isn't it? Everything is kind of dragging. Andy says there's a heap of discouragement abroad." Abruptly she turned to point down a side street. "Oh, Jenny, look at the crowd! Let's go see what's happening!"

The two women stood on the fringes of the crowd. Jenny stretched to look over the heads. "Why, there's Martin Harris, Oliver Cowdery, and David Whitmer talking to a young woman. Oh, Sally, can you see? She's dancing, spinning around like a top in the middle of the clearing."

"Sounds like one of those strange ones. The men will sure put a stop to that in a hurry. Let's go."

"Wait." Jenny put out a detaining hand and cocked her head. The crowd began to melt away, some with shamefaced glances at Harris, Cowdery, and Whitmer, others with snorts of disgust.

Jenny and Sally watched the three men press around the woman. Sally said, "Look at that silly girl; she's trying to get attention, and those men will give it. I'll bet she's pretending to be a witch or a sorceress."

"Let's go hear what she has to say." Jenny grasped Sally's arm.

"No!" Sally's voice was sharp and Jenny turned to look at her. "I've always been taught that's all of the devil, and my mother says the best way to avoid evil is to stay away from all such things. I'm going shoppin'." She turned on her heel and left Jenny standing in the street.

Jenny's intention was to follow, but curiosity won out. She moved close to the crowd and listened. The girl was still breathless from her frenzied dancing. She shoved aside her black cape and lifted a small dark stone. "Now who wants to hear the future read to him?"

For a moment Jenny teetered, eager to step forward, but she saw Martin Harris pushing his way toward her. Jenny shivered and slipped back into the crowd. She watched his tongue slip out to touch his lips, a symbol of his lust for the new and mysterious. Jenny turned and hurried away. Although years had passed since that last horrible encounter when he beat both her and his own wife, Jenny still found herself fleeing his presence, shuddering with terror.

In the weeks that followed, the young woman attracted further gatherings of Saints, those tired of the winter's problems and eager for a new thrill. Soon it was evident that the church was nearly evenly divided. Excitement swelled through the town like a tidal wave as the stranger gave forth revelations about the future after consulting the seer stone. At the end of July, Joseph Smith returned from his trip to Canada. Jenny settled back to watch him shake law and order back into the wayward church members.

Jenny's satisfaction was complete. Martin Harris was cut off from the church, and the repentant Cowdery and Whitmer were dispatched to Missouri.

Later at church conference time, Jenny listened to Joseph's rebuke, visualizing him wiping the dust of the whole affair from his hands as he talked. Once again Joseph Smith was sustained as president of the church.

Despite Sally's close companionship, restlessness was settling upon Jenny. She staggered under the burden of her loneliness and mourned Mark's absence. When she would come to the end of the labyrinth of her emotions, the anxious faces of Sally and Andy awaited her. And once again she became aware of the troubles around her.

In the golden days of autumn, at the Morgans' dinner table, Jenny heard Andy say, "Surely you've noticed."

"I've scarcely moved from my own doorstep."

"The steam mill isn't even operating. Land values are dropping out of sight, and every merchant in town is ready to go under. Jenny, if you'd walk the streets, you'd see half the houses empty. Families are moving west as fast as they can pack. It isn't just Kirtland; the whole country is in a depression. Soaring land prices no one can afford. Banks closing and shops going out of business."

"Well, at least that keeps Joseph from looking so bad," she said, lifting her spoon. Sally sighed and shook her head.

Andy said, "Joseph is leaving for Missouri. That's a smart move on his part. There are six suits pending against him. He's sent men around to the people to gather money for the church, but it'll have to come in a hurry if he's to save his skin."

As summer slipped into autumn, Jenny's spirits took a deeper plunge. The letters from England were short and businesslike. She eagerly scanned each one, looking for words of love, words which would assure her that the widening gulf was only in her mind.

Disappointed, she read the dutiful catalog of the daily activities of the missionaries. Only an occasional word added detail to the bleak picture, but the words reflected only confusion, questions, and more discouragement.

Eventually the letters ceased coming altogether.

On a dark, cold December evening Jenny took action. She went to Joseph, now back from Missouri.

The print shop was empty, but as she entered the building, she saw the door at the head of the stairs standing open. A light gleamed through the dusk. Quickly she climbed the stairs. Joseph sat slumped forward across his desk, coat discarded, hair rumpled.

All the worst tales Jenny had heard made her rush through the door to his side. When her hand fell on his shoulder, he lifted his startled face. His delighted grin made words unnecessary.

As he brought her a chair, and touched her arm, her shoulder, her chin, the unsaid things became more important. She was aware of his overwhelming manliness and that pleased smile. When he bent over her and she waved him away, they both knew it was not rejection.

As she watched the pulse in his throat settle to a steady beat, her own emotions calmed. But she was filled with dismay. The emotional protection her marriage had given was stripped away, and once more she stood weak and vulnerable before him.

"What brings you out this late?" He waited.

"I haven't heard from Mark for such a long time. The other wives have had letters." She was twisting her hands, and he glanced down at them.

When his eyes finally met hers, she saw the lines on his forehead, lines of concern. He spoke slowly and she read meaning into them. "Jenny, don't worry. We know Mark's a stable young man. You wives always start guessing. A missed letter doesn't mean your husband is chasing some young girl. Our men are dependable, and we must trust them."

His eyes! He didn't believe a word he said. "Why, Joseph! The thought never entered my head. I was supposing he might be ill. He left here tired and discouraged."

Joseph sighed. "Aren't we all."

"What is it, Joseph?" she whispered. "Where's the power? Why is everything suddenly all going awry?"

He leaned toward her. "Jenny, it isn't. Where's your faith? The Lord expects us to keep on plugging away without getting discouraged. For Mark's sake, be brave."

He touched her shoulder, at first timidly, then bravely. "Jenny, despite problems, these are great days for the church. We shall move onward and upward. The Lord plans for us to be the most holy people on earth, and that shall be accomplished as we obey Him. I have things to teach you about the priesthood. I—" They both heard a sound, and Jenny sighed with relief. She recognized she had been rescued.

The dark shop seemed silent again, and Joseph continued, speaking now in a low voice. "Jenny, I need you desperately." He hesitated, and a shadow touched his eyes. "These are difficult days; too often there's no one to listen. I can't understand any better than you why trouble surrounds us and the revelations fail. I do know we need power."

She nodded, momentarily forgetting the whisper of sound. "Joseph, I sense it, too. Once you asked me why I needed so desperately to join the church. The power, Joseph, that's why. But where is it?"

"Right now I'd settle for harmony." His voice held a touch of irony. "Come this Sabbath there will be a meeting in the temple. Be there if you care to see the power at work."

"The miracles, the strange speech, the visions," Jenny whispered. "Joseph, can anyone—"

"No, I mean—"

"Joseph," the woman's voice was tremulous as she swept into the room, "working late again! I need you to—Oh!"

"Emma!" At Joseph's exclamation, Jenny got to her feet, noticing that Emma Smith's expression was not one of surprise. She was busy taking in every detail of the room, including Joseph's discarded coat.

Jenny nodded. "Mrs. Smith, we've never met. I'm Mark Cartwright's wife; I stopped to inquire about him."

Jenny went on her way, feeling as if she had been caught with her hand in the candy jar. Guilt rode her steps all the way home, but looking back at that last scene, she was not without a measure of relief.

That first Sabbath after the new year, Jenny slipped into the pew beside Sally. Since her meeting in Joseph's office, she had made a point of visiting Andy to glean more information.

Sally's husband had been very serious. "More lawsuits, instigated by the faction fighting for control of the church. Jenny, I'm glad your husband isn't here to see this. Some of us old-timers can rock with the punches, but I'm afraid Mark's too idealistic."

Shaking his head, he continued, "Many of the elders, including Brigham Young, have been forced to flee to Missouri in order to avoid being sued. And Joseph is being followed. Just after he left the printing office the other evening, a bunch tried to get in and burn the press." Shame washed over Jenny as she thought of that evening. Did Andy know she had been there, too? His steady expression told her nothing.

Now, sitting in the pew with the Morgans, Jenny mused over that conversation with Andy and listened to the rustle of the crowd. A line of black-coated men marched into the temple and down to the front pew. Sally whispered, "That's the trouble-making bunch."

Now Joseph Smith and Sidney Rigdon were taking their places. Jenny looked from Joseph's face with its confident half-smile to Rigdon. Sally whispered, "That poor man looks nearly dead." Jenny could only agree as she watched the pallid Rigdon being assisted to the pulpit.

When Rigdon began his talk, his voice was weak, but as he continued, the momentum grew. "Liars, thieves, adulterers, counterfeiters, swindlers!" These were the words of a man who had kept his wrathful silence far too long. And in the end, while quietness gripped the temple, he was helped from the podium, through the auditorium and out the door. Abruptly the dissenters rose to their feet.

Appalled, Jenny watched and listened as charges and ugly countercharges echoed through the grand edifice.

Suddenly Joseph jumped to his feet. Shouting above the din, he commanded attention and called for a vote on excommunication. One of the black-coated men jumped to his feet and waving his arms, he bellowed, "Joseph Smith, you would cut off a man's head first and then ask to hear him afterward!"

Rising to their feet as one, the congregation watched their prophet stalk from their midst. His face wore defeat like an ill-fitting mask. For the first time, he was unable to regain control of his people, and it was obvious to everyone. Andy watched him go, muttering, "He is a broken man. All he has fought for is gone." Joseph, Jenny remembered, had promised her a display of power.

During the lonesome days that followed, Jenny spent a great deal of time pondering the situation. As she paced the floor in front of her cheery fire, she longed for Mark's calm, level-headed wisdom. She tried to recall his face, even his touch. All the while she was listening to a secret part of her heart advise her that Mark was gone from her life forever.

The January evening was bleak, snowy, and shadowed. Now her thoughts turned to Joseph, the bleakness coloring her picture of him also.

"Power!" she muttered, pacing the floor. "Power!" This time it was a plea. If she wanted power, there was still the sabbat. Jenny felt her spirit recoil in horror as she recalled the trampled cross and the chalice of blood. Momentarily she puzzled over the significance of denying the Christian faith, wondering why these dark promises Adela had tried to extract from her left her trembling with fear. Did it matter that she deny the baptism? Just thinking about it brought the brooding spirit world close, and she trembled at the sense of presence. "I will not!" she declared into the recesses of darkness. But then she contemplated Joseph's failure and found herself nearly ready to give up the church, her final hope of power.

There was a knock on her kitchen door. Glad to flee the gloomy thoughts, Jenny rushed to open it. Though the shadowy figure was covered with snow, she recognized him immediately. "Joseph!" Reaching for his arm, she pulled him in and closed the door. "Why are you out on a night like this?"

The snowy crown of his hat reminded her of the old white one he had been wearing the first time she saw him. He saw her smile and abruptly bent to brush his cold lips across her cheek. She stepped backward and shivered.

"I beg your pardon," he murmured. "Jenny, I'm leaving."

She helped him out of the coat and went to hang it by the stove. He followed. "Would you like tea?" He nodded, and she pulled her shiny teakettle over the fire, the kettle she had purchased for Mark. "Why are you leaving?"

Looking curiously about, he selected Mark's chair and pulled it close to the fire. "Grandison Newell has secured a warrant for my arrest, charging bank fraud."

"Where will you go?"

"Missouri, of course. Remember, we are still looking forward to Zion. Why the Lord chooses to beat us into submission before we go to the promised land, I don't know, but we must trust God." She had poured the water over the tea and he got to his feet. His eyes, curiously light, held hers. "May I depend on you, Jenny? Will you promise me that you will remain true to the church, and that as soon as possible you will move to Zion?"

He waited. Jenny, feeling compelled, trembled. "I promise, but—"

He interrupted, his voice nearly a whisper. "It seems I must again count my followers one by one." He sighed and lifted his head with a smile as if shaking off the somber mood. "I came to tell you good-bye, but also to ask if you had a message for your brother Tom."

She shook her head. "I've just written to him."

After Jenny closed the door behind Joseph, she still pondered his strange visit. She wondered whether the ties of the church or the magnetism of the Prophet had made her promise to follow him to Zion. Why did she feel as if the promise had been pulled from her against her will?

Immediately after Joseph left Kirtland, the dissenters seized the temple. Now the building rang with resolutions proclaiming his depravity.

Deep in the cold of the January night, the print shop caught fire and burned to the ground. The embers were hardly cold before Jenny, standing in front of Warren Parrish, heard him say, "He did it himself. Joseph fired the place to fulfill his prophecy that Kirtland would repent of its wickedness or the Lord would burn it to the ground." He continued, "These men are infidels; they have no fear of God before their eyes. They lie by revelation, run by revelation, and unless they themselves repent, I fear they will be damned by revelation."

4

SPRING SUNSHINE HAD everyone in Kirtland outside. Nettie had just left, and the familiar lonesome feeling settled on Jenny. She lingered on her steps, watching her neighbors shake rugs and pull weeds. They looked busy and content. Jenny tried to square her shoulders and fix a smile on her face; she failed dismally at both.

Slowly she went down the steps and walked around the house. "So you're disappointed, Jenny," she advised herself. "Stiffen your lip. What's to disappoint you except you haven't had a letter from Mark since Christmas, and now it's April. And you hear today that the Prophet has another little son and his wife is hale and hearty."

"Jenny." The quiet voice came from behind her. For a dizzy moment, Jenny recognized the voice, then rejected it. Again it came, "Jenny." This time she turned. "Mark!" For a moment it was impossible to move. She studied his face. At first he was only a stranger. There was a guarded question in his eyes, but there was also the beginning of a smile. She flew into his arms, stretching eagerly for his kisses. She knew it didn't matter— none of it, not the absence, the lack of letters, the hurts, the silences. Only Mark was necessary.

She held him, straining against him. Were all those tears hers? When she leaned back to look at his face and saw his tears, she sensed a newness in him. Jenny led him into the house, closing the door firmly behind them; she knew she couldn't be away from his touch for a moment until the gap of those long months was bridged.

Not until the next day could they sit together and face questions. Jenny had one question too tender to be probed—and that was *Why? Why wasn't love enough?*

"Jenny, I still don't understand it all." He paced restlessly and she was beginning to see the things Mark could never explain. Those agitated steps hinted at a torment his tired face had refused to admit last June. Momentarily, Jenny recalled the Mark she had glimpsed during their snowbound time in Cobleskill long ago.

She studied the new, tender smile and realized once again she was close to the hidden man. Unexpectedly Jenny was filled with an overwhelming desire to be one with that real Mark, but at the same time she was afraid.

He was ready to talk now, haltingly at first. "Jenny, I know only that I left here in bondage—to myself, to the church, most of all, to Joseph. I went to England trying to believe in all that I had been taught here. I went determined not to come back until I could honestly face your little-girl faith and say, 'I believe in Joseph Smith and his divine commission.' " His voice yearned for her understanding. "Did you sense how tired I had grown of pretending? Jenny, you'll never know how hard I tried to believe. I knew it was necessary if I was to come back here and live in the shadow of Joseph, following his teachings."

Jenny was distant and curious. "And what did you find?" she asked hesitantly. *Why wasn't love sufficient? Why must you have more?* her thoughts raced.

For a moment his glance wavered. And when he spoke, it was to himself. "How can I make you understand? I'm only just now beginning to comprehend all that's happened. I should have waited to come, but I knew I couldn't be away from you a moment longer." His hand was on her cheek, stroking, and his eyes were gentle, remembering her welcome.

Jenny's heart leaped. Surely their love would be all that was necessary! She knelt beside his chair, resting her head against his chest. When he pulled her onto his lap, she was satisfied that she had won. Love *was* sufficient.

Later he recalled his subject. "Jenny, for the first time I was put in a position where I had to understand Joseph's teachings and what his book says. I had to be out there ministering to people. I couldn't just say I had 'a burning in the bosom' like the rest of the fellows were doing. I had to *know*. I studied until my head was swimming. I talked with the brethren until we were all hoarse. Finally, Kimball let me borrow his Bible." He shot her a quick look. "Not the gold one."

She touched his cheek, and he turned his head to press a kiss into her hand. Taking a deep breath, he said, "Jenny, do you know God has promised that when we seek Him with our whole heart, He will allow us to find Him? I've come to understand what His message is."

"What message?"

"The Bible's message of salvation. What God is trying to get across to mankind. Jenny, it isn't as Joseph teaches at all. Before I could understand I had to read the whole book through several times. Essentially the message for man is the same now as it always has been. He's a sinner; from way back in the beginning that's so. There's no way on this earth a man can live good enough or wise enough to be righteous. There's love, too. I was overwhelmed by the message of love in the book."

His hands were holding hers now, pleading for her attention. "The words kept coming back at me. God loved us so much even while we were sinners that He provided a way for us to come to himself, not through doing good things, or being special set-apart ones, but simply through accepting the only possible way to bridge the gap between God and man."

Mark's voice broke. He dropped her hands, jumped up, and resumed his agitated pacing. "Jenny, I was raised in the church. You heard Mother talk about her beliefs. When I was young I heard the Bible read daily, and I heard my parents pray.

"Somehow, during all those years in Sunday school and church, the truth skimmed right over my head. I really didn't understand until I became so desperate that I was reduced to begging God to show me what I was failing to see.

"Jenny, Jesus Christ is God. Not *a* god, like Joseph has been telling us that all we men will become when we choose to accept the Mormon way. This Jesus is God. He came in human flesh, just like another man. But He did what none of us, including Joseph, has ever done; He lived His entire life without sinning once. He is God."

As he talked, every word Mark spoke became a brick in a wall between the two of them. Jenny's attempt to remain quiet, to hear him out, was knotting her stomach, chilling her hands, and setting her whole body to trembling.

Jenny jumped to her feet and whirled away from Mark. "I don't understand why I am feeling this way, Mark," she whispered through gritted teeth, "but all this talk is churning me up inside. If you say another word, I'll scream."

He came to her. "Jenny, I have no desire to upset you. I only needed to let you know what has been happening to me."

Abruptly he turned to pace the room and when he returned to her, he said, "My dearest Jenny, you know that I love you more than my own life. That's why the step I'm taking now is so necessary. I don't expect you to understand, just trust me." She looked up at his serious face, wondering. His smile wavered slightly as he said, "We're leaving Kirtland and Joseph's church just as soon as I can close up our affairs."

"Leave!" she gasped. "Leave the church and turn our backs on all that Joseph has taught us?" She was trembling, pressing her hands to her hot cheeks. "Mark, I can't begin to understand the strange things you've been heaping on me. I don't want you to quarrel with me about it, but can't you see? I can't leave the church. I—" she gulped and trembled. "I *dare* not.

I'm fully convinced that I will plunge myself into the deepest hell were I to do so."

Mark saw the fear in her eyes. "Let's just wait then, Jenny," was all he said.

One Sunday morning Nathaniel Taylor stood to his feet in the midst of Sabbath worship and waved his arm. "I'm for Zion!" he roared. "Everyone of like mind, prepare to go as soon as possible. Let's clear the town and make the biggest wagon train ever seen."

For the first time in weeks, Jenny felt her heart lift. She knew it was impossible to deny the challenge. With a smile, she turned to Mark sitting beside her. She saw his slight frown and watched him move uneasily. Her heart sank and she sighed. The past weeks had been full of strain. She admitted that the strain was on her part. Mark had been a sweet, tender lover, a patient husband, an understanding friend. Patience and understanding often kept him silent these days when she could see he yearned to talk.

While she couldn't understand this new Mark, the man with the tender smile and infinite patience, she was beginning to notice an underlying strength in him. In the face of her petulance, he was unmoving. Painfully conscious that neither one of them dare yield position, they both skirted the issue Mark had introduced.

Life resumed its old pattern, but there was a difference. Even while laughing together and loving, Jenny found herself desperately resisting this elusive new side of her husband.

On the day Jenny admitted that her church hadn't power to hold Mark, she finally acknowledged that which she had sensed all along. There was only one way she could win the struggle. Using charms and spells, Jenny redoubled her efforts to gain the power she so desperately needed to sway Mark completely under her control. And control him she must, or he would never consent to going to Missouri. With generous impartiality she prayed both to God and Luna, the moon goddess, begging help and favor.

As Kirtland prepared the wagon train for the trek to Zion, Jenny watched the activity of the families around them. She saw the loaded wagons and empty houses. Meanwhile, Mark was bringing his business in Kirtland to a close. Still fearful of facing the issue of leaving, still hoping for a miracle, Jenny began to sort and pack their belongings.

One day Sally Morgan came by. She surveyed the loaded barrels and said, "Mark's informed us of his new beliefs." The dismay was evident in her voice. "Reminds me of that Martin Harris. He's off again looking for another church to join." Jenny was stung by the comparison, but didn't answer.

Sally watched Jenny work, and finally she gave a heavy sigh. "Well, if he's going his way, you're welcome to join up with us. Andy can find a hand to drive for you."

Jenny threw the towels in a heap on the nearest trunk. "How can two people who love each other be separated by something as petty as religion?"

"Petty?" Sally echoed. "You mean that's the way you see your beliefs?"

"No," Jenny shivered. None of it was petty. At one time, Adela's decree had bound her with paralyzing fear as she searched for power. Now fear entwined her with Joseph and the church. How could an innocent search for power and knowledge bind her in fear? And what did she really fear? Hell?

Jenny thought about Mark and his new beliefs. Was hell the dark something lurking out there which had sent him seeking? If so, no wonder he was acting as he did!

That evening when he came into the house and looked at the trunks and barrels, she saw the questions in his somber eyes. But she must ask him a question first. "Mark, is it because of the terrible fear that you are pulling me away from here?"

"Fear? Jenny, my dear, my fear's resolved. It's because of truth I want this. Fear used to hold me, but not anymore."

She studied his face. He actually believed what he said. Anticipating the pain of further separation, she whispered, "Then you won't mind that we go to Missouri? It is for fear that we must."

"Jenny!" In desperation he grabbed her, digging his fingers into her forearms, commanding attention. "You don't understand!" He paused to steady his voice. "But you will someday. Until then, trust me. We must not go with Joseph."

"Someday," she whispered back. "Mark, there's no time to wait for someday. You've heard Joseph. Christ will be returning very soon and we must be in Zion waiting. There's no time to waste. Joseph's revelations say there will be destruction and death for all who refuse to accept the truth of this dispensation. All of the churches have been polluted; there is no other church with the truth. Joseph has shown us clearly that there is no other way." Mark turned away.

But now Jenny was caught by a clear, illuminated moment. Understanding suddenly dropped into her mind. Only by surrendering Mark would she have all things—and Mark, too. The key was obedience to the church. Before her loomed the promise of power. Joseph had said those words. Without power the dream could not be, and now the dream included Mark. Oh, how desperately it included Mark!

STAR LIGHT, STAR BRIGHT   273

She found herself whispering, "How blind, Mark, how blind can you be! Am I the only one who sees clearly?"

Mark turned his ravaged face toward her. Their eyes met, and in another moment they were in each other's arms. But even as Jenny lifted her lips and held him close, tears were streaming down her face. There was no turning back. The truth was *very* clear.

In the end Jenny, white-faced and rigid in her new wagon with a hired teamster, prepared to leave. Mark, equally white-faced, stood helpless and confused as he watched his wife, ready to ride out of Kirtland with her share of their marriage in the wagon.

And in the final moments, when it didn't seem possible for another word to be said, while Mark leaned against the wagon wheel, a flock of geese flew overhead. The quiet of the dawn was broken as their wings beat the air. Both Jenny and Mark lifted their faces, hearing a note of desperation in that honking as the geese flew on.

They watched the formation disappear into a tiny black check against the dawn. "Mark," Jenny whispered and her face came close to his, "that's just the way it is with me. I can do nothing other than go. I am compelled beyond my own personal desires, even the dearest longings of my heart. I prayed to understand my destiny, and I'm seeing it clearly."

The wagon train had just started to move when Mark walked away. He trudged through the silent streets, listening to the echo of his own footsteps. Old Matthew Lewis hailed him. "You're a fool." Lewis paused to spit contemptuously. "Joseph's taught these women that if their husbands refuse to join them, then their marriages are null and void. For the Saints, there's only one way—it's living up to the laws and revelations given in this dispensation under the Prophet. This new church has the keys to the kingdom; there's no other way."

Mark continued on to his lonely house. Still contemplating the half of his life that was left, he entered the house and witnessed Jenny's final act. She had left food prepared for his first lonely meal. He looked at the bread and milk, the cut of roast beef and the still warm apple pie.

Slowly he sat down and turned his back to the table. The door was open and he saw the shadow before he heard the knock. "I can't believe it— Tom!" Mark's lips moved woodenly as he got up to greet his brother-in-law.

Tom looked around the kitchen with a bewildered expression. "They told me most of Kirtland is gone, that even the troublemakers are headed for Zion." His eyes were wary. "Down at the stables, they gave me the story that my sister Jenny left her husband and has gone to Joseph's Zion."

Mark studied Tom's frowning face and shoved at a chair. "Look, you deserve a decent explanation. Sit down and eat this stuff while I talk."

Tom was eyeing the table as he said, "I met the wagon train just as I pulled into town. Didn't have an idea Jenny was on it, or I'd have looked for her."

Mark watched Tom cut into the roast. "I guess the only way to make myself understood is to start at the beginning." He noticed that Tom was picking at the meat in a half-hearted manner and he hunched his chair closer to his brother-in-law.

"See, in the beginning," he said, "back when Jenny and I were married, I didn't give a fig for any kind of religion. I joined the church because I wanted your sister. Also, I intended to keep it that way. I suppose if this were just another church, I would have."

"What do you mean?"

"I wasn't around Joseph long before I began to notice the blind adoration of his followers. I tried to ignore it, but I began to see an unquestioning obedience that bothered me. Somehow it all seemed wrong. I couldn't reconcile it with what I'd been taught about God."

"Mark, face it. All religions are like this. People are scared to death of losin' out and gettin' kicked out of the church." There was a touch of pride in his voice. "Joe inspires these people to give it their best if they want to make it in the hereafter."

"Is that it? I was beginning to think Joseph had some strange power over these people. Maybe it is fear. Fear of God and hell, of being left on the outside. At least Jenny talked like that. Tom, I'm seeing man's mindless groping. I find myself wishing there could be more than one way to God."

Tom lifted his head and slowly put down his spoon. "What do you mean, Mark? What are you gettin' at?"

"I went to England as a missionary. About the first week out in the countryside, while I was trying to tell the people about the new religion and how this was the latest thing and how the Lord was coming soon and they'd better join up and go build up Zion, it hit me.

"I saw those faces believing me and hanging on to every word. They were wanting what I had to offer. You should have seen them. Dirt-poor, without a chance of improving their lot. Sure, they were ready for anything sounding as good as Zion. But I was feeling bad about it. You see, I wasn't the least convinced."

Tom winced. "So what did you do?"

"I started reading the Bible. After all, the Mormons are supposed to believe that's God's Word, too."

"That's right," Tom nodded. "Brigham Young said he believed there was enough in the Bible to lead a man into finding salvation."

Mark paused and then continued, "Well, I decided to borrow Heber's Bible and have a go at reading it."

"To be fair, you should have read the *Book of Mormon.*"

"I have. I've also read the Prophet's revelations and some of the other writings." Mark paused and watched Tom eat Jenny's apple pie. Finally Mark got to his feet and paced the kitchen.

He was thinking about Tom's statement. Confusion and excitement mingled in him and finally he sat in front of Tom again. "So Brig said that. Tom, have you read the Bible?" He shook his head and Mark continued, his excitement growing. "Tom, do you consider me a fairly intelligent person?"

Tom looked up surprised. "Well, certainly, man. I've never doubted that. You know I've always respected your mind. Why do you ask?"

"There's a couple of things I came up with in my reading that just won't let me alone. One is that God is unchangeable. The *Book of Mormon* says that. Another is that the Bible says Jesus Christ is really God, come to this earth and born just like any other man except that His conception was a miracle from the Holy Spirit—not the result of a union of Adam and Mary. But here's the rub. The Bible teaches that sin caused separation between God and man, and the only way the separation can be bridged in a decent and honorable way is by the blood sacrifice provided by God Himself."

Tom's face was thoughtful, and Mark added, "Mormonism teaches Christ's death does not bring righteousness, but instead only another chance at life for everyone. It teaches that righteousness and holiness are to be earned. It says man can work his way into good standing with God simply by following Joseph's new church with its rules and regulations. I don't get the idea from watching people that this church is all that holy."

Tom sighed and sat back, "Now you've hit the nail on the head. There's stuff goin' on that even an ignorant blacksmith like me can figure out as bein' all wrong." His forehead puckered and slowly he spoke again. "If you're feelin' like this, what caused the big fight between you and Jenny that sent her runnin' to Missouri?"

Mark sighed and for a moment he dropped his head into his hands. "Tom, can you believe that I love your sister with all my heart and that I want nothing more than to spend the rest of my life with her?" He paused. "First, I tried to make her understand all I've told you and she rejected it. Then, like a complete dummy, I put my foot down and announced we were leaving the church and Kirtland. That did it. If I'd left well enough alone instead of trying to push my way on her, everything could maybe have been settled between us."

"So what happened?"

"She said she was scared to death of not going. That the second coming of Christ is so near, she didn't dare risk changing her belief. Tom, I could see she was running on account of fear. I just didn't know how to handle it." He looked imploringly at his brother-in-law and waited.

Tom slouched back in his chair and pushed his hat over his eyes. Mark waited while May's sweet perfume drifted through the door, reminding him that life was moving on. Finally Tom straightened and tossed his hat in the corner. "You say she's scared? I suppose you're just as scared God'll get you for not being in the right place at the right time."

"Tom," Mark protested, "that's not it at all. There's not one thing I can do to earn righteousness, but I don't see—"

"It's simple. Go to Missouri and wait this out. Seems if you're followin' God while the others aren't, you ought to be around to pick up the pieces when Zion falls apart. Besides, Jenny needs you—even if she won't admit it. Mark, she needs you more'n I can let on right now." Mark watched the troubled expression settle down across Tom's face, and as he pondered the heaviness of Tom's statement, new hope made him straighten up in his chair.

He was beginning to grin when Tom stood up and asked, "Gotta horse?"

He blinked, "Well, yes, but—"

"You can catch up with that wagon train if you hustle." He was addressing Mark's back. "Better take your duds. I'll pack up the rest of the furniture and see you in a couple weeks."

The wagon train was curving its way slowly out of Kirtland like a serpent, its tail still touching the edge of town while the head stretched in a cloud of dust south and west toward the prairie. He paused only a moment to measure the line of wagons and pick the one with the billowing top pressing toward the crest of the hill.

Mark rode his horse hard, pushing through the line of wagons and the surge of cattle. Winding out of the trail, spurred by impatience, he cut through the trees and headed for the spot where he knew Jenny's wagon would crest the hill.

He winced as he put the whip to the horse's flanks and leaned into the wind. That billowing top would blow loose before the week was out. What poor excuse for a driver had she found, a tad who couldn't even fasten a canvas?

Now Mark was beside the wagon, shrouded in dust, watching it lurch through the ruts. The driver was indeed a boy, straining at the reins. Jenny, tense and pale, clung to her seat.

Mark's yell was a mixture of triumph and anger. He had the reins in his hands before the youth could move. With one leap Mark was on the seat, dropping down between Jenny and the boy. "Here." Mark shoved some silver coins into the hands of the youth. "Now, get that horse and take it back to the stables. Tell Tom Timmons I sent you."

His hand urged the startled lad into action, and Mark settled into the seat and straightened the reins. He dared not glance at Jenny. "Didn't like the looks of that top. Decided I'd better come along and do the driving myself."

Mark leaned over and carefully wrapped the reins around the seat bracing. There was still no sound from her, but their silence shattered the first stone in the wall between them. For a moment he shivered with fear. What if she wouldn't have him back? When he turned, Mark was conscious only of amazement as he looked into her face. It took a while before he summoned the strength to draw that deep, ragged breath he needed, but when he did, Jenny moved and blinked. Slowly color began to touch her cheeks.

He could only whisper; even then he felt words were unnecessary. And over the creaking and groaning of the wagon, the lowing of the oxen and the crack of the canvas, they both knew the miracle. "Jenny, I'm here to go with you—all the way." Her eyes were speaking back, saying she could accept and there would be no questions. But he must say it. "Remember those words? I promised to love you as long as we both shall live."

Her lips moved stiffly and he leaned closer to hear. "Mark," she was pleading, "I know it is a strange love, but truly I do love you."

He couldn't speak, but when he bent to kiss her, he caught a glimpse of the shadows in her eyes. She didn't know that his lips moving against hers were promising, "In sickness, in health, I pledge you my love."

5

IT WAS HOT in the Cartwright wagon. Jenny brushed at the dampness on her face and shifted on the wagon seat. She glanced at Mark, studying the new beard and the wide-brimmed hat shading his face. Instead of his usual white shirt and silk tie, he was wearing the coarse homespun of a frontiersman. She touched his sleeve, enjoying the feel of the hard muscle tightening as he flicked the reins across the back of Sammy. "Get along there, girl, do your part of the pulling," he urged mildly.

Jenny smiled as she watched the errant mare quicken her step. "Poor dear," she said, "this is beneath their dignity, pulling this creaking wagon with all that canvas popping behind them. They're much more suited to cantering down a country lane with nary a rut, pulling a smart little buggy. But then I suppose you would have fitted me out with oxen like the rest of them had you known at the time that—" Her voice trailed away as she was caught up in the memory of that last fearful day when she had left Ohio, thinking that never again would she see Mark. She shivered even as she dabbed at the moisture on her forehead.

Mark's hand quickly clasped hers. When he looked at her, she saw the dark expression, but his light words bore no relation to that shared memory. "Might yet," he said with a grin, flicking the reins. "Do you hear that, gals? Might trade the two of you for one good ox."

His hand still cuddled hers and they rode in companionable silence. When Jenny finally stirred, she turned to Mark and commented, "They told me it was eight hundred miles to Missouri." She was feeling the late afternoon sun press against her like a heavy hand, blotting out all except the weary heat.

Mark shoved his hat back from his eyes and grinned at her. She studied his face, thinking she had never seen him so tanned. There was a band of white across his forehead and below it his face was mahogany brown. Rivulets of moisture drew lines through the dust on his cheeks and dampened his beard. With a sigh, she pushed her heavy hair away from her forehead, rubbing at the sweat, guessing that dust streaked her own face as well.

Jenny tried to stifle the weary yawn rising up within her even as she searched his expression looking again for some indication that he regretted being here on this lonesome road to Missouri. How constantly aware she was of the tiptoe feeling in her heart. Knowing how close she had come to forfeiting forever Mark's presence beside her was a memory that would be with her the rest of her life. She twisted her hands in her lap and felt the talisman snugged securely in the pocket of her dusty frock.

For a moment her lips trembled with a half smile. How much she would give to know just what power had won her husband back when she had given up all hopes of ever seeing him again!

She fingered the talisman again. Either this charmed metal with its secret spirit powers had done the trick, or praying to Luna and God had worked in her favor. For a moment, remembering Mark's new beliefs, she was filled with shame. She moved uneasily on the hard wooden seat of the wagon and wondered at the feeling. Was it because she knew the powers had worked for her against Mark's will?

Mark was speaking and she realized with a start how far afield her thoughts had wandered. "What did you say?" she asked, moving around to look at him.

"It *is* eight hundred miles," he repeated, "and divided into the twelve or fifteen miles we'll make a day, it'll be a miracle if we're there by Independence Day."

"Is it important?" Jenny murmured, thinking now of the isolation this wagon and this dusty road had thrown about their lives. She lifted her head and grinned at him. "At least while you're driving this wagon, Joseph can't be sending you off to kingdom come."

"That's good?"

She searched his eyes for the reason behind the question, even as she nodded. He started to add more and then hesitated. Jenny realized how often nowadays he had been doing that. Impatience boiled up within her, but immediately she trembled, thinking of all the things he might say. It was those very things which had nearly torn them apart—his new beliefs that seemed at odds with everything the church taught. She felt his hand on her arm and covered it with her own.

The next day the wagon train left Ohio behind, and the road turned south. Each day now they watched as the land became more arid. Jenny noticed even the smallest villages were miles apart. Slowly they moved from one watering hole to the next.

Indiana was a short stretch, and across the flat lands, the wagon train sometimes pressed through twenty miles in one day.

Again the way became hot and dusty; tired animals strayed and bawled for water, fretful children quarreled, and the menfolk snapped at each other. When the food supply dwindled, the wagon captains chafed while a day was snatched by the women for laundry and bread-baking.

One evening in June, the wagon train circled late in the evening on the prairie close to the Wabash River.

Their camp was hot and dusty and it didn't help at all, Jenny thought, to hear the distant crash of waterfalls and the shouts of the youths who had taken the cattle to water and then managed to fall in themselves.

Jenny sighed over her supper fire as she moved slowly about preparing a meal. She was recalling the day's travel. Her memory was full of gentle scenes: the clear fresh water of a brook cutting through an orchard, a log cabin with the yard dotted with people waving at the wagon train. She recalled the parents and children—tousle-haired, in stairstep order. Later in the day there had been glimpses of refreshing color on the prairie, masses of flowers growing wild. Jenny yearned after them. She paused, and the memory of it all tilted and tipped, thrusting the components of the day into order and serving up a dream of a home that didn't move every morning. And children.

She sighed and spread a cloth across rough boxes. Mark was watching and she asked, "Do you suppose we'll ever have a family like that?" At his puzzled frown she explained, "Those young'uns who were waving as we passed."

"I expect so." His grin was intimate, and for a moment she forgot their home moved every morning.

After a supper of salty, tough meat and leathery potatoes, Mark disappeared. Jenny spread their blankets under the wagon while she slapped at the buzzing flies and gnats. Thinking longingly of a cool bath, she swished the water around in the bucket. It barely covered the bottom of the pail.

When the embers of the supper fires had cooled and the mosquitoes moved in, Jenny retreated to her bed. She seldom allowed herself the luxury of tears, but tonight they couldn't be ignored. She dabbed at her eyes as she swatted insects and fanned away the heat and smoke.

Jenny heard Mark's step, but before she had time to mop the tears away, he was beside her. "Come," he whispered, pulling at her hand. "Don't make a sound." His hand urged her on as he guided her through the dark, sleeping camp.

When they were through the bushes she whispered, "Mark, they'll think we're Indians and shoot! Besides, you know we're not to leave camp." He tightened his grasp, and she silently followed.

They went up a slope and down a steep bank. In front of them the river shimmered in the moonlight. That dim gurgle of sound she had heard became a roar as they walked upstream toward the falls. Cool spray reached Jenny, and she lifted her face to the moisture. Beyond the mist, the moon was rising over the trees.

"Look," he whispered, pulling her close. "There're deer on the far bank. In a moment you'll see them outlined against the moonlight."

"After that terrible supper you'll *look* at deer instead of shooting?" she hissed.

He turned to answer and instead bent close. His hand touched her cheek. "Tears. Is it so bad? You know we can always—"

Hastily she interrupted, "Mark, it's the heat. I want to bathe."

"Aw!" he exclaimed, "my next surprise. Come." Down the next bend of the river she saw the inlet where the water was calm and shallow. "Perchance the sun has even warmed it," he said with a mock bow. He dug in his pocket and held up a bar of soap.

After the first shock the water was nearly warm. Jenny soaped her hair, then dived and swam the width of the inlet, leaving a trail of suds behind. Mark was beside her. Moonlight gleamed on his wet bare arm. She watched the muscles knot and relax as he floated lazy circles around her.

When he circled her one more time, she touched his wet arm and said, "I've never seen a marble statue, but I've seen pictures. They always look wet and smooth like this. But not warm." He slipped his arm under her shoulders and together they floated, gently rocked by the waves and lulled by river sounds. The moon was misting over with lazy clouds, and above their heads the stars became brilliant. Now center stage, they sparkled; occasionally one shot across the horizon.

Dreamily she said, "Mark, the Saints in Missouri saw a meteor shower. It came at a bad time. A good omen. Maybe tonight's such an omen for us. Maybe—" He bent over her and kissed her gently.

"I don't think we need an omen, do we?"

When morning came and Jenny rolled over in her nest of musty blankets, she couldn't believe the dream of water and star-shot sky, with Mark's wet shoulder against hers. She was ready with a sigh until she saw his smile; then she once more snuggled her face against his shoulder before the day began.

Just as the dusty miles piled up behind the wagon train and became greater than the miles that lay ahead, the sense of excitement began building. The Saints spent more and more of the evenings around the fire.

Some of the men had traveled this route before. Now they were the center of attention. In the evening, after Jenny and the other women washed their supper dishes, they joined the group around the fire, leaning close to watch as the men knelt on the ground and used a stick to draw maps in the soil. Eager questions were fired at them. "Are there mountains ahead?" "Are the Indians ornery in Missouri?" "When do we cross the Mississippi?"

As more miles passed beneath the wagon wheels, the questions changed. Jenny guessed from the anxiety in her own heart that the Saints were wondering as much she did. Finally the question was asked, "What will our new home be like? Will we have all the promises of Zion right off?"

Some of the answers given by the group captains were vague and left an uneasy feeling; she was especially aware of it in Mark's restlessness. Again the fear of losing him crept upon her, as she listened while some of the old-timers compared Jackson County to the new land farther north. She couldn't forget the night beside the fire when Matt Miller talked about Jackson.

The fire had burned down to sputtering coals and the figures about the fire were shadowy outlines against the star-filled sky. Old Matt had been one of the first group to settle in Missouri back in 1832. His voice was dreamy as he described the land. "Gentle acres, they was. Easy to set a plow to, and the seeds sprung up almost before you could get them settled and the soil patted down. Never had to worry about your next meal; the land was teeming with wild turkey, rabbit, deer and sage hen."

A question interrupted his reminiscence. "We've heard how the Missouri settlers mistreated the Saints. Is that a fact?"

He sighed before he answered and he spoke reluctantly. "It's a fact. Seems it hadn't ought to have been. There's room for all who want to work the land. With the Indian problems 'twas to their advantage to have a few more around."

"What was the problem?" Jenny recognized Thompson's heavy voice.

Miller replied, "Ya got to understand the old settlers. They's a rough breed, to be sure. But more'n anything, even more'n minding having us around, they objected to some of the lot informing them that the Lord had given the land to the Saints, and that no matter what, they'd get it all in the end." He sighed and passed his hand across his face wearily.

He added, "There's a bunch of us who grew mighty fond of the land. We'd a been glad to keep our mouths shut and work our hands to the bone just to get to stay there." His voice trailed away. When he spoke again his voice was matter-of-fact. "We left gentle, rich acres and growing towns. Our homes and farms we had to give up for unplowed prairie and barren wastes. A mighty price to pay because we believed the revelation and spoke out our belief. Now I hope we keep our mouths shut and live like any other man on this earth." He paused for a moment, and in the silence the last of the fire sputtered and snapped. His voice was filled with sorrow, and Jenny shivered as he said, "If we don't we'll be a running again. Only this time, could be we'll all pay with our lives."

During the following day, Jenny lined up the comments and questions, sorting and discarding the nerve-tender ones and pushing others at Mark. "It's nothing but rumbles; we've been hearing them all winter," she remarked, ignoring Mark's somber expression. "Missouri problems. Back then, back in the beginning, how could Joseph be expected to keep things moving smooth as stirred gravy when he wasn't around to tend to the stirring?"

Mark's smile was tentative as he said, "At least the fellows feel free to chew over the facts."

"That's because Joseph and the twelve aren't around to thunder at their grumbles." She saw his expression and regretted her words. She tried to smooth them over. "No one has a right to dispute when the Prophet has the keys of the kingdom and his word is scripture."

He ducked his head, but not before Jenny saw the white line around his mouth and heard him say, "Jenny, my dear, remember that statement. I'm certain I'll have occasion to remind you of it. But for now, there are problems. All the rumbles I've heard about the difficulties in Jackson County back in the beginning points to a rocky road once we reach Caldwell County."

"You're referring to the treatment the Saints had when they first went into Jackson. Well, that's persecution."

"Can you call it persecution when a fellow balances an apple on his head and dares his buddy to knock it off?"

"Meaning?" Jenny asked.

"For one thing, the articles Phelps published. For another, the Saints going around telling the people of Missouri God has given them the land, and that He'd promised the riches of the Gentiles would be theirs." Jenny opened her mouth to reply and Mark said, "How would you feel if someone told you all your work was for naught, that the Lord was going to pass it all on to someone else?"

"They *pushed* them out of Jackson. Now, up north the land isn't fertile."

"Don't forget what Miller said. Also, consider, they've found a home— and from all reports, they'll be welcome to stay if they try to get along with their neighbors." Mark was silent a moment, then thoughtfully said, "I think I'm going to make it a point to get acquainted with Phelps."

"Why?"

He was frowning slightly as he looked up. "I think I want to find out what makes the man tick."

"Mark," Jenny said slowly, recalling the troubled man she had lived with that first year of their marriage, "I'm thinking you're back to carrying the whole lot on your shoulders again. Some call it trouble-making, and the Prophet doesn't abide that."

His voice was sober as he replied, "Call it as you wish. I'd be less than a—a man if I didn't try to help those around me." Mark flicked the reins along the backs of the horses.

Suddenly Mark lifted his head and grinned. "Hey, you're talking about the *they's*. Do you realize we're going to be some of the *they's*? Think you'll like being a farmer's wife?"

"Mark!" Jenny looked down at his smooth hands. "Have you ever milked a cow in your life?"

"When I was about six."

Jenny laughed. "Finally, there's something I know better'n you. I'll be your teacher. I even know how to clean a pig sty."

But it wasn't the discontented rumbles, or the uneasy questions Jenny was thinking about that first evening they stopped on the border of Missouri. Jenny was remembering that star-studded night and the misty moonlit bath they'd had in the Wabash River in Indiana. What had there been about that time to make her think back wistfully? Was it the isolation of that spot and Mark all to herself? Why did that scene make her think of peace and restoration?

Mark had called it an Ebenezer night and when she tried to get him to explain, he'd grinned and said it was like climbing a hill and passing a post marking the halfway place. Then he added softly, "It means we've come thus far." She searched his face and that light in his eyes reassured even more than the strange words. *Thus far.* She hugged the words to herself and hoped.

It was soon evident that they were inside Missouri's borders. Here there weren't any tidy clusters of homes decorated with borders of flower gardens. Instead, tiny log cabins marked towns where there were nearly as many saloons as homes.

There were other things, too. She saw black men working the fields, while white men bunched around the saloons. She also saw the number of men was far greater than the women and children. While Jenny was still adjusting to this, she became aware that it was commonplace to find in every hamlet curious lines of people gathered to watch their wagons move through.

Sometimes there were friendly waves and children shouting, but often there were hostile, suspicious stares. On one occasion an old man called, "Be ye Mormons?" At Jenny's nod, he called, "Weren't Jackson enough? Bogg is too lily-livered about stopping ya, but we know some who will.

"We ain't forgettin' the past when yer men marched in with arms. 'Tis 'gainst the law. We ain't forgettin' yer men said the Lord gave them this land. Well, we get different information from the Lord."

Jenny murmured, "They aren't very friendly."

Mark replied, "But that woman waved and smiled."

"Then I should make friends of the women?" He nodded, but for a moment she wondered at the shadow in his eyes.

The wagon train pressed deeper into Missouri, heading farther north and west. The terrain was changing nearly daily. Jenny saw the mountains flattened into prairies of luxuriant grass. While trees clustered the valleys and bordered the creeks and rivers, the dense forests had disappeared.

On the days that it was their turn to ride near the lead of the wagon train, Jenny could watch the deer leaping away in the distance as the wagons approached. The quail and partridges would seek cover in the tall grasses until at last their courage failed. Too often they would rise to confront musket fire, and that night there would be fresh meat for supper.

The night talk around the fire became excited chatter when it was circulated that they were now close to the place where Joseph Smith had settled. Jenny felt contentment in the cozy talk of the women, suddenly happy with life and sure of the future.

While the men talked about this new land they would settle, and about the crops they would plant, the women had their heads together. Jenny listened to the news. Emma Smith had produced another boy child. "My, the Prophet's outfitting his farm proper-like."

A tart tongue added, "Likely those young'uns 'll have life easier than ours."

Once again the women rehashed the old story of the conflict in Jackson. As they weighed the chances of success in this new endeavor, some of the men joined their group. Jenny heard the derision in one voice as the man said, "After being turned out of Jackson County, the big-hearted Missouri legislature thought they were doing us a favor by giving all the Mormons Caldwell County. They don't know it, but Saints will be swarming over the whole state in a year or so." Jenny and Mark's eyes met, and she watched him turn away. For some unknown reason the June night seemed suddenly chilled.

Now, around the fire, the men who knew chortled, "They drew a line, but Joe's already stepped over it. Saints have moved into Daviess and Carroll as well as Ray counties."

The answer given was smug, and Jenny mentally squirmed over it, even as she acknowledged the truth of it. The woman sitting beside her said, " 'Tis true. The Lord's promised the land to us. Zion it will be, and already we're knowing that it's going to have to be taken, most likely by the sword, since they're resisting. 'Twill be a difficult time for us, but the promise of the lands and houses being ours as well as the gold and silver, well, that helps."

Jenny felt Mark stirring restlessly, but wisely she chose to hold her tongue.

6

JENNY HAD BEEN asleep when the stealthy rustle reached through her dreams. With eyes wide, she listened. In the silence of the camp, she was aware of the freshening air. The last of the smoke was gone and the circle of wagons was dark. She guessed it was very late. Again the rustle came. Slowly she reached for Mark. At the quick pressure of his hand she allowed herself a sigh of relief.

As Mark left her side she heard a clink of metal and a muffled curse. There was Mark's low voice and an answering voice. It must be just one of the men. After listening a moment longer, Jenny snuggled into the blankets. Her eyelids had begun to droop when she realized the tenor of voices had changed, and another voice was added.

For a moment more she strained to hear the muffled words. Finally she slipped out of the blankets and crouched behind the wagon wheel. Although she couldn't understand the words, she recognized that voice.

Crawling out from under the wagon she moved toward the men and whispered, "Oliver Cowdery, whatever are you doing here?"

Mark turned to pull her close, saying, "Be quiet and just listen. These men have come from Far West."

"Far West? That's in Caldwell County where we're headed, isn't it? What do they want?"

"Food for their families and anything else we can spare. They are destitute."

"There's bread and cold beans, dried meat and apples. We still have flour and—" Mark's words began to sink. She turned to Cowdery. "Destitute! Whatever has happened?"

Now she became conscious of other dark shadows in the background.

Cowdery sighed deeply and wiped a hand slowly across his face. Impatiently Mark said, "Jenny, don't we have extra quilts and dishes?"

"Quilts! It's nearly July. Dishes . . ." Mark's hand urged her toward the wagon and the men followed.

Inside the wagon Jenny tumbled through bundles, her mind in as much confusion as the jumble before her. The men pressed into the wagon.

"Four of you," she said in surprise. Slowly she reached for plates and forks and found an extra skillet. Her mind was busy bringing up facts about the men while their haunted, lined faces were giving out information that bewildered her. She paused to peer at the men. Surely she was mistaken—they couldn't be fleeing Zion!

There was Oliver Cowdery, schoolteacher and newspaper editor, but most importantly, one of the witnesses to the *Book of Mormon*. What could have forced him to leave? And Johnson. She knew nothing about him. Could he possibly be the brother of the Nancy Miranda whose name had been linked with Joseph's? They said the man Eli had led a mob against the Prophet. Jenny bit her lip. What trouble was being raised against the Prophet now? The man beside him, David Whitmer, was also a witness to the *Book of Mormon*. His brother John was the fourth member of the group. At their father's home Joseph had completed the translation of the golden plates. She ventured a peek at the stony faces, and her questions grew.

As she pulled out the flour and bacon, she cast a bewildered glance at Mark.

"They haven't had anything to eat since early morning," Mark said. "They've obtained wagons, but not much else. Whitmer says that now the word's passed, some are afraid to be seen talking with them, let alone give help. That's why they've come at night."

"Like common criminals," Cowdery said bitterly. "Rigdon's been after my neck since I came to Missouri. Just once too often I aired my feelings. Said I blamed him for the troubles the Saints are in. He'll never forgive us for being disheartened when the bank failed in Kirtland."

One of the Whitmers said, "I can see him gloating now that we've been reduced to running like rats, and begging like the scum of the earth instead of Israel's chosen."

Jenny studied the lined faces as the men talked. She was conscious of the germ of uneasiness growing inside. When she turned, Mark's serious face multiplied the feeling.

Mark gathered up the quilts and food. "You've told me enough to convince me the whole lot of us need to hear your story first thing in the morning. For now, let's take these things to your families and have you settled for the night."

As the group filed silently out of sight, Jenny was remembering the last time she had seen Cowdery. He, David Whitmer, and Martin Harris had been watching the black-robed girl as she had whirled on the streets and promised to read their futures. For a time the three men had been leaders in the group that followed the seeress with her black stone—the dissenters, as they'd been called.

Everyone knew how Joseph Smith had shaken them loose from their folly. Shortly after the Prophet returned to Kirtland, he had sent Whitmer and Cowdery to Missouri; Martin Harris had left the church completely.

When Mark came back to the wagon and crawled into bed, he murmured, "They've told me little. I know only that they've been run out of Zion on threat of their lives. I could see they were exhausted. I've promised to listen to their story tomorrow."

For a long time after Mark's even breathing told her he was asleep, Jenny lay wide-eyed staring into the darkness, wondering what portent was being heralded. Certainly evil was stalking into her life again. She sensed that when the men had talked.

Tossing and turning on her hard pallet, Jenny became convinced that the hints of happiness she had felt for the past few weeks were again being threatened. She tightened her hands around the talisman and vowed to renew her search for power and success. Success? She rolled onto her elbow and looked down at Mark. She thought of those empty days just before she had left Kirtland. Never again would she risk losing him.

Jenny tightened her grasp on the talisman and silently her lips moved through the incantations, invoking peace, happiness, and safety. Now she was holding her breath, willing stillness, waiting for intimations of peace; but in the quietness, a new vision pressed itself across her mind. There was Jenny on a seesaw, rising high only to plunge earthward. But even as she swooped down, she knew she could scoot to the middle and ride both sides. With a pleased grin, she turned on her side and snuggled against Mark. Little did it matter that both sides of the seesaw were books, one green and the other gold; she would use them both.

The next morning the four men and their families trailed into the wagon train's enclosure. Silent, questioning faces were turned toward them. Jenny was well aware of the tension moving through the group. The very air vibrated with it.

Early this morning, before breakfast, Mark had met with the men in command of the wagon train. She had watched that silent group as they had been called into council. She watched the hunched figures around the fire and listened to the low murmur of conversation. She saw the worried frown, the glances toward the strangers' wagons, and she felt her own skin prickle with an unidentified apprehension. She knew others were feeling it, too. She saw it in the worried faces of the women as they tried to busy themselves around camp.

As Jenny went about her tasks, from the camp next to them, Libby Taylor straightened her back and groaned, "Why do we have to get mixed up with dissenters before we've even a chance to settle in this new land?" The woman who answered her in a murmur looked in Jenny's direction.

Libby said loudly, "I don't care if she does. I intend to stay in the good graces of the presidency." Jenny paused, towel in hand, thinking back to those statements Matt had made. It was while she still agonized over his concern that this same woman had skimmed over it all with her words, saying, *"The Lord promised the land to us. Zion it will be—most likely by the sword."* This same woman's husband had said, *"They drew a line, but Joe's already stepped over it."*

Still staring at the woman, Jenny wrapped the towel around her shoulders and murmured, "Dear Lord, what are we getting ourselves into?" Immediately the incongruity of her statement swept over her. Jenny sighed as she turned back to the pan of dishes.

By midmorning the wagon train was still circled beside the trail. The group around the men had been growing since breakfast time. The men's story had been repeated, analyzed, and passed around the group. Jenny watched as they shifted uneasily from one foot to another, while the women stood apart in a miserable group.

She watched Mark's face. That furrowed brow made her uneasy. It held the expression she had seen often during the first winter of their marriage. Mark was being pulled asunder by things he didn't understand.

Now Mark's voice rose, "What started this? Was it talk over the Fannie Alger affair?"

Jenny looked at him in surprise. Mark wasn't prone to listen to gossip, and since the incident Nettie had reported to her had happened while Mark was in England, she supposed he knew nothing of the affair. While the excited babble surrounded her, Jenny was studying Mark's face, surprised by the play of expression, as his frown gave way to distaste, then anger.

The man spoke slowly, "I suppose it was partly to blame. You don't question Joseph and stay in his good graces."

Jenny couldn't keep the hard note out of her voice as she walked up to the group and addressed Johnson. "You were making terrible accusations against the Prophet right there in the temple. Everyone knows that."

Ignoring her, Cowdery said, "What really caused the problem was buying land here in Missouri and not deeding it to the church."

"The United Order," a knowing voice added. "Just like we had in Kirtland, only out here it seems the only takers were those who didn't have anything to consecrate to the church."

Another rough voice on the fringe of the group broke in. "I say, leave these men to their own devices. I'm feeling we're picking up a quarrel we've no need to. All who's for heading for Far West today, fall in behind me."

Jenny watched the string of men and women snaking along after the man; bemused, she recalled his name was Daniels.

Abruptly Jenny realized she was still standing beside the fire, clinging to Mark's arm. The midnight thieves, Oliver Cowdery, Lyman Johnson, David Whitmer, and John Whitmer, were standing there, too. But there were others.

Mark was saying, "You realize what you're doing? You're saying you believe these men and that you want to help their families. That could put you in bad with Joseph and Ridgon right off. Are you willing to stick your neck out like that?" In a moment he broke the silence, saying slowly, "Your reputation will tarnish before you even settle in Zion. Do you want to run the risk of being labeled as dissenters?"

Matt spoke up. "You know, I left Missouri just long enough to fetch my young'uns from Kirtland. I believe in the land. Maybe I don't believe enough in Joseph right now, but I like it here enough to fight for what I want."

"And what's that?" Mark asked slowly.

"A home in Missouri, freedom. Joe's gotta let us have more head room. He's gotta give us a chance to act like men, with minds to think and choose. Some of us are gettin' tired of being treated like bad little boys, havin' our hands smacked for havin' our say."

There was an uneasy ripple through the crowd, but Jenny's quick glance around the circle told her many were approving of Matt's words.

She had just a quick glance in Mark's direction, noting the relief on his face, when Silas Jenson quickly added, "But there's other reasons. The Whitmers have been good friends of ours since the church began. Take year before last. My wife nearly died birthin' and Missus Whitmer was right there long as we needed her. It pains me to think of what she's feelin' right now."

From the back of the circle a thoughtful voice added, "I can't believe Joseph's meanin' those things he said. Sure I believe Cowdery's telling the truth when he repeated the story, but I'd like to hear some more."

"Everybody knows Rigdon's a rant and raver. Everybody takes him with a grain of salt." There was a wave of nervous laughter.

Jenny said, "I've just finished the dishes. I didn't hear the men talk, neither did Clara or Betsy. Seems like, if we're to be following the men-folk into who knows what, then maybe we should be hearing their story."

"We don't have time. Let's get these wagons on the road."

There was a snort behind Jenny and she turned. Bella Partridge folded her arms across her ample body and stretched to her full height. She was nearly as tall as the tallest man in the group. The silence lasted another second and Jenny saw Bella's chin jut out while the flesh under her chin quivered. Words were unnecessary. Her husband sighed, "Might as well tell the whole story over again, or we ain't goin' no place."

The day was heating up rapidly. Mark led the way to a shady grove. As they settled in the shade of the trees, Jenny noticed most of the group were middle-aged and somber.

Cowdery spoke first. "I'm convinced Joseph is a prophet holding the keys of the kingdom. You know I'm wanting to obey the Lord and make it in the hereafter, or I'd not be out here in Missouri, following the Prophet."

David Whitmer was speaking now. "It goes against the grain to give up on a project. But a man's got to have some say about his life."

Cowdery continued, "Rigdon particularly is wanting us outta the state. He's made up his mind and won't rest until he's driven us out. Me particularly. I've made no bones about my feelings. Rigdon's the troublemaker. He's responsible for the Danites. They are his baby. Missourians are a tough lot, I grant, but Rigdon made up his mind he'll be tougher."

John Whitmer added, "They'd been putting the screws into me to give over all my property to the church. Rigdon was the one who started the tide of feeling against me. He did it with his preaching when he gave out that salt sermon on last June 17. Since then feelings were running high."

" 'Ye are the salt of the earth,' " Cowdery quoted bitterly, "and if the salt's lost its savor, it's to be trodden underfoot. The Saints were duty-bound to trample underfoot those who wouldn't go along with all the church taught."

Whitmer continued, "Corrill came to me secret-like, saying it was Rigdon's signal to the Danites to get me. He advised I hightail right then. I didn't want to give up everything I'd worked for because of that feeling, so I went to Joe."

Mark interrupted, "Did Joe sanction Rigdon's sermon?"

"He didn't come right out and say so, but he did say that the Lord revealed to him it was Peter who done in Judas." There was silence and Jenny pondered Joseph's statement.

The mild voice from the back of the crowd spoke again, "I ain't heard more'n whispers about the Danites. Some of you fellas explain."

David Whitmer faced the man and spoke tersely, "You're not the only one. Information is thin, but the bald facts are it's a band of cutthroats pledged to enforce the laws."

"What laws?"

"Anything the Prophet says is to be. Don't bother quoting me; it won't do no good. They're denying the bunch even exist. But they do, and you don't have to be too smart to know one of their first jobs is to get rid of dissenters."

Whitmer was speaking again. "We had enough trouble with money in Kirtland. The United Order didn't work there, and it failed out here. But they're getting set to try it again. You mark my words. Getting my hunk of land is the first step."

From out of the crowd a man spoke, and his voice reflected his abiding doubt. "They call you dissenters, saying you're fighting against council. We'll never get anywhere 'til men pull together."

"Depends on which direction you're pullin'." John Whitmer was sober. "There's other things; you haven't heard the end of our story yet."

When he paused, Jenny asked, "What brought on the salt sermon?" The men turned to look at Jenny.

Cowdery replied, "Well, it started up when Corrill and Marsh objected to the decision council reached on our case. Corrill reported back that I was faulted for objecting to the way things were running. In truth, it was the Danites and Avard with his cutthroat tactics I was against. But council decided we four best be done in."

"Corrill and Marsh," John Whitmer took up the story, "objected and then argued the matter needed to be brought before the whole body of Saints."

"So," Cowdery continued, "the sermon. Rigdon took it from the Bible, in Matthew about the salt having lost its savor; therefore it was good for nothing but to be cast out. He laid it out that the duty of the Saints is to take anybody that loses his faith and trample him under their feet. He went on to say there was a group of men in the bunch who had dissented from the church and were a doin' all in their power to destroy the presidency, laying plans to take their lives. He laid out accusations of counterfeiting, lying, cheating, and anything else you could name. He said it was the duty of the Saints to trample them into the ground, and he would construct a gallows in the middle of Far West to hang them."

Jenny shivered and rubbed her chilly arms; she looked at the faces around her, seeing the disbelief and shock she was feeling. The memory of Rigdon's scathing address to the people in the Kirtland temple flashed before her. She was seeing his pale face contorted with rage.

John Whitmer's words were nearly lost to her. "That's when the Prophet said what he did about the Lord telling him Peter did old Judas in. So then I tried to right things by going to Joseph and asking what I should do, and he said it would help if I were to give my property into the church—that way there would be good feelings about me, and the men would have confidence in me again."

" 'Twere only a couple of days until we got the letter," David Whitmer said, pausing to look around the circle of faces. "It was signed by eighty-three of the men of the church. It was in Rigdon's fine words, though. He was saying all kinds of dirt, and addin' that the citizens of Caldwell County had borne the abuse long enough; then he gave us three days to pack up our families to get out of the state."

"We had too much invested to walk out on it all," Cowdery said, glowering. "Land, cattle, furniture. So we headed for Liberty over in Clay County to hire us a Gentile lawyer. We knew a Mormon one daren't listen to us. When we headed back we met the womenfolk riding down the trail to meet us. Mind you, they had been sent out of their homes with only a team and a little bedding and their clothes. It was the Danites that did it. They surrounded the place, ordered them to leave, and threatened to kill any one of the bunch who would dare return."

It took Mark and the fragment of the wagon train two days to escort the dissenters to the Missouri state line. There they were stocked with food and fresh teams. Jenny saw Mark pressing money into David Whitmer's hand.

When the fragment of the wagon train turned again, pointing their teams toward Far West, Mark was the chosen leader. His first task was to open the crude map and outline the route. "We've worked farther north, see. The rest of our train is still pressing west along the southern route. I suggest we cut straight across on this trail." He traced his finger along the map. "We are small and can move faster; if we are fortunate, perhaps we'll arrive at the same time the other bunch does."

Jenny saw the level glances the men exchanged; she also saw the puckered frowns and worried eyes of the women.

She didn't need to question further. Mark knew how important it was to be in Far West when the other group arrived. How well aware she was of all those wagging tongues primed and ready to challenge Mark's humanitarian actions! Without a doubt, his help to those four families would be taken to mean he supported the dissenters. But then, didn't he? She studied his serene face and decided that, right or wrong, Mark would help those people.

Back in the wagon, Jenny moved closer to Mark and touched the coarse texture of his shirt sleeve. Beneath the fabric she could feel hard muscle flexing with each movement of his arm. She looked at his sunburned face, noting that the deep color intensified the curious blue-green of his eyes. "Do you know you have a million more freckles?" she asked.

He looked at her and the wary expression in his eyes disappeared. "And do you know that your curious owl eyes are twice as big today, and that they are very wise?"

"Because you are being the Mark I expected you to be?" She closed her eyes for a moment, and from far out of the past rose a vision of the long-ago Mark, somehow glowing and set apart, with a quality of life she didn't understand.

7

DURING THE REMAINDER of their trip across Missouri, Jenny was torn by the need to see Joseph. Torn because in her innermost heart, she sensed a hint of disloyalty in her decision. But try as she might, she couldn't identify the reason. Joseph needed to know the fears, even the gossip about the Danites. He also needed to be warned against Rigdon. What could be wrong about her decision to search him out at first opportunity? Jenny glanced at Mark and couldn't help feeling a touch of guilt.

True to Mark's prediction, the smaller train of wagons had moved quickly through Missouri, bending north and west through the prairie land.

When the news was passed through the line of wagons, Jenny leaned over the wagon seat to survey her new home. "So this is Far West," she said slowly as their wagon creaked down the main street until they reached the town square.

Mark stopped in front of a building—log, like the cabins, she noted, comparing the scattering of dwellings fanning out from the square. But most certainly, with that size, it was more than a house.

The last of the wagons pulled into the square and Jenny waited for the dust to settle before turning to study this place they were to call home—Zion. She thought of the awe that word had built in her and, with a sinking heart, compared the emotion with reality.

It was only another frontier town, just like all the other Missouri towns they had passed through. There were no neat door yards with tumbling flowers and shady trees, no houses of milled lumber or quarried stone. Crude log shelters, tiny and raw, were the only buildings.

Then she began to notice other things. The streets were wide. Half of their little wagon train could travel abreast down this avenue, half of the twelve wagons.

Remembering, Jenny looked around for the rest of the original wagon train. "Mark, have we arrived first?"

"I doubt it," he said casually as he knotted the reins to the seat. "They've probably been sent on to settle another area. It's not likely everyone would find enough land right around here."

As he jumped to the ground, the door of the crude log building opened. The man in the doorway was a stranger, a curious one. "Welcome to Far West. The Prophet is out of town right now. He's left instructions to head your bunch up Grand River way. Gallatin is Gentile, but beyond, up off Honey Creek, there's good land and a townsite picked." Jenny's heart sank. Joseph wasn't here.

The men from Mark's wagon train had gathered around him. The man looked pleased. Jenny saw him take a deep breath as he shifted his hat to the back of his head and say, "Now, folks, you're going to like it up there. The Prophet has bought a big parcel of land, and he's prepared to give you a good price on a nice little farm. Right now he has his agent up there to take your money or your notes and lead you on to your own lot. I predict that within the week, you'll all be settled on your own section."

The mingled voices and the man's instructions blocked out Mark's question. Jenny watched him lean back against the wagon wheel until he could gain an audience.

While they waited, Jenny got out of the wagon and joined the women forming a circle in the middle of the wide road.

"And to think we left Ohio for this!" The woman dabbed at her eyes as she peered around.

Jenny said, "But it's new. Far West has only been here for a year. Look at all they've done. It's a shock to me too, if I just look at the raw dirt and log huts. But look yonder. From here you can see the plowed fields. That building—it's surely a schoolhouse. That house over there in the middle of the big plot has a window with a curtain. There's corn nearly ready for eating." Even as she spoke, she wondered why she must defend Joseph's Zion.

"I hear there's Indians and snakes. Rattlers. They're poisonous. I had a cousin, came out here in '34. Died from snake bite."

"They're shippin' us on. I heard the fella say up north to Daviess County. The town—I've never heard such a name; he's calling it Adam-ondi-Ahman. All I want is a spot where I can put my feet up and call home."

The group of men broke up, all heading for their wagons.

Jenny joined Mark on the crude porch of the log building. She was breathing deeply of the air, noting the smells around her. The building still oozed resinous sap, and its pungent odor was only a backdrop for the sweet freshness of the towering evergreens, beginning just now to move with the evening breezes. Supper fires threw their own homey scent into the air. Again Jenny sniffed deeply and the fearful knot in her stomach loosened. Surely in such a place there could be only peace.

Then she thought of the people they had met fleeing for their lives. Again she studied Far West. This time she was convinced: Cowdery and his bunch were lying.

Behind her Mark was speaking to the man on the porch. "Where do I find David Whitmer's house?"

The man paused for a moment. Now his eyes grew cold as he studied Mark's face and said slowly. "Whitmer isn't around here no more. How's come you want him?"

"I don't. I have agreed to buy his house." Jenny caught her breath and Mark gave her a sharp glance as he waited for the man's answer.

"Sorry, but it isn't his to sell. Rigdon's living there now. Take it up with him." He started to turn away, but then he paused. "If you want to be happy in Far West, you best forget you even know that bunch of dissenters. They've caused enough trouble around here. The first presidency has suffered enough grief at their hands, and they're not making any bones about the purge. The purge will continue as long as we get men who can do nothing except buck the presidency."

"The purge?"

"The salt that has lost its savor is fit only to be trampled. Or hung."

Mark and Jenny slowly eased back into the line of wagons already heading out of Far West, cutting north toward the Grand River.

Jenny tried to keep her troubled thoughts to herself and concentrate on the changing scenery, but over and over the words moved through her thoughts. *Purge. If the salt has lost its savor* . . .

They were on the prairie again, and the view before her caught her attention. In this place the tall grasses were filled with color. Like a giant carpet, the wild flowers had painted a design that changed with every fancy of the wind. First blue, then sunrise rose pushed through, and finally golden blossoms of varying intensity became evident.

Startled wildlife fled the area, protesting with honks and crashing hoofbeats. Mark pointed his whip at the awkward rush of a wild turkey.

True to the man's word, in less than a week, Mark and Jenny were settling on their own acreage.

On the northern bank of Grand River, close to the little town with the strange name, Mark and Jenny found the section allotted to them. No matter that Joseph didn't appear and give them a choice. Like the others, they took their place in line and waited to be led to their homes.

They pulled their wagon into the clearing facing the river, and that first morning Jenny stood looking over her domain. She was still deeply conscious of the little stone cottage they had left behind, but now she was being caught up in the poetry of this place.

From undulating grasses to dark-hued trees, from rolling prairie to rearing stony cliffs, there was a theme that wrapped itself around Jenny leaving her wide-eyed and on emotional tiptoe.

As she faced the west, behind her the water of Grand River crashed and roared, while before her the dark trees whispered in the gentle breeze. Even now, in the beginning days, she felt she knew it all as a soul-deep experience.

"Oh, Mark," she whispered, "may we stay forever?"

When he turned she saw first his puzzled expression and then as he looked across the water, the deepening quiet began moving into his eyes. Looking out over the tumbling river he said softly, "It seems like heaven; but, my dear, we will be hard-pressed to make it so."

As if loathe to move away from the spot, for the two weeks which followed, Mark and Jenny stirred about their acres, learning it all, loving each tree and bush.

One day, watching Mark in his beginning efforts to clear land for a cabin, Jenny giggled, and when he looked at her, she said, "I was thinking, we're making a nest as if we're reluctant to move a twig out of its precious spot."

Mark wiped perspiration out of his eyes and nodded. His only answer was a kiss pressed quickly against her cheek as he reached for the axe.

While Mark continued to cut trees and tried to hide the crime, Jenny stacked river stones into a beehive of an oven. She reordered her wagon into a home while Mark removed its wheels and fashioned them and part of the box into a reasonable buggy.

And then it was Independence Day. From the first day of their arrival in Far West, they had been regaled with the glory of the celebration planned for Far West.

Jenny and Mark took a holiday from their house building, and early the morning of July Fourth, they joined the crowd moving toward Far West.

"Mrs. Cartwright, how festive you look!" Mark grinned down at her as he guided the crude buggy on its maiden voyage. "You look fresh out of *Harper's Bazaar*. No one will guess you've bathed in river water, with a laundry tub for a bathtub."

"And despite your calluses, you look more the fine gentleman than a bumbling farmer."

"I'm not even a bumbling farmer yet. And I won't be that for long if I can help it."

"You think there will be a place for you with Joseph?"

He shrugged and eased the buggy onto the main road heading toward Far West. They were silent until the road smoothed and then Jenny asked, "Have you heard about the program for the day?"

"Only hints. I know the ground-breaking for the temple is to take place. I know there will be speeches and food and quite a little horsing around. I'd almost guarantee you that Joseph will start a wrestling match and that someone will grease the new flagpole and wager against anyone climbing it."

Jenny patted the bundle covered with a tablecloth. "I hope this cake is good. I've never before baked a cake in a stone oven."

"I doubt you are alone in that. At least you have the sugar and flour—some don't have that."

"Seems strange to see stores so empty of food—and everything else except shovels and scythes, harnesses and ammunition. Joseph must plan for us to kill our daily bread." She leaned forward to look at Mark's face. "Mark, are things bad for people?"

"Of course, but then what would you expect? Many have expended themselves completely in order to make this journey."

They had nearly reached the outskirts of Far West when Jenny realized the line of buggies and wagons in front of them had slowed. "What is the problem?" she asked, stretching to see ahead.

"People," Mark replied. "In this one spot there're more people than we've seen in a long time."

"All Saints?" Mark didn't answer; he was leaning over the edge of the buggy to talk to the man who had run forward.

"You people Saints?" At Mark's nod, the man continued, "Joseph's having us all in the parade. Join the group ahead and go to the edge of town. We're marching to the temple site for the laying of the cornerstone. There's a pack of Gentiles here, and he's set on giving them an eye- and earful. Let no man doubt the strength of the Saints after today."

When Mark and Jenny joined the crowd, Jenny began eagerly scanning the group, looking for Kirtland friends.

Then she saw the trio of dark-coated men and unexpectedly her heart quickened its beat. While she was seeking out Joseph's face, she frowned, dismayed by the unexpected response of her errant heart. But her attention was quickly captured as Joseph turned his face toward her.

She studied the tall figure and bright hair. Beside him stood his brother Hyrum, and Sidney Rigdon. As she watched, a group of men stepped in front of the trio. She looked them over and asked, "Who are those men standing just in front of the first presidency? Those ragged-looking fellows with the guns?"

"I don't know," Mark murmured.

"Them's the infantry," the old fellow beside Mark said proudly. "Gideon's band, the Danites, whatever you want to call them. They look right ready to defend the Prophet, don't they?"

Mark's answer was drowned by the shouts of the horsemen cantering toward them. The old man added, "The cavalry's to bring up the end, so's we best be getting in line or they'll go off and leave us."

As they marched through the streets, Jenny was deeply aware of the line of men standing at the edge of the road. She knew they were not Saints. They not only looked rough, she decided, observing their scowling frowns; they also didn't look as if they had come to enjoy the celebration. She noted several kept their hands fastened firmly around the guns they carried. Jenny's uneasiness grew as they continued down the street.

Only a few of these Gentiles were women. She spotted them dotting the crowd. As she studied them, Jenny realized they varied from the weather-beaten ones wearing homespun and bewildered faces, to hard-faced women, corseted and wearing flamboyant hats decorated with plumes.

Jenny was so caught staring at these women that she stubbed her toe on a rock. Mark grasped her arm and with a grin asked, "Haven't you ever seen a fancy lady before?"

They had reached the end of the parade route and people clumped together. Jenny had only begun to recognize some of her Kirtland friends when the mass of people parted and Jenny saw they stood on the rim of a large hole.

She arched her eyebrows and Mark whispered, "The excavation for the temple."

When the silence became oppressive, a solemn-faced Rigdon took his place and spread his crackling papers. "Better, far better," he cried, lifting his face toward the sky, "to sleep with the dead than to be oppressed among the living."

The shock of his words swept through the crowd. Jenny felt it and was caught by the expression and murmurs of those around her. Soon she realized that after his glorious beginning, she had nearly lost the thread of the speech until she heard, "Our cheeks have been given to the smiters—time after time, again and again. I advise you, this we will do no more. Let there be a mob come upon us to disturb us again and I advise you"—he paused and leaned forward to fasten the crowd with an unwavering stare—"that mob we will follow until the last drop of their blood is shed. It will be a war of extermination. We will carry the war to them, one and all. One or the other of us will cease to exist. We will, remember, my men, not be the aggressors, but we'll stand for our own kind until death." His voice was hoarse and cracking as he concluded, "On this day we proclaim ourselves free—our determination will never, no, never be broken."

The crowd cheered and shouted, "Hosanna, hosanna to God and to the Lamb!" Jenny stood transfixed, watching as the Gentiles, hands on guns, melted away in the crowd and disappeared. For a moment, as she shivered and hugged her arms, Mark looked at her. She saw the darkness in his eyes and turned away.

But the shouting crowd had set the holiday mood. Joseph built upon it with his address, although secretly Jenny thought only his presence was necessary to bring his people to a state of adoring frenzy.

Nevertheless, there were his words, giving out the revelation in slow majestic tones that seemed to roll over the people, building in volume. He stood, hands clasped behind his black-clad figure, his head thrown back, saying, "My beloved Saints, I want you to hear from the Lord just how precious in His sight are the events transpiring here today. First off, He has instructed me of a name change. Henceforth the church is to be known as the Church of Jesus Christ of the Latter-Day Saints. His word to me is that the city of Far West is holy and consecrated land. It shall be called most holy. The very ground whereon it stands is holy. Next, He commands that we build a house to Him. Today we laid the cornerstone. In one year from last April 26, He commands that we commence building. From that time until it is finished, the work must continue. The counsel of men has been thwarted, but now is the appointed time. Saints from all over the world are commanded to assist in the building."

He paused and looked over the crowd. "Our Lord instructs us in the manner in which He will allow His house to be built. This most holy place will be acceptable to Him only if we carefully follow His instructions in the building of it. He has laid careful plans for the financing of our building."

When the last speech was ended, the crowd broke, separated, and re-grouped. For many of the new settlers, this was the first occasion for visiting. As they moved through the crowd, Jenny and Mark were seeing many of their Kirtland friends for the first time since the wagon train had divided. At the time, a hint of coolness in the reunion was overlooked in the excitement of being together again. Only in looking back was Jenny able to identify it.

Just as Mark had promised, there were all the foolish, lighthearted displays of valor. It was very late before Mark and Jenny started their return trip the thirteen miles home, and then Jenny mulled over the slight.

Mark answered her question with a short comment. "Could be, not that they were shunning, but that there's a fear abroad of being labeled dissenter. You've heard the talk. There's fierce and abiding loyalty demanded here. Jenny, already I detect a touch of cynicism in the Prophet." Slowly Mark added, "He's no longer the jolly Prophet I first met. I would say he's felt badly used and will try his best to avoid being seen as soft."

"Soft?" she repeated.

"The opposite of hard as nails," he said in a teasing voice. In the twilight he looked at her thoughtfully and in a gentle voice he added, "Perhaps it's just that Joseph has lost some of the stars in his eyes. Might be that now he sees himself and others in a more realistic way."

Three days later a storm tore through Far West. Some said the Lord was hurling his thunderbolts at the city. Saints shivered in their cabins, wondering at the fury of the Lord's actions. And when the storm was over, the liberty pole in the center of Far West's town square was shattered on the ground. Some whispered it was an evil omen and they couldn't help thinking it was signaling the end of freedom in Missouri.

In Adam-ondi-Ahman there was a rumor abroad. Mark reported it to Jenny. "They're saying Joseph is getting ready to reveal revelations from the Lord regarding the new United Order. You know Cowdery and Whitmer predicted this. They're giving out hints that indicate there's a significant benefit for us all."

Jenny looked up at him and said, "You're not believing that, are you?"

"No, like the dissenters, I believe every man should hold his own land. Besides, I believe Joseph and Rigdon are assuming too much control. If this keeps up, we'll all be wooden puppets."

Far West had scarcely time enough to settle into the post–Independence Day routine when Joseph announced the new order.

On July 8, he called together the church members. Standing before the assembled people, he read the revelation, calling upon the Saints to deed their property to the church. As she listened, Jenny was thinking of all the land just purchased by the Kirtland wagon train.

From behind her came a mutter, "This is a fine time to pull that. The bunch from Kirtland's just sunk a big bundle into land over at Adam-ondi-Ahman. The Saints pay Missouri for land and then turn around and give it to the Prophet."

Jenny moved her shoulders restlessly and tried to ignore the man behind her. She glanced around the vast group, trying to pick out her friends in that sea of faces. Where were Sally and Andy? She hadn't seen them on Independence Day. What had happened to those disgruntled foes of Cowdery, Johnson, and the Whitmers? What about old Mrs. Applewaite? Joseph surely wouldn't be asking for the property of the old and poor!

Now the Prophet was explaining that in return for their deed of property, each Saint would receive a deed for an everlasting inheritance. "The real property," Joseph called it. The surplus property—which was the Saints' donation to the church—was to remain in the hands of the bishop, to be used in building the temple and for supporting the church presidency, as well as laying the foundation of Zion.

In front of Jenny a man in a tattered shirt snorted and said, "And then on top of that there's the tithing we'll be having to pay on the everlasting inheritance. I can't give my family a decent life now, and look at the Prophet in his pretty black coat. He's never had it so good. I remember when he was a barefoot boy like my young'uns. Propheting is good business."

There was a low voice coming from behind Jenny. "Hansen, watch your complaints; even the ground has ears." The complainer drifted away as Rigdon stood to speak.

Jenny was watching Hansen as he limped away, but she turned back as Sidney Rigdon's voice rose. "I prophesy, just as surely as I stand here, those who fail to heed the warnings from the Lord will lose their property to Gentile thieves and robbers. I can assure you"—his voice dropped and he leaned across the podium—"sooner or later, those who refuse to comply will be surrendered to the brothers of Gideon."

From behind Jenny came the hiss, "The Danites."

Later, when the vote was taken, the Saints had voted unanimously to consecrate their property to the church.

On the way home, Jenny broke the silence. "Mark, what do you know about these Danites, or brothers of Gideon?"

Quietly, he replied, "I don't know, Jenny. But I intend to investigate the matter."

Thinking of the dissenters, Jenny whispered, "Mark, be careful." For a moment, as she continued to watch him, Jenny thought again of her resolve to see Joseph. With a sigh she turned away, wondering why she felt as if she were being pulled in two.

"What?" She questioned, realizing she hadn't been listening to Mark.

He was shaking his head, and then with a frown he added, "I will be careful, Jenny, my girl."

And then in another moment, she added with a sigh, "At least you voted to consecrate your property to the church."

He chuckled, "I haven't given a bride price yet—I think it will be worth it. Besides, right now, they aren't getting much. I've done little to improve the place except to pull out a few trees to clear a place for our cabin."

"It will be wonderful to have a cozy home before winter. That storm two weeks ago was an awful warning of what the winter will hold. Right now I just wish Tom would get here with the furniture. I'm worried about him."

"I think Tom can take care of himself. It isn't the first trip he's made out here." Mark was quiet for a moment and then slowly, thoughtfully, he said, "So the Prophet plans to acquire all land in a twelve-mile radius around each stake of Zion. That's our property, in the name of the church."

8

WHEN TOM PULLED the heavily loaded wagon into Far West, the place seemed little like the sleepy western town he had left at spring planting time.

Tom had been in on the birth-pains of this village just one year ago when Jackson County Mormons had moved into the area. From a clearing marked with tiny, crude cabins, Far West had grown into a presentable town with sturdy cabins and acres of tilled land. Even the first season crops had been good.

Although it wasn't until this spring that Joseph Smith had finally moved to Far West from Kirtland, Ohio, he had been responsible for the planning of the town. Wisely, Tom admitted with pride, Joseph had laid out the town with large lots and wide streets.

Tom knew that initially the area had been settled with fifteen hundred citizens. Since the exodus from Kirtland, Ohio, had begun, he had lost all count of the emigrants who had moved into Caldwell County and subsequently settled in the surrounding counties.

Looking around, Tom decided any man would find Far West a town to be proud of. Tom knew the Saints' industry had aroused the envy of Gentile neighbors. Besides the one large building serving multiple purposes and the scattering of little log huts, stocked with a goodly supply of every commodity necessary on the frontier, the Saints had also built a schoolhouse. Just this spring the basement of the temple had been excavated shortly before Joseph had moved his family to Far West.

Now Tom guided his team toward the town square, sawed on the reins, and scratched his head. The once-towering liberty pole in the center of the square was a splintery stub the size of a fence post. "Me thinks," he said slowly, "that the town of Far West has had some interesting life lately."

He headed for the long, low-slung log building which housed post office, saloon, and general store.

When he settled himself at the bar and ordered bacon and eggs, he said, "So, Mike, what's been happening in Caldwell County since I left? Specifically, who tore the flagpole down?"

Mike shrugged. "They're saying the Almighty. But 'twas lightning."

When Mike went back to polishing glasses, Tom concluded his question had been answered and went on to the next. "Wagon train from Kirtland arrive?"

Mike nodded. "While back Joseph completed dickering for land over Adam-ondi-Ahman way. He sent them up that way to buy their lots. Some of the die-hards in the bunch objected to being pointed in the direction Joe wanted them to go. Seems they wanted to settle closer to Far West."

"Spring Hill area, huh?"

"Don't let Joe hear you call it that. He's trying hard to get the Jackson crowd to calling it by its new name, seein' the place has something to do with Adam building that altar up the hill aways." His voice was dry.

"How do the Gentiles feel?"

"Excepting me?"

"I keep forgetting you're a Gentile—fact, I think you'd make a pretty good Mormon. Wanna join?"

Mike chuckled and shook his head. "More interesting just to watch. Them others? Mad. More mad because it was Joe sayin' that's where old Adam came out of the Garden of Eden and built an altar to worship Jehovah; he advised us 'tis prophesied through Joseph that Adam, the ancient of days, will return there to visit his people, sittin' on a fiery throne of flame, like is predicted by Daniel."

Mike snorted softly. "Old Handley, he's a Gentile, he's been tellin' me that Ancient of Days means God, and ole Adam sure ain't God." He shrugged, and his eyes were carefully examining Tom. "Where you been, watcha been doin'?"

Tom had just started on his plate of eggs when the door behind him creaked open. Mike's face brightened. "Joe!"

Tom stood and pumped the large hand of the Prophet. "Hey, Joe, it's good to see you!"

Joseph slid onto the stool beside Tom and accepted the glass Mike shoved toward him. "So, you've been gone a long time. How's things in Kirtland?"

"Ghost town."

"I can't feel sorry; they've brought the troubles upon themselves. Now I know how deep a man's loyalty goes—just as deep as his pocket. Satan buffeted me sorely there with the money problems, but now that's all behind me—why did it take you so long to get back?"

Tom waved toward the town square. "I brought back a load of furniture for my brother-in-law. Also, I tried to sell their house while I was there. There's just no buyers."

"I gave specific instructions concerning that." Joseph's voice was sharp. "The Lord said just leave the places if they couldn't be sold. I know it seems hard to us, but if that's His will—" He shrugged. In another moment he asked, "Mark, huh? He and his wife moved out this way? I didn't know they were here. I'll have to see them."

"Mark going to be working for you again?"

There was a long pause, then Joe slowly said, "He's a lawyer, isn't he? I'm thinking myself that Rigdon and I should be studying law. Sure's anything, we're going to need all the law knowledge we can get. We've been thrown a few loops already. We need to be on our toes."

Tom finished his egg. "Where you livin'?"

Joe looked as if he'd just come back into the room; he slowly focused on Tom and said, "Living? With the George Harris family, just a couple of miles outta town. Emma's just produced another son for me. Things are going well, and I plan on building my own place pretty soon."

"Harris," Tom said slowly. "Is his wife that pretty gal who used to be married to the anti-mason fella who got murdered? Think Morgan was his name."

"That's the one."

"She's a right pretty gal." Tom stood up and reached for coins. "This is quite an interesting place. Looks like the biggest building in Far West now, since that section was added on."

"It is. Come look around." Tom followed Joseph to the other end of the long dark building. Rows of shelves and piles of barrels formed narrow aisles which, Tom saw with surprise, unexpectedly opened into a wide space in front of a second stone fireplace. There was a table littered with papers and books. An easy chair was drawn close to the fireplace.

Tom said, "I'm guessing I've just discovered your hideout."

"And it will be until there's time to build a proper office building."

They walked back to the bar and Joseph pointed to the line of pigeon holes. " 'Tis a post office too." He turned to Tom. "What's your plan now?"

"Find Mark and get rid of my load. Then look for a way to occupy my time."

"I've got you tagged."

"What d' ya mean?"

Joe jerked his head toward the door and with a shrug toward Mike, Tom followed him out the door.

Behind him he heard Mike say, "Looks like Joe's tagged another one for his Danite group."

Jenny stood in the clearing and looked around. Although it was only the second week in August, on their bluff overlooking the Grand River she sensed a touch of autumn coolness in the air.

Behind her the neat little cabin was rising in the clearing Mark had hacked out of the woods. He had hired two men to help him with the construction. Just today the three of them finished lifting the last log into place. Jenny was hoping that by tomorrow they would be ready to use the pile of shingles Mark had been cutting and stacking to dry.

She raised her hands to her mouth and called, "Mark! Men! Come to dinner!" She knew she needn't call a second time. With a smile she turned back to her stone oven and checked the bread browning within.

"Miz Cartwright, that bread sure smells good."

It was John, the youngest member of the building team. Jenny had known his family in Kirtland; in fact, his mother had been Jenny's greatest nursing failure. She still winced thinking about Annie. With a sigh, Jenny turned away from the thoughts and went to lift the pot of meat and vegetables from the fire.

Mark was beside her now, carrying the heavy pot to the crude table. When he brought the jug of milk from the stream cutting through their property he said, "Jenny, you won't even have a chance to get your nose nipped by frost before you move into your new castle. By the way, you can start chinking anytime now."

Jenny wrinkled her nose in pretended disdain. "I'd thought myself too old to play in the mud."

Homer cleared his throat. The older man was graying and bent, but after watching him wrestle the heavy logs, Jenny realized he was still powerful. His words were so few that when he spoke everyone took notice. Today he said, "I hear the election in Gallatin didn't go well."

"That's the county seat of Daviess County," John informed Jenny.

She passed him the bread and replied, "I know. We've been there. Not much of a town for a county seat. Ten houses, and three of them saloons. I couldn't even buy a hank of thread there."

Mark's words were overlapping hers, and she heard the tension in them. "What do you mean, Homer?"

"The Saints round about decided to vote. First time in five years, since that time in Jackson County. They weren't supposed to."

"One of the stipulations?"

He nodded and continued. "Now Joseph Smith's moved out here from Ohio, things are different."

"How's that?"

With his head to one side, he paused to think. Casting a quick, almost apologetic glance at Mark he said, "I don't rightly know. Don't want to pin any blame on the presidency, but we were all treadin' lightly.

"Seems in general, since this place was to be Zion, we needed to be making the best of the situation. People movin' from Jackson to Caldwell County had one desire—that was to make a go of clearing their land and buildin' up their places. They were tryin' hard to get along with everyone."

He paused for a moment while he used bread to sop up the last of his gravy. "It's like peace fled since he came. Take the Danites. None of us gave a thought to such a thing—an army to scourge those who disagreed, sending them fleein' for their lives?"

Mark was leaning forward now. "What about Jared Carter?"

The man's expression was wary but he answered Mark, "Started out to be the big shot in the Danite group. See, you have to understand the oaths they take."

John's eyes were focused on Homer as he slowly said, "But the Lord's raised up a prophet. 'Tis only right we give him the best."

Homer's eyes were steely as he leaned across the table and demanded, "Boy, did you join up?"

John shook his head. "My pa wouldn't let me. But one of my friends who joined says with all the fussin' and rumbling goin' on, soon all the fellas will be *required.*"

Homer's eyes were still holding John's as he said, "The oaths instruct that a man not question nothin', not even the orders given, whether they agree or not. No one is to speak evil of the presidency, every fella's to be completely subject to their control. The secrets of the bunch are not to be let out on pain of death."

When the silence became uneasy Mark prompted, "Carter?"

"He complained to Joseph about something Rigdon said." Homer paused for a moment before he added, "He was dumped as leader. According to Danite principles he should have been killed. Peck told me himself that Carter deserved death according to the oaths. Joe admitted he should have cut his throat but didn't do it. They had a trial in front of the Danites, and Huntington said at the trial he came within a hair of losing his head."

The memory of that conversation was still with Jenny that next week when Tom came.

"How did you find us?" Jenny cried. "I'd nearly given up on you."

"Joe gave me a clue. It'd help if you were a little more friendly with the neighbors. Nobody in Adam-ondi-Ahman had heard about you."

"But they are mostly Gentile."

"Not now. There's several families from Kirtland livin' just a couple of miles away. The Hansens, and the Lewis family."

Jenny could see Tom was thin, and he looked strained and tired. Jenny led him into her house and seated him at the table. "You can live with us. There's not much room, but you could sleep in the loft."

He was shaking his head as he helped himself to the bread Jenny placed in front of him. "Too far for me to be travelin' back and forth."

"What are you doing?"

"Shoeing a few horses, pounding some nails, and plowing a few acres."

"You bought land?"

"Naw, just helping my friends."

"It doesn't sound like much."

He finished eating his slice of bread and drained the cup of milk. "You got yourselves a cow?"

"Yes, chickens too." There was laughter in her voice. "Oh, Tom, you should have seen Mark struggling to be a farmer. He didn't know how to milk a cow. He's just not cut out for the plowing and such."

"I 'spect Joe'll be tappin' him on the shoulder. Way things are goin' around here, there'll be clashes, and Joe needs all the legal help he can get."

Jenny stopped to look at Tom, her eyes searching for clues in his face as she said, "It seems all we've been hearing the past few weeks is fearful rumbles about trouble between the Saints and the Gentiles. What is causing this? All the Saints I know want nothing but peace and a chance to have a decent life." She paused, but when he didn't answer, she asked, "How do you know Joe needs legal help?"

He didn't pretend innocence. "I've joined the Danites." When he saw that she understood, he added, "We're keepin' busy, such as the Gallatin affair."

"Old Homer Thompson mentioned Gallatin when he was over helping Mark build the cabin. The conversation got sidetracked and I didn't realize until later that he'd never finished his story. What happened when the Mormons tried to vote?"

Tom leaned back and whistled softly. "You *are* isolated up here." He got to his feet and paced to the fireplace and back. "In Gallatin not too much happened. Oh, there were a few heads cracked and then the Saints were allowed to vote. It was the stories that circulated afterward that did the damage. It's like there's a bunch of soreheads out there just waitin' to swing their fists."

"Mormons, too?"

"Yes, I believe so." He was quiet for a moment. Jenny watched him chew at his lip, but she couldn't guess the reason behind it. "Though there were only a few heads that got knocked and a few insults spilled, rumor was there were men killed. I talked to John Lee later while he was busy tryin' to calm Joe down before he did more damage."

"More damage," Jenny said in a low voice. "What did he do?"

"Joe was told that Justice of the Peace, Adam Black, was gettin' together the Gentiles to chase the Mormons out of Adam-ondi-Ahman."

"But that's us!" Jenny's hand clenched over her mouth.

Tom continued. "Result was, Joe took his army and headed for Gallatin. The beggars took to the woods like scared chickens. But Joe couldn't be content to let sleepin' dogs lie, and he strong-armed his way into Black's cabin."

He paused before saying soberly, "This took place after he went to Adam-ondi-Ahman and found out the rumors were false." Tom took up his pacing again.

Finally he said, "Shoulda had sense to head for home. Anyhow, he forced Black to sign a paper sayin' there would be peace. As soon as he was out the door, things started rollin'. Old Black went a stompin' out of there and got up a warrant for Joseph's arrest."

"I—" Jenny paused listening. "That must be Mark. He's been into town." She moved to the door just as Mark appeared in the doorway. "What's wrong?" Jenny whispered.

Mark was still frowning as he lifted his face and looked around the room. "Tom, I'd heard that you were back in the state." He threw a quick glance at Jenny and answered, "I've just come from the miller's. Things are bad. Joseph was arrested for strong-arming Justice Black the other day. There was a trial but he got off with only a fine. They could have done much worse. It was brought out that the Saints were crossing county lines with arms. That's a pretty serious offense in Missouri."

Tom responded, "Yes, we were there, tucked just over the county line to make sure no one tried to do in our Prophet."

Jenny moved impatiently, "Oh, Tom! No one's going to kill the Prophet. Don't be so morbid."

Mark's steady eyes moved from one to the other. Finally he spoke. "Perhaps not do him in, but he's causing trouble for the rest of us. There's not a miller in this end of the state who'll grind a sack of wheat for us."

After Tom had left, Jenny faced Mark and said, "I didn't realize we were so cut off from all that's been going on. It's my fault. I like being up here alone, feeling like I was part of the whole universe, and that only we existed in this whole world—" Jenny paused, realizing Mark was looking at her with a strange expression.

In a moment he said, "It's my fault. Partly it's because there's not a newspaper in the area. But I don't intend to be left in the dust again. First thing, lady, we're going into Far West and see Joseph or someone who'll tell us what's going on."

"Tom told me Joseph and Sidney Rigdon are intending to study law. They've talked to Doniphan and believe that with hard work they'll be able to—to accomplish this within a year. He also said Joseph indicated he'd probably be seeing you, because he thought they'd be needing all the legal help they could get."

It was a long time before Mark's resolution to see Joseph was carried out. But late that same night Tom again paid them a visit.

He faced the groggy couple and said, "If I'd been a Missourian intending to take your life or steal your goods, you'd be easy prey. Get out, Mark and Jenny. Do you understand? The Gentiles are heading this way. Soon DeWitt and Adam-ondi-Ahman will be under attack."

While Jenny shivered in her shawl, Mark passed his hands over his face and sighed. Going to the fireplace, he pushed at the slumbering log and then turned. Slowly Mark said, "Tom, this is unbelievable. Things just don't happen like this. Under attack? Surely you're overrating a hot-headed fisticuffs."

Tom was shaking his head. Jenny could see her brother was trying to remain calm, and that was even more frightening. Tom said, "It's all because a bunch of hot-headed Missourians want the Saints to get out of their precious state and leave them alone. It started years ago with them fearin' that Mormons would work to free all the slaves in the state; from then it snowballed into fearin' we'd shove the Missourians out. All we want is peace and quiet."

"All?" Mark asked softly. "What about Zion? What about the Saints making no bones about saying the lands and riches of the Gentiles had been given to them by the Lord?"

Tom was quiet for a moment. Now calm, he answered thoughtfully, "It's the truth. We are the people of God and the place is ours. But I guess you're right. Comin' in here and—" He sighed deeply and said, "We've got ourselves into a fix. I'm supposin' we'll end up fightin' ourselves outta it."

While they watched him, Tom paced nervously back and forth. Now his voice rose again. "These madmen will not be satisfied until every home is burned and every Mormon driven into the wilderness." He whirled on Mark. "It's the Gentiles turned against us, just like it was in Jackson County." He paused to take a deep, ragged breath and then in a low voice said, "Mark, take her and go. Guard my sister. She's all I've got."

9

JENNY STOOD IN her doorway and breathed deeply of the crisp morning air. In the distance she could hear the crash of Grand River. Its turbulence was intimidating, but on the bluff high above the river, surrounded by the pine forest, Jenny felt safe.

Mark had chosen to build the cabin on a slight rise, where the morning sun drenched the logs with warmth and the one large window with light. This morning she felt the warmth of the sun on her face as she tilted her head to see the birds. They were disrupting the quiet of the forest, filling the air with their feisty complaints. Now she saw that the squirrels were causing the upset. She chuckled as a jay swooped down on his adversary.

Behind Jenny the pine fire was crackling in the fireplace and the kettle began to steam. With contented eyes, she turned to look around the room. "Not a bad job of chinking for a beginner," she murmured, but she was measuring the effect of bright quilts and shiny china against the rough bark of the walls.

The aroma of fresh wood still lingered about the cabin. Often at the most unexpected times, Jenny found herself touching fresh pitch, but it was a minor inconvenience.

She was happily aware of harmony in the mix of her belongings, Mark's saddle and rifle, and the polished rocking chair. She heaved a contented sigh. It was good to be in Zion and settled in her own home. " 'Tis a spot of heaven on earth."

Mark pushed through the open door with an armload of milled lumber. "Oh, there you are," Jenny said turning with a smile. "I heard the axe. You've been out there for ages. What is that?"

He was leaning the planks against the wall beside the window. "I'm building shutters." He began making marks on the log walls.

Jenny watched another moment and then said, "I'd rather have them outside. They are terribly heavy, but hang them on the casing. It seems more fitting. Also, could we paint them blue?"

When Mark turned, she saw him take a deep patient breath before he said, "Jenny, these shutters aren't for beauty. They are to—to keep people out."

"Mark!"

He rushed on before she could say more. "I was in Adam-ondi-Ahman yesterday long enough to hear some things that kept me awake most of the night. Jenny, there's going to be trouble very soon. I don't understand it all, but I'm making this place just as safe as possible. That window is big enough to let an army through. These shutters will at least slow them down."

Jenny blinked at Mark's serious face, and all the silly, lighthearted words that had tumbled to her lips were forgotten.

She watched the distant expression steal over his eyes. It was a look most apt to leave Jenny feeling left out, separated by unseen barriers. She whispered, "What is it, Mark? What are you thinking?"

He looked at her in surprise, and as she watched the change in his eyes, she realized he didn't recognize these times when his spirit fled away to an unknown place she couldn't follow. She touched his arm, feeling the familiar warmth, very conscious of knowing the man but not the soul of him.

She saw the caution, the hesitation, and then he said softly, "You really want to know? Jenny, can you—" He paused and walked a step away. When he turned to face her, his eyes were bright with an expression she couldn't understand. Mute, she waited.

"I was just thinking about homes, shelter. I suppose, back in the beginning, man's initial need for shelter was *against* wild animals and *for* his family. Here I'm getting ready to put up shutters, not to keep out the wild animals, but my fellowman. Jenny, that ought not to be. Anywhere. But it seems to me that in the Lord's Zion, it hadn't ought to be at all. Aren't you a mite disappointed in Zion?"

Jenny reluctantly said, "Well, yes. But Mark, didn't we have false hopes?"

"What was your hope?"

She spoke slowly, trying to pull deeply buried disappointments out to study them. "First, I suppose, since it's the Lord's place, and we are *commanded* to build it up, and we've all the revelations saying the land is ours and the wealth is ours, well—" She met his eyes and took a deep breath. "Oh, Mark, nothing is going right! It's scary! Since we've been here, there's more grumbling and fears than I've ever heard before in my life."

She stared at him silently, wanting to point at the fearful times in Kirtland just before Joseph had left. But Mark didn't know about those times. Surely it wouldn't do to mention it now. Also, it wasn't possible to tell him about the dreadful need for power, because he wouldn't approve of her power source.

Now she spoke quickly, wanting only to divert Mark's questions away from herself. "But you were thinking. What is it?"

"I was comparing all this with what I've been learning about God." Jenny moved impatiently and Mark spoke quickly, his voice sharp, "You've asked, and I think you need to hear me out. Jenny, I've been reading about a God of love, about a Savior named Jesus Christ who says if you love Me, prove it by your love for others. Where's Joseph's love? Why are the old-timers in the state—those Joseph sent out here in the early thirties to settle in Jackson County—saying that things were calming down and getting peaceful until Joseph came? Why were these same people content with life until he came? Jenny, I'm comparing my Bible with Joseph's golden one, and I don't like the difference. I fail to see where his gold book and his revelations have produced a holy people." He turned to pace the floor and his voice was low. "Jenny, these people around us matter. It isn't right to take their land and goods, to consign them to hell just because they disagree with us. Even Jesus Christ didn't force people to accept Him, and He was God, with the holy mission of dying for our sins."

Jenny heard Mark's words, but more than the words, she felt the impact of his expression: the sudden heavy lines twisting his face, the shadows in his eyes, the imploring hands that he lifted before shaking his head helplessly; Jenny saw clearly for one moment a strange darkness surrounding them.

But his words were lost as she shivered and turned away. Briefly she felt as if a curtain had been lifted, and she didn't like what she had seen. He whispered, "Jenny, forgive me. It's a load you aren't able to bear. The dear Lord himself wants me to restrain my hand." She looked and he was holding out his arms. Because there was no place to flee, she ran into them. And in another moment she lifted her face. "Mark," she whispered urgently, "please don't repeat this—I don't want you to be labeled a dissenter. That's what you are when you talk like Joseph isn't really a prophet from the Lord."

After breakfast, when the dishes had been washed and Mark was busy fastening heavy hinges to the wall, Jenny took her place beside him and reached for the screws. Trying desperately to forget his fearful words, with her voice low, she said, "Don't you think you'd better tell me all you've heard?"

When he turned to study her face, he said slowly, "I've been trying to think of some way to get out of the state without causing alarm among our neighbors or outrage in Joseph's camp."

"Mark, we've been here only two and a half months!" Even as she spoke, she was hastily pushing Mark's words and the black picture out of her mind. "How silly to give up before we've even tried to make a success of settling Zion. I know neither one of us is the adventuresome type, but, after all, the Prophet has said God commanded we settle and build up Zion." Her voice was dreamy as she continued, "This is God's kingdom; we will have power—"

"Jenny, every once in a while you mention having power. I am growing curious; just what do you mean?"

Jenny opened her eyes wide and looked at the frown on Mark's face. For a moment she felt trapped. "Oh," she said quickly, "it's not *political*, it's spiritual. Mark," she added brightly, "at times I feel we're miles apart spiritually."

"Yes," he said slowly, "I feel the same way." He turned back to his work.

Jenny watched for a time before saying, "Besides, I love it here in our cozy cabin, away from the push of people. I like having you all to myself. I like nature and the quiet. It makes me come alive."

He turned to pinch her cheek, "You really are part owl, aren't you?"

"If you weren't fearful for me, you'd stay, wouldn't you?"

Without answering her question, he said, "There were a bunch of strangers in town yesterday. Men I didn't recognize. From the expressions on their faces, I don't think they were interested in making my acquaintance."

When she remained silent, he added, "There are other things—rumbles, discontentment. You know the agreement between the Saints and the state of Missouri, set up to settle the Jackson problem. The stipulation was that the Mormons were to move to Caldwell County. Now Joseph's strongarmed himself into this place, Daviess County. The old settlers around here are angry because of the large number of Saints emigrating into the area. I can't say I blame them. The Gallatin situation, with the Missourians fighting our men when they came to vote, shows how fearful they are of the type of control Joseph has placed on the people."

"They'll just have to learn to like it," Jenny said impatiently. "I'm convinced, Mark, that Joseph is obeying the Lord." She lifted her chin, and when he said nothing, she continued, "It's His will that Joseph be leader in temporal as well as kingdom affairs."

"But in truth it's going against the constitutional right of man to think and act for himself. That was the whole problem at Gallatin. The Missourians knew the Saints weren't voting any conscience except Joseph's."

"Mark, that is a harsh statement. You best make certain that the walls haven't ears to carry the news back to Joseph."

"And that, my dear wife, is precisely what I mean." Mark turned away, shoulders hunched.

Jenny stated, "You might as well say it. Agree or disagree, it's better'n stewing over it. It didn't take your conversation with Tom to tell me we don't see eye to eye."

"Jenny, let's leave. I feel the Lord urging this on me."

She looked at him curiously for a moment before asking, "How can you say God is putting this on you when you know Joseph'll object?" Mark's long look was thoughtful. Jenny watched as he pressed his lips tightly together.

He turned back to the shutters and she watched him work silently. When he finally turned with an exasperated sigh, she had guessed the problem. "They are too heavy for those hinges, aren't they?"

"Looks like I need to make another trip into Adam-ondi-Ahman for hinges."

"Oh, Mark, take me with you." She saw his eyebrows raise at the unusual request. "I need thread, besides—"

"I was going to ride Sammy. I suppose we could take the wagon."

"I don't mind riding Patches," Jenny protested.

The memory of the look Mark gave her stayed with Jenny as they rode into the small village. He hadn't questioned her, and Jenny couldn't explain the need to push herself back into life and discover for herself just what was happening. It wasn't that she doubted the stories she had been hearing, she insisted to herself as she hurried the mare along.

"Adam-ondi-Ahman," she murmured to herself as they entered town, "the place where Adam settled after being expelled from the garden." It was different. From a pleasant village with Gentiles and Saints on nodding acquaintance, it had become a city of strangers.

She noticed them immediately: the hard-faced men carrying guns. She also noticed the absence of women. Without the usual cluster of wives visiting in the door yards, the neighborly feeling was missing. Now she realized no children played in the streets.

Mark dismounted in front of the general store, and Jenny slipped from her horse, handing the reins to him. "Mark," she whispered, "where are the families?"

"I don't know," he murmured. "It wasn't like this last week. Get your thread and stick close to me. I don't like the feel of this."

Inside the store the proprietor, Ned Wilson, greeted them with a level stare. He filled Jenny's order and when he turned to the back of the store after the hinges, Mark followed.

"What's going on?" Mark was speaking softly as he glanced in Jenny's direction.

"Not much." He hedged and then glanced at Mark with a worried frown. "You folks would be wise to stay on your own acres." Wilson murmured, glancing around. "The rumors are flying and I don't know which one to believe. God knows that most of us just want things to settle down. If you Mormons would just quit scratching the dust, it could happen. Right now everything you do gets the dander up.

"There's fellas moving in from all over the state. Rumor has it they're tired of waiting for the state militia to settle the scrappin'; and they're scared that if they don't take things into their own hands, you Mormons will run them outta the state before the year's out."

Jenny waited beside the long counter heaped with a jumble of tools, nails, and kitchen utensils. She noticed that the hooks which had held hams were empty, as was the flour bin and the barrel which had brimmed with dried beans just a month ago.

Just as she glanced at Mark and Ned Wilson, wondering whether she dared join them, a wagon creaked to a halt in front of the store. She moved to the open door as Moses Thornton stepped through. She smiled, and as she moved toward the man, a former neighbor from Kirtland, there was a rustle and a sharp voice behind her.

Jenny turned as the woman swished through the store from the living quarters in the rear. She was wiping her hands as she took her place behind the counter and leaned toward Moses. "Just don't you bother coming in here with your sad stories. We don't want the likes of you around. You and the missus will just have to do your buying where you're more welcome."

Moses' voice matched hers in hardness. "Look, ma'am, my money's just as good as the next fella's even if he happens to be Gentile." Jenny cringed at the contempt in his voice and turned away.

"The likes of you can't understand, can you?" There was scorn in her voice. "It isn't the money; though the chances of its being counterfeit is bigger'n I want to take. The reason you Mormons can't get a body willin' to sell to you is because there's a move to starve you outta the state. Now, what do you think of that?"

Jenny watched Moses as he straightened and threw back his head. His lips curled as he said, "Ma'am I think you're wastin' your time. Through the Prophet, Joseph Smith, the land and all the riches of the Gentiles have been promised to us. There's not one thing you can do to prevent the hand of the Lord, nor thwart His purposes."

Ned was standing beside his wife now. Jenny turned from listening to Moses, as Ned's hand on his wife's shoulder squeezed her into silence. His voice was heavy and loud. "The truth is, Thornton, there's no goods to be had—food or materials."

He paused, "Truth is, you Saints have descended like a horde of grass-hoppers and just about cleaned us outta everything."

Out in the dusty road beside the wagon, Moses said, "There's news that the governor has begun to sit up and take notice of our cries for mercy."

Mark took a deep breath and Jenny knew he was getting ready to say hard things. She watched with interest as Mark carefully untied Sammy's reins and just as carefully turned to the man. "Thornton, you weren't in the state when the Jackson County problems took place. Governor Dun-klin was negotiating a settlement which would have benefited the Saints. Joseph's marching on Missouri with an army ruined all hopes for a peace-ful settlement. Things aren't much better now.

"Through a grudging concession to the constitutional freedoms of every man, Governor Boggs is trying to be fair, even giving us an opportunity to settle the differences neighbor-like. I'd say we're seeing the hands of the clock of Missouri's patience just about to midnight."

Moses didn't reply, but Jenny couldn't help her outburst. "Mr. Thorn-ton, can't you see? You're saying the same things those people did—that God's on our side, not theirs. We know it's so, but doesn't faith mean we keep our mouths shut and wait for the Lord to *dump* the riches into our laps?"

During the week that followed, Jenny and Mark continued to work around their acreage, improving and preparing for winter. They didn't talk much about the things heavy on their minds. But as Jenny watched Mark fasten the last hinge to the shutters, she wondered if by *not* talking they were willing the problems to disappear.

Mark was still working on the corral the day Jenny found her hands idle for the first time in weeks. After washing the dishes that noontime, she said to Mark, "I'm going to walk over the hill and visit the Durfees. I've promised nosey old Mrs. Durfee I would, and though I don't like spending a beautiful day with her, I'll keep my promises."

Mark's eyes were twinkling, " 'Tis a lesson, young lady. Don't make promises you'll regret." Now the laughter faded from his eyes. "Jen, I worry. Don't stay into the dusk."

"I won't, my husband," she murmured, standing on tiptoe to press her lips to his cheek.

The way to the Durfee farm was a short walk downstream. Jenny chose to walk the river path instead of using the road. Avoiding the tangle of trees and bushes, Jenny climbed the high riverbank and was rewarded with a new view.

At Durfees', the older woman shoved the only chair close to the table before sitting down on the crude bench. Jenny threw aside her shawl and said, "The walk was wonderful—so warm I didn't need my shawl. Have you taken the river path? I could see for miles. Who owns the little ferry I saw chugging across the river?"

"Lyman Wight. Take it you've been fording the river?" Jenny nodded and the woman continued. "He's Joseph's right-hand man when it comes to running the battle."

"You think we'll be fighting?" Jenny asked slowly.

"If Wight has his say." The woman's answer was smug and her expression complacent. "Right now Joseph's got him moving his men into Adam-ondi-Ahman just as fast as the Gentiles can gather here."

Jenny shivered. "I'm beginning to wonder if we're safe."

The woman shrugged. "We are. But I'm hearing things are getting worse in town every day. The women and children daren't move outta their cabins, and food's mighty short."

"Where's Joseph?"

The woman's glance was sharp. She studied Jenny's face for a moment before answering slowly. "Most likely he's either still in Far West or moving this way. Could be he's at the ferry conferring with Wight. Why do you ask?"

Jenny's thoughts were on all the things churning around inside of her, all the things she needed desperately to say to Joseph now before it was too late. Abruptly she came back to the present. "I—I just need to talk to him."

"You and fifty other young ladies," the woman said dryly. "Seems you could wait until the bad times are over and things are settling down for Zion."

Later, as Jenny walked homeward, she thought about the things Mrs. Durfee had intimated. "Me and fifty others!" she snorted. The classification rankled.

Jenny thought back on her unique relationship with the Prophet, and then she smiled. What a long time it had been since she had locked horns with the man! She chuckled, suddenly wistfully aware of the lack in her life.

It was Joseph the man she was missing. She thought back on all those scenes with him—the verbal sparring, the times when she had bested him when he'd tried to pressure her into line with the rest of the females in his camp. She snorted, "Relief Society, my eye! Namby-pamby women trotting along to obey the Prophet."

And there was that unique request Joseph had made of her: to be his friend, to report the pulsebeat of the people. Again she was filled with the need to see Joseph. He must know of every rumble among the Saints.

These poor people had placed him on such a high pedestal that they dare not approach him even with information that might save Zion!

Now Jenny stood on the riverbank, looking downstream to the cluster of log cabins and the little ferry boat moving slowly across the Grand River.

"Joseph, I must see you," she murmured; and as the gentle breeze rippled across her hair, rumpling its smoothness like a careless hand, she shivered. Rubbing her arms, she contemplated the fear rising up, tightening her throat and speeding her pulse. "I didn't know he still had the power to frighten me. Obey the Prophet or be damned! Joseph, it's been such a long time since I've seen you, touched your hand. Now, I must rid myself of this fear and this nameless something, or I will be a slave again, trembling with fear lest I fail to keep the word of the Prophet." Her hand tightened on the talisman pinned to her pocket. "Adela, how desperately I need you now!"

Jenny turned away from the river and slowly walked homeward. She was studying the ground, even now searching for the fresh herbs Adela would demand before a suitable charm could be concocted.

She had forgotten the dangers, forgotten everything except the need to see Adela. When she heard the snap of dry branches and lifted her head in time to see the flash of red, there was only one thought in mind, and she ran forward.

"Adela!" The woman turned to face her as Jenny plunged through the forest. Now panting, Jenny stopped abruptly and walked slowly toward the stranger. The woman was dressed in red, a vivid slash of crimson satin, stretched tightly over every curve of her ample body, revealing so much bosom that Jenny blinked in surprise. Even as she spoke she was guessing the woman was one of the fancy ladies. "Oh, I'm sorry. I thought I'd recognized my friend."

The woman smiled cheerfully, "Well, you didn't. Since you frightened off my friend, you might as well tell me about her. She's around here? What's her last name? Sounds like she should be a friend of mine with a name like Adela."

"I—I don't know her last name. At least I'm not certain. It could be Martindale."

The woman frowned and settled down on a fallen log. "Don't think I recognize Martindale. What's she look like?"

"Well, she's dark and slender, about as tall as you are." The woman was frowning and Jenny realized her description said nothing. "I've mostly seen her in red chiffon, all floaty. You'd see her in the woods looking for moss and herbs. Sometimes she gathers swamp water in a jug that's shaped like—"

The woman was shaking her head while an amused smile lighted her eyes. "Baby!" She exclaimed. "Babe in the woods. You look at the wrong bunch of ladies. What you're running after is a witch." Now her glance was shrewd. "You're a Saint, aren't you? Things are getting pretty bad when the Saints have to consult the witches." Before Jenny could think of an answer, the woman continued, "I can't claim to be the best Christian in the world, but I know enough about religion to see through this business of Joe's. He's gotta good thing going and you're all just tagging along behind."

Jenny's voice was level, flat, as she said, "We happen to have enough faith to believe he's a prophet sent from God. God's revelations to him are guiding us all."

"Like the revelation that God's given Missouri to him for Zion, and that the riches of the Gentiles are for the Saints?" She waited a moment, before softly adding, "Then if it doesn't happen, who you going to believe?"

Jenny was still readying an answer when the woman spoke again. Now her voice was thoughtful, not jeering, and when Jenny looked into her face, she saw a flash of pity in the woman's eyes as she said, "You know, the whole of Missouri was watchin' last summer. It was reported back to us, the things that fella Rigdon had to say back in June when he was rilin' at the fellas. I think their names were Cowdery and Whitmer." Jenny nodded, and the woman continued, " 'Twas strong language he used." Now there was a sneer in her voice as she said, "Talking like 'twas best to kill your people 'cause they don't agree with ya."

At Jenny's gasp of dismay, the woman bobbed her head and continued, "Now you and me know that's just what he was meanin' when he preached that sermon about salt losin' its savor and 'twas fit only to be trampled underfoot. He was making it clear the Mormons had a duty to trample these men under their feet." She paused to snort. "We knew he meant kill, 'specially when he said he'd be willin' to erect gallows in the middle of Far West and hang them himself."

Jenny searched for words to defend even as the churning inside was turning her sick from the ugly words. Hotly she burst out, "You're blaming the whole of the people because of the wild words of that man. Don't believe his words were the words of the Prophet. We're not proud of the bad feeling Rigdon stirred up that day."

"No?" the woman questioned softly. "Then why didn't your prophet smack him down? Seems I recall him comin' back with one of those glorious revelations sayin' the Apostle Peter had informed Joseph that Judas hadn't hung himself. It was instead Peter, himself, that hung him."

She started to turn away then faced Jenny again. "Little girl, there's goin' to be trouble. Take yourself outta Zion before the state crumbles in on your head. And don't go outta here saying it's persecution like they did down south. There's as much ugly goin' on in Zion's camp as there is in ours." She paused again. "Now take a message to your prophet. Tell him Frances said forget it. Forget the whole shenanigans and hightail outta here before the militia stitches his hide to the liberty pole God broke in two, just trying to tell him something." Again she paused before adding, "See, we believe in God, too. And I'm thinking we're just as holy."

10

JENNY WANDERED AIMLESSLY toward home. She was no longer conscious of the autumn glory and the desires which had spurred her out into the day. She was recalling the woman, Frances. Everything about her, from the red satin dress straining over her bulk to the dirty creases on her fat neck, was sending a message, and Jenny didn't like the message.

That woman seemed to know too much about the Saints, and the advice she had asked be passed on to Joseph had left an implication as gritty as sand in the teeth.

Jenny hurried her feet along the path, but she was remembering the expression in the woman's eyes. She *pitied* Jenny!

As she entered the silent, empty cabin, Jenny was uneasily aware of the woman's words. They were lying against her heart like a lump of ice.

Jenny restlessly paced the floor of her home. The fire was only a glow of embers, and Mark seemed to have vanished. She cocked her head, listening for the sound of the axe, the thud of the hammer. There was only silence, and in the silence Jenny became uneasy.

Once again she paced the room, chafing at the echo of the woman's words. Still wondering and now worrying, Jenny began searching the cabin, fretting over Mark's absence. His coat was missing but his hat was beside the rocking chair, as was the harness he had been mending. His gun was in the corner, but there was something missing. Jenny frowned, carefully studying the room.

Her gaze traveled over the table with its lamp centered on the circle of embroidered linen. His Bible had lain there this morning; it was gone now.

Puzzled, Jenny slowly pulled the shawl across her shoulders. Had Mark been troubled this morning? She couldn't recall. With a nagging sense of need, Jenny left the cabin and began to wander across their land, first to the far edge of the clearing, past the makeshift corral.

The sense of need had become worry. She paused and listened. There was only the high swish of wind in the trees and the distant crash of Grand River. With a shiver she turned and ran back across the clearing, past the cabin.

On the edge of the heavily timbered area, she paused to glance behind herself, shivering at the strange sensation of being both repelled and attracted by the dark woods.

As she fought her way through the tangle of brush, the setting sun cast its last glow and allowed the gray of twilight to dominate. The shadows were deepening and Jenny fought back a sob. She turned to go back, and the naked branch of a sapling clung to her shawl.

Her trembling fingers were snatching at the soft wool when she heard the sound. Motionless she listened, unable to identify what she was hearing.

Frantically Jenny tugged at the captive shawl as she turned away from the tree. Then she saw the figure. Most surely that sprawled man was Mark, face down, with arms outstretched! As she watched, she saw him moving in agony. All of her fears became real; that was her Mark down the hill, and he had to be badly injured! She was powerless to move, caught in despair that overwhelmed and paralyzed her.

Now her trembling fingers tugged weakly at the imprisoned shawl. As she watched she saw Mark rise to a kneeling position. His shoulders shook as he bent over something in his hands.

Now Jenny's grip on the shawl loosened and her fear turned to astonishment. Never had she seen her husband like this. She clung to the tree for support as she looked down the glade and listened as Mark lifted his hands; he was holding his Bible! She heard him shout, "My God, I praise You, I adore You. Maker of heaven and earth, Redeemer of all the universe, how glorious You are, how worthy of praise!"

Jenny's dismay turned to relief. With a final tug at her shawl, she started toward Mark, and then without understanding why, she stopped.

Now Mark was on his feet. With agitated steps he paced the glade. When he paused, she watched him lift the book. She could hear low murmurs as if he were reading aloud and she strained to hear. But the words became unimportant as she saw him turn, clasp the open book to his chest and lift his face. Were those tears on his face—surely the twilight was deceiving!

For a long time, Jenny continued to watch, twisted by an emotion she didn't understand. Was it envy informing her that she was seeing more joy, love, and happiness on that face than she had ever seen in their most intimate, loving moments? She had moved to leave when she heard him pray, and again she was powerless to leave the spot while she listened.

His voice had changed, becoming vibrant and deeper. "Father, God of truth! How conscious I am of Your own dear self. How firmly do I feel Your hand, constraining me, reminding me of Your love. I know You are all-powerful. You have reminded me that You hold my most dear treasure in Your hand and that You have heard my prayer." There was silence for a moment and Jenny watched his shoulders once more transmitting agony.

Could she believe that her strong husband wept? Still she waited and Mark was speaking again. "I know Your power, Your promises," he was saying in a broken, humble voice. "You have never failed to keep one promise. I trust Your love as I have never trusted before."

Jenny's hand crept to her throat. Suddenly she turned and crashed through the bushes, running away from Mark. When she stood in her cabin, panting and trembling, she pressed her hand against her pounding heart and closed her eyes. Strangely the scene in the forest had left her feeling as if she were teetering on a high, crumbling shelf of rock. Slowly she crossed the room and reached behind the chest, fumbling until her hand touched the green book.

Changes were taking place in Daviess County. Jenny mentioned it to Mark. "Suddenly we are having a horde of visitors. Why? These are the folks we traveled with from Kirtland. For a time they were shunning us; I'm guessing it was because we helped the dissenters. Now they're acting like they can't get enough of us."

Mark leaned on the hoe and pinched her cheek. "Hey," he said gently. She bit her catty tongue and Mark nodded at the pile of firewood. "Probably, like us, people have been too busy fixing up before the winter cold sets in."

She wandered off the subject, saying with a tired sigh, "There's still much to be done. Passing down the road, we've seen people still living in wagons or poor bark shanties. There are garden plots to clear and trees to cut. Even with us—we've got to get that corral built."

"Haven't you heard misery likes company?" Mark grinned in answer to her original question while he turned back to his task of hoisting sacks of grain to the rafters in the lean-to.

"Do you really think you'll keep the squirrels and mice out of those sacks?" Jenny asked, although her thoughts were elsewhere. His smile reminded her of the Mark she spied upon in the forest. She sighed and turned her attention back to him.

"I'd better get this grain milled soon or you'll be reduced to scraping corn and baking it with pumpkin like they're doing down the valley," he said, heaving the last sack overhead.

She watched the muscles ripple across his shoulders and compared their power with that moment of weakness she had glimpsed in the forest. Weakness? Somehow that word didn't describe the scene she had happened upon, no matter that tears had been raining down his cheeks.

Later that evening Jenny thought of Mark's statement as she pulled the loaf of bread out of the oven and thumped its crusty top. It sounded hollow and she nodded with satisfaction as she put it on the table to cool. The aroma filled the cabin.

"Mark, the little stone oven you built in the corner of the fireplace does a good job. This bread's nigh perfect."

"Smells wonderful," he responded. He concentrated on his task of splicing the leather harness together. "By the way, I'm thinking the Andersens and the Guffries will be here this evening. Might be they'll bring a few others."

"What's the problem now?"

"Do or don't do, stay or go," he said wearily. Jenny turned away with a sigh.

One thing she knew, there wouldn't be bread by morning. Thinking of the shrinking mound of flour in the tin, she tried to set her mind in a charitable mood.

Jenny had barely time to cover the bread and set it aside before she heard the knock. Mark's glance at her was full of concern as he stood to open the door to his neighbors.

Jenny was right about the bread, but she didn't realize how fast it would disappear, or how hungry these people would be.

While the men huddled over the table, the women gathered by the fire and folded idle hands over the piles of mending they had carried with them.

Dora slanted a worried glance at the men and said, "I wish things would settle. Little Ruth Campbell is about to deliver, and she doesn't look able."

After the silence had stretched again, Lila straightened and said, "Late last night my Tyler heard a ruckus out yonder. He sneaked out there and found a fella settin' a fire in the hay. Tyler fired a load of buckshot at him."

There was more silence and Maudy gave a belated nervous laugh and said, "I just wish they'd do something. This waiting, for who knows what, is killin' me."

Now the women were listening to the low murmur of voices from the men. They were seeing the worried expressions and hearing the occasional angry outburst.

Dora whispered, "You know, the Prophet's said if we're living right, there's to be no harm done us, but I still worry." She had opened her mouth to add more when the low murmuring of the men caught their attention.

They had been sitting with their heads together around the table. Abruptly Tyler pushed back his stool and jumped to his feet. "I don't care what you're sayin', I intend stickin' with him. Seems if we're bent on believing he has the keys of the kingdom, then there's no other choice but this."

"Right or wrong? How about the way he goes at it?" Mark's voice was low; only Jenny caught the sharp edge of controlled anger in it.

"I'm with Tyler," Guffrie said slowly. "I'm in too far to back out. Maybe I just don't have the sense to figure out for myself whether I oughta run."

"Yes," Mark spoke heavily, "when you don't have a better reason, it's hard to choose."

When they moved to the door to leave, Mark and Jenny stood together watching them. The circle of lamplight highlighted the women's faces. Their eyes were darkening pools, shadowing away the fears.

In the morning Jenny stirred cornmeal into the boiling water and addressed Mark. "Missus Hardy said Tyler found a fella trying to fire their hay."

"They're also stealing horses and cattle," Mark said slowly. He was thinking of the other things he had heard. When he turned to face her, Mark found he was being forced into saying some things he had been keeping from her.

He took a deep breath, waiting for the guidance of the Holy Spirit. He was still fearful of probing the tender spots in their relationship which he had created with his criticism of Joseph Smith.

"This is getting to be more than just persecution." He paced the room as he spoke. "The Saints are in on it, too; and, on their part, it's a good case of retaliation."

She faced him squarely. From the expression in her eyes, he guessed that she was struggling to accept a new way of looking at the situation.

For a moment he felt like applauding her, but he must push one step more. She was well aware of all that was happening, that he knew, but he must go over the events again. "In the first place, this is an ongoing fight. It started way back when Joseph sent his men into Missouri in 1831, with the prophecy that the Lord had ordained Missouri to be the new Zion. This land, he told them, was to be the site of the New Jerusalem, coming down out of heaven. The people under Joseph were to claim the state and build up Zion, an acceptable land getting ready for the Lord to return. How do you think that set with the people? Especially when the Saints made no bones about fighting to gain their objective if necessary?"

She was still thinking as she said, "I can see them not being pleased, maybe angry, but—"

"Remember these were and are still rough frontiersmen. You saw the people on Independence Day."

Jenny nodded hesitantly. "The women were either fancy ladies or they were as tough as the men." She frowned, remembering that woman and feeling uneasy about her. It was starting to look as if she couldn't delay seeking out Joseph. There was that message.

Mark continued, "Things were starting to settle down a mite. The Saints from Jackson moved to Caldwell, just like the state legislature told them to. You recall I told you what some of the old settlers told me? They were talking about how it was until Joseph came to town last spring. The word was *peaceful.*

"This one fella told me the Jacksonites have one desire and that is to build a place up, get in a crop and live at peace with their neighbors. Sounds good as far as it goes, but peace is out of the question. Why? Now along with the information that hordes of Mormons are moving into the area, the Gentiles hear Joseph is building up an army with the intent to take the state, the country, and eventually the whole world."

He heard her protest. For a moment Mark paused to study Jenny's face. There was bewilderment and disbelief on it. He took a deep breath, conscious of the sure feeling that now was the time to face his wife with the facts she had chosen to ignore.

"Jenny," he pleaded, "right now I'm not asking you to judge his merits; instead, just try to put yourself in the Missourians' shoes. Their state isn't taking the action they feel is needed so the men are scared. They've resorted to mobbing, trying to make things miserable for the Saints, hoping they will leave on their own. Of course it isn't working, not under Joseph's hand. These people dare not leave under threat of being labeled *dissenter.* But in addition, some of the Saints are thieving and burning right back. For every bad tale you hear about the Missourians, there's another one about the Saints."

"Mark, I don't believe that. They say—" she paused and lifted her chin. It was at that moment Mark realized the change in Jenny.

His despair overrode his good sense and he whispered, "Jenny, what is happening to you? From the very beginning I saw what a wonderful mind you had. I watched you because I knew you were special, and I fell in love with that special person. You're closing your mind! Don't let others do your thinking for you—not now, not after all these hard years of scrapping for room to stand tall."

She was caught, and her eyes widened. She was wondering as she looked into his face. Was it possible Mark was seeing something she didn't? For a moment she toyed with the idea that at times she did feel as if her thoughts were only echoes of some other voice.

In another moment she shook her head. Whispering, she said, "Mark, you're wrong. My ability to think, to grasp what is right, that's just the very thing that's bringing me along the way to be a strong person." He pulled her close. For a moment, just before Mark bent to press his face against hers, she saw the shock in his eyes and the white line his lips had become.

11

LATE THAT SAME afternoon Mark thought about Tom again. That bleak conversation with Jenny had pushed the incident from his mind, and now he knew he couldn't discuss his unexpected meeting with Tom.

In Adam-ondi-Ahman, Tom and some of his fellow Danites had been assigned the task of building a fort in the middle of town.

What a shock, walking into the town square and finding the crude fortification! The silent streets, the sullen expressions on the faces of his Gentile neighbors hurrying about their business had alerted him to change, but when he heard the pounding of hammers, his heart sank.

When he confronted his brother-in-law, Tom's crooked grin hadn't cancelled the dark, hard look in his eyes. Tersely he said, "We're building Joseph a fort. Under siege, we are. Gentiles are banding together, moving this way. Like locusts, they're comin'. Like tender grass, we're moving. Joseph says head for Far West or Adam-ondi-Ahman."

His eyes followed the movement of the Gentile crossing the road, hurrying toward his horse. "We'll run 'em out. Next year this time there'll be only Saints about. The Lord's goin' to fight our battles for us."

Today Mark paced his lean-to, cracking his knuckles and reviewing Tom's statements. That expression in his brother-in-law's eyes! The angry frown that had underlined the words made it impossible to dismiss the unbelievable statements. But he was wondering what was twisting his brother-in-law's placid disposition.

Tom was talking as if the Danites were the Lord's avenging instrument, a sword to be lifted against the Missourians.

But it was the anger in Tom which had bothered Mark the most. Mark had been about to point out that the Danites' being in town would make it impossible to live in peace with these Missourians. He was about to point out that Gentiles owned as much of the town as the Saints did, when Tom's tight-lipped statement had cut off the conversation. Tom snapped, "Remember Rigdon's speech. Your concern comes too late." Mark knew Tom was referring to the Independence Day speech when Rigdon had thrown down the gauntlet.

Mark watched Jenny walk slowly down the path toward the tumble of wildflowers still vibrant with color. She bent to bury her face in the blossoms and his heart constricted with fear. "Dear Jesus," he murmured in agony, "help me. I'll never forgive myself if I stay here one moment past the time it takes Jenny to get her eyes open to the truth. I know it could mean the difference between life and death. My Lord," he pleaded, "I can't lose her now!"

In the following week, Mark and Jenny watched events pile up and then tumble like a rock slide, growing, crashing, sweeping up everything in its path.

The bands of desperados continued to plunder; the Saints daily reported new losses.

After visiting the nearest neighbors, Jenny brought the latest stories to Mark. "The Andersens are saying the mobs are concentrating on DeWitt and Adam-ondi-Ahman because they've made up their minds to rid the county of Mormons. There're only two Mormon families in DeWitt, the poor souls. If nothing else, they'll die of fright."

And still he was silent. But it was a troubled silence as he recalled Tom's angry face and the sound of hammers in the streets of Adam-ondi-Ahman.

In the middle of September, on the day Mark returned home with news of Joseph's petition for redress, Jenny had noticed the touch of autumn. Distant hills, rolling up and away from Grand River, were touched with a new glow of color. She also saw the grasses in the valley turning golden.

While Mark sat at the table and hungrily spooned up the wild plum preserves, Jenny ladled out bowls of barley soup. Mark commented, "The honey with plums gives a good flavor. I like it better than sugar."

He finished the soup, and Jenny said, "I can tell by your face that there's something brewing."

Startled he looked up. "Oh, I was pondering it all, trying to understand." He was silent while Jenny waited. Finally, "I've just heard Joseph has petitioned the judge of Ray County. I suppose he just didn't know what else to do. It's on behalf of those of us in Daviess County who are being threatened with expulsion."

"Are *we* being threatened with expulsion?" Jenny asked slowly. Then she added, "Is that what they call the mob action against us?" She waited, then asked, "There's more?"

He nodded soberly, speaking reluctantly, "Word's run ahead of them. General Lucas has dispatched Generals Atchison and Doniphan to settle our differences. They are headed this way with five hundred men under them. Quite a bunch to keep peace in a county this size."

"What does Joseph's petition ask?"

"He's complained about the treatment the Saints are receiving at the hands of the Missourians. About the fights, the looting, the harassment."

"When will these men arrive," Jenny whispered, "and, Mark, what shall we do?"

"I don't know." When he threw her a worried glance, her hand crept to her throat. "Don't start worrying yet. We're far enough from town; probably won't even know they're there. Besides, these men represent the state. They're coming to settle the differences, not start a war." He grinned at her.

He was picking at a piece of cornbread when Jenny stated, "Mark, you're not saying, but you're thinking the Saints are making a mistake."

"Yes," he said slowly, "it's just a feeling, but seems Joe would be smart to do his best to keep the peace by cooperating instead of pushing his luck. I can't help thinking the old settlers in the county are seeing it in the same light as a youngster running to his pa to complain because he's being mistreated, when in truth his teasing caused the problem in the beginning."

Jenny lifted her head. "I hear a horse." They both went to the window. As the horseman turned off the road, Jenny exclaimed, "It's Tom!"

And when he was standing in their cabin, holding out his bowl for soup, he said, with a grin, "Mind if I call this home for a spell?"

"What's that to mean?" Jenny asked, searching his face.

"I've just come from Far West. Seems Joe's sent a petition askin' for help to—"

"So we've heard," Mark interrupted.

Tom sat down at the table and added, "Well, then you know that Doniphan stopped in Far West with orders for that place."

"What were they?"

He piled plum preserves on his cornbread before looking up with a pleased grin. "To disband all parties found under arms. And he found a heap of us, even caught us totin' our guns around. We were ordered to clear out of there and head for our homes."

"Like little boys with their hands slapped."

"Aw, Sis. You've never seen a bunch of fellas so glad to go. We're hopin' this means the end of havin' to snatch up a gun and run when there's orders."

Mark was studying Tom with keen eyes. Slowly he said, "That surprises me. From all I've heard about the Danites, I had it figured you were all spoiling for a fight. I thought you were reconciled to having to take Zion by force, and the sooner the better."

"Mark, you have it wrong. Given our druthers, you'd find most of us a peaceful bunch. Oh, sure, there's a few hotheads in the group. But we fight because our salvation's at stake."

"Obey the Prophet or be damned," Mark said slowly, and Tom nodded.

Jenny sighed deeply. "I'm glad to have you. Seems we need all the kin we can get. Even Mark's worried about affairs around here."

"Well, they're not good," Tom continued soberly. "The bunch of Danites holed up here'bouts, they tell me, has been livin' on cattle, hogs and honey. They're callin' it bear, buffalo, and sweet oil. But they're not foolin' a soul. There's bound to be more'n a few heads cracked when the old settlers get fed up with havin' their stock feedin' the bunch fightin' them." Jenny saw the look the two men exchanged, and shivered; she dared not question further.

Tom stayed on with Mark and Jenny. In reflecting on the whole uneasy situation, Jenny decided that had Tom taken up whittling or fishing—anything except running about the country, she would have been able to dismiss the strange visit as loneliness.

Her worst fears were confirmed late one evening when Tom came home long after supper was cleared away, when the evening mists were creeping down the crimson hillsides.

He dug into her stew of venison and dumplings made of corn as if only it stood between him and starvation.

Sensing his troubled spirit, Mark and Jenny waited until he had finished eating. He drank the last of the milk and said, "I've been over Far West way. I'm mighty uneasy about how things are goin' to set. Joseph's got his ire up and it's bound to cause trouble."

"Haven't the troops Joe stationed in Daviess returned to Far West?"

Tom nodded. "It's DeWitt now. The old settlers have been tryin' their hardest to get those two Mormon families out of there. Finally they drew up a resolution statin' they couldn't live with Mormons. We found out it was decided they would use force to get rid of them. But before they could get goin' on it, Joseph moved a big bunch of Canadians into the area. He was mighty set on keepin' a foothold in DeWitt, since it's a good river port."

Mark got to his feet and paced the room. "Tom," he said thoughtfully, "Doniphan's been trying to negotiate a settlement in Adam-ondi-Ahman. Things were starting to look pretty good for us." Jenny listened to the growing excitement in his voice and looked at him in astonishment. She was beginning to understand his frequent and unexplained trips into town as he talked.

He was saying, "The way things were going, the Missourians were ready to sell out to us. I was ready to plunk down money myself. How's this new event going to set?"

"Not good," Tom said slowly. "That's why I've come back."

"I don't understand," Jenny said dully, her heart sinking in response to the anger and discouragement on Mark's face.

Tom continued and his voice was level, emotionless. "I'm a Danite. Joe's ordered us to DeWitt as soon as we can get there. I'm not here for arms, like Joseph's thinkin'; I'm here, Mark, to beg you to get my sister out of Missouri. Even if you have to leave without a thing and on horseback, just go!"

"What about you?" Jenny whispered.

Tom's face twisted in a half grin. "Accordin' to the promises Joe's given us, there's nothin' that can touch the Lord's anointed. He's promised God will send angels to do the fightin' for us."

Tom gathered up heavy clothing and took the gun Mark pressed upon him. Your life may depend on it," Mark added; "besides, I'll have yours."

"Just don't go to DeWitt. The Missouri mobs are gatherin' as fast as they can."

"Whatever for?" Jenny cried. "Surely a few families of Saints couldn't have brought that on."

"I forgot to tell you the Canadians have a breastwork of wagons stationed down the middle of town. That doesn't sound like innocent settlers bent on plantin' wheat."

It was dawn when Tom rode his horse into DeWitt. From the bluff overlooking the town he saw the peaceful river port, gently touched by the light of the rising sun. But he also noticed only a few trails of smoke rising from the chimneys of the log cabins clustered along the wharf.

Until his gaze moved to the center of the community, he had nearly convinced himself that this *was* a peaceful little river town. Then he saw, stretching down the middle of town, a barricade of wagons. Beyond the breastwork, he saw the Mormon camp and caught his breath in surprise. This was no mild response to the burning of one Mormon house and a few stray gunshots—this was a major offensive. In the pale light of dawn, the positioned Mormon troops were spread, as far as he could see, the length and breadth of the open space.

Carefully Tom made his way down into town and into Israel's camp. He found Joseph and his men ensconced with the Canadians behind the breastwork of wagons. Joseph's usually smiling face was creased into a worried frown.

He greeted Tom. "We didn't have any trouble marching into town, but I'm afraid we're in trouble now." Bewildered, Tom looked around. He could hear children's voices overlapping the voices of women, but the area around the fires was empty.

Joseph was pacing rapidly back and forth. "The settlers from Canada have suffered severely at the hands of the mob. Now the mob won't give us freedom to leave. What a trick! They let us in while they were pulling reinforcements from every county in the area. They'll all be down our necks—but we'll fool them. We've only to sit it out."

"Not fight!" Joe and Tom turned. Lyman Wight had been listening; his face was red with anger. "We've the Lord to fight our battles; march on!"

But in the end, Joe's will prevailed. An express was dispatched to the governor, but this time there was nothing of encouragement in the answer.

Joseph wadded the paper and threw it to the ground. Tersely he said, "The governor informs us that since we got ourselves into this fix, we should get ourselves out."

Tom slowly turned. Just beyond the fringe of town, away from the threat of the Canadians' guns, he could see the cluster of Gentiles with rifles raised. "Is that a cannon?" Tom asked. Joseph nodded briefly; then the Prophet slumped wearily.

Tom squatted in front of Joseph and said softly, "Joe, these people are in a bad way. The mob's been goin' through the bunch beating them. I guess they were in the wrong, out tryin' to find something to eat."

"I know," Joseph said slowly. He got to his feet. "For the sake of these people, I guess I have to admit we're licked for now. Get me a flag of truce."

Wight's face contorted with rage. "You are a fool! Not only are you backing down on the promises of God, but think of the message the Gentiles will get! I promised the Danites would take these people. You'll make a fool outta me."

Tom faced Wight and stated, "I can't believe you have a better plan."

Wight spun on his heel and flung his arm toward DeWitt. "See this little town? They'll boast they sent us crawling out of here on our bellies."

Joseph was still impassive, but he was watching as Wight whirled toward him. Tom cringed as Wight yelled, "You're embracing defeat like a friend!"

But Joseph shook his head. Under a flag of truce, the starving, beaten settlers were led to Far West.

A short time later, Tom was there when Joseph received the dispatch from Adam-ondi-Ahman.

When the ragged man with the message stood before Joseph, his voice was dull and discouragement bowed his shoulders. "They're saying up yonder—the Gentiles are—that if Carroll County can turn out the Saints, then Daviess County can too.

"General Doniphan's sent word negotiations have broken down and the settlers aren't going to sell out to the Saints. Sir, we've lost more'n De-Witt." He started to turn away, then added, "They're saying a mob of eight hundred's moving toward Adam-ondi-Ahman."

12

JENNY STOOD IN the one room of her home, bewildered. All of it was unbelievable: one moment the little cabin had seemed a bit of heaven, her place forever; now it was being wrenched out of her life.

"Mark, we've been here such a short time. It seems we've just settled in and now you're saying we must go."

"Little owl-eyes, don't look so sober. This isn't the end of the world, and we will be back. If you like your little cabin that much, we'll return to stay forever." Mark's finger flicked the tears off Jenny's cheeks before he bent to kiss her.

"Oh, Mark," she wrapped her arms around him and held him. "It's just that I can't understand all this. Why is it necessary we leave now?"

"Because I trust your brother, even the things he doesn't say. Now stop your fretting. We'll be back soon. Pretend that all along we've planned this trip to visit my mother. We'll have to do a little night travel to avoid causing offense to some of—of the militia." He held her away to see her face.

"Mark—" she studied his face and he tried to snuggle her against his shoulder again, lest she see the fear. She resisted him, and he faced the intensity of those gray eyes. Her next question surprised him. "Does it trouble you that because of me you must go, and that you aren't able to fight with the other men?"

Carefully he asked, "Why the questions?" She shook her head without answering, and he pushed her head under his chin and considered the question. "First of all, I'm not sold on fighting as a way to settle differences. Second, I think Joseph's in the wrong. Third, I'm a follower of Jesus Christ, and He says love your enemies, pray for them, and turn the other cheek." She fought away from his restraining arms. He was aware of resistance throughout her whole body. Again her eyes reminded him of an owl, a creature of the dark, with thought and feeling hidden away.

He sighed and said, "I'm not convinced we'll make it through with this buggy, but pack as much as you can in the way of food and clothing. Wrap

the luggage in quilts. I intend to grease those wheels until they are completely soundless." He saw her shiver as she turned away.

With a heavy heart, Mark went out to the lean-to and gathered up his
tools. He again felt that nudge reminding him time was fleeting. If only
they had left a week ago when Tom had urged them to action!

Dawn was just a smudge of color in the sky when Mark bundled Jenny
into the crude buggy and turned his team down the trail toward Adam-
ondi-Ahman.

As they rode through the town, Jenny gasped with dismay. "Mark, it's
been such a short time since we were here, but look at the difference!
Look at the trash lying about. It troubles me. And there's scarcely a sign of
a breakfast fire."

Mark had been aware of the forboding air of the town, but he said
nothing as he studied the area, looking for signs of change. Someone was
sweeping the steps of the general store—that was very ordinary. He recognized the owner, Wilson, a long-time resident, and a Gentile.

As they passed, the man paused and leaned on his broom. "Good morning, Wilson," Mark called. The man turned and headed back into his store.

Jenny was shivering. "Don't worry," Mark said, "Silence doesn't mean
anything. Mormon sympathizers aren't popular."

They continued on down the road toward Far West. The buggy wheels
were nearly soundless, and the pleasant clop-clop of the mare's hooves
sounded reassuring, normal.

It was nearly noon when they met the horsemen. Mark recognized several of them. Lyman Wight was leading the group, and Mark recalled
hearing that the man owned the ferry on Grand River, just a short distance downstream. "Hello," Mark called as they reined in their horses.

Wight asked, "You've come from Adam-ondi-Ahman?" Mark nodded
and Wight said, "Then you've probably seen the bunch with the cannon."

Mark felt Jenny's grasp tighten. "I haven't seen any group of men, let
alone a group with a cannon. When we left town this morning the place
seemed peaceful. Not many residents though—there was hardly a breakfast fire in the village."

The men rode on. Mark and Jenny continued south over the prairie,
mulling over the terse statements the men had made. "So the Danites are
going to rescue Daviess County from the DeWitt mob, which is moving
this way pulling a cannon."

"Do you believe them?"

"I believe they *think* they'll find a cannon and a skirmish." Jenny relaxed
and smiled for the first time in two days. Mark leaned over to kiss her.
"That's my girl. Now let's just concentrate on getting back to Ohio."

"Is there any way possible to avoid Far West?" Jenny asked.

"Not that I know of, but if there's anyone I dare ask, I will. Right now it would be nice to run into Tom."

Her face brightened, "Oh, would that be possible?"

He chuckled, heartened by her mood swing. "In this state anything is possible." Then he added slowly, "Particularly if they're calling out the Danites to go to Adam-ondi-Ahman."

Within an hour they again heard the sound of approaching horsemen. Mark frowned. "Jenny, I don't like this. These horses are coming too fast to be pulling a cannon; it's more like they're intent on catching up with the others."

"Let's get off the road!" Jenny exclaimed. But Mark was shaking his head, and she realized it was too late. Across the prairie a cloud of dust was moving toward them. In all that expanse there was not one tree to shield them from sight.

For a moment it seemed the troops would pass them by; but at the last moment there was a shout and the horses veered toward them. The man in front wore the fraying clothing of a farmer, but he carried himself like a general.

Jenny watched him leave his men behind and canter forward. "Why, you're Mark Cartwright!" the man exclaimed. "You don't know me, but I heard about you, back Kirtland way. Name's Lewis."

His expression was quizzical as he continued, "We've reason to believe a mob of Gentiles from DeWitt is headed up toward Daviess County, towing a cannon. They're intending to run the Saints out of Daviess. Have you seen or heard of them?"

Mark shook his head, "No, but just over an hour ago we met Wight and your men heading toward Grand River." His voice became thoughtful as he said, "This is starting to look pretty serious."

Nodding, the man squinted down at Mark. "You best believe it. I suppose the word's been spread and you're headed for Far West."

Jenny chimed in, "Actually, we're hoping to avoid Far West. Is there another road?"

He was grinning at Mark. "Missus have the last word? Ma'am, orders is orders. Don't try to talk him out of it. Don't you worry your pretty little head. There's plenty of company for you ladyfolks while the men are away."

There was a horse pressing through the troops behind Mark and Jenny, and then a familiar whinny. "Mark! Jenny!" Tom's face peering around the buggy was filled with dismay. "You should have stayed at home," he said carefully. "It isn't safe with those cutthroats on the loose."

Jenny opened her mouth to question, but Mark's hand squeezed hers tightly in an unmistakable message. Hastily he said, "Tom, I'm glad to see you. What's going on in Far West?"

"You mean Lewis here didn't tell you? The Prophet's called for all the men to assemble there." His voice was level and deliberate as he informed them. "We understand nearly all the men in Caldwell County are heading there right now. They are called under arms."

Even Jenny caught the message. She shivered, saying with a glance at Lewis, "Then I guess that's where we'll be going."

Lewis gave Jenny a pitying look. Turning to Mark he said, "I see you aren't fitted out for livin' in your rig. Better head for my house. Tell the missus I sent you. We've a good-sized loft and are expectin' to have it full by morning. Joseph's going to have to build a hotel if he intends to keep up this kinda thing."

In the morning, after the two of them had spent a restless night tossing on a straw pallet spread in the Lewis cabin, Mark faced Jenny and whispered, "I've every intention of getting out of this if it is possible. I can't believe Joseph will demand I fight. He knows how I feel about the whole affair. I'll let him know our plans are to return to Ohio right now."

Jenny's face brightened, but he saw her bite her lip. "Mark, you have more confidence than I do. I hope you are right."

"I want you to stay here until you find out just what is going to happen. Last night I found Andy Morgan. He's as reluctant to join this army as I am. He did say that Sally is alone and would welcome you. I've written the directions to their section; it isn't difficult to find. If I must leave, go to Sally and stay there until this mess is over." She stared up at him. His voice was flat and his eyes shadowed.

Then she understood. Mark had no hopes of leaving. She clenched her hands behind her back; he mustn't see them trembling.

Later that morning when the two of them joined the crowd of men and women pressing toward the town square, Mark looked at the sky and murmured, "That sky is promising nothing good. If it were December instead of the fifteenth of October, I'd expect snow." Jenny shivered in her shawl and decided that even snow couldn't make her feel worse. Mark left her with the group of men and women standing on the gentle slope facing the town square. She looked around at the somber faces and reminded herself that these women were feeling the same misery she was experiencing. There were some she recognized from Kirtland days, but they seemed as disinclined to talk as she.

Down below, in the crowd of men, there were a few excited voices; but for the most part only uneasy silence held the group as they waited for the Prophet to appear.

When the women began to stir restlessly, Jenny stood on tiptoe, guessing there was something of interest happening on the square. Far down the street she spotted a group of men coming. It was easy to guess who the dark-coated figure was. Dressed in somber black, Joseph towered above the men around him.

The pulse of the crowd quickened. By the time Joseph stood before them in the town square, the murmur of excitement had changed to a rumble, then a roar of welcome.

His voice was quiet and controlled as he began to speak. Wearily he began cataloging the events and listing the offenses of the Missourians against the Saints. To all the people listening to him it was a familiar tale, and they shifted restlessly.

Now his voice rose as he said, "We have heard from Governor Boggs in answer to our demand for relief." His voice rose, "We innocent people have suffered at the hands of the citizens of this state. Misunderstood and abused until our souls are sick within us, we have petitioned only for peace and fairness at the hands of our enemies."

His hand trembled as he lifted a paper above his head. "And what is our answer from the governor?" He paused, and silence gripped the group. Sardonically he said, "Our governor has advised us to fight our own battles." Leaning forward, he stated, "And that, my brethren, is just what we intend to do."

Amid the uproar, he continued, "We have tried to keep the law long enough. What has it gained us? It has been administered against us, never for us."

Over the cries of assent, Joseph raised his arm and with a shout said, "Hereafter, I do not intend to keep the law. We shall take affairs into our own hands and manage without Boggs or his laws."

When the roar of the crowd again subsided, he continued, "In DeWitt we yielded to the mob. Now they are heading for the homes of our people in Daviess County. I have determined that we shall not give another foot to them. No matter how many shall come against us, ten or a thousand of them, God will send His angels to our deliverance. We will be the victors, whether we fight one or a thousand of them."

Joseph started to move away, then with a grin he turned back. "There are those wondering how we shall supply the needs of our troops. Some will say I have told you to steal, but I have not. That isn't necessary when you can get plenty without. In closing I will tell you about a Dutchman and his field of potatoes. A colonel with his men was quartered nearby, and going to the old man, he offered to buy the field of potatoes. The old Dutchman refused to sell. When the colonel returned to his regiment with the tale of woe, he stated, 'Now remember, don't *let* a man of you *be caught* stealing potatoes.' " Joseph paused and then added, "In the morning there wasn't a potato in the patch." There was a moment of silence and then a few chuckled. The relief from tension was contagious and the rumble of laughter grew.

Joseph was still standing and waiting. From Jenny's position she could see the change taking place on his face. The half-smile slid away, and as the excited babble increased, rage contorted his face. Leaning forward, he cried, "If only they would leave us alone! Then we could preach the gospel in peace. But if there's an attempt to molest us, we shall establish our religion by the sword."

Sidney Rigdon stepped to the front and said, "We have a group of '*Oh, don't*' men in our midst. They are those who decry the order to support our right, saying, 'You are breaking the law, you will bring ruin to the society.'

"While others are fighting, these men are bringing division and disturbances to our midst. We must have unity. I say that blood must first run in the streets of Far West before we are worthy men to venture forth to fight the enemy. Is it fair for these *Oh, don't* men to stay behind while their brothers risk their lives? Should these men attempt to leave the county, their lives shall be forfeited and their property confiscated. I say these men should be rounded up, pitched on their horses with bayonets and placed in front as you go to battle." As Rigdon moved away, the crowd erupted in a frenzy of shouting.

From where Jenny stood the next words were only cacophony, but as she watched, men separated into groups and moved among the assembly. She saw men singled out, and led off one by one. Frowning, Jenny tried to find meaning in the actions. When two men surrounded Mark and led him away, she clenched one fist against her mouth, the other against her pounding heart. The meaning was clear. Mark had been labeled an *Oh don't* man.

After the men had been lined up and marched away, the women began to move. Just as Jenny was doing, they staggered like sleep-walkers. There was an occasional sob as they picked their way over the rutted streets of Far West and headed for the warmth of the general store. But Jenny lingered behind. That dark-cloaked figure was still in the town square, talking to the cluster of excited men pressing close. She waited until he broke free and headed down the street.

The sound of her feet pounding on the road made him turn. Staring up into his cold face, she could only stutter, "J—Joe, I—I must see you."

For a moment his face cleared, he nearly smiled. "Little Missus Cartwright," he drawled. "If you've come to plead for your husband, don't. We need every man we can get. Jenny, my beautiful dear, neither tears nor promises will get your heart's desire. This is war."

He turned and moved away while Jenny stood stricken and trembling, first with anger and then with fear. When she had recovered, he had rounded the corner and disappeared.

She whirled around. A young man standing just behind her was watching with a sympathetic smile. "Begging your pardon, but please don't trouble the Prophet. Seems he's wearied by all the women who think they have a special place—"

"No, no!" Jenny cried impatiently. "I need to see Joseph. I have information he needs to hear."

The man's expression was totally disbelieving, and she snapped, "Where's the Prophet's home?"

He spoke slowly, still looking at her with doubting eyes, "He lives with the George Harris family. If you look yonder, right through those trees, you can see the chimney. But don't expect to be seein' him right away. He doesn't have the time to spare." Jenny turned away. For a few minutes longer she lingered in the square, wondering what to do.

It was growing colder, and she rubbed her numb hands. Finally, with a sigh of frustration, she turned to follow the women to the store.

Until evening, the group of chilled, pinched-face women lingered on in Far West. Huddled around the fire in the general store, they waited, only to hear that the men had been divided into companies. Jenny watched their misery as they paced before the fire. Later they heard the first company of horsemen had started on their way to Adam-ondi-Ahman.

It was Tuesday afternoon before Jenny gave up hope of seeing Mark sprinting across the town square toward the Lewis cabin, saying he had been released.

Mrs. Lewis, sitting before the fire, knitting and keeping tabs on the affairs of Far West, said, " 'Tis life, my dear. Go about your business just like the rest of us. You heard the Prophet. There's no doubt about it; our men will be the victors, and soon this land of Zion will be free from the taint of the cursed ones."

Jenny's hands were trembling and tears burned her eyelids as she unfolded the paper and read directions to Sally's farm. At the end of the paper, Mark had written, *I love you; remember, I'll be back—we've promised.*

She closed her eyes, thinking back that long-ago time when he had pressed his lips against her hair. He had thought she didn't hear the whispered, *In sickness or in health,* but she did, and her heart had added, *'Til death, I promise you.*

Jenny picked up the bag which had been packed for Ohio and went to the stable to find the awkward buggy Mark had designed from scraps of their wagon.

It was dusk by the time Jenny followed the lamplight to Sally's door. And Sally, with Tamara beside her, stood wide-eyed and pale, waiting to welcome her.

13

THAT FIRST DAY at Sally's home, Jenny voiced her fears. She was drying the dishes as Sally washed. Slowly turning the cup in her hand, she said, "Sally, do you *really* believe Joseph's prophccy?" She glanced at Sally's face and protested, "Don't look at me like that. I'm not a tattletale. I'm scared, and I just wish you'd make me feel better about all this."

"You're just missing Mark," Sally protested, but her eyes were on the dish she was holding, and Jenny was caught by the feebleness of her reply. Her heart sank. Sally was knowing the fears, too.

Later beside the fire, with Sally cuddling Tamara on her lap, Jenny faced the pair. She pushed aside her uneasiness for a moment, thinking instead how much a miniature of her mother little Tamara was. As Jenny reached out to touch the child's cheek, Sally glanced down at her daughter and said, "Too bad you haven't produced a young'un; that'd help the time pass for you." She sighed. "Jenny, I know it's bad. I hate it all just as much as you, but dwelling on it and chewing over all the things we shouldn't even been thinking about—well, that doesn't help at all. Can't you leave the fussin' to the menfolk? It'll all work out."

Tamara held up her arms and Jenny took the child. "Sally, I know just what you'll be saying next. You're going to start chiding me because my faith is feeble and you'll tell me again that to question is to doubt, and that doubt is sin. Somehow I can't just accept anything in life without giving it a few questions. Why did God make me this way if asking questions is wrong?"

"Tell me what sense it makes to question?"

"Well, for one thing, I suppose it gives a person a good desire to change what ought to be changed."

Sally picked up her mending and asked, "Just what would you change in this affair if you could?"

Jenny looked around the little cabin. There were things from their past which had been disturbing her for some time. She had been recalling Kirtland. Closing her eyes she could see the Morgan home with its spacious rooms and big windows. She pictured the flower garden, the white picket fence, and the flock of chickens picking at sunflower seeds.

"Sally, don't you pine for that lovely house in Kirtland?"

Sally sighed and nodded, "And the furniture we couldn't bring with us." She stopped abruptly and Jenny saw her press her lips tightly together before she continued. "Jenny, we can't be fussing over *things*. Every one of us is called upon to make sacrifices for Zion."

"I don't know why I'm thinking like this right now," Jenny said slowly. "Maybe it is not having Mark around. Up Adam-ondi-Ahman way I could see the poor lot we had, but somehow it seemed to be just a passing thing; I expected it to be better tomorrow. Now—maybe it is just missing Mark."

Sally shook her head over her sewing. Her voice sounded wistful as she said, "No, it isn't just that. Seems you can take anything if you believe in it. I guess what you're trying to tell me is that maybe you no longer believe?" She lifted her head and searched Jenny's face. "Doesn't it make you feel terrible to *not* believe?"

Jenny stared thoughtfully at Sally, seeing the worried frown on her face, the anxious lines that had replaced the smiles. Sally didn't seem to know how she had changed. Finally Jenny said, "Sally, you wanted to know what I'd change. It's the helpless feeling."

"Helpless? Jenny, we're to be praying, trusting the Prophet to bring the word of the Lord to us. We're to believe everything will work out just the way Joseph prophesied it would."

"And if it doesn't?" For a moment fear spread across Sally's face and then she straightened on her stool and opened her mouth to speak. Hastily Jenny said, "See, deep down you're scared to death it won't. Well, that's where we're different. You'll sit and shake in your shoes. I intend to get out and make certain it does happen."

Jenny began to grin. She could see from the sparkle of hope in Sally's eyes that she had her attention. "And," she leaned forward, "one of these days, I'm going to say, 'Joseph, remember the hard times in Missouri's beginning days, back before we really became Zion with all these riches? Remember when we lived in log cabins instead of these white mansions? Remember when it looked like we were losing? Well, Joseph, that's when I—' "

Jenny stopped abruptly. It was as if she had suddenly dropped back into Sally's presence, and here was this weak, timid woman waiting for her to change the world.

Sally was holding her breath, waiting. Now Jenny didn't dare say those final things. Sally's little-girl eyes gazed at her with eyes so much like Tamara's. She wouldn't understand. For a moment Jenny felt as if she were Sally's mother. Her heart swelled with love for the timid little one, and then she knew, for one brief moment, the surge of power.

But even now it seemed life was falling back into a pattern of failure. She was very aware of a spirit of powerlessness and fear twisting around her, like the fear mirrored in Sally's eyes and echoed in Tamara's whimpers.

For a moment she teetered, powerless to help either herself or her friend, and then she remembered her resolve. She must see Joseph, now. She must tell him about all that was going amiss in his church. But would he listen to her?

Just two days ago he had brushed off her words as of no account. She puzzled over that; what had happened to the Joseph she had known in Kirtland, the man who had seemed eager to keep his finger upon the pulse of the church?

Then she realized the connections. She needed power at her disposal before she could be successful with Joseph. Jenny looked down at her hands lying limp and useless in her lap.

Was it all a dream, a useless, futile dream, or was there really power out there for the having? She waited, checking the response of her own spirit. There was that time, just before coming to Missouri, when she had *known* the only hope for power was through Joseph's church, through obedience to the Prophet.

For the rest of the day the two women tried to skirt the fearful things they had conjured and content themselves about the fire. But in the night, when chatter was done, Jenny's mind was filled with that painful picture of Mark, seeing him again as he was surrounded and marched out of her life.

During the dark lonesome hours, Jenny did a great deal of thinking, and she came to a single conclusion. She knew, with a deep-down spirit conviction, that Joseph was doomed to failure unless much more power were brought to bear upon the forces fighting him.

Now Jenny moaned softly as she twisted her face into the pillow. What careless folly! During the rush of the day, just before leaving their cabin at Adam-ondi-Ahman, Jenny had forgotten to pin the talisman into the folds of her fresh dress. It was still pinned to her work frock, left hanging behind the door of the cabin. And the green book. At the last moment she dared not hide it in the buggy lest Mark stumble across it. She whispered into the pillow, "No matter what the cost, I must go after the talisman and the book!"

The next day, as soon as she dared, Jenny was into the forest, searching the undergrowth for the power-filled mushrooms and herbs to round out her dwindling supply. The memory of the charms and chants in the green book were as fresh and alive in her thoughts as they had been the last time she had used them.

Unfortunately, there were many sections of the book she had never had the occasion to use. She thought of the book secreted back at the little cabin perched above the rapids of Grand River. How desperately she needed that book! And Adela. How badly she needed that woman's wisdom and counsel now, before it was too late!

With renewed passion, Jenny fought desperately for spirit power and the strength to know the secret vibrations of the other world. The following day she spent hours in the forest, while a listless Sally rocked beside the hearth and played with her child.

When Jenny returned to Sally's cabin, there was a strange discontent wrapping itself around her heart. Coming out of her meditations in the forest, she felt as if she were trading reality for a misty world without substance.

But that night, when the faint glow of the fire touched the shadowy room, Jenny felt herself alive to the spirit influence. She beamed her prayers toward the full moon and directed her spirit energy toward pleasing those fearful spirit entities.

Just two days after the men marched out of Far West, heading toward Adam-ondi-Ahman, an unseasonable snowstorm paralyzed Missouri for a brief time.

Jenny watched the snow from Sally's window and fretted about Mark, but at the same time she was taking credit for the storm. The influences from the spirit world knew better than she just what power must be used.

Heartened by victory, she redoubled her efforts, now adding incantations that left her shivery with the sense of power flowing through the universe. Meanwhile, Jenny watched Sally's fears and doubts grow day by day. But Jenny observed her friend's anxieties with an oblique sense of detachment, aware of her own power growing.

On the day that the snow melted back enough to reveal the crushed grasses and brown-earth path, Jenny rode Patches into Far West. Her plans were vague, but she knew she must try to find Joseph, even if it entailed walking up to the Harrises' front door and facing Emma Smith with her demands.

As she rode slowly through the deserted streets, she felt the air of desolation, even abandonment, and she shivered in response. In front of the sprawling log building, Jenny slid from the horse and tethered her beside the only other horse. She measured the gelding with a critical eye. Black, several hands taller than her mare, with a deep, powerful chest. As she headed for the door, she smiled to herself. That could be Joseph's horse. Just possibly she would have him to herself!

Inside, the man behind the high counter was polishing glasses. "Hello, Mike," she said, pulling the mittens from her hands.

"Miz Cartwright." His genial face crumpled into a frown. "No matter what you're a wantin', we probably don't have it."

She cocked her head and nodded with a pleased smile. "Yes you do. I hear Joseph's voice, and it's him I want."

Mike's eyebrows arched in surprise, "Well—"

Another voice roared through Joseph's murmured words; both Jenny and Mike faced the jumble of shelves and boxes that shielded the far end of the building. Jenny didn't recognize the voice, but she forgot that as she listened.

"I tell you, there's no other way. We will prevail. We will win! The Lord himself has given us this plan; you've said so yourself. The law of consecration will not support the building of the temple. These people are too poor. We must convince them that this new plan will work. Think of it— everyone divided into four companies, everyone placing their property under his company for the good of all. Everyone with a task to do, and we'll all prosper."

The roar subsided to a low rumble and Jenny looked at Mike. "Who is that?"

He cast her a pitying glance. "You best get acquainted. That fella is a big shot who's gonna get bigger. That's Avard, the wheel that runs the Danites."

"Avard!" She'd only time for a gasp of surprise when the man thumped his way into the room. He elbowed past her and slapped the bar.

"Mike, a stiff one." Now he turned with a sardonic grin, and she guessed he had been fully aware of her presence when he pushed into the room. "Well, well. A camp follower?"

"I'll thank you, sir, to watch your manners. I am a wife."

He slapped his knee and howled with laughter. "Aw, got your temper up, didn't I? Now you see me, what do you want?"

"Want? Nothing, I—" Stepping closer she peered up at him, "So you're the famous Avard who runs the Danites. I've heard about you. Why must you have such a fearful, secret army? Isn't it more proper to be all out in the open? I mean, if you're in the right and there's to be a fight, why the secret?"

"Well, now," he scratched his head and then grinned. "I guess 'cause the fellas like it."

"That's no reason. I've heard the menfolk are frightened, scared to step a toe over the line. They're talking about you having absolute control of the men. Why, I've heard that even Joseph Smith doesn't know what you're doing behind all that secrecy—"

"I've heard," he mimicked, with a snort of a laugh. "That ain't so. Joe knows what's goin' on. When we organized, he came before us to bless us. The presidency gave us to realize we're here to do a marvelous work on this earth. It's promised to us that we'll have glorious military victory, and it will be by the power of God. The revelation said that one of us will put a thousand to flight; besides that, we'll be assisted by angels in the work of the Lord as we go out to battle."

"You think you will?" Jenny's voice was only a whisper. She was thinking of Mark and Tom.

His glance was shrewd. "He prophesied that the time has come for us to take up arms in our defense. Joseph even promised that if trusting in him fails, we can use his head for a football." He was studying her face with eyes so sharp that Jenny steeled herself to endure the scrutiny.

Slowly he spoke, "You know what the worst thing on this earth is for a Saint?" She shook her head and he added, "To disbelieve or go against the Prophet and his men."

In a moment she recovered enough to say, "I heard you talking about the companies of workers."

He nodded, his gaze was still piercing as he said, "All persons who attempt to cheat by deception, holding back some of their property from the church, will meet the same fate as Ananias and Sapphira did. Peter killed them."

He turned back to the bar and lifted the glass. But Jenny was caught motionless. When he faced her again, she was still waiting. "There'll be a fight lady, whether you and the *Oh, don'ts* want it or not. I do, and well see the matter out; there's no other way." He finished his drink; without another word, he headed out the door.

Jenny heard his shout and the sharp whinny of his horse before she recalled the reason she was here. She turned to Mike. "Joseph. I must see him."

Mike was still polishing glasses. His look was level as he said, "Went out the back way 'bout five minutes ago. He's headed home and walkin'. I suppose you could catch him."

By the time Jenny was back on her mare and headed for the edge of town, she could see the dark figure cutting away from the road and moving into the trees. She was certain it was Joseph. That fellow had pointed out the George Harris home just beyond those trees.

As Jenny guided the mare away from the road and into the trees, she lost sight of Joseph. "Oh dear," she murmured, "one second and he's disappeared. I was certain he was moving that direction, and now—" Jenny blinked.

The path in front of her had been empty, but now there was a figure moving toward her. She had guessed it was a woman wearing a dark cloak, and now she saw a flash of red with every step the woman took. Red. Surely not.

Jenny leaned over the horse's neck and peered through the shadows. Was her silly heart playing tricks again? Had her deep need conjured an apparition? "Adela," she whispered. Her heart was pounding in confirmation of what she was seeing.

At the moment Jenny straightened and screamed, "Adela!" she brought the reins down across Patches' flanks. The horse lunged and reared. Jenny fought for control as they plunged through the bushes.

When Jenny had calmed the horse, she slipped from Patches' back, still trembling.

Joseph came loping through the bushes. "Jenny Cartwright, is that really you?" He reached for her with a pleased grin, then exclaimed, "What happened?"

"Nothing, really. This mare took off like a scared rabbit when I yelled."

"That was you? Who were you calling?"

"The woman. Did you see her?" Jenny ran past him to the path and stopped. "That's strange. She's completely disappeared. I would have expected that—" She shrugged and turned back to Joseph. "But it's you I've come to see."

He was frowning, looking around uneasily. When he turned back she saw he was puzzled, lost in thought. She studied his uneasy grin, saw how hard he tried to concentrate on her words, and, surprisingly, a crushing disappointment settled over her.

"Joseph, remember a long time ago in Kirtland, you said you needed me." She saw the astonishment flare in his eyes and paused only to wonder as she continued. "You said you needed a friend, to—to let you know what was going on. Do you still need me? I've been hearing so much—she faltered when she saw the thundercloud expression.

"Of course," he said hastily. "What is it?"

"The people. Please give them a chance. They grumble and argue, but they daren't tell you what they are thinking. Joseph, it hadn't ought to be." For a moment she was lost in reflection, and then recovering, she added, "Even I miss the old Joseph. You were so much fun, and they adored you."

His eyes softened for a moment and then with a sigh, he said, "Those were the old days, Jenny. How I wish I could have held them forever in that way. But no! It is not that I wished differently; it was them."

His eyes were blazing and he grasped the hand she held outstretched. "Jenny, I've found how deep their devotion goes. It's only as deep as their pockets. If I am a cynic, it is because I have discovered I can trust no man. They want to own me, shape me to their image. I will be owned by none. I am the Lord's anointed. I hold the keys of the kingdom. If I must control these people with an iron hand in order to bring them into the kingdom of heaven, then I will do so."

"Love?"

It was a question, and he stared into her eyes as he slowly asked, "What do you mean?"

"Mark says God is love. He thinks it is possible for people to be controlled by love." Joseph's mouth was twisting in amusement, and hastily Jenny continued, "I don't agree. I think it's power." She recalled the woman. "That's why I was so excited when I saw her. Do you still have the talisman and the seer stone? Do you still believe—"

Now Joseph threw his head back and laughed heartily, "Jenny, my dear! Do you mean to tell me that you haven't outgrown those childish ways? How have you escaped the pious clutches of your husband's holy fervor?" Now he leaned close and whispered, "Don't be foolish, my dear! Of course I don't believe the old witching tales. I am Prophet, Seer, and Revelator. I am the anointed. What I say is the Word of God to my people. Don't forget that. When I say jump, my people must jump. When I say a thing will happen, it will happen."

"Like the riches of the Gentiles will be ours?" She was staring into his face. Without wavering, his eyes met hers. Slowly, she whispered, "Joseph, I wish with all my heart that I could believe as surely as you do. Then maybe it wouldn't make any difference whether I ever saw Adela again, whether I got back my talisman and the book."

He blinked. "What's happened?"

"Nothing. Silly-like, I left them in Adam-ondi-Ahman."

And then in another moment he said thoughtfully, "So the people aren't happy. What do they want from me?"

"They want you to stay your hand. They want to live in peace with these people in this state. It can't happen as long as you insist on crushing everyone around you, Saints included."

"Jenny, my dear." His voice was sorrowful. "It is for their own good. Have you not heard enough of the revelations to know that when the people disobey, God will punish them? It is my unhappy lot to be standing between the two as prophet. I get blamed for all the Lord does to His people." He paused before adding, "Now go. When the questioners come to you, tell them that when they quit sinning, they will experience all the fullness of the blessings of the Lord. If they refuse to consecrate their property and do the work of the Lord, well, they'll suffer for their sins."

His shiver was tiny and controlled, but Jenny turned away with a new seed of despair in her heart.

Joseph lifted Jenny to her horse. Once again he was distant, cold. She rode away with a heavy heart. Back on the road to Far West, she allowed the mare to amble along while she thought about the things Joseph had said.

She was deeply conscious of sin and failure. As she headed up the road to Morgans' little cabin, she murmured, "I went expecting to improve the Saints' lot, and I've come back crushed to the ground by all our faults. No wonder the Lord can't bless us. I'm guessing I'd do well to quit blaming Joseph for something he can't help and go to work on changing things."

She rode silently for a time and then with a grin, she straightened and lifted her face. "Seems it really is hopeless, Joseph. You told me not to be childish, but you don't know what you're talking about. No sense advertising to you, but I intend to get that book and the talisman. But I don't expect you to thank me for saving your neck!"

Joseph watched until Jenny was out of sight and then he turned. "All right, Lucinda, come out of those bushes. I know you are there."

She raised her arms and Joseph caught her close. "But you are a witch, of the very best kind. Miss me?" He bent to kiss her before she could answer.

Lucinda leaned back to study his face, saying, "For a moment I thought I had competition." His grin wasn't reassuring. As she snuggled close, she stifled a sigh.

14

As MARK LEFT Far West with the newly formed militia, now called the Armies of Israel, he soon discovered that he was part of the derided group. Rigdon had referred to them as the *Oh, don't* men. Right now they were called the "bayonet outfit" by the old timers. As nearly as he could determine, the name either had reference to the position of the men in battle line—right out front—or because it took the urging of a bayonet to get them on the horses.

His chagrin over the stigma was short-lived when he met his illustrious companions. "John Corrill, Phelps, Cleminson, and Reed Peck!" he exclaimed when the men were forced into line in front of the foot soldiers as they prepared to march to Adam-ondi-Ahman.

The first day their march extended into the cool autumn dusk. The troops passed up the road he and Jenny had traveled just a few days previously. Toward evening Mark and his companions talked in low voices while the remainder of the army abandoned caution and sang one song after another.

The morning of the second day of march, the troops began seeing caravans of people heading down the valley toward them. Mark pointed them out to Corrill and asked, "What do you make of that?"

He didn't get an answer until the group had passed, and then Corrill's answer confirmed his guess. "From the looks of those poor beggars, I'm guessin' we've routed the rest of the Gentiles out of Daviess County. I recognize some faces. They don't impress me as goin' on a pleasure trip."

The troops watched the exodus of the Gentiles as they passed with wagons piled high with furniture and stuffed with people. The oxen were having a hard time of it and the wagons moved slowly. Mark saw the pinched-faced women staring stoically ahead, while solemn children watched wide-eyed.

"It's enough to make you feel like a perfect rotter," Peck muttered.

"Can't say I'm too proud of myself running a neighbor outta his home," Corrill added.

When the exhausted men reached Adam-ondi-Ahman late Tuesday evening, Mark discovered the character of the small town had undergone a radical change. True, he and Jenny had sensed abandonment as they had ridden through, but now the Gentile settlers seemed to have vanished. As Mark studied the half-finished fortress in the middle of town, he recalled his conversation with Tom, and how, at the time, the bunker had seemed like a feeble joke. But clearly the Danites were in control now.

Mark turned in that night, crowded between the other dissenters and placed under guard. Corrill murmured, "One advantage to being labeled an *Oh, don't* man is that we get to sleep inside the stable on the hay instead of outside with the tough ones, and, man, is it getting cold out there!"

By the morning it was snowing heavily. The men clustered around the campfires and shifted from one soggy foot to another. A chosen group was sent out to hunt dinner. Seeing Tom in the group, Mark hailed him and was surprised to see his curt salute as he turned away.

All that day, as the snow continued to pile high in Adam-ondi-Ahman, the men huddled around the fire. Mark's thoughts were gloomy as he recalled Jenny's white face and terror-filled eyes. When he caught Phelps' eye and the man gave him a twisted grin, he decided his thoughts weren't much different than the ones others were having.

Moving closer to Mark, Phelps murmured, "I'm not liking it either. My family isn't faring better; fact is," he gave a twisted grin, "I'm out of favor, too. Guess I did too much thinking out loud." After a moment he added, "I'm not a man to be out totin' a gun, but when pushed in the corner, I guess I fight."

As the morning wore on, the small talk around the fire dwindled to discontented murmuring, given with eyes slanted toward the known Danites in the group.

The men's restlessness carried them back and forth between the livery stable, the stockade, and the fire. Mark was eyeing Phelps as he moved back into the circle of the fire about noontime. He pulled a log close to Mark's and grunted, "Some status, from newspaper editor to Joseph's flunky. Still, I guess that means living your religion, and I'm not too much different than the others. You're an attorney, aren't you?" Mark nodded.

While Phelps stared into the fire, he spoke slowly, as if thinking aloud, "I still believe in Joseph. There's too many indications that his revelations are truth."

"What are you referring to?"

He looked up. "I was thinking about all the Indians being moved this way by Andy Jackson." He chuckled and shook his head. "He'd a pushed them into the Atlantic rather than serve the Lord's and Joseph's purposes by gathering Israel so close to Zion." He paused and then added, "I predicted then that the second coming was less than nine years away."

"The deadline is close," Mark observed, studying the man. Phelps shrugged, and Mark asked, "What did you do to rate the title of an *Oh, don't* man?"

"Just what any decent newspaper man would do. I was sticking up for the rights of those unjustly persecuted."

"You mean you think the dissenters were persecuted?"

"Isn't that right? They spoke out against oppression and lost position, favor, property, and were forced to run for their lives. It was fortunate that they survived the interview with the Danites," he murmured, glancing quickly around.

Mark looked too, and then said, "That's plenty. I did less and got myself in hot water."

"Yes, I know. You helped them out of the state and then flapped your big mouth over Whitmer's house when you knew Rigdon had confiscated it for himself."

"And Joseph sanctioned all this by his silence." Phelps' eyebrows raised, but he nodded. Deliberately pushing now, Mark added, "And no law, nothing, is superior to the Word of the Lord given through the Prophet."

"When you say it like that, the whole thing sounds ridiculous."

"Phelps, you're a thinking man. You can't continue to follow a man so obviously wrong in his dealings with his fellowman."

The man looked at Mark for a long time, studying his face thoughtfully. Finally he sighed and shifted his weight on the log. "You're overlooking the most important thing. I believe he has the keys to the kingdom, that he has given us the sacred Word of God."

"What about all those things that happened back in the early days before he had a following? What about the South Bainbridge days, the money digging and witching? Surely a thinking man wouldn't accept without questioning."

"You're right," Phelps said. "I did question. It was an advantage to do my questioning *first* instead of as an afterthought."

"You did?" Mark knew his surprise and disappointment was showing, but he must ask. "How did that happen?"

"Just after the founding of the church I heard about Joseph and his men and decided to inquire.

"And you were satisfied?"

He moved restlessly and looked away from Mark. For a moment he was silent, and Mark saw the uncertainty on his face. When he squared his shoulders and looked at Mark, he grinned. "I guess we all have our moments of doubt—but to doubt is wrong. I was curious and looking. At the time, I'd been involved with my soapbox, Masonry. When I found out how dead set Joseph was against the secret societies, and how he'd had revelations showing God commanding against them, well, that just sealed my determination to be a part of the group."

Mark moved restlessly. Then Phelps was speaking again. "From the beginning, Joseph's spirit was consistent with what we see now—a man of God."

"Tell me more."

"You know the rest of the story. About the finding of the gold plates."

"Phelps, can you believe his holy calling on the basis of this?"

"I told you, I'd worked my way through belief and disbelief. It was hard; the story was incredulous. But just like the others, I had to ask for a sign from God, and He gave me a burning in the bosom in confirmation." He was silent a moment and then added, "Besides, there's something about the man. Sometimes I get angry at him, but I can't help it; I've got to believe his calling. There is a divine cord about me which will not let me go."

Mark found he couldn't control the ridiculous question: "Are you afraid?"

Phelps looked up in surprise. "Of course! Mark, don't you realize eternal salvation for you will depend on whether Joseph *approves*? I've heard him myself, saying that he will stand at the entrance of heaven and turn back those who haven't won his approval."

They were still standing in front of the fire, silent with their own thoughts, when they heard the clatter of hooves on the river road. The men around the fire turned to watch. It was a lone horseman, and Phelps muttered. "The Ram of the mountain. It's Colonel Wight—wonder what his problem is?"

Mark watched the man dismount. He was wearing only a light jacket with his hairy chest open to the snow. His long, heavy hair was tied back with a soiled red kerchief.

Wight impatiently flipped the bearskin covering his saddle, and strode to the fire waving a cutlass. Watching him swish the short curved blade as he impatiently kicked a log into the fire, Mark murmured, "The name fits."

One of the Danites who had just approached the fire slanted a glance at Mark and Phelps. "Second to Avard, he's a man the Gentiles fear. There's trouble on the Millport road. I heard them talking last night. We all just might be called out there yet unless the rest of the army in Far West is moved this way."

"What's the problem?" Mark asked, turning from the fire to meet the man's frown.

"Yesterday Wight was addressing the men in camp. I was there and, I'll tell you, it was a speech to put fire in the veins of a dead man. He was in the midst of telling us how the Lord had made us invincible and that there's not an army around who can defeat us when this fella up and cut out of there, riding like his life was on the line. And it would have been if we'd known who he was.

"Information leaking back later let us know it was a dispatch from the other side. He'd been sent from the Missouri militia, mind you, to advise that their group was mutinous and that they were joining the DeWitt mob.

"Later we heard more from one of the spies. He told us this fella, the one we saw bust and run, carried back the report that Wight had fifteen thousand men under him and would be in their camp in two hours. Intelligence said they broke camp and left, but Joseph's sweating it out, getting ready to send more men this way."

It was late in the afternoon before the men took up the thread of conversation again. Mark heard Pratt reviewing the Lord's plan for Missouri, but he paid little attention until the man sat up and declared, "There's coming a day when the Lord will give these people a chance to accept the *Book of Mormon.* If they refuse to hearken to it, the remnant of Jacob, that's the Indians, will go through here and tear these people to pieces."

"Do you really reckon it will happen, Pratt?" came a wistful voice from the far side of the fire.

Pratt got to his feet and paced back and forth. His hands were linked behind his back. Mark was thinking that Pratt was a fellow who would catch anyone's attention. When Pratt answered, his sonorous voice made the hair on Mark's neck prickle. "I prophesy," he said, "that there will not be an unbelieving Gentile on this continent in fifty years' time. Furthermore, if they aren't to a great extent scourged and overthrown in five or ten years from now—this year of 1838—then I say the *Book of Mormon* will have proved itself to be false. I intend to write this prophecy for posterity. I may not be suited to fighting, but I have the ability to prophesy."

Late that evening the hunters returned. Mark was still mulling over Pratt's statement when he heard the questions shouted to the men. "Same old fare," they called back. "Bear, buffalo, and sweet oil."

Phelps rubbed his cold chin and said, "That means we dine on Gentile cows, pigs, and honey. I just hope this doesn't mean someone's going hungry."

Cleminson answered, "I was on one of these thieving missions when the fellows helped themselves. Some old lady was left to watch her only cow being led away to feed Mormon bellies. I tell you, I felt like a rotter."

Phelps said in a soft voice, "Better keep your thoughts to yourself if you don't want to join the group tomorrow night."

The men were eating the roasted beef, cooked over the open fire, when a lone man rode into their encampment. "Lee, come have something to eat," Pratt called, waving his chunk of beef. "You have news?"

He nodded. After taking the stick impaled with chunks of roasted meat, he said, "I'm here to round up volunteers to ride out with us in the morning."

Mark studied his furrowed brow as Franklin asked, "What's the mission?"

"Joseph, Wight, and Patten have cooked up a plan. You'll hear about it tomorrow." He looked around the group and said, "Just give me some men. About forty will do."

15

AFTER BEING HOUSEBOUND by the snow, Jenny's restless spirit couldn't get enough of roaming. The snow, still piled under the trees, and the paths, a soggy mat of torn branches and snow-packed grass, didn't stop her. However, she did spend one day dragging her skirts through the soggy mess and dampening her boots almost beyond saving before resorting to Patches.

One day she was thinking, as she rode into Far West, that she would much rather crash through the deserted woods than ride the trails around town, but riding was better than nothing—and there were advantages.

She had just let her restless horse shy away from Anna Briton. She chalked up the first advantage with a sly grin. A horse made it possible to escape busybody neighbors whose total enjoyment was checking out how others were living their religion.

Jenny dug her heels into the horse's ribs and refused to rescue her hair when the wind caught it and flung it over her shoulders.

She was riding helter-skelter through Far West when the difference in the town caught her attention. More than just a sprinkling of frightened women were on the street, there were men as well—tattered, dirty, but jubilant. And the men and women who surrounded them were either frowning and backing away or pressing forward with eager hands and welcoming cries.

Jenny watched the milling crowd, realizing now that the focus of their attention wasn't the returning warriors home from battle. Instead, all eyes were on the loaded wagons in the town square.

Slipping from her horse, she joined the group, where Mrs. Lewis greeted her with a smile. Jenny returned her greeting and turned to watch the eager hands pulling furniture—feather beds, a churn, even a mirror— from the wagon.

When Mrs. Lewis stopped beside her, Jenny asked, "What is this?"

The man tossing down bundles of clothing answered, " 'Tis the riches of the Gentiles. Come get your share." He tossed an embroidered shawl to her, and Jenny held it away to study it.

It was of soft creamy wool, gently scented with lavender. She could see it was old; the folds were yellow with age. Closing her eyes, she could nearly see the woman who had cherished the shawl. "Her mother," she murmured. "I'm sure it was her mother's shawl, and she's grieving the loss!"

"What did you say?" Mrs. Lewis was looking into her face.

"I shall keep it," Jenny declared. "And when this nightmare is over, I shall return it to its owner. It belonged to her dead mother. We've no right to take it."

The man on the wagon roared, " 'Tis the Gentiles. They'll be consigned to hell and there's no need for shawls there!" The laughter spilled around Jenny, and she backed away, still clutching the shawl.

Mrs. Lewis was chiding gently, "Child, are you disputing the word of the Lord through Joseph? You know the revelation. You know that now is the time for the riches of the Gentiles to become our inheritance. Come, don't sound like a dissenter." Her fingers were grasping the shawl, prying it out of Jenny's hands. She added, "If you've no need for it, I can use a new one. I wonder if the yellow streaks will come out."

After watching the Saints rummage through the wagons and cart off their choices, Jenny shook her head and turned her horse away. "Atta girl." She heard the soft comment and glanced up. Jake was grinning at her. Then she noticed others leaving the town square empty-handed.

Guiding Patches away from the main streets, Jenny worked her way slowly toward the fringes of town. She was passing the cluster of log cabins, noticing, with a sharp stab of surprise, the number which had been deserted.

She was uneasy, still pondering that discovery as she rode past the schoolhouse. A group of men stood close to the steps, one of them Sidney Rigdon. With a casual glance, Jenny had started on when the sharp voices caught her attention.

She pulled on the reins and turned Patches. Rigdon was standing on the steps, looking out over the men. His face was contorted with rage as he waved his arm and shouted, "The last Saint has fled Far West! So you don't like the directions of the Lord? We'll see to it that you do! The next to leave will be chased, brought back—dead or alive. I bring before you a resolution: if a man attempts to pack his belongings, take his family, and leave, I propose that the man who sees this happening shall, without revealing his intentions to any other, kill the fleeing Saint and hide his body in the bushes." He paused and in the silence added, "Yesterday about this time, one man from Far West slipped his wind and was dragged into the bushes to die. Now, I warn you, any man lisping a word of this shall have the same happen to him."

That evening as Jenny sat beside the fire, poking at the tumble of yarn in her lap, she thought about the afternoon scene around the wagon. The memory had become doubly troubling since she had heard Rigdon's tirade.

Under the ripple of conversation Sally was releasing, Jenny was thinking. It hurt to imagine these people deprived of their possessions, but that wasn't the reason she was hearing warning bells in her soul. It was something deeper.

With a sigh, Jenny straightened on her stool and said, "Sally, I've got to go back to Adam-ondi-Ahman." As she described the afternoon's events, she saw Sally's expression change from placid content to shock and disbelief.

"Jenny, how ridiculous! You risk your life to go fuss at Joseph. I'm certain he knows how Rigdon feels. I don't understand it all, but where'd we be if every man fled Far West? As for being in danger, they're not. They are doing just what the Lord's commanded them to do. How could He fail to keep them safe? Besides, they'd never listen to a woman."

There was an urgency, an underlying current of fear in Sally's voice. Jenny searched her friend's face and could see the dark circles under her eyes, the weary lines on her face. Without a doubt Sally needed her, but Jenny's need to get the talisman and the green book was growing deeper every day. This afternoon's ride had confirmed the uneasy impression that something very wrong was happening in Zion. She needed all the power she could possibly conjure if she were to help these people.

As she studied Sally's face, Jenny had the distinct impression that she alone sensed disaster moving close.

Jenny dropped to her knees beside Sally and clasped her hands. Even now she guessed that Sally would let her go, but she couldn't endure leaving her without hope.

"Sally, listen to me. It isn't just what happened this afternoon. There's something else. When I went into Far West that first time, I met that horrible Samson Avard."

"The leader of the Danites?" Sally whispered. Jenny could see she had her attention. She nodded. Sally was still speaking softly, as if she expected the walls to hear. "He's terrible. I've heard whispers about how he's deceiving Joseph and how he's so cruel."

"That's why I must go. Surely Joseph doesn't know of his influence with the men and the terrible things he's planning. Sally, do you see? I *must* go."

She watched the woman's countenance fall and lunged for the nearest word. "Faith. Sally, you must have faith. You're going to be ill if you continue in this hopeless way." *Faith.* The word mocked Jenny, and she nearly thought she could hear the spirit's laughter.

"You heard Joseph and Rigdon and the others. They've promised that the Lord will fight for the men and that not a hair on their heads will be lost. Don't you believe it?" Sally studied her face without answering, but now there was a spark of a question in her dull eyes.

"Faith is just believing when your good sense tells you it's all wrong," Sally finally whispered.

Tamara was holding up her arms and Jenny lifted the child. She buried her face in the toddler's hair and hoped Sally wouldn't ask her for her own definition. How could she convince Sally of the faith she had professed? Faith was having a green book with instructions for living. Faith was having charms and the sure knowledge of power.

Jenny's lips twisted as she imagined this woman, a devout follower of the Prophet, being exposed to Jenny's beliefs. She closed her eyes and imagined the horrified expression on Sally's face were she to know how she really believed. But still, faith was faith. "God of nature, God of all," Jenny murmured, "bring me power to help this woman."

"Jenny, I—I," Sally stopped with a gulp. "I'm so fearful. It isn't just about Andy. That's part, but not all. I—I keep thinking that if I don't do something soon—" She was silent for a long minute and Jenny, busy with her own thoughts, wondered how she could give Sally hope without shattering her tenuous faith in the Prophet.

"Jenny," it was a timid attempt, and Jenny raised her head. "I—it's been so long since we've seen each other to really talk and now I feel so-—so bound up that I dare not say a thing."

"Sally, I'm sorry. I didn't mean to make you feel that way."

"Oh no," Sally said quickly. "It isn't that, it's just that I've been entrusted with secret things—responsibilities. I dare not say more. It's just that I feel the weight of it all so deeply." She dropped her face into her hands, and Jenny saw her press her lips with a gesture of despair.

When Sally lifted her face she said, "The Prophet says we must obey if we are to have the assurance that the Lord will take care of us. Jenny, it's a fearful responsibility."

Slowly Jenny said, "You're talking as if having faith is similar to lifting a sack of potatoes. Hard." She looked curiously at her and thought of her own faith. And when she had examined it, she decided Sally's definition just might fit.

Early the following morning Jenny rode through the woods. She headed north, away from Log Creek where Sally and Andy Morgan had built their cabin close to Haun's Mill. As she approached Far West, she walked the horse deeper into the woods, making it appear as if she were out for a leisurely ride. She was also thinking it might be a good idea to have an excuse ready to offer since she would be traveling into forbidden territory.

As she rode, Jenny was still thinking about Sally. Momentarily she frowned, wondering at the depths of the woman's agony. Finally Jenny's lips twisted in amusement. To think she had once thought herself shackled to Joseph's church, fearful and duty-bound to obey. Now Sally's face served as a tonic, freeing her of the past.

She chuckled as she rode on, secure with her decision to win power, all the power the church boasted, plus more. "I've come full circle," she reminded herself in a pleased whisper. "All I need now is Pa's green book."

North of Far West, Jenny turned back to the road and whipped her horse on toward Gallatin. Effortlessly, the horse flew with the wind, carrying Jenny's light body.

At Gallatin she again left the road and cut around town at an easy walk. This was Gentile territory, and it was wise to avoid strangers these days. She began to relax, to enjoy the day and the ride.

She was on the far side of town, beyond the store and stables, when she met the man. The trail was dim and shadowed, and she was picking her way carefully when she heard his horse. Her heart began to pound, pressed by all those fearful stories.

Raising her whip, she waited for him to approach. He dismounted. Jenny jerked the reins and the man leaped for them. "Take it easy, ma'am, I mean no harm. Gentile or Saint, it isn't safe for pretty young women to be out."

She thought he looked familiar. "Saint, and I've business in Adam-ondi-Ahman."

"Aren't you Mark Cartwright's wife? I'm John Lee. The missus and I met you at the last meeting. If you're headin' for home, I say don't. Go back the way you've come."

"But why?"

He turned to point toward the north. "See that and that? Them ain't supper fires. The Gentiles are burnin' and the Mormons are burnin'. Both are snitchin' everything they can and burnin' what they can't."

"Mr. Lee, that's terrible! Burning! If we treat them that way, we'll never learn to live with these people. What will happen if this keeps up?"

He shrugged his shoulders. "Joe says this is civil war, and by the rules each of us is justified in spoilin' the enemy."

"Mark would call that wrong—lawlessness. Where does it end when we're all doing that?"

"I'd guess it ends when there's nobody left to fight." It was a light answer, but peering up at him in the dusk, Jenny saw his brow was furrowed and his eyes unhappy. Thoughtfully he said, "I'm seein' men becomin' perfect demons as they spoil and waste each other. Seems to be the natural inclination of men to steal and plunder. But the thing that surprises me most is that these men got religion in the only true church left in the world. I'd expect there's somethin' wrong when religion's not got the power to subdue the animal passion in man."

"Animal?" she asked thoughtfully.

He nodded. "That's what they're like. The church takes its restrictions off, and they're animals. Seems the ideal would be you wouldn't have to pressure a man with fear of death to get him to act right."

"But how do you learn what's right? Don't people have different ideas of right?"

He scratched his head and looked thoughtfully at Jenny. "Seems strange to be philosophizin' beside the road with a pretty lady—but, no." Jenny's horse snorted and pawed restlessly. "Seems there's some kinda standard built into a person. But I'm thinkin' some squash it down, 'til you'd never know the man had a right idea." Lee straightened and sighed. "But now. You can't ride on to Adam-ondi-Ahman today. These men are roamin' the countryside, doin' all the damage they can. Go back."

"I must go on," Jenny insisted; "besides, it's as dangerous to go back."

He thought a moment and then admitted, "That's true." In another moment, he added, "I have a friend up the way here. Name's McBrier. An old gentleman who's been mighty good to me regardless of being Gentile. I'll point you in the way. You go stay with McBrier until you don't see smoke comin' up around the place; then you high-tail for home, get your business done, and then get back to Far West."

"How long will that be?"

"Day or so. Right now things are bad. While back, they pulled the state militia out here." He shook his head. "The Saints sent them on back, saying they could handle the situation. Don't know why they did it, seein's Joseph called for help in the first place. So the fellas mobbing on both sides are gettin' mighty brave about doing anything they want.

"In a day or so the squabbling will be coolin'." While his restless horse pawed and snorted, Lee said, "Come along, I'll point you in the right direction." And Jenny knew it was useless to argue.

When Lee stopped at the end of the lane leading to the low log house, it was dusk. There was a faint glow of light coming from the windows. Jenny thanked the man and slowly rode toward the light. The house was pleasant, she could see that. She could also see the corrals and barn, the cows and horses, and she could hear the contented barnyard sounds. For the first time since Mark had left, the tightness around Jenny's heart eased.

The gray-haired woman who opened the door at Jenny's knock stood staring in shock. Then reaching out she pulled Jenny through the door. "My dear!" she exclaimed. "Whatever are you doing out alone?"

"Well, I thought I was safe," Jenny explained, "until I met Mr. John Lee. He scolded me and brought me up here. Said I should stay until the fighting is over."

As Mrs. McBrier bustled out to call her husband, Jenny unwound her shawl and looked around the large room. As she had ridden onto the farm, she had noticed the mellow look as if it had been here a long time. Inside there was a settled, homey look. Heavy timbers crossed the room, and a stone fireplace covered an end wall. A spinning wheel with carded wool stood close to the polished rocking chair. Comfortable chairs cushioned with colorful quilts edged the room. Jenny was admiring the walnut table and chairs and stroking the tall cherry cabinet when the McBriers came into the room.

The old gentleman had a twinkly smile, and his bright blue eyes seemed kin to his wife's. He held out his hand. "Mother tells me John sent you. Any friend of John's is our friend, too. You are welcome to stay until it is safe to travel again. My, such carryin' on!" He continued shaking his head sadly as he led her to the fireplace. "We've put your horse up. Now, you just take this chair and let us offer you tea." He paused; looking confused, he said, "I'm forgetting, if you're—"

Jenny hastily said, "Tea! Oh, that would be wonderful."

Before the evening was over, Jenny felt as if she had known these people for years. It seemed they had a story for every treasure in their home. Even the furniture was rich with family heritage. She handled the black-bound Book they held with such reverence and listened to them explain the list of names written on a page in the middle.

While they talked, Jenny was thinking of her mother's black Book. Was her name written into it? Thoughtfuly she thumbed through the pages, recalling how her mother had held that book as if it were precious. And Mark. He had a Book just like this. On occasion he had taken it out and tried to read it to her.

Abruptly the picture of Jenny preparing to shove the Book into the stove flashed across her memory. She cringed as she recalled the fearful time of headaches and oppression that year in Kirtland just before Mark had left. She had blamed the Book for causing them. Just briefly, as she held McBrier's Book, guilt touched her, and she could only wonder why. As she considered that time, curiosity was born in her.

She interrupted Mrs. McBrier's story, asking, "Have you read this Book?"

"Oh my, yes." The woman patted the pages comfortably. "When I was just a youngster I won a medal for reading it through in less than a year. It was hard at times, keeping awake through Chronicles and Numbers, but I made it."

She paused and studied Jenny for a moment before saying, "The Mormons say they believe it is a holy book. Do they expect their young people to read it?"

Jenny cocked her head and thought. Slowly she said, "I don't know. In fact, I don't know any of the young people. I do know the twelve and the first presidency sometimes talk about the things that the Bible says. At times they read it aloud."

"Then you hear it preached about how to know Jesus. About how He died for our sins in order to give us God's righteousness and provide a way for us to be with Him for eternity."

Jenny studied her curiously, "No, that's not the way we heard it. But, then, it doesn't matter, does it? There's only one God; how we choose to worship Him doesn't really matter. It's the worship that's important."

From the far side of the fireplace, Mr. McBrier cleared his throat and with a twinkle in his eyes he said, "Well, I'm not up to talking theology with anyone, especially with a young lady looking as smart as you do. One thing I do know; reading God's Word was like having Him rope me in.

"Just like a rebellious calf, fighting the branding iron and the rope, I was. But do you know, after getting a good exposure to the words, I found out I *liked* it. It made a change in me, sure. Can't read about Jesus Christ without being attracted.

"But, sure enough, the first part of being attracted is being made mighty uncomfortable. You read about all that He went through, the spitting on Him and pulling His beard, the crown of thorns and such; then without complaining He gets killed. I really sat up straight when I found out about Him rising from the dead." He stared thoughtfully into the fire for a long moment before he again faced Jenny and said, "I can remember how I used to feel inside. Reading made me churn around like a creek in spring thaw. I wanted to quit the reading, but by then I couldn't. Now I'm glad."

Jenny waited a moment and then asked, "Why?"

He looked directly at her and said, "Because I soon found out that this man is God, and that He came here to this earth just to die for us."

"That seems like such a waste. I can't understand why He'd do that," Jenny mused as she stared into the fire.

"Well, He did it because He loved us enough to want us with Him forever. See, we couldn't go to heaven on our own, because of sin. Sin, well, that makes everybody squirm just thinking about it. Until we finally accept what God did to get rid of sin." He looked at her while Jenny wished he would talk of something else. "It's like this. Sin's so terrible man can't ever undo it. He can't ever make up for it. So God did. His dying made it possible for people to actually be holy themselves."

"So everyone is holy," Jenny said thoughtfully.

"Only if you believe it and accept Jesus' death for yourself. That's called faith, believing what God says to man in the Book."

Later as Mrs. McBrier led Jenny to the spare bedroom and turned back the colorful quilt, Jenny was thinking about the conversation around the fire. She found herself sighing, and that surprised her.

16

ON OCTOBER 18 when David Patten and forty men galloped into Adam-ondi-Ahman, the Saints were still spending most of their time huddled around the fire, just watching the snow melt and run down the road. Mark had been thinking how good it was to see the unseasonable snow melting rapidly.

The sunshine inspired hope and confidence, and Mark's secret hope was that Boggs would send his troops back and peace would reign. But the truth of the matter was that the Mormon troops from Far West were still waiting for the Gentile mob from DeWitt, and not with hopes for peace.

Mark was still brooding over the alternatives when he heard the sound of hooves pounding the sodden road. The men around him flew to their stations, and he slowly got up to follow.

When Patten rounded the corner, Lee went forward to meet him. His scowl changed to surprise as he addressed Patten. "What's the meaning of this? Where's the mob we're supposed to be fighting?"

"They're still headed this way, dragging that cannon behind. That isn't why we've come. I could use a few more good men." He paused to look around the group. "You, Tom Timmons. Got a good horse and rifle? Come on."

Patten pointed out other men and waved at them to follow him. Mark watched Tom jump to his feet, glad for activity. As he left the fire, one of the men growled, "Why the secrecy?" Tom looked up; when he met Mark's questioning gaze he shrugged. The fellow muttered, "Don't much care *what* they do, long's they're moving."

Patten got off his horse and the men clustered around him. Mark watched Patten's restless eyes as he looked over the men, saying, "Joseph and Wight sent me out to do a little business. We're headed to Gallatin to give the folks there a little shake-up."

"Wait a minute!" Hansen exclaimed. "They haven't given us trouble."

"Isn't a matter of trouble," Patten said shortly. "The Prophet has said that now is the time for the riches of the Gentiles to be consecrated to Israel. Come on, men."

"So Joseph sent 'em."

"And the riches of the Gentiles are about to be reaped," the speaker chuckled.

Mark turned and saw Phelps watching him. As Mark hesitated, the man dropped his gaze. Mark waited a moment longer before he shoved his hands into his pockets and strolled down the road.

Rivulets of brown water cut down the length of the roadbed, deepening the ruts. Mark eyed them, wondering how the Gentiles would manage to pull their cannon up the hill into Adam-ondi-Ahman. Another horse was coming. From the sound Mark guessed that leisurely trot wasn't threatening. He leaned against a tree and waited.

It was Joseph. Seeing Mark, he wheeled his horse toward him. His grin was challenging, mocking; and Mark realized it was the first time he had seen the Prophet since, along with the other *Oh, don't* men, he had been sent into exile.

As Mark watched the man dismount, he realized his opportunity. He had the Prophet all to himself, and now was the time for his appeal.

He studied the broad-shouldered figure, admiring the athletic stride, the commanding air. But when his eyes met that sardonic grin, he nearly abandoned his mission. No matter that his racing pulse reminded him that it was now or never.

"You're on guard? Where's your gun?" Joseph snapped.

Softly Mark replied, "No. Seems there's no need. Patten rode in with his men just an hour ago. Says you sent him out."

"Did he tell you why?" The grin was still there; his light blue eyes challenged Mark. But Mark waited. The eyes wavered slightly. "I know your Puritan soul can't accept the way the Lord is working in our midst. I wonder why you haven't gone long ago, like the others." He was moving restlessly, slapping his fine leather gloves against his palm.

Mark's eyes were on the gloves, thinking of the shabby Saints with adoration in their eyes. "Joseph, I think it's time you and I do a little talking. Man to man. Don't pull that prophet business on me." Without waiting for Joseph's reply he plunged on. "Things are bad in the Mormon camp. They are getting worse. You can't hope to continue to hold these people. They are scared, they're hungry, and their children are suffering. At one time you offered these people a beautiful dream. You called it Zion. I call it heaven on earth. But that's not to be, and you know it.

"Now, Joseph, you have a big bunch of people under your control. Have you thought about them? Where does this all lead? Right now they want nothing more than to settle down, have a few acres, and feed their families. You won't let them. Last summer when these people should have been planting their acres, they were preparing to defend Far West. You've a fortified town, but no food. You have people without a heart. You've frightened them with the fear of hell-fire if they think or act for the interests of their families. And if they're willing to risk hell, and head for the state line, you've got the Danites on their trail. Are you going to fight for an impossible dream until the blood of your last faithful one is shed?"

Mark paused to take a breath and pace across his muddy platform. When he turned, he said, "For the sake of these people, be man enough to back down before any more damage is done. For the sake of their very lives, get out." Now Mark raised his head. Joseph's face was white, twisted into lines of suffering and Mark's heart leaped in hope.

Slowly Joseph turned and paced the muddy road and Mark waited. When the Prophet returned he lifted sorrowful eyes. "Mark, my friend," he said heavily, "you break my heart. Will you be another Judas? You know I dare not deny my God. What you are suggesting is impossible. We'll all die if we refuse to follow the commands placed before us. To obey is the only recourse we have."

"Joseph," Mark asked slowly, "where's love? Since I've been a Mormon I've heard a great deal about cursing our enemies, revenge, damning to hell. Now I'm hearing we're to plunder our enemies, steal their cattle and furniture, burn their houses. I'm seeing men with their faces contorted with rage lifting arms against a people we should be able to live with in peace. It's beginning to look as if wherever you are, Joseph, there is no peace. In every place you have gone there's been strife.

"I've been reading my Bible, that Book which you say is all wrong because it hasn't been translated by the power of God. I like what it says. I don't have to shed my blood in Missouri for a cause that any thinking man realizes is all wrong. Jesus Christ shed His blood for me. For all my sins, I only need to accept that gift, humbly, recognizing there is nothing I can do to earn salvation. It's by grace. My Bible says God loves, forgives, restores, guides, makes holy with a righteousness that has discernible fruits of righteousness. Joseph, if you are close to God, where are your discernible fruits of righteousness?"

The sorrow on Joseph's face had disappeared. Now his eyes were alight and his face glowed. Softly he said, "Wait around, Mark; you'll see."

As they cantered toward Gallatin Tom's thoughts were in turmoil. He soon discovered others shared his feelings. Beside him Arnold Johnson shot a quick glance his direction. In a low voice he said, "I'm having feelings inside telling me this isn't right, even though we're taught to accept Joseph's word like God himself."

"You can't question," Tom said roughly; "that isn't faith. You make up your mind to do what Joseph says or be an apostate."

"Just try to leave," the man said bitterly. "It's our neck if we do. It's beyond a man having a chance to talk or think for himself."

Patten halted his men in the last grove of trees before they reached Gallatin. Tersely he explained, "I don't know what we'll find here—maybe the DeWitt bunch, maybe nothing. All right, men, go to it."

With a yell echoing through the ranks, the men galloped through the town. Tom deliberately slowed his horse. Under cover of the shouts, he yelled, "Johnson, ease up and give the people a chance to escape."

When they reached the main street of Gallatin, Tom saw that not a soul stirred. Patten shouted a command to halt and dropped from his horse. When the men clustered around him, he said, "Fresh tracks, but the place is deserted. All right men, get busy." Tom hesitated, bewildered by the strange command.

Patten turned back and said, "Timmons, get in that store and start carrying the goods out. Check out the post office; could be money there. The fellas will be pulling up wagons. We want them filled double time, with everything of value." Tom started to speak, but Patten turned his flinty face to Tom and waited. Tom shrugged and headed for the store.

When the men finally rode out of town, Patten turned to survey the scene behind them. Tom saw the satisfaction on the man's face as he looked from the blazing store and post office to the still-smoldering ruins of a log cabin. He waved toward the wagons his men were driving and said, "Pretty profitable day."

"What are we going to do with all this stuff?" the man riding beside Tom asked. Pointing toward Adam-ondi-Ahman, Patten said, "We're taking it back and putting it in the bishop's storehouse. We've plenty of poor people who could use the spoils of the Gentiles."

They had nearly reached town when Patten wheeled back and said, "Timmons, you know the Millport road. Head down that way and see what you can find out. Don't go into town without cover. There could be a skirmish."

As Tom pulled away from the group, Hansen asked, "More of the same?"

Tom saw Patten's grin and heard him say, "Yes, the fur company's been out that way today."

Tom had just turned down the road leading to the little town of Millport when he met Lyman Wight and a group of men heading toward Adam-ondi-Ahman. Wight hailed him and waved his men on as Tom approached.

"Where are you headed?"

"Patton directed me toward Millport to see what's going on."

"Not a thing. We've come from there. The place's deserted. I'm headed into town to report to Joseph. Come along. I'm thinking we'll need you to carry a message before the night's over."

"Joe wasn't in Adam-ondi-Ahman when we left this morning."

"Well, he and Hyrum should be there by now." They rode the rest of the way in silence. When the two reached town, Tom discovered changes had been made during the day. The Gentile store was now the company head-quarters for the Army of Israel.

When Tom entered the building, Joseph and Hyrum were there. But, more surprising, he found Mark talking to the men.

Wight sat down close to the open fire and stretched his feet toward the blaze. "Millport's deserted. I get the feeling the Gentiles are running like scared chickens. Sure seems like the fight's gone outta them all of a sudden."

Hyrum said, "God's put the dread of the Israelites into them."

"Well, they're sure gone," Wight continued. "Left everything, but there's not a soul around."

Joseph leaned forward, "Left their goods, huh? We'd better see to it."

"Never mind," Wight said getting to his feet. "We'll have a private council and take care of the whole situation." Tom saw the look the men exchanged before Wight turned to him. "Come along, Tom. I've a job for you."

It was dusk as they left the building. Wight turned abruptly and cocked his head toward the road. "There's a bunch of wagons coming up that road," he said slowly. "Guess we'd better mosey down and see what's up." At that moment Joseph, Hyrum, and Mark came out the door.

"Wagons?" Joseph questioned.

A lone horseman cantered into town. He circled around and came up to the group. It was John Lee. "Met these men down the road a piece; they wanted me to find out what you want done with the goods."

"Who are they?" Hyrum asked.

A sardonic grin creased Lee's face, "They said to tell you they were the fur company."

Joseph laughed and said, "Tell them to head for the bishop's store-house."

As Joseph turned aside, Lee turned to Mark and said, "Met your wife yesterday. She was heading this way. Said she had to go to the house. I told her it wasn't safe and directed her to go over to McBriers' and stay until the worst of this mess is over."

"Jenny out roaming while this is going on?" Mark muttered, distressed. Tom saw him clench his fist and bang it against the hitching post. Watching him, Tom was remembering all the tales of horror that had been surfacing. He swallowed hard and took a step toward Mark.

Joseph turned back and said, "Might be you could be spared to hunt for her." He paused and there was an awkward silence as he studied Mark, still smiling that strange smile. Tom guessed Joseph was recalling the reason Mark was up here. The smile became cold as Joseph added, "But then, 'twould be better to send Tom once he gets back from Far West."

Mark opened his mouth, but abruptly he turned away, his shoulders sagging.

Tom muttered, "Seems a decent man'd trust his friend enough to let him go find his wife."

17

Tom AND LYMAN Wight rode to Israel's camp where Wight called out a youth to accompany them to Far West. The trio left immediately, riding hard for the meeting.

They splashed across Grand River at the shallow ford, and cut away from the gorge, out onto the open prairie. As they rode, Tom was wondering just what Wight would expect of him. He had to admit to the awe he was feeling. This would be his first meeting with the Danite leaders.

"Don't much like hob-nobbing with the big shots," he muttered to the silent fellow beside him. The youth shrugged and didn't answer.

The road became hard-packed, smoothed by the passage of the settlers. The only sound in the night was the thud of hooves and the clink of harnesses. As the horses settled into a steady lope, Tom found himself caught up again in thinking about Jenny and Mark. His own fears for his sister seemed feeble compared to the pain he had seen in Mark's face. He shook his head in bewilderment. "Sure don't make sense, her takin' off like that," he muttered. The youth beside him grunted and nodded.

It was a clear night. A scythe-shaped moon was rising, outlining the clouds with slices of brightness. Frost was beginning to spread a diamond gleam on bare branches and grass still crushed and matted by the snow. Just beyond Gallatin the trio paused to rest their horses and let them drink in the last fork of the Grand River. As they waited they ate a cold supper of bread and meat.

Only once did Wight bring up the subject of the meeting. He said, "A wise move it would be to keep the details under your hat. You two are young in the Danites group, and there's those who will have your neck if you can't keep the secret paths and the mission of the Danites to yourselves." He turned in his saddle to look squarely at the two. "We're pledged to support the presidency and obey them under penalty of death. We're not called upon to agree, only obey, don't forget that."

By the time they reached Far West, the meeting was well under way. Wight and Tom eased themselves onto the crowded bench in the rear of the building while the silent youth took charge of the horses. Avard, the

Danite leader, was pacing back and forth across the front of the room. He paused briefly, saluted Wight and continued with his speech.

"For you who just came in, this is my word to you tonight. Even this very day the word to you has been put into action. You are commanded to take to yourselves the spoils of the Gentiles. It is written, given by the Lord himself to his servant Joseph, that the riches of the Gentiles are to be yours. You will waste away the Gentiles by robbing them and plundering them of their property. In this manner we will build up the house of Israel, the kingdom of God, and thus we'll roll forth the little stone of Daniel's time, which he saw cut out of the mountain. It will roll out until it fills the whole earth. My men, this is the way God plans to build up His kingdom in these last days. If we're seen, what does it matter? We will defend each other, lie for each other. If this won't do it, we'll put our accuser under the sand just as Joseph did the Egyptian. And I promise you, if one of this society reveals any of this, I'll put him where the dogs can't bite."

Abruptly he whirled and, pointing his finger, he said, "If I meet one of you cursing the presidency, I'll feed him a bowl of brandy, get him into the bushes, and be into his guts in a minute."

The murmur of voices ceased and Avard continued, "Now, we are here tonight to appoint a committee called the Destruction Company. The purpose will be to burn and destroy. You will go against any people who would do us mischief here in Caldwell. If the people of Ray and Clay move against us, you are to burn their towns of Liberty and Richmond. This will be done secretly."

After Avard had appointed the chosen twelve, he turned back to other matters. "I have a decree I want you to vote upon. This statement reads as follows: *Be it resolved, no Mormon dissenter shall leave Caldwell County alive. All such ones who attempt to do so shall be shot down.*" Carefully Tom controlled his shiver as he recalled the advice he had given to Mark.

The formal meeting was called to a close. Some of the men left the room, while Tom and Wight joined the others pressing toward the front.

As they elbowed their way forward, Tom could hear Avard saying, "I propose to start a pestilence among the Gentiles. I have in mind poison. We'll do their corn, their fruit, anything else that grows. We'll say the Lord done it."

There was another question and Tom heard Avard say, "The plan of the Prophet is to take this state, the whole United States, and finally the whole world." There was a murmur with Avard's reply cutting through it. "Joseph's prophecies are superior to the law of the land. I have heard him say that if he was let alone, he would be a second Mahomet for this generation. He would make a gore of blood from the Atlantic to the Pacific."

Each day since the afternoon Jenny met John Lee and had been sent to the McBrier farm, there was evidence of new fires. Often during the day, Jenny heard distant gun shots. Mr. McBrier would emphatically shake his head when Jenny mentioned leaving. Although she was impatient to be on her way, secretly she was relieved at his insistent "just one more day." She knew he had been visiting with neighbors, and she saw his concern and frustration continue to grow.

One evening as he hung his hat and coat behind the door, he said, "I can't pretend to be hopeful about the situation. Since the state militia's pulled out, the Mormons and the old settlers are acting like they're trying to outdo each other in devilment. First one side burns a barn, the next does one better—he takes the cattle and burns the barn."

He snorted in disgust as he sat down to the table. Bowing his head, he prayed, "Bless, O Lord, this food. We thank You for the bounty of this good land." He cleared his throat, "Please set Your hand upon these people and restrain the wicked one. Thy kingdom come, thy will be done. And help our good sister here to be guided by Your Spirit. She has a need to know about You. Supply her need. In Jesus' name, Amen."

As Jenny looked curiously at him, he sliced the meat and held out his hand for her plate. "Not a bit better." He was answering her unspoken question. He said, "Riding toward Gallatin today I saw at least ten fires over the valley."

"Oh." Jenny took her plate and slowly said, "I *must* be going home. Just being there, well, it might help. Surely they wouldn't burn it down while I am there."

Mrs. McBrier shook her head, chiding, "Child, you don't realize how dangerous it is. The stories rollin' in here don't promise a thing for the strongest man, let alone a little woman like you."

They ate in silence, and then Jenny broached the subject which had caught her attention during the prayer. "Sir, you said I had a need to know God. I do know God, perhaps even better than you."

"Why do you say that?"

"Because we have Joseph's book and he has the keys to the kingdom. Besides that, I've been studying out the secrets and the power through—" Suddenly she stopped.

Looking around the room she was seeing it as if for the first time. By the glow of delicately shaded china lamps, she was seeing things she had missed before. The comfort of the surroundings was more than material. There was a serenity about the home; she saw reflections of it in the polished wood and colorful quilts. She also noticed the black-bound Book on the table beside Mr. McBrier's chair. Her thoughts overlapped it with the picture of the green and gold book, and unexpectedly she saw the garish contrast. She looked at the McBriers; they were still waiting.

While Jenny fumbled for words, Mr. McBrier said sharply, "And I suppose you've decided to join the Protestants and the Catholics as well as the Mormons. Jenny, wee girl, it's reading God's Holy Bible and letting God Himself have a dwelling place in your heart that makes you know something about Himself." He studied her face for a moment and the twinkle came back into his eyes. "Besides, I've been on the way of following Jesus for these past forty years, and I know myself less learned and less worthy each year I live."

Two days later Jenny decided to take matters in her own hands. In her restlessness, she felt that these good people were determined to smother her with kindness when there wasn't a need.

After breakfast she packed her valise and headed for the barn. With her horse saddled and wearing her cloak, she searched out the McBriers and announced her intention. "I do appreciate your goodness to me, but I simply must push on. Don't worry about me."

She could see from their expression that they realized the futility of arguing further. With a sigh, old Mr. McBrier said, "Then go, we pray, with God's blessing and His care." At the end of the lane, she turned to wave to them.

Jenny knew the direction she must ride to reach Adam-ondi-Ahman before pressing on to the farm. First she headed toward the main road and then turned north. Between the McBriers' home and the road the trees were thick and tall. A screen, she thought, between herself and the rest of the world.

As she started out, Jenny realized sight was blocked, but not sound. She had not yet reached the road when she began to hear gunfire. Pulling on the reins, she hesitated. Suddenly there was the sound of pounding hooves. But only when Jenny heard shouts and the crash of horses, only as her own mount snorted with terror, did she wheel her horse and slap her with the reins. Jenny dug her heels into Patches' ribs, forcing her into the undergrowth beside the trail.

Before Jenny had time to dismount the riders galloped past her hiding place and disappeared. She saw they were going in the direction of the McBriers' home.

She hesitated, wondering, yet not believing those gentle people would suffer at the hands of these men.

At the moment she heard the crack of the whip, Jenny's horse was rearing, snorting with pain.

Over her shoulder she saw the man as he lifted the whip again. "Be off, you Gentile! The Army of the Lord is here and the wealth of the Gentiles is ours. Begone, or we'll have your horse, too!"

Jenny vainly tried to control the fleeing animal under her; she clung to the mare and was conscious only of the roar of wind in her ears. At last the horse stood quivering and snorting. Jenny realized they were in a clearing looking down over the McBriers' homestead.

As she swallowed the dryness in her throat and pressed her hand against the pounding of her heart, her attention was drawn to the activity far down the hill.

She watched a wagon being drawn close to the house. Soon men were running in and out of the McBriers' house, carrying bundles. She caught the gleam of dark wood. The dining table. The pile of brightness was Mrs. McBrier's colorful quilts. The sun glinted off a shiny lamp. Jenny pressed her hand against her mouth and moaned. The words that man had yelled were still with her.

Powerless, Jenny watched from her lookout. After the cattle were led from the barn, it was set ablaze. She was numb with shock as she watched the fire. In a short time, the wagon pulled away, leaving the house burning in an explosion of flame and smoke.

The last timber had crashed with a shower of sparks flying up from the blackened ruins before Jenny tore her fascinated gaze away from the scene and rubbed life into her numb arms and face. The McBriers—where were they? Had they perished in the blaze?

Jenny dug her heels into the horse's ribs and wheeled back the way she had come. When she rode up the McBriers' lane, she found the couple standing in their yard, shivering under wraps too scanty to cut the chill of the afternoon. Throwing herself from the horse, Jenny rushed to them.

They moved like wooden figures. Mrs. McBrier said, "Why, Jenny, you're crying."

It was the old gray-haired gentleman who wiped the tears from her face and listened as she screamed, "I hate them for what they've done to you! Hate, hate, hate! They are animals!"

"Come, child." They both drew her close and the three of them settled on the log beside the watering trough. Jenny saw bits of charred wood floating in the water. At her feet a hen pecked listlessly as if she must concentrate on that tiny portion of her world.

The tears had dried on Jenny's cheeks. She had wrapped her cloak around Mrs. McBrier, and now the old gentleman patted his wife's hand and said, "There, there, Mother. It's going to be all right. God's in His heaven and He's never failed us yet."

Mrs. McBrier pressed her face against her husband's shoulder. Jenny was surprised to see serenity in the midst of tragedy reflected on those old faces as the couple rested on the log. Mrs. McBrier spoke slowly, heavily, "I guess I can't complain; we're no better than the others, and many have lost as much."

"Our men have been guilty, too," Mr. McBrier said slowly. "I just can't reconcile the causes. Seems people ought to be able to live in peace, regardless."

Jenny watched his boot push at the charred wood and needed badly to say *live where?* but the fearful question wouldn't come. Suddenly he lifted his head and smiled. It was like a ray of sunshine in the dark, and Jenny watched him wordlessly wondering how it was possible.

Mrs. McBrier squeezed her husband's hand and he smiled down at her, saying, "One good thing has come out of this." They waited patiently and finally he continued. "Seems every man who's ever searched for God ends up desiring more of Him. Makes a body prone to *not* want to wait for eternity. Right now we're wanting new visions and glimpses of heaven. Some claim to have them.

"I've not envied a man's horses or cattle, but I've wanted to be one of those privileged to sit in God's presence. For a time, listening to them talk about the visions of glory, their calling to build a city for God; hearing about the gold plates and the angels, well, my heart went yearning. Almost I was ready to run after these Mormons.

"But even while looking at this, I recall hearing that Joseph Smith said these people are the most righteous people who ever lived. And no other religion has the keys of the kingdom. Then, sitting here, I got to thinking about what the Holy Bible says about love. You know, Jenny and Mother, God's Word is full of love. It says without love even the prophecies are nothing. Even if we give up ourselves to be burned, if we don't have love, the sacrifice is nothing. And the Bible says God *is* love, that He loved us so much He gave His Son for us."

He was silent a moment; then he lifted his head and looked at Jenny with his gentle blue eyes. "Sister, I guess it was worth losing everything to find out that love isn't in the Mormon camp." He shuddered slowly, shaking his head. "I came close to being enticed into making a terrible mistake."

Jenny was pondering his statement, wondering, ready to ask her question when she heard the sound of hoofbeats. A lone horseman was coming fast, and Jenny slowly got to her feet.

Dread filled her as she faced the road. When the man jumped down from his horse and hurried toward them, Jenny recognized the man who had sent her here, John Lee. Still waiting beside the McBriers, she watched his face twist with disbelief, then settle into a mask of grief.

Going to Mr. McBrier he said, "I'd heard. I just couldn't believe they'd do such a thing after the way you've befriended so many of 'em."

Crossing his hands behind his back he paced restlessly back and forth across the yard. When he stopped in front of them he said, "This trouble-making is wrong. I've told Joseph this has got to stop! It can only lead to disaster for the whole camp. You can rest assured that your neighbors will avenge you for this."

Mr. McBrier was shaking his head even as Lee spoke. "I don't want revenge. I want to see no more hurt on either side. Oh, God," he mur-mured, "what will be the outcome?"

Lee paced again and when he stopped, shoving his hat back on his head, Jenny saw the sadness in his eyes. Slowly he shook his head. "I don't understand, but I see clearly that religion hasn't the power to subdue this passion in man. It ought not be this way. As soon as the church takes its thumb outta their backs, these men become beasts. They're as bad as if they'd spent all of their lives being the most degraded of criminals."

Lee's words sank deep into Jenny's mind—confusing at first, then sham-ing her with a nameless guilt. Later she helped John Lee gather up the small bundle of belongings the McBriers managed to salvage and the two of them took the McBriers to the nearest Gentile neighbor.

Late in the afternoon Jenny and John Lee turned their horses toward Adam-ondi-Ahman.

Lee said, "Your husband was quartered in town until two days ago. Joseph called for him to go into Far West. It was something to do with legal questions."

Jenny's heart sank, but she bravely said, "No matter. I'll just ride up to our farm. You might tell him I'm going there when you see him."

"You'll be safer in town. We'll find a place for you to stay."

Jenny shook her head. "I'm not afraid. I'll be doing what needs to be done up there, pack up a few things and go back to Far West."

Finally he shrugged and watched as she turned her horse off the road and headed up the trail to the cabin overlooking the Grand River.

18

WHEN TOM PUSHED open the door of the general store in Far West, the first person he saw was Mark. His brother-in-law was sitting close to the fireplace, his leg propped high on a stool.

"What's the matter with you?" Tom stopped in front of the leg and studied it.

"Got it banged up a bit fooling around with the horses. What are you doing back in town?"

"Called back. Them up there insisted they don't need all the troops. Mostly scared of having so many to feed. So they sent a pack of us back here."

"Could I get you to hunt for Jenny?"

Tom raised his eyebrows, "You here all this time and haven't seen your bride?"

Mark's grin was twisted. "Don't forget, I've a bad name, they're calling us the *Oh, don't* men. That's as bad as being a dissenter; they just didn't have the evidence to hang *that* on me. Meanwhile, I'm being shunned. Twisted my leg bad enough I can't take sitting on a horse right now, and I can't get a soul to ride out to the McBrier place and bring Jenny back for me."

"Sorry, old man. I've a little job to do, so Jenny'll have to stay out there another day or so."

Tom grinned at Mark's frown and then asked, "I'd heard you were here. What's Joe got you up to?"

"I don't know yet. He sent me ahead, promising he'd be back here in a couple of days. He mentioned law problems. Seems to feel his friends Atchison and Doniphan don't understand the ramifications of the war problems. I'll worry about that later."

"Worry? Sounds like you aren't too sold on Joe's problems and the need for a body to counsel him."

"Tom, you know that." His voice was low. "A fellow wanting to make it in the legal profession would find plenty here to make him squirm if his intentions were to play the game fair and square."

Tom said slowly, "You know they captured the cannon taken out of DeWitt. Found it over in Livingston County."

Mark sighed wearily. "That's just one more in the catalog of wrongs, on both sides. It's an offense to carry arms from county to county, and it's pretty hard to overlook a cannon."

It was the next day that Corrill came into the store and found Mark. "Well, you've pulled a soft assignment," he joked. "Almost as soft as the Prophet."

"What's he doing?"

"When I left Adam-ondi-Ahman he was wrestling in the mud."

Mark snorted, "Corrill, even I won't swallow that one."

"It's the truth. I was there; just ask him."

"When's Joseph coming back? When he sent me down here, he said he'd be along shortly."

Corrill looked surprised and then he frowned. He shot Mark a quick look and said, "Did Lee tell you that your wife has gone back to your place?"

Mark sat up straight, "Jenny in Adam-ondi-Ahman? Lee mentioned that he found her out on the road and took her to the McBriers' place to stay until things settled down. I'd no idea she had left. When did she leave for our place?"

"Well, I overheard Lee telling Joseph to pass the message on to you. I expected him to be here by now." Corrill paused for a moment and then said, "Sorry, old man."

The door closed behind him. Mark sat staring at the door while the man's words rolled through his thoughts. What did Corrill mean? Abruptly Mark heaved himself to his feet and tested his weight on his lame leg.

Wincing, he walked slowly around the room and then he approached the counter where Mike was polishing glasses and watching him. "If someone asks for me, tell them I had to take a quick trip to Adam-ondi-Ahman."

"Anyone? Even Joe?"

"Particularly Joe." Mark knew his voice was bitter as he pushed open the door.

It was late when Jenny approached her own front door. For a moment she sat on her horse, feeling the quiet and thinking that the forest stillness seemed to have taken possession of her home.

In another moment she realized the silence meant the chickens and cow were gone. "Tyler was to be caring for them," she whispered. "Could he have taken them?" The door of the makeshift barn hung open. It was evident the bags of grain were missing from the rafters of the lean-to.

Filled with dread, she slowly slipped from the mare, led her to a grassy spot, and then went to the house.

Surprisingly she found the one-room cabin as she had left it—with one notable exception. Standing in the middle of the room was a handsome walnut grandfather clock. She moved slowly toward it. Was it another spirit trick?

The polished surface was cool and real under her fingers. As she ran her fingers over the wood, the clock chimed out the hour. Six o'clock. "That must be pretty close to accurate," she murmured. "Whoever brought you here was interested in seeing whether or not you still worked."

She frowned in the effort to think through all the implications of the clock's being there. It was John D. Lee who had told the McBriers that stolen goods were being spread around in order to avoid any one person being blamed should they be discovered. Jenny lifted her head. Slowly she said, "If that is so, Mark Cartwright, attorney-at-law, could be charged."

Jenny slowly sat down and studied the clock. Obviously it was costly. She sighed and tried to find a solution to the situation. Of course, it would be too heavy for her to lift. She cringed, thinking of the neighbor's reaction were she to ask for help. Finally she got up and shrugged off the problem. She found flour, several eggs and some moldy bacon in her larder, and went to start a fire in the fireplace. After sliding Mark's shutters into position and fastening them securely, she prepared her supper. While she was frying the bacon she addressed the clock, "I think it is a very good thing I came up here. You are beautiful and I would love to have you, but, too bad. I think I need to find some way to shove you into the Grand River."

As she ate her lonely meal, Jenny's thought was full of the unbelievable events of the day. The memory of the McBriers' faces knotted her throat into a miserable lump; but at the same time, she was accepting the conviction that once she left this house, she would never see it again.

Would she see Mark? For a moment her spirit plunged and then soared: there was Joseph's prophecy and there was her commitment. Only by obeying the Prophet completely would there be a surety of having her wishes granted. Too often she had heard him remind the Saints that there was no safety except in obeying the Prophet. But there was another thing, too—all the promises of power through the green book. And she intended to use every one of them.

Jenny spent a restless night tossing in the bed which suddenly seemed too big and very cold. Her dreams were filled with dark shadows and Jenny running, searching the sky as she ran, looking for the first star of the

evening, the wishing star. And in her half-waking state, she was murmuring, "Star light, star bright, first star I see tonight—"

She sat up. "I should be praying for power instead of chanting childish
wishes." Silently she searched her heart, wondering if she were failing the
Prophet. Her guilty conscience informed her that she was. As she sighed
and settled back in bed, she couldn't help wondering how much her sins
were dragging down the cause of Zion.

When morning came, she threw back the shutters. As the giant clock
again pounded out the hours with an intensity that reverberated from the
walls of the tiny cabin, Jenny greeted the dawn eagerly. She studied the
line of coral rimming the sky beyond the trees which marked the distant
bluffs of the river and wondered how many of these lonely nights she
could endure without going mad. She shivered.

Quickly now she flew about, stirring up the fire, boiling water, and stirring in a meager handful of meal. By the time Jenny had finished her
breakfast, she knew she must find the green book and the talisman.

With a sense of finality, she knew she must go through the cabin searching out each valued item. Had Mark not left behind another rifle and
ammunition? What about his Bible? She could tie the extra shawl behind
the saddle. It would cover the green book, and if she were to see Mark in
Adam-ondi-Ahman, then there would be no need to explain her strange
trip.

Late in the morning, Jenny was nearly ready to leave. She wrapped the
book in the shawl and was ready to pin the talisman in her frock when the
pin-prick of alarm touched her. At that moment the clock gonged out the
hours. Ten. In the silence, with only gentle seconds ticking off, her world
pressed in. The scenes of yesterday's fire and those stricken faces held her
for a moment, and then the heightened sense of need sent her flying to the
door.

Jenny guessed what she would find before she reached the spot where
she had left the mare tethered. As she stared at the bare pasture, her heart
sank. She was totally alone.

There was a broken branch. Jenny fingered it. In dismay she declared,
"Since when have you forgotten horses aren't above breaking a dry limb
when they're looking for something to eat?" She kicked at the grass
chewed down to stubble, and turned to trail the mare.

The sun was directly overhead when Jenny gave up in frustration. "A
thief. Right now I wish I could take a gun to that fella!" she cried, smack-
ing one palm with the other as she kicked at a crumbling log. The words
she muttered under her breath would have more nearly suited Lyman
Wight than the wife of Mark Cartwright; and despite her fear and dismay,
she was instantly seized with shame.

For reasons she couldn't guess, she leaned against a tree and allowed bitter tears to flow. As she cried, John Lee's face flashed across her thoughts. She was seeing the sadness in his eyes as he looked at the charred ruins of the McBriers' house and said, "It seems religion's not got the power to subdue the animal passion in a man."

She shoved her head against the tree, pounded her fist against the rough bark and said, "And the passion's taken my horse." But a quiet finger underlined the soul-deep anger she was feeling toward that nameless man, and at the same moment she murmured, "Why, Jenny, that makes you no better'n the bunch that burned out the McBriers."

Again the tears began. For a long time, Jenny leaned against the tree and cried without understanding the reason behind her tears.

Finally Jenny slumped down to rest against the tree. The sun had burned out the last of the night's chill and she rested in the warm spot. When the last of her sobs ended, she heard a gentle nicker nearby.

Raising her head, she listened for a moment, then with a glad cry she jumped to her feet and crashed through the bushes to throw her arms around the mare. Rubbing the horse's neck as she wrapped reins securely around her hand, Jenny looked around, trying to get her bearings. "Old girl, you've wandered a far piece from home. I'm thinking we'll have a time getting back there."

At midmorning Mark took the cutoff outside Adam-ondi-Ahman and headed up the road to his home. He was riding fast, as hard as he dared push his horse, but despite his anxiety, he was seeing things that sent disturbing signals to him.

There was an air of neglect and desolation around the cabins he had been passing. The smell of charred wood and the acrid scorch of burning grass lingered in the air. More frequently now he was passing bands of people heading south and east. Several times he met a wagon, but most often he was seeing women and children walking. He discovered that as he approached, the groups turned and scattered into the bushes. After one attempt to search them out and ask questions, he gave up and pressed harder for home.

When Mark turned down his own lane, he slowed his horse to a walk. The pricked ears of his mare had already alerted him to the presence of another horse. He eyed the gelding as he circled the cabin and stopped at the door.

A sound caught his attention, and before Mark could move, the man, still in the shadows, called, "Well, Mark, I'll ask you into your own house." Joseph Smith stepped through the doorway.

Mark's tumbling emotions held him motionless. When he got off the horse, he took time to pull the saddle from the mare and lead her to grass. Inside the cabin he faced Joseph Smith and tersely asked, "Where's Jenny?"

"I have no way of knowing, Mark. And what gives you the idea that I came here to see your wife?"

For a moment Mark studied the expression of complete candor and his resisting the impulse to squirm like a youngster caught with his hand in the cookie jar. Deliberately he held Joseph's gaze with his own and said, "Let's not play games, or I'll be tempted to do some prophesying on my own."

Joseph's eyes began to twinkle. "You're taking liberties."

"I was ready to say the same about you. There's just too much talk going around about you and some of the womenfolk. First it was Fannie Alger, then Nancy Johnson. Now they're talking about Lucinda Harris. I don't want it to be my wife next."

Joseph chuckled. "Look, Mark, you're a nice-looking fella, don't tell me the girls haven't cast eyes at you."

"Cut it out, Joe, this isn't about innocent flirtations and hero worship. If it is all foolish gossip, why do you feel called upon to denounce the rumors? A prophet ought to be above having to answer these kind of questions."

Now Mark noticed the walnut clock. Jerking his head toward it, he asked, "Where did that come from?"

"If you can't answer that question, then ask your wife."

"No doubt someone's stashed it here with the intention of returning. Joseph, it's all for naught."

"What do you mean?"

"Any sympathy you might have gained in a search for religious freedom has been swept away by total anarchy. You might justify it to your men, but that attitude won't prevail with either Governor Boggs or Washington."

"Are you prophesying again?"

"I'm warning," Mark growled. "These are the things I've been waiting to say all week. Are you taking into consideration the before-Joseph and after-Joseph climate of the state of Missouri? Since I talked to you last, I've had numerous Jacksonites come to me and beg me to get you to back down. They're not mincing words when they say you'll bring down the government on all our heads."

"You forget, Mark, I am above the law. You've seen the revelations. You've heard the promises. God has ordained that we possess the land either by purchase or by sword. That is a *command*. It is only through complete obedience to God through his Prophet in these last days that we can expect to see the promises fulfilled.

"If you or any of the others fail to obey the least of the commands, you'll bring disaster upon the people. I warned you of this before. Mark, don't blame me if this group of people fails to occupy the land. Blame those who are too weak and feeble to stand upon His Word in these latter days."

Joseph took a deep breath and paced the room. As he circled the clock again, he shot a glance at Mark and said, "Mark, I need your help and your loyalty, but right now you are close to apostasy. You've heard the counsel against the dissenters."

Mark watched Joseph's lips tighten as he continued, "Since the very day you entered Missouri, you've been fighting against the presidency."

"What do you mean?" Mark asked, already guessing.

"You've been a troublemaker. You shielded the dissenters, siding with the Whitmers, Cowdery, and Johnson."

Mark didn't bother answering, but he was fully aware of the position Joseph was forcing upon him as he spoke again. "Do you realize I could have shot you when you walked up to the door? And I would have been justified, because you left Caldwell County without permission. I am willing to forget the ugly accusations you've made against me in the past and today, but in return I'll expect more of you."

"Or," Mark said with a tight smile, "it will be like Avard says. I'll be in the bushes with a knife in my guts."

Softly Joseph replied, "You said it, Mark, I didn't."

And then after a moment of quiet reflection, Mark raised his head with a start. "Joseph, Far West is rumbling with all kinds of trouble right now. And in the midst of it, the men are milling around like lost sheep saying 'where's Joseph?' " He moved about the room restlessly. "I think you'd better quit your womanizing and get back to Far West this afternoon before that hot-headed Avard does us all in."

Joseph stared at Mark and Mark returned the look without flinching. He had nearly decided he was the victor in this round when Joseph said, "If that is the case, my trusted attorney, Mark Cartwright, will need to come with me. Seems Atchison and Doniphan aren't being of much help right now, and I have a *compelling* need for all my men to be close at hand."

Mark sighed and surrendered, "Much as I wanted to see my wife, I'm thinking you're right. Let's be off."

Just as the two men started out the door, Mark noticed the pair of blue mittens lying on the mantel. Beside them was a strange medal. He reached out to finger it. Seeing the unfamiliar symbols, he frowned and bent closer to study them. Finally he replaced the medal and examined the mittens again. Surely those were the mittens Jenny had been wearing the last time he had seen her. She had brushed them lightly across his face just before he had marched away from her.

Outside, Mark looked at Joseph standing beside the gelding waiting. He felt his throat tighten.

In the bushes beside the lean-to Jenny watched in amazement. From the moment she had heard the impatient horses stomping beside her door, she had been hiding in the bushes, fearfully expecting to see the thief who had deposited the clock in her cabin.

The sight of Joseph had frozen her beyond voice or movement. While her thoughts had churned out reasons for his being there, Mark had come out the door.

But Jenny still hesitated, wondering and fearful. When the men disappeared from sight, reason returned and Jenny jumped to her feet to run after them. Then suddenly she remembered her purpose for coming to the cabin. The book and the talisman.

She stood poised for flight. There were all those reasons why she needed power, but the most pressing reason was Mark.

While her heart still yearned after him, she rushed into the cabin and began to gather her precious bundle together. "Hurry, Jenny," she ordered herself, as she prepared to ride after the men, even then anticipating their surprise. But Jenny knew nothing of the messenger who met them just outside of town, nor of the hurried conference that sent them pounding down the road, beyond chance of being overtaken.

19

"WHERE'S THE PROPHET?" Tom turned to face the agitated man. For some time, Tom had been leaning against the door of the stable; in this position he was able to see down the main street of Far West. During the past week he had been watching men and their families pouring into the town. Every nook and cranny in the place was crowded, and still the people continued to arrive.

Tom looked at the man and sighed. "I don't rightly know. If it's lodging you want, you'll just have to—"

The man interrupted, "It's Joe I want. Our men caught a fella comin' out of Liberty. Seems he was carryin' a letter to Boggs."

"Militia?"

"Naw. Jest a ragged Gentile."

Slowly Tom said, "A fella could get into trouble snitchin' letters bound for the governor's office."

"We just wanted a look-see. He could be bought, and after we read it, he went on his way. That's the problem."

"Well, tell me the problem. I might be motivated to go take a look for Joe."

"It was from Atchison." He paused to let the import of that name sink in.

"Joe's good lawyer friend," Tom said slowly. "Well, what was the gist of the letter?"

"It were a letter of complaint. First off he listed a bunch of stuff. Talked about the goings on up in Daviess County. He were fair, that I gotta say for the man. He mentioned the old settlers doing damage to the Saints, too."

"And?"

"Atchison was sounding like we were doing mob violence, and said he won't disgrace himself by being part of a mob, too. Therefore he wouldn't lead out the militia. Sounds like he was suggesting the governor take his hands off, look the other way, and let us and the mobs cut each other's throats."

"In other words, we don't have a lick of protection anymore."

"On top of that, there's more of them than there is of us."

"Sounds like we need to be tightenin' up the ship." Tom chewed at his lip for a moment, pondering the situation. Getting to his feet, he reached for the bridle, saying, "Guess I'll mosey up Adam-ondi-Ahman way and see if I can round up Joe."

As he started out the door, the man said, "Ah—tell him the Gentile fella said he'd heard General Atchison order out a bunch of his militia to guard the line between Caldwell and Ray counties. He was saying they'd heard the Mormons were fixin' to attack Richmond. Tom, are we fixin' to fight out there?"

"Not that I'd know anything about, but then I don't know everything going on." Tom didn't look at him as he led his horse out and reached for the saddle. He was muttering to himself, "I'm guessin' things are boiling up to a full head of steam; seems it's time Joseph starts actin' like a prophet again."

He turned his horse toward the north and slapped her hard with the reins.

Tom met Mark and Joseph Smith just outside of Gallatin. He delivered the information and the three men headed for Far West at a hard run.

After Jenny left her cabin and turned onto the main road, she hurried her horse along as fast as she dared, hoping to catch up with Mark and Joseph Smith. Just beyond Gallatin she met a group of women and children walking along the road toward her.

Sliding from the mare, Jenny approached the group. "Please, can you tell me," she asked, "have you seen the Prophet and another man riding this way?"

"Were three men," came the terse answer. "The way they tore outta here I'm guessing it's meanin' more trouble."

Jenny studied their tired, worried faces. "Why are you walking along the road without your menfolk?"

"Just like you—they've run off and left us." The woman gave a bitter snort and added, "The Missourians have had enough of the thievin' and burnin', and they're riled up. The menfolk are running for their lives, and we're left to make do the best we can. The Missourians won't do nothin' to a bunch of women alone. They're after the men."

Another woman joined the group. After listening quietly, she said, "I've been against this squabble all along. Don't make sense to go in and disrupt." She squinted at Jenny. "Seems people learnt their lessons in Jackson. We found we had to keep still about Missouri being Zion, and just go on like common folk." There was an accusing note in her voice, and Jenny began understanding how the Jacksonites were viewing the newcomers from Ohio.

The first woman took up the conversation again. "Like a bird in the hand, most of us were willing to shelve the Zion idea if they'd just leave us alone and let us homestead."

The wistful words remained with Jenny as she rode on toward Far West.

It was dusk when Jenny reached town. Holding her horse down to a walk, she studied the changes which had taken place in the week since she had left. Now Far West was filled with people and wagons. Campfires dotted the town square and children played in the street. On every corner people teemed restlessly about.

Jenny pulled on the reins. Looking around, she tried to guess where Mark and Joseph would be.

A woman stopped beside her. "You be lookin' for someone?"

"Joseph Smith and another—no, two more men."

"Well, things are rilin'. I expect you'll find all the men at the general store."

Jenny thanked her and gratefully slid from the horse. With a tired sigh she tied the horse to the hitching post and entered the store. Spotting the cluster of men gathered around the bar, she headed for them.

Joseph, leaning close to the men, was saying, "Now, fellas, here's what we'll do," he stopped and lifted his head as she approached. Mark turned, jumped up, hobbled quickly toward her.

"Jenny, where've you been?" his voice was strained and his hand grasped her arm until she winced.

"Oh, Mark, I'm so glad—"

"Never mind. I can't leave now, but Tom'll see you back to the Morgans. This time, don't leave until I come after you. Promise me?" She looked up into his face, seeing the lines of strain, the pale circle around his mouth. She nodded and he turned to beckon Tom to them.

When Jenny and Tom stood on the street, he studied her with narrowed, suspicious eyes and asked, "Where you been?"

"Oh, Tom, don't look at me that way." She tried to speak lightly. "I'm not a spy."

"I wasn't thinking spy," his voice was slow, deliberate. She paused with her hand on the saddle horn and turned to look up at him. "Oh, please, Tom. I am so tired."

"I think a lot of Mark," he continued, stressing each word. "And I won't let you make a fool of him."

"Tom!" she gasped. "I love that man with all my heart—why did you say such a thing?" She watched the frown clear from his face as he continued to study her.

"Lee said he met you on the trail a couple of days ago, with you saying that you had to go to your place. He said you were pretty insistent, but that he talked you into going to the McBriers' 'til things settled a mite. Mark went up there looking for you and found Joseph instead."

She thought about that for a moment and then pushed aside the questions. "I did go to McBriers'." Tom continued to study her. Realizing he wouldn't be satisfied until she told the truth, she said, "Come on, I'll explain as we head toward Sally's."

They were out of town when Jenny reined her horse and waited for Tom. "I guess no matter how long we live, I'll still be 'little sister,' won't I?"

"You want it otherwise?"

"No, Tom. I can't get along without you, especially now. I need you to be my friend, too." She frowned, wondering how much she should reveal. After all, Tom was a staunch member of Joseph's church. She slanted a look at him and discovered his frown was returning.

"Tom," she said hastily, "no matter how badly you think of me, I must admit it. I was on my way to the cabin to get Pa's green book."

His jaw dropped and he stared. "What—you have *Pa's book*? Even after all these years it's meanin' something to you?" He sighed and scratched his head. Suddenly he leaned forward. "That's *all* you went after?"

"All? Of course *all.*" She dared not admit having a talisman, even to Tom. "Whatever else could pry me away from Sally's place with the turmoil going on?"

A happy grin took over his face. He wiped it away with a shaky hand; frowning again he said, "It's a surprise to know you've had the book all these years. What does Mark think of it?"

Jenny gasped. "Oh, Tom, I'd never tell him about it."

"Why? He's your husband."

"Because, because—" She stopped and could only visualize the horror and the disillusionment on Mark's face were he to find out about the book. "Can you imagine Mark understanding all we shared in South Bainbridge?"

"No. But that's in the past. Jenny, even Joseph doesn't believe like that anymore."

"Yes, he does. No matter what he says, it keeps cropping up. If it were otherwise, then why does he carry a talisman?"

"It's probably just a good-luck piece. Besides, how do you know?"

"I've seen it," Jenny answered shortly. "I'll just make a bet with you about the craft. I know for a fact that his pa was looking for money with the witching stick while we were in Kirtland."

"What his pa *does* has nothing to do with Joe's having the book and the keys to the kingdom."

"His pa is patriarch of the church. That's pretty holy."

"Jenny," Tom warned, ignoring her statement, "if you don't start exercising faith, there'll be no success for the people."

There was her sin again, and she faced it bleakly before saying, "I am. In my own way I'm exercising all the faith and power possible. If there's a way to win out over all the bad things that's happening in this place, I'll find it, even if—" She stopped and searched his face. Even to Tom she dared not say the word that rolled around in her head: *sabbat.*

As they rode on down the trail, Jenny was thinking of Adela and the strange vibration she had on the day Mrs. Martindale had walked out of Joseph's office. Deep inside Jenny the conviction was growing that Adela Martindale was *her* Adela.

When Tom and Jenny reached Morgans' cabin, Sally rushed out to meet them. Weeping, she threw her arms around Jenny, and the terror of the past days suddenly swept over her. Jenny found herself clinging to Sally, trembling and crying.

Tom followed the two women into the cabin. Tamara, seeing her mother's tears, began to cry. While Jenny was mopping her eyes, she discovered Tom looking embarrassed while he thumped both of the Morgans on the back.

"Oh, Tom, you've missed your calling," Jenny said with an attempt to appear lighthearted.

"No, I haven't; I'm heading back to the smithy." He said, looking relieved when Sally managed a smile.

Jenny got to her feet and wandered around the cabin. "I don't know why I'm acting like this. It's silly. Never once was I in danger, yet—" She stopped, remembering the man with the whip. He had called her a Gentile.

After Tom left there was Sally's storm of tearful questions. Didn't Jenny know how dangerous it was? Daily the stories were pouring into Far West, and as often as Andy was able to be home he carried his own tales.

Sally knew all about the Gentiles torturing the Saints, killing their animals and ravaging the crops. She knew of the mass of Saints moving out of their homes, rushing into Adam-ondi-Ahman or Far West, rushing to save their very lives when all other hope was gone.

And when Sally was calm again, Jenny told her story. Sharp memory of the gentle McBriers made her give an honest assessment. "Sally, those people had befriended the Saints. They were willing to be good neighbors, and they were trusting."

Now Jenny's question was for herself. Slowly she said, "How do you measure their story against the other stories we're hearing? I'm thinking there's a lot of wrong going on—on both sides. It troubles me, but also I feel as if just seeing all this forces me into admitting I'm a part of it. Somehow I'm less proud to be a member of the church."

"Jenny," Sally was whispering, grasping Jenny's arm, "don't give up on your faith. You've accepted the revelation in these latter days. You know Joseph is a prophet of God. You also know our only hope in these times is to obey the Prophet in everything he says."

"Sally, you keep reminding me of my duty. But do you really believe what you're saying?" Sally dropped her head. Jenny watched Sally's trembling fingers pick at a fraying spot on her dress.

That night decisions were made that started the battle of Crooked River.

Mark had gone out to walk the streets of Far West. The crisp, clear air hinted of another hard frost before morning, but the sting of cold was preferable to the damp, musty hay that was serving as his bed in the loft of the livery stable. He knew he was brooding over the situation, perhaps feeling sorry for himself. He tried to concentrate on Jenny's lonely state. But there were painful implications if that chance encounter with Joseph Smith at his cabin meant what seemed to be obvious.

Mark limped along, kicking at the clumps of freezing grass and wishing that faith had visible strings which he could yank up tight. He was deeply conscious that the most important decision he could make right now was to do nothing except hang on to his confused, limp faith. He tried to find joy in reminding himself that Jenny was in his Lord's hands.

But there were other things to think about. He watched the sentry walking off the measured limits of his post. The night seemed serene, but he felt it was only an illusion.

Mark hunched his shoulders against the cold and reflected on the nebulous sensation of danger moving closer with each tick of the clock. He knew he wasn't alone in this feeling. He was seeing the troubled frowns, the dark eyes of fear staring at him every day.

From out on the prairie the cry of the night owls went up. Then came the warning call of the wolves as they stalked their territory and terrorized their enemies with their heart-stopping howls.

Even the hair on the back of Mark's neck stiffened in response as he stood in his lonely place, listening to the wolves' message that chilled the blood with its threat.

Peering out across the pale prairie, he was conscious of a parallel between the animal world and the little town of Far West. Wasn't the little town a hedge, staking a claim against the wild; marking with a threat that was all too similar to the wolves' territorial claim?

The wild call and the threat seemed the same. He moved uneasily, suddenly conscious of threat moving closer, just as those roving wolves now sniffed at the outskirts of Far West.

Shaking off the mood, he turned. The only visible light in Far West came from the window over Joseph's work table. For a moment Mark stared at that bright spot. Then with a sigh of surrender, he began to walk toward the store.

Joseph was hunched over the table; he glanced up in surprise as Mark walked into the circle of his lamplight. While Joseph waited in silence, Mark realized he was being forced into position. Aware of the irritation in his voice, he said, "Look, Joseph, I've been thinking. We're all in this together. One falls, we all lose.

"I meant everything I said to you, but then you're a man. I guess you can handle a person liking you even while disagreeing with just about everything you believe in, can't you?"

He could see Joseph struggling. Mark sensed that he knew, even better than Joseph himself, just how far the Prophet would have to come down to accept Mark's terms.

Finally he spoke. "Of course, Mark. I need your help pulling these people out of a bad spot. Someday you'll realize how badly you need me. Until that day, we'll forget the past. Right now—" He paused, and as Mark stifled his one last urge to correct the man, the front door banged.

"Joseph, you there?"

It was Wight. He charged into the enclosure, spewing words as he came. "Long-faced dupes, hob-goblins, devils, what have you. The whole lot is to be damned and sent to hell." Joseph was on his feet and Wight explained. "The Gentiles."

"What now? Calm down and give us the facts."

"Mob. Gentile mob. Sent to Boggs, they did, reporting lies about us. Comes out that in fact it was them. They won't stay away from that county line, when they've been ordered just as much as we have. Came over the county line they did, and snatched three of our men. Now we're hearing they're fixin' to shoot them at sunrise."

Mark watched Joseph's face turn deathly pale. Quietly he asked, "Mob you say; are you certain?"

"Mob."

"We've got to recover our men. This is a job for Patten." He turned to Mark. "I have two things for you to do. First, get Patten and send him here. Then," he paused to take a deep breath, "we've got to have intelligence from behind their lines. We've got to know just what we're facing. Mark, I want you behind those lines, finding out who's where and what they are doing. Get a lead on whether or not the state's behind them, and how many men are milling around with guns."

Immediately Mark got the clear picture. He needn't see the challenge in Joseph's eyes to be reminded that despite their truce, Mark was still a Saint in disfavor. But he must justify with one last word. "Mark, your face is unknown. Being laid up with that leg's kept you out of sight. That's a big advantage to us right now."

In the livery stable Mark aroused Patten, and the other men crowded around. He delivered Joseph's message. Looking around at the other men, he added, "I guess you'll all be called out before the night's over."

Tom was at his elbow. "What about you?"

Briefly Mark explained his mission and Tom exploded, "That's foolish! Doesn't make no difference now. We just fight regardless. You'll be a loser no matter which way you go. I'm sayin' just split, Mark."

There were averted eyes around the circle. Patten was dressed and pulling on his white coat. His voice was hard as he said, "Tom, that's going against counsel. I'll forget I heard it this time, but don't *you* forget that God is protecting us. There's no bullet, no knife can touch those the Lord is protecting. We may be small in number, but we shall expect the holy angels to fight our battles for us. Don't fear, Cartwright. You'll come back safely."

"Captain Fearnought!" exclaimed a youth affectionately. "You cheer us all with your faith!"

Tom was to recall that scene vividly just a few short hours later. He followed as the men scurried along behind Patten striding toward the store.

Joseph was pacing the floor in front of the fire. He lifted his head, gave a short nod of approval as the men clustered in behind Patten. "Here's the information I have now," he said tersely, moving behind his table. "There's a Gentile mob just south of here on the line between Caldwell and Ray counties. From what we can determine right now, they are down in this draw, holding three of our men. Their intentions—the poor devils—are to shoot our men at sunrise. Need I say more?"

Tom found himself adding his growl of rage to the chorus around him.

It was nearly dawn by the time Patten and his sixty men reached the slough at Crooked River. They had spent the pre-dawn hours creeping soundlessly through the rough terrain. Now nerves were taut with strain as eager men, confident of victory, pressed to the battle.

With his men around him, Patten pointed out the final hill. "Just over this rise is the mob's camp. We've smelled their fires, heard their dogs. Now, before it is daylight we rush over the hill and have them in our hands before they can think." There was a ripple of excitement through the troops.

"Captain, sir," a cautious voice whispered, " 'tis nearly dawn. I suggest you remove that white coat. It gleams like a flag of truce, and we don't want them making a dreadful mistake."

There was a choked howl of mirth and Patten responded, "Well said, my lad. However, we've nothing to fear, either of being taken too lightly or too seriously. The coat? Well, the Lord's on our side. His angels wear white. Perchance they'll see me as another angel."

When they reached the last hill Tom saw that hickory trees blanketing the slope made an unexpected obstacle, dragging at the Saints and slowing their progress. Tom realized the threat immediately, and looking at the sky felt his first uneasiness. But there wasn't time for fear; it was too near sunrise.

Flat on their bellies, the Saints squirmed into position. Patten's word passed down the line. The Gentile camp was safely ensconced behind a sheltering line of thick oaks. But daylight was already upon them, and Patten's strategy was in disarray. Reluctantly the order was given. There was no recourse but to dash down that hill.

Patten's men were on their feet; then came that cautious change of position. Muscles tensed, rifles readied.

"Halt! Who goes there?"

"Friends," Patten yelled.

"Armed?"

"Yes."

"Lay them down."

"Fire," Patten snapped. He was on his feet, leading the men, surging with them down the hill.

Tom heard the shots. In the next second, there was return fire. He heard a startled grunt. The Saint in front of him dropped and rolled limply down the hill. With a growl Tom was on his feet, shooting as he ran; but that scene of the rag doll figure, rolling away with arms like useless ropes, stayed with him.

When the Saints charged into the Gentile camp, Tom was still on the hill, bending over the man, knowing suddenly the reality of war. Nothing but that man was important. But his help was useless. As he got to his feet he saw the Gentiles fleeing their camp, running like startled partridges.

He was still staring at the scene when he saw the one Gentile who didn't flee but instead ducked behind the tree. When the crack of the rifle came, Tom was looking at Captain Fearnought and saw him fall.

They carried him back to Far West to die. Tom, in the frozen emotion of the moment, could only focus on the white coat smeared with blood.

It was late morning when Jenny and Sally learned of the battle. Jenny and Tamara had gone for a walk, with the toddler happily leading the way. They had circled through the woods, following Log Creek nearly to the settlement of Haun's Mill. When Tamara was tired, her tearful face won a ride on Jenny's shoulders.

Homeward they went, with Tamara sagging against Jenny, and Jenny feeling every vibration of the forest, drinking in every fragrant whiff of moss and wood, seeing every shade of green, brown, and dampened gray.

There they met Andy Morgan, sagging, white-faced, and bone-weary from battle. Jenny led him home, but before he could rest, they found he had to relieve his soul.

He described the battle. "Patten died early this morning," he added. "I was down there with the others. Danites. It was a lark. Nothing could touch us." His voice was bitter, his eyes bleak. Jenny and Sally clung to each other, shivering.

"Patten, foolish man. He'd heard so long that we were invincible. Didn't take ordinary precautions. In his white coat, he yelled, 'Charge, in the name of Lazarus!' I could see we were outlined against the morning sky."

He got to his feet to pace the floor, and when Jenny tried to comfort him, he said. "I'm ashamed. I could have reasoned with the man. But it's hard when you've been taught not to question. Not to even think they mightn't have all the right answers." Later his voice was bleak as he said, "I'm the one who'll have to live with my uneasy conscience. It's too late to change what has happened."

And then Jenny remembered. She could only say, "Mark?"

Andy turned quickly. "Oh, I'm sorry. Mark was sent on another assignment."

At that moment Mark was facing Joseph in the office behind the shelves and barrels. Did Joseph seem surprised to see him?

Mark rubbed a weary hand across his face. "I found out that all of Richmond is running like scared rabbits. They're moving the women and children out, preparing for siege."

Mark was seeing the pleased smile on Joseph's face. "But that isn't the most significant fact I discovered. Sorry I didn't find out in time to warn you, but—"

"Warn?" Joseph was leaning forward now.

"Yes. That wasn't a mob Patten and his men attacked; it was men sent out by the state militia."

Joseph Smith leaned back in his chair and the smile disappeared from his face.

Mark had to say the obvious. "Joseph, there's bound to be trouble over this."

20

THE DAY WAS cold and moisture hung in the air like the draperies of mourning. *Fitting,* Jenny thought as she left Morgans' cabin to join Andy and Sally for the ride into town. She commented, "Looks like the eternities themselves are mourning for Captain Patten. The sky seems ready to weep."

Sally pulled her shawl close, shoved the black bonnet more securely on her blonde hair and turned a tear-reddened face to Jenny. Jenny shivered. Sally's sad, hopeless face was the epitome of the collective emotions in Far West today.

There were a few wagons moving into town for the funeral. But when they reached Far West, Jenny saw the mass of people swarming into town from the cluster of campsites on its fringes.

Tom and Mark joined them as they stepped out of the wagon. Jenny clung to Mark and tried to believe his unresponsiveness was related to the occasion.

Jerking his head toward the group just driving into town, Tom said, "That's the bunch from Haun's Mill. I was at the store earlier today when Jacob Haun came in to protest Joe's order to evacuate all the settlements and move into Far West. Seems he doesn't want to give up the mill. Can't say I blame him. The Gentiles won't grind our grain for us, and we can't live on dry corn all winter."

"Joseph did hear him out," Mark said soberly. "He left the decision up to Haun, saying it was better to lose the mill rather than their lives. He told me later that he was confident they'd sacrifice their lives for their decision."

Jenny shivered. "Why didn't he insist they come?" And when Mark didn't answer, she asked, "Will those from Adam-ondi-Ahman be coming for the funeral?"

He was avoiding her eyes as he answered tersely. "Most of the men are already here, called in to guard Far West. It's best the remainder of them stay there." He looked squarely at her for the first time, and she saw the shadows in his eyes. "Since we've left they've been building siegeworks in the middle of town."

"Then it *is* bad," she said slowly.

Again he met her eyes and said, "Jenny, we're getting very close to being in a real skirmish. The men Patten attacked weren't a mob. They were militia sent out by Boggs, part of Atchison's company. Do you realize this is part of the company sent out to make peace?"

Jenny shivered, "Mark, what is going to happen next?"

His voice was weary as he slowly said, "I don't know. I've tried to get Joseph to come to his senses. I—"

Abruptly he stopped. Jenny searched his eyes and what she saw there made her shiver again. "Are we really safe at the Morgans' place?"

"Andy insists so. But he did promise me that he'll make plans to move you and Sally out by the first of November. I'll try to be free to join you then." He pressed her fingers and her heart lifted, but in the next moment, the somber notes of the bugle drew their attention to the crude coffin in front of the schoolhouse.

As Joseph took his place beside the coffin, a pale wintry gleam of sunlight pierced the clouds and shed a glow about the dark-suited man. Jenny looked curiously at Joseph, wondering briefly why he had stopped by their cabin.

The light against his hair seemed momentarily to bring back its youthful brightness. Although his features were heavy with strain and sorrow today, she was reminded of the long-ago boy. For a moment her heart yearned for that peaceful yesterday, filled with foolish, girlish dreams. Abruptly his words began to filter through her thoughts.

"The missiles of death will cut down a Saint, just like any other man," he was saying. "You have not the right to believe that just because we are the Lord's chosen, we will never escape the judgment of the Lord. We have not got a magic circle drawn about us, protecting us from what folly we have chosen to bring upon ourselves."

He paused and the group standing before him shifted restlessly, and Jenny was piercingly aware of the wooden coffin. She clung more tightly to Mark's arm while Joseph's words continued to build fear in her.

His voice was sad as he continued, "I have been communing with the Lord these days, seeking wisdom. Now I must advise you that the Lord is angry with these people, yea, even the chosen of the Lord. They have been unbelieving and faithless. A stubborn generation this is, refusing to give to the Lord the use of their earthly treasure. How can any one of you expect the blessings of the Lord in the face of disobedience?

"To expect the favor of God, we must learn to blindly trust Him. I tell you, my people, if you would do so, the very windows of heaven would be opened and showers of blessings would be poured upon you. All that the people could contain of blessings will be the reward of obedience to the will of God given to mankind through the prophet of God. Verily, I say, when you are obedient, you will enjoy all the wealth of the world. God will consecrate the riches of the Gentiles to you."

The mood of the crowd changed from outrage to excited hope. When the flutter of excitement passed, he added, "I have been charged with the restoration of the house of Israel in these last days. Called of God, I have been given the power and authority from God to accomplish His purposes. I can help that power to rest upon all who will do His will. Again I remind you that Saints from the four corners of this earth will be gathered to Zion, this holy land. We shall set up the kingdom of God, ready for the second coming of Christ in these last days. This is the Word of the Lord to you."

Jenny and Sally went home with the chastisement and the future promise of blessing still swirling in their thoughts.

Briefly Mark and Andy lingered before returning to their posts. As they were preparing to leave, a wagon stopped beside the cabin door. From the conversation, Jenny realized it was a man who had been at Crooked River. She could see a bandage showing under the rim of his hat.

Carefully tilting his hat, he nodded as Andy introduced Sally and Jenny, still standing in the doorway. Then addressing Andy, the man, Byman, said, "Hyde, Tom Marsh, and a couple of others slipped outta Missouri during the night. Joseph sent a bunch after them, but they never did catch up with them. Had their families with them, but they were sure traveling light to have slipped the bunch trailing them."

"Fortunate for them," Mark said heavily. Jenny pressed her fingers against her eyes, trying to crowd out the memory of Rigdon's face and the words he had shouted from the steps of the schoolhouse.

Byman nodded soberly. "And after Joseph's threat today, there's not many men who'd dare. They were brave."

Andy added, "I don't know. Things are getting sticky enough around here; maybe it's worth the chance." His brooding eyes studied Sally and Tamara.

Mark and Andy Morgan rode away together. Mark was shaking his head soberly as he said, "It makes me uneasy to leave the women there alone."

"Well, if yours would just stay put, they'd be safe enough," Andy drawled.

Mark threw him a quick glance, saying, "She's promised. I don't know what got into her, but I think she's convinced it isn't safe."

He was thinking about the mittens and talisman when Andy added, "That Gentile mob out there is crowding us close. And Doniphan's not far behind. 'Tisn't that I'm really fearing him, but that's the reason I'm reluctant to move the women at this time."

Mark added, "Haun's Mill is a mighty attractive target. I keep hoping the Gentiles don't take it into their heads to latch on to it. Maybe it hasn't occurred to them that they'd about starve us out if they controlled the mill."

The next morning, like a chess game subjected to a gentle, seemingly harmless maneuver, the whole scene started to change. What had been a contest of will and power had begun to develop into open war. That which had seemed insignificant had become strategic. Strangely, dissenters from the Mormon camp made the move.

Mark and Tom were with the men in the town square when the fellow rode in. Mark recognized him as the man sent out to spy when he had returned from Richmond.

Tom grasped his arm and spoke softly, "Mark, something's wrong. Tucker looks half-dead, and that horse is lathered. I'll take care of his mount; you get Tucker in to Joseph."

In Joseph's office, Tucker drained the mug of water, wiped his hand across his face and gasped, "Joe, it's bad. Soon as I found out Marsh and Hyde had dispatched a message to Boggs, I tried to intercept it. Couldn't catch up with the kid carryin' it. Musta had a twenty-mile start on me.

"I laid around Boggs' stable, hopin' to have a little chat with the fella later. Found out he'd left before I got there. But the whole place was buzzin' with the talk."

Mark interrupted impatiently, "What makes you think they leveled with you?"

"They weren't talkin' to me. 'Twas all between themselves as they were preparing to move out."

"Where?" Joseph's voice was taut.

"Here. Seems troops were layin' over near Jefferson City, and their commander was called in to confer with Boggs when he got the dispatch."

"So it was from Marsh and Hyde. What did they pass on to Boggs?"

"First off, they gave him the details about the Danites. Told about spoilin' Gallatin and backed up their comments by giving the details of your Mahomet talk, when ya said you'd take your sword and make a gore of blood from coast to coast. Seems they also said something about the Danites planning to burn Richmond, 'cause they mentioned that and something about them poisoning the wells of the old settlers to start a pestilence."

When Tucker finally got to his feet and headed for the door, he turned. "Joseph, I forgot to tell you—Atchison's real mad." He hesitated and then left.

Mark was watching the play of expression across Joseph's face. When he spoke, his voice was bitter. "So even my friend Atchison has turned against me."

But in another moment, Joseph started for the door, saying, "Come on, there's lots to do. Spread the word that all the Saints from all the outlying areas are to move into Far West as quick as they can get here. Could be their lives will depend on it. I'm going to start those lazy fellas around the fire building a fortress in the middle of town, even if they have to tear down every house to get wood."

It was the next day, the Sabbath, before Mark finished contacting the outlying communities and put in motion the exodus to Far West.

When he rode back into town, he was feeling the effects of the gloomy day and the cold drizzle of rain; he was also brooding over Jenny and dismally accepting the sense of loss which was slowly wrapping itself around everyone. He had seen it on the faces of the men and women, and he had been unable to offer hope.

He stopped first to warm himself at the fire burning feebly in the center of the square. He noticed that in just a day's time the fortification had grown to a haphazard, rearing chunk. Looking at the barricade, feeling the message of hopelessness it transmitted, Mark shook his head and turned his back.

The men grouped around the fire looked as dismal as their handiwork. Shifting from foot to foot, they blew on their reddened hands and kicked at the embers. Mark's terse greeting was acknowledged by a grunt. He rubbed his hands and searched for something to say.

"Hey, you fellas there!" Mark heard the angry growl and recognized the Prophet's voice. Joseph strode up to the fire. Like the others, his coat was damp and his hands red, but he didn't slow his stride. Moving from man to man, he grasped them by the shoulders and spun them away from the fire. "Come on!" he roared. "Move, jump, run! Anthing but mope. Let's wrestle! A soldier will win at anything."

Joseph was still moving, shoving the men into a ring. Stepping into the middle he threw back his head and laughed. The challenge was out. Within seconds, Joseph was the center of a laughing, brawling group.

With a smile, Mark stepped back to watch as the men, one by one, tried to throw Joseph.

"Stop, stop!" Mark turned and watched Sidney Rigdon charge into the midst of the wrestling match. He was waving his sword. Astonished, Mark noticed the man's face was contorted with rage. "You will not break the Sabbath in this manner! I forbid any more of this! I will not suffer it!"

Instantly the men were subdued, scuffling their feet and glancing at Joseph from the corners of their eyes. A braver one exclaimed, "Brother Joe, you put us up to this! Now clear our names."

Joseph moved. "Brother Sidney," he said in a low, deliberate drawl, "you best get out of here and leave the fellas alone. It's my orders putting life into them. You are an old man. Go get ready for meeting and leave them be." Suddenly he moved. Mark had only time for a choked protest as he watched Joseph knock the sword from Rigdon's hand, spinning him around. A pleased grin swept across Joseph's face, and with another quick movement, he swept the hat from the smaller man's head, and dragged him bodily from the ring. Now grasping his fine coat, he gave one quick yank, ripping it in two.

Rigdon's voice rose in protest, but Joseph turned to his men. Breathing heavily, he said, "My lads, don't ever say I got you into something that I couldn't get you out of."

On that day when the first of the troops stationed outside of town trickled back, Mark was in the square. He saw their crestfallen faces and asked, "What's happening out there?"

With a dejected sigh a young fellow said, "We've been called into retreat. We were guarding the county line. Captain said, 'Head for Far West'; and we did." Even as the man spoke, Mark saw the picket guards and scouts coming into town. From their drooping shoulders and slow steps, it was easy to guess that the rest of the men had been ordered in.

The men were still milling around in the town square when a scout and Joseph came out of the grocery store. "They're mobbers," the scout declared as the men began pressing around Joseph.

"Are you certain?"

"Couldn't be no other. Every Gentile in the state's gathered out there, just waitin' for us to make a crooked move. Chased us in here. I wanted to stay'n fight. The Lord's promised—"

An angry voice rose, "There's a multitude out there. We've only a handful. Don't even have sufficient arms."

Excited voices rose as the restless crowd jostled the men about. Joseph abruptly turned and leaped upon the line of barricades the men had been erecting. The silence of the crowd caught Mark's attention, and he turned to study the faces of the men as Joseph addressed them. Those hungry faces devoured every word their leader said.

But Mark's despair grew as he watched their emotions change to hope.

Someone cheered, and Mark turned to listen to Joseph's charge to valor. "We must fight for everything we hold dear—our homes, our Zion. God is for us!"

While Joseph was speaking, Mark's attention had been caught by the dark line of the Gentile mob moving slowly across the prairie toward Far West.

When the final cheer was over, Joseph's men took formation and moved to the edge of the prairie.

Mark climbed to the top of the breastwork to watch the confrontation. Cautiously the Saints moved across the prairie toward that dark mass of Gentiles waiting for them.

Mark winced and started to jump from the breastwork when something caught his eye. It was a dot of white being hoisted.

He could hardly believe his eyes as he watched the flag of truce waving in the Gentile ranks. Frowning, he strained to see, trying to comprehend the significance. "Surely that big bunch of Gentiles isn't giving in to Joseph's men without a fight. There's something very strange going on," Mark muttered to himself.

Mark had only begun to limp his way toward the store when some of the men started to trickle back into town. He called to the nearest soldier, "What's going on out there?"

Joseph came out of the store in time to see the man's stricken face. Together they heard the words. "Them's not the mob we've been after; it's Doniphan's militia. Won't be easy straightening this out, taking after the state militia when we thought it was mobbers. I'm feelin' like we got our hands smacked good."

Mark followed the Prophet back into the store. He watched Joseph drop heavily into his chair. Head in hands, he sat beside his fire. Mark held his silence, waiting.

Later, when the scout came, Mark was there to listen as Joseph received the news. The man spoke heavily, "It's Doniphan's troops." He ran his finger along the crude map spread on the counter. "He's positioned them between Haun's Mill and Far West, just one mile out of town."

When the ragged soldier turned and left the store, Mark wheeled, "I'm going to the Morgans' for the women."

Joseph stepped in front of him. "No, you are not. If one Saint sees you leave, he'll shoot without asking questions. Simpson's said every Gentile in the state has surrounded the town, and they're all holding their guns on Far West. Maybe that's so, maybe it isn't. But I'm not making a move until I figure out what's going on. If you want activity, then start praying." He paused, then added, "I'll shoot that lame leg out from under you just to save your life if I must."

Mark turned to leave and collided with a man standing in the shadows behind a stack of barrels. "Beg your—" He saw the uniform. Instantly

Mark grabbed the man. "Spy!" he cried, and Joseph was towering over the man, gripping the dirty uniform around his neck like a noose.

The man gasped, "Doniphan sent me. Message."

Joseph released the man and shoved him against the wall. "Hand it over."

The man trembled as he smoothed out the sheets of paper and handed them to Joseph. While Mark kept his gaze on the soldier, Joseph moved close to the lamp.

Mark heard the exclamation as Joseph whirled around, smashing the papers between his hands. His voice was thick as he yelled, "Get out!"

The youth trembled. "No message?"

Joseph shook his head and paced the floor until the soldier had disappeared. Stopping in front of Mark, he shoved the papers at him. "You are a lawyer; read these. Tell me what it means."

Mark scanned the letter from Doniphan. Slowly he said, "He's enclosing an order from Governor Boggs and he's suggesting that you take action quickly since Lucas and General Clark are headed for Far West with six thousand men, and with instructions to enforce this order."

Mark sat down and spread the second paper across his knees. "The order from Boggs is dated October 27, 1838, from Jefferson City." He glanced up at Joseph. "It appears he's had a change of mind from some previous decision—"

Joseph interrupted, "Previously he'd ordered troops to Daviess County to reinstate the Gentile residents. I'd received word that Doniphan's men were to be the ones sent to Daviess County."

Mark glanced at the paper he held. "Well, now he states that he has information just received that has changed the whole face of things. This new information indicates to him that the Mormons are in defiance of the laws of the state. He accuses us of 'having made open war upon the people of the state.'" Mark was silent for a moment and then said slowly, "He advises that the Mormons are to be treated as enemies and must be exterminated or else driven from the state."

Looking up at Joseph, Mark winced. "Exterminated. That's an unusual word. Do you suppose he's planned revenge, using the very word Rigdon proposed in his Independence Day speech? I remember hearing him use it."

Joseph shook his head and sighed. Mark watched him again drop his head into his hands. With a strange sensation of detachment, Mark wondered if the whole scene, even the alarming papers Joseph still held, were real. But he couldn't help measuring the reaction of Joseph Smith, and he decided he was seeing a defeated man.

As he hesitated, a conviction gripped him that it was no accident he was sitting here beside Joseph in this one quiet moment before a decision must be made.

On the far wall of the long, dimly lighted building, a clock ticked off the minutes. For a moment Mark recalled the unexpected sight of the walnut clock standing in the middle of his cabin. Immediately the impulse to warn Joseph was overlapped with the memory of Jenny's blue mittens and the talisman. He stopped.

His jaw tightened as he stared down at Joseph. *The man deserves whatever Boggs plans to give him.* Mark clenched his fist and then relaxed.

Pushing aside his own angry feeling, he squatted in front of the Prophet. "Joe, there's the people to think about. You've got to save them; it's your responsibility as leader. Do you see? Joe, it's starting to look tough out there. I think you'll have a chance if you get out and level with your men. Admit you've no heaven-stamped guarantee that your troops will be victors. Admit that God's not playing favorites with you. The riches and lands of the Gentiles aren't going to be handed to you on a silver platter. Pull your men in. I saw them facing off out there on the prairie. They're still thinking they're obligated to fight because God's ordered it. You know there's only a handful compared to Doniphan's men. Plead with Hinkel, Wight, Avard, and the rest to get back here, and then surrender. Admit—"

Joseph jumped to his feet. "Mark, I'm not seeking advice. I'm a prophet of the Lord, *I* give the orders."

"And you haven't a chance in the world to succeed if you follow this track. Joseph, in God's name, can't you see what your childish play-acting has led you into? You have no more audience with God than—" Joseph turned away and stomped toward the bar at the end of the building. Heavily Mark followed him. His voice was controlled and low now. "I could say all the things like repent, accept God on His terms, quit trying to be God; but I don't think you intend to listen."

Mark started for the door and Joseph called, "You might stay around to pick up the pieces. One of these days, just maybe—"

The door burst open. Lyman Wight and Colonel Hinkel charged into the room. "You've got communication," Hinkel said. "Let's see it."

Joseph clenched the papers and glared at Hinkel. "Who's in command?" he snapped. The men dropped back and Joseph stepped forward. "What's going on out there?"

"It's Doniphan. His troops have moved closer. Don't think they're more'n a mile outta town. We're using the breastwork down the middle of town. The men are lined up, just dancing with excitement, daring Doniphan's bunch to get close enough so's they can take a shot at 'em. Joseph, our men are straining at the bit. When do I give them the word?"

Joseph's voice was deliberately slow as he said, "Not until *I* give the word. We're going to play hell with their apple carts."

Mark grabbed up his coat and left the store, shaking his head in dismay. For some time he walked around the camp, watching the men, listening to their subdued conversations. More than once he saw their quick glances in his direction. It was easy to guess they were seeing him as a spy for Joseph. No wonder they turned away, with expressions very nearly like fear on their faces. Mark sighed heavily.

Later when he picked up his tin plate and joined the others around the mess fire, he discovered that the men were silent, but the air of depression was real. In the absence of conversation, he found himself mulling over all that had happened that day. Measuring events against the feeling that Joseph's decisions were wrong, he picked at his food and admitted the obvious. Not only were Joe's decisions wrong, Mark's legal mind admitted uneasily, but the decisions must be challenged or the constitution of the state, as well as law and justice, were impotent vessels.

One statement Joseph had made still rang in Mark's ears: "I am above the law."

Mark sighed, gave up on the plate of cold food, and headed for his bunk.

Mark knew it was late when the armed guard touched his shoulder. He knew it because he had known how long he had tossed on his mat before going to sleep. When he raised himself to one elbow, the man's grip tightened. "Mr. Cartwright," he said respectfully, "Joseph bids me tell you that you are under arrest. Please, sir, this is for your own protection." The man's grip had become steely. "Come with me; Haun's Mill has been attacked."

21

OCTOBER 30 DAWNED with the promise of being a nice day, and Jenny immediately seized on the promise. "Sally, let's get out. We've been cooped up here like a bunch of chickens. Let's walk over to Haun's Mill; it's only a good stroll down the creek. You've made friends over that way, and there's a woman I want to inquire after."

Sally lifted dull eyes and moved restlessly on her bench. "I suppose so—anything's better than sitting here, fearing what's happening to the menfolk. We haven't heard a word for days."

"I suppose I should have walked into town," Jenny said slowly. "But they say no news is good news. With Mark riding Sammy, and Patches with a lame foot, it's been easier to sit and wait on the fellows."

"I did promise Mrs. Harris I'd visit," Sally added.

After breakfast, Jenny bundled Tamara into warm clothing and hurried Sally along.

The heavy, unseasonable snow earlier in the month had broken branches and stripped leaves from the trees before they had completed their cycle of autumn glory. Snow still lingered in the heavy shadows, and the leaves were a soggy cushion underfoot.

While Sally shivered, Jenny enjoyed the pungent forest smells—the pine and the acrid odor of ancient foliage. She gloried in the scurry of squirrels and the raucous complaint of jays. With Tamara beside her, she was seeing with new eyes the wonder of twigs and shiny rocks. They followed Log Creek into the settlement.

Haun's Mill was a tidy circle in the midst of forest. In addition to the mill and a cluster of cabins, there was the blacksmith shop and corrals. Over all lay order and neatness. Jenny studied the garden patches, saying, "I like it here. It would be a pleasant place to live. Seems there's such a haphazard air to Adam-ondi-Ahman."

Sally lifted her head and looked surprised. "Why the difference?"

Jenny shrugged, "Probably because up that way the settlements are new." Abruptly she changed the subject. "I've been hearing things about Far West that surprised me. Mrs. Harris said everything's topsy-turvy. She was blaming most of it on the disorder of the breastworks they're putting up for defense in case the fighting gets into town. She was telling me she heard one woman complaining that Joseph has had them building block houses for defense for such a long time, they didn't even get a chance to put in crops. She told Mrs. Harris, confidential-like, that they'd all be thieving for their grain before spring—and from what she says, there's plenty of that going on right now."

Sally poked at a pile of leaves with the stick she carried, saying, "What difference does it make? The Prophet's promised that the cattle on a thousand hills belong to the Lord, and that means it belongs to us, too. Why worry about planting when there's more important things to do?"

As it turned out, both Sally and Jenny found many of their Kirtland friends living at Haun's Mill. The day passed quickly as they visited from cabin to cabin. Women, as isolated as they, were eager to talk. Jenny was only vaguely conscious of how quickly the time passed as they worried together over the latest news and the fearful things taking place.

Jane Laney shivered and said, "I'm right grateful we settled down here in Caldwell County instead of in Daviess. I don't think the Gentiles will ever give in to the Saints up there."

Later on their way down the lane they met old Thomas McBride. He leaned on his cane and waited until they reached him. There was concern in his eyes as he said, "Now don't you young ladies linger until dark. I've been listenin' to the troops all day."

"They're just shooting rabbits," Jenny said with a laugh. "The McLaughlin boy crept up on them. It's just a bunch of men from down the way. They're not the militia, and they're not any more serious about this business than we are."

"What makes you think that way?" His eyes were piercingly intent. "You're too young to know war and suffering and you're thinking it can't happen to you. I fought in the Revolutionary War, and I know it's not that way at all."

For a moment Jenny was caught by the memory of the McBriers' home—both before and after. She shivered, saying, "Yes, I know it can happen." Suddenly sober, she added, "Sally, perhaps we'd better go."

The always-present fear settled back down over Sally's gentle face. As her eyes darkened, Jenny added hastily, "Oh, it can't be that bad. We'll finish our walk to Matilda's and then go home."

She turned to wave at Mr. McBride and then took Tamara's hand.

The afternoon was far gone when they left Matilda's cabin. Jenny said with a sigh, "We've still not asked about the Martindales."

"Martindales?" Sally said wrinkling her nose. "Why do you want to visit that stuffy old lady? She's the biggest bore I've ever met."

Jenny stopped abruptly. "She is?" she said slowly, thinking back to the whirling red-clad Adela with her sparkling smile and mysterious lilting voice. "I wonder if I'm mistaken—" She looked at the heavy clouds overhead and sighed. "It's going to darken quickly tonight. Those clouds promise a storm."

They were still hesitating in the path when the gunfire began. At first Jenny thought *rabbits,* but then she heard the screams.

For a moment she could almost dismiss it as a bad dream. Looking around the clearing at the solid cabins and rustling cornstalks, she thought, *It seems so ordinary and peaceful.* Then she heard Tamara's whimpers and felt Sally's frantic hands grasping at her.

Turning slowly, Jenny looked at the scene behind them. The gunfire was coming again. She saw people running; women and children streamed toward the woods, while men with guns were running, shooting, and running again toward the blacksmith shop standing in the middle of the clearing.

In the space of one hard breath, Jenny saw men swarming up the creek bank toward them—strangers, dirty and ragged. Jenny caught a glimpse of their faces, some leering, some contorted in rage, waving rifles over their heads.

Still with a sense of idle detachment, Jenny saw them turn on the running figures, chasing the women and children, herding the silent racing figures into the woods.

Until the screams penetrated Jenny's confusion, she didn't comprehend what was happening. But even while Jenny watched, she saw them kneel and lift their rifles. Dust pricked upward in puffs.

Once again the men laughed and aimed their rifles at the women fleeing toward the trees. In the brief silence after the women disappeared, the men turned back.

Hands were shoving at Jenny and she moved in response. Now aware of gunfire coming from behind her, Jenny forced her numb body to move, stepping backward into the sheltering trees.

Now she could see a ring of men gathered around the blacksmith shop, shooting, waiting, and shooting again.

Then Jenny realized that she and Sally were clinging to each other. With every blast of gunfire, Sally cringed, her body jerking as if she felt those bullets. In a brief, silent interval, she cried, "Will it go on forever?" Jenny could only shake her head.

Darkness was nearly upon them when the rapid volley trailed into an occasional burst of gunfire. Jenny became aware of Sally's strangling sobs. They were still clinging to each other with Tamara wedged between them.

Jenny found mind enough to be glad the child stayed motionless and soundless.

Later Jenny began to breathe easier. A few shadowy figures pulled themselves upright and came to huddle in the trees. The silence was alive with fear. Once more men pounded past, circled, and returned. With every sound of their searching feet, the women cringed deeper into the trees.

When the footsteps faded and the eerie quiet grew, Jenny began to realize that their total, mindless fear had saved them. In the trees she discovered others had survived too. Much later, like Jenny and Sally, they came creeping out of the woods. Together they huddled in the clearing, stunned and wondering.

That gunfire. They saw the silent shop and remembered the men and boys who had fled into the blacksmith shop. Finally Matilda spoke, and for moments Jenny could only compare the strong, confident woman she knew with this trembling, weak creature who was clinging to the tree beside her.

Jenny spoke out of memory she didn't know she had. "Those—those, they knelt down and shot through the spaces between the logs. It was like—they didn't have a place to run."

The women continued to huddle on the edge of the clearing. The last gun had long been silent. The final shadowy figure slipped away, and the scent of gunpowder disappeared. They were still motionless when a lone shadow moved hesitantly toward them, stood, and stumbled to fall again.

One of the group, braver than the rest, said slowly, "It's a woman." Her voice unshackled the others and slowly they began to come forward. They surrounded the trembling figure and waited, powerless to act.

She spoke in a faltering voice, "I was hiding in the wagon. Old Thomas, he surrendered his rifle, and one of those men—" she choked and they heard her ragged breath—"one of those men hacked him to pieces with a corn knife." Her voice became shrill, "The others—" She shook her head, but it was enough.

They turned and faced the blacksmith shop. First one and then the others began moving hesitantly toward it.

Mark pulled on his clothes. As the guard instructed, he picked up his rifle and coat. The man's voice had been heavy; that should have been enough to alert Mark, but even now the information, still seeping into his mind, seemed unreal.

When they reached the store, the facts began to add up and make sense. Joseph was sitting behind a table. His arms rested on the piles of paper; his hands clasped the base of the smoking oil lamp. When the guard spoke, Joseph sighed and got to his feet. Now his face was shadowed, and Mark found himself leaning forward to peer into his eyes.

Joseph spoke as if stunned. "We've just received communication from Haun's Mill. One of the wounded made it in with the information that they had been fired upon this afternoon. Seventeen are dead and fifteen wounded."

"But why am I arrested?" Mark questioned.

"I need you and I can't have you running off to Log Creek to be shot like a hero."

The final fact sank in: Haun's Mill was fearfully close to Morgans' cabin. He had to moisten his lips before he could ask, "Then you think the outlying cabins were attacked too?"

"It's possible." As Joseph paced the floor, Mark watched him, his heart thudding; but he dared not allow his thoughts to probe further.

The door opened. Corrill and Reed Peck entered the store. When they walked into the circle of lamplight, Joseph returned to his chair behind the table. He pulled a pile of papers toward him and said, "I've a mission for you men. I want you to find Doniphan and beg like a dog for peace."

The three men facing him stood motionless, silent. Mark moved first, and with a puzzled frown, glanced at the other faces. Then the realization struck him. Joseph had chosen dissenters to carry his message. He was speaking again and his voice was level, emotionless. "Yesterday it was Haun's Mill. God knows what it will be tomorrow. I'm getting new information almost every hour. The militia is moving in from all directions. We're outnumbered five to one. By this time tomorrow there'll be ten thousand men surrounding the town."

And Mark knew why they had been chosen. Wight, Avard, and all the other men who had been brainwashed by Joseph's doctrine would never back down now. He could almost hear Avard's cry: *Charge, Danites, charge! The Lord will fight our battles for us!*

Dawn was breaking over the horizon when the three saddled up and pointed their horses in the direction in which they believed Doniphan's camp lay.

Already Israel's army was stirring, moving toward the town square. When Mark heard the cheer, he muttered to Corrill and Peck, "Wait up, fellows; let's hear what Joseph has to say to the men."

They watched the lithe figure vault to the top of the breastwork and face the men. "The Gentiles are coming." His voice rang through the crisp morning air. "I care not a fig. For years we've tried to please them. Their lawlessness spells out their belief that 'might makes right.' And mighty they are. But we have God on our side. They are a damned set and God will blast them into hell."

Corrill shivered and said, "Come on, fellas."

As they wheeled their horses, Joseph's voice followed them: "All we lack in number the Lord will match. He'll send angels to fight."

When they reached the road, Reed Peck looked at Mark. "Lee told me confidentially he doesn't believe that Joseph has the least conviction that his little band of men can stand off the army coming against him."

"Then we'd better get going before Joseph's battle cry leads his men where his faith can't take them."

At noon, Peck reined in his horse and waited until Mark and Corrill halted. "Men, we've seen plenty of evidence that Doniphan's been traveling this route; but at the rate we're trailing him, we won't catch up with him until midnight."

"Any suggestions?" Mark asked.

"We're under orders!" Corrill snapped. "There's not one thing we can do except continue to trail him and hope we reach his camp before it's too late."

"From the way this trail is leading, I suspect he's received communication and is going in the back door of Far West."

"Then let's stretch these horses' legs."

The light of supper fires in Doniphan's camp informed the three they had reached their destination. Peck stopped and scratched his head. "Well, I'll be—look at that, we've ended up in our own backyard, just like you said, Cartwright. As late as it is, Peck, I suggest you pay Joseph a visit, tell him where we found the camp, and ask if there's a message. We'll keep our eye on the place."

When Peck returned, Mark and Corrill had a small fire burning and supper simmering in a pot. Corrill heard the horse first. He looked up from his work and cocked his head. "If that's Peck, he's not riding the horse he left on."

They stepped back in the trees and waited until they could identify Peck. Corrill stepped out. "Whose horse?"

"Joseph's."

"You sure? If you ride into camp on some Missourian's horse, there could be trouble."

"I asked Joe if it were consecrated property and he said no."

Later, as Peck held out his bowl for the stew, he shook his head and said, "In Far West there's men lined along the edge of town, facing the militia. They looked ready for a fight."

"Still?"

He nodded. "But then, before I left, I met men on the street wandering around looking like they'd been kicked in the stomach."

"I'm trying to figure out whether that means Joseph's leveled with the fellas and told them what's going on, or if they're just looking at the bunch out here, scared to death of what could happen."

He shrugged, and Corrill said, "Well, finish up that stew and let's get on down to camp with Joseph's message."

When they were close to Doniphan's camp, Corrill said, "Get those white rags up high before they decide to shoot first and ask later."

They had gone another fifteen yards when a guard challenged them. Stepping from behind a tree, he waved a gun and yelled, "Halt!"

Peck called, "We're from Joseph Smith with a message for General Doniphan."

"Well, he's not taking communications tonight."

"I've an idea if you tell him that Reed Peck is wanting to see him, he'll be mighty glad to know about it."

The guard spoke to someone behind him and then addressed Peck. "Might as well settle down and stack your arms. Could be a while, if ever."

To the tired, impatient men it seemed a long time before the guard stood in front of them and nodded, saying, "Follow me."

As they walked through the Gentile camp, Mark was aware of Peck's heavy mood. He tried to ponder the meaning of it, but it wasn't until they stood before General Doniphan that he began to understand.

Peck handed over the folded paper bearing Joseph Smith's message. Mark watched the change of expression on Doniphan's face as he read and slowly refolded the paper.

Then Peck spoke, hesitantly at first. Soon his words began to tumble over each other eagerly.

There was a thoughtful expression on Doniphan's face; Mark watched him nod in agreement. Stepping closer to listen to Peck, Mark took a deep breath and felt the burden on his heart grow lighter.

Peck was saying, "We're not all the way you've been seeing us. Don't forget we're under obligation to obey the Prophet, but there's some who's been doing a little thinking for themselves. Many of the people are warmly opposed to the wickedness taking place in Daviess, the plundering and slaughter and burning. They're also opposed to the oppression being put upon them by the church. Just as much as any man in your army would be. But they're compelled, even to the place where they must stand and let their blood be shed for measures they don't approve."

General Doniphan jumped to his feet. With a muttered oath, he linked his hands behind his back and paced back and forth in front of the fire.

When he stopped and faced the three, Mark could see the line of pale faces circling the far side of the fire.

Now Doniphan's words caught him with their intensity. He was saying, "I promise you that these people will not be endangered when they turn to us for protection." His voice rose to a subdued roar. "Without a doubt, society must be restructured within this state. It must be the people who will determine whether or not they will be governed by priestcraft. If the people are too weak to fight off the oppression which surrounds them, I promise you they will be protected in their flight out of the state."

As the three men prepared to leave, a shadow of a smile softened the face of the white-haired general. "We're here to enforce peace, not to destroy a helpless people. You realize, don't you, that our numbers make the Mormon force look ridiculous. You might say our strength is only a statement designed for wise people." As he turned to go, he spoke over his shoulder. "I want to see the leaders of these people early in the morning."

Mark could hold his tongue no longer. "Sir, Haun's Mill—"

"Unfortunate," Doniphan rumbled. "That mob wasn't under orders. You must believe that."

Mark, Reed Peck, and John Corrill mounted and headed back to Far West. The men rode silently, each busy with his own thoughts. Mark was feeling a new appreciation for Peck and wondering if his statements would swing the tide of feeling for the Saints.

Corrill turned to Mark, saying, "I know you share the good feelings of the Prophet. I can't bind you to silence about what was said this evening."

"No, you can't," Mark answered thoughtfully. "If I felt Joseph needed to know, I would tell him. Right now I see it would serve no purpose whatsoever. Both of you are to be commended for your concern for the people."

Far West seemed to be sleeping as they rode through the streets. Silently they separated. They didn't need to remind each other of their early morning meeting with Joseph.

22

IN THE MORNING Joseph's men were waiting. It was very early as Mark walked down the street toward the store and their meeting with Joseph.

He noticed how the November frost rimmed the mud puddles as he passed the group of ragged soldiers pacing before their breakfast fires. Their faces turned toward him; he saw the questions in their eyes, the lines on their haggard faces.

As he walked, he reminded himself that these were family men. They had children and wives waiting for them, and, without a doubt, they were going to lose everything they owned. His heart squeezed with pity and he turned his face away, lest they asked the questions he dared not answer.

Later in the morning, when Joseph received a dispatch from Doniphan, Mark was there to hear him read it. "Says, 'No settlement can be approached until the arrival of orders from Governor Boggs, which we expect immediately.' That's that." His voice was filled with despair. "We know how those orders read. He said exterminate."

Mark watched him crumple the paper and pace the floor of the store. A fire burned, cheerfully crackling under the spider on the hearth. Joseph faced Reed Peck and said, "A compromise must be made, honorable or dishonorable."

Peck's gaze met Mark's, and again Mark recalled Peck's statement to Doniphan. He was also remembering his own heartening reaction. Just now he felt his heart lift in a wordless prayer, and at the same time he was accepting the calling. Those men out there must be warned, rescued.

Now Mark could no longer hold back the question. "Have you heard any more from Haun's Mill?"

"A woman was injured; it wasn't your wife. I believe Andy Morgan has gone looking for them. I'll send him to you at first convenience." He turned impatiently away.

Late in the afternoon the lookout passed the information down. Mark hurried back to the store as soon as he heard the shout. Joseph turned when Mark entered. Slowly he moved and sighed. "I know," he said heavily. "A runner brought the news ten minutes ago. I guess he expected me to duck out the back door." There was a touch of bitter irony in his voice. "It's Lucas out there. That won't help our cause in the least."

Mark thought of all the things which could be said, but he knew he was looking at a beaten man and he turned away as Joseph added, "There are several other generals out there too. Boggs is going to make certain his order is delivered and enforced." He nodded his head toward the door. "I've sent Corrill, Phelps, Cleminson, Peck, and Hinkel. I hope they'll use their heads."

There was a stir at the door. "Sir," the youth said timidly, "I have a request here from General Lucas. He requests that Joseph Smith, Sidney Rigdon, George Robinson, Parley Pratt, and Lyman Wight present themselves as hostages until tomorrow morning." He took a deep breath and lifted his chin. "At such time, if a treaty is not forthcoming, these men will be returned. Also I am sent to inform you that if such men are not forthcoming, the army will be forced to march into Far West and take them."

Joseph winced. "Kindly inform Lucas that we shall be there shortly."

They watched the door close softly. Mark sighed. "You realize that the first term of the treaty will likely call for the immediate removal of the Saints from the state."

Joseph turned and said, "I don't care. I'll be most happy to get out of this damnable state." After a pause he added, "There's not much point in resisting the militia acting under Boggs' orders. The church is over a barrel, and it'll have to comply."

Mark stood at the window, watching the men mill restlessly about the streets, but again he recalled Joseph's brave words, *I am above the law.* He turned. "Joseph, those men out there don't know what's going on. How much longer are you going to leave them in the dark?"

Joseph didn't answer. Neither did he move from his position at the table. Uneasy now, Mark sat down and waited. When Mark finally spoke again, he tried to keep his voice light. "It's getting late; do you want me to round up the men?"

"No."

At the sound of footsteps, Joseph raised his head and waited. Mark was relieved to see Corrill and Peck, but he also saw they looked as worried as he felt. "Joseph, Lucas is getting mighty edgy. He meant what he said. They're prepared to march in here and take you if you don't come along."

Joseph's grin was ragged, and Mark turned back to the window. He was busy thinking, and it was a moment before the flurry of activity began to have meaning. When the drums and bugles sounded, he sprang away from the window. "Joe, the fellows are preparing to fight. That means the militia's heading this way."

Corrill whirled, "Haven't you told the men what's going on?" When Joseph didn't answer, Corrill and Peck ran out the door. Mark watched them dashing toward the oncoming troops.

He took Joseph's arm and snapped, "Get out there right now before there's more bloodshed. I'll round up the rest of the men."

As Mark ran into the street, he collided with George Robinson. "Get Rigdon and head for Lucas' camp. Where's Wight? Bring Pratt. He's got to come, too."

When Mark reached the conference grounds with Pratt and Wight, Joseph was still talking to Lucas. Mark winced as he heard Joseph pleading for permission to stay the night with his family. He saw the general shake his head, and immediately the troops surrounded the men. As they were escorted away, the militia began to shout.

Slowly Mark walked back to Far West. He was aware of the silent, staring men as he entered the store. Mike was behind the counter. "Wanna stiff one?" Mark shook his head and wandered aimlessly about the store, worried and confused. Mike, his sleeves bunched above muscular arms, stopped in front of him. "Have they included you in on it?"

"I'm not certain I know what you're talking about."

"The bunch who fought at Crooked River are running scared. Have been since they found out they were fighting Doniphan's men. Avard, too." Mark frowned and Mike said hastily, "They're gone."

"Just pulling out, leaving?"

Mike nodded and said, "Joe told them to head out."

Slowly Mark said, "They're family men. How are they getting their women and children out?"

"They aren't. Sounds like they're leaving their families to take care of themselves. Might be it's the only way," he said apologetically. "By the way, Andy Morgan was in last night and said to tell you the womenfolk are all right. They'll be coming in as soon as they can safely pass the troops."

"Jenny, she's safe?" At Mike's nod, Mark turned away with a deep, thankful sigh.

The next day, after another sleepless night, Mark was back in the store office at dawn.

As he had walked toward the store, he realized that Far West had become a restless camp, bearing the marks of fear and discouragement. For the first time, he noticed that the tidy cabins and gardens looked neglected, while wagons and cattle still crowded the streets. It seemed the breastwork erected about the town was the only sign of real activity. He studied the block houses Joseph had ordered built. As he marveled at the extensive fortification, he couldn't help thinking that the breastwork had become the most significant landmark in the town.

"Mister?" Mark turned to face the woman picking at his sleeve with nervous fingers. "What's going to become of us?"

He took a deep breath. "Ma'am, I don't know. There's to be a meeting between our men and the generals in charge. Right now there's nothing I can tell you."

She swallowed with difficulty and whispered, "What's going to happen to Joseph?"

"I don't know." Mark saw the darkening of her eyes, the fear. Hastily he added, "All you can do is hope that Governor Boggs will be compassionate."

She wrinkled her brow, thinking. Slowly she said, "Some's saying we'll be sent out of state, losing our homes, ever'thing we've worked for. Mister, I've been here since '32. We've been pushed around for so long. Seems the revelations about Zion are amiss. Begging your pardon. But could you just tell Joseph we're tired of it all? Please, just let us go home."

She started to move away and then looked back. "We can stand to lose our homes, Zion. But how'd we ever get along without Joseph? We'd not have much to hope for. Seems we'd be adrift, not knowing which way to turn."

"But you'd still have God."

She looked blank. "That's true, but we did before, too. Seems kinda pale to go back."

At midmorning Colonel Hinkel came into the store carrying a sheet of paper. "Since you seem to be the only one around with a part of his mind left; here, read it."

It was a copy of the treaty. Mark ticked off the items. The Mormons were to deliver up their leaders for trial. Those who had carried arms were to surrender their property in payment of war debts. Arms were to be surrendered immediately, and the Mormons were to leave the state.

Thinking of the people, Mark sadly shook his head. Hinkel said, "It could have been worse. Lucas turned out to be fair-minded. He said he thought treaty could be had instead of the route Governor Boggs had advocated. It was fortunate for us all that he was willing to overlook even Joseph's last high-handedness."

Mark looked at the man and remembered the talk of the men. They had called Hinkel a fair-weather Saint, saying that in the thick of battle they had seen him turn his coat inside out. Studying the man, Mark saw only the elegant figure, the charming smile. He seemed every bit the southern gentleman. "What a motley group we Mormons are," he said softly and watched Hinkel blink in surprise.

Hinkel moved toward the door. Then he stopped and turned. "By the way, the charge against Joseph is treason."

"Of course, it must be," Mark murmured, "I—" he stopped, realizing that he had been hearing sounds of activity, and suddenly he understood. The militia was moving. Those were shouted orders, the thud of feet. He started for the door, and Hinkel said, "They've come."

Standing on the steps, they watched the army of Israel march out of town. Slowly they followed. Out on the prairie, where November had left the landscape a blank page, the army of Israel stopped and the state militia surrounded the men on three sides.

Distance blurred the shouted command, but Mark saw the men slowly surrender their arms. Within a short time, the men were marched back into Far West and placed under guard. "Well, that's that for the day," Hinkel said. For a moment Mark wondered if he detected a note of satisfaction in his voice.

Jenny had no clear remembrance of the walk from Haun's Mill back to Morgans' cabin. But sharp images had been etched on her mind: a mass of people, suddenly all kin in tragedy; the wounded and the dead. And she had found it impossible to shrink away from the ugliness and the need.

Much later there was the sensation of stumbling through the darkness with someone leading the way. And now, with soiled frock and blood-stained hands, Jenny knelt on the hearth in Morgans' cabin and blew life into the slumbering coals.

Intently, patiently, she fed bits of bark into the fire. When there was a glow and a touch of warmth, she got to her feet. Sally still stood beside the door with the sleeping toddler in her arms.

Jenny found she must ignore those haunted eyes and concentrate on Tamara. Slipping her arms under the wonderfully warm, limp child, Jenny carried her to the cot tucked back in the corner. There was a streak of dirt on the child's cheek, marked through with the water-course of tears.

As Jenny pulled the coverlet over her, Tamara curled one hand across her forehead. The blood on her hand must have come from Jenny's own. She winced as she looked down at herself and wondered whose blood it was.

Sally knelt beside the fire, shivering and weeping silently. The kettle of water was beginning to steam, and Jenny went to her precious store of herbs. Mindlessly she murmured the chant, stirred the herbs together and poured the hot water over them.

When Sally had drunk the last of the pungent mixture, color returned to her face. She placed the cup on the table and whispered, "What's to happen to us all? Will we be next?"

"Laney said no, that they have gone."

Sally shivered again, and from the horror in her eyes, Jenny knew she would talk. "I'll never forget the smell of blood, those cold, limp bodies. Why did those men shoot that little boy?" Jenny shook her head and closed her eyes against the memory of the backsmith shop and the smell of death. Her spirit shrank in horror even as taunting voices bound her thoughts and sent prickles of meaning into the scene at Haun's Mill.

The words had to be said, and Jenny gave them voice. "Good and evil. The one is wrapped in the other, and never can they be escaped. The spirits laugh with glee. How can I believe in anything good when such horror abounds?"

Jumping to her feet she dashed for the jar of herbs. Pouring a handful of the mixture into the skillet, she bent over the fire and waited until the dried leaves began to smolder and smoke. Shivering with fear and urgency, Jenny began the chant against death and disaster. When the leaves spiralled into flame, she slowly stood and, holding the skillet high, walked about the room, lifting the purifying smoke into every corner of the room.

From her place on the hearth, Sally watched. When the last wisp of smoke had dissipated, she whispered, "You really believe those charms work, don't you?"

"They are working on you—see how calm you've become?"

"I thought it was the drink." She paused and then asked, "What will the smoke do?"

"Dispel the bad spirits and give us peace."

"If that is so, why does your hand still shake?" Soundlessly Jenny shook her head. With new horror, she felt the tears rolling down her face.

Later, when the fire had burned to coals and Jenny slept, the dreams came. She awakened in terror. Sitting up in bed she stared at her hands in the pearly light of dawn. In her dream they had dripped with blood. Everything she touched became tainted with human blood, even Mark. And he had slipped from her grasping hands, disappearing in darkness.

As she huddled in her bed, trembling at the memory scent of blood and wondering why the herbs hadn't dispelled the spirits, she recalled the rest of the dream. Jenny had been wearing the crown of a high priestess. It had been shiny, glittering with jewels, but when she had stretched out her regal hand to confer blessings and power, the hand dripped blood. Looking down at her robe, she discovered it filthy and covered with blood.

Jenny and Sally dragged themselves about their morning tasks, and then at high noon, Andy came.

Seeing their faces, he slowly sat down and pulled Tamara to his lap. After listening to their experiences, Jenny saw their own horror reflected on his face. She saw the concern as he looked from her to his wife. It was an expression she couldn't understand.

It was several days before Andy began to talk about all that had been happening. Jenny learned about the siege in Far West and Adam-ondi-Ahman. He described that final disheartening scene when the men yielded their arms and their Prophet was marched away under guard. "It makes a person wonder and question. Especially when all the promises seem to be failing."

Sally's reaction forced Jenny to grasp the seriousness of it all. "No!" Sally cried, clasping her hands against her face. "That cannot be. He is the Lord's anointed in this dispensation. God's will and promises to him must not fail. Oh, where have we failed the Prophet?

"We must not allow his hands to be tied. He assured us that if we were faithful to obey, then the blessings of the Lord would shower upon us. Blessings from heaven!"

She dropped her hands and lifted her chin. "I have not failed him. I shall be obedient to the Lord's anointed until death." For a moment her face flushed and her eyes sparkled, but Jenny was caught by the expression in Andy's eyes. It was disturbing to her, but she did not understand why until much later when she was to see that same expression in Mark's eyes.

23

"TOM TIMMONS, LYMAN Wight's sent for you. Hurry, they're rounding up the men right now." Tom dumped the handful of horseshoes he had been holding and turned. Mike looked at him curiously. "What have you been doing? Folks were beginning to think you'd left with the rest of the fellas."

"Trying to salvage this bunch of old shoes. A body's got to have something to do to keep from going crazy." Mike nodded sympathetically, but Tom knew his concern was only skin deep. Mike was a Gentile, an easygoing fellow who liked everyone and refused to side with any.

Mike continued, "Joseph and all the other Mormon big shots are being pulled in. Wight sent me to find you. He wants you to be sticking as close to Joe as you can. Says follow the bunch, bend an ear and, whatever you do, watch out for Avard."

Tom frowned, "Why did you say that? Is Joe fearing Avard will turn traitor?"

"I'm in the dark," Mike said with a shrug. "I only know what Wight said. He was talking about a paper Avard didn't dispose of. Joe had told him if the Gentiles got a hold of that paper, it would give them information about the Danites that would be grounds for charging him with treason." Mike studied Tom thoughtfully before adding, "Looks like your bunch is knee-high in hot water right now." He was still shaking his head when he left the stable.

Late in the day, following the orders he had been given, Tom eased through the militia lines and nosed around until he discovered the open area where the prisoners were bedded down. It had begun to rain about the time Tom left Far West. The cold drizzle continued all night.

Crouched close to the guards placed around the men, Tom shivered in his wet clothes. He couldn't help wondering who was more miserable—Joe and the other prisoners, the guards, or himself.

Late that night, he heard the low murmur of voices coming from the guards. Cautiously Tom crept closer to listen. The rumble of conversation was punctuated by an occasional word and a mocking laugh. As Tom listened, he realized the guards were betting each other on the outcome of Joseph's trial. Tom moved restlessly in his hiding place. Only his promise to Wight kept him quiet. All instinct demanded he attempt to rescue the Prophet.

He had nearly dozed when the clink of metal stirrups startled him. Inching forward, Tom immediately recognized General Lucas' cold voice speaking to Wight. "You are sentenced to be shot to death at eight tomorrow morning," he was saying. "You and the rest of the men."

Just as Tom moaned and ducked his head into his folded arms, Wight's voice thundered back, "Shoot and be damned."

And Lucas admonished, "We were hoping you would come out against Joseph Smith. It would save your hide. I fear your fate is settled."

When Lucas turned and strode away, Tom moved back in the shelter of the willows; the rain was dripping down his back. All talk had ceased, even the guards were silent except for sober monosyllables. Tom was left to his thoughts as he crouched, shivering, under the willows. He tried to imagine the Saints without Joseph, and could feel only despair.

Without a doubt, every person in Israel's camp would feel the rending. Tom tried to analyze his faith and compare it with some of the strong ones. His gloom deepened when he finally acknowledged his feelings. Without Joseph there didn't seem to be anything to have faith in. Shaking with cold, he waited for the dawn.

The sky was just beginning to lighten when Tom managed to mingle with the men around the corrals. Later he discovered he had a ringside seat. When the restless milling of the crowd ceased, there was a roll of drums. General Doniphan and his brigade marched in and took formation.

Slowly the crowd parted. Tom watched the bedraggled prisoners being brought to face Doniphan. Tom studied the impassive faces of the dark-clad Joseph Smith and his tattered men. Remembering Lucas' statement last night, he felt his heart tighten in horror and pity. He felt that somehow all life had been suspended. Even the early sunlight touching the faces of the men seemed to pause before moving on.

There was silence and a hushed expectancy as Doniphan walked regally toward the line of prisoners. For a moment his figure outlined against the dawn seemed larger than life. His roar filled the arena. "You have been sentenced by court-martial to be shot!" He paused until the echo of his voice died away. "Your actions have not been the actions of honorable men. But I have indicated in the past that I will not disgrace myself or my men by sinking to mob tactics, and that is just what I deem today's order. My brigade is here, not to carry out those orders, but instead to take up a line of march out of this camp. I refuse to be a part of cold-blooded murder."

General Doniphan turned and held out a white paper. For a moment a vagrant pencil of sunlight touched the paper, and Tom was filled with a sense of good omen. With awe he watched the orderly run across the field carrying the paper, which he thrust into General Lucas' hand. Tom watched the confusion of expression and sound as General Lucas quickly gathered his men about him and retired from the field.

Stealthily Tom made his way behind the line of tents, seeking a place to listen as Lucas called the court to order and read the paper to them. In addition to the declaration which he had made on the field, Doniphan had included his instructions, which Lucas slowly read aloud. "If you follow through with the execution of these men, I promise you I shall hold you responsible before the courts."

Before Tom had a chance to bring his news to Far West, the message was carried by Lucas and his men. When Tom reached the town square, it was packed with Saints. He studied the tired, careworn faces gathered to listen as General Lucas delivered the verdict in a cold, passionless voice.

Tom was watching the people as the man delivered his speech in ringing tones that filled the square and echoed back, underscoring the finality of the situation.

It took another Saint to understand the quiet expressions on these faces—the softening of the men's furrowed brows, the tears on the faces of Joseph's parents, Emma's tightly closed eyes. These things might not seem like high emotion to Lucas; but Tom knew what it meant.

These people were not only hearing that the lives of Joseph and his men had been spared, but they were hearing a vindication for themselves. Once again they were to be given an opportunity to pick up the staff of their religion; and through obeying their Prophet, they would give God a chance to fulfill His promises to them. That was hope reborn.

Tom turned away. Most surely there would be prison and trial, but that bridge would be crossed later. He grinned. Joseph had survived the death sentence; didn't that prove the Lord was on his side?

Before the glad tears had dried on the faces of the Saints, there was another order. All of those who had participated in the war were to surrender their arms and prepare to yield their property to pay for the expenses of the war.

When Lucas paraded the prisoners through the streets of Far West, Tom was there. He had spotted Mark in the crowd and edged close. Together they watched the prison wagon move slowly through the streets, carrying Joseph Smith and his men.

Right at the last, in the confusion created as the wives and mothers of the prisoners pressed close to the wagon for a final word with their loved ones, Tom hissed in Mark's ear, "Get Jenny and head for the state line.

You won't be in the wrong; that leg kept you out of the battle. But if you don't leave, they'll find some way to get to you. Be off, get my sister, and go."

"Since Haun's Mill I've been trying to reach her. Once Joseph's men broke and ran, we were placed under heavy guard, and I can't get out of town. But Andy's been with the women nearly all the time, so they're safe."

"You don't understand, Mark. It's for you I'm fearing."

"I'll see," Mark answered slowly. "You know Joseph asked me to keep a hand on the affairs around here until Brigham Young can help out. I'm about the only one of the bunch left. Brigham and Heber Kimball have left the state. Avard and most of the other Danites who didn't get caught have left, too." He paused and then asked, "What about you?"

"Right now I'm the only smithy around. I'm better known for hanging around the stable than for my Danite activities. If I'm lucky they'll be concentrating on their list of names and leave me alone."

Despite Tom's warning, Mark lingered on, trying to reassure the bewildered people. But within the next week the town of Far West crumbled. With the surrender, rioting mobs freely entered the town, destroying and looting. Tom couldn't help wondering if the Gentiles had gained new confidence since they knew the remnant of the army of Israel—those who had been forced to yield their arms and surrender property—were being held prisoner in Far West.

A committee had been assigned to investigate the affairs of the Saints, to determine what property would be assigned to them in order to enable them to leave the state. But for now rioting intensified, and the spirit of lawlessness grew.

In the end, in the midst of the confusion, Mark simply walked out of Far West. He was only one more restless prisoner managing to escape.

That evening when he walked through the Morgans' door, Jenny stood staring at him, unbelieving and without hope. When he held her, he knew the difference. With his hand under her chin, he lifted her face. "My dear, we are going to leave this place as soon as possible." Studying her face, he saw all the horror of Haun's Mill reflected in her shadowed eyes.

Mark turned and led her to a bench. She sagged helplessly against him. "Tell me all," she said. "I know only Haun's Mill and Andy's view of the troubles. It isn't that bad, is it?" He couldn't understand the expression in her eyes. Had she lost all hope?

He was silent a moment, thinking of his hope and wishing desperately that she would listen to him. He sighed restlessly, trying once again to be patient.

"It is total. Jenny, Missouri has crushed us. All Joseph's people are paupers. If we escape with our lives, it will be a miracle." He couldn't withhold the truth of the situation; Jenny was too intelligent to stand for anything except the truth. But at the same time, he clung to her hand and tried to reassure her with a smile.

"All because we would not obey the Prophet," she said. Mark looked deeply into her eyes and saw still another shadow but could not name it, except to say that it resembled failure.

Their flight was aborted before it began. Andy brought the news. "General Clark is in town. Tomorrow every Mormon man is to be in Far West to receive orders." He eyed Mark disapprovingly, knowing his plan to leave.

Mark saw that look, but there was nothing he could say. In Andy's eyes he was apostate, another Judas to deny Joseph.

The next day Jenny, Sally, and Tamara went with Mark and Andy. While Andy drove the team, he told them that General Clark was the commander and chief of the Missouri Militia. Andy faced the women and said, "You see, this is getting to be very serious."

"It's snowballed," Mark added. "The whole situation has just been getting bigger since Joseph moved to Missouri. First it was the run-in with the local justices; then it became an unpleasant game with the militia. That built until now we have the commander and chief of the state militia out against us." Mark saw Jenny shiver, and knew she was beginning to understand the seriousness of the situation. Mark himself began thinking of Tom's advice. What possible evidences of guilt could be brought against him? Then he remembered the walnut clock at the cabin and winced.

In town there was an additional stir of excitement. Avard had been captured as he attempted to flee the state. When Mark heard, he carried the news back to Andy, saying, "Every man here is shaking in his boots. No one has the slightest idea what'll happen now."

"I don't understand," Jenny said slowly.

Mark said, "Rumor's such that it's looking like Avard had Joseph wrapped around his finger. It's Avard who's supposed to be responsible for the Danites. If they manage to pull out all the information about their activities, there're many men who could be ruined."

The air of dread and excitement was rising in the town as the people waited. All the Caldwell County Saints were in Far West, crammed into the town square when General Clark and his men arrived.

While their families huddled miserably, shivering in the cold wind, fifty-six men were separated from the others. Now prisoners of the state, they were advised they were to be sent to Richmond for trial.

As the charges were read against the group, General Clark paused to look out over the town. "The citizens of Daviess County are faced with the task of trying to restore a measure of order to their lives." His voice was dry. "It has been ascertained that prior to his surrender to General Lucas, Joseph Smith ordered that the plunder taken from the citizens of both Caldwell and Daviess counties be gathered and stored in one area in order to avoid any one person being charged with the particular crime. This attempt to shield his people has expedited the recovery of goods. It has also enabled us to honor the request of some of your past churchmen, now referred to as dissenters. We have been able to recover some of the household goods belonging to David and John Whitmer, Oliver Cowdery, and a Mr. Johnson. These goods will be returned to them." There was a stir among the people and for a brief moment, Mark grinned.

The final business of settling the disposition of the Mormon's property was handled before General Clark rose to address the people. His stern voice rang with authority, and his message settled into the hearts of the people. "This state has suffered irreparably because of the character, conduct, and influence of these Latter-Day Saints. We have endeavored to restore our state to the best of our ability by the actions we have chosen to take against you. As you know, the orders of the governor of this state were that you be exterminated and not allowed to remain in the area. Had your leaders not surrendered, we would have, of necessity, been forced to follow through. Now I say you must leave.

"I don't ask that you leave before spring, but do not delay for another season. The doom of your leaders is sealed. You have been the aggressors; these difficulties have been brought upon you by yourselves. I advise you to take it upon yourselves to become citizens of decent standing wherever you choose to live. To follow any other course will bring ruin upon you."

Tom lingered beside Mark and Jenny while the Saints wandered about the town. There was confusion, disbelief and, on several faces, relief.

"Yes, people do look stunned," Mark remarked softly to Tom. "I can hardly believe it myself. But it feels like the end of an era to me. Joseph's church can't endure this punishment and survive."

Tom looked slowly around, studying the faces of his friends. He was thoughtful as he spoke. "Mark, religion aside, these people are fighters. They're where they are today because they have no better sense than to dream big and not think about the consequences. Sure, they're confused, but change?" He was shaking his head. "Once you pick a way to live, it becomes mighty hard to change. If by some fluke Joseph manages to survive this, he'll land on his feet. Might come up with a better idea to make the whole promise of Zion even more attractive." He paused for a moment, then added, "Joe's still my friend, and I'm bettin' on him. Right now I feel mighty sorry for the fella. I guess I'll go sympathize and give him the latest news."

Tom rode away as Mark and Jenny, Andy and Sally climbed back into their wagon. When Andy picked up the reins, Tom circled back to them. "By the way, Mark, don't bother going back to your place. Them Missourians aren't gettin' much outta you."

"What do you mean?"

"Burnt. Was up there last week and everything's a big ash heap." Tom turned his horse toward Richmond. "Going to visit the jail; gotta see the Prophet."

When Tom was led into the enclosure which served as home and office to Joseph, he remarked, "Sure's not many around; what's happened to the others?"

Joseph stood up, saying, "Some had bailable offenses. I understand they posted bond." He grinned slowly.

Tom said, "I'm guessin' the state'll see no more of them, right?"

"I 'spect." After a moment, Joseph added, "We'll be moving on to Liberty jail pretty soon." Again he was silent, and Tom watched his features settle into a countenance of defeat.

"You're thinkin' this is the end of the road, no matter that you said in your brave speech?"

"It hurts to see men I trusted turning from me to save their own hides. I should've known I couldn't trust a man as blood-thirsty as Avard. He told everything he could think of in court. All about setting up the Danites, even showed around the constitution. There's things in it that makes the lawyers think they have grounds for charging treason against me. Judge King's trying hard to prove we're setting up a kingdom. A man without a speck of religion can't even think like a man of God," Joe said, moving restlessly about his small quarters.

Tom admitted, "There's things we talked about in meetin' that an outsider wouldn't understand. Like how we swore to protect the secrets of the society."

"He charged me with being the prime organizer of the Danites, and went on to say they were set up first to take care of the dissenters, then to fight the Gentiles and take over their property."

"I can see where if a man wasn't in the kingdom, he wouldn't understand the Danites bein' necessary." He shot a glance at Joseph and continued, "I suppose he told all about how the first presidency was made up of all the officers, and how in your blessing you prophesied that the Danites would be the means of usherin' in the millennial kingdom with God's help. I'm supposin' they wouldn't be understandin' a man feelin' so strong about all this that he would swear his life to be forfeit if he was to reveal the secrets of the society?" Joseph didn't answer, but Tom knew it wasn't necessary.

Tom had a question that had burned in his mind for weeks. "Joe, mind if I ask you something? I've been strugglin' with my faith. It seems the spirit's tellin' me to ask you. You've been preachin' how the Lord's askin' us to set up Zion, and how we're goin' to be successful and how the Lord's goin' to be fightin' our battles for us." He paused to take a deep breath; looking up at Joseph he said, "Joe, we've had one big pile of failure. How are we to believe now?" Tom watched the big man sitting opposite him. He was slumped forward, resting his arms on his legs and staring at the floor.

When Joseph lifted his face, Tom saw the despair. "Tom," he spoke slowly and carefully. "I want you to understand what all this means. Simply, I've been betrayed. These men—not just Avard, but Wight, Pratt, Robinson, Marsh, Stout, Rich—you name them, from one end of the roster to the other, they've betrayed me. The church has betrayed me just like Christ was betrayed by Judas."

Tom got to his feet, standing awkwardly and wondering how to take his leave. Joe looked at him. "Remember, Tom, no matter how you judge me, God intended for the army of Israel to be victorious, but these men were just not perfect enough to withstand so large an army."

Joseph followed Tom to the door. "You know some of the things that contributed to the failure. There were those who wouldn't consecrate their property, who wouldn't obey council." He added, "Come back. The Lord's still working. I have a feeling that there's still important things ahead for us." A half-smile lit Joseph's face, and Tom saw the dreamy expression in his eyes. For just a moment a tingling excitement, a promise of hope reached out to touch Tom, and he nearly forgot his disappointment.

24

MARK PULLED JENNY'S hand through his arm and cuddled it close to his side. The day was clear and pleasantly warm for November. "I'm glad you agreed to a walk this Sabbath day," he murmured. "Seems the Morgan cabin is getting more crowded every day. Jenny, we need to be pushing out of the state."

She raised troubled eyes and studied his face. "Mark, what did you think of all we were hearing this morning?"

"Are you talking about the letters Joseph wrote to us from prison?"

She nodded and then added, "Brigham Young is being a good fill-in for him. But he admitted he'd carried news to Joseph. I wish he hadn't told him that some of the Saints are calling Joseph a fallen prophet. I wish he hadn't troubled him with the news."

"And you didn't care for Joseph calling Hinkel a traitor, saying there was a parallel between him and the way the Savior was led into the camp of enemies? I saw you frown."

"Well, something about it made me uneasy. I keep wondering who he will denounce next." She was thinking of the label *Oh, don't* men as she looked up at Mark. But he didn't seem uneasy, and she sighed with relief. Then she added, "It couldn't help Joseph to be spreading information about Isaac Russell's setting up a little church of his own. And it's too bad Brother Young had to admit to defending the Prophet before the high council of the church. Seems right now it would be best if we didn't have to be airing our linen in front of the Gentiles." She sighed.

"Well, there's not much being aired, compared to what could be—" Mark abruptly ended his sentence and headed Jenny down the trail, away from the turnoff to Haun's Mill.

"Do you suppose Brigham's let Joseph know how his brother William's going around telling people that if he'd had his way, Joseph would have been hung years ago? What ever does he mean by that? I know there's been trouble. William's just jealous that Joseph is the Lord's anointed."

Slowly Mark said, "There's some whisper of talk that Joseph has the position William was to have held."

Jenny was silent for long minutes. When she spoke it was slowly and thoughtfully. "Are you saying that William was supposed to have been the anointed one instead of Joseph?" She turned away. Her shoulders drooped and Mark wondered what she was thinking.

They continued their walk, quietly, arms linked together as they wandered down the winter-crushed path. When Mark pulled Jenny to a halt under the spreading branches of a giant oak, he lifted her chin and studied her eyes. When he bent to kiss her, there was only a sad, dutiful pressure from her lips. He wrapped his arms around her and snuggled her close, but it was minutes before she relaxed against him.

He found himself wondering if repeating the gossip about Joseph had hammered a new wedge between the two of them. He thought of the cabin they had shared, and immediately the memory of Joseph standing in front of their fireplace intruded. Mark pressed his lips tightly together and tried to shove the picture out of his mind.

"Jenny, let's go now, before the rest of the Saints start trailing out of here with their wagons. I'll get a buggy to take us to the river. From there we can take a steamer to Saint Louis. I've a mind to look around Springfield, Illinois."

She pulled back and looked up at him. Her eyes seemed to probe the very depths, making him uneasy with all his unspoken thoughts. He was aware that both of them were carrying problems they dared not discuss with the other. Mark found himself wondering if there would ever be a day when all of those questions could be faced.

She spoke, but she was ignoring his plea. "Why did Joseph say those things in the letter Brigham Young read today?"

"Well," Mark said hesitantly, "I suppose he was apologizing, but he was also defending himself. I'm glad he had the manhood not to deny responsibility for the Danites. I suppose saying Avard was responsible for teaching erroneous things is justifiable."

Jenny interrupted, "But why did he bring up the subject of polygamy? No one has accused him of any such thing."

Mark was surprised to hear sadness in her voice, not the indignation he expected. He studied her open, questioning expression. "Because," he spoke slowly, deliberately, waiting for a change in her eyes, "there's talk. Always the taint has followed Joseph."

Jenny frowned slightly but she was still gazing steadily at Mark. "I don't believe it. I can nearly assure you those are lies."

He must push one last time. "Do you know Cowdery has stated that you visited Joseph in his office on more than one occasion?"

She reacted, but before the flush touched her face, astonishment flooded her features. "The office! I went there to get books, to—" She paused and then said, "Did he talk about all the *old* women who went in there too?"

"Jenny," he caught himself, but he had her attention. When she looked up, he said, "Then you won't mind settling in Springfield, will you?"

Mark's question stayed with Jenny during the weeks that followed. But even more than the question was the dark expression in his eyes.

The little cabin was crowded. Its one room offered not the slightest privacy, and as winter settled in, even the quilt serving as a curtain between the bunks was discarded in an attempt to keep the occupants warm.

The pressures of living under those circumstances forced a routine on the two families. During the day the men were gone, mostly listening to the latest news from the state legislature concerning the Mormon problems. Just lately they carried back tales of Corrill's attempt to win concessions with a petition to the legislature from the Mormon people.

Andy added, "After all the trouble Joseph and the people heaped upon Corrill, I'd have expected him to be gone without troubling himself anymore with the woes of the Saints. But he was right in there, bending the ear of anyone who would listen to him. It didn't do any good, though, and the restrictions remain. We must all be gone before another spring planting."

Mark retorted, "In his plea he was rather rough on Joseph and the Danite leaders, but all the talk didn't do much. However, from reports drifting back it's beginning to look as if there's a good chance the legislature will grant a little stipend to help the Saints get out of the territory. I'm thinking it's starting to look as if we might as well pull out as soon as we can."

"Might as well," Andy replied. "I intend to go as soon as I dispose of this place, and for what they're offering, I'd be well off just to dump it."

Several days later, while the men were in town, the two women were sewing. Their conversation had dwindled away and Jenny was busy with her own thoughts. While half-heartedly stitching together scraps of cloth to mend a torn quilt, she recalled the Sabbath walk and Mark's conversation.

She was still remembering how he had looked at her. She was sure he believed she was lying to him. Her heart was sore. But, then, it had been for a long time. To discover he doubted her was only the capstone on the troubled feelings she had been having for months.

Never would she be able to explain to him all that was on her mind. One thing was very certain—she had discovered it in the cloudy, jumbled thoughts. There was no hope. Joseph's dream of Zion had failed. Not even in the green book had she found one concrete evidence of hope. Looking back, she realized that since the day she had retrieved the green book from the cabin, life had begun to crumble around her.

She had not quit trying, but everything she had attempted had failed. All the herbs and charms, all the incantations and chants had failed. Even the final promise of contacting Adela for help had disappeared. Adela Martindale was not Adela of the red chiffon.

"Ouch!" Jenny stared at her pricked finger and watched the blood drip onto her sewing. Blood. Sabbat. Was she receiving a message? The memory swirled before her. She hadn't thought of the event for many, many months. But suddenly without warning the sickening memory of the sabbat made her jump to her feet.

For a moment she stood paralyzed as the remembered smell of blood overwhelmed her. Against her closed eyelids she saw the silver chalice floating in front of her.

"Jenny!" Sally's needle was poised. "It isn't fatal," she said dryly. Her attempt at wit didn't touch Jenny, and she added, "Jenny, what's the problem? I've been watching you and Mark for a week now. You won't even look at each other."

Jenny sat down and squeezed her finger. She tried to think of an answer, but there was only truth. "Mark thinks I've been unfaithful to him."

Cautiously Sally asked, "What has made him say that?"

When she lifted her head, their eyes met and Jenny whispered, "Sally, don't look at me like that. I've done nothing. It isn't what he said, it's the way he looks. There's Cowdery's story about my going to the office in Kirtland. I saw then that Mark believed me unfaithful. Sally, before all this, we would have laughed. Now everything is twisted and ugly."

Sally's hands were limp and motionless in her lap. Slowly a strange expression crossed her face. She focused on Jenny and said, "You mustn't let it discourage you. Regardless of what Mark says, you must be true to your religion. Your whole eternity depends upon that."

Puzzled, Jenny studied the curious expression and tried to pick sense out of the pieces of information being thrust at her. "Sally, you know Mark's apostate from the one true religion, but he didn't bring religion into it. It was us. Me—he was doubting me. I love Mark with all my heart. It hurts terribly to have him treat me this way."

Abruptly Sally crossed the room and knelt beside Jenny. Clasping her arm in a surprisingly strong grasp, she said, "Look at me, Jenny. You must give him up. I've heard him pressuring you to go to Springfield. He's trying to get you to leave the church. He's thinking that now's the time to force you to go." Abruptly she dropped her hands and rocked back on her heels. "Or do you?"

"Do I what?"

"Believe, like some of the others, that Joseph is a prophet fallen from grace, that he no longer holds the keys of the kingdom. You know what his letter said. The Lord himself assured Joseph that he still holds the keys of the kingdom, and, furthermore, Zion is not dead but alive!"

Sally's voice rose in a cry of triumph that sent prickles of excitement over Jenny. She searched her friend's face. "Sally, if only I could recapture my faith. I'm so dead inside. After Haun's Mill I didn't believe you would ever be happy again. Now I'm the one whose faith is faltering and whose hope is gone."

Sally threw her arms around Jenny. "Oh, I will pray for you that the Lord will make you strong enough to do His will, even if it means you must renounce Mark himself."

Jenny leaned back and slowly asked, "Do you remember what Joseph has taught? That God has put the right way within us, and that it is natural and easy to follow along the way we should go, that God will make us have a witness to the way?"

Sally leaned forward, her face was shining as she whispered, "Yes, Jenny. I remember. I really believe it. We are to follow that inner light. Sometimes it comes across only as a big desire, but I know it is right."

Jenny looked at her curiously for a moment. Now cocking her head, she was lost in a response that surprised herself. Slowly she said, "Sally, I don't think that's totally correct. At least right now, this moment, I'm feeling some strange tuggings taking me every which direction.

"For a moment, mostly because I loved so much and because I know Mark is so wrong, I believed that I must give him up, run forever from the pull he has on my life. But there's something else."

She paused and lifted her face. It was Sally who said with awe in her voice, "Your face is shining like an angel. I didn't believe before that you could see things. Now I'm sure of it. Tell me, what do you see?"

Jenny's eyes were wide. Slowly she said, "I'm seeing, I'm remembering. Our wedding. There were yellow roses and—" now she was whispering, "so much spirit feeling there. I'd never experienced it that way. I still smell the roses, I still know those promises I made to Mark were the most important words I've ever said. Sally, it was like the whole heaven and earth witnessed our vows. But there was more, someone or something that transcended every influence I've ever known. I know it was there when I said, *Mark, I promise you.*"

Now Sally whispered, "Was it God?"

Jenny opened her eyes wide. "Oh no. It wasn't God. I know the god influence." Unexpectedly she shivered and looked at Sally. "God is fearsome. This was like love with eyes. Do you know what I mean?" Obviously Sally didn't.

Thinking hard now, trying to understand her deepest feelings, Jenny said, "Well, I'm believing that my inner self is telling me to follow Mark. But it isn't easy to decide that. It's as if there are two Jennys inside arguing that out. I want badly to be here waiting for a miracle to happen to Joseph, but that isn't to be. Somehow, I know that the only right way is to go with Mark. Perhaps he will be won to the only true church through my going with him now."

"Jenny, that's not possible. He's taking you away from the church!"

But Jenny wasn't listening. She hugged herself and sighed with relief. For the first time in months she had a strong, sure sense that she was making a right decision. She couldn't wait for Mark to come.

"Sally!" Jenny jumped to her feet and tossed aside the sewing. "I want to go meet the men."

She was nearly to Far West before she saw the lone horseman. It was Mark. When she ran to him, he slid off the horse and stood waiting. His face was clouded with worry, but when he saw her open arms and lifted face, he began to grin.

"Oh, Mark! I'm ready; let's go now!" His arms were tight about her and Jenny sighed with contentment. Nothing else was necessary. She didn't see his lips move or hear the whisper, "Thank you, Lord Jesus."

MORNING
STAR

INTRODUCTION

JENNY TIMMONS' STORY begins in the first book of this trilogy, *The Wishing Star.* As an eleven-year-old child from a poor family, living on the fringes of South Bainbridge, New York, Jenny becomes acquainted with Joseph Smith. Jenny's brother, Tom, introduces the mysterious youth who is engaged in searching for money with his peep stone while working for Josiah Stowell.

Life for a poor child living in a small New York town in 1825 could have been insipid were it not for Joseph Smith, the curious stone, the money diggings, and the strange, shivery feeling of excitement it all gave Jenny. There was Pa's green book, too.

That first year Joseph's money digging nets him trouble and the town of South Bainbridge, excitement. After it is all over, Joseph moves on, but Jenny doesn't forget him.

The next summer Jenny's father starts his westward trek, and the first leg of the journey lands the family in Manchester, New York. The following year the Timmons family—except for Tom and Jenny—move farther west. The brother and sister gain employment with Martin Harris—Tom at the livery stable, and Jenny as a hired girl in the Harris home.

Lucy Harris is good to Jenny and she learns to *do* for Mrs. Harris, developing skills she had not learned at home. Jenny also attends school and becomes friends of Joseph Smith's family. Again the paths of their lives cross.

Honoring a promise to Jenny's mother, Mrs. Harris sees to Jenny's religious education. Jenny joins the Presbyterian church, but at the same time delves into the mysteries of the green book that she has stolen from her father.

Also, during this period Joseph Smith marries and comes to live in the Palmyra-Manchester area just long enough to find the gold Bible.

Martin Harris, one of the first three witnesses to the *Book of Mormon,* soon becomes deeply involved in the gold Bible work. This new interest quickly pulls life down around Jenny's head. As the Harris home is broken apart by his new interests, Jenny and Tom are forced to move on.

Mark Cartwright, a youth both Jenny and Tom knew from the South Bainbridge days, steps into their life with an offer which takes them to eastern New York State.

Jenny's maturing years are spent away from Tom while she works and finishes school. During this time the whole focus of her life is wrapped in a twisted desire to have life on her own terms. This desire is fed through her friendship with Clara and the secret green book.

Meanwhile, Tom, who has never lost interest in Joseph Smith, follows the fledgling prophet to Kirtland, Ohio. When Jenny visits Tom, all the old fascination is reborn, and Jenny moves to Ohio to become a member of Joseph's church.

It isn't long until Jenny discovers that to be a follower of Joseph Smith demands total obedience. When he instructs her to marry, and tells her whom to marry, she proposes to Mark Cartwright.

The second book of the trilogy, *Star Light, Star Bright,* begins with hope and promise as Jenny and Mark celebrate their marriage and start their life together in Kirtland, Ohio.

There is the promise, and by rights it should be fulfilled. It is the promise of young love, the "true" church, and a life together which is to extend throughout eternity.

But promises require obedience. Soon Mark is tapped for the first major missionary endeavor to England. Jenny is left behind. The letters dwindle, but that was the result of problems surfacing in the young couple's life.

Problems are surfacing in the young church, too. With every quarrel and painful misunderstanding seen between the young couple, the counterpart is mirrored in the uneasy marriage of church and people. But for both, life struggles on. Problems are resolved and an uneasy peace effected.

That next spring Mark returns from his missionary journey with news so shocking that Jenny nearly surrenders her marriage. Mark has become a Christian and he makes certain that Jenny knows this is something world-shattering and totally different than the message Joseph has given to his followers.

It is Mark who surrenders and follows Jenny as she joins the exodus to Zion. He surrenders, not because of Jenny's strengths, but because of her weakness and fear.

Even before Joseph's church was established, the young prophet had received revelations commanding the people to set up an earthly Zion, to be founded in the state of Missouri. Immediately after the church was organized, a group of converts migrated to the state and settled in Jackson County. Unfortunately, the Missourians didn't accept the command of the Lord given through Joseph. From the beginning there were serious problems.

Long before the expedient removal of the Kirtland Saints to the state of Missouri, the difficulties in Missouri between the Saints and the Gentiles had forced the governor of the state to step into the affair. The Saints were subsequently ordered to leave Jackson County and move farther north to Caldwell County.

But shortly after Joseph's move to Caldwell County from Ohio, life became just as difficult in this new area. Once again the prophet stepped over the boundary set for his people.

It is no wonder that Jenny, fearful and sensing the greater dangers lying ahead, turned from her new religion back into the ancient religion of nature. No wonder, that is, since she was certain *her* understanding of God was right and Mark's was wrong.

Before long the troubled issue resulted in bloodshed, and finally the Mormons were forced to leave Missouri. Once again they were driven out, penniless and homeless, while their prophet, Joseph Smith, remained behind in jail.

1

JENNY THRASHED HER head on the pillow and moaned. The movement sent pain stabbing through her head. Eyes closed, she groped for the pillow beside her. She felt an empty expanse of smooth linen, and her eyes flew open. Sunshine flooded the room and shot arrows of pain into her eyes. Covering her face, she moaned and rolled over.

It was at least ten o'clock; the sun glared into her bedroom. The white curtains hanging over the open window were motionless.

Mark must have left hours ago, moving quietly to allow her to sleep. Her lips twisted in a perverse grin. Strange that a man as intelligent as Mark should so readily accept her excuses, even giving credence to her midnight tryst by his gentle trust and unquestioning acceptance.

Especially strange, since he claimed a special place with God. He called it being born again, redeemed. Her claim to religious devotion was as genuine as his. But never would she try to explain that the rituals and traditions she practiced with a select group of women were rooted in the ancient worship to the true god of nature. She was still wondering about Mark when she fell asleep again.

When Jenny awakened later, the sun had shifted off Mark's pillow, and the white curtains moved just enough to allow the summer scents of the garden to invade her rest.

As she slowly bathed in tepid water and dressed, she felt the last traces of her headache leave. By the time she left the bedroom she was hungry, and life began to press in with its demands.

Jenny paused at the head of the stairs and admired her home. This Springfield, Illinois, home contrasted sharply with the little log hut in Missouri—and even with the stone house in Kirtland, Ohio. She kissed the tips of her fingers and flung kisses about the house.

"Beautiful one!" she cried. "Good morning to you, fair walls and shiny floors. Polished furniture and gleaming windows, how silently you keep your distance until I'm ready to be your mistress again!" As she walked down the stairs, she continued to admire the ivy-sprigged wallpaper, the plush furniture in the newest shade of plum. She cocked her head for just a moment. Were the green and plum really suited to the deep rose of the new carpet?

Jenny crossed the hall and went through the shaded dining room with its dark mahogany, feeling again the urge to shake the room into life. But the room seemed alien no matter how she polished the furniture and shifted the china. Perhaps it was the china.

She frowned at the rose pattern, a duplicate of the dishes Mark had purchased for their first home. They did make her think of the possessions destroyed in the fire in Missouri. She looked at the grandfather clock just as it began to boom out the hours in its authoritative bass. Noon?

With a sigh Jenny hurried toward the kitchen, still rubbing her arms, conscious of the chill of the room. If the spirits were active, they weren't friendly ones. Why would the room goad her into an unwilling memory of those terror-filled months in Missouri?

In the kitchen the cold remains of Mark's lonely breakfast sat on the table. She chewed her lip, reading the message of the room. Mark usually tidied up after himself. Today a smear of cold beans crusted the single plate. A crumbled slice of bread lay beside an untouched glass of milk.

Guilt touched her. She saw in the scene symbols of her neglect as well as a touch of uncharacteristic absentmindedness in Mark.

As she cleared the table and began to heat water, her thoughts were busy tossing the guilt back and forth. *But the coven called, and they can't be denied,* she defended herself. As she ate bread and drank milk, she was thinking of the group of witches. Was it luck, or was it spirit need that had sent petite, dark-eyed Crystal into her life?

Soon after arriving here, just when Mark's associates had undertaken the task of introducing them to Springfield society, Jenny had met Crystal Matison, wife of a newly appointed state representative, Haddon Matison.

As Jenny cleared the table and poured hot water over the dishes, she pondered the events that had drawn her into the coven over which Crystal had charge. What joy, what sisterhood after the barren years with only occasional contact with Adela!

Chuckling, Jenny recalled Crystal's daring move. Very shortly after becoming acquainted, Crystal had casually dropped a talisman at Jenny's feet.

Jenny sighed, straightened her shoulders, and looked around the kitchen. Only a practicing witch would recognize the signs: the wisp of rosemary, the crossed twigs, the hint of lavender. Now she frowned and moved her shoulders uneasily.

It had been a year since she and Mark had moved to Springfield—a year of being back into the craft on a practicing basis—and still she felt the familiar void in her life. The powerlessness, the lack of growth and direction in her life filled her with frustration.

Just last night, after the coven had held their solstice ritual, Jenny had confided to Crystal her disappointment. After listening, Crystal had shrugged and wiped at the perspiration on her face, saying abruptly, "I've no sympathy. You've been advised to go to sabbat. You knew when you started meeting with us that we were no more than white witches. If you want more, you know what must be done."

In frustration Jenny had cried, "And you—why will you be content to be a powerless white witch?"

The woman had looked at her with a stony face. "I might wonder what you have in mind. I enjoy the craft, but I intend to be master of my own fate. You might say I'm frightened enough to accept my own limitations. I have all the power I need. I enjoy our coven and the ritual of worship. *I am,* and that is all I need."

Jenny slowly dried the dishes and returned them to the cupboard. She was frowning, puzzling over Crystal's statement and the strange icy blast her words had left.

Restlessly, Jenny took up her trowel and walked slowly out the back door and down the garden path. It was past noon. The herb garden was shadowed and cool. Perhaps digging through the soil would straighten out her muddled thoughts.

As Jenny ducked under the chestnut tree, her hair tangled in the branches. Impatiently she shook the branch and picked at the pins in her hair. When the coil of her hair slipped down her back, she was freed. But the action immediately plunged her into being more than Jenny.

Kneeling in the soil, breathing deeply of the mingled odor of pungent herbs and moist earth, Jenny thought again of those words. *I am.* Jenny sensed a hidden meaning, and knew only that she was left curious and vaguely uneasy.

Jenny pulled weeds from her herb garden and dug into the loam with her fingers. The crumbled soil smelled faintly of last autumn's leaves. As she lifted her hand to sniff at it, her mind immediately filled with scenes of their life in Missouri.

Though the events had happened eighteen months ago, the damp earth scent bridged the gap as if it were yesterday she and little Tamara had walked the woodland paths as serene and happy as woodland nymphs. But the serenity was an illusion.

She winced, remembering the ugliness and death at Haun's Mill. Closing her eyes she saw the tortured faces of the Saints. Homes, family, even faith were stripped from them.

Settling back on her heels, she stared up at the sun-dappled trees and wondered about the people. Were they happy now? How easy it had been to drop the faith as soon as she left Missouri! But what about them? If their new life was not better than hers, they were in a desperate situation.

And what about Joseph? He had escaped from his Missouri prison, and his flock had settled across the river in Illinois. What a commotion that had caused! She grinned. Good old Joseph had landed on his feet just as she expected. The newspapers had been full of the stories. Illinois had welcomed the Saints with open arms.

A twig snapped behind Jenny. Without raising her head she murmured, "Is that you, my husband?"

"Is that a disappointment?" Mark's voice was heavy, bitter. Jenny got to her feet and turned. He looked at her soiled hands and the tumble of hair spilling down her back, and she saw the frown and his tightened lips.

"You're angry because I went last night," she whispered, widening her eyes to allow him to see the pain. It worked; the cold expression softened a bit and he bent to press a kiss against her forehead. But he turned away, and she knew the matter wasn't resolved.

She had tried to tell him the truth about her nature worship, about God, but that had failed. He didn't understand, and discussing it only fortified this stony wall between them.

She tried the dimpled grin, and that won out. As she carefully held her soiled hands away from his dark suit and lifted her face, he murmured, "At least my rival is a bunch of women, dotty with their strange ideas. It could be worse."

He stepped back and pulled a black lace scarf from his pocket. "Letty Harrison asked her husband to pass this on to you. So now Letty is a member of your group! I am amazed that Lew takes it so lightly—he's a deacon at the First Presbyterian Church."

Jenny's voice was throaty, "Everyone takes it lightly except my husband. True, most of the husbands are being indulgent, but some are seeing the value in it all."

"Value?"

Jenny ticked off the list. "How do you suppose Lew Harrison won a seat to the senate? He knows. Remember the ulcerated leg of Mather Johnson? It wasn't that addle-pated doctor who cured him. Mark, I could go on and on—the storm that broke up the rioting last month, as well as the reversed finances of William Frank that kept him from running for the House of Representatives."

"And your group is taking credit for all of this?" Mark turned away. "Come, let's see if there's anything for dinner. After these meetings of yours the Cartwright household suffers for a week."

As Mark followed Jenny to the house, he stuffed his hand in his pocket and felt the letter. He pushed it down out of sight, deciding he needed more time to think about it. The outrageous letter had initially evoked a solid *no,* but now, strange as it seemed, it was causing him to have second thoughts. Most certainly those second thoughts would never have been necessary had it not been for the scarf and those midnight meetings deep in the forest.

Mark turned away from the door and went instead to sit on the porch swing. The pleasant street reflected all the values of a prospering, growing city. Just recently the city had become the seat of state government. Springfield was attracting settlers with money and influence. In response to demands, the small city was quickly assuming a cosmopolitan atmosphere.

Up and down the wide, tree-lined street, houses similar to the Cartwright home had been built during the year since Mark and Jenny had arrived.

He contemplated Jenny's reaction if he dared propose leaving this comfortable white bungalow. With a sigh Mark shook his head.

"Mister Cartwright, sir—" A woman stood at the gate, peering up at him. "I've come from the post office. They gave me a letter to deliver to the missus." She still hesitated at the gate, glancing uneasily beyond him.

"Mrs. Callon, if I remember correctly," Mark said, going down the steps toward the elderly woman clutching her shawl about her head. "I haven't seen you for some time. I understand your husband is ailing."

" 'Tis, but I intend taking him to the doctor. I don't believe in the likes of this witchin'." She watched him stuff the letter in beside the first and glanced sharply at him. He opened his mouth to speak, but she hurriedly continued.

"Good thing you were accepted by the Supreme Court to practice law in the state of Illinois before it come out that your wife is in the witchin' business."

Mark heard Jenny's step behind him as she answered, "Why, Mrs. Callon! You talk as if it's bad. I'm a white witch. I'm not out to harm a soul. You need to investigate the craft. We witches are intent on helping people, doing good to all mankind. See, someone's in need of the power to move nature in response to our needs. If you'd like, I'll come past with some things to help your husband."

With a snort of alarm, the woman backed toward the street. " 'Tis using the devil's powers to do the devil's work and then lay claim to the powers of heaven."

Jenny watched the woman leave, then in a bemused voice she said, "Mark, your dinner is ready." Mark pulled the flap of his pocket down over the letters and followed his wife into the house.

After dinner, while Jenny was washing the dishes, Mark took out the letter Mrs. Callon had given him. "Jenny, here's a letter. Mrs. Callon brought it from the post office."

With her hands in suds, Jenny exclaimed, "Letter! Who ever could be writing to me?"

"Don't you want the surprise of discovering on your own?" he teased. "Here, I'll dry dishes for you. There are dark circles under your eyes. I know you're tired."

"And no one believes it's anything except a silly lark," Jenny brooded. He knew from the shadow in her eyes that Mrs. Callon's words had disturbed her.

When she had dried her hands, she took the thin folded sheet and carefully opened it. "Oh, it's from Sally. How did she ever know where to find us?"

"We told her before we left Missouri that we'd be going to Springfield."

"It's been so long. Why did she delay writing?"

Mark had to admit, "Likely she needed confirmation. I didn't tell you, but Joseph Smith was through Springfield last autumn. He stopped to see me at my office. I'm sure he carried the news back to Sally."

He saw the brief flare of anger in her eyes and watched as she chewed her lip. "If Joseph was here, it was for a reason. Why didn't you tell me?"

"I didn't think it important to the welfare of the Cartwright home." He said lightly, "He was on his way to Washington and hadn't time to spare on us."

"Washington," she mused. "Whatever for?"

"He was just following up on his campaign for national notice and sympathy. You saw the newspaper articles. You know the Nauvoo newspaper, *Times and Seasons,* had published accounts of the Haun's Mill massacre as well as a complete story of the Saints' expulsion from the state."

"I also know of the nationwide interest and sympathy," she said soberly. " 'Tis only fair."

For a moment Mark was silent. He was thinking of the reply to those articles given by the editor of the *Chicago Democrat.* That editor had stated that the stories were being used to the profit of the Saints. Given more bloody marks in their history by Illinois or any other state, he predicted, the sympathy generated would insure that the Mormon religion would become firmly entrenched in the land. Mark sighed and reviewed his unwilling involvement in it all.

He looked at Jenny. "Joseph carried hundreds of affidavits and petitions to Washington seeking redress for Missouri's persecutions. Right off he bumped into what we've been hearing so much about lately—states' rights."

Jenny nodded. "I remember, but I thought it mostly dealt with slavery."

"No, it's a touchy situation. The state's constitution makes the legal entanglements far-reaching. Washington couldn't afford to get involved. There're too many out there just waiting to see how far Washington and the Constitution can be pushed."

"So they wouldn't do anything for him."

"Not only that, but seems Joseph let the cat out of the woodshed. Since he's gone home, Missouri sent a few notes of their own. Boggs furnished Washington a complete transcript of the Mormon problem in Missouri. That didn't set well, and Washington told Joseph's lawyer, Higbee, to take the case to Missouri."

"I guess that settles that," Jenny said soberly.

"If Joseph is inclined to leave it there," Mark replied. "I hope he will."

Jenny was reading her letter. "Sally mentions Joseph in Washington. That's how she knew we were here." She read silently and then said, . "There's much happening. Oh, Mark, I feel so out of touch!"

He couldn't help asking, "You'd trade this for another frontier town?"

She looked around her home for a moment and with a sigh lifted the letter and began to read aloud:

"Nauvoo is a lovely place. The name means a beautiful plantation in Hebrew—the Gentiles had called it Commerce. We were here from the beginning and have watched the struggle from a plague-infested swamp with a handful of poor houses to what it is today. In just one year's time it has grown to a place to be proud of. Joseph laid it out in nice square blocks. There's a goodly lot for each home. We started out with log houses, like Missouri, but already there's brick and limestone buildings going up.

"But we'll not forget our past. Already Joseph says Nauvoo is just a stopping place until we are strong enough to claim our inheritance. Now the army is being built up. The temple will be set high on the hill. Plans are in the making, including the temple, a grist mill, and other such businesses. In another year we'll be on our feet again.

"Which comes to the purpose of my letter. Jenny, I fear for your soul. It's going on two years, and you need to be thinking of Zion. There's to be a gathering. The prophecies still hold: Joseph warns us that destruction still awaits this nation. Only the true church will be saved."

Jenny lifted her face and Mark watched her rub at the tears. "There,"
he chided, "there's nothing in that letter to make you cry."

"Oh, Mark, you'll never understand!" She was shivering, and now his
thoughts were on the past. Jenny's fear was a reminder: at one time her
brother Tom had asked if his fear of God was keeping him from following
Jenny to Missouri. And when he had joined the wagon train, he had given
her his whispered promise, *In sickness, in health, I pledge you my love.*
Could those dark shadows in her eyes reflect a soul sickness?

With a sigh, Mark slowly pulled the other letter out of his pocket. "I've
had a letter from Joseph asking me to come to Nauvoo. Seems he needs
another lawyer, and he knows Illinois has granted me a license to practice
law in the state."

2

MARK STOOD AT the window of his second-floor law office looking down on Springfield's busy main thoroughfare. Accustomed as he was to the brisk passage of buggies and wagons, and the cluster of women visiting on the streets while their parasols and billowing skirts forced a detour upon the male pedestrians, today's unusual activity kept him glued to the window despite the piles of paper on his desk.

When he heard the quick steps on the stairs, Mark turned to face the door. It was Aaron Turnbull, his partner.

Aaron nodded at the case of books on the floor. "You've settled your affairs to the point you must pack law books?"

"Yes." Mark said with a note of regret in his voice. "The house has been sold and Jennifer has begun to pack our belongings."

"I still can't quite convince myself you'll really do this. Certainly I can't believe it's a wise decision." His curious eyes held that wary expression Mark had come to expect since he had admitted his connection with Joseph Smith, the Mormon prophet. Mark sighed and turned toward his desk.

"By the way," Aaron said, "is there any possibility you're related to the evangelist, Peter Cartwright?"

"Yes, he's a brother of my father. Why do you ask?"

"Well, he's a part of the reason the streets are nearly impassable. He's holed up in the lobby of the Continental Hotel."

"I should pay him my respects," Mark murmured, shuffling through the papers on his desk.

"The other reason is that the esteemed prophet is in town. I understand he's the guest of Judge Adams. That makes me question his religion."

"Joseph's in town?" Mark said in surprise. "I didn't know. I'm sure he'll want to dine with us. You say he's staying with Judge Adams? That really surprises me, although I know little about the man. It's just—"

"Well, let me fill you in." Aaron said shortly.

"If it's only conjecture—"

"It isn't. You need to know if you intend to make Nauvoo your home and practice law there. Abe Lincoln has circulated a handbill. I'll try to get you a copy of it, but for now, Lincoln's charged him with being a forger and swindler."

"I wonder what the connection can be?"

"Since he's involved with the Masons, I'd guess it has something to do with that."

"That's impossible. Joseph is dead set against the Masonic Lodge, always has been. His gold book strongly teaches against secret societies."

Aaron shrugged and went to his desk. Mark closed his desk drawer and said, "Well, I'll head for the hotel and then try to find Joseph."

"That won't be difficult," Aaron replied in a muffled voice. "When I left the hotel they were having a shouting match in the lobby. If you look out the window, you'll notice their audience is streaming inside. I doubt you'll get a ringside seat."

For a moment Mark weighed speed against dignity and decided that speed was the more important. He headed for the hotel.

Aaron was correct; the lobby was full. Mark elbowed his way through the crowd. Although he hadn't seen his uncle Peter for years, he recognized the man.

Joseph was talking. Both men were seated in comfortable chairs in the lobby, but only Joseph looked the gentleman at ease and sounded—Mark winced—like the same old Joseph. His clothes were costly, elegant and rumpled. Peter Cartwright looked the part of a circuit rider—dusty, threadbare, and careworn. The man leaned forward with hands on knees and gave Joseph his undivided attention.

Joseph's eyes flicked across the crowd, lighted up when he spied Mark, and then returned to the evangelist. He was saying, "I'm convinced, sir, that of all the sects in existence today, we'd find the Methodist to be the closest to being correct." His broad palm warded off Peter's words as he said, "Now mind me, they are not correct right now, but if the sect would advance in the knowledge, they would take the world."

Peter moved impatiently and said, "Sir, you see us all wrong; we've no intention or desire to take the world. I'm not spending my life on horseback to preach the gospel of human endeavor. I'm here to preach Jesus Christ as Savior of each individual who comes to Him looking for grace to rescue him from the wrath of God. You, sir, are advertised as living a life of sin. If you would be great in God's eyes, you must repent."

Joseph's voice rose, overlapping Peter's, and Mark squirmed. When Mark realized it was Joseph's voice spewing out the curses, he began backing away, and then the voice stopped him. Joseph was on his feet; with clenched fist raised he shouted, "I proclaim that I am here to raise up a

government in this country of America, these very states, which will overthrow our present form of government! I promise you, I will lift high a
religion which shall overcome every form of religion in these United
States!"

There was a moment of silence and Peter Cartwright lifted his shaggy
head. Slowly he said, "The Bible tells us that bold and deceitful men will
not live out half their days. I venture to say that the Lord will send the
devil after you one of these days unless you repent."

"No," Joseph's voice overlapped Peter's again. Breathing heavily he
added, "I prophesy that I shall live and prosper while you die in your sins."

In the weeks that followed, Mark often thought of the exchange between his uncle and Joseph Smith. He hadn't told Jenny of the encounter
and didn't intend to. Right now, recalling that incident, Mark looked at
their new home and shook his head.

Jenny and Mark stood on the tiny porch of a weatherbeaten house,
nestled in the woods halfway between Warsaw and Nauvoo, Illinois. Mark
looked at Jenny's dismal face and said, "It could be worse."

"You mean Missouri. I loved the little cabin."

"I'm rejoicing right now. After paying off the mortgage, the money we
realized from the sale of our home in Springfield completely paid for this
little patch of earth and shabby cottage. Besides, the agent promised that
when—I say if—the railroad comes through here, they'll want to buy our
land."

His toe nudged at the boxes and barrels clustered on the porch.
"Frankly, given the condition of the state, it'll be years before that can
happen. Right now I'm just happy to be out of debt."

"Oh yes, I remember the battle cry back home." Jenny's voice dropped
to mock the well-worn refrain. " 'Thirteen hundred citizens and fifty miles
of railroad.' And all we've seen are molehill piles of dirt."

"But given everything, you've had your wish. We are now residents—or
nearly so—of Nauvoo, Illinois."

"Do you suppose we've been wise to choose the country instead of
waiting to build in Nauvoo?"

"Are you fond of sleeping in a tent? Few homes are finished, and
they're mostly little Missouri-style log cabins. Even Joseph's house is small
and cramped. Don't forget, my dear, Nauvoo has been in existence for
only one year and a few months.

"Now shall we go inside and see what surprises await a couple who grab
up real estate, sight unseen, just in order to have a roof over their heads?"
Mark opened the door and led the way.

Jenny sighed and said, "At least it looks as if it has been occupied recently."

"By folks fleeing the Mormons. No cause, that's certain, but nevertheless—" his voice trailed away.

Jenny ignored him and marched through the rooms. "There's a good kitchen with a decent stove. The floors are clean but terrible. The walls need to be papered, the stairs are in need of repair. Oh, for a clothes press!"

"Unless our furniture arrives before nightfall, we'll be forced to spend the night on the floor."

"Bless my precious brother for volunteering to drive the wagon so we could ride the stage together." Jenny's voice was warm. "Since he left long before we did, surely he'll be finding us shortly."

"Then I'll bring in these barrels and find firewood," Mark said as he removed his coat and hung it on a nail beside the door. Jenny eyed the coat and shook her head in amusement as she rolled up her sleeves.

Nauvoo, even in late August, was hot—and much different than Jenny had anticipated. True, the mighty Mississippi did wind like a circling arm around that rearing bluff of their land, but she hadn't expected to find forest treading nearly on the toes of Nauvoo's residents.

And the riverport was a disappointment—a rattletrap wharf, a ferry, and a tumble of shabby dinghies. In her mind she had imagined a real port with steamers. In truth, the real port was in Warren, close to Warsaw.

That next week, she had a chance to view the river and town from the high point. The land already showed activity in preparation for building; Jenny looked downstream to the line that was Warsaw. "Why?" she turned on the seat of the wagon to address Mark. "With all this water, why go beyond Warsaw for a port?"

"The river rapids keep the big ships downstream. Joseph plans to build a wing dam which should take care of the problem. But Warsaw has trouble with sandbars."

Jenny shrugged and turned back to study Nauvoo. Mark said, "Homes are to be built much as Joseph planned in Zion, with large lots and wide streets. I understand some of the poorer Saints have been given land for farming on the outskirts of town. Right now Joseph's selling off parcels of land in town. I hear he's given some of the parcels to the favored ones."

"Will we be out of favor by buying through the agent instead of going to Joseph?"

Mark shrugged. "Joseph's lots are expensive. There are big interest payments on his land purchases. I've also been investigating this man, Galland, who's sold the land to the Saints. Part of his dealings has involved forged deeds. I preferred not taking any chances, and fortunately I found this little house and land just out of town."

"Gentile property," Jenny said. She sighed and continued, "This new place is a poor substitute for what we've given up. But Joseph has reminded us again and again that the Lord expects us to sacrifice for Zion. Also he's promising us something much better than we've left behind. Why does Joseph need another lawyer in Nauvoo? Is it something to do with the land problem?"

Mark shook his head. "He didn't give me any details, just offered me a good position."

He turned away and Jenny continued, "I wonder where we'll find Tom. I haven't seen him since he left the furniture."

"He isn't in town," Mark replied. "I have been doing a little asking around. I know where Andy and Sally Morgan are living. If we hurry, after we visit Joseph's store we'll have time to stop by their place." He turned the wagon and flicked the reins across the horses' backs.

Slowly they made their way down Nauvoo's main street. Mark pointed out a two-story log house with a white clapboard addition. "That's Joseph's home. I don't know who owns the other houses on this street, but there's evidence of building going on all over town. I've seen brick and limestone buildings going up. From the size of them I'd guess them to be businesses."

Jenny was still silent as Mark pointed to another building under construction. "I understand that building is to be the *Times and Seasons* office." At her questioning look he added, "Newspaper and printing office. I just heard Joseph's men made a covert trip back to Missouri to recover the press and type they'd buried in Far West. The next place is Joseph's store. Looks like he has a good-sized office upstairs."

He looked at her drooping mouth. "Cheer up, dear wife; in another year this little town will compete with the best of them. Just the sheer force of numbers will guarantee that."

"What do you mean by that?" Jenny asked slowly as she turned to face him.

"Progress. I hear the latest missionary endeavor to England has netted two hundred converts. Right now they're on the way to Nauvoo. And more Canadian converts are coming. It's whispered that the army's being reorganized. That's bound to put heart into the Saints. See that hill? It's been marked out as the spot for the new temple."

"There was a revelation that the temple in Missouri was to be commenced in 1839. I haven't forgotten that. Has Joseph?"

Mark studied her face. For just a moment he wished his answer could be yes. "Jenny, in April of last year, Brigham Young and several of the other brethren slipped across into Missouri and rolled a log into place at the temple excavations, thus starting construction on it." She grinned with delight. Mark jumped from the wagon and looped the reins over the hitching post.

As Mark turned to help Jenny from the wagon, he was caught motionless for a second, seeing sharply the contrast between this Jenny and the Jenny he had known in Springfield for the past year. Now neat in her dark calico dress with its demure white collar, serene with smiling lips and neatly coiled dark hair, she was a wife to make any man proud.

He frowned, for a moment caught up with that vivid picture of last year's Jenny. With troubled eyes and drawn face, wearing a frown that seemed to indicate she was miles away in thought, her hair tumbled and her home looking as if she'd forgotten it existed, Jenny had sent signals to Mark which filled him with despair.

Mark now took Jenny's arm and smiled down at her. Her eyes danced with anticipation, and the contentment on her face told him she knew herself at home once again. But that same contentment made Mark sigh. He need not remind himself that his experiment had failed. In Missouri he had been confident that once they moved to Springfield, all Jenny's strange ideas would disappear. Once under the teaching of a Bible-believing church, Jenny would see the truth. Since her early years he had sensed her forthrightness and intelligence, and that had led him to believe in her desire for knowledge and truth. But belief was not enough. His silent waiting for time to right the wrongs wasn't working.

As Mark mulled over the past year, he briefly wondered if moving to Nauvoo represented a decision not to wait for God to act in Jenny's life. Did the decisions he made reflect a lack of trust in his life?

When they stepped through the door of the general store, Mark and Jenny were struck by the mingled odors. "It's obviously a store carrying everything," Mark muttered. He could identify smoked ham, pickled herring, even sour pickles crowding the open barrel. The smell of leather goods, and the nose-prickling lint and dye wafted from the far corner. But the line of black books caught his attention.

As Jenny swung her basket and headed for the dry goods, Mark stopped in front of the display of books. "Them's just Bibles, we're outta the *Book of Mormon*," the youth behind the counter advised him.

The excitement was growing in Mark, but he carefully picked up the book and slowly turned. "Jenny, you don't have a Bible, do you? No good Mormon should be without one."

As she stopped and turned, he saw the wary expression in her eyes, and for a long moment those gray-brown eyes held him as if searching out deep thought. Did her ivory cheeks pale even more? He waited. "No,

Mark, I don't," she said slowly. "I've never felt the need—maybe the curiosity, but not the need."

"Curiosity should be enough," he said, reaching into his pocket for coins. "Besides, we're reforming."

Again there was that stillness as she waited. "We haven't been as faithful about attending the Sabbath services as we ought. Now I intend to take my wife to church each Sabbath," he said, looking into her eyes. "And you'll need this black book to go with your new dress."

Her dimples broke through and she laughed up at him. Coming to him, she said, "Then, my husband, it seems I need a new bonnet with a plume of ostrich feathers to make the costume complete."

With a grin he answered, "You may have two if you can find them here."

She wrinkled her nose. "I win. Not here, but I've seen them already. Down the street a home has a display with a sign advertising bonnets made to order."

The clerk was nodding his head vigorously as he accepted Mark's coins. "That's Hannah Ells; she's a dressmaker."

Jenny finished her shopping and the clerk accepted more of Mark's money, saying, "You're new, but Nauvoo's a goodly town already."

Curiously Mark questioned, "How do you know we are new? Nauvoo is growing too fast for you to know everyone."

The clerk looked surprised, then cautious. "Seems the careful thing's to make a point to know your neighbor. I must say, there's a good feeling about the state. Sir, you don't know, but when we first came from Missouri, we were a sorry lot—hungry and nearly naked. But the folks in Quincy were right good about taking us in and giving us a hand until we got on our feet. We'll not be forgetting their kindness. Makes a person take a deep sigh of relief after Missouri."

3

Jᴇɴɴʏ HAD MADE her curtains, scrubbed the worn floors, and stocked the large pantry. She polished the banister on the stairs that led to the two bedrooms on the second floor, and bemoaned the lack of a clothes press.

Mark pruned apple and pear trees, cut underbrush, and pulled weeds. He also grinned mysteriously at Jenny but said nothing until the day Tom came and the two of them harnessed the team.

At her questioning frown, he responded, "It's a surprise. We'll be needing a hot apple pie. I put a basket of early pippins in the kitchen."

The pie was fresh from the oven and Jenny's cheeks still flushed with the heat when the team returned. She reached the front door in time to see Mark and Tom wrestling a blanket-shrouded bundle out of the wagon. On the porch they paused to wipe their sweating faces and unwrap the blankets.

Jenny caught her breath and reached out to touch the satiny wood. "Cherry," Mark informed her. "It was the only clothes press to be had in town, and because we're Mormons, it cost twice what it should. There're some carpets too."

Jenny was still stroking the wood, remembering for an unaccountable reason the gleam of the McBriers' furniture as it was being carried out of their home and loaded into a wagon. For a moment she wanted to gather the clothes press into her arms.

Tom snorted in disgust and Jenny looked up at him. "After what happened today, I'm guessing the Missouri stories have made their way to Illinois. The things they said!"

"Weren't overly friendly," Mark agreed mildly.

With a sinking heart, Jenny whispered, "Tom, tell me. Don't keep anything away, that's worse than not knowing, even if it's only stories."

"Oh, they started in on Joseph for what he gave out at conference time. Said if that's the case, they wouldn't be extending credit."

"Tom, what are you talking about? We weren't here in April and we've no way of knowing—"

"Joseph cancelled all the Saints' Missouri debts. He just plain outlawed them, saying it was unchristian to demand payment, anyhow."

Jenny was still staring at Tom incredulously when Mark said, "That's only one thing we heard. Right now it seems they're looking for offense, and there have been other irritations. The people of Hancock and Adams counties are fussing about the Legion, and they're also saying Ripley has been running surveys.

"The charge today in Warsaw is that Ripley has been plotting out the whole countryside for Mormon territory. Seems a Mormon community to be called Zarahemla is being plotted to take in Montrose County across the river. Most certainly Ripley and his men didn't win friends for the cause when they drew up street and property lines running right through the homes of the Gentiles living there. The townfolk took it to be a pretty good hint that they should pack up and leave." Mark was silent for a moment, then said thoughtfully, "I hadn't realized there was a move to create a new territory of this section of the state."

Tom shrugged and added, "Now they're blaming us for runnin' off their cattle, stealin' their tools and everything else. Boats get cut loose and we get blamed. A store is robbed and they look at the Mormons. Now they're a-callin' the Nauvoo Ferry the horse thieves' ferry."

Mark nodded soberly. "I'd heard back in Springfield that Nauvoo is a haven for criminals from three states. I discount that, but since we've arrived, it seems obvious there's an undue amount of traffic in stolen horses."

Mark saw Jenny's stricken face and reached for her. "Now, don't fret. Surely you didn't think we'd be free of problems, did you?" He circled her with his arms and looked at Tom. "Come on, let's go have some of that pie."

"Let's get this monster upstairs first," he grunted. "I'd enjoy my pie more knowing we've lived through the task."

The next day while Mark was dressing for his first meeting with Joseph, Jenny picked up the conversation. "In Springfield they were talking well of the Saints."

"Springfield's not neighboring with the Saints. Right here we're close; in fact, you might say we're sitting on the fence between the Mormons and the Gentiles." He paused to grin, but Jenny saw the mirth didn't reach his eyes as he added, "We might need to adjust to having them heaving rotten pumpkins back and forth over the fence."

"Things can't be that bad?"

"I don't suppose they are, but the talk won't help. The Saints'll get their back up and then there'll be trouble. Right now, Illinois is in big trouble with her finances. There's also the political side. Every fella with dollar signs or votes in front of his eyes will be currying the favor of Joseph. That won't help his cause with his neighbors.

"When Joseph first landed in Quincy in '39, a bunch of politicians were there, among them Stephen A. Douglas. Joseph lost no time in getting acquainted and extracting promises from him to get the state legislature to guarantee protection for the Saints."

Jenny was wearing a thoughtful expression when he turned from the mirror. "Look, I'll be in a meeting with Joseph all day. Put on your bonnet and come along. You can visit with Sally, and I'll join you there this afternoon."

When Mark slowly climbed the stairs to Joseph's office, he was thinking of the last time he had seen the prophet. He winced and his steps faltered. "Mark Cartwright, whatever possessed you to show that letter to Jenny?" he muttered to himself.

Surprisingly, as Mark walked into the room, Joseph stood and leaned across his desk with his hand outstretched. "Mark Cartwright! Am I ever glad to have you join our staff! I'll need all the legal advice I can get during the next few years. As you can see, the Lord has important plans for the people. Granted, when we were in Missouri, everything looked hopeless. Little did I dream we'd have to take the Illinois route to accomplish the Lord's designs."

His grin was disarming and his expression frankly curious. But Mark decided to avoid mentioning the last time he had seen Joseph.

Mark took a deep breath and said, "I must admit, it is because of Jenny that I've agreed to come."

"At least I've one loyal Saint in the family," Joseph said with a faint shrug. "You challenge me. I'll trust the Lord to make a loyal follower of you."

He turned to pick up a sheaf of papers and Mark realized the Prophet was once more in control. He winced abruptly as he realized Joseph was also his employer once again.

"You've no doubt kept informed of all that's gone on in Nauvoo. You can see the progress we're making in building up the city. Now let me tell you about what's going on behind the scenes. I trust you're aware of the conversion of Dr. John C. Bennett."

"No, but from your voice I gather I'm supposed to know something about the man."

"He's a doctor, a physician, but he's also informed about politics. We need help on that score. Right now he's working hard to get the Nauvoo Charter through the state legislature."

Mark frowned, "I'd heard the Mormons were asking for preferential status. I discounted that just as I have most of the other rumors, such as asking the Nauvoo area be designated as a separate territory."

Joseph grinned, "Rumors do fly about. That's all right—doesn't hurt people to know we have a little power."

For a moment Joseph's eyes were fastened on Mark's. A growing question loomed in those eyes, and for a moment Mark thought he should throw all the rumors out before the Prophet. But Joseph returned to the sheaf of papers.

"I'll have you meet Bennett later and go over the charter. Right now it reads just the way I want it to read, and I don't want an item changed. I just want you to check the spots which might cause problems. Don't bother to say all the goody things. I know the Lord will work out the details."

"Then why do you want me to look at it?"

He paused and straightened in his chair. "Because if there are problems, I want to be able to say, 'The esteemed Springfield attorney, Mark Cartwright, has checked the charter and approves of it.' Do you get the picture?"

"I get the impression that you are trying to buy me. What's the price?"

"Only a place in the kingdom. I promise you, Mark, your sins are forgiven. You shall inherit the kingdom along with the best of my men. Eternal kingdoms are yours."

"You mean I can skip the other steps? The surrender of property, the obeying of the laws, the—well, whatever you come up with tomorrow. You know you've done a lot of that. In the beginning I had to join the church or be damned. Now I have to do this, that, and whatever else you say, or I'll be damned."

"Mark, I can't make special concessions to you. I don't know what the Lord will demand of us tomorrow. Remember, I'm in this just like you are. He demands obedience of me and I can't buck Him on that."

Joseph jumped to his feet and paced quickly back and forth in front of Mark. "Prison was a humbling experience to me. I grew closer to the Lord, more holy than I've ever been before. He showed me the order of things. Mark, you've no idea of all the Lord has in store. I can't reveal it all now; there just isn't time. Besides, some things must wait—the Lord hasn't given me the complete plan yet."

"Joseph, I'm not wagering for a part in your kingdom. You know how I feel about all this. I didn't hide my feelings when we were in Missouri."

"Not my kingdom—it's the Lord's kingdom. Besides, Mark, you love your wife. You wouldn't want to make decisions that would completely cut you off from her, both now and for eternity."

Mark was still pondering the last statement of Joseph's as he walked back to the Morgan home. There had been an underlying note of excitement in the man's voice, an excitement which stirred uneasiness in Mark.

The Morgans' log house was little better than their Missouri home. Sally opened the door to him and immediately turned back to Jenny. With amusement, Mark studied the sparkle on her face and realized that Sally and Jenny were scarcely conscious of his presence. Playfully Andy clapped his hands over his ears and grinned at Mark.

Sally interrupted her discourse long enough to push around Andy. "Oh, Mark, stay for dinner—we need to talk."

"With me?" he asked in surprise.

"No, Jenny and I. It's been so long."

"I hope we survive this meal," Andy said gloomily. "Let's take a walk. I want to show you a few things."

"No," Sally declared. "Dinner is ready. Here, Jenny, put the plates on."

Andy raised his voice. "Did Joseph tell you about the writ?"

"Sit down, Mark," Sally ordered. "Here's the applesauce."

"What writ?" Mark asked cautiously.

"Then he didn't, or you'd know."

"Andy, don't talk business."

After dinner they walked through Nauvoo's streets. Sally and Jenny chattered; under the cover of their talk, Andy muttered, "Joseph's been served with a writ from the new Missouri governor, Reynolds. The Missouri problems have reared their head again." He glanced at Mark. "I knew he'd got wind of it this afternoon. Must have hightailed outta there just after you left his office."

"Hightailed? You mean the sheriff didn't catch up with him?"

"That's right. I suppose it'll be a while before we see much of the Prophet." Mark looked at Andy, hardly believing the grin of amusement he was seeing.

Sally scooted back to them. As Andy lifted little Tamara, Sally leaned close to Mark. "Did Andy tell you what that place is?" She pointed to the little white frame building across the road.

Mark surveyed the building, "No, but I'd guess it's a store of some kind."

Sally leaned closer. "A brothel!" she hissed. "Some say it's Bennett's idea. I can't believe the Prophet will tolerate that once he gets wind of it."

"I can't believe Joseph would have that under his nose and *not* know about it," Jenny said slowly, looking quizzically from Sally to Andy.

Mark watched Jenny for a moment, at first feeling elation; then the questions began. They were back in Joseph's territory. With a tired sigh, he waited until the women moved ahead before he took up the conversation with Andy.

"Have you any idea what the charges were in the writ?"

"No, but you know Joseph and Hyrum escaped from prison. On Missouri's books they are fugitives. You didn't think the Legion was just for show, did you?"

"I'd heard the army was back in business," Mark answered slowly. "Frankly, I hoped it was just a result of Joseph's boyish desire for the theatrical."

"It isn't. You know he hasn't given up on Zion."

"I know that in Springfield he was expending a lot of energy cursing the Missourians, especially Boggs."

Mark took a deep breath and turned to face his friend. The passing years had changed Andy. The boyish exuberance was gone, and Andy's mouth had settled into a grim line of determination. Besides the unexpected touch of gray in his hair, Mark had noticed the shadows in his eyes.

"Andy, how's it with you? Do you still believe Joseph is a prophet?" Andy hesitated only a moment before nodding. Mark pushed, "With the keys of the kingdom, that he's the Christ for this dispensation? Do you really, Andy?"

They walked in silence. The mid-September evening was full of the clarion echoes of life. They were hearing the shouts, the ring of a horse's hooves against stone. There was a distant sound of a waterfall, the faraway toot of the ferry and, close at hand, the innocent laughter of their wives.

Mark sighed and said slowly, "Andy, I believe a man's relationship with his God is the most important part of life. Not just from man's viewpoint, but from God's, too. This makes me believe God'll do more'n we could ever hope to make Himself known to man. The information is there if man will go about getting it in the right way. Part of it is believing that God's not going to strike a man down for having an honest question about what the Lord expects of him."

"Well and good," Andy said slowly, "but there's got to be a point of contact. Where does that begin? Sometimes us humans are so poor and ignorant we have to let someone else do our thinking and make contact with God for us. Surely God won't fault a man for that."

"He'll fault a man for stumbling over truth and refusing to acknowledge it is truth. There's a verse in the Bible that's been burning into me. I can't quote it, but the gist of it is that there's a way that seems right to man but it ends up leading to death."

"How can God fault a fellow for doing his best?"

He shook his head. "Only, seems to me, if the fella is ignoring the obvious . . ."

"How's that?"

"God wouldn't put out two books with completely different instructions."

"You're back on that old tack, about not believing that the Bible is translated correctly."

"No, I'm talking about the *Book of Mormon* contradicting the relevations Joseph's giving out as from the Lord."

Andy turned and grasped Mark's arm. "Who told you about the revelation? Who's been talking? This is not to be spread around right now. With the other problems, we can't afford to let it leak."

Mark knew his face gave him away. Andy dropped his hands and shoved them into his pockets. He watched Andy hunch his shoulders as he muttered. "Forget it, Mark; forget I even mentioned it. Do me a favor and pretend this conversation didn't happen, huh?"

Mark promised, but Andy's excitement made him ponder the question he had so innocently raised. Whatever the secret, the revelation must be very important.

4

Monday DAWNED—A bright, clear September morning. Mark had just left for Nauvoo. Jenny sat on her front steps, enjoying the morning and waiting for the wash water to boil. In the kitchen the sheets and towels waited beside the stove, along with a bar of brown soap shaved into wafers to dissolve quickly in the boiling water.

Jenny's front door faced east; to the south, beyond the pasture, the forest pressed close. To the west, the trees and the craggy slope of their land dipped down into the deep river gorge. When the night silence held the land, Jenny could hear the water crashing over the rocks upstream, and she could imagine it gentling, moving into the shallow basin at the bottom of the gorge before taking up its rapid trip down the Mississippi River.

The gorge was a separator—only a minor gouge in the terrain of the land and water, but a deep chasm between neighbors. She knew Gentiles owned the land on the bluff across the basin. Beyond them was the Gentile town of Warsaw, and already Jenny was learning they best be shunned.

Turning her face to the south, feeling the sun and hearing the peaceful morning song of the birds, Jenny brooded. Was Nauvoo to be only another Missouri? But nature said *no,* and she tried to take heart from the message.

The water was beginning to simmer. Jenny went to stir in the soap and push her sheets and towels into the tub.

When she came back to the porch, the mood of her thoughts had broken. The steps needed to be swept, and the apple tree had released a shower of fruit to the prying fingers of last night's wind.

For a brief moment, she was caught and separated from the familiar pattern of her thoughts and the demanding spirit-tug which so often held her captive for days at a time. She thought of yesterday; the Sabbath-day worship had broken the tide of spirit control. But it was more than that.

On the Saturday before, the day she and Mark had shopped in Nauvoo before visiting Andy and Sally, she had felt the nudge.

The linens were threatening to boil themselves out of the tub. Jenny pushed herself off the step and hurried into the kitchen.

When the last of the clothes were pinned to the line, Jenny returned to the step, realizing now her need to do some serious thinking. What about the contrast between Springfield and Nauvoo, between those women who had been her friends and Sally?

She frowned and bit her finger. "Same old thing," she muttered. "It's Sally. From Kirtland time, even when I've not been seeking the craft, I've always had Sally to remind me of all I'm not. She's holy. Doesn't take much to realize that. She's living her religion, and I can't even call the power down."

With a snort of exasperation, Jenny got up and went into the house. The talisman was still pinned to her Sunday frock. She smiled at the memory as she released the medal and slipped it into the pocket of her apron. "All spiffy I was," she said with a chuckle. "Me in my best calico with the talisman and the Bible and the *Book of Mormon* going to meeting with my apostate husband."

She paused to sigh over Mark and her thoughts fled back to Springfield—how fruitless that time had turned out to be! In the beginning there had been such promise of winning Mark to the true gospel.

"I can't be held totally responsible," she murmured, moving about the living room. She assembled the pile of charms and opened the green book to a new and untried way of calling down the spirits. Dutifully they had gone to church, not the one true church but one which Mark had selected.

He would never know the churning inside, the nerve-tearing anguish of hearing those words read when she knew they were all wrong. *After Joseph teaching us the Bible wasn't translated by men gifted to handle the job,* she thought, *how nigh I was to pushing my hands over my ears; trying to keep from hearing the words contradicting everything Joseph's been teaching!*

Jenny paused to clear the table between the two chairs. Her lips twisted. Mark had it all planned. The pretty new table with the lamp centered there and the Bibles on each side, his and hers. She stacked the Bibles on his chair and opened the green book.

For the next hour Jenny murmured the words and mixed the charms; when she finally stood to her feet, her heart was pounding. Already she was sensing the swirling forces moving nearer and she slipped easily into the trance, chanting with determination, then feeling her body slipping into the disjointed, released world of the spirits. The room about her receded and grew dim.

Coming back to her world was a shock. She knew it first in a moment of disappointment and nausea as she stood trembling and blinking in the noontime sun. She was outside, but she couldn't recall getting there. Her frock was soaked with perspiration and her hair streamed down her back.

A sense of awe gripped Jenny as she walked slowly into the house. The mood she had wrapped about herself with the chants and charms had become the most intense experience she had ever felt. As she moved slowly across the room, she caught the reflected image in the mirror and turned to study herself. But could that image be Jenny?

The room seemed dark. She stepped close and leaned toward the mirror. A smoky floating cloud surrounded the image she was seeing. She blinked and pressed closer. The image twisted, her own familiar features distorting, warping. In horror she saw the familiar becoming strange and repelling. The dark cloud was tearing at her hair, poking her eyes until they were only black pits. The scene before her became the forest. Tree branches grew into torturing hands and dug into her face, her body, wound in her hair and held her suspended, helpless.

Jenny's heart was pounding—a drum of thumping, compelling anxiety. Suspended, perspiring, at the mercy of nature, she swung. Life returned. Not seeping, trickling back, but life rushing, demanding. The distorted face remained, but in the background, beyond the trees, a dot of red was growing, moving.

"No!" On tiptoe, Jenny surged forward, her fists pounding, shredding the image into slivers of meaningless light that for one moment glowed deeply purple.

The heavy frame with its fragments of glass crashing against the floor broke the spell. Jenny was flung back into life. In awe she looked at the floor and then at her bleeding fists. Blood. Trembling, horrified, for one clear moment Jenny saw herself at the mercy of the unknown.

When Mark returned home, a serene wife was moving about the kitchen. The pile of fresh laundry wafted woodland perfume from its wicker basket. Mark kissed the freshly washed and coiled mass of dark hair, nuzzled the pale cheek and noticed the bandaged hands.

"Now what have you butchered or broken?"

"Oh, Mark, the mirror! I'm so sorry. It just happened."

Mark captured her hands and she saw him pale. "My dear, you could have been badly hurt!" He studied her face and pushed her into the chair. She allowed him to fuss about the kitchen and later wash the dishes.

The next day Jenny made her decision. Again Mark had gone to Joseph, and she was left alone. She sat on the steps and studied her bandaged hands. "It could have been worse." She shuddered. Blood. That was bad.

She was still shivering, now at the memory of that shadowy image in the mirror. She dared not say it aloud lest the spirits hear, but the words trembled through her being—*I am done with them, forever.* She knew the emotion she felt was fear, but it was also acceptance of defeat.

Jenny closed her eyes and leaned against the porch railing. The warm breeze ruffled her hair while the river crashed and the birds sang in the trees. It was a lonesome feeling to be the only human in this place. Even the birds seemed confident and at peace in their world.

"If only I could tell Mark," she whispered. But she visualized the horror on his face and shivered. Never would Mark understand, even if she were to explain that the power was really for his sake.

Then she felt a nudge inside, and she returned to the contemplation of the Sabbath meeting, held at the place called the temple grove. Sally had pointed out the hill, telling her it would be the site of the new temple. But for now, the grassy plot circled with trees would be the temple and meetinghouse.

Joseph's unexpected appearance had made the meeting special. Over the cheering and shouting, the tears and clinging hands, Joseph had stood before his people.

"Governor Reynolds of Missouri—" he began, then paused to grin while the boos and cat-calls filled the arena, "has issued a writ for my arrest. I needn't be reminded that I'm a fugitive from the wrath of Missouri, so I went for a little walk by myself while the sheriff's posse visited our friendly city." He paused, waiting for the laughter to end.

"Seems he didn't like the general atmosphere of the city and therefore gave up and went home. Brethren, hopefully that will be the last of them. I think he may have been motivated by fear of the Legion and the goodly number of people who are a great deal more friendly to me than they are to him."

Jenny had lost ears for the rest of the sermon. The movement of people and the tide of emotion had her attention. She was overwhelmed by the contrasts—the careworn and the excited, the old and the young. But all alike were reflecting back to Jenny a mood much different from what she had felt in Missouri.

Once again she saw Joseph's people as proud, confident, and very holy. She knew herself scrubby, poor, and unholy in comparison. Her gaze had fastened on Sally standing in front of her. Her blonde hair had been captured under a smoky-gray bonnet which shaded her face and shadowed her wide blue eyes into a mysteriously regal expression.

The wind rose, but Jenny remained huddled on the steps, powerless to move. The air was filled with autumn's treasure of brilliant leaves. They swirled, lifted on the wings of the wind. When one brown missile was flung against her cheek, Jenny lifted her face. The air was full of the brilliance of the leaves. Wind-borne, they circled high.

Abruptly the sun broke through the clouds, lighting the fire of scarlet leaves, and Jenny saw the scene again: red, grasping branches, smoky clouds. Jenny's heart began to pound. Scrambling to her feet she fled into the house and stood pressed against the closed door, knowing again the horror of the mirrored vision.

The room was darkening, but Jenny was conscious only of the alien wind and the amplified horror of the mirror. The wind buffeted the door as she pushed against it. Did she hear her name thrown into the wind? As she strained to hear, there was an anguished groan and crash. Now the door strained against her.

"Jenny, it's me, Mark. Let me in."

She stepped backward and pressed trembling hands at her tumbling hair. Biting her lips, she fought for calmness, knowing it wasn't working. His eyes widened and his hands were moving over her. "Are you hurt? Jenny, what is it? Answer me."

She gulped, but her voice came out a thin whisper. "Whatever is wrong? I'm not hurt; why do you ask?"

He held her close and then looked into her eyes. She saw his jaw tighten. "It was a mistake, wasn't it? I should never have brought you this far away."

"From Springfield? Nonsense, Mark. I wanted to come." Now she knew her voice sounded threadbare, without substance. He led her to the kitchen and poured hot water over the tea leaves. His face was still pale and lined, but the expression he turned on her was level, demanding.

"Jenny, why don't you tell me what is happening to you? From the time we decided to move to Nauvoo, you became a different person. You came back to life—the old Jenny. But for the past six weeks you've been wandering around in a cloud."

Her voice was deliberate, flat even to her own ears: "You are saying this because I've become a slothful housewife. But I've been bored by it all. Mark, if only we had a child. If only—"

For a moment his face relaxed, "If that's all, I'd—" In his silence he paced the kitchen floor. "Jenny, I'm going on instinct. I know you are deeply troubled—perhaps it is our childlessness. I'm willing to abide by that for now. But why do I feel as if I can no longer touch the real Jenny? I was certain that bringing you to the shelter of the church—to Joseph's Nauvoo—would be the answer to your problems."

He fell silent, and Jenny sensed the hesitancy in his statement. Painfully she gripped her wounded hands and pressed them against her. The temptation to pour it all out was nearly more than she could bear. But looking up at her husband, she saw not concern and questions, but instead horror, shrinking away, even outrage if she were to tell him the truth.

She studied his face, saw his attempt to smile as he said, "I suppose you miss those silly games you and the senator's wife were playing with the scarves and herbs. Jenny, I must insist—"

She was breathless. "What?"

"You're going to be ill unless you break this tide. As soon as it is possible, we are going to move into town. But until we can, I insist you make every effort to get acquainted with the women of Nauvoo. There's Sarah Pratt, Sally, Eliza Snow. Miss Snow teaches school; perhaps you could help her with the children."

Jenny jumped to her feet, "Mark! I don't want—"

"All right, I won't tell you what must be done. You decide for yourself— just don't stay out here alone day after day. I heard that group of women inviting you to be part of their sewing circle. I also heard your answer. You sounded haughty; no wonder they haven't asked again." He moved away, saying as he turned, "I intend to buy you a light buggy as soon as I can find one. Jenny, I am worried about you and I intend to act on your best interests. Even if that means returning to Springfield."

5

JENNY SNUGGLED HER face into the warm folds of her shawl and flicked the reins across the mare's back. It was only Mark's insistence that had her out of the house today. The January sky was slowly releasing snowflakes, nearly as reluctantly as Jenny was to receive them.

The mare's pace quickened. As many times as she had taken this trip in the past two months, she need not be urged toward the livery stable.

Tom was there to take the reins from her. He frowned and studied her face. "Still a mite peaked. Mark's worried; thinks you're fretting yourself sick."

"Mark's bothering himself for no reason," she answered smartly. She took Tom's hand and stepped down. "He can't stand for a body to think or feel a bit different than he does."

Tom's brow unfurled itself and he grinned. "He's pokin' you about religion again?" She gave him a level look and said nothing. "Oh, been into the book again! Tryin' to raise up a storm?"

"Tom, for the years you spent following the Prophet while he did his money digging, you are a mite sarcastic. I'd expect more sympathy. Would you like me to give you a love potion?" He reddened, and Jenny pressed on, "I intend to have the power, no matter how it must come about."

"What you want power for?" Jenny closed her eyes for a moment and tried to line up the reasons, but saw only that vision of Sally, assured and confident. "Jen," he said impatiently, "why is it you can never be satisfied with anything?"

"It goes deeper than being satisfied. I suppose I'm just tired of being a nothing."

Tom's eyes widened. "Married to one of the most important men in town outside Joseph and his twelve, and she calls it nothing."

"It's how I feel." Now the new thought came, Jenny contemplated the visions of Joseph. "Maybe," she said slowly, "I need to go talk religion with Joseph."

Tom frowned again. "Meaning?" His eyes were watchful.

"Meaning, I can't spend all my time with the sewing circle or at Sally's. Meaning, sometimes I have serious thoughts in my head."

She knew he was still watching her as she headed down the street toward Joseph's office. Her heart was heavy as she contemplated the lonely figure of her brother—silent, faithful, undemanding. She couldn't help wondering whether he ever had experienced this brooding need to split through the seams of life and discover something for himself.

Unexpectedly, her latest discovery burst into her mind and she shivered. Would autumn's terrible vision ever leave her? Again she murmured, "I'm through with the craft forever." The familiar discontent settled upon her. All the spirit-world's promises of power and knowledge had come to naught. Except for the bid for higher status offered only through the dreaded sabbat, she had tried every trick of the craft, and still she was only weak Jenny.

As Jenny approached Joseph's store, she began to wonder how she would win an audience with the Prophet alone. Surely Mark—or at least some of the twelve—would be with him.

She hesitated at the bottom of the long flight of stairs stretching up the exterior brick wall of the store. She was self-conscious, aware that every eye on the street would take stock of Jenny Cartwright going to Joseph's office. "And every Saint in town will be chewing over Jenny, wondering what problem has sent her running to the Prophet for advice." Jenny abruptly decided she needed a bit of cloth to stitch.

Joseph was inside, in his shirt sleeves, stocking shelves as casually as a junior clerk. When he noticed her he said, "Mark's gone to Carthage for me. Business. You could buy a ham or a nice new plow while you are here."

After greeting him she lowered her voice. "Joseph, it's you I must see."

His hands slowed among the boxes and rolls of twine. She nearly squirmed under the questions in his eyes, the faint smile. "I need advice. Joseph, it's important. There's no other place to go."

"Have you seen Dr. Bennett? Surely he can help you out."

"What? Joseph, not medical. I want to talk about the craft and—religion."

He frowned, then his face cleared in a smile. "Then wait by the stove." He jerked his head toward the women in the store. "They'll soon be gone."

When the store was empty, he came back to her. Sitting down on the bench beside her, he clasped his hands and leaned forward. "Jenny, my dear, what seems to be the problem?"

She backed away, too conscious of the small space between them and the warmth of him reaching through her chill. Caught by the significance, she frowned in annoyance. For a moment she studied his face, wondering again at the magnetism of this man. His smile was encouraging.

"Joseph," she groped for a beginning. "Do you still have the talisman?"

"Yes, but I'm wise this time; I'll not take it out for you to see."

"I'd forgotten that," she said, and his grin flashed, underscoring the lie while she blushed. "Joseph, I didn't forget. I just didn't want you getting the best of me right off."

"Right off?"

She ignored the thrust. "I need to know. Do you remember in Missouri at Captain Patten's funeral you said that you had the power to give to those who wanted it? I want that power."

He was silent for a long time. In the dim building, the fire snapped in the stove and the red light of it shone through the open door, reminding Jenny of the mirror and the spirit world she had seen. She shivered, and he lifted his head. Now shadows from the threatening storm were hiding Joseph's eyes.

"Jenny," he said slowly, while she peered at him, "I believe you are serious; but let me ask you some questions. You mentioned the talisman. I've told you I'd renounced the craft. No longer do I get my power from this source. It is through the church and the promise given to the priesthood that I now know power. Are you unaware that the promise of the priesthood is only for men and, through them, their wives?"

"I don't understand the priesthood, I've heard little about it. Seems no one knows enough to talk about it now."

"That's good. Most of the details haven't yet been revealed. It shall be soon. I'm waiting for my people to purify themselves through the ordinances; then the Lord has promised the fullness of the gospel will be given."

"But, power!" Her voice broke. "Joseph, the need is destroying me. How long can a person take the promise without the fulfillment? I tremble with fear of my inadequacy. Please—"

"Don't push. There's nothing I can do unless you meet the requirements of the gospel. Have you prepared yourself by reading the Scriptures? Are you paying your tithing, doing your part to build up the Saints?"

"I . . . I don't know. There's much I don't know right now."

"I suggest you become a learner. I've plans to have some of the older women teach the younger all the ordinances of the faith. Until we can do this, just do your work at home."

"What do you mean?"

Joseph took a deep breath and reached for her hand. "Jenny, your husband is as nearly apostate as I can tolerate. He's always given me a difficult time. Without disclosing the details of our talk, my instruction to you is that you win him to the church by your saintly life. This is very important. Without a husband to take you to the highest degree of heaven, you'll never receive the power on this earth, never be more than a slave in the hereafter."

It was snowing hard when Jenny left the store, but she was so deep in thought that she was unconscious of the wet, cold flakes against her face. She was also unaware of Mark dismounting and walking toward the store just as she hurried away.

Looking after her retreating back, he frowned and faced Joseph. "That was Jenny. Why was she here?"

"Mark, remember, I'm Jenny's spiritual advisor. Why else would she be here? I've told her to pull up tight the reins around home and in time she will inherit all the blessings of the Lord, which she so desperately longs for."

For a moment he frowned at Mark and then he clapped him on the shoulder. "Come in and tell me what you've been able to come up with in Carthage."

Mark reached the livery stable just as Jenny stepped back in her buggy. Tom was beside her, and Mark handed the reins of his mount to him. "Old Nell's had enough for the day. Put her up for the night. I'll drive Jenny home."

Jenny slid over and Mark said, "Your nose is like a cherry already, and we've nearly five miles to go. Why did you venture out in such a storm?"

"There were only a few flakes when I left—besides, I was taking your advice. I was sick of my own company."

"Did Joseph give you some good *advice*?" He stressed the word slightly and Jenny glanced up at him. She frowned, and Mark was instantly sorry. He settled into his overcoat and reached for the lap robe.

He was still berating himself for allowing his jealousy to show as he tucked the robe around Jenny. "Now, let's see how fast this rig will move," he said lightly.

He flicked the reins across the back of the mare and headed through Nauvoo. Glancing at Jenny he saw the faint smile on her lips and felt that twinge again. Was it related to the angry scene he had interrupted in Joseph's office this morning?

Jenny turned her head toward him and asked, "Did you have a good trip to Carthage?"

He shook his head. "So Joseph told you. Actually, I could see no reason to have gone. The fellow I was to contact has been out of the state for a month. His business partner looked at me as if I were slightly deranged when I asked after him." He was silent, thinking again about the confrontation between the two men that morning. Those words had capped all the ugly rumors he had been hearing. He knew a confrontation with Joseph was fast approaching.

Mark shot another glance at Jenny. The faint smile was still on her lips. "You look pleased," he stated. "That must mean *your* meeting went well."

She turned to him with a puzzled look. "It was the snow I was smiling about. It's pleasant now that I needn't ride home alone. I don't know what to think about my meeting with Joseph. I'm feeling more was left unsaid than was said."

"How's that?" he asked cautiously.

"There are so many gaps in my religion. So much I don't understand, and so much more I need. Joseph put me off by saying there's new revelations to be made to the church in the future. He didn't give me any help except to tell me to go home and read the Scriptures."

Mark straightened and turned to study Jenny's face intently. She was busy flicking snow off her shawl and drawing it more tightly around her head, and she didn't see his excitement. Carefully he settled back and compared this with the information rolling around in his mind. *So Jenny isn't happy with her religion!* he mused.

He felt his grin disappearing. New revelations. That seemed to fit in with the scene he had interrupted between Joseph and his brother, Don Carlos.

This morning he had arrived early at the office over the grocery store. Obviously neither man had anticipated an audience to their angry scene. He had heard Don Carlos as he walked in. The man's flushed, angry face had emphasized his words, and his wrath had delivered the rest of them. Turning to Joseph, he shouted, "I don't care if you are my brother and the Prophet of the living God. Sure as I stand here, you'll go to hell if you preach the spiritual wife doctrine. Hyrum feels the same. He told me last night that he's confident it will break up the church."

The angry red left Don Carlos' face, and he paused on his way to the door. Mark saw the anguish in his eyes. "Hyrum said it could cost your life. I don't know what he meant by that unless—" Suddenly he noticed Mark. He ducked his head and hurried out the door.

Mark became aware that Jenny was throwing worried glances at his frowns, and he snatched up the conversation again. "Jen, tell me where your church has failed you." He saw the startled expression and watched her shrug.

In the morning, Jenny was still wondering how to answer Mark. As she broke eggs into the sizzling fat, Mark came into the kitchen. "One thing I did find out yesterday," he said, as he turned the bread toasting on the stove, "Joseph has had communication from Dr. Bennett."

"Isn't he in Springfield?"

"Yes. He wrote that the Nauvoo Charter passed the house without being read."

Jenny dropped the knife she held. "You mean after all the fearing you and Joseph went through over that charter, they didn't even read it?"

"That's right." She studied his frown and waited. "Seems like careless legislation. I have a hard time reconciling that with my friend, Lincoln. But those are the facts. The state has granted the little Mormon municipality a charter that, if it goes unchallenged, virtually makes us a state within a state."

"Well, tell me what the charter is all about."

"I can give you a copy to read, but for now here are the facts: Besides the expected items such as incorporating the city, even providing for a university, there's the clause calling for a militia to be called the Nauvoo Legion.

"The charter will give the city council power to make and execute ordinances not repugnant to the state or United States Constitution." He paused, adding, "Note this, my dear, it is an ambiguous statement wide open to all kinds of interpretation.

"Among other items, the mayor of the city will be chief justice of the municipal court, empowered to issue writs of habeas corpus, with the power to try those issued from other courts, including trying the original actions in the case. In effect, the court has the power to cast out everything that goes against the desires of—you guessed it—Joseph. I don't think he'll have to worry about Missouri as long as the charter is in effect."

"This is the first big step toward getting approval to be designated a territory." Jenny's eyes were wide, and Mark winced. "That's not good?"

"It will be impossible. I just wish he would give up on his foolish dream. Jen, if I'd any idea Joseph hadn't learned his lesson in Missouri, I would never have accepted his job offer."

"The people here have been so good to us, except for those in Warsaw, Warren and—"

"And anyone else close enough to be touched by the Saints." He followed Jenny to the table. He had only taken two bites of his breakfast when he said, "Lincoln made a statement concerning the law that goes something like this: municipal law, that is, local law, is a standard for conduct approved by the state governing bodies, and it's for the purpose of fostering right and correcting wrong."

"But you're talking about law—not about a community set up to live under God's holy Prophet and kingdom rules."

"Jenny, my dear, you sound too Mormon."

"What do you mean by that?"

"I can practically quote chapter and verse. You don't really believe that. Why don't you think it through? Why don't you read and question, even argue just as you have done in the past?"

"I suppose because I am an adult now. I should have the questions settled. It isn't mature to go through life fussing over everything."

"It isn't mature *not* to, if you know a question deep down inside."

She was slowly lowering the dishes into the dishpan when he came back into the kitchen. He was wearing his coat and drawing on the mittens she had knit for him. "Jenny, what's wrong? Why don't you bring your questions to me instead of to Joseph? I saw how torn you were in Springfield when you were practicing what you called your nature religion, worshiping in the forest by the light of the moon. That didn't satisfy you—as a matter of fact, it was destroying you. Now I'm seeing the same dissatisfaction. Will you let me help you?"

"Mark, you are apostate."

"Perhaps. Yet Joseph values my judgment enough to offer this position."

6

EVENTS CONCERNING THE Mormons seemed to move just as rapidly as spring was moving upon the country. Jenny stood on her front porch watching the birds flitting back and forth across the pasture, carrying twigs to the large oak tree beside the barn. Some of the events taking place in Nauvoo were puzzling to her.

The town was growing rapidly. Just this month ten thousand had gathered at the temple for the ceremony of laying the cornerstone. Nearly every Sabbath, the meeting in the temple clearing produced a larger crowd and new faces. She thought of last week's sermon and winced. Even Mark didn't know the reason behind Brigham Young's sermon. His face had been very sober as he had watched the stranger turn and slip out of the crowd just as Brigham Young had put his pistol back inside his coat.

Now Jenny shook her head. "Brigham, I don't know you very well, but I'd always credited you with more intelligence than that," she murmured to herself. "In the past Joseph's always made the wild statements, but you nearly capped them all when you said what you did."

Shivering, Jenny whispered the words Brigham had roared at the crowd: " 'The earth is the Lord's and therefore it belongs to the Saints!' But Brig, you shouldn't have waved that pistol and said this is the way we intend to take it."

Walking back to the house, she stopped at the pasture to look at the lambs. The chickens were nesting, and there was another new lamb in the pasture. Mark predicted the cow would be freshening soon. Even the women of Nauvoo seemed to be blossoming with expected life.

Everyone except Jenny. It was becoming increasingly painful to go to the weekly sewing circle—except that it was a good place to pick up the latest gossip. She chuckled, shaking her head.

"Jenny." Mark came down the stairs two at a time. He paused to finish tucking his tie under his collar and then said, "There's a parade and speeches in town today; want to ride in with me?"

"Oh, I suppose so. I've nothing much else to do."

"It isn't that bad, is it? It's spring and the world is blossoming out all over, even in our pasture."

"Everywhere except in me," she sighed, turning away.

He nuzzled the back of her neck. "Don't give up yet," he murmured.

"Do you suppose I should see Dr. Bennett?" she turned.

Mark's head snapped, his answer explosive. "No!"

"What is the problem? Mark, he's the only real doctor in town and you should see the way people—"

"People, or only women?"

"Well, the women at the sewing circle. I must say I can't understand them. Just mention his name and there are all kinds of funny reactions. Still, it seems safer to go to a qualified doctor instead of the fellow who just hands out herbs."

He looked at her quizzically. "A couple of years ago you were handing out the herbs."

"True." She paused, frowning over the things she had heard. "There're whispers of Dr. Bennett misbehaving with some questionable women— those fancy ladies living down by the wharf. I heard he's responsible for that brothel. Remember? Sally pointed it out to us."

"And you want to see *him*? Why don't you just talk to Patty Sessions? I've a feeling she'll just tell you to stop worrying."

"Mark! We've been married nearly five years. I would think—"

She turned away, and he came to put his arms around her. "Hey, tears won't help. Come on now, you need Nauvoo today."

The parade had begun by the time Mark and Jenny arrived in Nauvoo. In silence they sat in their buggy and listened to the brass band and the shouts of the people. When the first line of men appeared after the band had passed, Mark whispered, "The Legion. See, there's Joseph standing in the wagon waving to the people."

"What an elegant uniform!" Jenny exclaimed. "Look at the men dressed in white. Why there's John D. Lee."

"That's Joseph's special contingent of body guards," Mark muttered, and she wondered at the note of irony in his voice.

With a glance at him she asked, "What is the significance of the white?"

"I think it's supposed to project the idea of protecting angels."

Jenny snickered. "I don't think Porter Rockwell looks like an angel."

Mark turned the buggy in behind the parade and followed it to the clearing beside the temple grove. By the time Mark had found a place for the buggy and they made their way to the clearing, the band was playing again. But this wasn't marching music.

"Dancing!" Jenny gasped when they stepped into the clearing. "In Kirtland it was expressly forbidden."

The young man in front of Jenny turned with a cheerful grin. "Ma'am, this isn't Ohio. Be glad the Prophet's relaxing a bit."

"Are there going to be speeches?" Mark asked.

"Seems." The young man moved impatiently. "Mostly it's a rallying cry to get started building the Nauvoo House."

"Oh," Jenny said. "That's to be the boarding house the Lord ordered built, isn't it? Is that all?"

"No, they're saying he's going to lay the polygamy rumor to rest again, and he's going to give instruction about baptism for the dead. Already Brigham Young's declaring it is a great and mighty work we are to be doing for the Lord." The fellow's face wore a pensive grin for a moment and then he aroused himself, "Personally, I'd rather be dancing and—" He looked at Jenny and, with a teasing salute, walked away.

"Why, Phelps!" Jenny looked up at Mark's exclamation. Mark was holding up his hand, and his glad surprise seemed to embarrass the man. "You've rejoined Zion's camp?"

With a wry grin, Phelps nodded. "Only I'm hearing the Zion part has been put on hold."

"Then you've been informed about the revelation that Joseph received from the Lord in January?" Jenny asked, nodding at the woman beside him. "My, you missed something; that revelation was chockful of direction for the Saints."

"I've heard a little about warning the kings and rulers of their prophesied end, and about how Zion must wait until the proper time." He shook his head sadly. "I'd already started for Nauvoo when I learned Joseph had to drop his plans to begin building up an army to march on Missouri immediately."

Mrs. Phelps stepped forward, eyeing Jenny curiously. "We heard there are converts streaming in from Canada and England, also that there's a temple to be built here. My, there's excitement in store for the people of God!"

"I don't understand about baptisms for the dead," Jenny said, "but I hear they've already started. Someone said they heard one fellow got baptized for George Washington."

"There's going to be great days ahead," Phelps said.

"But there's much to be done," Mark warned. "Right now we're having financial problems. Seems the real estate sold to Saints in Iowa was based on fraudulent deeds. A large number of poor Saints are even poorer now. I hear Joseph intends to give some of them work in construction of the temple."

"Have you heard rumors about the new bankruptcy law?"

"It hasn't passed the house yet," Mark said shortly.

"Well," Phelps said lamely, "seems it's an answer to the claims Missouri's been making against us."

"Oh," Jenny said brightly, "then you haven't heard that Joseph dismissed those debts a year ago."

"Jenny," Mark interrupted, "I must go to the office. I'll take you to Sally's home first." As they turned to go, Jenny saw the expression on Phelps' face—an incomprehensible question. Phelps didn't trust Mark.

The year 1841 snowballed with one event after another, and through it all the new Mormon community grew at a rate that left Jenny giddy. From a village with two hundred and fifty homes, a straggle of shops and a temple lot gouged enough for a cornerstone, Nauvoo was now spreading into a modest-sized city. From generous lots in town to the farms clustering like timid chicks around their mother hen, Nauvoo was making her presence known in Illinois.

During that first year Mark and Jenny lived in Nauvoo, they watched with trepidation as the bold prophet continued to lay claim to more territory.

While Jenny had held her breath because of the daring of the Nauvoo Charter, Mark cringed at the political machinery of the Saints released upon the state. The influence of the Saints' solid voting bloc caused Illinois to tremble.

In 1840 when the Saints voted as a man, their unified action helped place the Whigs in power. Again in 1841, Joseph Smith boldly declared the Mormon vote would shine most brightly on the party willing to extend favors.

It would have been a daring move for any group of people; but for the Prophet it seemed the ordinary, logical result of seeking the will of the Lord.

Nearly as soon as the Nauvoo Charter passed the House, Saints and Gentiles became increasingly aware of the role John C. Bennett was playing in Nauvoo—and not only in politics.

Rigdon, ill since the Missouri days, was replaced with Dr. Bennett as Joseph's right-hand man. Mark carried home the news to Jenny.

"Mark," she said slowly, studying the frown on his face, "this should be good news—after all, Rigdon was a drag on the heels of everything happening in Nauvoo. Why are you so troubled?"

As he hung up his coat, he responded, "I distrust that man's ambition. Joseph seems entirely blind to a personality that is causing most of his friends to shudder."

He took a deep breath and paced the floor of their kitchen. "There are letters. From the beginning Bennett has had some of us puzzled and worried. He's just too smooth. Now Joseph's had letters saying he's held in disrepute back east. The letters state he's abandoned a family, and the Masonic Lodge expelled him. I have no idea what the charges are." Mark paced the floor and then turned to Jenny. "All of this mess is enough to make me want to quit, to get out of Nauvoo while I still have my sanity."

"Oh, Mark, you wouldn't, surely!"

He looked at her pleading face close to his shoulder and tried to grin. "No, my sweet, I wouldn't." He watched her brow smooth and tried to guess her secret desires.

Mark still carried the churning need to help others understand the mystery of Jesus Christ. The compulsion pressed against his heart each time he saw the confusion on Tom's face. And what about Jenny? He turned away with a sigh. How true it was that the most difficult burden was the one nearest a person's heart!

7

MAY HAD ARRIVED, and in the temple grove the air was warm and heavy. Brigham's voice droned on. Some of the other women moved restlessly, no doubt thinking—as Jenny was—of the basket dinner. Jenny wondered whether she had remembered to pack butter.

When Mark moved impatiently and yanked at his collar, Jenny realized her mind had been wandering. She glanced at him as he began chewing at the corner of his mouth. Brigham Young's voice carried clearly over the crowd; she tried to listen as her gaze skimmed the crowd pressing as close as possible to the speaker.

Nancy Rigdon turned her head and flashed a dimpled smile at Jenny. She was standing close to Sarah Pratt, and it was Sarah's turn to glance at Jenny.

As Jenny smiled toward the women, she was thinking of the sewing circle. In the past months, since spring had offered more diversions, the crowd had dwindled. Recalling with amusement the fun she had shared with Sarah and Nancy, Jenny couldn't regret the change.

What a strange pair the two were! Nancy, the youngest daughter of Sidney Rigdon, was all spice and froth. Much younger than Sarah, she obviously adored the graceful, attractive woman. Sarah was married to Orson Pratt, one of the twelve. Jenny knew they had one small child.

Mark stirred again, now frowning. Jenny tried to fasten her wandering mind on the sermon. Brigham's monologue poured out more words and Jenny sifted through them, looking for the ones irritating Mark. She heard, "Our religion is founded upon the priesthood of the Son of God."

Jenny was still puzzling over Mark's reaction when she heard more: "The Son of God labors to build up, exalt, create, purify all things on the earth, bringing it to His standard of glory, perfection, and greatness. I want you to know, my friends, that we are to be helping Him. When the fullness of time has come, we will have been partakers in the task of bringing the kingdom to perfection. Those who buck this perfection will just have to go. Also, I want you to understand that Jesus Christ can't return to this earth until we have the kingdom prepared for Him."

It was midafternoon before Jenny and Mark left Nauvoo. Jenny was thinking about Nancy's new frock when she recalled Mark's reaction to the sermon. She studied his face, saw that he was miles away in thought, and said, "Who was the man standing beside you? He's as big as Joseph and looks nearly as important."

"He's a Canadian; William Law is his name. Was converted to the church in Canada and has just arrived this spring. Seems to be an enthusiastic person, full of ideas. More than willing to do his share around here."

She waited a moment and then asked, "Why were you so irritated by Brigham Young's sermon?"

Mark looked surprised. "I'm displeased because what he had to say doesn't line up with what the Bible teaches. I'm hearing more of this all the time, particularly slanted toward an idea that's being whispered about."

"What's that?"

He moved restlessly and glanced at her. "A kingdom of God that is going to take over—and I'm quoting current whispers—'Illinois, Missouri, Iowa, and finally all the states and then the world.' Now you are frowning—why?"

"I'm wondering how you've come to know so much about what the Bible teaches."

"Jenny, I've been reading. It's right there just as plain as it can be for anyone who cares to read."

"Joseph told me to read the Scriptures. I think he meant both the Bible and the *Book of Mormon*. But then the sermons tell me so much, it seems foolish to waste time reading."

"You read to check it out—to make certain what you're hearing lines up with God's Word. Matter of fact, if you *don't* compare the revelations and the *Book of Mormon* with the Bible, how do you know you aren't being—" He stopped and both of them looked up as they heard the horse rapidly approaching.

"It's Tom!" Jenny exclaimed. "Is he coming from our house?"

"Well, he wasn't in Nauvoo this morning."

When Tom wheeled his horse around, Jenny noticed the lines of strain around his mouth. "I'd given up waiting for you and decided to head for Nauvoo."

"Sabbath meeting," Mark said tersely, then waited.

"Joe's in big trouble. I've been sticking with him, fearin' to leave him for a minute until today. Thank goodness he finally was able to get a writ of habeas corpus."

"What's happened?"

"Joseph had a meeting with Governor Carlin. On the way back to Nauvoo, a sheriff from Missouri with his posse appeared on the scene. 'Twas so well-timed I'm thinkin' it was planned higher up."

"So Joseph's wild prophecy has reached the ears of Missouri, particularly Boggs."

"You mean the prophecy he gave out a couple of months ago, sayin' that within a year Boggs would die? Mark, that was from the Lord. Did you expect Joseph would fail to give the warning? Of course he wanted Missouri to hear." Tom shrugged. "They nabbed Joe, and I just tagged along, tryin' to figure out what to do."

"And?" Mark prodded.

"They hauled him clear to Quincy before there was a chance to take a breath. That's gettin' mighty close to Missouri. We tried several places to get a writ and not a soul would issue one. Don't think they'd a done it in Quincy but for the fact his old friend Stephen A. Douglas was in town hearing a case."

"Douglas is on the Supreme Court," Mark said thoughtfully. "That should mean something."

"You're tooting right. Word barely leaked about Douglas stickin' his neck out for Joe when a couple of Whig lawyers scooted for Quincy to offer *their* services. Douglas being Democrat and political himself done the trick. We're about ready to have a caucus over there."

"For once Joe's politics is standing him in good stead," Mark remarked dryly.

"Yes, but he needs all the help he can get. He told me to fetch you."

Mark sighed and glanced at Jenny. "I don't like leaving Jen alone; also there's a pile of paper work at the office."

"Can't be as important as this."

"It could be more important. There's going to be a real storm if we don't get Joseph's financial affairs in order before the next meeting of the district court."

Tom's horse pawed impatiently. "Head back for Quincy," Mark said. "I'll ride over, but if things are under control, I won't stay."

"I'm to alert the men."

Mark winced. "The Danites. That's the worst order Joe could have given."

"Not the Danites," Tom stressed the words, "nor even the Legion. His *bodyguard*." He wheeled away without waiting for a reply.

Jenny couldn't restrain her dismal words. "It's like Missouri all over again."

Mark took a deep breath and said, "We can leave any time you give the word."

Jenny considered and shuddered, remembering that shadowy image. Only to herself did she dare admit the alternative was unthinkable. She said, "You'll be away tonight."

"Do you want me to take you to Sally?"

"It's so far, and you need to hurry. Is there a chance you'll be back tonight?"

She felt him studying her face. Slowly he said, "I'm of a mind to make certain I'll be back."

"Oh, Mark," she whispered, "thank you." She blinked tears out of her eyes as she smiled at him.

She saw the concern. Always it was there, but sometimes it nearly forced the words she didn't know how to say. "Jenny," he began, then gave a feeble grin. "Lock the doors and read your Bible. That'll keep the spooks away. I promise I'll be back before midnight."

He helped her from the buggy and went to saddle up. She was still staring after him, wondering whether the light words carried a hidden message. What a strange way to tease!

When Mark disappeared down the road, Jenny went into the house. She dropped the latch into place on both doors and pulled the curtains over the windows. Although the late spring afternoon was warm, she stirred up the coals in the stove and added wood, still thinking about Mark's statement.

Since the afternoon she had broken the mirror with her bare fists, Jenny had not made another attempt to use the charms and book. At times she trembled with a fearful urgency to be back into the craft. But the memory of those contorted images was stronger.

When the water was boiling, Jenny brewed tea for herself and settled down in the rocking chair. As she sipped her tea, she studied the smooth leather cover of the Bible Mark had given her. "Like a talisman," she mused, "he wants me to read it to keep away the spirits. Only read, not rub it like I would the medal."

Suddenly she began to giggle. "How silly!" The picture was strong in front of her—Jenny briskly buffing the black cover and chanting the prayer to Luna the moon goddess. Now a new thought took over. Was it any sillier than stroking the medal and burning the herbs?"

She shivered. "I may not be seeing the power I hope for," she murmured. "But certain as I sit here, there's something out there, and I'm finding it very frightening."

Jenny silently explored all the reaches of her thoughts, knowing with certainty that a question was being forced upon her. "It was the green book in the beginning that opened it all up, but then Clara taught me more. And Joseph."

She closed her eyes and relived the excitement of South Bainbridge. With the digging and witching that went on that year, with the sure thread of strange excitement moving through them all, there could be no doubt. An idea presented itself, and she must consider it. Would she go back to it all? It was strangely attractive, drawing with an appeal that was more real than the chair under her.

But even as she was slipping into a floating sense of ease, being drawn gently in, Jenny abruptly faced reality. She remembered that day with the mirror—her own face, twisting into ugliness. And the sabbat awaited her—a threat which would never leave as long as she poked into the spirits' territory.

She jumped to her feet and reached for the black Book. Holding it tightly against herself, she waited for her wildly beating heart to slow. But she couldn't stop the forbidden thought and the wish. "I wish I could see Adela; she was so beautiful! She could tell me what has gone wrong." Once verbalized, the wish was an uneasy cold spot against her heart.

The afternoon light was becoming dim; ahead lay all those dark hours before Mark would come. Jenny picked up the Bible and her empty teacup.

Back in the kitchen she lighted the lamp, stirred up the fire and cooked an egg, which she didn't eat. The Book lay on the table in front of her.

"Funny," she mused. "Since I could say the alphabet I've wanted to read everything in sight. Now I have this Book, and no desire for it."

Outside the wind was rising. Jenny could hear the moaning in the trees and she tried to force her mind away from the curious question: Was it wind? She reached for the Book and held it tightly.

The wind continued. Abruptly she envisioned Mark fighting the wind. Darkness was total now, and it was too early for the fragment of moonlight. Jenny peered through the curtains and hoped the chickens were safe, and the lambs. There had been wolves sighted. Were there Indians? But no matter—at least Indians were flesh and blood.

With a shiver she went back to her chair and opened the black Book to the middle.

"The Lord is my shepherd," she read slowly, then paused. The picture that came before her eyes was not the same kind of picture she saw when Joseph preached about the Lord commanding the Saints to avenge Him of His enemies.

Jenny flipped the pages, looking for the messages Joseph had been preaching. Words caught her eyes and she lifted the Book to study the pages. "*I am.*" Jenny thought back to Springfield and the woman who had said those words. Why did they still make her shiver? She moved her finger down the page and read, "Stand now with thine enchantments and with the multitude of thy sorceries, wherein thou hast laboured from thy youth. . . . Now let the astrologers, the stargazers, the monthly prognosticators, stand up, and save thee from these things that shall come upon thee. . . . They shall not deliver themselves from the power of the flame: . . . None shall save thee." She shivered and flipped more pages.

Another word caught her eye: *blood.* She went back. "But your iniquities have separated between you and your God, and your sins have hid His face from you, that He will not hear. For your hands are defiled with blood. . . ."

She remembered that dream after the day at Haun's Mill. "But I didn't shed blood!" she cried, and then was caught by more words: "Your lips have spoken lies, your tongue hath muttered perverseness. None calleth for justice, nor any pleadeth for truth: . . ." Could other things be as bad as shedding blood when God looked at the sins?

Carefully Jenny folded the page so that the words were hidden.

She was still sitting beside the stove when Mark came. Jenny had returned the Book to the parlor table. She had combed her hair and washed her hands, but the words were still there.

8

MARK NOTICED JENNY standing at the parlor window as he rode out of the yard, past the puddles in the road. The rain had flattened March's dandelions, and the road was a mirror reflecting sky and clouds.

As soon as the horse had cantered beyond Jenny's vision, Mark tightened the mare's reins. "Hold it, girl, there's no sense getting to Nauvoo a minute sooner than necessary."

He slumped in the saddle, grateful for his lonely ride into town. For the past two months his face ached continually from the cheerful grin he forced himself to wear.

This morning bone-weariness, his constant companion, helped him discount the misery of the moisture hanging in the air. Once again, as he rode, he found himself reviewing all the facts and considering the two options open to him: stay and endure, or leave Nauvoo.

It had been a year since Joseph Smith had first laid all his cards on the table. In the beginning, Mark had been grateful. It had signaled a change in their relationship and indicated a chance to help Joseph.

From the beginning, Mark had been uncomfortable with Joseph's role. This feeling, coupled with the tension created by the man's "prophet" image, had grated against his nerves. The image was supported by all those around Joseph, reminding Mark that *he* was the sore thumb in Nauvoo.

Mark had become tired of tiptoeing around in deference to Joseph and yearned for the relationship they had shared in Missouri. Open warfare seemed preferable to some of the pussyfooting he was seeing. Mark thought of Clayton, the man who had recently begun serving as Joseph's recording secretary. He wanted to tell the fellow it was all right to sneeze once in a while.

Mark winced. Open warfare? That left no alternatives—it was an all-or-nothing situation. But he couldn't help feeling that either all or nothing merited the same results.

With a sigh Mark acknowledged a showdown in the offing. But could he explain this to Jenny? There was too much forbidden territory in their marriage.

She wouldn't tolerate talk about Jesus Christ and all the Bible had to say about a personal relationship with the Lord. But was her dabbling in the occult a constant statement of her need for God? She evidently found no satisfaction in Joseph's church.

As Mark rode, he reminded himself that he should be rejoicing in this fact. But for some reason he couldn't identify, knowing only this much left him shaking with fear for Jenny, and this unknown made him fearful of leaving Nauvoo.

With a sigh, he murmured, "Oh, Lord, I know I'm to be leaving this in Your hands, but I must admit, I'm shaking in my boots. There's just too much going on that I know nothing about."

Mark went back to mulling over Joseph's problems. From the Kirtland and Missouri years, Mark had known of the chaotic state of Joseph's financial affairs. He also knew the step Brigham Young had taken just after returning from his mission to England.

Mark had heard of Brigham's despair back in 1840 when he saw the condition of the church finances. Young had immediately set himself to the task of convincing Joseph he must turn over the financial affairs of the church to the twelve apostles.

Brigham's success had encouraged Mark when he received Joseph's offer of a position in Nauvoo as his attorney. But a complicating situation had now surfaced.

During the summer of 1841, Congress had passed a personal bankruptcy law; then just two months ago, Joseph threw all his financial problems before Mark.

As Mark shuffled through the pile of debts with a sinking heart, Joseph's countenance had become more cheerful. Quickly Mark realized that Joseph was depending on the new statute to work a miracle in his finances.

Last week the situation had climaxed in a heated argument between Mark and Joseph. Unfortunately, it had served only to remove the last polite hedge between them.

On that morning, Joseph had dumped the pile of paper on Mark's desk and declared, "See here, this is what I intend to do. I'll declare total bankruptcy. I'm insolvent."

"No, you are not!" Mark had snapped back. "Let me show you. See this and this?" His finger flicked through all the items. "To begin with, you've taken upon yourself the position as sole trustee of the church, which you know is illegal. In the state of Illinois the church act requires a board of five trustees. Besides that detail, which is bound to be questioned, you've set yourself up to handle all the real estate dealings in the community. According to the books, you've made yourself a bundle."

Joseph had opened his mouth to protest when Mark interrupted. "Your words are working against you. More than one man in the state can point to the statement you made recently, remember?"

"Yes, I shot my big mouth off, saying I own a million dollars' worth of property hereabouts."

"Joseph, I've seen the books. I happen to know that you've acquired city lots for a few dollars and are selling them for a thousand. And you expect *me* to be party to this fraud?"

"I'll transfer the titles. My young'uns will inherit it all anyway—might as well do it now."

"Joseph, need I remind you that the bankruptcy law will allow no transfer of goods to take advantage of this law? You can't transfer the property to the church either. The state law allows a church to own only five acres of land."

Shaking his head as he recalled that interview, Mark straightened in the saddle and took a deep breath. Jenny was right—he was prone to carry everyone's load on his own shoulders. He tried to shove away the oppressive feeling that he must do something—and quickly.

The rain clouds had moved on. Looking around, noting the signs of spring, he dug his heels into the mare's ribs and tightened his grip on the reins.

This road between Warsaw and Nauvoo had been a lonesome road just last year, but now with the influx of the English settlers as well as the addition of more Canadians, the countryside was becoming dotted with farms. Neat fences bordered the road. Trees had been cleared and the plow had been set to the virgin acres.

As Mark studied the landscape, he thought of his Gentile neighbors. At times when Mark listened to the grumbles and studied the hostile stares of the Gentiles living around the area, he wondered where the discontent would lead. What he saw and heard made him uneasy.

Back in 1839, that first traumatic year of the exodus, the people of Illinois, living close to the old town of Commerce, had welcomed the Saints with compassion and tolerance.

But the feeling was fast disappearing, for several reasons. One was the disappearance of prime farm land from the market. Nearly all the prairie land had been purchased. And the fact that the deeds were in Joseph's hand, waiting for new converts to claim them, didn't help.

But Joseph chose to see only the pleasant side of life right now. Mark writhed under the Prophet's arrogant confidence, even though he realized he should have expected it. How could he have forgotten even for one minute Joseph's reaction to the hordes of visitors streaming into Nauvoo?

The rapt audience of strangers listening to him, and the admiring throng of people there to watch the Nauvoo Legion parade through the streets, worked like blinders on Joseph. Finally, with a sigh, Mark tried to dismiss Joseph from his thoughts.

The early morning sun slanted light across the plowed acres. Mark watched it tunneling under the cluster of clouds capping the forest. Birds pecked at the fresh-turned soil, while across the meadow a thin spire of smoke marked a cabin. The trees showed fresh color, splashing yellow-green, pink, and white against the dark pine.

Mark's appreciation was forming into a prayer when he heard the creaking wagon wheels behind him. Pulling the mare aside, he turned as the wagon reached him.

"Mornin'," said Daniels, the Gentile who lived across the ravine. The old man pointed his whip toward the sky. "Right pretty with the clouds and sunshine. God's in His heaven, all's right down below."

"I hope that is so," Mark said soberly. "If it isn't, I expect we've been responsible." The man considered, nodded his head, and passed on.

At the next break in the fence, another rider met Mark—Orson Pratt. He pulled his mount even with Mark and turned a worried frown on him. "What do you think about this getting the Lodge in Nauvoo?"

Mark studied the apostle for a moment before replying, "Seems a bad time to be taking a poll. The installation is to be next week. Pratt, you know my feelings, and I haven't backed down. I expressed my view last fall when things first started rolling that direction. I'm against the secret societies in general. However, I'm not the best informed about masonry because I've never considered it.

"The *Book of Mormon* talks enough about the Lord being against secret—is it called murderous combinations? Can't believe Joseph would go against the gold book."

Pratt's frown deepened. "That's what bothers me. Seems I can't reconcile Joseph allowing it, either." He shot Mark a quick look, and for a moment Mark felt as if he were being measured by some unseen rule.

Jenny had returned to her kitchen and was washing the dishes when the tap came on her window. Tom was grinning at her and she went to unlatch the door. "Am I in time for breakfast?"

She gave him a quick hug and pulled him into the room. "I'll have some ready immediately. Eggs?"

He nodded. "Mark left?"

She sighed. "Yes, 'twas awfully early, but he acted as if he couldn't wait to get out of the house. Tom, there's something troubling him. I wish he'd feel free to talk it out."

She turned from the stove and saw the curious expression on Tom's face. "Now you look a dark brown study yourself. Tom, what's going on? No one's said a thing to me—won't, in fact, though I've tried to find out. Seems I've no friend to trust me with a lick of gossip."

He snorted. "With Joseph starting up that Relief Society meeting this month, there's bound to be lots of loose gossip floatin' around."

"Well, there isn't," Jenny sniffed. "However, I'm put out at him. In the first place, we women would like to do the organizing. Most of us were well content with having a small sewing group so we could share a little refreshment and the latest stitching patterns. But no, Joseph's pushing every woman in town to be a part of it."

"Aw, that's it. He found out you ladies were sipping tea and breakin' the word of wisdom, so he's had to sic Emma on you."

"Mind your tongue," Jenny said with real irritation. "Emma's nice enough if a body doesn't cross her. It's just the bossiness of it all."

"Now, Jenny, you know a female isn't goin' to make it to heaven at all without a man to take her there. No sense in buckin' the Word of the Lord. We've got the priesthood, and there's no sense in wanting the old ways."

"Tom, did you just come to fuss? Besides, when are you going to do your part and get married?"

She watched the play of expression on his face—fear, puzzlement, then embarrassment. He ignored the question. "Not to fuss. Wanted to ride in with Mark." He was silent for a moment. Turning, she was surprised to see the scowl again. "I've been over Warsaw way, listening to more of the rumbles. Sure's discontent when they talk about things."

"Like what?"

"Oh, to start, the Nauvoo Charter. Seems they're thinkin' we Mormons are uppity. The rumbles over the charter makes me believe Missouri's tossing out information. I heard talk about wantin' to see Joe go back for trial. Also there's the prophecy he gave out last year, about Boggs and Carlin both dying."

"Well, I guess they can take that with a grain of salt unless it comes true."

"Jen, the way you said that surprises me." Tom paused for a moment to scratch his head. Slowly he said, "Seems in the past you shivered over all the prophecies; now it's 'wait and see.' Are you not believing anymore?"

"In Joseph? Of course. I have to believe; there's nothing else. It's just . . ." Her voice trailed away and she chewed at her lip for a moment. "It's just that I've been counting up in my mind all Joseph's said that hasn't come to pass."

"What possessed you to do that?"

Slowly she said, "I've been reading the Bible." His eyebrows went up. "Joseph's been urging me to read the Scriptures, so I do. One day it's the *Book of Mormon* and the next it's the Holy Bible. Just yesterday I read about God telling how to distinguish a true prophet. The Bible says if a fellow is a prophet from the Lord, then all his prophecies come to pass, and if they don't, well, then he's a false prophet and he's to be taken out and killed."

"Jen, that's the Old Testament."

"But everything else we believe comes from there, doesn't it? The law and the sacrifices? Joseph himself said that the sacrifices of animals is to start up again soon as the temple is finished. I know for a fact that they did some sacrifices in Kirtland temple."

"Well, 'tis so, the law and sacrifices." Tom paused to scratch his head. "But there's Jesus Christ. He's New Testament."

"So far I can't understand where He fits in. Mark talks about Jesus being the only important part. The Atonement, he calls it."

After Tom left, Jenny sat in the rocker beside the window and watched the robins building their nest. Her dishwater was cooling, but she couldn't move away from the thoughts. She sighed. Her reading was bringing up questions, some of them as irritating as pebbles in her shoe.

When Jenny finally returned to her tasks, she was thinking about the melodious words she had read; they sang through her, and she wondered why she'd never discovered the beauty in the Bible before. At the very back of the book, she had found the words, "And he that overcometh, and keepeth my works unto the end, to him will I give power over the nations: . . . And I will give him the morning star."

As she went to dust the table holding the Bibles, she whispered, "The morning star. I've seen it—bright, promising, I—" She stopped and cocked her head. "That section talks about power over the nations, but I like the part about the morning star."

She was sweeping the porch when she began to ponder the rest of the verse. Leaning on the broom, she murmured, "I wonder if that's where Joseph got his power. I'd like to ask him what works it's talking about."

9

THE WARMTH OF the April sunshine made the clearing in front of the temple uncomfortably hot. Jenny loosened the shawl from her shoulders and shifted her feet.

She nudged Mark with her elbow. "There's Dr. Bennett. With all the fuss he's generated, I'm surprised to see him."

He frowned. "Are you referring to the newspaper articles?"

Jenny tilted her head to see his face. "Then there's something else?" The muscle in his jaw tightened, and she recalled the gossip, most of it unsavory, that had started at Relief Society. "There are whispers at Society about the way he takes advantage of women," she murmured.

"Jenny, let's talk later," he whispered, looking uncomfortable.

William Law stopped beside him. Jenny looked up into his stern face as he touched his hat, "Ma'am." Then addressing Mark, he asked, "Have you succeeded with Joseph?"

Mark started to reply just as the line of dark-coated men walked toward the crowd. He paused and said, "Law, why don't you stop by this afternoon? Seems best, considering."

He nodded and moved away as Heber C. Kimball began to address the crowd. Jenny's attention wandered away. She watched as William Law returned to his place beside his wife. Jane Law gave Jenny a quick glance and nod.

Jenny's gaze shifted across the crowd, nodding to the other restless ones, and then she studied the pile of limestone which would be the temple.

She thought of the promises Joseph had made about the temple—the promises and the warning. Baptism for the dead. Although she'd heard often enough about the rite from Brigham Young, she still felt uneasy.

Heber C. Kimball's words caught her attention. "Brethren, sisters, in the Lord. We are all concerned with how we get right with our God. But don't let this uneasiness possess your soul. I will tell you—it is knowledge. We must all increase in wisdom in order to gain salvation. The very act of believing in another man's testimony helps us increase in knowledge.

Thereby we gain wisdom and the power of God. As for your leaders, my advice is simply this: Whatever you are told to do—do it. If our advice leads you astray, the burden will be upon our shoulders, not yours."

Joseph Smith stepped forward and Jenny felt the tension and excitement grow. Unexpectedly Jenny found herself responding, leaning forward to catch his words.

More soft-spoken today, Joseph repeated words they had all heard before, but even Jenny acknowledged the need to hear them again. "My people, I must remind you that the ordinances you have received, and more, will be multiplied and increased for your good in the days which lie before you. But these are not new. In the beginning, the ordinances of the priesthood were passed on to Adam. This sacred trust was given to him at the creation, even before the world was formed. Remember that Adam is Michael, the archangel. Do not forget that Noah himself is Gabriel. When Daniel speaks of the Ancient of Days, he is referring to the oldest man who lives, our Father Adam. I will not keep you long this Sabbath day. I want only to remind you again that Father Adam presides over the spirits of mankind. He is our God."

The crowd was breaking apart, drifting homeward, when Sally and Andy hurried toward them. Sally threw her invitation across the people. "Come home with us?"

Mark shook his head and Jenny called, "You come with us; there's chicken in the oven."

When the Laws arrived, Sally and Jenny had just finished the dishes. As they came into the house, Jenny stood awkwardly in the doorway, suddenly shy and inadequate. She spoke tentatively, "Shall I prepare tea?" Jane Law glanced at her husband as she slowly drew off her gloves.

William frowned, but Mark said, "Some of us will enjoy a cup."

As Jenny turned into the kitchen, she was very conscious of Sally's trill of excited laughter. *"Kitchen maid,"* she muttered to herself, cringing as she reached for the teacups. She had heard that Jane and William Law were wealthy. She peeked through the doorway. The Canadians' British accent was nearly as intimidating as their fine clothes. Jenny eyed the fluffy gray fur edging Jane's brocade cape before she turned to load her tray.

Graciously Jane accepted the cup of tea. "Lovely china," she murmured with a smile. "My favorite pattern."

Tamara cuddled close to her mother, and her solemn blue eyes watched every move Jane made.

The conversation between the men cut through Jenny's thoughts. As she brought Mark tea, she lingered beside his chair. William was saying, "I'm fearful of what will happen if Bennett's excesses aren't curbed. I've tried talking to the man."

"Bennett?" Sally's laughter interrupted and the men turned. "But the council took care of him when they pushed his brothel into the gully last autumn!"

"Unfortunately that isn't the scope of his endeavors." William rumbled on. "Women aside, his biggest threat right now is the image he's projecting of the Saints."

"You're referring to the articles?" Mark asked. Jenny knew he was talking about the series the *Times and Seasons* had published.

Jenny couldn't hold back the words, "I wondered why the Saints' newspaper printed them."

William scrutinized Jenny before he said, "I wondered too—certainly there was nothing good to be accomplished."

"What were they about?" Sally asked.

"Well," Jane replied, "most certainly he informed the world at large that Joseph is a power to be reckoned with, that he now has at his disposal the power to avenge the wrongs inflicted upon his people in Missouri. He has demanded satisfaction for wrongs, and hinted Missouri land must be restored to the Saints."

William added, "We weren't in the States when this all happened and, to be certain, the information we've had is limited, but nevertheless we saw it as a war cry."

Heavily Mark said, "I'm afraid it was intended to be. I tried to get Joseph to stay Bennett's hand, but . . ."

Andy continued, "He's too powerful. He had Joseph eating out of his hand. Now it's too late to curb the man. Our only hope is that he will tire of the game and go home."

William frowned. "You seem convinced the man is insincere. Is there a possibility he's warping the mind of the Prophet?"

"A man of God being warped by a mere mortal?" Mark snorted, and Jenny, studying his face, saw how ludicrous the idea was. A secret question which had its birth in the articles slipped away and she sighed with relief. Obviously Joseph didn't support the articles. She caught Mark's sharp glance; then William began speaking again, his voice rumbling slowly and thoughtfully.

"Mark, it's a different problem that plagues me today. You know Foster and I are engaged in trying to put up homes in Nauvoo as quickly as possible. Some of these poor people spent the winter in wagons and shanties. That ought not be so. You also know Joseph is determined the temple and his precious Nauvoo House will be built first. There's a real tug-of-war taking place. I'm here to ask your intervention."

Mark replied bitterly, "What makes you think I have any more influence with Joseph Smith than you?"

The man sighed, "I'd hoped." When he spoke again his voice was thoughtful. "He threatened to excommunicate any man who bought land without consulting him. I don't like some of his financial ventures, such as publishing his revised Bible. I honestly feel he's misusing the money he has collected to build the temple and the Nauvoo House."

Mark's shoulders straightened. "Law," he said sharply, "that's a serious charge."

"I know. Right now I wouldn't make it in court, but there're indications he's invested the funds in real estate and then sold at a profit."

"Is that all that's bothering you?" Mark asked.

"No. I'm deeply disturbed because of the workers on the temple site. They're living on parched corn. There's no income for the work, and they're practically starving."

Andy added, "These are the men who bought land on the Iowa side and then lost everything when the deeds proved to be fraudulent."

"Foster and I are fighting to get the materials to erect houses before winter. Now Joseph is saying the Nauvoo House must be built, that our salvation depends upon this happening." For a time, William sat with his head bowed to his chest. When he finally sighed and straightened, he looked around the room and muttered, "I tried to remonstrate with him about some other things. I can't tell you all, but I was sorely tried when he informed me in a lighthearted manner that if the results were as I feared, we could both go to hell, and that hell is by no means the bad place it's been pictured. To the contrary, Joseph thought it was a pretty agreeable place."

Jenny felt the shock of the statement, but Mark's eyes holding hers made her shiver even more. The question in their depths could not be avoided: he was challenging her commitment to Joseph. She turned away from them all with a tired sigh, but even then she knew the questions couldn't be avoided any longer.

That Monday when Mark guided his mare out to the main road, he had put William Law's conversation behind him. As he faced the sunshine cresting the rolling hills of Nauvoo, he thought of the blank page of the week stretching out before him. He knew of the items that needed to be placed on the page, he also knew of the problems that were pressing him, demanding their rightful place. His lips twisted in a rueful smile as he thought of the Prophet. With his usual pleasant smile, he would sweep Mark's page clean and dump another load upon it.

When Mark reached the office, Joseph was there. He was sitting behind his desk, and Mark immediately recognized that this was the day for confrontation. Joseph's suit for bankruptcy had been pushed aside for the last time.

After the polite words had passed between them, Mark took a deep breath and said, "The answer is *no*. Morally, for you to declare bankruptcy is wrong. If you insist on this line of action, you'll need to find another attorney to represent you."

Joseph's level gaze was unwavering. Mark was conscious of all the implications of his decision. What about Jenny's spiritual groping? Would her wavering spirit be crushed by leaving Nauvoo with her questions still unanswered?

Even as Mark realized he must push the hard questions at Joseph, he was aware of the risk he was taking. *Excommunication.* "Joseph, I feel I must warn you that there's a great risk to be taken in following this course of declaring bankruptcy. Are you prepared to subject your personal life to legal scrutiny?"

Joseph leaned back and grinned. "I see you've been listening to gossip."

"Is it gossip? I thought it common knowledge that you've begun teaching something the brethren are calling the spiritual wife doctrine. I—"

Joseph's chair thumped to the floor and with a scowl, he leaned toward Mark. "I've inquired of the Lord. Of course I knew the gossip. The Lord assures me that I *have not* committed adultery. Mark, judge not. If you are to remain in the good graces of the church, sooner or later you must receive this doctrine. The spirit tells me you are not sufficiently righteous to receive it now. Until that time, I suggest you join the Lodge and take up your religion."

"What are you referring to?"

"I've been advised you display no interest in becoming acquainted with the endowments and, specifically, baptism for the dead."

"You know I don't believe that way."

For a moment Mark was pierced by Joseph's questioning look. Then the Prophet said, "Mark, I'm considering sending out another group of missionaries. It's being made clear to me that I'm to gather money from all the people before the Nauvoo House can be completed."

Mark jumped to his feet, anger surging through him. Joseph's message was very clear. As Mark opened his mouth, there came the clear picture of Jenny's ravaged face and terror-filled eyes. Slowly he turned to pace the room.

On his second trip back across the room, there was a tap on the door as it was shoved open. William Smith stood there, wearing a wide, lazy grin. "Gentleman wantin' to see my esteemed brother, the Prophet. Better not keep him waiting; he looks important."

Joseph hurried out of the room and Mark slowly extended his hand. "Hello, William. I don't believe I've had a chance to talk to you since Missouri days. Is your family well?"

William nodded. There was a question in his eyes as he turned to survey the room. "I hear you're Joseph's lawyer. Didn't know you were here. Sorry for exploding in." A low grin moved across his face. "Keep hoping I'll catch him teaching some lovelies the secrets of the kingdom."

Mark ignored the remark and said, "I understand you've been involved in mission work. What do you think about the climate out there? Are people being attracted to Joseph, or is it the promise of land and freedom?"

William shrugged, still wearing his gleeful grin, and pushed on. "What do you think about the new doctrine?"

Mark replied, "I know absolutely nothing about it."

For a moment he looked disappointed and the glee disappeared, leaving his face surprisingly thoughtful. "Hyrum was terribly against it in the beginning. Don Carlos told me before he died that Joseph had prophesied to Hyrum there would be a witness given to him about the rightness of the doctrine. Well, sure enough, he got it." He paused to scratch his shaggy thatch of hair and pace the room.

His face was now very sober, nearly frighteningly so, Mark saw with surprise. Fastening Mark with a steely gaze he said, " 'Tis upsetting to say the least, but the *Book of Mormon*—"

Joseph stepped through the door. He eyed William as the unfinished sentence hung in the silence. Glancing sharply from William to Mark, he said, with his voice cold and level, "And just what about the *Book of Mormon,* my dearly beloved brother? Just what had you in mind to say to Attorney Cartwright?"

Astonished, Mark looked at William and saw the sober expression replaced with wicked glee. His lips were twisted in derision. Abruptly he laughed and turned toward the door.

With a quick movement, Joseph was there. "Not so fast." His hand grasped William's shirt and twisted, pulling the big man closer. "William, you are not keeping your part of the bargain. I suggest you snug up your religion good and tight. You may need it more than you think you do." With a thrust he propelled his brother out the door and slammed it behind him.

Joseph was still trembling with anger as he turned around. Mark watched him take a careful breath, settle his collar, and move behind the desk. After another breath he said, "Just a little problem with Judge Adams. Mark, I'm afraid I'll be involved the rest of the day."

Mark could see that Joseph was in control now. He also saw the curiosity in his eyes, a deeper expression Mark didn't understand. Joseph spoke slowly, "I hope you didn't get the wrong idea. I wasn't thinking of sending you on a mission. I'm certain of your loyalty and I know you'd be willing, but I need you here."

Mark was on the street before he could identify that look in Joseph's eyes. It was fear. As he walked toward the stable he muttered, "Just maybe there's something to those rumors about William having something on Joseph. More than maybe, I'd say. Seems the words *Book of Mormon* has something to do with it."

Mark's thoughts were full of the scripture he had read that morning. It had excited him with a mysterious promise. When he had read it aloud to Jenny, she had just looked puzzled. Now Mark murmured the words, "So they shall make their own tongue to fall upon themselves."

10

THE SPRING MORNING was lovely enough of itself, Jenny thought, but another joy wound itself around her heart this late April day. She flicked the reins along the mare's back and smiled to herself. It was Mark. For the past two weeks he had acted like a man who'd dropped his sack of potatoes.

"God's in his heaven, and it's all right in the world," Jenny happily misquoted to the blue sky and wild plum trees.

A creaking, groaning wagon was approaching and she looked over her shoulder. "Morning, ma'am." The white-haired farmer yanked on the reins as they drew abreast. The apple-cheeked woman beside him nodded brightly. "You be Mark Cartwright's wife?"

Jenny nodded. "Saints?"

"No." For just a moment the smile dimmed and then she added, "We met your husband a-goin' into town when we're on our way with the milk. Nice, friendly fella." With another smile they were on their way, and Jenny realized they hadn't introduced themselves.

Snapping the reins across the horse's back Jenny said, "Must be our Gentile neighbors across the ravine, the Daniels." She rode on.

The Pratt farm was just ahead. Jenny studied the log house tucked back in the curve of trees and felt her curiosity welling up again. Sarah Pratt had become the object of gossip for the past two Relief Society meetings. Strange things those women could find to pick over—talking about her and Dr. Bennett. Thinking of Sarah's winsome face, her honest smile, Jenny shook her head and her curiosity grew.

The lane leading to the Pratt home was coming up. Jenny compared the story of Sarah's unhappy husband to her own cheerful Mark. They said he nearly committed suicide when he came back from his mission and heard the gossip.

Abruptly giving way to impulse, Jenny tugged the reins and wheeled the buggy into Pratts' lane. She had only a few troubled minutes to sort the things she might say to Sarah, and then she was at the house.

Sarah was standing in the doorway and Jenny called. "Just passing this way. I wonder, would you like to go into Nauvoo for the Relief Society meeting with me?"

Slowly Sarah came down to the buggy and lifted her face. Jenny saw the frown, the questions in the clear gray eyes and waited. "I heard there's a bit of talk. Would it help or hinder if I were to go? I understand Emma's a mite sharp."

Jenny frowned. For a moment she was caught up in wondering why Emma was involved in the gossip. "Sharp? At times she seems so," Jenny said slowly. "I was thinking not of the gossip, but of your husband. I know he's better now, but remembering how unhappy my Mark has been, I wanted to encourage you."

Sarah's eyebrows arched in surprise. "I'm sure it isn't for the same reason."

"Reason?" Jenny frowned, beginning now to regret her hasty decision. She slanted a glance at the woman and saw her unexpected smile.

"Yes, I would like to be out this day. I've felt house-bound. If you could come in while I dress the tyke and smooth my hair—"

Jenny hopped from the buggy. "Wonderful!"

Sarah's little boy, Aaron, was nearly the same age as Sally's Tamara. He carried his boots to Jenny as Sarah went to change her frock. Over the little fellow's chatter, Jenny heard her horse nicker and Sarah said, "There's someone. Please—while I finish dressing."

Jenny opened the door and with surprise said, "Why, Dr. Bennett!"

He bent over her hand in a way that warmed Jenny's cheeks, saying, "We've not been introduced, but I'm certain you are Mark Cartwright's wife."

"And I know you only through—" she hesitated, and he grinned.

Sarah came into the room, looking startled as she saw the visitor. "Why, Dr. Bennett, what brings you this way?"

"I've a task out this way and I decided to check on my friend." He turned to lift the child. Over little Aaron's head he asked, "I haven't seen Orson. Is it well with him?"

Sarah paused only briefly. "Aye. But there's so much inquiry this morning, I'm beginning to worry. Is there a new story afloat?"

Dr. Bennett glanced at Jenny with surprise. "Oh, no," Jenny said hastily; she took a deep breath and felt she had much to explain. "See, Mark's been so . . ." They waited. "Well, not himself. Remembering what they said about Orson, I just felt . . ." The two faces were changing. Jenny saw Sarah's stony expression and saw the lines crinkling across Dr. Bennett's. He was amused!

"I assure you, my dear," he chuckled, taking Jenny's hand, "Sarah is just as virtuous as she claims to be. If you have a problem, let's just sit down and discuss it. You won't be able to shock me. Is it Joseph?"

Sarah interrupted, "Dr. Bennett, I do believe—"

He glanced at her and Jenny watched his face change. When he faced Jenny again, he said, "I'm on my way to do another task." Again he paused and studied Jenny's face. "I can assure you, my dear. At any stage in the problem, I can take care of the situation. There will be no danger to the mother and this will not prevent future increases, if she so desires."

"What—where?"

Sarah interrupted, "He has a kind of—hospital. Surely you've noticed the little building out on the flats. It's only about a mile and a half from town. But I can't believe that you've—"

Jenny was shaking her head furiously. "You're talking about taking a baby out, aren't you?"

"Abortion." Sarah's voice was flat. " 'Tis a common task in town." Her voice was bitter. "And a very common need."

"I can't believe that," Jenny said dully, thinking of her own great need. Now she lifted her head, realizing the unstated questions. "Dr. Bennett, I wanted to come to you for advice on *how* I could—And you think it's just the contrary situation!"

Sarah put her arms around Jenny. Now the hard lines were gone and she smiled. "Oh, Jenny, I'm so sorry. Seems we all think the worst of each other around here."

After Dr. Bennett left, Sarah seated Jenny at the table and made tea. "I do not condone all that's going on in the name of religion," she said as she sat beside Jenny. "The reason Dr. Bennett and I are friends is because he has been a friend to me in my need." Jenny watched her compress her lips as she picked at the lint on her sleeve.

When she lifted her head she smiled. "I don't want to hurt people or hurt the Saints' cause, but I have been misunderstood by people—" Again she paused and then took a deep breath. "Just this one thing. I was hungry and nearly destitute while my husband was on a mission. Dr. Bennett befriended me. Contrary to the gossip, he was never my lover. Even if it weren't for my husband, whom I love dearly, John Bennett and I are too close friends for that."

Jenny, recovering from the shock she had felt, was beginning to understand the dark looks, the hinted questions of the women at Relief Society. "Sarah," she whispered, "I would like very much to be your friend. Perhaps in time, if you'll go with me, the others will forget the terrible stories and we'll all be friends."

She hesitated a moment and then continued, "But will you please tell me about Dr. Bennett? I know nearly nothing about the man except mentioning him makes the women giggle."

"Well, there are a few things I don't know. I haven't questioned him about his morals, and I don't know much about his past. He is a doctor. In the beginning he contacted Joseph. Some call him an opportunist, and it could look that way when you consider the way he eagerly walked into the church and started taking control of everything.

"But then, I have a feeling Joseph really needed him. There is a flair, a sophistication about the man. But he's also capable of being a sincere friend.

"He was secretary of the Illinois Medical Association at the time he came to Nauvoo. I don't condone the abortions he's doing, if you are wondering about that.

"Bennett wrote the Nauvoo city charter, and with his influence was responsible for getting it through the state legislature. He became mayor of Nauvoo, assistant to Joseph in the church, chancellor of the university, brigadier-general of the Legion and even had a revelation addressed to him, calling him blessed. You know about his brothel and how it was shoved over the hill. Dr. Bennett is also quartermaster general for the state militia; that influence enabled him to win concessions for Joseph's Legion, including cannon.

"His newspaper articles make me uneasy. I feel there's more to Dr. Bennett's aspirations than we know about. But then, I'm not a man and needn't worry myself on that score.

"I do believe that he and Joseph aren't nearly as much in agreement as they have been in the past," she finished thoughtfully as she gathered up little Aaron and smiled at Jenny. "I'm ready to go."

Mark was nearly to Carthage when he realized he'd forgotten to pick up the papers from Joseph's office over the store. Disgusted with himself, he wheeled his mount and headed back to Nauvoo. As he rode he realized it would be too late to return to the land title office in Carthage that afternoon, but he pressed on, muttering, "I'll get the papers and head for home. Tomorrow I'll take the shortcut and save an hour. Don't know why Joseph couldn't have held off until the end of the week when Clayton makes his usual trip. It would save my going."

He was still feeling like a disgruntled errand boy when he reached the store and took the back stairs two at a time.

The door at the top of the stairs was opening as Mark reached for the knob. He nearly collided with the scarlet-cheeked woman rushing past.

"Beg your pardon, ma'am!" he exclaimed, stepping back.

She paused and turned to him. "*I* should apologize," she insisted, attempting a smile.

Mark saw the compressed lips, the shadowed eyes. With dismay he said, "I've offended you; I'm terribly sorry."

"No, sir." Her reply was sharp and her hand descended on his arm. "But, if you will be so kind, please escort me."

Mark accompanied the young lady to her front porch. He was frowning as he started down the path to the office. "Miss Martha Brotherton," he muttered to himself. "You've been seeking counsel from Brother Joseph, and I don't think he's helped you at all. It's been a long time since I've escorted a young woman who galloped down the street in such a huff. I can't believe a grizzly bear would have failed to take to the bushes under that threat."

Within a week, Mark's questions about the encounter were explained, but all Nauvoo seemed to know before the information reached Mark. As he rode homeward, hashing over the story, he mused, "Of all the gossip that's circulating around about Nauvoo concerning Joseph and the twelve misbehaving, I suppose I've come as close as possible to having the evidence squashed in my face by an irate victim."

He paused, then reflected aloud, "So this is the little English lady who dared refuse the Prophet and Brigham, and even published their indecent proposals! The world knows now that there's one woman in Zion who didn't like the idea of being married to Brigham Young in this world or the next, especially since she wasn't the first one he'd approached with the same proposal."

He continued on his way home, pondering the advisability of telling Jenny the story. She had a nebulous feeling of change about her. He considered again and then regretfully shook his head with a wry grin. "Hands off," he muttered. "Much as I want to do it my way, I'll keep my mouth shut. Just as I was tenderly instructed by love, so Jenny must be."

11

ON THE DAY that news about the Boggs' shooting reached Jenny, she was with Sally.

After completing her shopping, Jenny had walked to Sally's home. For an hour she followed Sally around the kitchen as she worked, and it was nearly time for Andy to be home for his noon meal.

Jenny's chatter initially kept her from noticing how quiet her friend was. Finally, when Sally paused with hands on hips, Jenny asked, "What is it?"

Sally looked startled. "I was thinking—all this food, and only the two of us. Why don't you go after Mark?"

"Well, I suppose I could. He's carried a snack with him, but—" She paused, contemplating. "That's nice, Sally. I'll be back with him shortly." Jenny swung out the door. With a sigh of relief, Sally followed her to the door.

Jane Law was just coming up the path and Sally saw her hold out the packet of papers. Jenny shook her head, pointing to Sally. Jane walked up the steps. "Jenny said to give these papers to you. She'll return with Mark."

"Oh." Sally looked from the papers to Jane, searching the face of the older woman. She took a deep breath. "Have you heard the latest?" She was surprised at the waver in her voice.

Jane glanced at her sharply. "No," she said slowly. "Seems it's something you need to say."

"Could be it's nothing more than gossip, but there's a letter."

Jane's head came up. "From whom?"

Slowly Sally said, "Joseph. To Nancy Rigdon."

Now Jane's curiosity surfaced. "What's in it?"

"Well, first, Ann Eliza told me she'd seen it herself."

"They are friends," Jane said slowly as she carried her tea to the table.

"Right off, Nancy Rigdon told her that Dr. Bennett warned her that Joseph was going to approach her with a proposal to become his spiritual wife." Sally glanced sharply at Jane. She could see by the older woman's nod that she was familiar with the doctrine.

She took up her story. "Ann Eliza said when Joseph came to Mrs. Hyde's place—you know, the printing office where she and Dr. Richards live—"

"Together?" Jane was surprised. Sally took time to nod, and she began to wonder how much she should tell this woman. Right now she decided, eyeing her, it wouldn't be wise to tell her deepest secrets.

"Well, Nancy came to the printing office, but Joseph was busy. He had Richards tell her to come to the store later. But one of the men there leveled with her, told her what was going on and suggested she go ahead and find out.

"I'm guessing she didn't believe the fella at the time. Poor girl. Had confidence in him—Joseph."

"What do you mean?"

"According to Ann Eliza, Joseph took Nancy into the office and locked the door. That kinda scared her. She told Ann Eliza she was glad Mrs. Hyde had gone with her. He started in about how the Lord had given Nancy to him, and so on. There sat Nancy, crying and fussing. He tried to kiss her and she told him to stop or she'd scream and get the whole town there. Seems to have done the trick, 'cause he unlocked the door for her.

"Ann Eliza told me confidential-like that if it weren't for the letter, she wouldn't have believed such an outlandish story. Have you ever heard the like?"

Jane shook her head. "What about the letter?"

"Well, first off, Nancy told her pa and he confronted Joseph. Then Ann Eliza said Joseph kept denying everything until they waved the letter in front of him.

"First, the letter said that happiness was the object of existence, and that the path to happiness is virtue, faithfulness and holiness, and so on, including keeping all the commandments of God—which led him to explain *the* commandment. He also said a thing which was wrong under one circumstance was right under another. Ann Eliza said he was meaning you-know-what. So then he said everything God requires is right, no matter what it is. And that God is more liberal than we are ready to believe.

"Nancy told Ann Eliza this was all explaining what he'd told her in the office, about how she was to be his wife, because God had given her to him." Sally stopped and looked at Jane who was staring into her teacup.

After a long moment Jane lifted her head. "I don't know what to say; it's just so unbelievable." As Jane stood to leave, Sally saw again the dark question in her eyes.

Leaning against the doorjamb, waiting for Jenny and the men, Sally whispered, "She doesn't believe me!" But as she turned back to the kitchen, the ache around Sally's heart was easier. She wondered, if in time, she also would come to disbelieve the story.

Jenny was through the door first, "Oh, Sally, you just can't imagine! The prophecy has come to pass!"

Sally turned with the tureen of soup in her hands. Carefully placing it on the table she asked, "What?"

"Boggs has been shot. Already they're blaming Joseph."

Andy came through the door as Sally cried, "Oh, is he in trouble?"

The men were both shaking their heads and Andy said, "Joseph's preparing a statement for the newspaper. He'll admit to the prophecy—after all, he's a prophet. His statement will show his belief that Boggs was a victim of a political opponent, backing it up with the declaration that his hands are free from the stain of murder."

As they ate the soup, Mark said, "There are rumbles that Porter Rockwell is missing. If he's innocent of Boggs' blood, he'll save a lot of trouble for the Prophet if he just stays missing."

Later, Mark and Andy headed back to town together. They walked over the hill and through the temple grove, pausing to inspect the work at the site. Andy had recently been appointed as superintendent of the temple construction. Mark turned to Andy and said, "I know that Law's working independently, on houses and such. Is there a conflict between you?"

"Naw, my tasks keep me close to the office." Slowly Andy said, "I often wonder how long Joseph will tolerate a man of Law's stature. He's closer to being real competition than any other man around, even Brig."

As the men walked around the excavation, Mark remarked, "Since you and Law were at the house, you've been appointed to supervise the temple work. How do the complaints Law made that day affect you?"

"That's a strange question. You know I dare not let them if I am to work in peace and harmony with the Prophet."

"Does that disturb you?"

"No. I value my standing. Also, Joseph is ultimately responsible both to God and the people for any wrongdoing."

"That's small comfort when a man's hungry and can't provide for his children."

"Seems Joseph's doing the best he can."

"Seems—if you don't look at his resources and the comfort of his own life."

"Mark, he said, for all to hear, that if a man's hungry he can come to the Mansion House for dinner."

The two turned away from the temple and started down the hill. Mark was lost in thought when Andy said, "The temple reminds me that I need to say something to you.

"Mark, when do you intend to follow through? You realize, being as close to Joseph as you are, that everybody's watching your life. It doesn't speak well for a man's success when his attorney doesn't go along with the teaching."

"You're saying?"

"Every man in town who amounts to a hill of beans has joined the Lodge. Except for you."

Mark moved his shoulders uneasily. "Andy, I know. I'll admit I don't know too much about the Masons, but the Holy Spirit is warning me that something's wrong. I know it's a secret organization, but if you're my friend and you're serious about my joining, I need to know what I'm getting into."

"Well, it can't be bad," Andy's voice was rueful. "The ritual closely parallels the temple endowments."

Mark frowned. "That seems strange, particularly since the endowments came soon after the Lodge was started. Are you saying there's real religious influence in Masonry?"

"Of course, in a kind of oblique way. It's about God. It's religion without being a religion. It focuses on an individual helping himself, not keeping churchy rules."

Mark studied Andy's face for another moment. There was that second unanswered question. He plunged. "Andy, tell me about the Council of Fifty."

His lips twisted, "John D. Lee refers to it as the council of gods. Mark, it's all related to the kingdom." He paused and studied Mark's face intently before saying, "You know Joseph's received the revelation about setting up the kingdom. Nothing official's been done. There's a need to wait. Right now the time isn't ripe to reveal it.

"You'd have been in on it all, just like I've been, except you've bucked authority. It's common knowledge that Joseph's favorite attorney's saying things that makes it hard to talk to him. In a place like Nauvoo, particularly after the troubles the Saints have gone through, the disagreements are hard to take."

Mark sighed, "Andy, going back to the Masonic Lodge, I don't know the teachings. I only buck it because the *Book of Mormon* is against secret societies. Seems there's an awful lot of secrets suddenly cropping up in Joseph's church. If what Joseph claims about the *Book of Mormon* is true, then how dare he teach something that goes against God's Word to him?"

"But there are other things that stick in the man's craw about you."

"Name a few."

"For one, why does it trouble you that Joseph wants to be called *General Smith* instead of *president*? The men were calling him *squire* while we were in Missouri. And why buck the Nauvoo Charter? Seems if Joseph's going to push the kingdom in another year or so, we might as well have the legal advantage to begin with."

Mark knew his face was reflecting surprise, and Andy studied him thoughtfully for a moment. "You know I'm talking when I have no business doing so."

Nodding, Mark said, "I don't ask you to betray confidence. But all this muttering and rumbling I hear in the background makes me uneasy. From a legal point of view, the charter's passing is nearly ludicrous. I can't believe the state legislators did that."

The two men finished the walk in silence and parted at the store. Mark slowly climbed the stairs. Joseph lifted his head as Mark walked into the room. "Must have been a heavy meal you had. Sounded like you weighed a ton walking up those stairs."

Abruptly Mark said, "Tell me about the Lodge. Why did you apply for a lodge in Nauvoo? I'm aware of the *Book of Mormon* stance against secret societies. What advantage is there to your going against it?"

Joseph leaned back in his chair and tented his fingers together while he gazed out the window. He was silent for so long, Mark thought he had forgotten him. When he finally glanced up, he wore a brisk, friendly grin.

"Mark, you're nearly apostate, you've bucked me so much. Do you realize what would happen to your family if I were to follow through according to what you deserve?"

Frowning Mark said, "I don't believe I understand you."

"You've questioned my judgment for years, even during the times I've functioned as a prophet. You won't go along with council to join the Lodge like the rest of the men. Your walking behind light is crippling your chance to gain the power of the priesthood."

"I am aware you are initiating some of the men into the higher teachings of the priesthood," Mark responded, "but Joseph, I haven't asked for that concession. In truth, just like Masonry, I'd question it deeply before I'd consent to being a part of it. It goes against the grain to say yes and then find out I don't like what I bargained for."

Joseph said heavily, "That isn't faith—either in the Lord or in me as prophet. If all of my members were like you, where would the church be?"

"If all the church members had the freedom to question and even make an ecclesiastical error without endangering their salvation," Mark countered, "perhaps you'd have an exhibit of more love and less fear."

Joseph thought for a minute and then settled back. The dreamy expression was back on his face. "All right, I'll tell you. I've felt for some time that the Lord was leading me to investigate Masonry. You saw me in

Springfield. I was talking with Grand Master Jonas. I've discovered more than I'd guessed."

Again he was silent. When he looked up his face was radiant and for a moment Mark was caught, understanding for a clear moment the compelling charm of the man.

Joseph leaned forward and his voice was soft as he said, "Mark, my friend, for one thing I've discovered that just as God's Word has been distorted and filled with errors by the hand of those transcribers who had not the gift and calling from God, so Masonry has suffered.

"You know that I have preached of Adam receiving the priesthood back in the beginning days of creation. Now I will tell you something which is not common knowledge—Masonry is degenerate from the priesthood."

"Then how can you allow the Lodge in Nauvoo?"

"Oh, the first principles are trustworthy. Masonry is a steppingstone for something more."

"What are you referring to?"

Joseph glanced at Mark. "First, the principles. By the time I finish, you'll be wanting to join. We are beings lost to perfection. It is the business of living to make us into perfection, completeness. This is done through seeking the elder brother, first off. Now in Masonry, this isn't church—in fact, the belief is that there are many paths upward. Nowadays we have the understanding that there's only one true church, containing the keys to the kingdom. But it is still our cognizance to build upon these principles."

"What special knowledge do you have?" Mark asked slowly.

"That intelligence will save; that knowledge will lead to the eternities. When a man takes and builds upon what the Lord has given him, he begins to grow into communion with God—verily, even into a god himself.

"Granted, Mark, I see in your face the disbelief, but even Masonry supports the idea that it is by striving and working at the task of controlling our humanity and all the passions which must be perfected that we arrive at this state."

"I hear you say Masonry has taught you to become a god?"

"That and more. There's a certain center to it that allows a man to learn all there is to know, to understand and think like god. There is a light and knowledge hidden in this universe which we are obligated to obtain. I warn you, Mark, there's a very real danger for you to try to obtain these mysteries of knowledge apart from the true church.

"I also warn you that moral suicide awaits the man who tastes of the things the Lord offers through the church, particularly the priesthood, and then turns aside. You've gotten enough that you are in danger of this. I admonish you, enter the secret center where truth abides forever."

Mark got to his feet. "Joseph, I can't say I'm convinced. I've never had a desire to be a god. I don't even consider myself a good follower of the Lord Jesus Christ." He turned to go, but Joseph's words stopped him.

"Mark, you're near to being an apostate. I suggest you pull the reins up tight within these next few weeks. The Lord Himself has led me to understand that for an apostate spouse there is nothing.

"If you leave Nauvoo, Jenny will stay behind. I know she's trying with all her heart to be a good Saint. If you leave—" he paused, and his eyes were curiously light, "your marriage contract will be null and void."

12

IT WAS RAINING—not the usual summer rain, but instead a cold drizzle that chilled the bones. Mark had left for Nauvoo looking as dismal as Jenny felt. She pushed more wood into the kitchen stove and went to the window.

"Here it's June, and I should be weeding the garden and gathering peas," she advised herself, rubbing her chilled arms. "Instead, I shiver and look for something to do."

She was caught with remembering, muttering, "If Clara were here, she could help me drive the clouds away. Or Adela." The thoughts threw open the door she had firmly closed that dismal day of the broken mirror.

Restlessly Jenny paced the floor, troubled but unable to stop the probing questions surfacing in her mind. After thinking she had moved beyond the book and charms, why did she still feel the pull?

"I've lived my religion," she whispered into the silent room. "Why is there no contentment? The others seem to be happy with their lot in life. I still feel like the young'un with my nose against the window of the candy store."

Jenny slowly pulled the broom across the floor, looking for a stray particle of dust. Reasons for feeling this way began to surface. "Power," she muttered. "I need to know what's out there. I want to do something that will make me feel a part of the whole universe. I liked the mystery, the charms. I enjoyed Adela's company. Now there's nothing."

She had taken her broom into the parlor. Pausing to lean on it, she looked at the table centered between the two chairs. Carefully arranged on opposite sides of the china lamp were the Bibles, hers and Mark's. Jenny's rested on top of another black book—the *Book of Mormon.*

Jenny went after the dustcloth. As she moved it over the table and around the pink roses on the lamp, she noticed the differences in the books. Mark's Bible was scuffed, and the pages curled invitingly outward. *It's almost as if the words were trying to escape,* Jenny thought with amusement as she looked at the smooth leather of her own Bible, still shiny with newness.

Joseph Smith told me to study the Scriptures, she thought. She had started, but somewhere along the way too many days had passed between the readings.

"I know why," she said thoughtfully. "I was just plain tired of reading about Nephi, and the books in the Old Testament were either listing a bunch of men I didn't know or saying things I didn't like. The wrath of God. The people getting swallowed up for doing a little stealing. If the Lord were around hereabouts, there'd be a mighty big hole in the ground. Leastwise, Joseph preaches a lot about thieving."

Her dustcloth slowed. What would happen if she were to read the New Testament first? She looked at Mark's Bible and couldn't keep from wondering why it looked as it did.

She put away the broom and dustcloth, washed her hands and settled into the rocking chair.

Jenny looked up when she heard the horse. She recognized Tom's shout and saw him riding to the barn. By the time he reached the back door, Jenny had pulled the teakettle over the fire.

Tom hung his coat on the hook behind the door and carefully tilted his hat against the stove to dry.

"What brings you out today?" Jenny asked, reaching for the skillet.

"Carried a message to Mrs. Pratt for the Prophet and thought I'd come this way before headin' back to town."

"Is her husband away?"

"Yes, but he's due back shortly. I think that was the information in the letter." He shook his shaggy head. "Don't like being mistrusted."

"How's that?"

"Joseph. He sealed the letter, like he wanted to make sure I wouldn't read it."

"That's strange." Jenny began placing dishes upon the table.

Tom picked up the open Bible she had placed there and looked at the page. "How's come you put all these lines under the words?"

"I didn't. That's Mark's Bible. I've been reading it."

"Don't you have one of your own?"

"Yes. I'd only intended seeing why the pages bulge. He has pieces of paper inside and all these marks around verses. I had to discover why."

"Could ask."

"No." She took a deep breath and faced Tom. "Seems when we get off on religion, Mark and I disagree something terrible. I think he knows now how I feel about his picking at me. Every once in a while I see that look in his eyes, telling me he's all ready to give it all out and then suddenly he just closes his mouth and goes off."

"Guess if that's what you want—"

"I do and I don't. Tom, I don't want him shoving his ideas at me. Besides, they're scary."

"Why do you feel that? I've listened to him. Sure it's different, what he has to say; but somehow the strange things are almost believable when Mark says them. I'd expect him to back them up." Tom fell silent as he picked up his fork and stabbed at the potatoes and bacon. "I've been feelin' a mite disappointed in my religion lately."

Jenny studied him for a moment before saying, "Kinda like it isn't satisfying?"

Tom nodded. "I expect I'd not feel that way if it weren't for listenin' to Mark talk about his, and seein' he feels so different." He nodded toward the Book. "What did you read today?"

"Oh, lots. I got bored with Chronicles, so I started in with the New Testament. Just opened it to John. It was like a cow swallowing a pile of hay in one gulp. Now I find I'm back to chewing my cud. Some things stick, and I need to think about them for a time."

"Like what?" He reached for the bread.

"I read quite a bit in the first chapter before I discovered the *He* the fellow was talking about was Jesus. I get the feeling this all doesn't line up with Joseph's teachings. Guess I need to ask him. Tom," she continued slowly, "there's some things I really like about this man—Jesus. He seems so loving, but then He can be hard."

She fell silent, watching Tom eat. Then unable to hold back the words, she rushed on. "Mark had things written down on pieces of paper. Some I couldn't understand. On one piece he'd written references. I looked them up, and the thoughts all strung together were strange. According to them, God calls us into fellowship with His Son, and with love. God adopted us as sons through Jesus.

"Today I read in the first part of John that we have power to become the sons of God if we believe in Jesus. I wonder what that means, because I believe He's God's Son and I don't feel any power. Right now I'd settle for enough power to get rid of the rain."

Tom's brow furrowed in a frown. "Somehow I get the feelin' that isn't the kind of power the Book is talkin' about. Better go ask Joseph."

Jenny had forgotten the Legion was parading on the day she rode into Nauvoo to see Joseph. After she left the horse and buggy at the livery stable, she joined the throng of Saints lining the streets.

It was a clear, bright day, the beginning of summer. Despite the upheaval of construction the city was beginning to wear the homey look of grass, flowers, and garden patches. Neat picket fences and young fruit trees gave Nauvoo a look of permanence which had never existed in Far West.

As Jenny nodded to the Saints she recognized, smiled at the strangers, and studied it all, she was aware of more in the Saints' favor. The beginning of prosperity was evident in round cheeks blooming with health. Jenny also noticed bright parasols and bonnets with lace and plumes. More men wore black frock coats and tall dark hats.

The band was coming into view. The children surrounding Jenny were jumping up and down with excitement. Their dancing steps mimicked the prancing steps of the band and the smart steps of the Nauvoo Legion. She watched one youngster toot his imaginary trumpet while another swished a sword made of two crossed boards.

Jenny shouted across the blaring trumpets, "Your sons will make good soldiers."

"Aye!" their proud mother exclaimed, "both are members of the youth military corps. Joseph will have a fine army. 'Tis between four and six hundred young'uns right now."

The woman beside the mother said, "Did you hear how they nearly captured Nauvoo?" Mystified, Jenny shook her head. "Well, Joseph's oldest boy dreamed it up."

The mother took up the story. "The Prophet got wind of their intentions and routed the Legion to play at their own game."

"But unbeknown to the Prophet," her friend chimed in, "the boys were armed with every pot and pan in Nauvoo. When they came out of the woods, the Legion rushed them. The little fellas set up such a clatter with their ma's pots and big spoons that all the horses spooked except for old Charlie, and he daren't with the Prophet on his back."

She paused and cried, "And look, there comes the Prophet now!"

Jenny turned as the prancing black stallion moved into view. She was hearing the excitement sweeping the crowd, watching the people waving and shouting as he drew abreast. Jenny blinked at the glory of his uniform of blue and buff, decorated with gold braid and punctuated with the flashing sword and brace of pistols.

The shouting dwindled to a murmur as the Legion marched down the street. Beside Jenny the dark stranger moved and muttered, "I've never in my life seen anything like this."

"You know nothing of armies?"

He looked at her. "Madam, I am an officer in the United States Artillery. I simply mean there's no troops on the state level that could meet their match." Jenny couldn't control her pride, and his shrewd eyes saw it.

"Why this strict discipline, the ardor? Do they intend to conquer the world? I've not seen such enthusiasm even in our ranks." He turned to stare down the street, murmuring, "General Smith, the Prophet, huh? At this rate, in a few years they'll be thirty or fifty thousand—and that's a formidable foe, capable of instigating a religious crusade. I hope they don't intend to subvert the Constitution of the United States while we sit back and look on." He took one last glance at Jenny. "The fortifications Bennett's planning for this little monarchy are impressive. But I understand the Prophet is trying to oust him. Too bad for Joseph. Bennett seems to be an intelligent man with a great deal of courage. He'll be hard to replace. So Joseph's talking about an earthly kingdom of God, huh?" Without waiting for an answer, the man turned and strode down the street.

13

"WHO IS THIS Jesus?" Jenny whispered into her pan of soapy dishwater. Her hands were moving slowly through the dishes, washing and lifting the china cups adorned with pink roses.

Her hands rested in the water as she questioned herself, "Matter-of-fact, Jenny, why are you so caught up with all of this wondering?" Her nagging curiosity had, during the past weeks, led her to complete neglect of the *Book of Mormon*.

What would Joseph say to that? Or Mark? His notes had aroused her curiosity. What would he think of his wife running to his Bible every morning as soon as she was alone, searching out the newly scribbled references and the intriguing words he had inserted?

"Mystery, mystery of Christ," Jenny murmured, acknowledging the tingle of excitement and wonder the words caused. Quickly she reached for the skillet, eager to finish her work and take up Mark's Bible again.

But she had other thoughts as well, ones she had discovered on her own. "Who *is* this Jesus? Joseph says He's a son of God just like we are; that Lucifer is His brother. The only unique thing about Him is that when He and Lucifer volunteered to go save the world because of original sin, He was chosen instead. Because of that, He had a special body, which God was responsible for when He came down to sleep with Mary."

Jenny gave a troubled sigh. She poured hot water over the cups and reached for the towel. "The only thing is, when I heard *that*, it didn't give me a turn at all. But now every time I pick up the Bible and read about Jesus living on this earth, healing people and telling them stories, even giving out strict sermons, I just get more curious."

Jenny held a teacup up to the sunshine and admired the way light rays put rainbows of pastel color through the milky china. "Hold it up to the light, you see more," she mused, rubbing her thumb across the cup.

She turned away to stack the clean dishes in the cupboard, but her hands were slow. In her reading, the word *believe* was causing the problem. *Seems I keep falling over it,* she thought.

As she picked up the broom and headed for the parlor, she addressed the empty room. "I find myself wishing more for Tom. I have a better time trying out my questions on him 'cause he knows enough about me that I can't get scared out of questioning. It's been a long time since he reminded me it's a sin to ask questions, or to doubt. Could be he's having some questions too."

By the time Jenny finished sweeping and dusting, she had decided to seek Joseph's advice. The decision left her satisfied, and she carried the Bibles to the kitchen table.

Yesterday she had found the paper marked "mystery of Christ," but after being caught up with all the *believe* verses in the book of St. John, she had put it back in Mark's Bible, carefully, lest he guess she was looking through his notes.

As Jenny thumbed through her Bible, she mused over her need for secrecy. "Mark shoves so much at me I can't accept. I'd rather find out for myself. I'm fearing he's been led astray. Like atonement."

Moving carefully through the Book, discovering she could now more easily find the references, Jenny followed Mark's notes leading her to Ephesians. She read, and then leaned back in her chair, slowly putting her thoughts into words. "This Paul is talking about having a knowledge of the mystery of Christ. Seems from his words, the mystery is that the Gentiles can have the same promises the children of Israel have—through Christ."

Now her eyes caught two things on the page in front of her, the first was a drift of words across the page—the *unsearchable riches of Christ.* The second was a scripture notation—Mark had written in: *Romans 9:30–32; 10:2–4.*

Jenny didn't know about Romans, and it took her a long time to find the passage; when she did, she read and then puzzled over it. The implications filled her with dismay. "It says the Gentiles who aren't even related to the children of Israel found righteousness by faith, but that the children of Israel didn't have righteousness because instead of using faith, they were using works of law," she murmured.

"Why, Joseph says we're the children of Israel by baptism, whereby the Holy Spirit changes our blood into children of Israel blood, and he teaches we're righteous by keeping the law and by doing the works of the church."

She was thoughtful for a moment before returning to Romans. Then she read: " 'For Christ *is* the end of the law for righteousness to every one that believeth.' " She closed the Book, saying, "There's that *believe* again. I wonder what it means?" All the other verses stacked up in her mind, like a towering pile of library books.

With a sigh she went back to the final verse Mark had listed, 1 Corinthians 2:7. "More mystery," she muttered. "Now it's talking about the wisdom of God being a mystery, and that if it weren't, the princes of this world wouldn't have crucified the Lord of glory." For a long time she struggled with the words *princes of this world* and *the Lord of glory.*

When she finally closed the Bible, it was with an impatient snap and a sigh of frustration. The verses she read told her that God was calling her into fellowship with His Son Jesus Christ. And all those other verses said the same. But they didn't tell her *how.*

Jenny replaced the Bibles, straight, just the way Mark had placed them. She cocked her head, looking at them, then decided. "I'm going to have to visit Joseph, even if I must chase him clear to Carthage.

"I don't understand all those verses, and some of them he's not been reading himself. I wonder if my saying carries enough weight to change the church. *By faith.*"

She grinned at the foolish picture of Joseph leading Jenny to the front and dramatically acknowledging the new revelation.

"Silly. Joseph thinks women are to be seen, not heard; and besides, it isn't a new revelation; it's been there all along."

On Relief Society day, Jenny decided again to approach Joseph with her questions. The meeting itself had spurred on the idea.

Since the day Jenny first urged Sarah Pratt to accompany her, the two had been riding together. Jenny was beginning to enjoy Sarah's company, but since that first time together, Jenny sensed there were many deep and hidden places in the woman's life.

Not daring to probe with questions which might raise the specter of gossip again, Jenny listened and learned. She guessed there were deep hurts, but she also saw Sarah's loyalty.

Sarah's references to her husband were guarded. Jenny knew he had been cut off from his apostleship. Soon she realized that part of the gossip was correct. Orson's quarrel with the Prophet had been responsible, but surely it wasn't because of the rumor of Sarah's adultery.

This fine June day, Sarah loaded Aaron into Jenny's buggy, saying, "I'll not be riding back with you. Orson has a meeting with Joseph this morning and he will take me home from the meeting."

Her face was radiant with pride and Jenny said, "That's good, isn't it?"

Sarah looked astonished, paused, and then said, "Seems you don't know that we've both been rebaptized. Joseph has accepted us back into full fellowship."

"I wonder why he had to rebaptize you?" Jenny saw the embarrassment on Sarah's face and hurried on. "I was baptized in the Presbyterian church years ago. At that time I learned that just one baptism was necessary. When I joined this church I went along with the Prophet since he told me my former baptism was to be nullified by being baptized into the Latter-day Saints Church. Apparently the first was not any good to begin with."

Abruptly the symbols of sacrament and baptism surfaced in Jenny's mind. She was again seeing the sun-shot window with its glorious brilliance, and a finger of purple light beamed at the chalice of wine. Just as abruptly, overlapping the picture, came the same chalice—now dark and shadowed, bearing the horror of blood.

Jenny shivered and Sarah looked at her in concern. "Are you coming down with the ague? I'd thought we'd put that behind us."

"No," Jenny shook her head, "I was just thinking about baptisms and such. It's scary—this not being sure of things, only doing the best you can, and then wondering."

"You're talking about the church?" Sarah frowned and slowly said, "I know what you mean. The troubles of the past year have left me wondering. Might of been, if Orson hadn't needed so badly to be restored to fellowship, I'd have been gone forever."

Jenny studied her, remembering the talk she'd heard in Kirtland. "Then you don't really think Joseph is the Christ of this dispensation?"

Sarah thought and then sighed. "I've got to—there's nothing else to lean on, seeing the Bible's polluted and the true Christian church has been gone for fourteen hundred years. I felt the witness confirming it all, or I'd never have joined in the first place."

She looked curiously at Jenny and then asked, "Looking at your face, I'm thinking you need to be asking, too. Mostly you look like you've more questions than a person should be asked to handle."

"Are you talking about the burning in the bosom like Tom talks about?"

She nodded. "Have you been into the museum since it was finished? The mummies are on display." She paused and added, "You know, if you aren't interested in the burning of the bosom, there's the writings.

"You know the translation of the text they found with the mummies turned out to be the writings of Abraham. Did you know Joseph has finished the book and it's being printed now?"

They had reached Nauvoo; the horses slowed in the press of traffic. Sarah said, "There's Joseph's Nauvoo Mansion. Just looks like a nice home to me. Wish he could be satisfied for a time. This building a hotel seems a little too grand right now when we're still so poor."

"Mark says there's many visitors coming to the city." Jenny turned to look at the neat home, adding, "Sure, it's bigger than most of us will ever have. I suppose his needs are greater."

"I hear Emma's expecting again." Sarah sighed. "Poor woman, I'm really sorry for her with feeling so badly and then having to contend—"

She glanced sharply at Jenny, looking embarrassed. "I—where are we going for meeting today?"

"Rooms over the printshop. Good thing there's places like that. Our need for meeting places is getting bigger."

"Soon as they get Joseph and the twelve moved into their offices in the temple things will open up for us. Meanwhile, the men come first."

"It will be soon?"

"Before the winter's out, at the rate the building's going on."

Jenny left the buggy at the livery stable and the pair walked the short distance to the printing office.

As soon as they entered the meeting hall over the pressroom, Jenny realized Emma was in one of her unpleasant moods. With a sigh she whispered to Sarah, "Looks like no sewing today. Shall we wager the subject she has on her mind?"

"I just object to her personal questions. For the past month she's been after information. Everyone is squirming."

"Why? Certainly there's nothing to worry about." Astonishment was in Sarah's eyes, "You haven't heard—" but before she could finish, Sally approached.

"I hope you've been keeping a tight ship," she cautioned Sarah and Jenny. "Emma's got everyone on the carpet today.

"You've heard all the outrageous things Dr. Bennett's been saying— that horrible confession Joseph insisted he make before the brethren in the Masonic Hall. Andy says the men were ready to take him apart, limb by limb when Joseph started pleading for him. So much for that confession. That man's going to be—" she gulped as Emma Smith approached.

"Sally, my dear, must we have gossip? Are you really criticizing the Prophet for moving with compassion and interest in the salvation of one soul? Joseph will be here in just a few minutes. Will you women please be seated?"

She turned away. Before Jenny had time to react to Sarah's raised eyebrows, Joseph came into the room. Jenny felt the excitement sweep through the room. She felt it touch herself even as she studied the faces of the women around her. Sarah Pratt was the only woman not viewing the Prophet with eyes filled with adoration. That troubled Jenny as she settled herself to listen to Joseph.

Wearing a slight frown, Joseph was terse, to the point. "All of you women have heard of the confessions of Dr. Bennett. I consider you representative of the city's virtuous women. I've come to beg your help. The disclosures Dr. Bennett has made are a reflection upon his character, but they will be damaging to the virtue of this city and to the Saints who are living their religion and seeking to please God.

"Remember, a little tale will travel many miles, and it can set the world on fire, particularly our world. I urge you, my dear Saints, please listen to me. At the present time a truth involving the guilty must not be aired. We are attempting to hold our influence with the world, and spare ourselves extermination. The brethren wish me to caution you to be prudent, wise, virtuous. If there is a need to repent, then reform, and do so in a way which will not destroy those about you." With a quick wave of his hand, the Prophet was gone and the room was silent.

Jenny was aware only of Emma's stern gaze. Although the woman was studying every person in the room, Jenny felt as if she were on trial. All too clearly she was remembering Emma's interruption the evening Jenny approached Joseph in his office while Mark was in England. Today Emma was wearing that same expression.

Sarah and Jenny walked down to the street together. When Orson arrived Jenny watched him bundle his wife and son into the buggy before she made up her mind. She turned back to the printing office, saying, "I'll just pick up a copy of the *Book of Abraham* while I'm here."

Jenny could hear the press running as she stepped through the doorway. The door leading into the pressroom was open and Jenny walked toward it.

Willard Richards and Mrs. Hyde were facing the press. Just as Jenny stepped forward, Mrs. Hyde slipped her arms around the man's shoulders and lifted her face. Jenny watched the kiss and all the implications burned through her. She started to turn and bumped against the table.

Nancy Hyde dropped her arms and turned with a smile. "Oh, sorry, I didn't hear you." The smile faded and she studied Jenny with a quizzical look. "You've been listening to Joseph's talk?"

"Yes," Jenny said slowly. "About—I thought it was all gossip."

"Remember what he said," Nancy replied sharply. "The Prophet's interested in keeping things nice and smooth around Nauvoo. Now, what do you want?"

Jenny blinked and through stiff lips murmured, "Oh, Sarah Pratt mentioned the *Book of Abraham* is finished. I thought I'd just pick up a copy."

"Joseph's just taken the entire batch. You'll have to see him for a copy." With a flounce she moved away and because Jenny couldn't think of anything to say, she turned and left the office.

On the street she realized her mind was a jumble of confusion. Bible verses were flying around in her head, along with the sure decision that she must tell Joseph about the ones he hadn't read. And she thought of

Nancy Marinda Hyde kissing Willard Richards right under Joseph's feet as he talked. Jenny's forehead pricked into a troubled frown.

Slowly she whispered, "I'd thought all the gossip was just a way to pass the time of day. Now I wonder. How do I tell Joseph without getting Nancy into trouble?"

14

JENNY STILL HESITATED on the street, her mind a jumble of confusion. But as the beauty of the summer day intruded, she took a deep breath and looked around, delighting in what she was seeing. The buildings revealed the mix of brick and lumber, the smell of old and new; on the streets she saw the contrast of growing greenery and busy people.

Nauvoo was becoming a respectable city. Respectable? She cringed. The new brewery was being built under the sanction of Joseph Smith, while in the background the temple was being erected as quickly as possible.

At Relief Society, when Emma wasn't within hearing distance, there had been a great deal of criticism of the brewery. Mrs. Ingersoll had summed up the discussion by saying, " 'Tis either right or wrong. According to the word of wisdom, 'tis wrong. We'll have to throw out the brewery or the temple."

Jenny looked at the lorries and buggies moving briskly down the street and tried to forget the problem of the brewery. The lumber and kegs of hardware the lorries carried spelled prosperity, as did the buggies loaded with gaily dressed women and serious men.

On the bluff overlooking the river the Nauvoo House was rising. Very soon the hotel would be ready for the first occupants—the Prophet and his family.

At the other end of town, on the hill overlooking the city, the new temple was being built. The limestone gleamed in the noon brilliance, making Jenny blink.

As she shaded her eyes and turned away, Joseph Smith came out of the store and started up the stairs to his office. She hurried after him. Hearing her steps, he turned to wait. "I've sent Mark to Carthage to register land sales."

"It's you I've come to see." Jenny was surprised when his face brightened.

In his office, she was suddenly caught by memories. Silently she studied the room, thinking of the poor cubbyhole of an office in Kirtland. This office was spacious, and there were other rooms on this floor—probably offices for Mark and Mr. Clayton.

Jenny turned to meet Joseph's quizzical expression and blurted out, "It's been a long time, hasn't it—that we've known each other. Since Bainbridge days."

"Yes, Jenny it has. You were such a scrawny thing, bony legs and arms and big eyes." He looked around his office with satisfaction. "We've both come a long way. I'm here with more of this world's goods than I ever expected to have and you—" He studied her until she felt her face warm.

"Little Jenny has become a beautiful woman, a very beautiful one, who, I imagine, could have anything she wanted. What do you want, Jenny?"

"The *Book of Abraham.*"

For a moment he looked astonished and then began to laugh. "How in character, and how much I've forgotten! Are you still the serious little girl inside?"

Jenny considered and finally admitted, "I suppose I am. Somehow there's never been that much to laugh and frolic over." She thought for another moment and the jumble of her mind began straightening itself. "I guess I'm too much caught up with the things happening under the surface of life."

"What do you mean?"

"The wondering about all that makes life move on—God, and what He's about. More than anything, what I can do about it all. Power. You used to be like this; don't you ever think this way anymore?"

He settled lower in his chair and seemed to forget her presence. "Yes, but the whole situation is changing for me. The power is there; now my problem is learning how to harness it up like an old team and plow my own field just the way I want it. Jenny, I have power in abundance."

"Do you still want to give it out to people?"

"It isn't so much giving it out; it's teaching people how to lay hold of it for themselves." He shot her a quick look.

"You said once that knowledge leads to salvation. I think that was what you were referring to when you told me to read the Scriptures. But power—" She stopped abruptly.

Joseph sat up and leaned forward. "What is it, Jenny?"

"I'm saying all the things I *didn't* want to say. I came here to talk about the Scriptures and all that's going on in Nauvoo, not about power."

"Have you been reading? Tell me what's troubling you."

"The Bible, Joseph. It says that having Christ doesn't do us any good if we're justified by law; it only means we've fallen from grace. Then I found something about the mystery of Christ which I don't quite understand. The Bible talks about the Israelites trying to establish their own righteousness by law instead of by faith. The same section says the Gentiles have reached righteousness through faith in Jesus Christ. Joseph, it's so confusing! It all seems just the opposite of what we are learning."

"Then it's obvious, my dear, if it's confusing you, it's wrong. I've told you the Bible hasn't been correctly translated. Why don't you just follow the teachings of the *Book of Mormon* and forget about the confusion?"

"But you said to read the Scriptures, and that's what the Bible is. There's even parts of it in the *Book of Mormon* and the church accepts it. And something else. The Bible talks about our being adopted by God. That doesn't sound like we're children of God to begin with. Then it talks about how the law can't clear the conscience, that the law isn't reality; it's only a shadow of reality. Joseph, sometimes I feel so confused and frightened."

"Seems you need some help understanding."

"I suppose."

"Maybe for right now you'd better stop the reading."

"But the strange part is," Jenny said slowly, "that as confusing as it is, it is also very appealing. I *want* to read it. If you could just answer my questions."

"Which ones?"

"Well, these. But I want to bring more. I want to read the new book and then talk about it."

Jenny got to her feet and moved restlessly around the room. "Joseph, I must admit, I just don't fit in around here. I've tried to belong. But the rest of the women, well, they seem so serene and happy in their religion. All my religion does for me is send me looking for more. I guess besides power I want to be content like these women, feeling like they do, like the queens of heaven."

"Jenny, be patient! The Lord has given us much in the priesthood that will help you reach the contentment you desire." For a moment he studied her with a frown and abruptly Jenny was aware of her impudence. This was the Prophet Joseph Smith and she was treating him like the young'un in South Bainbridge.

She moved to apologize, but he continued, "What you are referring to will in these last days be realized, but not in an abstract way." He leaned forward and placed his hand on hers. "Jenny, it isn't a vision or a promise on paper. Our kingdom and the manifestation of it will be real. You talked about the law being a shadow of reality. Well, very soon the reality of the unseen next world will be revealed to you.

"Jenny, God will make me to be God to you in His stead. Now, will that suffice? I will take you to heaven with me if you will keep all the ordinances of the gospel. I will be your salvation and you shall be queen of heaven."

He got to his feet and paced around the room. "Jenny, I am certain that the Lord is preparing you to accept the teaching; the evidence of that is indicated by your restless spirit. Remember, the Lord wants to show you the way to feel like a queen of heaven. Let this suffice for now."

When Jenny left Joseph's office, she carried a copy of the *Book of Abraham* under her arm. Her head was still full of all Joseph had said, particularly the exciting story the new book carried.

She had nearly reached home before she realized that all Joseph had told her had completely chased the puzzling scriptures from her mind.

It was midafternoon when Mark returned to Nauvoo. He carried the receipts directly to Joseph's office. Walking into the room, he found the Prophet pacing his office. With a nod, he said, "Come in, Mark, give me some advice."

After Mark settled in the chair, Joseph said, "I've been going over this Bennett situation. The tide of feeling is arising against the Saints in an alarming fashion."

"Like Missouri?" Mark asked, watching the man's face. Today Joseph was dressed in a manner befitting his prophet role. Mark noticed that his stiff white collar pointed to the beginnings of a fleshy second chin. He also decided that Joseph's sensuous lips and smooth hands were more noticeable when his face was relaxed and his usual dominant nature bent to another voice.

Joseph didn't answer Mark's question. As he continued to pace the room, he picked up a newspaper and said, "I've been so caught up reading the good articles about myself that I've nearly been caught short."

"What do you mean?"

He struck the newspaper. "Since Bennett was ousted, he's gone to fighting through the papers. I fear that vile tongue. All lies, but we can't afford the luxury of letting them poison the minds of the public. We've too much at stake."

"You're speaking of the upcoming state election?"

"Yes, that and more. Perhaps I was too hasty back in January when I let it drop that we'd vote Whig this election. There's much to risk." He paused to look at Mark and added, "If only you were part of the Lodge and the planning committee, I'd feel free to confide in you."

With amusement, Mark said, "I thought attorneys enjoyed a higher level of confidentiality."

He was shaking his head, "Not when matters of the Lord are at hand."

Mark decided to level. "You know, Joseph, it's that very thing which seems so wrong to me—perhaps the biggest reason why I can't go along with this. A church should be the last institution on earth to be restricted or secret."

"That isn't the only problem." He tossed the newspaper to Mark. "See this? Seems we had a military officer witness the drilling of the Legion. He questions our excellence as if it were monstrous, asking if we intend to take over the States. He goes on to prophesy that we'll be a fearful host with the intent of subverting the Constitution of the United States, imply-ing we'll roll over them all. He's calling us religious fanatics, intent on shaking the country to its center."

Joseph reached for more papers, and Mark said, "You've been saving these?"

"Of course. Now, listen to this one. This is a January 1842 paper from Springfield. I won't read it all, but the important criticisms are against the Army of Israel with the warning that I should let someone else lead the army, and stick to church business. Here's the quote: 'His situation in Illinois is . . . more dangerous than ever it was in Missouri. . . .' " He lowered the paper. "Mark that's a threat. Do you see? I have a job for you.

"Now here's another. The *Alton Telegraph* is complaining about my issu-ing a proclamation. They're saying: 'commanding his followers to vote . . . bold stride against despotism.' " The expression he turned on Mark for just a moment was one of bewilderment. In that brief flash, Mark was astonished. Joseph didn't see in himself any of the attributes of a despot.

With a sigh, Mark said, "I suppose you've decided I should write rebut-tals to all these articles."

"No," Joseph folded the papers and tucked them in a drawer. When he stood up, he looked at Mark and said, "I want you to go on a goodwill tour for me. There're a few things I have on my mind that need to be presented to Washington before next session. You might as well deliver these papers in person. Stop in Springfield and anywhere else you think this is neces-sary. Just let it be known you are the attorney of General Joseph Smith and then let them do the talking and the questioning. A goodwill trip like this will be more valuable to me right now than a million dollars." Mark was still staring at him, not believing what he was hearing. Joseph contin-ued, "Go talk to John D. Lee; he might have some suggestions for you."

Mark's voice was flat and even as he said, "You command me to go on a goodwill trip for you, to dig up all the information I can about how people are seeing the Mormon movement. You expect *that* when you know what my views are? Joseph, I suppose you expect me to defend you and build up your cause in Washington and Springfield and every hamlet in between."

"I expect it," Joseph said calmly.

"Then you listen to me first. Laying aside all the stories about the vi-sions and the gold plates and the revelations, you haven't a leg to stand on in front of God. Yet you want me to build up the church in the eyes of those fellows out there."

Curiously Joseph looked at Mark, "Why do you say I haven't a leg to stand on?"

Mark reached across Joseph's desk and picked up the Prophet's Bible. "Listen to what God's Word says and then compare it to what you are saying God says." He took a deep breath and turned the pages of the Bible.

"For a starter, Matthew 5:44 says: 'Love your enemies, bless them that curse you, do good to them that hate you . . . that ye may be the children of your Father which is in heaven.' And then the words of Jesus in 7:17, 'Every good tree bringeth forth good fruit; but a corrupt tree bringeth forth evil fruit.' A few verses on He says the corrupt tree will be burned.

"Joseph, I could stand here all night reading until my voice gives out. This Book is full of verses saying that Jesus Christ is God in the flesh, come to this earth to die for our sins. Jesus also tells us that 'God is spirit: and they that worship him must worship him in spirit and in truth.' "

Mark closed the Book and replaced it on Joseph's desk. Then he faced the Prophet. "There's another section, found in Romans 9 and 10. Paul is talking to the Gentiles about his countrymen, the Israelites, and the words show his heart is nearly breaking as he says Israel has pursued a law of righteousness, but it isn't working for them because they are doing it by works instead of faith. With their own proud hands they think they're working their way up to God. Paul admits the children of Israel are zealous for God, but their zeal isn't based on knowledge. Somehow they missed the point. We don't *make* righteousness; we *submit* to God's righteousness. Paul is practically shouting out the words on paper, 'Christ is the end of the law so that there may be righteousness for everyone who believes.' "

Leaning forward Mark continued, "Prophet, the Bible clearly says Christ delivers us from the law, yet you not only want the law, but you even want the sacrifice. What a kick in the face to the God who came to die on the cross!

"While we were in Missouri, Joseph, I began to understand that Jesus Christ wanted me to stick around the Mormon camp and say to everyone who would listen that Jesus Christ is Lord, the Lord bearing salvation to all who will *believe*. I'll go, Joseph, but I'll talk on my own terms, saying what I want to say. I'm just as curious as you to know what the people think."

15

IT WAS LATE when Mark rode home. The long rays of the afternoon sun cut through the outcropping of trees bordering the bluff. The light laid bars of yellow across the pasture green, pointing to the cattle grazing there.

Still stunned by Joseph's order, he could think only of the unimportant. Who would plow the garden patch for Jenny when the last of the pumpkin was harvested? What would she do with the extra milk? What about her night fears?

And in the end, just before he reached his own lane, Mark knew his responsibility to Jenny demanded that the hard things, the unspoken, must be said before he could leave.

Jenny was reading when he walked in, so deeply absorbed she scarcely lifted her head. He saw the table set and the supper pot simmering on the back of the stove.

Taking a deep breath, Mark asked, "What are you reading?" He carried the kettle to the table as she lifted her face. He bent to kiss the bemused expression away.

She finally eluded his lips and said, "Oh, Mark, it's so fascinating! See, here's a drawing from the parchment. And right here's a list telling all about the meanings of the illustration."

She pulled him over to the rocking chair, placed herself on his lap and began to point out the pictures and tell about them. Mark nuzzled her neck and tried to push aside the numbness in his mind.

"See?" Jenny pointed. "Did you know this star Kolob is a *governing* star? I didn't know there was such a thing. It's nearest to the place where God lives. Oh, Mark, think of that! It makes me feel high and lifted up, almost there beside God. Isn't that what people really want deep down inside? Joseph didn't say as much today, but I'm sure that's what he's feeling. Not just the need to know about God, but the need to be right there close to Him."

Mark rested his head against the back of the rocker and watched Jenny's animated face. It was full of the sweep of mystery he had seen so often, but today there was a brightness, even hope, in the depths of her eyes. For a moment he felt his spirit move with uneasiness and then she pressed her cheek against his.

Holding her close, thinking of all that needed to be said, he mused aloud. "There's a section in Jeremiah that's running in my mind. God tells the people a man isn't to boast about riches or any such thing, but instead to boast that we know and understand God."

Her curious eyes questioned, examining his face, and then she returned to the subject, saying, "There's more: I saw illustrations about Shinehah, the sun; Kokob, a star; Olea, the moon; the Kokaubeam, which stands for stars. Think of that! Not the stars so much, but that God and Abraham talked together, just like a couple of men. In fact, Abraham said he talked face-to-face with God. I guess that's one more instance where man saw God."

"One more?" he asked puzzled.

"Well, Joseph saw God and His Son, Jesus Christ."

"In several places in the Bible, it says no man has seen God; in fact, no man can see God *and live.* Jenny, doesn't it bother you that Joseph teaches so much that is in contradiction to the Book which he claims to accept as God's Word?"

"But he believes only insofar as it is correctly translated."

"Jenny, we've gone over that before. Joseph is saying that the *Book of Mormon* is the most correct book on earth. It contains much from the Bible. Isn't he contradicting himself? It seems strange to think a God of power unable to keep His word safe for mankind. Seems particularly strange when that Book says His word will never pass away. I find myself having to accept either Joseph's word or God's Word; I can't have both because they disagree."

Jenny moved restlessly and he knew he was crossing the unseen line which they both knew existed. "Jenny, my dearest wife—" He paused to cup her chin in his hand and force her to meet his gaze. "I must tell you that Jesus Christ is God. He is God come to this earth for the purpose of reconciling men to Himself. He did it by paying the blood sacrifice required for sin. Jenny, do you see? Sin is terrible—it isn't something we recover from, or overcome, it is something from which we must be rescued. God must swoop down like an eagle and snatch us up to Himself."

Jenny got off Mark's lap and walked to the stove. "Mark, I don't want to hear your ideas. You are throwing me into complete confusion. I've got to believe that God has put the right way within me and all I need to do is follow. Joseph has been helping me understand. I must admit, I've been miserably aware of my need for God. It started as a realization that I didn't have the power to control my life at all. Most certainly, I'll admit

I've gone a curious route searching for God and the happiness which is my due. But in all my groping, I know I've found the right way now."

He looked at her curiously, "What has convinced you it's right?"

"Because my spirit and his spirit are in harmony. There's none of this turmoil inside when he speaks."

"Is it possible your spirits really are the same spirit? It sounds that way. If so, it's probable Joseph is just as unhappy and miserable on the inside as you are. Jenny, I've lived with you long enough to see the agony of your life. I've held back my words because you've rejected everything I've said to you, but now I must point out something you'll have to consider."

Getting out of the rocking chair and going into the parlor, Mark picked up his Bible and returned to the kitchen. He murmured, "That's strange. I had a piece of paper here; it must have fallen out. No matter, I know the section well enough." He thumbed through the pages, and read aloud. "It's in 2 Corinthians 11:4, 'For if he that cometh preacheth another Jesus, whom we have not received, or *if* ye receive another spirit, which ye have not received, or another gospel, which ye have not accepted, ye might well bear with *him*.' Then Paul goes on in verse 13 to say, 'For such are false apostles, deceitful workers, transforming themselves into the apostles of Christ.' The next verse says that Satan himself is transformed into an angel of light." He closed his Bible and looked up.

Jenny was trembling, tears running down her cheeks, but her hands were clenched into fists. "Mark, you are trying to destroy every bit of soul peace I have. I will not allow you to tear me apart in this way."

"Jenny!" He came and caught her hands. "I'm not forcing you. I have only this tremendous desire to say to you these words. You do with them as you see fit. God himself will not insist you take the right way, worship the right Christ. He gives you the freedom to choose, and I can do no less."

Her eyes were moving, studying his face, seeking a confirmation, and he gave it. "Jenny, I love you, and I'll always stick by you, no matter what."

"But why are you saying these things now, while our dinner is getting cold?"

"Jenny, Joseph has given me a job to do which will take me out of Nauvoo for a time."

She was silent for a while, searching his face. "Will I be able to go with you?"

"No. I'll probably be gone for months. There are still two weeks of July left, and he wants me to leave immediately. He mentioned my being back by December."

He watched a cloud of dread move over her face. "We could go back to Springfield," he said gently.

She was shaking her head, managing a smile. "No, Mark, it's best. Without Joseph's help and counsel, I am fearful I'll miss the way. Soon they'll have the baptismal font open at the temple. You know how they feel about this ordinance. I must be here to participate. Besides I—" Her chin trembled and she flew into his arms. "Mark, oh, Mark, please—"

She could say no more, and Mark folded her close. The time was so short.

Within the week Mark had settled his affairs at the office. He turned over detail work to Clayton, Joseph's secretary. The legal affairs went to Higbee, who would handle Joseph's petition for bankruptcy.

Tom volunteered to move in with Jenny. Still heart-sore, Mark saw the arrangement satisfactory to the point where he wondered whether he would be missed.

Finally at the stage stop, Jenny's white face and trembling hands made him turn to Tom with genuine warmth. "I don't know what I'd do without you."

Tom grumped around the farm for the first few days, and Jenny was grateful for his sympathy as she listened to his discourse on the subject. " 'Church widows,' they call them," he said. "Seems like every man in the church gets the tap sooner or later. Take John Lee. He'd only been back in the area a couple of months. Didn't even have time to complete his house before the presidency was tapping him on the shoulder ready to send him out. He went, too."

"I'm surprised they haven't sent you out."

"I'm too dumb to talk and convince."

"That group waiting for the stage didn't impress me as being overly educated. Seems all it takes is a *Book of Mormon* under the arm." Jenny sighed and turned away, but she was grateful for Tom's presence.

Mark had been gone only a week when Jenny took the horse and buggy into Nauvoo. She was scheduled for another meeting with Joseph Smith in his office. As she set out, she glanced at her satchel to make certain it held the list of questions, the *Book of Mormon* and the new *Book of Abraham.*

Continuing on her way, she mulled over the questions. *What was Jesus referring to when He said He'd come so that we might have life more abundantly?* Jenny sighed and addressed the horse's back. "There I go again, asking questions about the Bible when I should be remembering he said—"

As Jenny went up the stairs to Joseph's office, she tried to put a pleasant smile on her face, tried to feel anticipation. Her thoughts were wrapped around Mark, wondering where he was and what he was doing. She swallowed the miserable lump in her throat.

She tapped on Joseph's door and heard a feminine voice call, "Come."
Jenny stepped into the room. There was a tiny woman in Joseph's chair.

She grinned impishly at Jenny, saying, "Surprise! The Prophet had to be
out of town today, seeing it's time for his petition for bankruptcy to be
filed. Since he said I could do the job as well as he could, well, here I am."

"Oh," Jenny said, disappointed. "We were to be studying the doctrine of
the church and the books. I could come later."

She shook her head, saying, "I'm Patty Sessions, midwife and mother in
Israel."

"What does that mean?"

Taking a deep breath, Patty said, "Well, the job's a new one, but Joseph's expecting those of us who have the teaching to start instruction with
the young women of the church who will be learning the doctrine of the
priesthood."

"I thought that was for the men only."

"Well, the priesthood is, but some of the ordinances involve the
women."

Jenny placed her satchel on the floor and sat down. "I've been hearing
from Sarah and some of the others that the men are being initiated into
the endowments right now. Seems it's not fair, when the women want the
privileges, too."

"Won't be much longer before the women are included. One of the rites
is what I want to talk to you about today."

She came around the desk and Jenny studied her, remembering that she
had seen her at the Relief Society meetings. Patty was a tiny, slender
woman; with her quick movements and bright eyes, she reminded Jenny of
a sparrow.

She smoothed her graying hair and then folded her delicate hands over
her gray calico dress. "Much of what I'll teach today has already been said
from the pulpit and discussed at Society meeting. Jenny, there are three
degrees of heaven. You know that in order for a man to enter into the
highest degree and thereby be granted the privilege of having his own
kingdom, he must enter the new and everlasting covenant of marriage. If
he does not, there will be no possibility of having a kingdom and he shall
have no increase."

"What of those who won't live up to their religion?" Jenny asked softly,
thinking of Mark.

Patty shrugged. "There's no possibility. If it's your spouse and there's no
chance of winning him to the church, you best be looking farther afield;
otherwise you'll be left out, too."

"You're suggesting I leave my husband?"

"Yes. It's been revealed to the Prophet that since these marriages weren't preached over by an elder having the priesthood, meaning the ordination from God, then they are invalid anyway."

"But not under the Constitution of the United states," Jenny protested.

Patty shrugged. "Jenny, the kingdom of God will be around long after the United States ceases to exist."

For a moment Jenny closed her eyes. She saw the white lace and the yellow roses, and heard her vows echo through her mind: *I will cleave to no other as long as we both shall live.*

Patty was speaking again, but her words held no meaning. Jenny stored them in her mind without giving them further thought.

When the meeting with Patty finished and Jenny turned to leave, Patty reminded her, "Next week at the same time; the Prophet promised he'd be back by then. Don't worry, he'll have some good advice for you."

Later, on her way home, Jenny impatiently flicked the reins across the horse's back and the words crowded to the surface of her mind. Patty called it the spiritual wife doctrine. Funny, she'd heard the term, but it had always been mentioned with snickers.

So a woman couldn't go to heaven without her husband taking her there! Several women referred to their husbands as their saviors. Curiously Jenny considered the thoughts Patty had planted. She hadn't snickered when she spoke the words. Her earnest eyes had sparkled with a zeal Jenny couldn't doubt. The unbelievable became real. Some of the men in the community really had been selected by God. Jenny shivered at the memory, just as Patty shivered, saying, " 'Tis a privilege a man can't take lightly, and a woman daren't refuse."

Jenny thought of Mark and sighed. She spoke her troubled words into the afternoon air. "Mark says he loves me, but he never will consent to this." She trembled, remembering Patty's advice.

16

WHEN JENNY DROVE her rig into the yard, she saw Tom's horse in the pasture. Surprised, she glanced at the sun. It was only midafternoon. She stepped out of the buggy just as Tom appeared.

"I'll handle it," he muttered. He started to lead the horse into the barn.

"Tom, it's so early. Is something wrong?"

"Tell you in a minute," he growled. She watched him unharness the horse and lead it to pasture. When he returned he took her arm.

The unusual gesture alerted Jenny. Wheeling around, she grasped his sleeve, saying, "Mark? Is something wrong with him?"

"Naw," he growled. "Joseph stopped by the stable on his way to his bankruptcy meeting and told me I was picked for a mission."

"Tom, when?"

"There's a bunch leaving in less than a week and I'm to be going with them. He's calling it a training session—intends to make me into a missionary. Says I'll only be gone for a month, but that isn't the point. I'm no more missionary material than a hog is."

"What'll I do?" Jenny whispered, looking around the barn, seeing the half-completed pig sty and the hay that needed to be stacked. But deep inside she was thinking of the dark night hours.

"That's what I said. But Joseph, seein' he's responsible, said he'll send a boy to take care of the chores until I get back."

Later that evening when they were seated at the table, Tom said, "I feel you fear being alone more than the work."

"I do. Oh, Tom, it's so far to the nearest neighbor! At night I hear the coyotes howl. Even the screech-owls in the forest make me nervous."

"Aw, you're a big girl," he chided with a grin, but she saw the worried frown and nearly confided in him her dark night visions and the strange laughter. "Dreams," he would say. Dreams they might be, but dreams didn't walk through the house. She shivered as she fingered the talisman tucked in her pocket.

And that next week when she went to her meeting with Joseph, he looked at her and frowned. "You're all alone out there. I see you're troubled. If being alone is that bad, I think I'd best take you home with me."

He turned and she followed him up the stairs to his office. "Just a minute; I've an order to write," he murmured.

As she waited, Jenny moved quietly around his office, looking at the display of arrowheads and bones, the fragments of pottery marked with strange figures. She studied the line of books and pulled one down to read.

The windows were open to the summer breezes. She watched the curtains move and listened to the clop of horses, the shouts of playing children. With the sudden shock of awareness, Jenny turned to look at Joseph.

Now it seemed the sounds of life beyond the room marked their isolation while the intimacy of their surroundings pressed in upon her.

She watched him write. He had discarded his coat, and his heavy shoulders strained at the light linen of his shirt. His hair curled across the back of his neck, and she felt her throat tighten.

Abruptly he lifted his head and grinned. As their eyes met she saw the grin disappear. She turned away, disturbed and ashamed of her response to him. Sitting down, she fingered the book and wondered if she dared beg off today's meeting. Would a headache do?

"I'm sorry I've kept you waiting." His voice was brisk and businesslike. Jenny turned as he pulled a chair close to the desk. "Patty Sessions told me that you had a good meeting last week, but that you've questions you want to ask. Well, I've a little instructing to do; then I need to step out for a time. Do you wish to ask your questions first?" She shook her head, realizing she couldn't remember them.

Joseph continued after a sharp glance at her. "Patty said she began by instructing you in the covenant of marriage, given to the priesthood. You understand that the covenant of marriage is eternal, unchanging, don't you? The Lord has asked me to unfold the covenant to the people a small portion at a time. In due time, all of the church will be involved, but for now only a favored few. Also, I must instruct you, that the specific privileges are assigned by the Lord."

"But Mark won't follow the church!" Jenny burst out in torment. "That means I'll never have a chance to fulfill my calling. Talking about my being a queen of heaven is as bitter as gall. I've no chance. Why are you instructing me in the way when Mark is the one who must be convinced?"

Joseph was very sober as he shook his head and sighed. "Jenny, I've tried. One of the most important reasons I offered him the position as my attorney was in order to bring him back into the fold and allow him the privilege of the priesthood. Just before he left for Washington I had a most unpleasant interview with him. There is no doubt in my mind that Mark is apostate at heart."

Jenny bit her lip and tried desperately to control her tears. Joseph put his hand on her arm, "I know, my dear, it is a difficult situation. We can only pray the Lord will give him opportunity to see the error of his ways. Meanwhile, there's you to think about."

Getting to his feet, Joseph went to his bookcase and removed a large leatherbound book. He put it on the desk and opened the cover. Jenny attempted to put aside her own personal unhappiness. Trying to show interest, she leaned forward to watch.

Inside the book was a collection of heavy paper packets, folded and sealed with wax. She tried to see the imprint on the seal as Joseph thumbed through the sections. When he reached the packet labeled *Armyeo,* he stopped and sat down.

Folding his hands across the open book he began to speak again. "Jenny, I want you to know that the presidency and the council have met together to pray over these most solemn matters. The Lord's blessing must rest upon each decision, but there's more to it than that. We have His personal instructions as to His will. Now what I am going to say will seem to you to be lacking, but in the press of time and circumstances—" He paused and a flicker of amusement touched his face. "I must say, the Lord is much more abrupt and to the point than we humans are." He turned back to the book.

"Before me is this document, containing His special blessings for a number of women in the community who have been selected to be initiated into the covenant of eternal marriage. Jenny, your name, the secret name given by the Lord himself, is on the front of this packet. What is inside is to be revealed to you by the Lord's instructions. When you are ready to obey the Lord and accept your responsibility in this ordinance, I will allow you to break this seal."

"What will I have to do?" Jenny whispered.

"You will be taken to the Masonic Hall, where you will be united with me for eternity. This ceremony will provide for a spiritual, eternal marriage relationship between the two of us. Do you understand this? It is God's will. He has given me the responsibility of assuring your place in glory." He paused until she nodded and then continued, "The conclusion of the matter is this: For you this means a union complete, with worlds and kingdoms and powers forever. Amen."

For a long time, Jenny stared at the packet on the desk. She was only vaguely aware of Joseph leaving the room.

The curtains moved and Jenny looked at the curious seal and the name, *Armyeo.* For some undefined reason, the strange name stirred a mysterious response in her. As she concentrated on it, her thoughts winged backward in time.

There was that scrawny little girl proclaiming to the world that she intended to marry Joseph Smith. And then there was the talisman and the wax.

Abruptly Jenny threw back her head and laughed. "Through the powers given I nearly settled for an earthly marriage. Now he's offering to marry me for all eternity. I'll have the best of heaven and earth. Here my darling Mark and there—" Again she was laughing, trying to strangle her giggles in her hands.

When Joseph came into the room, Jenny was composed, sitting rigidly upright, with her hands folded. At his question she said, "Of course, Joseph. I'll be proud to be your queen. What must I do?"

Together they walked down the street and climbed the stairs to the Masonic Hall, located in the second floor of Brigham Young's store.

The large chamber was dim and gloomy, with strange emblems and symbols decorating the walls and the long table spread across the front of the room. A solemn line of dark-coated men stood at the end of the room with hands clasped before them.

As Jenny took her place in front of them, their quietness made them seem unreal, nearly unearthly, until she saw the quizzical gleam in Brigham Young's eyes.

It was a strange ceremony. The book holding her name linked to Joseph Smith's was spread between them. With her hand resting lightly on his, they listened to Brigham Young's sonorous voice lifting to the ceiling. "Brethren, and sister Jenny, we are gathered here in the sight of God to join in eternal union Joseph Smith and Jenny Cartwright. This marriage, decreed by heaven, was commanded of the Prophet by an angel bearing an unsheathed sword. Dare mortal man fight heaven's command? Let no mere human challenge the edicts of the eternal. What God has joined in this ceremony is to remain throughout eternity; the consequences of shattering this union will result in eternal damnation. Amen."

As soon as the ceremony ended, Jenny collected her horse and buggy from the livery stable and started for home. She did not need Joseph's warning of secrecy. That strange ceremony scarcely penetrated her mind with reality.

Even if she were so inclined to talk, who could be expected to believe it had truly happened? She murmured, "Neither token or script to indicate the transaction. Seems I can only whisper my confidences to Luna."

In the days that immediately followed, the heat of July blasted into August. The first day of August in Jenny's hot little house she was miserably aware of the deficiencies in her life. First, there had been no letter from Mark, and Jenny was consumed with fear for him. Joseph's promised boy hadn't come to milk the cows and cart the product away. The profusion of the garden begged for attention. And there was only Jenny to face the task.

Standing on her back steps, wiping a weary hand across her brow, Jenny irritably tugged at her sticky cotton dress and wondered why she couldn't button the bodice.

She heard the crunch of feet on the path paved with river pebbles and turned. It was Joseph Smith, smiling, immaculate, and confident.

She met his happy greeting with crossness. "Where is that fellow who's to do the chores? I milked three cows and poured it all as slop for the pigs. Milk in this hot weather is nauseous."

His grin disappeared, "Jenny! I'd forgotten! I promise you, there'll be someone here tomorrow." He came up the steps, saying, "You'll have a sunstroke out here. Come inside."

"I should be saying that, Joseph!" she snapped. He looked startled and immediately she apologized. "I'm sorry. Nothing is going right today." He stared at her gaping bodice and she yanked at it.

He was following her into the house as she said, "I was ready to wrestle with the pail at the well. The rope's frayed. There's not even water to offer." Without a word, he picked up the pail and went out the door.

Jenny was smoothing her hands over her hair as he came in with the water. She splashed water against her hot cheeks. "Thank you, Joseph."

Puzzled, she watched him over the top of the towel as he set the pail on the bench. Taking a deep breath, she said, "What brings you out this way so early this morning?"

"You." She blinked, and he continued. "I haven't been able to get away. With the press of things right now, it seems we'll have to snatch our moments when we can. Fortunately, both Mark and Tom will be gone for some time."

She hung the towel and faced him. Rubbing at the frown she felt forming, she said, "What on earth are you talking about, Joseph? I didn't call for you. If it's just to discuss Scripture, I'll gladly forego that pleasure until cool weather."

"You are uppity today, my dear. Unfortunately I haven't all day to tease you back into good humor. Come now."

He reached for her hand and she backed away, slowly saying, "Joseph, you're talking like a husband of twenty years, reminding a willful wife of her duty. Do I hear you correctly?"

He looked astonished. "That's one way of looking at the situation. Unfortunately my station leaves neither the time nor energy for the niceties of life." She was still backing away, too shocked to think. He studied her face closely and, turning, went to sit in the rocking chair. "We'll have it your way. Come here."

Jenny focused on the rocking chair and she saw herself and Mark there. For a moment, as she smiled over the memory, her heart was twisted with loneliness.

Joseph was reaching for her hand, and reason returned. She stepped backward and said, "Joseph, you have no right to come into my house in this manner."

"But I do. Have you forgotten that day just one week ago?"

Suddenly she saw the total picture. All the fragments of gossip and innuendo began to have meaning. But surely not! She looked at him. Seeing the guileless smile, she could not doubt him.

"Joseph, our marriage is a spiritual marriage, one for eternity only. That's right, isn't it?"

"No, Jenny. That is only part of it; there is a very real earthly marriage too, and I want you as my wife, now."

She closed her eyes briefly and he said, "I know what you are thinking. It isn't adultery. The Lord has told me so. It is all right for us to have our fun as long as we don't tell anyone about it."

As she pressed her hands against her eyes, she felt his hand upon her arm. She put her fingers against the pulse in her throat and tried to sort through the jumble of thought and emotion. Abruptly a word filled her mind—*talisman.*

Blinking, Jenny looked around, "Did you say—"

"I said, come here."

Thrusting her hand into her pocket she felt the medal burning against her skin. Slowly she began backing toward the door. The knowledge of what she must do was there—not accepted or questioned, just there. She must rid herself of the talisman if she were ever to be free of Joseph's power over her.

The rocking chair creaked. She looked at Joseph, just beginning to push himself up out of the chair.

Jenny had just put her hand on the doorjamb when she saw the chair slip backward on her polished floor, flying out from under the surprised prophet. One second she hesitated; then she ran.

She threw herself over the pasture fence, sobbing as she streaked across the pasture toward the trees. Only one thought filled her mind. *The talisman—get rid of the talisman!* From where had that thought appeared?

The dark trees edging the bluff were coming close. She ran into them, feeling their branches snatch at her hair as their roots tripped. Jenny flew on, only guessing Joseph would be behind her.

Nearly fainting now, Jenny reached the edge of the bluff and felt the wind tear at her as she gasped for breath. Far below was the surging water of the inlet. For a moment, as dizziness swept over her, Jenny braced herself against a tree, groping in her pocket with trembling fingers. The talisman. She felt the hot, burning link and knew what she must do.

Taking a quick step to the tall bank, Jenny raised her arm to throw the talisman. "Jenny!" She knew his call. She hesitated. Again his voice echoed off the trees, coming nearer. Quickly she spun, and immediately the earth gave way.

She felt the swoop of air. Trees spiraled past; grass, water, and then sunshot sky. The cold shock of water took her, swirling her downward.

She was engulfed in a flood of purple. As the water broke over her, she saw the chalice, tipping, throwing purple wine over her body.

17

JENNY HEARD HIS voice before she opened her eyes, saying, "Like a shooting star she came over the bluff, whirling with the black hair streaming out. How she ever managed to hit the one deep spot in the river, I'll never know. Could have been the rocks."

A woman's voice answered him, and Jenny opened her eyes. There was a giant's wet boots and britches planted beside her and a white-haired woman kneeling over her. The woman said, "Why, you're Mark Cartwright's wife."

Jenny tried to speak and choked. The whole of the giant emerged. He knelt and rolled her over. "Get that water out." When he helped her into a sitting position, she met his worried blue eyes and saw a question in their depths.

"A miracle!" he added. "There's rocks along the river. A miracle Pa and I were fishing." Now she saw the old gentleman hovering in the background—Mr. Daniels.

He stepped forward and she saw the same troubled question. She was still wondering about their expression when Mrs. Daniels said, "Lands, child, you're shivering!"

"And this morning is hotter'n blazes." Jenny could only nod at the giant as he lifted her to her feet. "Ken ya walk or shall I pack ya?"

"Walk," she managed; taking a deep, choking breath, she set her feet to follow Mrs. Daniels. In the cabin, beside the remnants of the breakfast fire, Jenny dried herself. She donned the cotton dress belonging to the little woman moving around the kitchen, and then Jenny sat down to watch her.

Shaking her head, Mrs. Daniels was stirring up the fire and caring for Jenny's clothing as she talked. " 'Twere a miracle. I heard the splash and the menfolk yelling." She paused to cast that questioning look at Jenny.

With a sigh Jenny started her explanation. "I was running, in this heat, dizzy. I had something in my hand and I was trying to throw it in the river. I slipped," she finished lamely.

Mrs. Daniels had been reheating the breakfast coffee and she carried a cup to Jenny. With the first sip, Jenny's stomach went into immediate revolt. She jumped to her feet and fled to the door.

When she returned, dizzy and trembling, Mrs. Daniels led her to the bedroom. "You caught?" she asked as she wiped Jenny's face.

Jenny puzzled over the strange statement and finally pushed herself upright. Mrs. Daniels was saying, "Could be because you're not used to coffee."

"Could be," Jenny murmured, remembering the smell; then she asked, "What do you mean, *caught*?"

"With a young'un," Mrs. Daniels said, sounding as surprised as Jenny was feeling.

"A baby! After all these years!" She grasped Mrs. Daniels' arm. "Could it be? We've been married six years and we've given up hoping. Could it?"

Mrs. Daniels' face relaxed and she was smiling back at Jenny. "Could be cause for being dizzy, too. Now you just lie back and rest a time. The menfolk had to take the milk into town, but I suspect they'll be looking for your husband without being told."

Jenny's excitement withered. Dully she said, "He's gone." Then she rallied. "But if it's so, then I'm not really alone. Oh, I can hardly believe it! If only he'd come soon," she added wistfully.

Late that afternoon the young giant took her home. For a minute, considering the events leading up to that plunge over the bluff, Jenny longingly considered the invitation to stay. But there was only the loft where the giant, Alson, slept, and the tiny bedroom where she had rested.

As the wagon rumbled down her own lane, Jenny found herself glad for the long afternoon shadows. Joseph would be at home with his family.

When Alson lifted her from the wagon and said, "Ma'am, those cows and pigs are needing attention. I'd be happy to oblige you."

"Oh, would you? I am still shaky. And if you'd care for the job, I'll hire you to do the chores until Tom returns."

He nodded with a pleased grin. "I'm obliged."

When Jenny entered the kitchen, she immediately noticed the rocker upside-down. For a moment she hesitated in the doorway while the words and the emotions of the morning tumbled through her. Guilt surged over her as she recalled her strange, unwilling response to Joseph.

Frowning now, she righted the chair and sat down. *Why the guilt, if this is God's will for me?*

No answer came, and it was late when Jenny left the rocking chair and went to lock the doors and close the curtains against the night.

During the past lonesome nights, Jenny had formed the habit of murmuring a chant against evil as she went about the evening ritual of preparing for bed. Tonight the words began to slip easily from her lips. "God of light, protector of the hearth, spread circles of power—"

Abruptly she stopped. She was in the parlor, looking down at the table where her Bible lay. Would there be more power if she were to find words from it to recite each evening? The scenes from the morning flashed across her memory. With a shiver she picked up the Book and carried it into the kitchen.

She placed the lighted lamp on the table and bent over the Book. Her fingers were hesitant, unsure as they turned pages, first one way and then the other.

One word caught her attention and her fingers found the beginning. Isaiah 8. She read slowly, " 'And when they shall say unto you, Seek unto them that have familiar spirits, . . . should not a people seek unto their God? . . . To the law and to the testimony: if they speak not according to this word, *it is* because *there is* no light in them.' " And farther down, the phrase, " '. . . and *they* shall be driven to darkness.' "

"Familiar spirits," she murmured slowly, remembering there was talk of such in the green book—spirits sent to help those seeking power. For a moment another thought pricked her mind and then was gone. "Light, darkness," she puzzled as she went up the stairs to bed.

The words were with her in the morning. Now she could look at the previous day and marvel.

The heat was still upon the Mississippi lowlands. Jenny saw it in the mists rising from the river to cloud the forest. Alson Daniels came; she heard the clank of his bucket.

When he left, she went out to gather from her garden, sharply conscious that busy barnyard sounds contrasted with her silent house. She washed the vegetables at the well and sat in the shade to eat them. Her stomach was in revolt again, but today she welcomed the sign. She also welcomed the tight frock and hugged herself with excitement.

"If only Mark would write!" she sighed. "I want so badly to tell him." She stood bemused, drawing a memory picture of his face and painting it with delight. Suppose there were a letter at the post office right now? She nearly gave in to her impulse to go to town, then quickly changed her mind at the thought of a chance meeting with Joseph.

A plaintive cry came from the pasture, and Jenny went to lean across the fence. "Oh, you scamp," she said with a sigh. The tiniest lamb had crawled through the pasture fence. Now he was bawling his fear from the dark forest side of the fence. "You baby," she called, crawling over the fence and heading across the pasture. The remainder of the flock contentedly chewed their cud in the shade of the apple tree.

Jenny paused before jumping the creek. She was hearing the murmur of water washing over smooth stones. It was peaceful, all of it. Again she heaved a contended sigh and started after the lamb.

"Come, little scamp," she called, stretching beseeching fingers through the fence. The pink mouth wailed his protest while his spindly legs wobbled. With a sigh of exasperation, Jenny went over the fence.

The woods were dim and cool. After pushing the lamb through the fence, she followed the creek into the trees.

The rock she selected was flat and inviting. Bracing her shoulders against a tree, Jenny settled back to listen to the brook and the birds. A tiny warm breeze touched her face; she closed her eyes against the flickering pattern of leaves, and the sounds grew faint.

When Jenny opened her eyes it seemed darker. Getting to her feet she stretched, surprised at the sense of well-being that enveloped her. Her dream had been filled with yesterday's kaleidoscope of purple and silver.

Until the dream, she had forgotten the images of yesterday. Only now the memory surfaced, stamped upon her mind. Never would she forget that spiraling downward while purple light and flashing silver surrounded her.

Now settling back on the rock, she allowed the memory to flow through her, wondering at the meaning. "Purple—the church window. At the time I was baptized there was that window and the chalice and the wine."

Suddenly, as if yesterday's water swept over her, she intoned, "I baptize thee—" Jenny frowned. The words wouldn't come. But there, as if caught in a balance scale, she recalled the baptism in Joseph's church compared with that first baptism. There were no purple-shot images, no hint of a hovering just beyond her touch. She recalled only mud and river slime, and meaningless words.

Jenny got to her feet, still trying to remember that word and tie it to the fleeting impressions. She finally shrugged and turned away from the creek. As she bent to pick the graceful frond of fern at her feet, she heard, "Jenny." It was the lilt of the wind. "Jenny."

She turned and searched the dark shadows shifting with wind-born light. "Jenny!" The call was louder, insistent, and she looked beyond. A flash of red shone through the trees. Dropping the ferns, Jenny ran, not thinking, merely triggered by her deep need.

The shadows grew darker and Jenny slowed, picking her way through bushes and rocks. The figure in red was waiting on the next rise. "Adela!" Jenny called, and when she repeated the name, it was a scream of frenzy.

"Oh, how I've longed to see you!" Jenny stopped. Now pressing fingers against her forehead, she tried to remember why she must see Adela.

The woman moved, her smile familiar and warm. The same red chiffon floated softly about her figure, lifting with the breeze. Jenny took a step and hesitated.

Her words were stilted as she said, "You look so familiar in that old red dress, why—"

The lost words were before her. "That's it. The name of Jesus. In the name of Jesus I was baptized." She raised her delighted smile to Adela. "I was—" The red figure seemed to be retreating, dimming.

Jenny hurried forward, across the rocks, up the slope. Now sunlight slanted through the trees and she stopped. The light clearly outlined the scene before her. The red chiffon still swirled, the woman still smiled. Jenny blinked and passed her hands across her eyes.

The dress was the same, but those perfect features were sagging, twisting. Before her eyes, Adela became a wizened figure, fading, disappearing. Stunned, Jenny whispered, "Jesus."

Then she was brought back to herself by a clap of thunder. In terror she listened to it growing, exploding, then rumbling away. While the air was still filled with the sharp odor of sulphur, the rain burst upon Jenny, and she ran.

In the days that followed, Jenny doubted the vision her memory periodically cast before her, but she didn't forget running into the house, panting and crying. She also recalled groping through the storm-dimmed room until she found her Bible. And in the days that followed, she didn't forget the comfort she felt simply from holding the book.

18

OVER THE DISHPAN Jenny murmured, " 'Jesus saith unto him, I am the way, the truth, and the life: no man cometh unto the Father, but by me.' " She lifted the cups and watched the soap bubbles burst and disappear. "Adela said there were many ways to worship God. Why did she disappear like these bubbles?" The truth was clear, and Jenny could only whisper in awe, "Jesus."

Very sober as she continued to wash dishes, Jenny pieced together in her mind all that she had refused to consider before. Did it matter that Adela was a familiar spirit? With a sigh Jenny said, "Yes, it does matter. I thought she was a friend. She was everything I admired—beautiful and strong."

Jenny's mind nudged her with another fact. Adela had power, and if she were a spirit instead of a real person, this meant the promise of power for herself was a lie—or was it? Could there be something she didn't understand?

Jenny moved uneasily and stared out the window. Was power to order life beyond the scope of human beings? Immediately Jenny remembered the pressure Adela had used to get her to take the vows at sabbat. That oath, the blood in the chalice—even now they made her shiver. But there was another thought. Jenny whispered it to herself, her voice filled with awe. "I simply said the name of Jesus. I wasn't even thinking of Adela— my head was full of baptism and purple light. I said 'Jesus,' and Adela disappeared." Abruptly Jenny was trembling.

As soon as the kitchen was tidied, Jenny fled to the only comforting presence in the house, her Bible.

She read the Gospels, feeling as if she were looking over Jesus' shoulder. With awe she watched and listened, as thirsty as the woman at the well.

Daily Jenny flew about her work and then settled to read, conscious only of her desperate need. But the reading was not without pain. There were hard words which caused days of uneasiness and questioning: *sin, the wrath of God, judgment; believe, trust, the blood of Jesus.*

In her silent house she brooded in isolation and then fled, desperate for companionship. One hot August day she took her light buggy to Sarah Pratt's home.

As she let the mare amble down Sarah's shady lane, Jenny was thinking the trees looked as limp as she felt. But then she had a reason. She grinned and flicked the reins.

Instead of taking the mare to the house, Jenny stopped the buggy in the shade of a tree and left the horse to graze. Just as Jenny reached the front door, she heard Sarah's voice coming from the shady side yard and circled around the house.

Hearing a strange voice, she hesitated momentarily. Then, with a shrug she stepped forward just as the woman laughed and said, "Sarah, such outrage! Why do you make a fuss about a little gossip. Even if it isn't true, people will speculate. Besides, you should consider it an honor. Why, I've been his mistress for four years now."

Jenny gasped and as the women turned, said, "Oh, I . . . I'm sorry. I didn't mean to sneak up on you."

The stranger threw back her head and laughed. "Don't look so appalled. I'm not."

Looking surprisingly relieved, Sarah hurried toward Jenny. Taking Jenny's hand she said, "Do come sit in the shade. This is Lucinda Harris."

While Jenny frowned, wondering why the face was familiar, Lucinda drawled, "Yes, I was in Far West while you were there. Seems we didn't have time to get acquainted. I suppose I knew most everyone because we were part of the early settlement. Your husband is the attorney. Didn't I hear that Joseph sent him to Washington to present another bill?" She turned to Sarah. "Do you suppose that's where Joseph's gone?"

Sarah shrugged and addressed Jenny. "I suppose you've heard the latest news, though it's been so long since I've seen you."

Jenny muttered, "I haven't heard any news for ages. I've not even had a letter from Mark."

"Oh," Sarah added quickly. "Then you don't know that Joseph's disappeared. Don't look so alarmed! It's that Boggs affair."

"If only he'd kept his mouth shut," Lucinda said. "Coming out with his prophecy about Boggs being shot and then broadcasting his views hither and yonder when it did happen."

"I'd heard about that," Jenny replied.

"Well," Sarah continued, "as you know, Boggs didn't die. Now Governor Carlin's issued a writ for Joseph's and Porter Rockwell's arrest."

Lucinda's smooth voice cut in. "The Nauvoo Charter came to the rescue again. They were released under a writ of habeas corpus and the city council stepped in and issued a new ordinance which required Nauvoo court to inquire into the validity of the writ."

Sarah said, "Well, I know the charter was designed to help Joseph's cause, that's obvious, considering the trouble in Missouri. Somehow it doesn't seem quite right. But by the time the sheriffs returned from seeing Carlin a second time, Joseph and Porter were both gone."

Jenny lost the thread of conversation; her mind was busy with the implications. She breathed a deep sigh of relief. Perhaps by the time the legal problems simmered down, Joseph would have forgotten all about that piece of paper in his office.

Jenny soon found an excuse to leave Sarah and her friend. She turned her rig onto the road and headed for Nauvoo, still hoping for a letter from Mark.

The afternoon Tom rode his horse back into Nauvoo, he was conscious only of being tired with the bone-weariness of discouragement and physical fatigue. He was so busy planning his speech to Joseph that he scarcely noticed the first hint of autumn this September day.

He was still mulling over his dilemma when he reached Joseph's Mansion House. Although it was still early afternoon, a peculiar crystal stillness held the deserted streets. The thread of smoke rising from the mansion's chimney was slender and wick-straight.

Now he noticed the horse hitched to Joseph's fence post. Slowly Tom dismounted and looped his reins around the post nearest a succulent patch of grass.

Pausing to scratch his head and flex his shoulders, Tom took time to notice the clear blue of the sky. A white cloud puffed across his vision like a ship under full sail.

Tom turned toward Joseph's front door just as it burst open. He recognized the Prophet's heavy voice as the two figures came through the door.

To Tom's astonishment, the first figure was hurrying and the second figure was kicking. Tom scratched his head while he waited until the rotund figure picked himself up out of the street, dusted off his suit, straightened his tie, and mounted his horse.

Joseph's face was flushed and he was still breathing heavily as he stepped close to Tom. He jerked his head at the departing figure. "Justin Butterfield, United States Attorney for Illinois. Came in here accusing me of misbehaving."

"How's that?"

"Bankruptcy petition. Says I transferred property illegally. Guess he won't do that again." Joseph was at ease as he led the way into the house. "State's in a hole financially, so they're going to take every advantage of a fellow they can to save a cent. What's on your mind? What are you doing back in Nauvoo?"

Tom gulped and cringed. That scene was too sharply etched on his mind. Feeling like a ten-year-old, he started his explanation. "Joseph, I'm just not cut out to be a missionary. Figured I was doin' more harm than good so I settled for comin' home. I was dragging the rest of the fellas down, honest." He braced himself and, surprisingly, Joseph only shook his head.

"I guess I wasn't much of a judge of character, Tom," he said. "You can do everything else, including putting out the best shoeing job in the state. Go back to the stable. I guess I might as well admit, we've been missing you sore.

"So's my horse. Take a look at him first thing in the morning, will you? It's the right front shoe."

Tom sighed with relief and started to get up. Joseph's hand stopped him. Tom settled back and was surprised to see the dark frown back on his face.

"Tom, I don't know how to tell you this. But Mark's gone and you're closest of kin. There's some talk that Jenny's been pretty unhappy. Alson Daniels and his pa fished her outta the river a couple of weeks back. When Alson came into town with the milk, he told me about it. Says she jumped off the bluff, clearly intent on ending it all."

Tom stared at Joseph, trying to put meaning into the words. "My sister? Jen's not the kind a person to do herself in."

Joseph shook his head and leaned forward. "Unfortunately, I've not had time to visit with her. It turned out that Porter and I had to take a little trip to avoid Missouri sheriffs with writs for our arrest. I didn't want the task of trying Nauvoo's charters in court right now, especially since I was being laid on the line."

Joseph settled back in his chair and studied his fists. When he spoke again, Tom thought it was as if the words were pulled from him. "Tom, from what I've heard, I'm really worried about your sister's mind. Sometimes women get all kinds of funny ideas. The suicide try indicates that to me.

"I realize you don't know much about females, being you're not married, but watch out for her. Let me know if there's anything I can do to help. I'll try to see her as soon as the pressure is off my neck."

Tom had started for the door when Joseph said, "One thing more, Tom. Since you're not hankering to be a missionary, I'll put the touch on you for the priesthood."

Tom was nearly to the farm before he was able to shake his mood. He straightened in the saddle and looked around. The Pratt farm was off to his left, and he could see Orson herding his cows into the barn. The apple trees were beginning to show color. He noticed that Orson had propped up the heaviest branches.

By the time he started down Jenny's lane, Tom was whistling. He saw Jenny turn and set her pail down. When he swung her up in his arms, he saw the tears on her face. "Jen, it's just your old brother."

"I'm just so glad to see you; it's been so lonely!"

He hugged her again and said, "Hey, you're treating yourself well— gettin' chunky, aren't ya?"

She leaned back grinning at him. "I'm going to have a baby."

"Well, I'll be switched," he said slowly, studying her face. Even as he spoke, he was putting facts together. "I'd about given up on hopin' you'd ever get around to that. What does Mark think about all this?"

He saw the cloud on her face. "He doesn't know. Tom, I haven't had one letter from him since he's left. Can he possibly be that busy? Why must he be gone so long?"

"I don't know," Tom said, troubled by what he was seeing. He was thinking of the way he had sloped out of a disagreeable job as he said, "I'm kinda wonderin' why Mark doesn't jump ship like I did."

"Does Joseph know you're back?"

"Yeah." Tom remembered the conversation as he searched Jenny's face. She looked pale and tired, but there was that happy smile. Surely, if circumstances were as he was thinking, she wouldn't be so happy about it.

Tom sighed and took up his conversation again. "He's lettin' me off easy. I expected to get sent to China, but he's sending me back to the stable. Might be he's had a report on my preachin'."

The next morning at breakfast Tom said, "One thing Joseph did do which surprised me; he's earmarked me for the high priesthood."

Jenny nearly dropped the skillet. Astonishment flooded her face as she turned to him. "That's nice, but it sure surprises me too. Seems such a limited group from what I'm hearing; guess I just didn't realize how special you were to Joseph." She hesitated and frowned. "Tom, there's lots of funny talk going on. Don't get yourself into something you'll regret."

"How's that?" he asked, chewing slowly.

She sighed and frowned, saying, "There's talk of building up the Legion more. Is it true Joseph's not given up on Missouri yet?" After a pause she turned to him and shrugged, shaking her head. "Oh, I just don't know; this Legion business worries me. I know there's rumbles around about it. I heard a fellow on the street. A stranger. He seemed uneasy. Just things floating around making us wonder. At Relief Society we talk."

"Gossip session?"

"I—I just don't know. One minute I get the feeling the women are all the best of friends; then next meeting I see the tides moving, telling me there's something going on underneath all the nice smiles. There's an undercurrent in Nauvoo I don't like."

19

JENNY WAS PULLING the curtains across the windows when Tom came into the house carrying the pail of milk. " 'Tis a mite nippy out there tonight; reminds me this nice October is about to bid us good-bye."

With a shiver, Jenny went to the stove and pushed the simmering pot to one side. "I keep worrying about Mark. Since that one letter I've heard no more, and I can't help wondering if it is well with him. It bothers me that there are letters I didn't receive."

"Mail service isn't the best out here," Tom reminded mildly. But Jenny was brooding over the note of alarm in Mark's letter. Was he doubting her love because he didn't receive a letter from her? She moved her shoulders irritably and saw Tom's glance.

"It's terrible to not know where to send a letter," she explained. "And he doesn't even know about this," she patted her stomach. "Tom, just think, his baby is poking at my ribs, and Mark doesn't even know about him."

Tom sat down at the table and grinned at Jenny as she pressed her hands across her thickening waist. "Might be it'll be a girl. Think he'll trade it off?"

"I doubt. After waiting this long, we'll take anything we get. Just, please God, let it be healthy."

She felt his quick look and knew he wondered about the prayer. Strange how it seemed the words came without thinking.

Jenny went to strain the milk and slice the bread. "You want milk with your stew?"

He nodded. "I 'spect I'd better. I'd rather have hot tea, but tonight's priesthood meeting. There's a little talk that Joseph'll be there. I'm not thinkin' it'll be likely though, since they're still lookin' for him."

"How do you know?"

He hesitated and looked sharply at her. "Remember those fellows we saw last time we went to shop?"

She frowned, "You're meaning the bunch sitting around in front of the store whittling with those terrible knives?"

Nodding, he added, "Those are Joseph's men. They make it a point to know what's going on. You needn't worry. There ain't no surprises around here."

Silently Jenny ladled the stew into a bowl and carried it to the table. When Tom reached for his third slice of bread, he added, "Bennett started all this with his running to Missouri. Seems all's fair—"

"How Joseph could have taken that fellow in, befriending him and making him the mayor of Nauvoo as well as being in charge of the Legion, well, it seems strange." Jenny slowly picked up her fork, thinking of the man she had met at Sarah Pratt's home. Thoughtfully she added, "Bennett seems nice enough. Mark hesitated over him though. Well, he's gone. Beyond making so much trouble for the Prophet now, I suppose we'll never know what's in the heart of the man. But no matter; I'm against the letters he's written to the press."

Jenny had just hung her dish towel to dry when they heard the tap at the door. Tom opened it and exclaimed, "Brother Joseph! Is there trouble?"

Joseph Smith came into the room, nodded briefly at Jenny and turned to Tom, saying, "Only that I need to get a message to Mark. He's to be in Springfield this week, but I don't trust a letter to reach him."

"Problems?" Tom took the packet of papers the Prophet offered and studied Joseph's face.

"I'm just covering every detail I can. Thomas Ford will be inaugurated as governor of the state come the first week in December. That's not much more'n a month away. I need to remind him of his promise to test the Missouri writ in court. Mark can fill him in on the details. He's got papers with him. But he mustn't come back here without seeing Ford and wringing a promise out of him. I can't spend the rest of the winter dodging the sheriff and posse from Missouri."

He paced the floor and added, "Tom, tonight is as good a time to start as tomorrow. So pack a grip and be off."

Tom threw a quick glance at Jenny. "Brother Joseph, think about my sister. I'm not of a mind to walk out on her right now."

"I'll have John Lee take her back to the Mansion House. Just be about your business; she'll be okay." Going to the door he said, "Lee's minding the horses. I'll speak to him and then be here to get you off."

Tom looked at Jenny. She swallowed hard and said, "Best do it, Tom. I'll be better in town than by myself. Could you stop past the Daniels' and have Alson do the milking? Tom, please tell Mark how miserably lonesome I am for him, tell him—please hurry home."

Jenny carried her valise downstairs just as she heard Tom close the door behind himself. Joseph was sprawled comfortably in Mark's chair. "The fire feels good tonight," he said, gesturing toward the fireplace. "Now come sit; I've a few things to say to you."

"Joseph," she warned, "this is my home."

"And you are my wife."

"I can't believe you are still talking in this manner," her voice was low, but she challenged him with her eyes. "When this took place, you indicated it was a marriage for eternity."

"And you thought that was all I meant? Jennifer, I didn't see that in your response. I see you are laboring under a lack of understanding. Seems Patty Sessions didn't do a thorough job of teaching."

He pointed to the chair. "I've some things to say to you. First, I must remind you of the very idea brought forth in the Bible. This is the idea that things change. Some things are wrong under one circumstance—and I remind you of the instances involving murder. The Bible says 'Thou shalt not murder' in one place, and in another advocates killing off the enemy. The same applies here."

"Are you referring to adultery?"

He continued, "You call it adultery? When I came for my rights, you named it thus. God doesn't. What might very well be adultery in one circumstance is commanded of God in another. Jenny, when God instructed me to take you as wife, the angel told me, with a sword in his hand, that I was to fulfill the command or die. I dare not disobey."

Jenny's heart sank. Feeling as if the weight of the universe rested upon her, she slowly got to her feet. She faced him and groped for words, murmuring the only word that was there, "Jesus."

He raised his head, "What did you say?"

She stepped forward and clasped her hands across the precious swelling. "Joseph, I regret that ceremony more than I can say. I sense there's no backing out of it unless I forfeit my eternal salvation. But this is earthly life. I can't understand mixing the two. Besides, I'm carrying Mark's child. To let you—"

She paused and took a shaky breath, weaving now through the maze of contradictory thoughts. "I don't have anything to go on. I don't know enough about God or even His Holy Bible—but I'm reading and trying very hard to learn. It's just—Joseph, it *feels* so wrong. There's Mark. I love him and I've always been taught you don't let another man touch you."

He looked up at Jenny, slowly shaking his head. "My dear, how twisted this has all become in your mind! I will pray for you.

"For now I'll just have to trust the Lord to protect you from the evil attack and spare your life until you have your eyes open to truth. But, Jenny, my dear, you must devote yourself to praying about this matter. God will give you a sure knowledge of the rightness of the message. Just as

I have seen Him, you'll see Him filling your room with such a brightness of His presence you'll never doubt again. Meanwhile, I must urge you to not speak of this to anyone. Keep it to yourself and pray lest you be tempted and lose the blessing to another."

With a sigh, Joseph got to his feet and went to the door. "Lee," he called and then turned back. "I'm running for my life. John will take you to the Mansion House. It's crowded, but Emma will make room for you. I'll try to get back into town soon."

It was very late when John D. Lee aroused Emma Smith and delivered the Prophet's message. He carried in Jenny's bag and took the buggy to the livery stable.

Jenny faced the woman swathed in a robe which didn't conceal her pregnancy. She studied Emma's weary, lined face and said, "I'm so sorry to disturb you. I wanted to wait until morning, but they said no."

With a terse nod, Emma led the way up the stairs and opened the door. "We're packed to the rafters. You'll have to push Julie over. Could be tomorrow I'll be able to settle you in a room."

It was late that next morning before Jenny went downstairs. She had been aroused early when the adopted daughter of Joseph and Emma slipped out of the room. Lying in bed, Jenny considered the twist of circumstances in her life—first, Joseph's visit the previous evening. Now, she considered with dismay the necessity of facing Emma as well as Joseph's children.

As she left the bedroom, Jenny looked about the house curiously. There was still that raw, unsettled air about the house, but the rooms seemed large and bright. In the upstairs hall she noticed the rooms opening off the hall had doors bearing numbered brass plaques.

When she reached the foot of the stairs, Jenny paused, confused. She peered through the first open door and saw the large room. It looked more like a lobby than a parlor. At one end there was an attractive fireplace and comfortable chairs.

Then she looked to the other end and frowned. It looked as if cabinets were being removed. As she considered the long bar, she nodded with understanding, remembering the stories she had heard. That was the bar Joseph had installed while Emma was away from home.

Jenny felt a spark of admiration for the woman as she chuckled over the story. Joseph had installed his bar and set up Porter Rockwell, pigtail and all, as bartender. Emma, so the story went, had taken one look and condemned the addition. Joseph, Porter, and all the liquor had speedily departed when Emma threatened to take the children and move back to the old cabin.

The next door Jenny tried led back to the kitchen. Hearing voices, she went in. Emma and her children, as well as several women, sat at the table.

As she sat down, Emma pointed out the children. "This is Julie, our daughter; she's twelve now and a big help. There's Joseph our firstborn, Frederick, and Alexander. This is Eliza Snow. Miss Snow is a school-teacher by profession. And Emily Partridge. Emily is living with us and earning her keep."

Jenny looked at the comely girl as she bobbed her head and went to the stove. "Mrs. Smith says you'll be staying for a time. There's little room right now. But two gentlemen just passin' through will doubtless be leaving in a day or so."

Jenny glanced at the shy Julie, and with a smile said, "I do appreciate the hospitality, but I'm imposing. I don't know why I didn't just stay at the farm. Surely Tom will be back soon." There were questions in the eyes of the women, but Jenny dismissed them as she accepted the bowl of por-ridge from Emily.

Emma was looking out the window, watching the procession of wagons and buggies on the street. Slowly she said, "I'll be happy just to have life back to normal again. Joseph's promised to be back for the birthin' in December. But it will take more'n that. There's this coming and going of all the strangers. There's the fear and unrest. These men they're calling the Whittling Deacons bother me. Seems holiness shouldn't have to worry people on either side of the fence."

Eliza Snow had pushed aside her breakfast dishes. With her arms propped on the table she folded her hands under her chin and dreamily addressed the ceiling. "There's little of holiness going on right now. It isn't the Prophet's fault. 'Tis the responsibility of the people to be holy in order to free the powers of God."

She paused to smile slowly at Emma. "You remember yourself all the promises. All the miracles expected at Kirtland had to be postponed until we had a temple in Missouri. That blessed event still hasn't happened. Therefore we wait until the people purify themselves and accept all the commandments of the Lord; then He will make our enemies live at peace with us."

Emma moved impatiently and said, "I suppose I'm too practical for Zion talk. I worry about the present, about the children and their future. They need their father at home. We all need to know we can depend on a surety."

Eliza was shaking her head. "Emma, dear woman, of all of us, I ex-pected you to have settled in. From the beginning, Joseph has taught us all that we know by the spirit, not by sight. You know that Joseph knows all things that will come to pass right up to the end of the world. Granted, he isn't allowed to reveal them yet."

Emma got to her feet and shooed the children out the door. "Now get your books and be off," she admonished them, then turned impatiently to Eliza.

With a quick cry she said, "I don't like the uncertain; I want to touch and see."

Jenny watched Eliza, the dreamy expression on her face and the slight smile as she raised her head. "I know, 'tis womanlike to want it so, but Emma, my dear friend, I must admit there's such a mysterious power when he speaks. It makes me willing to forego the material and draws me on to the spiritual."

For a moment Emma was caught. Jenny saw the wistful expression on her face and then she turned impatiently, " 'Tis not the spiritual that'll feed me and the young'uns."

When Emma had left the room, Eliza turned to Jenny with a gentle smile. "Emma needs to have the experience of being carried away by the spirit. She's too earthly-minded. 'Twill get us into trouble, I fear."

Jenny spent another uncomfortable night on the narrow cot with Julie, and then Sally came.

Eliza and Jenny were beside the fire, poking at needlework for Emma and probing, just as tentatively, each other's thoughts when Sally sailed into the room, crying, "Jenny, why didn't you come to me? I shall be angry if you don't pack and come now."

Jenny packed and came, but she did so wondering why, after months of neglect, Sally had appeared in such a rush of compassion.

The answer came out as Sally settled Jenny in the spare bedroom and confided, "Andy saw Tom just last week. We've learned of your good fortune. A baby." For a fleeting moment Jenny saw the question in her eyes before she added, "My, Mark will be surprised. Tom said he didn't know yet. All these years . . ." her voice trailed away.

Jenny turned from hanging her frock and said, "Is that too unusual? After all, there's only Tamara in your family."

In the silence Jenny turned and caught Sally twisting her hands together. She looked up and smiled. "I haven't told Andy yet, but there's to be another one. Not until next summer, though."

"Oh, Sally, that's wonderful! Now we can share this together. Do you want another little girl or a boy for Andy?"

There was a white line around Sally's mouth as she smiled and said, "A boy, of course. But please don't mention it to Andy just yet."

As they started down the stairs together, Sally impulsively hugged Jenny. "I'm glad you've come."

"I am, too," Jenny admitted. "For more than just the joy of being with you. After two days of Eliza I was starting to feel like a grubby child."

"Why?" Sally asked in surprise.

"Well, she talks so much. About her poetry and how she's complimented on it. She says things like 'the spirit told me,' and then she talks about how the spirit ministers to her. On and on.

"I think even Emma's annoyed by it all. Julie loves it. She hangs on to every word. But then Eliza's good with the boys, too. Seems to have time for cookies and things, even games with them."

20

IN THE DAYS that followed, Jenny settled in with Sally. The bond between the two had always made their friendship easy. Even after long separations, and despite their differences, Jenny and Sally quickly moved into an intimate relationship. Sally called it a sisterhood.

Now Sally was having morning sickness and Jenny asked, "You still haven't told Andy? Why?" A shadow crossed Sally's eyes, and she shrugged.

As Jenny resolved to mend her meddling ways, Sally said, "I suppose I'm fearin' and not believin' it true. But I will. I just don't like Andy fussing."

Jenny grinned, "But telling him means you don't have to sneak your sewing away when he comes." Jenny looked at Tamara playing beside the fire. The child was six now. "She needs to know just as much as Andy."

Sally's eyes were thoughtful as she frowned at Tamara. The child's angelic fairness had darkened until she now resembled her father. Smiling, Jenny watched her play with her dolls. To Sally she said, "At times I'm tempted to pinch myself just to make certain it's real. I can hardly wait."

There was a cynical twist to Sally's smile. "Let's hope Mark will feel the same. Seems it's always the woman who wants it the most."

"Mark isn't that way." She paused. "Sally, what's wrong? I don't understand, but there's something. Our friendship has just about slipped away this past year, we've seen each other so seldom. I don't like it at all. If you've got troubles, say them."

Sally looked surprised and then embarrassed. "I'm sorry, Jenny. It's just Andy. You know how jealous he's always been. I'm afraid with all the talk buzzing around that telling him I'm pregnant will just make matters worse."

"Oh, Sally, how could it?"

Sally didn't answer, but she got up from her chair and went to the desk. Picking up the newspapers there, she came to sit beside Jenny. "I suppose you've read the pamphlet put out by Udney Hay Jacobs called *The Peace Maker*?"

Jenny shook her head, "I haven't heard of it. Don't forget, I've scarcely been into town except for Relief Society meeting." Sally went back to the desk and opened a drawer. She carried the booklet to Jenny and dropped it in her lap. When Jenny picked it up, she noticed the front cover bore the name, *Joseph Smith, Printer.*

Jenny read quietly for a time, then she gasped and looked at Sally. "Have you read this? How terrible! It makes women sound like monsters."

Sally nodded and said, "I see you don't like being told you've enslaved your husband."

"Or that marriage has made him effeminate. I shall be afraid to ask a thing of him for fear—"

"He'll think he's in bondage to the law of the woman." Sally snorted. The dark shadows came back into her eyes. "What I can't understand is the purpose behind the thing. Do you suppose we'll risk having our husbands leave just because we ask them to take out the trash?"

"Oh, that's silly," Jenny protested and then studied the booklet. "Somehow I don't think that's the purpose," Jenny said slowly. "It seems to me it's coming down hard on women for being even a mite snippy. What woman hasn't had a headache?"

Sally was shivering and Jenny looked at her in concern. "You're chilling. Could you be catching something? Come to the fireside."

Settling in the rocker beside the fire, Sally said, "What did you get out of it—the meaning behind it all?"

Jenny picked up the paper and picked out sentences. "Says here that if a wife doesn't love her husband sufficiently and gets a young'un by him, the child's apt to be deficient. And that such a fact means the wife's committing fornication against her husband. He identifies fornication as lack of love and respect on the wife's part."

"Do I understand there's something about people like that not making it?"

"Well, it says the children of such don't make it into the congregation of the Lord. I suppose that means heaven." Jenny studied the paper again and then said slowly, "Sally, seems to me there's a lot of stuff in here just rolling around in circles, trying to hide the real message."

"What's the real message?"

"That in order for the women to keep from sinning and for the children to make it into eternity, it's best for a man to have more'n one wife. Mostly, I guess, laying up against those times when his wife's got a headache."

"Makes me so angry to hear them say a woman's a man's property, just like an old cow," Sally muttered.

"Seems this is egging a man on to have more'n one wife; here it's saying, oblique-like, to not do so just proves he's under the law of his wife."

"I'd like to get a hold on that Jacobs," Sally continued. "Like to shake some sense into him."

"And there you'd just be proving his point," Jenny added. "According to him, you're wrong if you're anything but a sweet little wife." Jenny returned to the pamphlet. She read more. He says that to outlaw polygamy shows the stupidity of modern Christianity. He's calling for us to restore the law of God, that's plural wives. I guess that's different from spiritual wives, isn't it?"

Sally began to have a coughing spell, and Jenny hurried to get water for her. "I believe you're coming down with the croup. Do go to bed for a rest."

She watched Sally go up the stairs and went to put away the pamphlet. As she folded the paper, she noticed the final line and stopped. "I should be grieved to see you slain before him," she read. *Strange,* she thought, *that phrase reminds me of what Joseph said. Could there be a connection between this and the spiritual wives' doctrine?*

As Jenny went to the desk with the pamphlet, she saw the newspaper lying there and picked it up to read. It was an old one. The pages had been turned back and the article on top was by Joseph Smith. Words caught her attention.

"In response to the protest over the Jacobs work, I must advise my innocence . . . Had I known, the paper would never have been printed. . . . It is nothing except a sensational piece of trash, designed to excite the minds of the uneducated."

Jenny was thoughtful as she replaced the paper. When she went into the kitchen to prepare dinner she was still thinking about Joseph's article, and only momentarily did she pause to wonder why Sally had kept the old paper.

That evening, at dinner, Andy told Sally and Jenny of his plans to go to St. Louis on Joseph's steamboat, *The Maid of Iowa.* "There's material to be ordered for the temple. It will be to my advantage to see to it personally," he added. With a smile he looked at Jenny and said, "You two can keep each other company. I'm glad to have you here, Jenny. Sally's been looking puny these last weeks."

Jenny looked quickly at Sally and said, "I'm thinking she's trying to catch the croup. She keeps this up, I'll be going back to doctorin' yet."

The first morning after Andy left, Sally came into the kitchen still wearing her nightgown and swathed in a shawl. Her voice was muffled as she said, "I don't care for breakfast. I've taken some medicine and will sleep. Why don't you take Tamara over to the Whitneys'? She's been wanting to play with Amy."

It was nearly noon when Jenny left the Whitney home, with the promise to return for Tamara before evening. As she started the short distance to Sally's home, Jenny stopped at Joseph's store for more flannel.

Back on the street, she began thinking about Sally. With a sigh she shook her head. Sally's strange silence was beginning to trouble her. Now she began to wonder about the medicine Sally had taken.

As soon as Jenny stepped into the house, she heard the moans, the weak call. When she rushed into the bedroom, Sally was on her knees beside the bed. "Oh, Sally, the blood! Is it the baby?"

That day and night was a nightmare. Patty Sessions came, and then the doctor. At the week's end, Andy returned.

His face was nearly as pale as Sally's, and Jenny was filled with guilt. She felt a pin-prick of knowledge, and had ignored the responsibility.

After the first bad days were past, Jenny showed the empty bottle to Sally and asked the question. Sally wore a guilty expression, and Jenny had to ask her, *Why?* She couldn't forget Sally's failure to answer.

During Sally's time of recuperation, Tom returned and went back to the farm, while Jenny lingered on with Andy and Sally.

On the day that Sally could face the dishes and broom again, Jenny said, "I need to go home. Soon Mark will be here." She hugged the joy to herself even as she felt the guilt Sally's pale face aroused.

Sally noticed and said, "Go. We can make it now. But today there's a storm a brewin'. If you go today, you'll travel in snow. Linger 'til tomorrow."

"My Mark will travel in snow, too, if he doesn't hurry." Jenny shook her head, packed her valise, and said, "First to the store for more—" she stopped.

Sally said, "You needn't fuss. I'm fine. You can't quit talking babies because of what happened." She hugged Jenny and sent her on her way.

Jenny did her shopping and then went on to the Mansion House to deliver the packet of candies she had bought for the children.

Emma was touched, and Jenny forgot her shyness as Emma pulled her into the kitchen and poured tea, saying, "Joseph doesn't keep the word of wisdom with his wine; neither will I withhold the tea on a blustery day."

She looked at Jenny. "So Sally Morgan has lost her baby. That's too bad. Is she well now?"

Jenny looked at Emma's drawn face and bulging figure and nodded. "Your time will be upon you soon. Will you need help?"

"Only my husband. I won't lack." She sighed and in a low voice said, "I've been poorly, I just hope—" For a moment Jenny saw her tortured eyes before she bent to pour the tea.

"I—I hope you'll be delivered of a fine, strong baby," she said.

The front door flew open and Joseph, Emma's eldest child, raced into the kitchen. "Snow!" he shouted. "By morning there'll be enough for a snowman."

"Oh," Jenny started up in dismay. "I must leave now."

"No, you shall not start out in this. You've no need to be at home this evening. Pray stay."

Emma went to look out the window. "Joseph came last night. He's been working at the office today, but he'll stay, too. Luckily the Missourians aren't prone to come this way in a snowstorm. We'll have a lovely dinner, all of us together. I'm guessing from the past, there'll be more guests before the evening is over."

The dinner was lovely and the crowd grew, just as Emma said it would. It was late when the last lamp was snuffed at the Mansion House. Jenny knew, as she tumbled into bed, that she would oversleep. Thinking of all she needed to do at home, she yawned and snuggled into the quilts.

When she awakened, Jenny guessed by the pale wash of light at the window that it was early. As she lay still, reluctant to face the day, she heard a whisper of sound outside her door, then the creak of floor boards. Thinking it was Emma, Jenny slipped from bed and went to open the door.

There was no one at the door and Jenny poked her head into the hall. Light from the window at the end of the corridor outlined the two figures as they met and merged. Jenny recognized Joseph and Eliza Snow, but surprise held her motionless.

Now the door across the hall flew open. Jenny saw Emma's face turned toward that scene at the end of the hall.

Jenny was still standing dumbfounded as Emma quietly turned, and snatched up the broom leaning against the wall. Moving swiftly despite her bulky body, Emma charged down the hall with broom flying.

Joseph stepped back, and Jenny saw the astonishment on his face. But Joseph was not the object of her wrath. Onward she ran, flailing the broom at the fleeing woman.

With a gasp, Jenny ran through the hall just as Emma's broom drove Eliza down the stairs. Jenny moaned and clasped her hands over her mouth as she heard the thump on the stairs.

Behind Jenny another door banged. "Mother, Mother, don't hurt Auntie Eliza." Pushing past her, young Joseph screamed and ran toward the stairs.

It was afternoon before Jenny collected her buggy and mare and headed for home. Still numb from the events, her mind held only the sights and sounds of horror.

The contorted faces were stamped on her mind—Emma's, Eliza's, and little Joseph's. The significance of all she had seen still eluded her, even though she had been there to hover in the hallway as the doctor came to attend Eliza.

Jenny pulled the buffalo robe about herself and flicked the reins across the mare's back.

21

MARK REACHED THE outskirts of Nauvoo on an early December afternoon. As he rode rapidly through the streets, his mind was clicking off the changes five months had made in the town. *City,* he reminded himself. The shops and sidewalks teemed with bustling people on this snowy afternoon. Lorries and carriages filled the streets. From factory, to shop, to the *Times and Seasons* newspaper office, the place was filled with activity.

Mark was noticing the strange faces, but he was also hailing friends. As he lifted his arm to salute Andy Morgan, he saw Phelps, William Law, and his brother Wilson.

To all he called, "Not now! I'm going home. I'll visit later."

Turning in at the livery stable he found Tom shoeing a horse. "I'm back," he clapped his brother-in-law on the shoulder. "I'm heading home as fast as I can go. Soon as you finish that horse, will you take this packet of papers to Joseph? Tell him I'll see him on Monday."

Tom recovered from his surprise and slowly said, "Can't ya take a bit to talk?"

Mark was backing out the door. "No. That's why I'm letting you deliver the papers. See ya later."

He met Orson Pratt at the door. The shock on his face had Mark apologizing. "Didn't mean to run you down."

" 'Tweren't that. Just surprised." He hesitated and studied Mark's face. "From the grin I'm guessing you're heading home. Give a half hour and I'll ride with you."

"Man, *give* me a break—I haven't been home for five months!" Pratt hesitated; Mark, sensing the unsaid, studied his face and waited, but Pratt shrugged and turned away.

Mark cut away from the main street of town. He followed the ravine down to the wharf and then cut south along the river road. The road was coarse and uneven from heavy wagons, but it was quick.

He touched his tired horse lightly with his heels and pondered again the futility of his mission. He was also mulling over the effect of the separation on Jenny. "Not one letter," he muttered, feeling a familiar sinking sensation which had dogged his life during the past months.

Again he reminded himself, "If I'd known what I know now, I'd never have gone. At times I think Joseph invents these missions just to prove his power."

When Mark cantered up his lane he saw the lonely figure. His Jenny, swathed in a shawl, was dragging a pail toward the barn. His throat tightened and it was a minute before he could shout her name.

He was off the horse and running toward her before she could move. When he finally released her, he said, "Give me a minute to pull the saddle off the mare, then let's get in the house. The tears are freezing on your face. I'll feed the pigs later."

Inside she pushed him into the rocking chair and knelt to pull off his boots. She could only smile and mop at the tears. When he lifted her, he asked, "Has it been that bad?"

"Oh, Mark, if only I could put it in words! But, yes. Please don't leave me again, ever—I'll die!"

"Jen." He held her close and pressed his cold face against her warm neck. "I won't. I can't take another separation either—no letters, nothing except that worthless time."

The afternoon light was a pale gleam when he stood, saying, "I've got to take care of the stock."

When he set her on her feet, she smiled and spread her arms. "Mark, look!"

It took a moment to understand the difference he had been feeling. "I'm pregnant. Oh, Mark, we're going to have a baby."

"Baby?" He knew his voice was stunned.

The smile faded and she whispered, "Aren't you glad? After all these years—"

"That's what I was thinking," he said slowly. "After all these years. Jen, it'll take me a spell to get used to the idea." Abruptly it sunk in. "We're going to have a child, a baby. My little boy!"

She was laughing. "That's the way I felt. I should have guessed before you left. But for Mrs. Daniels' guessing I don't think I could have believed even then." She was quiet for a moment and he watched the strange shadow momentarily mingle with the joy on her face.

Then she lifted her face and smiled as Mark said, "Be back in a few minutes." He went out to care for his horse and feed the pigs.

When Tom came, Mark was still in the barn, bemused, and lost in thought. Tom pulled down hay for the horses and said, "Well, what do you think about being a papa?"

Mark faced him and grinned, but he saw the expression on Tom's face as he avoided his eyes. "What's the problem? You don't look like you're crazy about being an uncle." Tom turned away, and Mark didn't press the question.

During the night Mark felt Jenny turning restlessly and he reached to pull her close. "Mark, I worry. It's such a responsibility."

"And you think about that now?"

She pressed his hand across her stomach. "But feel him; he's so tiny and alive!" Abruptly she asked, "Mark, who is Jesus?"

"God."

"Like Joseph says?" Her voice was flat.

"No." He raised to one elbow and tried to see her face in the dim moonlight. He was guessing a difference and wondering if it was the pregnancy. He felt his heart lift as he carefully answered, "Not the brother of Lucifer, not the child of Mary and Adam. Not the spirit brother of all good Mormons. Jenny, I've told you before that the Bible teaches there is only one God and that there will never be another God.

"If that is so, biblically there's only one answer. If Jesus is God, as the Bible says, then He is *the God.* Just as the Bible teaches. He is God come to earth to take upon Himself a human body, to live among men and to be their atonement for sin."

Later when Mark recalled that nighttime conversation, he held it as an extra blessing, crowning his first night home. But too soon it was forgotten.

By Monday evening, after his first day back in the office, Mark had garnered enough of covert glances and questioning eyes to become alarmed over Joseph's unusual arrogance. The uneasy questions began to grow in his mind.

When Tom reached home, Mark met him at the barn.

Tom started the conversation when he turned from his task of forking down hay to the cattle. Looking over his shoulder at Mark, he said, "Mark, there's been a heap of strange happenings since you've been gone. And some not so strange."

"That's what I came to ask you about. Joseph hinted at a couple. I tried to avoid showing my ignorance."

"Well, you know about the Boggs shooting, and how the Prophet's prediction about it nearly did him in." Mark was nodding and Tom went on. "Seems all that leaked back to Missouri. Unfortunately, Boggs didn't die.

"Just after you left a sheriff and posse from Missouri appeared with a writ for Joseph and Porter Rockwell's arrest. The Nauvoo court shoved it back to Governor Carlin. By the time they had satisfaction from Carlin and came back for him, he'd skipped."

"Where did he go?"

"Not far. Porter Rockwell headed for Pennsylvania, but Joseph's been layin' low. Couple of times the posse got pretty close. One time he was at home, havin' a nice dinner with friends when this knock came. Joseph ducked into his hidden room, went up to the roof and shinnied down the trees, all unbeknownst to the fellas at the door." Tom paused to chuckle, "Joseph sure had the gift of prophecy when he had that hidden staircase built to the roof."

Tom bent to pick up the pails of milk. "Don't think he's ever been farther than across the river. Plenty of friends around to hide him out. I saw him a couple of times."

"Today Joe mentioned he'd surrendered and is to stand trial in Springfield after the first of the year."

Tom nodded. "Kicking Bennett outta the church and all his positions sure turned him sour. Seems his contrite spirit didn't last long. I hear he's out stirrin' up things in Missouri. Guess you saw all the newspaper articles he's put out."

Mark nodded and Tom said, "Well, Carlin's out of office as of the first of the month and Ford's governor of Illinois. Joe has a lot of confidence in him. Says he isn't political. I think he means he won't be hard on the Saints."

Tom paused and looked at Mark as he asked, "What else has happened since I've been gone?"

"Just after you left, Orson Pratt had a bad time. Seems all the gossip about Sarah got to him."

"About the situation while Orson was in England?"

"Yes, there was a lot of rot. Gossip sproutin' both ways. First off, Bennett was sayin' Joseph was trying to starve her into submission to him, after promising her husband he'd see she had enough to eat and such. I did hear before you and Jenny moved to Nauvoo that she was in a bad way, not havin' enough to eat or fuel to keep warm. Finally heard she'd took to sewin' in order to have a livelihood.

"About the time Orson came back, the gossip surfaced that she'd been carryin' on with Dr. Bennett. Well, that kept gnawing on Orson. Some say he nearly did himself in. Took a bunch a fellas a while to talk him back to normal. I never heard him myself, but I understand he was walking the streets for a time, tellin' ever'body he met that Sarah was innocent."

"What else?"

Tom paused and hedged, scratching his head. "Well, I've been gone too. Joseph had me out on a couple of assignments. Weren't gone long. The Daniels' young'un took care of the stock." His voice trailed off and he looked at Mark.

"That isn't what I'm referring to."

"Aw, who's been talkin'?"

"Not a soul. It's the looks, and the way Pratt and Andy Morgan are dodging around avoiding me. It's a pile of impressions, and I think you can tell me about it. Does it have something to do with the baby?"

Tom winced. He lifted his head and Mark saw the dark questions. "Mark, I don't know. I just don't know what to make of the whole affair. Jen seems so happy now. When I got back in town after the first trip, Joseph came to give me the sad news that Jen had tried to do herself in.

"Says Daniels told him all about it. How she jumped in the river and they pulled her out. Joseph said he was right worried about her mind. Seemed to indicate she might not be remembering and able to hang life all together. I've not had that impression, but I've sure been watchin'."

Tom had been silent for some time before Mark realized it. Lifting his head out of his hands, he said, "Sorry, Tom. What did you say?" Tom shook his head, his expression bleak.

Silently they sat together. When Mark began shivering, he realized the last of the afternoon light was gone. With a sigh he said, "Well, guess I'd better be getting in the house."

That evening, while they were eating, Tom said, "Well, I can't see that you two need me around here, and I'm right anxious to get back to my cozy hole over the livery stable before the blizzards begin. I'll be movin' out tomorrow."

In the morning, as Mark prepared to leave, he kissed Jenny's cheek. He was still reflecting on all Tom had said. Last evening, he had tried to give Jenny every opportunity possible to talk about her fall in the river, but she had said nothing.

Mark was still brooding as he headed for Nauvoo. Orson Pratt rode down his lane; just as Mark passed, he hailed him.

Bringing his horse even with Mark's mare he said, "I suppose you're glad to be free of traveling for a time. Sarah says there's to be a little one at your house come spring."

Mark noticed the man's nervousness and recalled Tom's remarks as he acknowledged the news. "Yes, we're pretty proud."

In the silence he added, "I'm hoping to settle into that pile on my desk today. Whatever the Prophet's activities, he's managed to stack up enough work to keep me busy until spring."

"He tapped you for the council yet?"

"Priesthood?" Mark waited for Pratt's shrug before he shook his head. "I don't intend to be part of it."

"Mark," Pratt warned and then paused to take a deep breath. "Sarah's been talking about how deeply involved Jenny is in the church. I know you've had some trouble with the beliefs in the past, but if I can counsel you to accept Joseph's direction, I'd be glad to."

Orson continued, "I've been in disfavor because of my attitude. The Prophet's forgiven me, and there's not much I wouldn't do to help his cause right now. Without revealing any of the hidden doctrines, I must advise you that things are moving forward at a rapid pace. There's much to learn yet of the kingdom business. To deny Joseph endangers your soul. To refuse to progress means trouble for you with your wife."

"What do you mean by that?"

"You know Joseph is teaching now that an apostate spouse voids the marriage contract." Mark didn't reply, but he saw Pratt's troubled expression. In a moment Pratt continued with another line—at least Mark thought so as he listened to the gossip.

"They're saying Emma Smith sent Eliza Snow tumbling down the stairs after catching her with the Prophet. I know for a fact that Doc had a time with her. Seems she won't be having increase very soon." Again there was a pause, and Orson said, "In these latter days we're being called upon to pick up all the old ways of the church. It's our holiness and our salvation to do so."

While they were talking, the two had reached the main street in Nauvoo. They overtook a figure hunched nearly double on his horse. He straightened and turned. "Hello, Taylor," Pratt said, pulling on the reins. "I was just advising Mark he's about to be tapped on the shoulder."

Taylor nodded soberly and peered at Mark. "Joseph's declared that the church is at the crossroads. Unless these higher teachings are embraced wholeheartedly, there will be no further progression for the church. We must work to that end.

"Just last meeting Joseph was telling us that as soon as the temple is completed, there's instructions to be given out which are of the utmost importance. He says, for example, the keys of the kingdom are signs and words whereby false spirits and persons can be detected." His piercing gaze held Mark's for a moment before he bid them farewell.

Later Mark had reason to be grateful for the strange conversation with the two men.

By the time the Prophet had arrived at the office, Mark had pieced together all the facts and the ramifications of the invitation Joseph would extend to him.

Sitting at his desk he muttered, "Number one, my wife will forfeit our marriage before she will surrender her only hope of salvation. Number two, if I don't cooperate, I'll be forced to leave. My marriage vows still mean more to me than anything else in life. Joe's teachings aren't biblical. I can give in to the anger and frustration I feel, or I leave, standing no chance of being an influence for Jenny's salvation. Number three, the baby." He winced and tried to push out of his mind the dark thoughts that surfaced every time he saw the questions in the eyes of the brethren. He sighed and added, "Number four, even though I don't count with Jenny in these new circumstances, I love her more than—life."

When Joseph walked in Mark got to his feet. He looked at the smooth, smiling face of the Prophet, and found that the distance of five months allowed him to be objective.

Narrowing his eyes, he saw Joseph as a stranger would. In the rush of the Prophet's words, Mark tried to steel himself against the charm, against the bid to like the man.

In the back of his mind a picture was forming, compiled of the bits and pieces of six years' worth of scenes and words. While he stared at Joseph, he found himself wondering how he could know the man as intimately as he did, how he could add the new knowledge he was accumulating, without hating Joseph hopelessly.

Mark composed himself to listen to Joseph's smooth recital. He was seeing the words punctuated with the ethereal look on Joseph's face as he rehashed the events Tom had told him the night before.

Later Mark nodded his head, agreeing to become part of Joseph's inner kingdom workings, with the task of preparing to offer up to the world the lately revealed secrets; Mark did it with Jenny's heart-shaped face and shadowed eyes firmly before him.

22

ON CHRISTMAS EVE Tom came into the house, sniffing, bringing a cradle he had made. Jenny had been baking pies, and the savory odor of dressing for the goose mingled with the apple and mince and pumpkin.

"Oh, Tom, it is absolutely beautiful!" she cried, bending over the cradle. She fingered the carving and nudged it into rocking. "Mark, come see!"

There was a sigh of exasperation from the parlor, and Mark emerged from the depths of the teetering fir tree.

Tom eyed the tree sagging against the wall and said, "I see I have my work cut out for me. Mark, how come you still can't put a stand on straight?" Addressing Jenny he said, "Besides me, who's going to eat all those pies?"

"The Morgans are coming. Andy's sister is visiting them; she'll be here too."

"I suppose she's young and fat with buck teeth."

"You're going to have to start someplace," Mark said darkly.

Tom saw Jenny's sharp glance, but her voice was smooth as she said, "She's a nice girl. I met her at Relief Society meeting last week." As Jenny continued to talk up the virtues of Helene Morgan, Tom saw the shadows in Jenny's eyes.

When she paused for breath, he asked, "You ailin'?"

She threw him a startled glance and then the brooding expression shifted to Mark struggling with the tree. "No. It's just that—I guess I'm tired."

Mark was standing in the doorway. "Jen, let's put on candles for decoration, but don't light them. Can't see any sense in getting the house on fire. The red will look nice with the string of white popcorn."

She nodded without looking up. Addressing Tom she said, "I understand the Prophet's having a big party at the Mansion House. We were invited, but Mark didn't want to go." She sighed wistfully, "I would have loved to see their tree. And there's to be music."

Mark's voice was sharp as he said, "You shouldn't be traveling that far in the snow in a buggy." To Tom he added, "I've ordered a sleigh; unfortunately it hasn't been delivered yet. It's just too risky for her to be out in a buggy now. Sam Wright's family was stranded in a drift while he had to go for help."

Abruptly Mark turned back to the parlor. Tom was silent, struck by Mark's cold voice and impatient manner. He watched as his brother-in-law began struggling with the tree, then he went to help.

Late that evening, after a quick supper of bacon and corn chowder, more gifts were presented. Tom was still admiring his new muffler as he watched Jenny open the big box.

When the color slowly drained from her face, Tom looked at Mark and saw his frown. Jenny's face was strained as she lifted the brilliant red robe from the box. Tom saw the question in her eyes as she held the wool against her face.

Frowning, Mark said, "You don't like the color? I bought the heaviest one I could find. It's a boudoir gown. I thought with the baby—"

"Oh," she whispered, and Tom wondered at the relief in her voice and then he began to chuckle as she explained, "it's beautiful. I just wondered for a moment if I were to wear it to church." Mark began to laugh, but Tom saw she still wore the strange expression.

"With the size you are getting to be and the color," Tom shook his head, "you'd be a sensation!"

Mark was grinning as he went to kiss Jenny, saying, "Merry Christmas, my dear wife. I'm sorry the sleigh isn't here. I just can't risk you now."

"Young'uns don't grow on trees," Tom said dryly, feeling a relief he couldn't identify when Jenny lifted a radiant smile to Mark.

That relief stretched through the following day, and Tom discovered that Helene wasn't all that bad.

When Tom returned to Nauvoo Christmas night, he shook his head over the doings at the Mansion House.

Sitting horseback outside the house, looking at the line of carriages, and listening to the roar of masculine voices rising above the fiddles, he slowly said, "One thing, with the twirling and dipping going on, and the eating and drinking, I'd say the Lord's up to changing the emphasis again. Back in Kirtland days"—now he was addressing the white uniformed men standing guard at the gate—"back then there was no unholy frolic. 'Twas good business to be sober and holy. Times have changed."

Shaking his head, he rode toward the livery stable. But inside, Tom looked at the cold forge and with a troubled frown he said, "Leaves a body wondering. Will this church end up as cold and lifeless as all the others? I feel the high tide of excitement giving way to secret whispers which bode no good."

He went upstairs to his lonely room. With a sense of relief, he stoked the little sheet metal stove into cherry-red comfort.

He looked around his barren chamber and addressed the festoon of cobwebs. "Not likely I'll get married unless forced into it. Me and the dirt are comfortable. Even the smell of horses I don't object to. Besides, I can't afford a wife—or two or three." He glumly surveyed the *Book of Mormon* resting on the wooden crate beside his bed.

He was thinking of the barroom whispers the men were passing around along with the drinks. "Is having more'n one wife the way to beat the doldrums the church is having? Or is there a bigger reason for it?" He shook his head and wondered at the dismay in his own heart. There were shadows in Jenny's eyes, too. Could Mark have been touched for the teaching? With a regretful sigh Tom admitted to himself that he could very likely be next.

As he pulled the kettle of water over the heat, Tom was thinking of his initiation into Masonry last spring and now into this new council.

When he finally moved and sighed again, he said, "One thing's sure. Mark's joined up in Joseph's high priesthood, and they're teaching the way to earn salvation is through having more'n one wife. Right now he's not the most gladsome individual alive, and seems his confidence has slipped, but I guess I can trust him." He frowned. But what about Jenny's wan cheeks and her shadowy eyes?

Tom tried to imagine how his sister would feel about sharing her home with another woman. It was impossible, but he guessed her expression told him something. "Makes a body wish there were a different way to get into God's good graces." He shook his head and sighed. It was John Taylor himself who said the teaching would last forever because a revelation, once given, wouldn't ever be taken back.

The twenty-seventh of December dawned crystal clear, full of sunshine. As Mark rode into Nauvoo he considered the week before him. He knew Joseph would be leaving for the Springfield trial immediately.

The church had engaged the District Attorney for the state of Illinois to handle the case; when Mark found out, he breathed a sigh of relief. He now could easily decline Joseph's invitation to be part of the group traveling to the city.

Later in the day, Mark stood in the doorway of the office and watched the men set out for Springfield. Just as they had earlier escorted the Prophet to the office, now John Taylor and Orson Hyde, on either side of Joseph Smith, supported him as he cautiously stepped down the stairs.

Obviously the Prophet still suffered from his exuberant celebration of Christmas.

As the trio left, Mark found himself shaking his head over the picture. The subdued Prophet, with dark circles under his eyes, hung on Taylor's arm, walking as if each step jarred clear through his frame.

Mark walked back into his office, chuckling and shaking his head. Patty Sessions was waiting, and noting his humor, she released her sharp tongue. "Why are you rejoicing over his misery? Seems a body can always pick out a man who thinks he's abused by the Prophet. A body who loves him sure won't be gleeful over his misery."

"What makes you think I feel mistreated?" Mark asked, astonished. Without answering, she pressed her lips together. Mark began wondering why his bruised spirit was so evident to others. He thought it carefully hidden.

Jenny's new sleigh was delivered just after the first of the year, the day before Joseph and his men returned to Nauvoo.

Mark had been standing at his office window when he became aware of the surge of excited people, and the sound of drums and bugles.

Within hours all of Nauvoo knew of the victory, and the city reverberated with the sounds of celebration. The people continued to crowd the streets to welcome their Prophet, and Mark went down to join them.

Later Mark carried home an invitation to dinner at the Mansion House, explaining to Jenny that all the city notables and church leaders had been invited to a gala dinner the following evening.

When Mark gave his news, he couldn't help grinning at Jenny's bright-eyed joy. "Yes, my dear wife, we'll go. My neck was saved by the sleigh, wasn't it?"

"Did you join the parade? I suppose the Legion was out in all their glory. Will Sally and Andy be there? What about Emma? 'Tis so sad that her baby died." Now she was sober, and for a moment Mark responded to her secret fear.

For the first time in weeks, Mark scooped Jenny up to sit in the rocking chair with him. "Your questions? Yes, yes, and I don't know." He was forcing the grin, trying to seem lighthearted over the sudden awareness of the blue-veined fragility of her face, and weight of the child moving against him.

He resisted the desire to crush her to him and unburden himself of all the hidden fears. Lightly he said, "My dear, you need to rest if you intend being out half the night."

"Rest!" she wailed, "I *must* find something to wear that will fit around me. Oh, Mark, do I look awful?"

"You are beautiful," he said. With a sharp pang he added, "I don't want to risk you unnecessarily."

She leaned back and he saw the questions. "Is that why you—you are always busy?"

He pressed his lips to her forehead. "Am I too busy?" She was nodding and he felt the moisture against his face. "What shall I do for you?"

"Oh, Mark—talk." She leaned back to look into his face, but even as she lifted her hand to touch his lips, he remembered the shrinking away, the shadows. Because he feared those shadows as much as she, he held her close, hiding his face in her hair.

The next evening was crisp and the snow sang beneath the runners of the new sleigh. "Oh, Mark, it's wonderful!" Jenny cried from the depths of the buffalo robe. "It rides as smooth as ice skating. See, even Tupper loves it." She pointed at the mare swishing her tail.

Jenny's cheeks were pink and her eyes were sparkling, reminding him of a time long ago. "You remember ice skating."

She only nodded, but he could see her eyes were soft with gentle memories. He found himself wishing to hold the moment, but wishing even more desperately, to wing back through the years. "The beautiful young Jenny," he murmured. With a pang of regret, he saw his words brought back the shadows.

The Mansion House glowed with lamps in every window. There was music and the sound of laughter and clink of dishes. As Mark and Jenny stepped through the door, Jenny looked toward the stairwell.

The sweep of polished stairs was empty of all except memories. Jenny stared at that spot and remembered the horror of Eliza tumbling and screaming. She shivered under her shawl as she followed the crowd into the parlor.

A pale-faced Emma, isolated in her chair by the hearth, her figure swathed in black, was the only somber note in the room.

For several minutes, Jenny stood near the back of the crowded room and wrapped her shawl tightly around herself as she listened to Joseph. She wondered if her condition were making him seem a braggart. He was giving every detail of his trip to Springfield and the trial while his audience hung on every word. She found herself watching his face, but his words slipped passed her.

In a few minutes, Jenny moved slowly through the visitors to that dark-clad figure by the fire. As she walked, her attention was caught by the expressions of those around her.

Sarah Pratt blocked Jenny's path. She lifted her face, saw Jenny's figure, and smiled broadly. But Jenny was struck by that first expression.

Only Sarah's face, of all those in the room, reflected complete boredom. Their eyes met again and Sarah murmured, "Jenny, you are looking well." Then she turned abruptly, and Jenny went on.

Emma pointed to the chair beside her. "Oh, Emma," Jenny whispered under the cover of the excited outburst around them, "I'm so sorry you've lost your baby."

"Was it punishment? No." Her lips twisted, knowing that only she and Jenny shared the memory of that last time together. "I've had eight babies and only three survive. Jenny, I am getting to be an old woman. Where does it all end?" Jenny saw her fear and bowed her head. When she next looked, the small polite smile was back, and Emma was extending a limp, powerless hand to the gentleman beside her.

After dinner, when the group had reshifted and settled into new comfortable segments, Jenny found herself shuffled toward the end of the room. Wedging into a chair beside the door, she loosened the concealing shawl and picked up a book to use as a fan.

She heard a murmur of voices behind her, coming from the kitchen. Recognizing Mark's voice, she went into the hallway.

Joseph and Mark, with their backs to her, were in the kitchen talking to another man. As Jenny hesitated, Joseph reached out to take the paper extended toward him. The men shifted and Jenny saw Orson Pratt.

Before she could make her presence known, he was saying, "He considered me a dissenter. He's accused me of having designs of my own." The light flooded the expression on his face. Distaste filled Jenny at the overweening manner of the man as he continued, "Little did he dream I would use the letter to advantage."

Joseph was reading and murmuring, "Written at Springfield. Wonder if he was at the trial? It wouldn't surprise me at all. Addressed to you and Rigdon, huh? Well, let's see . . ."

In a moment he said thoughtfully, "Thank you, Pratt, you've done me a great favor. Mark, says here that Bennett's had contact with Missouri authorities. Now in the making is an attempt to revive the old charges. He's mentioning murder, arson, theft, larceny, and stealing. Well, well, my dear Dr. Bennett, seems we're one up on you."

Jenny was beside Mark when Joseph raised his head to study Pratt's face. "You've done me a favor, Pratt—is it more than just a bid for recognition? You've been rebaptized into the church, you and your wife. Is there something else you want?"

The man's voice was low, "Just my old position. I want to be back in the Quorum of Twelve. Might even be a good example, encouragement to others, seeing me back where I belong."

Joseph clapped him on the shoulder. "Wanting to be our gauge of philosophy again, eh, professor? Well, we need you nearly as much as you need us."

Jenny and Mark were silent as they rode homeward. Once Jenny roused herself to comment on the dinner. But she faced Mark's dark scowl and dared not reveal her own churning emotions.

23

"MARK. YOU'LL BE at the meeting tonight?"

Mark lifted his head and saw Joseph lounging in the doorway of the office. "Huh? Yes, Joseph, I'll be there. Sorry. I was in the middle of this and didn't hear you." He gestured toward the book he had been reading and got to his feet. Unexpectedly his eyes met those of William Clayton.

The hang-dog expression in the eyes of Joseph's secretary caught his attention. He hesitated, but Joseph jerked his head toward his own office and turned away. Mark sighed in frustration. Sharing office space with Clayton created problems; but, he had to admit as he shuffled the papers on his desk, the problems seemed related to Joseph's desire for secrecy.

Slowly Mark picked up the brief and started to follow the Prophet, but Clayton's expression nagged at his attention. Why was the man constantly in a state of tension?

Joseph was at his desk with his feet up, placed in the middle of the papers, and his hands clasped behind his head. "What's Clayton finding to complain about?"

"Why, I don't think he was." Mark frowned with the effort to remember the man's words. "Honestly, I wasn't paying him much attention. He does ramble at times. Oh, seems he was talking about your sermon. Joseph, you can't be checking on everything that's happening," he said in exasperation.

Then he continued, "Jenny and I didn't get out this last Sabbath. It was too cold, and her time is getting close." For a moment Mark saw interest flare in the Prophet's eyes. Anger surged through Mark, but holding his voice even he continued, "Clayton mentioned you'd talked about the kingdom of God, and I asked him to define *kingdom*. He said where the oracles of God are given, there is the kingdom. I guess my attention drifted after that."

"Do you agree?"

"Jesus Christ said His kingdom isn't of this world. *Oracles* is an Old Testament word I'm not very familiar with. Right now the only scripture I can think of dealing with oracle is where the prophets are warned against declaring their own words as oracles of the Lord."

Joseph paused for a moment and then nodded. " 'Tis a fearful thing to take upon one's self the burden of claiming the Lord's Word when it isn't."

He leaned forward. "About this priesthood meeting. I know you've bucked counsel, but I believe I can rescue you from apostasy. The Lord has shown me great and wonderful things which are to be unfolded before the Saints in the coming months and years."

Mark shifted restlessly. "You'll insist even when you know how I believe?"

"To your soul's salvation." As he continued speaking, Mark was caught in a moment of seeing Joseph through the eyes of a stranger. There was something very compelling about the man. His pale eyes gleamed with the new idea, while the expression lighting his face momentarily touched Mark with a tingle of excitement.

"Mark, there's lots about the priesthood meetings which is old hat. Business and the mundane of kingdom planning. But believe me, if you'll handle counsel, I promise you there'll be no regrets." Again Mark saw the flare of excitement. After a moment's hesitation Joseph said, "Might as well let a little of this slip. If I can't trust you to keep it quiet until the appointed time, then who—"

Mark watched Joseph flexing the steel letter opener until Mark expected to see it fly from his hands. It still held his fascinated gaze as Joseph continued, "The Lord's told me now's the time to begin the organization of the kingdom.

"There's been just a few of us in meeting, planning and discussing in preparation. It's all great and far-reaching; I must start by recruiting every man of intelligence and integrity in the church."

Mark was lining up all he had heard: the facts, the whispers, even the expressions of doubt and fear. He was readying his refusal when words thrown into air dropped into his mind with understanding: *rule the world, king, President of the United States.*

But Joseph wasn't waiting for his answer. He moved on to a new subject. "Mark, I know you started bucking this all when you heard about the Lodge coming to town. Man, I tell you, if you haven't vision and faith to grasp all this on your own, at least for your soul's welfare, be willing to accept on the faith of the others."

Joseph paused and leaned forward, searching Mark's face with those penetrating eyes. He whispered, "This is from God. Mark, I was utterly compelled to embrace the teaching. Would it help if I were to tell you God revealed to me new information about the order of Masons? He told me this is the ancient wisdom. The same priesthood was given to the first father, Adam. Later it was passed on to the great fathers, Noah and such.

By the time it reached Solomon, it had become corrupted. What has happened now is that God has restored it to us in all its pristine beauty and holiness. It is to be part of the deep inner workings of the kingdom."

"Including the secret rituals?" Mark added. "This is the type of thing the *Book of Mormon* speaks against." He paused and then added, "Why is it the church is departing from the original revelations?"

"It isn't."

"I ran into David Whitmer and William McLellin in Springfield last November. We had quite a talk. They had a lot of questions about the church and Nauvoo."

"Yeah?" Joseph's face brightened. "They coming back?"

"I doubt it. They brought up some pretty hard questions, and I couldn't find an answer that would satisfy you."

"What questions?"

"Well, for a starter, *they* answered a question I'd had since I heard about it, related to the big to-do when the Kirtland temple was dedicated. I knew you'd promised there would be a tremendous endowment for the men, particularly those who'd been part of the army sent to rescue the Saints in Jackson, Missouri. A few had told me the endowment was a great success. Both Whitmer and McLellin said it was a trumped-up farce. Not only a failed revelation but a sham of the lowest kind perpetuated by suggestion and wine."

"Anything else?" Joseph asked.

"Have you made the statement that the revelations are the recorded words of the Lord Jesus Christ?"

"That is so. You've heard me say that more than once in those words, more or less."

"McLellin told me he'd been closely connected with you at the time they were being prepared for publication. He mentioned that the revelations, just before printing, had been altered so much they scarcely resembled the original.

"Joseph, isn't it presumptuous—no, more than that—isn't it blasphemous to change the Lord's words?"

Before Joseph could answer, Mark added, "David Whitmer was troubled by the idea of even considering that God might change His mind. I feel the same way. If I can't depend upon God to say something and stick by His words, then what can I depend upon?"

Jenny draped the black cloth over the mirror while the herbs curled and crisped in the pan on the stove. They were beginning to smolder when she put on the red robe.

It had been the similarity between the robe and Adela's red dress that seized her attention at Christmastime. Had it been the spirits' urge to enable her to search once again for more power? Jenny knew how desperately she needed power for the months ahead.

Shaking off the strange foreboding that she knew signaled the gathering of the spirits, Jenny began walking about her house, holding high the pan of smoldering herbs. The chant she muttered rose and fell in the prescribed rhythm, corresponding to the dipping of the pan. She was in the bedroom when the pounding began.

She froze in horror, staring at the smoking pan in her trembling hands. Immediately her thoughts flew to that forest scene, seeing the twisting apparition and hearing the thunder.

Immediately the resolution born of that time flew into her face to confront her. The pounding came again, and she cried, "Oh, God! It is *wrong!*"

Just then she heard a voice, "Jen! Are you in there?"

It was Tom—not spirits, but a very human Tom. Trembling with relief, she placed the pan on the floor and stumbled down the stairs. "Tom, I'm coming!" she called.

Wrenching the back door open, she gasped, "Give a body time! I don't move as fast as before."

Tom came grinning into the room. He was carrying a small parcel which he handed to Jenny. "From Sally. Came into the livery stable with it, she did; said hurry, you might need it before she could get out."

"Oh." Jenny collapsed into the rocking chair and opened the package. It was a soft knitted shawl.

"That's as blue as the Prophet's eyes," Tom said admiringly.

Jenny dropped the shawl and stared at him, whispering, "Tom, whatever made you say that?"

"Why," he stammered, "I don't know. Jest seemed to be the same color."

She looked at it and said, "I may hate it because—"

Tom was sniffing. "What's that strange smell? It's nearly like burnt wood."

"Oh!" She was out of the chair, moving faster than she thought possible. When she reached the bedroom, Tom was right behind her.

He stared down at her kneeling on the floor as she gingerly lifted the pan. "Ugh. It's stuck to the floor, took some of the paint off. What'll Mark say?"

"I don't know. Is he that bad a fusser?"

"Seems lately—" her voice was faint as she scuffed at the spot with her fingernails.

"What were you trying to do?" Tom was holding up the pan and peering at the contents. "It couldn't be dinner. The whole house is full of the stink."

With a sigh, Jenny pulled herself to her feet and started wearily for the stairs. Suddenly the ritual seemed utterly foolish.

Tom was behind her and as they passed through the parlor, he paused. "You break this mirror, too?"

She turned and snatched at the scrap of cloth draped across the new mirror. The tears were starting down her face, and she tried to dab at them as she hurried back into the kitchen.

Tom took her shoulder and pulled her around. "Hey, give a little. What's got you so upset? So you were trying to cook supper in the bedroom and you burned the floor. Can't you jest level with your old brother?"

Jenny flew into his arms, crying and denying the need. "It's just being pregnant, I guess. I feel so ugly and everything."

He eased her into the rocking chair and said, "I thought females were supposed to feel just like they look—hey, I didn't mean that! Girls, women! Ah, Jenny, hush!"

She tried, and he added gloomily, "My first impressions are right. I'm not cut out to be a husband, and all this other. Regardless of what Joseph says, I just can't."

Abruptly Jenny was laughing through the tears. "Oh, Tom. I didn't mean to upset you. It's just that—"

Just as abruptly he said, "Okay, now level. What were you doing? Why the rag over the mirror?"

She stopped mopping her eyes and looked at his frown. The years had taught her evasion was impossible. "I've been using the charms and herbs."

"Mind telling me why?"

"Suddenly you nearly make it seem silly to believe—but Tom, I had to have something. Nothing works. I've tried to be a good Mormon, even reading the Bible like Mark does. The only thing I regret is throwing the talisman away."

"Talisman? What are you talking about?"

"I've had a talisman, like Joseph's. I bought it from Clara years ago. Well, in a tight spot I was thinking the power was working against me and I took it out and threw it in the river. Now I'd give anything to have it back."

The tears were starting up again and with a sigh of exasperation, Tom said, "Aw, Jen, I can't understand through the bawlin'. Lay off. Tell me why you want it back."

She was shaking her head and dabbing at her eyes. "No, Tom, you don't believe, and you'd just make fun of me."

He settled back on his heels beside the chair and said, "Got anyone else you can tell it to?" She shook her head and he continued, "Well, it seems to me you're going to spend the rest of your life a bawlin' unless you tell someone." Jenny was crying again. Tom waited. "Okay, let's hear it."

"Tom, I didn't realize it or I'd never have pitched the talisman. See, I had the talisman when Mark and I got married. I just didn't realize it was the power that was making him love me. Now that I've pitched it, there's nothing. He looks at me like he doesn't even see me. We used to talk so much—even when we were disagreeing there was something there. Now it's nothing. Tom, I'm so miserable I could die."

Tom was silent, chewing his lip thoughtfully. "I can't believe a little old medal could have that much power."

"I do. There's no doubt about it. Even I feel different about—" She paused and gulped, adding, "well, things."

"Could be he's just taking the responsibilities of bein' a pa pretty serious. I know he's kinda worried about you. Thinks you're looking puny. Would you want me to talk to him?"

"No! Tom, of course not. I told you only because you pushed at me. Please, don't say anything about this. Now I've got to get the smoke out of the house before he comes home."

"I'd pull a rug over that burned spot fer now." Tom headed for the door and then turned. "The mirror?"

"Oh." Jenny stared at her hands.

A strange expression filled his eyes, nearly like fear. "Something to do with the charms, huh? I've heard of spirits manifesting through mirrors. Jen, are you bitin' off more'n you can handle? Seems religion's safer."

Jenny was still sitting at the table long after Tom left. The afternoon was nearly over and soon Mark would be coming home. For a moment she felt her heart leap and then she contemplated the emotion. Perhaps it did help to talk to Tom.

She pushed herself out of the chair and went to find potatoes and carrots and onions. The pan was still full of the charred herbs and she began to scrub it clean. She shook her head and shuddered, "Land, what a start Tom gave me!"

Soberly she thought of those words, "Seems I said what I was denying all along. I have to admit, those words I was reading in the Bible just yesterday were speaking to me." She paused to consider, wondering why it took fear to strip away everything except the real need. Would she be able to follow after what was necessary?

Washing her hands, she went into the parlor and picked up the Bible. She sat in the rocking chair and turned to Isaiah, saying, "Seems I have to deal with the verses catching my attention first. This Isaiah 8:19 is talking about people seeking familiar spirits. That's me. I finally realized it when Adela just disappeared. What about her saying we could worship any way we pleased, 'cause there's only one god. Seems God doesn't like it, because He's saying in seeking God, if they don't speak according to God's Word, then there's no light in them." Silently she reread the words and had to admit that the truth was there.

Finding the other section in Isaiah 47:12, she read aloud, " 'Stand now with thine enchantments, and with the multitude of thy sorceries, wherein thou hast laboured from thy youth; if so be thou shalt be able to profit, if so be thou mayest prevail. . . . Let now the astrologers, the stargazers, the monthly prognosticators, stand up, and save thee from these things that shall come upon thee.' "

Slowly she closed the Book. "Jenny, it's saying right here, first, God doesn't like people seeking out the spirits." She was shivering now as she whispered, "I must admit, the spirits never helped a mite. I can't stand with them. Never has the green book led me to anything good. When this baby comes, the charms and herbs'll do me no good."

For a time she sat in silence while her thoughts drifted, searching for a sureness to believe in. "Funny how the words just popped out of me," she mused, recalling the day in the forest. "All those years, I never realized once that Adela was a familiar spirit." She shivered with awe. "I just said 'in the name of Jesus.' Adela couldn't stand against the Name, and she just disappeared like smoke."

Slowly Jenny closed her Bible and stood up. She needed to do something. Thinking a moment, she clasped the Bible to her bosom and looked up. "I renounce the way of the spirits. Because I'm fearing them—no, God, I fear what You'll do to me if I don't. I'm going to read my Bible and become a good Christian like Mark and Joseph Smith."

24

MARK STARED OUT the window of the municipal building, watching the water drip off the roof. Carriages sloshed down the main street of Nauvoo, flinging arcs of dirty slush into the air.

It was late February and the afternoon sun streamed through the windows of the city council chamber. As attorney, Mark had been asked to sit in on the council meeting which would begin just as soon as Joseph arrived.

Mark moved his shoulders restlessly and stretched his shirt collar. Pratt was watching him with amusement.

Joseph hurried into the room with a sharp salute and Hyde called, "General Smith!" With a friendly smile, Joseph bowed. Still impatient with waiting, Mark scowled. He could see only Joseph's arrogance and the lateness of the hour. He met the Prophet's smile with a frown.

Without ceremony, Joseph plunged into his prepared speech. "These are great days, my brethren. I feel the power of God upon me. The purposes of the Almighty shall prevail. I intend to see they happen. I am a man empowered by the great Jehovah, and this influence is not to be taken lightly. With the children of God the power does more with a handful than a million men could do without the power."

"Hear ye, hear ye!" shouted Kimball. Mark was gloomy as he listened to the upbeat tenor of the laughter greeting Kimball.

Joseph was into the heart of his message. "Do you see Nauvoo correctly? We are a state within a state. Soon we shall petition Congress for that recognition. The Nauvoo Charter, which passed the Illinois Legislature unanimously, signifies our relationship. We are to the union the same as a state."

He paused and leaned forward, saying in deliberately paced words, "You brethren know as well as I do that the laws of the state of Illinois are unconstitutional. We would be a pack of fools to keep such laws as our own."

"Prophet, General," came a voice from the back of the room. "I would like to remind the brethren that the charter provides that should any man

come into the city with a writ for your arrest, we shall arrest him and try
him. If he's found guilty of pushing the old Missouri offenses, he can be
sentenced to life imprisonment."

Amid the uproar, Clayton added, "And he can be pardoned by the
governor of the state only under the consent of the mayor of Nauvoo
himself, which is the prophet Joseph."

Mark was back in his office when Joseph came in. With effort, Mark
attempted to control himself as the Prophet entered the room. As he
looked at Joseph he was still thinking of Clayton's statement and wondering how many of the men of Nauvoo agreed with him.

"What's on your mind?" Joseph asked, flopping into Mark's chair.

"I was thinking of your slave Abel."

"He isn't a slave; he's a free man."

"Free when he dumps his money in your lap and is happy with shining
your shoes and being your valet?"

"That was his idea. Any suggestions?"

"It isn't just Abel," Mark admitted. "Nearly every man close to you has
this same shoe-licking air about him. I come near boiling every time I see
their blind adoration. Joseph, it isn't normal."

"You speak like a man who's never had a friend to love him. I'm able to
accept the love."

"Accept? The smiles and pats, yes—but what about those who disagree
with you? Why can't you allow criticism without labeling them dissenters
and chasing them out?"

"Have anyone in mind?"

"Last week, during the priesthood meeting I was listening to you lay on
us all the new teachings. Joseph, you know as well as I those teachings are
completely contrary to the Holy Bible, contrary to all we've been taught
through our growing-up years. Yet those men sat there and took it. I was
thinking, too, of David Whitmer.

"You remember I mentioned having a talk with him in Springfield. One
of the things that struck me so forcefully was his statement that some of
the men are so blinded to reason that they believe anything you say. I'm
beginning to think that's right."

"Mark, I'm called of God. I have the keys to the kingdom. Need I keep
reminding you of the fact?"

"And the fact that the revelations you've given are the very words of
Jesus Christ? Whitmer says you made changes in the *Book of Commandments* which ended up supporting you as a seer in the church. The same
changes also support the idea of the priesthood in the church. He charged
you with departing from the teachings of Jesus Christ revealed in the *Book*

of Mormon when you made these changes. If the Book is from God and is Scripture, how do you respond to his claim?"

Joseph got to his feet. "The reason I came in here, Mark, is because I don't like your arrogance. I came near to flogging you in city council meeting just to wipe the sneer off your face. I think the spirit of Satan is in your heart, and you'd better be getting it out. There're not many around here who can take such an attitude."

Joseph continued. "Funny you should be talking about men who displayed the same spirit. Better learn from them. They're out. They and their families have lost their estate in the hereafter. Mark, take the warning to heart."

Mark was still seething when he left the office and went to the livery stable to get his horse. It hadn't helped to have Clayton's counsel after Joseph left the room.

Joseph's secretary said, "I tremble with fear for you, Mark. You know Joseph has the keys of the kingdom. There's not a one of us who will make it in the hereafter without the Prophet meeting us and taking us in to be with him for eternity. If he says the word, there's damnation waiting for us."

As Mark prepared to mount his horse, Tom's staying hand gripped the bridle. "Something the matter?"

"Just irritated at Joseph."

"I rode out to see Jen. Mark, you know she's a bit teary right now."

Mark frowned. "Seems natural in her condition."

"I'm not an authority, but I'm guessing she's feeling as big as she looked in that red outfit. Might be just a hug or pat would let her know you still love her." Tom turned away.

Mark's black thoughts kept him company until he had nearly reached home. The first timid hints of spring were becoming evident. The snow had melted from the roadway and the water gurgled through ditches. Spikes of green tipped the branches of trees and bushes. He heard the burst of song from the robins, saw crocuses in the snow.

On the last stretch of road, he reined in the mare and let her browse as he tried to collect his thoughts and shake his dismal mood.

He regarded his commitment and scowled. What high hopes he had felt, what tide of need he had seen that day in Far West when he'd whispered, "Yes, Lord." He recalled thinking brave thoughts of bringing all the Mormons to an understanding of truth and a joyful acceptance of the way of Jesus Christ.

Now he slumped in his saddle. What had the dedication merited? Nothing except—Mark winced and as the pain grew inside of him, he began to face the fact he had been ignoring since December. The teaching at last week's priesthood meeting had linked together the gossip and innuendos. Could he admit it and carry on?

The mare grazed her way down the road and turned into the lane. When she stopped beside the barn, Mark was able to admit he had a problem. He pulled the saddle from the horse and carried it into the barn. "How do you say 'yes, Lord' when it means giving up your wife to Joseph's embraces and raising his son as your own?"

Mark was still sitting on the edge of the manger when the last of the sunlight touched the apple tree and disappeared. When he shivered with cold, he realized nothing had been resolved.

With a sigh, he headed for the house, muttering to himself, "One thing's certain. My lousy attitude has got to go. Didn't realize Jen was suffering the backwash." He winced and pressed his lips together. "Never will I deny her anything she wishes, even if it's that monster."

Jenny, wrapped in the red flannel robe, was huddled in the rocking chair beside the kitchen stove. She lifted her face as Mark walked in the door. "Oh," she whispered, "I didn't know you were home."

He saw her swollen face, the pile of newspapers and books on her lap as she attempted to get to her feet. "Jenny, is there something wrong?" The dread nearly held him motionless.

"No," she sighed. "Just lazy, I guess. I was trying to read and dropped off." Her brooding eyes watched as he took the books from her and carried them to the shelf.

As she removed the robe and folded it, he said, "I wondered if you were going to wear it. Is it warm?" She nodded. He forced the words, just then realizing how seldom he had mentioned the baby. "You'll be needing it soon. I understand new mothers spend lots of nights walking the floor with their babies." He saw the corners of her mouth lift as she went to the stove.

Thinking of the picture Tom had created with his accusation, Mark watched Jenny. Seeing the delicate curl on her neck, the soft curve of her chin, he felt as if his heart would explode.

She turned and met his eyes. "Mark, what is it?"

In the shadowy kitchen it was impossible to keep back the words. "Jenny, I can't get along without you."

She rushed at him and crowded close. "Oh, Mark, it isn't that bad. Not very many women—Mark, it'll soon be over, and then we'll be happy again, won't we?"

The words were almost worse than the silence, he decided as he held her. She had brought up a fear he hadn't even considered. "Jenny, hadn't you ought to have someone here? It's so far to town. What if you need me in a hurry?"

Serenity swept across her face. "Mark, first babies take forever to get here. Besides, I'm trusting the Lord to take care of it all. See, I've been reading the Bible, the *Book of Mormon* and the *Doctrine and Covenants*. I am obeying the ordinances; what can happen?"

For a dismayed moment he considered the things he might say and said instead, "Shall I take you in to Sally?"

"For a whole month? Mark, it might be nice, but let's wait."

That night when he awakened he saw her outlined against the moonlit window. "Jenny, come to bed; it's too cold for you to sit there."

When she turned he saw the pale oval of her face. "Mark, what was your father's name?"

"John."

"John Mark was a Bible name. Could we call him that?" The constant pain stabbed him afresh. He was silent as he considered it, wondering if having the baby here would diminish the hurt. "Maybe you'd better pick a girl's name as well."

She was beside him in the bed and her hands were on his face. "Mark, what is it?" He could only shake his head as she curled against him.

When she was breathing gently, again he thought of the revelation Hyrum Smith had given them in priesthood meeting—the revelation on everlasting marriage. Several of the men had winced when Hyrum revealed the section dealing with the righteousness of having more than one wife.

He delivered his final statement to all the members of the High Council. Mark had dared not look into the faces of those men as Hyrum said, *Now you have been delivered the revelation concerning the celestial marriage. You who accept and obey will be saved; those who reject the teaching shall be damned.*

25

"OH, MARK!" JENNY called as Mark ran down the stairs. "Come look—there's a new lamb."

She was standing at the kitchen window, the red robe not quite covering the bulge of her pregnancy. Mark looked at her pale face and shining eyes. "My dear, tomorrow you go to Sally. I've talked with her and she urged me to insist you come soon."

Her eyes were still shining as she turned. Now he saw the shine was tears as she whispered, "Just last spring I was pounding on heaven's gates because the sheep were having babies, while I was barren. Oh, Mark, it is too good to be true, isn't it?"

"Yes." His voice was flat, and he turned away.

The excitement was gone from her voice as she passed him, saying, "Your breakfast is ready. Are you staying for priesthood meeting tonight?"

"Yes, but Joseph's promised the important part will be brief, and then I will leave." He carried the coffeepot to the table. "Will you get your things together today? I'd like to leave early in the morning. There's a meeting I can't afford to miss."

"And the baby's." Her voice was smug.

"What? Oh." He stared at her. A baby would be coming back with them.

"Mark," her voice was timid and he looked up, "I've been reading—I have so many questions. How do we know we'll go to heaven when we die?"

"I've told you, Jenny. By trusting in Jesus' atonement."

"The books say so, too, but then there's more, and I get so confused. Seems everytime I turn around there's something else I must do." She sighed and rubbed her hand across her face.

Mark was caught by that gesture. It said more than her words, more than ever before.

Mark's day was busy—full of paperwork and Joseph's talk. Until later, during the High Council meeting, there hadn't been time to think about Jenny again.

But at the meeting, as Mark watched the man standing before Hyrum Smith and listened to the accusation, he recalled Jenny's question and the way her trembling hands had pressed her face. When the realization struck him, he could scarcely wait for the session to be over.

Jenny's questions were not idle curiosity. A fervent prayer welled up in him; it was the first hopeful prayer in weeks.

But now Hyrum was speaking again. "Brother Hoyt, we have heard testimony. Please face the council for instruction." The man moved, and Hyrum added, "You are ordered to cease using the divining rod. In addition, you will refrain from calling certain individuals witches or wizards, and in conjunction with this, no more are you to indulge in the burning of boards to heal or deliver those so-called witches from their bewitchment."

Old man Walker sitting in front of Mark muttered, "Some teaching. It's different than from the beginning of the church. Back in those days Cowdery got mentioned in a revelation, telling him he had the gift of using the divining rod."

When Mark left the meeting, Lewis Wilson, who had been sitting beside him, moved up to touch Walker on the elbow. Mark nearly collided with the two. Lewis was saying, "You ought not to talk against the Prophet. It isn't safe."

"Walls have ears?"

He shrugged and his voice dropped. "Joseph called me in and told me every word I said to Kimball last week when we were talking—" He glanced at Mark and nodded, drawing him close. "Joseph said the spirit told him ever'thing I said. So both of you, be watching what you say."

When Mark reached home, Jenny was back in the rocking chair. Her Bible and the *Book of Mormon* were in her lap, and folded on top was a newspaper.

He pulled a chair forward and sat down facing her. Today she seemed relaxed, her faint smile delivered as if from a great distance. "Jenny, you asked me what you were to believe. The Holy Bible says that Jesus is God, come to this earth for the purpose of redeeming us, reconciling us to God. He did it through dying on the cross as atonement for our sins. It is grace, Jenny. That's all.

"Jenny, believing, having faith in order to receive this glorious gift from God is simply taking God at His Word. Just believe, just accept the gift, and you'll never again have to wonder what you must do to please God."

She lifted her dreamy eyes to him and said, "Nothing, only believe? Mark, that doesn't seem right. Nothing? That's impossible. I must *do* something for God. I can't accept the *only believe* idea. Seems Joseph's more nearly right when he gives out the commandments, the rules and regulations."

She was quiet for a moment and then she added, "I don't believe there's a person in town who wouldn't rather do something to work for his salvation. That's love."

She picked up the paper. "Sometimes I do get a little confused, though."

"How's that?"

The glance she slanted at him was quick, and just as quickly it slid away, but not until he saw the wise-owl expression. "There's this article in the *Millennial Star.* It's an old one."

He leaned back. "Well, tell me about it."

"The writer says there are tales circulating saying that we Mormons have the practice of polygamy. But the writer is in a fuss about it. He is stating emphatically that no such practice exists among the people, nor will it ever be so, since our books are very strict about talking against it. Mark, did you know the *Book of Mormon* forbids polygamy, calling it adultery?"

Slowly he asked his question, dreading the answer. "Does that bother you?"

"Yes," she said slowly as she rolled the corner of the newspaper between her fingers. "It bothers me because there's something going on that makes the statement a lie." Now her eyes were questioning, looking directly at him. "Mark, you've joined the priesthood. Is there talk?"

"A little." He was considering the question and planning his answer when she spoke.

"I am fearful," she said with a troubled sigh. Glancing up at him, she added, "More'n I can say, the church means so much to me. I can't ever leave it—I'm fearful to do so. But—" Mark found himself holding his breath. Jenny sighed again and finally said, "I believe there are hard times ahead for the church."

Mark got to his feet, nearly stumbling in his haste. "I've got to milk the cows. Stay in the chair. I'll find something for us to eat when I bring the milk in."

Grabbing the milk buckets, he headed for the barn. Mark flung hay and corn until the effort sent perspiration pouring down his back. When he finished the milking and gathered the eggs, he still lingered on.

Finally he sighed and lifted his face. "God, I hear you. I can't. Somehow forgiving her when we had such love—somehow it's impossible."

He gave most of the milk to the pigs. Eyeing the remainder in the bottom of the pail, he was filled with heaviness as he considered the days ahead.

Jenny was asleep when Mark slipped out of bed the next morning. Moving quietly, he dressed and left to milk the cows and prepare breakfast.

He was still staring at the skillet and thinking of last night's conversation when Jenny came into the kitchen.

Dully, without looking up, he asked, "Got your things together?"

When there wasn't an answer he turned. Jenny was leaning against the doorjamb. Even her lips were colorless as she slowly bent against the pain.

Mark took a deep breath and shoved his hands into his pockets. "If you don't need breakfast, let's just get going."

"Mark," her breath ended in a gasp. "It's too late."

"Jenny," he implored, "we've got to go!" She was shaking her head. "Shall I go for Sarah, Mrs. Daniels?"

"Mark, don't leave. Hot water." She straightened and tried to smile. "I've delivered babies before, I—oh!"

He lifted her in his arms, wondering how his shaking legs would get him up the stairs.

Mark boiled the water, found the baby clothes, and watched the circle of sunlight move from the patchwork quilt to the middle of the rag rug. And when it was over, Jenny was in command.

Mark held the squalling, squirming boy and Jenny sponged him clean, wrapped the blanket around the child, and held him to her breast. She took a deep breath and leaned back against the pillows.

"It's done, it's happened. Mark, this is your little boy. John Mark." She looked at him and the smile disappeared from her face. "I think you'd better lie down, too."

The sun hid behind the clouds, and in the afternoon, Mark managed a meal and brought the diapers. He pulled the cradle close to the bed, and when Jenny's arms released the bundle, he lifted the child, feeling him stir. He watched the little fists uncurl and the eyelids flutter, and he felt the lump growing in his throat.

When he escaped to the barn, the tears had him stumbling, groping until the hay was under him. It was much later, nearly dark, when Mark dragged himself out of the hay and went to feed the stock. He tried to whistle and the sobs came again. "Jesus, Lord. I don't deserve Your forgiveness, even if I do forgive her. I don't care whose baby it is—I'll love him and raise him like my own. And I'll love Jenny more than ever before."

26

"How's THE LITTLE tyke?" Tom asked as Mark came into the stable.

Mark grinned. "For only being a month old, fine. I don't think he'll be playing ball with you before summer, but he has a good appetite and doesn't complain about sleeping most nights. Can I expect more?" As he led the mare out he added, "Tom, Joseph wants you at his office as soon as possible."

Tom watched Mark head down the street and slowly wiped his hands. "Seems fine now, even proud of the young'un. My brother-in-law just might have had the pre-baby grouch. Leastwise, he seems pretty happy." Tom frowned as he reached for his hat and headed for Joseph's store. There were enough rumors running around Nauvoo to scare any husband.

The Prophet was in the barroom at the back of the store. When he saw Tom he shoved the glass back and walked to the door. "Upstairs, Tom." He led the way.

They passed Clayton's office and the man lifted his head long enough to nod at Tom before he picked up his pen.

"Catching up," Joseph murmured as he opened the door for Tom. "Wish all my men were as eager to do their work."

Joseph dropped into the chair behind his desk and pointed to the chair opposite him. "John D. Lee's outta town. Will be for up to a month. Family problems. Something about his wife's sister; the whole family's headed to Vandalia.

"That's why I wanted to see you. You haven't been much involved in the Danites since Missouri, and I felt it best to start pulling up the reins tight. Never know when it's important to have trustworthy men close to you."

"Problems?" Tom asked.

"Nothing new. The Missourians keep me a little edgy. I hear Bennett's over that way trying to stir up trouble. It's just wise to prevent trouble before it happens. Lee's been serving as bodyguard since '41, all the time except when he's on mission work. Right now I need you to hang out around the Mansion House evenings. When I go out I need someone with me; that's where you'll fit in."

As Tom got up to leave, Joseph added, "By the way, Clayton had a conversation with Kimball. Seems he found out about a plot to trap members of the secret priesthood. Keep your ears open. Could be advisable to send the Whittling Deacons out that way. Don't know who's involved or what the motive. I've a hunch Bennett might be in back of the deal."

Tom left Joseph, wondering how he could manage working at the stable days and the Mansion House nights.

As he walked back to work, Tom mused on the changes in Nauvoo. As the weather warmed, hordes of strangers were making their way to the city. It was easy to spot the visitors, Tom thought as he stepped past the group on the sidewalk. The women seemed to all have that wide-eyed expression, while the men wore a curious, half-envious one.

By now Tom had adjusted to answering questions and to seeing a trail of people moving in and out of the museum, the unfinished Nauvoo House, and the temple. He was also accustomed to seeing Joseph on the street, discoursing with gusto on any topic.

He winced, recalling the last curbside speech Joseph had made. "Seems a mite hot-winded," Tom muttered, "comparing himself so high up, sayin' 'Is there not one greater than Solomon here? He built his temple with his father David's money, and I've had to do my building by myself.' Joe's not countin' the hours we donated to building and the money the Saints have dished out." He brooded for a moment and added, "Seems it's more *our* temple."

Just before Tom entered the stable, he raised his head to look at the temple rising on the highest city hill. "Sure going to look good with all that gold leaf on the dome, isn't it?" Tom turned to greet Andy Morgan.

"And you've done a great job on it," Tom complimented.

"We're moving as fast as possible. Joseph says we're not going to progress very fast until we get the temple done so we'll be able to move on with the endowments."

"He's also said our salvation depends on gettin' the Nauvoo House built," Tom added.

Andy sighed and shook his head. After a pause he added, "Saw you coming out of the store and wondered if you'd like a ride out to see the new baby. Sally and I will be leaving shortly."

Tom was already shaking his head. "Sorry, taking on a new job. Prophet's asked me to do guard duty at the Mansion House. Lee's outta town, maybe for a month."

"Is that so?" Andy studied Tom's face. "The job could be interesting."

"What do you mean by that?"

"Oh, nothing," Andy replied hastily. "Maybe we'll get together later."

Jenny had just started dinner when Mark arrived. She reached for his kisses and said, "Oh, I'm sorry. The baby's been fussy and I haven't started the potatoes yet." She paused, then asked, "Would you please hold him?" Mark nodded and bent over the cradle.

"Sarah was here. She came to bring some of Aaron's clothing and some little blankets. I'd expect her to be keeping them for the next one. Strange."

"What's strange?"

She looked startled. "Oh, it's not what she said. She just looked kinda sad when I asked if she'd like them back."

In a moment she added, "Sarah said the temple offices are nearly complete and that Joseph and the twelve will be moving in shortly. She's been in the Nauvoo House and says it's going to be beautiful when it's finished." Jenny paused and added, "A little bitter she was about it all."

"Sounds like Sarah's unhappy; do you know why?" Mark asked as he carefully shifted the fussing baby on his shoulder.

"There, did you hear that? No wonder John was unhappy. Takes pa to get the bubbles out, huh?"

"Nauvoo House. Because it is so luxurious. Sarah's that way. Worried about the poor emigrants coming in."

"It's a valid worry. But Joseph seems to think giving a good image of the Saints to the world is important."

"Sarah told me something else. Did you hear anything about a fellow named Wiley who lives at Kinderhook digging up some ancient plates?"

Mark looked up. "News travels fast. Clayton told me a week or so ago."

"And you didn't tell me?" Jenny wailed. "Sarah even had a newspaper clipping to show me. It says the plates prove the *Book of Mormon* is true."

Hastily Mark said, "Honestly, I didn't have much confidence in the tale."

"Sarah says Joseph has started to translate them."

Mark sat down in the rocking chair and watched John chew his fist. Finally he looked up and said, "Clayton was telling me about them last week. When Joseph walked into the office he verified the finding, saying there were six of them. Wiley cleaned them up and brought them to him for translation."

"And he's going to translate them?"

"Of course. Joseph said he'd started, and that so far he's discovered they contain the history of the person with whom they were found. Seems this fellow was a direct descendant of Ham through Pharaoh. He also said the man received his kingdom from the ruler of heaven and earth."

Jenny glanced sharply at Mark; as he grinned she said, "You aren't taking this very seriously, are you?"

"If those potatoes aren't done, I'll eat them raw."

"If Joseph could hear you, he'd run you out of town for an apostate."

"He's tried. I can't imagine why he keeps me here. Probably it's his pride."

"What do you mean?"

"He intends to humble me, make me another groveling Clayton."

"I do know from gossip that he considers you a plum," Jenny said slowly. "Even Orson knew of your reputation in Springfield. Do you suppose it's because Joseph is seeing how important it is to be on the good side of the governor?"

"That doesn't sound like a Saint," Mark said slowly, studying her. "You're starting to sound like a woman with her eyes wide open."

"Not like a good Mormon who believes God's going to drop everything in our laps, no matter what?" A thoughtful expression crossed Jenny's face, on which Mark hadn't seen for a long time. Still holding the baby, he went to kiss her.

On the Sabbath, the day sparkled like a jewel. When Mark drove the team out onto the road, he had difficulty holding Tupper back. "Frisky as a colt," he said, grinning down at Jenny. "And you look prettier than any married woman with a baby has any right to be."

"Oh, Mark, it's such a beautiful day and it's good to be out again. I can't wait to show little Mark to everyone."

"John," he said firmly.

"John Mark?" He studied her clear eyes and looked at the baby's blonde hair curling out from under his cap.

When they reached Nauvoo, Mark said, "Looks as if the service is going to be in the temple grove today. Shall I place the buggy under the trees, or do you want to sit down front on the benches?"

"Oh, on the benches. I want to see everyone. There's Tom. Sally and Tamara are over there."

Mark lifted Jenny and the baby from the buggy and settled them on a front bench. As he walked back to the buggy, the women began clustering around Jenny.

Leaving the rig and mare at the stable, Mark headed back to the grove. Although it was still early, crowds of people streamed toward the grove.

As he walked down the street, he saw Clayton and Joseph Smith on the sidewalk in front of Joseph's store. A crowd was gathering, and Mark paused to listen. Joseph was saying, "While I was praying, a voice said to me that if I live to be eighty-four, I'd see the Son of Man. Right now, I don't believe the Second Coming will be sooner."

"I've heard the Father is only spirit," said the stranger at Mark's right.

Joseph answered, "That, brethren, is a sectarian doctrine. It is completely false. Both the Father and the Son have bodies like ours. The idea that they dwell in a man's heart is false."

"Where does God dwell?"

"On a planet which is like crystal. There's a sea of glass before His throne." Joseph grinned and added, "You brethren are going to be smarter than me in another minute. But that's all right. Knowledge is power. The man who seeks knowledge will have power."

Then he added, "The earth, when it is purified, will become the same type of crystal. It will be a Urim and Thummim by which all things in regards to an inferior kingdom will be made manifest to those dwelling there. At the same time, this earth will be with Christ. Brethren, I could go on and on, but it behooves us to get to services."

He paused to add, "The principle of intelligence we garner in this life will rise with us in the resurrection. If a person gains knowledge here through diligence and obedience, so much better for him in the next world." Mark watched Joseph and his followers walk rapidly up the hill to the temple grove.

When Mark finally reached Jenny's side, the morning sermon was well underway. John Mark was sleeping with one pink fist curled like a rose bud. Examining the little face, Mark could not find a single feature resembling anyone he knew. He touched his finger against the tiny button of a nose, and gratitude welled up in him. That nose did not in the slightest resemble the beak of the Prophet.

Mark turned his attention to the sermon just as the Prophet said, "I want you to understand, the Holy Ghost is a personage, just as the Father and Son are personages. A man can receive all the gifts the Holy Ghost has to offer, and in addition, the Holy Ghost may descend upon a man, but will not tarry with him."

As the people around Mark and Jenny got to their feet, Jenny said, "Sally's invited us to go home with them."

"It may take all afternoon to get there," Mark said with a grin. "I've never seen such a crowd. And I think you've shown this baby to them all."

"For that, you carry him." She deposited the blue bundle in his lap and stood to her feet. "Oh, what a beautiful day! But in another month it will be hot. Mark, why have they taken so many of the trees out of the grove?"

"They need more room. Look at the mass of people."

"The Saints will be a multitude soon," Jenny murmured as she walked beside Mark with her hand tucked through his arm. "Seems the prophecies are being fulfilled. We will become a multitude."

"Sister, don't forget the rest," the wizened man beside her grinned. "It has been given that we shall take over the state, the whole country and finally the whole world. You mark my words, this young'un will be march-ing triumphantly around the world for the Lord."

Jenny watched the man limp away and said slowly, "All the war talk hits home with a different meaning when there's a baby." She looked at Mark, and her eyes were troubled.

27

"MARK, YOU CAN'T be serious!" Jenny exclaimed. "Take a three-month-old baby on a boat?"

"My dear, this isn't just a boat. It's Joseph's *Maid of Iowa*. Joseph, Clayton, and I need to make a trip to Quincy. The fastest way to go is by boat. Joseph suggested we make a party of it. Seems everyone except you is in favor of it."

"He won't get sunburned?" She looked anxiously at the baby in the cradle.

"Jenny, there are cabins and a big pavilion on the main deck. Joseph has invited a large group of the Saints. We're to leave early in the morning. We should arrive at Quincy with plenty of time to take care of business and allow you women to shop."

Jenny's excitement was rising. "Oh, Mark, it does sound fun!"

The following morning when the steamboat pulled away from John D. Lee's wharf, the sun was just topping the forested hills to the east of Nauvoo.

Jenny found that the pavilion was enclosed with glass and lined with benches. The festive air was immediately apparent. Children in Sabbath best romped about the deck. Women dressed in pastel calico and printed lawn scattered like blossoms around the room. From the galley came the fragrance of spicy cider and popping corn. The freed slave, Abel, now Joseph Smith's adoring, self-appointed slave, sat on the bulkhead watching the activities.

One young matron with a bulging middle and youngsters clinging to her skirts groaned, "Popcorn this early? My young'uns will be sick before they can get sunburned."

Several young girls began organizing games for the smaller children, and the women settled on the benches as their husbands disappeared below deck.

Mrs. Kimball grimaced. "Heber calls it work, but I saw the liquor and apple-jack they were loading. Oh, well, I suppose they'll work it off by nighttime."

Jenny allowed herself to be pushed into one of the few comfortable deck chairs. The boat was picking up speed now. Wide-eyed youngsters clung to the rail and Jenny caught her breath as the vessel trembled and groaned. Giving a sharp three-note toot, the craft slipped into the main current of the river, and a cooling breeze filled the pavilion. With a sigh of relief, Jenny snuggled John Mark close and curled his hair around her fingers as he began to nurse.

The women were settling into cozy groups. Some sat with their heads together, and their giggles punctuated the trip. Others pulled out satchels of handwork. When Jenny lifted the sleeping baby to her shoulder, Emma Smith caught her eye.

The older woman moved close and touched John Mark's soft curls. The dreamy expression on her face caused Jenny to bite her lip. "Don't look so," Emma said. "There will be more. I shall never give up that hope. Is there anything more comforting than the blessed weight of those soft little bodies in your arms?"

"I've waited a long time for this one," Jenny said softly. "Yes, you are right."

All too soon, it seemed, the boat was cutting speed. After a final bend in the river, the town of Quincy lay before them. While the women and children flocked to the rail, Jenny carried John Mark into the shelter of a cabin to change his diapers.

Mark came to the door. "The men are heading for the courthouse. Will you go with the women?"

"Yes, but tell them I'll come later. John Mark must be fed again before I join them."

The last of the children's shouts had faded away, leaving only the gentle slap of water against the hull. As Jenny went to lay the sleeping baby on the bunk, the sharp scent of alcohol reached her. Turning quickly she found Joseph filling the doorway.

"Jenny, my beautiful one," he murmured, and she realized it was his breath laden with alcohol. He came into the room and shut the door. "My wife."

Anger surged through Jenny, but she determined to remain calm as she turned away from him to button her frock. She fought for composure and finally turned to him. "Joseph, I refuse to even discuss this matter with you. Please leave now and say no more—ever."

He dropped heavily into the chair and said, "Move the baby to the top bunk." She folded her arms and stared at him. "Jenny, my dear, I earnestly desire con—connubial bliss." His tongue stumbled over the words.

"At one time, Joseph, had you snapped your fingers I would have come running. That was before you had a wife. Now I consider this tasteless seduction."

"The grand lady. You are my grand lady. Remember the ceremony witnessed by Brigham Young, Kimball, and Hyde? Remember the book? Jennifer, the book of the law of the Lord is His will written out for you timid females to see. Will you risk the wrath of the Lord by being coy?"

She could see he was fast losing his befuddled air, and she found herself fearing this cold-eyed man. Taking a deep breath, Jenny searched for words to answer him. Suddenly her world righted itself.

"Why, Joseph, I'm not afraid of the Lord near as much as you think. But tell me, what's there to fear?"

"The loss of your salvation. As your husband I will be god to you. I will take you to the heavenlies with me to reign as queen forever. Without me, you'll never have salvation."

Jenny was eyeing the door. The baby stirred and her heart sank. It was impossible to reach both John Mark and the door before Joseph would stop her.

He was speaking. "I must remind you that no marriage is valid until consummated."

"And I will remind you that this is adultery."

"The Lord has shown me it's all right to have fun; it isn't adultery unless we talk about it to others."

His words made Jenny pause, and curiosity picked at her. "Where did you get that idea? Of course it's adultery."

"The Lord has shown me that something can be wrong in one case, but not in another."

"If that is so, then how's a person ever to know what's right and what's wrong?"

"Jenny, you can take my word for it or you can try the spirits. Just pray for a sign. The Lord will pour out on you such a blessing as you've never had before. I will pray for you, but you must also earnestly ask the Lord for this manifestation."

Jenny was silent for a long time, then slowly she turned and paced the room, thinking hard. His words had pulled up deeply buried ideas and impressions, and she must study them out. *Manifestation*. Adela.

She studied him keenly, sensing now what had escaped her attention before. "Joseph, you should know better than to reveal your plan to me. Remember, I was there at the diggings. I know about spirits, too."

"Jennifer, you'll go to hell if you continue to act in this manner."

"Like Mr. Thompson? I've only heard gossip, but I wonder. What kind of temptation did Thompson give in to? Why did he have to die, and how? Is it possible to control the spirits to that extent?"

"Aren't you fearful?" he asked curiously.

She shook her head, saying, "I intend to talk. The first one I'll tell will be Emma." She saw him cringe. "Joseph, I am beginning to think I'm not the only woman in Nauvoo who has had to listen to this from you. If I ever find out anything to support that hunch, I'll make trouble. Remember, I saw you with Eliza Snow."

For a long time Joseph sat slumped in the chair. When he finally sighed and sat up, he said, "Jennifer, I honestly do love you and want you desperately; but more than that, I'm thinking of our future, the eternities, worlds without end. More than losing you here, I don't want to spend eternity without you. That's something, isn't it? I can have any woman I want just by snapping my fingers. Doesn't it matter to you that I *choose* you?"

"No."

She heard the sound of footsteps and Clayton's muffled, timid voice. "Joseph, you'll have to come before the probate judge." His voice was apologetic. "I've had to make out new papers, and you'll need to sign them."

Jenny couldn't understand the word he muttered, but Joseph pulled himself to his feet and left the room. As soon as the door closed, Jenny dropped into the chair. When her trembling ceased, she sat up and smoothed her hair.

By the time John Mark stirred, Jenny was smiling. "Joseph, I'll never be afraid of you again." She paused to wonder at the change in her response toward the Prophet. Finally she whispered, "Either getting rid of the talisman or reading the books has put a peck of religion into me. But somehow I know I need so much more." She shivered, remembering that mirrored image.

Tom found the late June day only pleasantly warm. He nudged his mount, urging the mare to keep up with the carriage moving smartly along the road to Dixon. As he flicked the reins, he glanced at the occupants. Joseph and Emma were visiting her sister in Dixon, Illinois, and from the Prophet's expression, Tom guessed he'd had enough of woman-talk. Emma's sister bobbed her head to emphasize each word.

Joseph caught Tom's eye and he mouthed, "Horse." Tom nodded. As the carriage turned up the lane, he noticed the mounted rider waiting and touched the gun on his hip.

"Hold it, Joseph," he warned, spurring his horse. Tom didn't recognize the man, but when he saw him eye the carriage and slip from his horse, Tom relaxed.

The man's voice was soft, "Judge Adams sent me. Governor Ford let it slip secret-like that he'd signed a writ from Missouri. They're coming after Joseph Smith."

Joseph was standing beside them as the fellow finished and touched his hat. "I'm to offer no advice, and to leave promptly." He touched his hat and turned.

Tom saw the pinched look on Emma's face as she asked, "What will you do? You can't continue to run from them."

Joseph studied her face and said slowly, "That's just what I was thinking. Emma, if you can stand it, I think now's the time to test the Nauvoo Charter." She paled and he turned to Tom. "I'm not inclined to leave just now. Go into town and nose around, see what you can find out and then get back here."

Two hours later Tom arrived back at the house to find two men with the Prophet. There was a sardonic smile on Joseph's face as he said, "These fellas are sheriffs from Missouri—Wilson and Reynolds. They suggest I come into Dixon with them."

"That's a good idea." Tom kept his voice level and relief brightened Joseph's eyes.

By the time Tom located Cyrus Walker and returned to the tavern, Joseph had an audience.

The top story of the tavern served as the jail. Now Tom saw that the upstairs window was open; Joseph was leaning out, thundering at the crowd gathered in the street below.

As the cheers and laughter swept through the crowd, Tom tightened the reins and paused to listen.

In his best Sabbath-morning voice, Joseph was delivering a discourse on marriage. As the fellow beside him roared, Tom said, "What's goin' on?"

"Aw, they shut him up and he's been leaning out the window scorching our ears with Missouri talk. Old Jake found out who he was and asked for a sermon. Funny, he is."

Joseph caught sight of Tom and the man behind him. Hastily he concluded his sermon and withdrew his head.

Walker was in good humor as he followed Tom up the back stairs. After introductions he said, "Timmons says you're looking for counsel."

"I want the best there is. Are you that man?"

"I'm campaigning for Congress. I don't have time to take on a criminal case now."

Joseph winced. "What's your price?"

"That you make it worth my time to give up campaigning. Ten thousand and the promise of your vote in the election. You gave it to the Democrats last election; the Whigs need it now."

Joseph nodded and Cryus got to his feet. "First I'll file suit for assault and false imprisonment against the Missouri fellas downstairs; then we'll head for Quincy. Judge Stephen A. Douglas is holding court there. It's going to be interesting. We'll have to trail out of here with the sheriffs from Missouri holding you while they're being held by a Dixon sheriff." He was chuckling as he left the room.

"Wouldn't be so funny if it was *his* ten thousand," Tom muttered.

Joseph grasped his arm and Tom saw the fear on the Prophet's face. "Tom, head outta here right this minute. I want you in Nauvoo to round up the Legion." Tom saw the beads of perspiration on Joseph's face as he paced the room.

"These fellas are going to do their best to slip me over the river to Missouri. I feel it in my bones. The only hope is to cut them off. First, get Wight and a few others to take the *Maid of Iowa* to Grafton. They're to head off any boats coming down the Illinois River. I know they're not in this alone. I'm too big a fish for just two men. I want the Legion to meet us at Monmouth."

"Joseph, that's nigh impossible!" Tom gasped.

"My life is at stake," Joseph said softly. "I feel it by the spirit."

Tom sprinted down the stairs. "Old girl, I hate to do this to you," he muttered as he jumped on the horse and dug in his heels.

The Legion had just crossed the Fox River when they caught up with the carriage carrying Joseph, Walker, and the two sheriffs. The bewildered sheriff from Dixon was still holding his gun and looking around when Tom reached the carriage.

He heard the Prophet's half-sob as he exclaimed, "These are my boys. We're not heading for Missouri!"

Tom tried to cover his embarrassment, saying, "There's more, but they ruined their horses gettin' here."

Within an hour Joseph had talked Walker into holding court in Nauvoo, while the Legion relaxed in the shade. "We need a rest tonight or we'll never make it," Taylor said when he heard the verdict, and Tom agreed.

It was two days before Joseph's caravan reached the outskirts of Nauvoo, but the Legion band and all the townfolk were there to meet them.

When Mark arrived home that afternoon, Jenny met him at the door. "Mark, I've been hearing guns. What's happened?"

"Nothing except the Prophet has come home, complete with Cyrus Walker, attorney and candidate for Congress, two sheriffs from Missouri and one from Dixon, as well as an escort of a hundred and fifty troops from Nauvoo."

"The guns?"

"Just celebration. The people and the band marched through town and the Legion popped off a few rounds. A little exuberance. The Prophet's to address the folks in the temple grove this afternoon. Put on your party clothes and dress up the little one. I'll take you in."

By the time Mark and Jenny arrived at the temple grove, people were moving in from all directions. "Mark, there are so many—will there be room for all?"

"Looks like thousands," Mark admitted. "It's good they cut those trees out of the grove. It'll be standing room only."

As they worked their way through the crowd, Jenny murmured, "It's hot already. Oh, look, there's Eliza Snow and Sarah Pratt. I see Sally and Andy on the other side of the Laws."

The crowd began to roar. Standing on her tiptoes, Jenny saw Joseph and several strangers moving toward the platform.

Joseph took his place and the crowd began to quiet. Jenny shifted the baby on her shoulder as she thought of the last time she had seen him. She found herself wondering, *Would he be wearing that happy, confident grin if I were to tell the truth about him?*

She shuddered. The speeches had begun, but Jenny was busy visualizing the horror on people's faces if she were to make her accusations. She glanced at her husband. Even Mark. Never would he believe that horrible story. She shifted uneasily and Mark took the baby from her.

Joseph was telling of his arrest. She listened. "The state of Illinois has given Nauvoo her charter. We have rights no one can take away. If our enemies will fight to suppress us or oppress us, they will fight against our rights. If the authorities of state and nation will not defend us, then we'll claim defense from higher powers."

A murmur swept through the crowd as he continued. "The persecution which I have suffered is not condoned by heaven. Before it happens again, I promise you I'll shed every drop of blood in my veins and, in the end, I'll see my enemies in hell."

"Mark," Jenny whispered, outraged, "he doesn't have enemies."

There was a hiss and they turned again to listen. Joseph was saying, "To bear the oppression of the enemy any longer is a sin. Shall we put up with sin?" The grove trembled and shook under the *No!* and Jenny was filled with the memories of Missouri. The Saints and the sad-faced people of Missouri all lined up to march across Jenny's imagination, and with the memory she felt a cold chill sweep through her.

She whispered, and Mark bent close to hear, "Will it come again, the fighting?"

Joseph's words swept across the crowd. "If Missouri refuses to hold back the hand of revenge, I will restrain you no longer."

The chanting was sweeping through the crowd as he said, "In the name of Jesus Christ, with my authority under the holy priesthood, I turn the key! No longer shall the heavens restrain your hands. I will lead you to battle if you are not afraid to die for our cause, or to shed blood. I ask you to pledge your lives and your energy for the cause of freedom. If you will help me, then lift high your hand for the cause." Bewildered, Jenny looked around at the sea of hands.

She glanced at Mark's ashen face and cried, "Oh, Mark, let's leave! This is Missouri all over again."

As she turned to make her way through the crowd, Jenny heard Joseph say, "It does my heart good to see your love and support. It is an honor to lead forth people so virtuous and honest."

The next day, July 1, Joseph appeared before the Municipal Court of Nauvoo. When Mark came home that evening, he sank into the rocking chair with a tired sigh. Shaking his head, he said, "Well, unless the courts find a way to challenge it, the matter's settled."

"The trial? What happened?"

"The sheriff from Missouri, Reynolds, did a lot of protesting, but the court, under the jurisdiction of Chief Justice William Marks, tried Joseph and discharged him.

"Under the Nauvoo Charter the Missouri charge of treason was dismissed. Testimony—all by Mormons—showed that Joseph suffered at the hands of the Missourians, rather than being, as they claimed, the aggressor."

"Mark, will that decision stand?" Jenny whispered.

He looked up. "Depends. There's too much of politics in it right now. This is an election year. If the past is any indicator, Joseph's church voting power will play a role in the outcome of the election. Right now he's committed to a Whig vote because of the trial."

28

Wɪᴛʜ ᴀ sɪɢʜ Mark pulled himself out of bed and went to the window. Dawn was a promise, but as he stood there, feeling as if all the wakeful hours of the past six weeks were pressing upon him, Mark didn't relish the promise.

He had heard the baby's whimper and had known when Jenny slipped out of bed, but that was just one more reminder of the problem heavy upon his mind.

Bracing his elbow against the window frame, Mark let his memories of that June day capture him again and pull him back into the problem. On the day he rushed into the office with the papers in his hands, Joseph, his brow furrowed with effort, was dictating to Clayton.

When Mark apologized and began to back out of the room, Joseph waved him to a chair, saying, "Stay. I'm nearly finished and I want you to hear this."

It was the revelation on marriage—the everlasting covenant of marriage. The words still knocked around in Mark's head, challenging him to deal with the issue. In the quiet of the night, with the press of Jenny's body close to him, he found the words a mockery.

He moved restlessly. He didn't believe in the revelations, or even in the Prophet's calling—but Jenny did, and that was the problem. He found himself whispering, "Lord Jesus, a long time ago You helped me realize the only honest way for me to deal with Jenny's need of You is to keep my mouth shut, never to force my deep desire for her salvation upon her. Lord, it's been difficult, and it's getting worse. I know pushing the truth on her makes me no different than Joseph, even when I *know* my truth is the Bible truth and his is not. Please help."

He waited in silence while the words from that revelation welled up in his mind: *I the Lord justified my servants Abraham, Isaac, Jacob . . . of their having many wives. . . . All those who have this law revealed to them must obey the same. . . . If ye abide not that covenant, then are ye damned; for no one can reject this covenant and be permitted to enter into my glory.*

Mark muttered, "And under the covenant, all these men will be gods, with power and angels in submission. And it's by doing the works of Abraham; in other words—as you are so fond of saying, Joseph—it's plural marriage that saves a man. And any good Mormon who won't go along with this is to be destroyed." Mark turned away from the window, once again affirming his commitment. "Lord, I must trust You to work this all out. You know, don't You? I wake up in a cold sweat thinking of the fearful *what ifs*."

In the kitchen Jenny saw the dawn touching the windows with light. The summer heat was only a misty warmth seeping through the open window.

She sat in the rocking chair holding John Mark against her breast. Deeply conscious of his warm weight, she pressed her lips to his fist and touched the tear on his cheek.

In the quiet she heard the beginning rustle of woodland creatures, the call of birds. From the pasture came the plaintive cry of the lambs. Jenny sighed deeply and snuggled the infant against her. "God's in His heaven and all's right—" she murmured, even then thinking of the imprint these early morning hours were making upon her.

" 'Tis impossible not to feel it," she added, looking out the window. "The beauty, the peace. The deeps. It's like it's being branded into me, all the goodness of God." She sat musing on a new fact. These early morning hours seemed to freshen her memory, and the words stored there surfaced.

"I didn't realize I was remembering the words while I was reading the Bible. Now if I could only find out the *whys* of it all."

"What why?" Mark was beside her, uttering the question as quietly as if the silence of morning rested in his soul, too. He sat on the woodbox at her feet, and their eyes were on the same level.

By the dawning light, she was seeing the curious flecks of blue-green in his eyes. Dreamily she thought to make mention that she had noticed John Mark's eyes changing to the same curious color, but it wasn't the time. Slowly she pressed out words, designed to fit the morning. "God, wrath, beauty. Jesus speaks of peace. Joseph preaches wrath. Jesus says, "Believe"; Joseph says, "Fear." Mark, my head whirls trying to remember the *do's*. Why does the Bible tell us that if righteousness comes by law, then Christ died for nothing?"

His eyes were changing, and for a moment she was caught up in the tenderness, wondering. Then he whispered, "Grace, Jenny. Jesus gives salvation as a gracious gift. Here we only glimpse the perfection of God, but we have hints. It's hinted through the love. He knows there's no way we can be holy, so He gives it."

"It doesn't seem right—to be ugly with all the sin we do, and then just get it." Her voice was brooding. "Seems more right to do something for God."

"There's no way we can *do* enough to be holy. It's like a coat. Through Jesus Christ's atonement, we have righteousness thrown about us. Only it isn't ours until we reach out and accept it."

In a moment she sighed and the words welled up: " 'To appoint unto them that mourn in Zion, to give unto them beauty for ashes, the oil of joy for mourning, the garment of praise for the spirit of heaviness; that they might be called trees of righteousness, the planting of the Lord, that he might be glorified.' " A moment later she quoted, " 'Who shall ascend into the hill of the Lord? or who shall stand in his holy place? He that hath clean hands, and a pure heart . . .' "

He gently prodded, "Why, Jenny?" She could only shake her head, whispering, "I don't know. Sometimes I get so weary for something." Then she whispered, "I love the phrase, 'Who is this king of glory?' It's a mystery, isn't it?" She got to her feet and carried the sleeping baby to his cradle. Now the sun was bright and she sighed with regret.

Mark rode to Nauvoo with sadness as heavy as cold iron resting upon his heart. Just before he left the house Jenny had whispered, " 'Lift up your heads, O ye gates; . . . and the king of glory shall come in.' " Her eyes had been dark pools of yearning.

He had said *Jenny* with gladness on his soul, and then he looked at the sleeping boy. With his vow of silence and forgiveness, how could he say *Jenny, not until* . . . ? With every mile he rode, Mark felt as if his heart was breaking with the desire to urge her confession.

He straightened in the saddle; once again he must face Joseph and the necessity of forgiving that man.

July was slipping away, but Joseph still basked in the glory of the Independence Day celebration. To Mark it seemed that nearly every day the Prophet found occasion to mention the crowds of strangers who had poured into Nauvoo to see the marvels and listen to the man who had bested the Missourians and escaped untainted from their grasp.

The newspaper articles that issued out of Springfield did little to dampen Joseph's joy, even though he recognized the heavy hand of Dr. John C. Bennett in them.

The sheriff from Missouri became the joke of Nauvoo when it was learned he had stomped his way to Springfield, demanding that Governor Ford furnish troops in order that he might march on Nauvoo and drag the Prophet out.

Today, when Mark reached the office, both Joseph and William Clayton were laughing with glee. Joseph waved the paper under Mark's nose and said, "See this? The gist of it is that if we vote Democrat, we've nothing more to fear from Governor Ford. We're home free as far as Missouri is concerned."

"It's to Ford's advantage to cooperate with the Lord," Joseph added. As for Washington, in the name of the Lord, I deliver unto you the prophecy that within a few years' time, this government will be overthrown and wasted away. This is judgment from the Lord for their wickedness in supporting the cause of Missouri. We are still an oppressed people, and our rights have not been upheld."

Joseph returned to his desk and began sorting through the papers there. As Clayton prepared to leave the room, Joseph said, "By the way, William, did you take care of the deeds?"

"I did. In June. They've been duly filed. Emma's share is sixty city lots."

"Joseph—" Mark paused and tried to control his anger. "I advised you a year ago that this wasn't to be done. The provisions of the bankruptcy law will not allow you to transfer any property. You're heading for trouble."

"I'll cross that bridge when I get to it!" Joseph snapped. "I'm not concerned. There are too many other things of first importance.

"Must I remind you again that it has been prophesied concerning the war which will soon break out? The Lord has given me to understand that the first outbreak with the shedding of blood will take place at South Carolina. Fear not, Mark, only be faithful to the will of the Lord revealed to you."

Jenny sighed and folded the scraps of calico spread across the kitchen table. "Sweet little John Mark; how about going for a ride with Mama?"

Jenny bent over the cradle. John Mark's arms and legs pounded out his enthusiasm while he crowed with delight. Jenny scooped him up, saying, "Oh, wet! We're going to visit that nice Sarah Pratt as soon as I make you presentable. I don't have a pattern for these quilt blocks."

Sarah answered Jenny's knock. "Oh," Jenny said in dismay as she looked at the woman's red eyes and blotched face. "I shouldn't have come. Are you ill?"

"No," Sarah sighed and stepped back to allow Jenny to enter the house. "I'm just feeling sorry for myself today."

"Is there anything I can do to help?" Jenny asked timidly.

Sarah started to shake her head, and the tears began. "I don't want to dump my troubles on you. Besides, what I'm going through is nothing more or less than what you'll all be called upon to endure sooner or later if the Prophet calls for the sacrifice."

"What do you mean?" Jenny asked.

"Then Mark hasn't been tapped to obey the priesthood?" she asked bitterly. "Well, just wait; it'll be soon." She glanced sharply at Jenny adding, "You act as if you don't know. Plural marriage, celestial marriage, the everlasting covenant of marriage which no man is allowed to refuse once it is given to him. To refuse is to be damned, and I assure you, my husband is not going to be damned."

Feeling as if she were being backed into a corner, Jenny reminded Sarah, "You know as well as I do that the Prophet's been preaching against the doctrine. There's the pamphlet he's come out against. From the pulpit he's denied the accusations."

"Out of one side of the mouth while he's promoting it with the other."

Jenny remembered that day over a year ago when she had met Dr. Bennett right here in this room. Questions nagged at her, and she had to know. Slowly she said, "Dr. Bennett, that time I met him here, was talking about abortion like it was something happening right here in Nauvoo. Is that true? Was he referring to Saints getting rid of their babies?"

"Yes, Jenny. Remember? He said he did this to prevent *exposure* of the parties involved. He meant Saints."

"I can't imagine anyone getting rid of a baby," Jenny said, cuddling John Mark. "Was it to keep people from knowing about polygamy? If that's so, how can the teaching be from God?"

"It isn't," she said bitterly. "Jenny, use your head. Is it even logical to think the Lord would advocate plural marriage as a means to holiness when the result is a tearing apart of the sweet union of husband and wife?"

For a moment Jenny teetered on the edge of understanding, but even then she knew this step would force her to face something within herself.

Sarah was speaking again. "Joseph sent my husband to England on a mission, with the promise that he would see I was provided with food and fuel for the winter. Shortly after he left, Joseph paid me a visit. He advised me that the Lord had given me to him as a *spiritual wife*. I didn't understand what he meant until he pulled himself up to the top of his dignity and in a stuffy voice said he desired *connubial bliss* with me and hoped I wouldn't deny him. Of course, by then I realized it was nothing except a ruse to get me to go to bed with him.

"I informed him I wouldn't disgrace the institution of marriage by calling his proposal *that*. Jenny, I dearly love my husband. Never could I be willing to sacrifice that sweet relationship. I didn't count on Joseph's insistence, though."

"Oh, no!" Jenny moaned.

Sarah frowned, paused, and then continued. "Joseph threatened to ruin my reputation if I told anyone. Well, you know the rest—how the story leaked out, how Dr. Bennett was accused by the Prophet of doing what he desired himself. You also remember what it did to my husband; when William Law, poor unsuspecting man, got up in the meeting and asked the Saints to lift their hands attesting to the righteousness of the Prophet, my Orson was the only one who voted against him."

"I know it was rumored about that he'd tried to do himself in." Jenny replied in a low voice. "But he's better now, isn't he?"

"Yes." Sarah's bitter voice cracked. In a moment she added, "Yes, Orson's better—and he's become an ardent follower of the Prophet. Seems he can't marry fast enough nowadays." She lifted her face, and finally Jenny understood the black despair in her eyes.

Jenny took a copy of Sarah's quilt pattern and climbed back in her buggy with John Mark. All the way home, while John Mark crowed his delight and waved his hands, Jenny thought about all Sarah had said. She measured Sarah's experience against her own, then compared her Mark with Sarah's Orson and shivered.

As she took the buggy to the barn and unhitched the horse, she said to herself, "One thing is certain in my mind. I must never tell Mark what has happened to me. I couldn't stand to have him become another Orson."

29

"I CAN'T IMAGINE anyone moving in August, at least this August!" Jenny exclaimed, fanning herself vigorously. "Even John Mark fusses when I hold him because it's so hot."

Mark threw her a quick glance. "Perhaps I shouldn't have brought you into town today. It'll be hotter there."

"Ah, but the picnic with Andy, Sally, and Tamara makes it worth the trip in the heat." Jenny tilted the parasol to shade the baby lying on his bed of blankets on the seat of the buggy. "If you will find a shady spot to leave the buggy, John Mark and I will have a pleasant wait while you take the papers up to Clayton."

She fanned herself again, saying, "And if you manage to drive past the Nauvoo House, I'll enjoy gawking at the men carrying in all the Prophet's belongings."

"I won't take the time to pass," he answered, smiling down at her, "but I shall leave the buggy close enough for you to watch the whole event."

Nauvoo House had been built west of the city on a point of land overlooking the wharf. Although it was not finished, the apartment for the Prophet had been readied, and Jenny knew today was moving day.

The three-story, L-shaped building was of red brick. The length and breadth of it started on Main Street and extended down Water Street.

From where Mark had parked the buggy, Jenny could feel the cooling breeze from the river and see the building. Beyond it were the stables and the wharf. She also saw the last load of furniture being taken in the front door.

Disappointed at having missed the excitement, Jenny studied the windows already draped with red velvet and opened to the cooling breezes. "Oh, John Mark, I do so want to see inside! If only Emma would stick her head out, I'd be tempted to go beg a look. I sure don't want to wait for months until the grand opening."

John Mark waved his fists and screwed up his face to cry. "It was early when you nursed," Jenny moaned in dismay, conscious of the lorries and workmen passing the buggy.

Looking around she frowned, saying, " 'Tis only a couple of blocks to the Mansion House. Could be Emma is there. If not, we could walk across the way to the old farmhouse and sit among the trees."

But before they reached Mansion House, John Mark balled up his little fists and complained heartily. Patting his sweaty little shoulders, Jenny sighed, "You win, tyke; we'll cut through the field and save some time."

Back in the trees, just beyond the old farmhouse, Jenny gratefully settled among the ferns and cuddled John Mark to her.

Here the cool woods formed an encircling arm around the old farmhouse and the stretch of Nauvoo beyond. Even the clamor of workmen and the shouts from the wharf were muffled. The house with its patchwork architecture—originally log, with a new addition of white frame was nearly lost in the tangle of lilac bushes. As she idly studied the house, Jenny recalled that the original building was part of the old town of Commerce.

Jenny's eyes were nearly closed when a movement near the house made them start open.

A woman dressed in pale summer colors was striding through the meadow toward the house. With scarcely a pause, she approached the door and slipped through. Jenny frowned, then said, "That's Emily Partridge, Emma's girl. I suppose she's been sent after something. If you hurry, babe, we'll go visit with her."

Only a few minutes later Jenny was laying John Mark down on his blanket when another figure approached. She recognized the tall, thin figure in the dark dress. "Well," Jenny said as she watched her enter the house, "seems we'll have our visit with Emma after all."

Jenny was nearly to the door of the house when she heard the angry cry. As she hesitated, Emma rushed through the door and started up the hill.

Jenny called, "Emma!" But the woman didn't stop until she reached the roadway. Her face was stony when Jenny reached her.

"Oh, you," she said in a lifeless voice, turning away. But Jenny had seen her face.

"Emma, you've hurt yourself!" She could scarcely believe her own words as she blurted out, "Why, someone hit you!"

Emma nodded and dabbed at her swelling eye. Jenny circled her shoulders with one arm and said, "You need a balm on that. The store's just down the street; come." As they started down the road, Jenny said, "I never would have expected Emily Partridge to behave like that."

"It wasn't Emily." She paused and then added, "You saw her. I suppose you saw Joseph, too."

"Joseph?" Jenny asked, then gasped. She was beginning to understand.

"It wasn't Emily. It was Joseph who struck me." They had reached the store. Jenny opened the door and together they went to find the oint- ment. By the time they had made their choice, the door banged open and Joseph rushed in. He paused to look around, and seeing Emma he came to her.

Seizing Emma in his arms, he kissed her. "I'm sorry," he said. "But, Emma, you know better than to follow me."

Speechless, Jenny stared after the two as they left the store, arm in arm.

Later that afternoon, Mark and Jenny met Andy and Sally in the temple grove. After their picnic supper the men and Tamara wandered away.

Sally was slowly repacking the hamper as she said, "Jenny, you've been terribly quiet today. Is there something wrong?"

Bemused, Jenny raised her head, "Oh, I'm sorry. Lost in thought, I guess."

"Has something happened between you and Mark?"

"Oh, no, Sally." Jenny bit her lip and then said, "I saw something today that I just can't understand. What would you think was happening if you saw a woman go into the old farmhouse, and in a few minutes be followed by Emma, who shortly comes out with a bruised eye, saying that Joseph did it?"

Sally looked startled. "I'd think she was lying."

"Even when Joseph came into the store later and apologized to her, saying she should know better than to follow?"

"I guess she wasn't lying."

Now Jenny saw the troubled look on Sally's face and said, "Yes, I too have a hard time believing Joseph is like that. Sally, I've heard rumors. Sarah Pratt admitted the Prophet's urging men to take other wives. When I think of Mark being pulled into that situation, I nearly become ill."

Sally burst into tears. Jenny turned on the blanket and put her arms around her friend. "Oh, Sally, I didn't dream Andy was involved. Please forgive me for hurting you. But I just can't understand—"

Her voice was very low. "It isn't Andy." More sobs muffled her words, and Jenny could only wait, beginning to fear her next words. Finally she straightened and mopped her eyes on Jenny's handkerchief.

"Do you mind if I tell you all about it? Jenny, I am going out of my mind soon if I don't confide in someone."

Reluctantly Jenny nodded. She glanced at the sleeping baby stretched on his blanket and listened to the laughing voices of their men punctuated by Tamara's shrill voice.

Looking into Sally's face, she nodded again, whispering, "If it will help. Sally, you know how I feel about you and Andy both, I—"

Sally bent forward and buried her face against her knees. "Oh, Jenny, don't say it. You'll hate me when I finish, but that's the chance I must take. See, I'm one of Joseph's wives."

Jenny gulped and took a deep breath. "Explain that."

"Since Kirtland. He began teaching me the doctrine of spiritual wives just after you and Mark were married in '36. That next year we took our endowments. I wanted to wait, but it was starting to look as if we'd be leaving for Missouri soon, and Joseph said the Lord had commanded the marriage to be sealed."

Her brave voice dropped to a whisper as she continued, "I didn't want to do it. But after he got through teaching the doctrine and bade me pray for direction, I dared not disobey the Lord."

"You had a *sign*?"

"Yes." For a moment Sally's face brightened. "I'd prayed and fasted, just like he told me to. One night late I awakened and went downstairs to pray. There I had the most wonderful vision, and I knew I had confirmation."

"What was it?"

She hesitated and fumbled for words. "A—sensation of brightness and a tremendous peace swept over me."

Jenny settled back on her heels and thought. "Well, Sally, I guess I can't quarrel with that. The Prophet's taught us to seek signs and wisdom. I've followed that course myself seeking for power and wisdom. I must confess, though, at times I don't like what I find, and the confusion that ends up inside of me nearly makes me sick. But, according to the teaching, that's Satan fighting against what is being given to us."

"I thought it was just the opposite. Once you said—"

"That they were saying the right way is within us, and that we follow it naturally." She stopped and stared at Sally. "I am getting so confused I don't know what I think. One thing is certain. All you're telling me leaves me churning around inside. Why is the way of salvation so difficult?"

"Shall I tell you more? I think I might be able to get rid of this terrible guilt if you would listen."

Jenny nodded and Sally continued. "That medicine. I think you guessed I'd tried to get rid of the baby. Jenny, I wasn't trying to cause an abortion. I wanted to die; that's why I took the medicine."

Now her sobs were soundless. Jenny watched the agony expressed in the trembling curve of her body. Her own arms felt leaden as she lifted them and pulled Sally close. One more rush of words from Sally explained it all. "I think it was Joseph's baby."

It was dusk. From down the hill came the mingled sounds of laughter from Mark and Andy. Jenny could control her bitterness no longer. "How could you do that to Andy?"

The silence lasted for a long time. Jenny could no longer see Sally's face.

Sally finally moved, sighed, and in the voice of an old, wise woman, she said, "Do you think I have not suffered over it? There hasn't been a day since the sealing that I haven't agonized over it. But I must bow to the wishes of the Prophet, pretending and deceiving my husband, when each deception is nearly the death of me." She was silent, and then as if she guessed Jenny's unspoken question, she added, "If I dared attempt death again, I would."

"Isn't there something you can do? Why don't you ask Andy to leave Nauvoo?"

Sally leaned over Jenny. Her fingers were digging into Jenny's arm shaking it. "Don't you understand? I dare not. My salvation is at stake. I would go to hell most surely. You know, Jenny, not a one of us will make it unless Joseph is there to admit us to heaven."

The men's voices were growing louder as they laughed and romped up the hill with Tamara. Seeing one last agonized glance from Sally, Jenny leaned forward and kissed her cheek. "Trust me; somehow I'll find a way to get you out of this mess."

30

JENNY LEFT THE Relief Society meeting and headed for Joseph's store, carrying a lunch of cold meat and vegetables to Mark.

With John Mark clutched tightly in one arm and the other hand holding the food pail, Jenny slowly made her way up the stairs, kicking her long skirt out of the way as she went.

Halfway up the stairs, she heard a door bang against the wall and Joseph's voice rose above the clatter. "Law, you'll be damned if you don't!"

The angry voice retorted, "And I'll be damned if I do! What a doctrine!"

Feet thundered on the stairs and William exclaimed, "Oh Mrs. Cartwright! I nearly swept you down the stairs. Here, let me help you." He took the pail and surveyed John Mark, whose face was beginning to pucker.

"Oh, he's shy," Jenny explained, pressing the baby's head against her shoulder. "I'm just bringing lunch to Mark."

"I think he's out. Here, I'll put the pail on his desk, and you can wait."

Clayton was at his desk, hunched over the notebook. Busily dipping his pen, he said, "Morning, ma'am. Mark'll be back in a minute." He wiped his pen and came to pat the baby and beam at him. "Little blessing. 'Tis for all of us if we only mind the Lord and keep His commandments. Now, that William is sure bucking counsel." He sighed gustily, with a wistful look in his eyes. Jenny recalled the Relief Society gossip of some trouble at home.

He continued, "My heart's desire is to fulfill the requirements of the gospel. I pray the great Elohim to bless us all with His will." He paused for a moment, searching Jenny's face, then said, "You know, we don't live to please ourselves. All of this is only to keep the covenants of our God and to earn the right to the eternities He's prepared for us." Clayton picked up his hat and with a smile headed for the door.

Mark arrived as Jenny was still pondering the veiled meaning of Clayton's remarks. They shared the lunch and Jenny left the office, saying, "I'm going to shop and then go home."

By the time Jenny was back in the buggy, she was brooding over the old problem. Halfway home, suddenly the obvious solution occurred to Jenny.

John Mark was asleep and she allowed the mare to amble along at her own pace. There was a touch of coolness in the breeze, and Jenny lifted her face to it. "Of course," she beamed, "how simple! Why didn't I think of it before?"

It was the solution to all the problems—Sarah's, Emma's, Sally's. "It's that talisman. You admitted yourself that it was the power in the talisman causing the problem with you. Is it too ridiculous to believe it's causing *their* problems, too? Granted, they don't have a talisman to pitch, like you did, but he does."

She recalled Sally's ravaged face and her heart squeezed tight. But how would she get Joseph's talisman? "One thing," she told herself, "you're going to have to see a lot more of the Prophet."

"Jenny!" Mark exclaimed, "you've been walking around this house all day looking as if you reside on a different planet. You've studied that potato as if you've never seen one before."

Jenny raised her head. "Oh, Mark, that isn't funny."

"Meaning?"

"I'm having a difficult time trying to understand all the Prophet says, and here you are picking at his sermons."

He frowned and then grinned. "Planet. That was a pun. Why don't you just read the Bible? You know he says he believes in it, too." He came to lean over her shoulder, to peer at the vegetables.

"But only as far as it is correctly translated." She hastily added, "I know, you're going to talk about having Bible sections in the *Book of Mormon.* You're going to say we don't know what *not* to believe."

"No, I'm going to kiss your neck and suggest you forget about the whole subject right now."

She saw his eyes as he bent to kiss her. The frown indicated that Mark wasn't as lighthearted as he seemed. For a moment she wished desperately that she could tell him all. But even with that wish, her soul withered in fear.

The next morning, while she was reading the book of John, she murmured, "Jesus, I still don't understand, but I wish I knew what I could believe about this Book.

"What does it mean when it says You've come to give life, and that if I follow You, I won't walk in darkness? Why am I condemned already if I don't believe? What does *believe* mean? I believe Mark will come home tonight; I believe the sun will rise tomorrow."

As Jenny stared at the Book, the thought occurred to her that she should believe it all. She shook her head, "Joseph—" The thought seemed suddenly illuminated. *Why believe Joseph?* She caught her breath and examined the question. So many problems would disappear if she *didn't* believe Joseph: that certificate in Joseph's office, salvation through the church. Now another thought came into her mind. It was so vivid that for a moment she felt as if she had literally heard the statement. *The power of the deed will be broken if you tell Mark.*

Aghast, she considered his reaction—the horror on his face, the disappointment, and finally the rejection. With regret she shook her head.

To be done with the guilt, even the possibility of being forced to honor that contract, was a temptation she dared not consider. As attractive as the thought was, she could not risk losing Mark. Taking a deep breath, she whispered, "Joseph has not one hold on me. He knows I would tell Emma. I am no longer afraid of him."

When Jenny heard Mark's horse late that afternoon, she knew he was angry. Standing in the doorway she watched Mark slide from the horse and yank off the saddle and bridle. He impatiently pulled open the gate and slapped the mare across the rump.

As he came up the steps she said, "What's wrong?"

"Speech in the temple grove. You know election is coming up next week. Joseph promised his vote to Cyrus Walker when he was arrested. Well, Hyrum had a revelation. He said he'd asked God how the people should vote. The answer was that God wanted the people to vote for Hoge, on the Democratic ticket. Quite a sensation, this abrupt reversal of what we'd been led to expect. Especially considering Hyrum had previously promised the Democrats the Mormon vote if they would promise him a seat in the state legislature next year."

Jenny paused to think for a moment; then with a sigh and shake of her head, she said, "Well, come have a cool drink and tell me more about it."

He pulled the buttermilk from the well where it had been chilling. She began preparing dinner as he talked.

"When Cyrus Walker took Joseph's case against the Missouri charge, it was done with Joseph's promise of support in the upcoming election. Well, Walker's the Whig candidate for Congress. Remember the rumor floating down from Springfield?"

Slowly Jenny said, "You mean the trip J. B. Backenstos made to confer with Ford? About the promise in exchange for the Mormons' vote on the Democratic ticket? Didn't they say Joseph would have nothing to fear from the governor? Mark, are you saying there's a possibility Joseph will be voting for the Democrats to keep from being arrested?"

"You know how strong the people lean on revelations." He went to pick up John Mark. "William Law was irate. He got to his feet and chewed out Hyrum, reminding everyone that only Joseph was entitled to have revelations. Then he reminded them Joseph had pledged Walker the Mormon support."

"So what did Joseph say?"

"Only that he was pledged to support Walker, and unless he had a revelation to the contrary, they should support him too.

"Oh, my," Jenny murmured. "Sabbath-day sermon should be interesting."

At the end of the sermon the following day, Mark leaned toward Jenny and said, "You were right, my dear."

She nodded, her eyes riveted on the pulpit. Joseph was saying, "I've no intention of telling you how to vote. I don't have a revelation concerning the election. Matter of fact, I don't believe in troubling the Lord about politics. I gave my word to Walker when I hired him to handle my case against Reynolds, but I didn't pledge him the votes of all the Saints. Now Hyrum advises us that he has a revelation from the Lord instructing that the Saints should vote for Hoge." He paused for a moment and then slowly said, "I must admit, I've never known Hyrum to have a revelation that failed."

William Law was standing beside Mark, and as the congregation began to move toward their wagons and carriages, William fell into step with Mark. Jenny saw his shoulders droop in discouragement as he said, "I wonder if he believes he can get away with this? I'm afraid Joseph's just garnered himself a pack of enemies." At Mark's quick glance he said, "Oh, I still believe in him. I just think he's making a terrible mistake right now."

Sarah and Orson Pratt caught up with them. Orson said, "Law, I heard what you said. Seems we ought to be discussing the situation. Maybe we could get together this afternoon?"

"If you've carried your dinner, bring it and come," Sarah invited. "We've plenty of trees for shade and the breeze off the river hits us just fine."

While the men stood in the shade of the trees on the Pratt farm, the women spread their food across the table.

Looking at the dishes, Sarah said slowly, "When I remember the time we had in Missouri, just getting wheat milled and enough to eat, I'd be grateful for just a speck of this."

Jenny looked at the table. There was snowy bread, creamy butter, ham, fried chicken, a joint of venison, garden vegetables baked into a thick custard, cucumbers floating in vinegar and spices, applesauce, and fried pumpkin chips. The pies looked like apple and peach. Jenny's spice cake, heavy with raisins, released a fragrance of molasses and cinnamon.

Jenny looked from Sarah to Jane. Addressing Jane, she said, "Except for what you've heard from the pulpit, you don't know what it was like."

"I've been fed a constant dose of the stories of the persecutions ever since we've arrived," she said; then she raised her head and added in a rush, "Seems Joseph is bound to not let it die. It cuts a picture of a man not big enough to let by-gones be. Will he hold a grudge forever? I was raised to believe in the importance of forgiving those who sin against us. Even though we're Latter-day Saints, seems there's still a few Christian virtues that need to be retained."

The men came to the table and the conversation turned lighthearted until the table had been cleared.

When William Law leaned back in his chair he addressed Pratt. "Orson, do you believe Joseph's statements today will have an effect on the election?"

"I should hope so," Orson replied. Jenny glanced at Mark. When he sighed heavily, she knew he had an objection, but she also guessed he would save his irritation for her ears. Pratt continued, "We've a responsibility toward these people. They need instruction until they've accepted all that will be given to them to achieve the knowledge necessary for salvation."

"You think knowledge gives salvation?" Mark asked, looking surprised.

"Of course. The Prophet gave that to us."

Mark was asking, "What about the truth concerning God as revealed in the Holy Bible?"

Orson moved impatiently. "In the Bible there's not a thing you can believe in with surety except what is contained in the original. What we have nowadays is a corrupted translation, given out by uninspired men without the authority to translate. I tell you, there's no part that we can accept with certainty as the Word of God. I declare to you that what we have is only the words of men, not the true Word. It is only the skeleton— the mutilated, the changed, the corrupted."

William Law was leaning forward; there was a perplexed frown on his face. "Then what do you trust?"

"The Prophet. He has been given the keys to the kingdom. Through the direct revelation of God himself, we know Joseph is to be trusted."

"But, Pratt, we have only Joseph's word for it," Mark said.

"That's true," Pratt admitted. "But he's also told us to ask God to give us a testimony of the rightness of all this. There's not a man in the church who's asked, who hasn't received."

Law's frown remained. Slowly he said, "One of the things that's really nagged at me has been the willingness of the people to rely on emotion. I've heard things like, 'I *feel* this is right. I know by the spirit, I've been caught up in the spirit. I saw a great light when I prayed. I felt a burning in the bosom.' I'm a practical man; I don't like to go by hunches. I want facts. Why can't we rely on the Word?"

"What word?" Mark asked. "If you're talking about the *Book of Mormon,* then please tell me what I should depend upon. I've been listening to Joseph long enough to realize little of his beliefs come from his holy book, the *Book of Mormon.*"

"Well, you can't rely upon the Bible. The *Book of Mormon* clearly sets forth that the Christian church, referred to as the 'abominable church' has taken from the Bible the most plain and precious parts of the gospel," William said.

"God deliver us from ever calling ourselves Christian," muttered Orson.

"I suppose there would be some merit in living by the doctrine of the *Book of Mormon,*" Mark added. "I saw in the second book of Nephi the thirteenth verse where old Nephi urges relying completely upon the merits of Jesus Christ for salvation, urging the people to feast upon the Word of Christ. It doesn't say a church will save us."

In the silence Mark continued, "But there's more. This hits right at the priesthood. Chapter one of the book of Jacob calls it a wicked practice, this having many wives."

Orson's voice was brittle. "Anything else, Brother Cartwright?"

"I've noticed the book refers to Christ as God, the Father of all things. That isn't consistent with Joseph's saying Christ is our elder brother. I kinda like it where it says God came down and took upon Himself flesh and blood and that He shall redeem His people. Sure beats any salvation I can earn for myself through the church."

William and Orson were on their feet when Mark added, "Have you noticed? The book of Alma says that Mary, the mother of Jesus, conceived by the power of the Holy Ghost."

Mark and Jenny were in the buggy headed for home before Jenny dared say, "Mark, you worry me. If Joseph were to hear about this—"

"I'd be labeled apostate." He turned to smile at her, saying, "But the strange thing is, although this goes against his teaching, I'm only giving his words back to him."

In a moment he added, "If I were to ask if—" The smile disappeared and he turned to flick the reins along the mare's back.

"Jenny, I believe there's a move on among the people to break out of the bondage Joseph has placed upon them. There're some intelligent men in the camp who are beginning to think for themselves. One of these days they are going to demand that Joseph give way and take stock of the teaching which he claims comes from God.

"Have you noticed? Back in Kirtland days there was a new revelation just about every time Joseph took a breath. Now it's seldom we get one. Nowadays it's just a matter of Joseph saying jump and the people jump. One of these days they won't."

31

"THE END OF August is as hot as July. Here in the temple grove this Sabbath, there's not a whisper of a breeze," Jenny murmured as she settled on the bench in front of the pulpit and tried to fan the squirming John Mark.

"You might as well forget that," Mark said. "He's generating more wind with his bouncing around. I don't think he's minding the heat as much as his mother."

"I nearly wish I'd stayed home with him. He's getting so strong, and I think he's going to have a tooth soon."

Jenny continued to struggle with the squirming baby as the Sabbath service began. She had nearly lost the thread of the message when John Mark went to sleep. While Mark adjusted the blanket across their legs and eased the baby onto his lap, Jenny became aware of the Prophet's words.

Briefly he referred to the death of the Higbee child, and then said, "The time of the endowments in the temple is drawing nigh. The sad death this past week shows the importance of this ordinance. When the parents of a child have been sealed in the temple, their posterity is secured. For all eternity this child is theirs, saved through the virtue of the covenant of the father."

Jenny was still mulling over that information when the Prophet moved on, proclaiming, "I received information which indicates that Sidney Rigdon has given oath to Governor Carlin of Missouri to bind over my life to the Missourians. At this time, I desire to withdraw the hand of fellowship from Sidney Rigdon, and I put this up to the vote of the people."

A rustle of indignation spread through the audience. Catcalls accompanied the lifting of hands. Joseph acknowledged their remarks with a smile and continued, "We've voted unanimously to remove his name, and we will revoke his license. I will advise you that, regardless of the schemer's plans, all the powers of hell or earth together cannot put down this old boy. I have promises from the eternal God."

John Mark awakened when the shouting began. Jenny was juggling him into quietness when Joseph began talking about the Melchizedek priesthood. "The sectarians have never professed to have the priesthood. In consequence, it is impossible for them to save anyone. They'll all be damned together. Only the priesthood gives power for endless lives."

He paused, and bending forward, said, "I will remind you of the power of the priesthood. You know the sacrifice of Abraham. These everlasting covenants cannot be broken! When God gives knowledge or blessing to a man and he refuses to accept, he shall be damned."

Service was over. Jenny got to her feet, stumbling as she followed Mark. Those words filled her mind. John Mark didn't have a chance to even begin to earn his position in the eternities unless his daddy would accept Joseph's way.

"Jenny, what are you thinking?"

"Oh . . ." Jenny blinked against the sunshine and looked up at Mark. The Sabbath day was nearly over. John Mark was still napping while the two of them leaned over the pasture fence.

"That the world is beautiful and that I love our farm." How conscious she was of evading the real thoughts, even as she turned to glance up at him!

She was aware of his eyes, with those curious flecks of color, watching her. Watching them, aware of their candor, she realized how often in these past weeks Mark had gently probed, urging her to talk. She began to giggle.

"What's that about?"

"I was thinking back to some of the silly talking we've been doing in the past weeks."

"About the girls who are trying to entrap Tom?"

"And the new fall fashions and whether poke bonnets should be allowed in the temple."

Mark's grin faded, "Like the unimportant."

The breeze swept a yellow leaf past Jenny and she whispered, "What, Mark? What is it you want—a piece of my soul?"

"Is that too much?"

"It is until I understand it myself."

"You've changed, you know. I find myself wondering."

She searched his face, not daring to ask: *for good or bad?* She simply said, "All of life is changing. It's nearly autumn. The tourists have gone. Joseph's church is still fumbling and restless. The Saints will soon be worshiping in the temple. There will be new teachings, the endowments." She was still watching him as he turned away.

Softly now she said, "Do you realize, Mark, even between us there's so much that *can't* be said? We had new teaching today. Joseph said that if we're to be having little John Mark for eternity, if he's even to have a chance at eternity, you must fulfill the requirements of the gospel. There must be endowment."

He turned away. "I'm sorry, Jenny. When a person doesn't believe, he can't live a lie—even for the dearest person on earth."

Jenny contemplated the pasture, the brilliance of the day. All too soon the bronze, copper and gold of autumn would be here, and then the snow. Where were their lives together leading them? She couldn't face that answer.

The peeled log railing of the fence had whitened with age. She ran her hand over the smooth surface, wondering how long it would be until the smoothness turned to slivers.

"So?"

"See, so smooth now. You peel back the bark and it's vulnerable, Mark, like us. How long before it all turns to splinters?" Watching she realized, in the darkening of his eyes, there was pain in the unprobed depths of her husband. Deeply she felt the answer from her own heart even as she bit her lips and turned away.

He held out his arms, and in them she was conscious of passion drowned in a desire for union deeper than physical. It must be the call for endowment. Her sigh was as heavy as she felt. When he finally dropped his arms, she heard his sigh of regret. "We'd better see if the tyke is awake."

That evening, when Mark stepped into the circle of her lamplight, he asked, "What are you reading?"

She brought her thoughts back and lifted her face. "The Bible. Mark, what is God's love?"

He came into the light and sat down. "I suppose what we see of God and understand as love. Salvation instead of what we deserve. Even just holding the world together. If He were to take away His hand, we'd disappear. Certainly considering sin and disobedience, we don't deserve more than that. But He handles us very gently. This should bring us running into His love. I guess God's love is a place where we are to dwell."

In a moment he quoted, " 'But God commendeth His love toward us, in that, while we were yet sinners, Christ died for us. Much more then, being now justified by his blood, we shall be saved from wrath through Him.' Jenny, this chapter in Romans says we're justified by faith, not works like Joseph says. It tells us this is a free gift."

She knew he saw her trembling hands. As she shook her head he stopped abruptly. "Mark, it sounds so nice, but I am afraid. Now there's another one to fear for. The fear sends me running; I'll be faithful to my church to the best of my ability. I'll also work to bring some of these teachings of the Bible into our church. We need the best of both. But, please don't ask me to give up the security of this. I've already given up so much."

She saw the curiosity in his eyes and braced herself to answer the words which she had unintentionally let slip.

"Do you regret it?"

Jenny caught her breath. It wasn't what she had expected. He meant unsaid things they had never talked about. The craft. For a moment she looked at Mark, seeing clearly how much he had comprehended even while he held his silence. She whispered, "No, never. I've traded ugliness for God's church." Mark turned away and Jenny returned to the Book.

She bent her head over it. "It says here in John that a man who doesn't love Jesus doesn't obey His teaching." Looking out the window, she asked, "Do you suppose Joseph doesn't know about that verse?"

"Why do you ask?"

"Because I sense so much of fear and fighting in him. Seems it's in him more than the rest of us."

He sat down beside her, and she felt his excitement. "You've caught that? What else have you seen?"

"I'm thinking of a verse, a question. 'Are you foolish? After beginning with the spirit, are you made perfect by works?' Then it goes on to say it was faith that saved Abraham, not doing, and that no man is justified by the law—yet this very day, Joseph talked about the *sacrifice* of Abraham."

She studied her hands for a moment, then said, "There's more. It says if you're led by the spirit, you're not under law. Mark, does it possibly mean even the type of law in the church—all the doing and . . ."

She couldn't finish. Mark took her hands and pulled her close. "Jen—" He stopped. She saw the joyful expression on his face fade. Then caution swept over his features as he carefully said, "Even Joseph couldn't object to the reading and learning you are doing. One of these days he'll have to allow us to do some thinking on our own."

Now she was brave enough to try the verse. "Mark, there's something else. I think it's a verse even you don't know about."

"What does it say?"

"That in Jesus there isn't such as Jew or Greek, even men and women—we're all the same."

"I know about it."

"Then you see what it means. Oh, Mark, I can hardly believe it!"

"That Jesus Christ doesn't see you as less than me?"

She frowned and regarded him thoughtfully for a moment before slipping away from her original intention into the other thought the verse held. Slowly she said, "No, Mark, I was thinking of the baptism. Joseph teaches that baptism changes all of us who aren't the literal descendants of the children of Israel, so that we have their Jewish blood in our veins."

When Jenny slowly followed Mark up the stairs to their bedroom, she was wistfully thinking of the verse, wondering why she couldn't push aside that amazing thought. *All are alike in Jesus' eyes. All have the same rights— to enjoy eternity, without having a man take them there.*

What would Mark think of that? And what about having a man look at her with respect in his eyes, as if what she had to say was important?

As Jenny slipped into bed beside Mark, she saw the expression in his eyes and paused. Sometimes she felt as if Mark might feel that way. But what would he say right now if she were to pound her pillow and demand he say what he was thinking?

32

"WHAT IS THE mystery of God, of Christ?" Jenny pondered as she slowly turned the pages in her Bible. "In here there's talk about the hidden wisdom which God set up before He created the world. Oh, what does this mean? 'Which none of the princes of this world knew: for had they known it, they would not have crucified the Lord of glory.' Why? There's something here so big, and I can't understand it!"

She sat staring at the Book. "The Lord of glory, that's Jesus Christ." As she read further, the puzzle became more complex. When she put aside the Book and started her morning tasks, she mulled over the words which had dropped into her mind. "Eyes haven't seen and ears haven't heard. God has prepared great things for us who love Him! That means even Joseph doesn't know—or does he?"

Those who love God. Did she love God? What did that mean? Joseph didn't talk about *doing* because of love. He talked about earning eternal life by the righteousness of deeds.

Later as Jenny bathed John Mark and dressed him, a verse jumped into her mind whole, impossible to forget. At the most unexpected moments it bounded into her thoughts. " 'Now we have received, not the spirit of the world,' " she murmured, " 'but the spirit which is of God; that we might know the things that are freely given to us of God.' " As she sat down to feed the baby, she considered the words that followed: " 'So the natural man does not receive the things of the Spirit because they are foolish to him. Spiritually discerned.' That's why Joseph is so far above us."

It was afternoon when Jenny carried the sleeping infant to the buggy. Feeling the sweet weight of him brought tears to her eyes. She squeezed him tight and he flung a tiny arm against her. When she bent to kiss the hand, her tears dampened it.

When Jenny reached Joseph's office, Clayton was just leaving. He closed the door carefully and said, "Mark isn't here right now. He's made a trip to Carthage today."

"I know. It's Joseph I want to see." The man looked uneasy and Jenny explained, "It's religious counsel." He reddened.

Joseph opened the door. "Come in, Jenny." His eyes brightened, and for just one moment Jenny remembered the last time she had been alone with him.

"I need instruction," she said loudly as she entered. She heard the shuffle of feet as Clayton went back to his office. Joseph closed the door and motioned for Jenny to be seated.

"Your sermon. About sealing for posterity's sake."

"Yes, what about it?"

She bit her lip. "Mark won't. He says he doesn't believe in it. What shall I do?"

"Jenny, you don't understand the teachings. You've already been sealed to me. When there's a sealing for eternity, the offspring of the wife is automatically credited to the spiritual mate. Your baby belongs to me for all eternity."

The facts lined up in Jenny's mind as she looked at Joseph. John Mark was safe for all eternity. He would have an opportunity for eternal progression, under Joseph. John Mark no longer belonged to Mark; in the sight of God he was Joseph's baby.

She could only stare at Joseph as he leaned back in his chair and made a tent of his fingers. His face was pulled down into a troubled frown. "However, Jenny, I must remind you. Our marriage, with all the rights attested to it, still awaits validation. Until it is consummated, your little one is no better off than an infidel."

John Mark pulled her finger into his mouth and began to suck on it. As she stared down at him, he grinned and waved a pudgy fist. Her heart sank. "Joseph, I must think some more."

She rose to leave. He was still watching and she thought of all she had been saving to ask him. Slowly Jenny said, "I've had so many questions. You are our contact with God. The spirit tells you, and the rest of us only wonder."

"Perhaps you'd understand better if you were to obey the light you have. Jenny, you are not obedient to the gospel."

"The Bible says the blood of Jesus frees us from things the law couldn't. What?"

"The crucifixion purchases resurrection from the dead. This is for all people."

"Is that all?"

"Yes. It is only through obedience to the true church that we have the right to the highest heaven and all that implies: kingdoms, godhood, eternal progress. It makes the troubles we endure down here seem insignificant, doesn't it?"

"Then, Joseph, what is the mystery of Christ?"

Jenny felt as if her head whirled with knowledge. But her heart was even heavier than it had been when she had first entered the office.

She shifted John Mark to her other arm and hesitated. Joseph waited. "You tell us the Bible isn't translated correctly," Jenny said. "You give us so much wisdom and knowledge, spirit direction. But, Joseph, I don't understand it all.

"Why is it that when I read the Bible, the words sing through me? I can't forget some of them. God so loved us that He gave, that whosoever might have eternal life just by believing in Jesus. Aren't we 'whosoever'? Joseph, who was Jesus? Why does He say we must be born again?"

Clayton was at the door waiting to come in. Apologetically he said, "I don't mean to bother, if you need more time." Jenny shook her head, but her eyes were studying the books and the large charts he held. He shuffled through them and lifted one. " 'Tis of the heavens. The Prophet and I have been seeking the ancient knowledge of the heavens. My, what amazing things we've discovered."

"About the universe?" Jenny questioned.

"No, about the influence of energy and the stars. Of their magnetic force released on the people of the earth. Did you know we are under these influences?"

Feeling even more confused, Jenny shook her head and left the office. As she got into the buggy she murmured, "I still don't understand the mystery of Christ. Why wouldn't the princes have crucified Him?"

"Being a mama is harder on a lady than I thought."

Jenny looked up. Tom was standing beside the buggy, grinning at her and reaching for his nephew. "Hey, big fella. When we goin' huntin' together?" John Mark drooled and reached for Tom's beard.

"I'm sorry; I just didn't see you. Where are you headed? Do you want a ride?"

"Going up to Nauvoo House. Emma's all set to take off on the steamboat, bound for St. Louis to buy some fancies for the place."

Jenny exclaimed, "Oh, the luck! I wish I were going, too. New clothes and new furniture, oh, my! But where do you fit in?"

"Joseph just wants me to settle the lady in. So I'll go up and drive her in the carriage to the wharf."

"Come out for supper with Mark."

He shook his head. "Lee's outta town. Joseph's tapped me for duty at the house tonight. I do want to see Mark; you might let the word drop. I got a lot on my mind, and I want his advice."

"Love or finances?" Jenny teased. Tom glared, and she laughed. "Well, come when you can. It's been a month since you've been out."

"Yeah." He paused. "I heard Mark ruffled Pratt's feathers a couple of weeks ago."

"It's been around," Jenny mused. "Seems Mark's having a harder time keeping quiet lately. Tom, I'm worried for him. He won't sign up for the endowments. You heard the sermon. What does that mean to John Mark?"

"Maybe nothing at all."

Tom stood watching his sister drive out of sight. Her slender figure in the dark calico seemed especially vulnerable, fragile; he wondered at his uneasiness.

Walking back to the stables behind Nauvoo House, Tom was pondering the effect of the summer's assignment on his feelings. "A body can't help being influenced by it all." He muttered, thinking of what he had seen and heard during the past months.

"One thing's for sure. I'll be very happy to chuck this job and go back to tending horses. They don't give me no surprises."

But later, as Tom settled himself on the cot in the back hall of Nauvoo House, he advised himself, "Can't complain about this assignment." Joseph had been finished with his calls early. The two of them had been back at Nauvoo House before ten o'clock. After a quick nightcap, Joseph had gone upstairs, leaving Tom to the devices of the kitchen maids.

New ones, they were, and he missed the friendly Partridge girls. He was still chuckling over the two as he settled himself to sleep close to the foot of the stairs.

The creak of the stairs awakened Tom. Dawn touched the windows with a rosy glow. As he sat up on the cot, Tom saw the heels of Brother Rushton, the steward, disappearing up the stairs. Realizing the man was going after the keys, Tom started up the stairs after him.

By the time Tom reached Joseph's door, Rushton had already tapped and pushed open the door. Tom was behind Rushton as the startled young woman sat up in bed. "Oh!" She pulled the sheet higher and smiled at the two. "My, you startled me nearly as much as I startled you!" She turned and reached for the keys. "Well, for this week, you'll just have to pretend I'm Sister Emma."

Tom saw the bedcovers heave, and another head appeared. Joseph sat up. Tom's fascinated gaze froze on the brilliant red nightshirt the Prophet was wearing. After several silent seconds, the Prophet added, "You heard the lady—now be off."

He was still glaring at Tom as Brother Rushton closed the door behind them. "Tom," Brother Rushton said, "I have an idea the General would rather we didn't mention seeing him under these circumstances. Particu-

larly since we'll have to put up with Sister Emma being gone all week."
Tom watched him go slowly down the stairs, shaking his head.

When Tom reached the farm the next evening, Mark was in the barn
milking. He said, "For a young fella without the burden of land and family,
you sure do look down in the mouth."

"Might say I am. Might be 'cause I'm fearing what you've indicated."

"Aw, it isn't so bad, dear brother-in-law," Mark was laughing until he
lifted his head from the cow's flank. Then his face sobered and he said, "It
is? Better pull up a log and tell me about it."

"It's this priesthood thing. I suppose you've heard the rumors, even if
you haven't been tapped for it yet."

"I'm on the council. I'm guessing. It's the everlasting covenant of marriage, isn't it?"

Tom nodded. "I don't even have one wife, and can't say I'm overanxious
for one. Now Joseph is saying I do or be damned. Mark, I've been right
happy with the church all along, seemed a jolly way to have religion, even
in the rough times."

"Even in Missouri?"

"Aw, that was rough on the women and children. But most of the fellas
managed to tough it through."

"Not minding it?"

"How do I say it? When you listen to a fella like Joseph, you manage to
swallow the questions and just get on with it." He looked at Mark. "Sure, I
know with a family there's fears a body wouldn't have otherwise."

"Tom," Mark said slowly, "do you ever get the idea we might be heading
in the same direction now?"

"As Missouri? I hate having you put it out in words."

"Maybe it's time for all of us to get our heads out of the sand." Mark
had finished the milking and fed the pigs before he asked, "What's on your
mind?"

Tom looked astonished, "I thought I said."

"I had the feeling it was something more."

"Aw, I busted in on Joseph and the wife of one of the elders." Mark said
nothing, and so Tom added, "At six in the morning they weren't discussing
the doctrine of the church."

"I understand there's quite a bit of that thing going on." Mark's voice
was muffled as he pitched straw into the corner of the barn.

"You don't act too concerned."

"Let's say there's little one fellow can do. If you want to join a committee for reform, you just might find a bunch of husbands around who are
willing."

Tom shook his head. "I have the feeling Joseph will be converting the husbands faster than we can."

"Meanwhile, there's your problem," Mark said soberly. "You want to make it in the hereafter, but on your own terms—which differ somewhat from the Prophet's."

"Aw," Tom grinned sheepishly, "you don't make me sound so good. Matter-of-fact, I guess my big problem is I'm starting to have some questions about the whole deal. I guess I'll just have to find somewhere to sit tight until I get a few answers. I'd hate to decide I'd made a big mistake about Joseph, the church, and his new ideas about the kingdom of God, and wake up to find I have four wives and sixteen kids."

"Matter-of-fact, Tom, that's about the wisest thing I've ever heard you say." He slapped Tom on the shoulder. "Let's go have some supper."

33

JENNY WAS PEERING out the window when Mark came into the kitchen. "Last night's storm blew the rest of the leaves off the trees," she said, "and now it looks like it's going to snow."

"I'm not too crazy about you and tyke out on the road, especially just for Relief Society meeting."

"I hate to miss. Not just the quilting for Nauvoo House, but the gossip. I never imagined this fall and winter would be shoving up such things to talk about."

"Like?"

"Orson Pratt and another fellow are headed for Washington, carrying a petition to Congress. Sarah told me a little about it. She says it's pushing our plea to be made into an independent federal territory. Joseph's also asked that the Nauvoo Legion be incorporated into the United States Army and that the mayor of the Nauvoo be given authority to call out the United States troops whenever necessary." She stopped suddenly and Mark looked up. "You know all this; why are you getting me to talk?"

"Maybe I wanted to hear what was going around in Relief Society."

"Do you think we're getting things differently?"

"Yes. In fact, I have a feeling you ladies are adoring slaves of the Prophet, and that he can convince you to say anything."

Speechless, Jenny looked at Mark. Finally she said, "It's a good thing your eyes are twinkling, otherwise—"

"What?" Now she saw his eyes were very serious.

"Mark!" She rushed to him, and he caught her tight against him. "Oh, Mark, what's happening to us? It isn't just to us two, it's everyone."

"You tell me." His voice was flat, and she leaned back to look at him. Slowly she raised herself on tiptoe and put her arms around his neck. He met her lips, but she saw the shadows in his eyes. He was first to turn away. "Maybe this early storm has more significance than we guessed. Could be a barometer of Nauvoo."

"A gathering storm in Nauvoo?" She paused, then insisted, "But—loyalty to the church. Mark, you just don't give up on a thing because the going is rough."

"Jenny, are you trying to convince yourself?"

She whispered, "Let's have a happy Christmas. Last year was wonderful because of the excitement of a baby coming. This year let's celebrate and celebrate. Let's invite everyone we can think of."

"Jenny," he chided with a smile, "this isn't Nauvoo House. There are limits to the number of people who'll fit into this house."

Jenny made her Christmas plans. But life in Nauvoo continued to change. Before Christmas Joseph Smith's petition to Congress had been rejected.

Mark had been there with the other members of the council when Joseph had received the news and then got to his feet to speak. "I prophesy," he roared, "through virtue of the office of the priesthood, in the name of the Lord, that if Congress chooses to deny our petition, they shall suffer destruction! They will be broken up as a government—God will damn them. There shall be nothing left of them, not even a spot of grease!"

Later Mark explained it to Jenny as he sampled the Christmas cookies. "It was like an explosion of gunpowder. Nearly blew us all off our seats. I guess some of us had our hopes higher than we thought. But I expect by the beginning of the year, something new will be brewing in the fertile mind of the Prophet."

He was thoughtful as he studied the disappointed droop to Jenny's lips, deciding he couldn't admit to her just how little he knew about the unrest in Nauvoo right now. But he admitted to himself that not knowing was downright frightening. One thing was certain. The words *apostate* and *dissenter* were becoming common words in Nauvoo.

Mark had other things on his mind. As he watched Jenny cutting Christmas cookies, he found himself thinking he would like to be a mouse in the corner of Relief Society meeting.

Last summer he had first become aware of the cloak of secrecy being thrown up around the society. But last summer, Mark admitted, the whole town writhed under the weight of submerged feelings. The Prophet had started it when he had introduced the revelation on everlasting marriage to some of the elders.

Then in August Joseph Smith had begun mentioning *emigration.* In September Tom had been one of a group of men who suddenly disappeared. Only Mark, the Prophet, and a sprinkling of others knew the men had been sent on an expedition by the Prophet.

Mark had been in council meeting the day the Prophet had faced the men. His usual jovial air was only slightly dampened as he spread the map

on the table and began pointing out territories. "This here is Texas; right now it doesn't belong to the United States. It's land for grabs. I want Lucian Woodworth to go see what it'll take to get a big hunk of land."
With his finger he sketched out an area from the big river in Texas to the Gulf of Mexico, from the Rio Grande River to the territorial boundary of the United States.

"But we're not going to lap up the first offer. We want to investigate every alternative. Fellas—" he paused to fix a commanding gaze on them all, one by one, "Things are getting tight."

In a moment he continued, "This here is Oregon. And this area around the Rocky Mountains is barren—worthless, but empty.

"There are high mountains, according to a fella I've been talking to. Good places for a people to hide out and live their lives without the kind of oppression that's been our lot." His voice had been brooding as he said, "Never will we as a people escape persecution. It's a fact that the holier a people are, the more they're bound to suffer for their religion."

And as the men prepared to go, the Prophet ordered them to check out all the locations he had earmarked. Before they left the room Joseph had fastened them with a stern eye and commanded their vow of silence. "We don't know what the next few years will hold for us. I'm not saying we're leaving, but I want all options checked out. Be a Joshua and Caleb, but don't put your heads too high in the clouds.

"We want a reasonable solution for the Saints. We want a decent place to live out our lives where we never again will be persecuted and hounded to death because we choose to follow God."

But Mark couldn't tell Jenny, he decided, as he continued to eat cookies. There was a dark shadow in her eyes these days.

Jenny's attention was on a different country. She was thinking of her interview with Joseph. She continued to make cookies, while her heart was heavy with his words. Little John Mark didn't have a place with her in the eternities until she obeyed the Prophet.

This year Mark made certain the Christmas tree stand was sturdy. The tree stood straight and brave under its burden of popcorn, candy canes and shiny tin stars. Tom came carrying a wooden horse and cow for John Mark.

The Morgans came with Andy's sister, Helene. A determined gleam lit Helene's eyes as she smiled at Tom. The Orson Pratts came, with Orson full of his disappointment with the Washington trip.

Late in the afternoon they all returned to town for a reception at Nauvoo House. It was nearly dusk when they reached the red brick edifice.

"It's like a painting!" Jenny exclaimed to Mark as she hugged John Mark to her. The snow was falling gently in large fluffy flakes. "Just look!"

she said, pointing to the sleighs with their graceful lines and bright bells. "Even the Saints are bright in their new Christmas mufflers and mittens." Every window on the lower floor of the hotel glowed with light, completing the Christmas picture.

Inside, Jenny discovered Emma's fat china lamps sporting new red glass shades. Wreaths of holly and garlands of evergreen festooned the polished banister of the staircase, and the red carpeting of the lobby beckoned toward the fireplace and blazing fire.

Sally stopped beside Jenny and whispered, "Look at the chandelier; it glitters like diamonds." In awe they stared up at the prisms, made alive with every fresh gust of wintry air. "It's grand, isn't it?" Sally stroked the marble-topped table and studied the shiny horsehair and red velvet upholstery. "Doesn't Emma look elegant in brocade? My, we Saints are going to be something special yet."

Together Mark and Jenny made their way through the rooms, greeting the guests. There were the twelve, Brigham Young and his wife, Lyman Wight, both of the Pratt brothers, Hiram Kimball, and his wife. Later they found William Phelps and Joseph's younger brother, William Smith.

Jenny lost the thread of conversation moving around them. She was busy thinking about this powerful, tall brother of Joseph's. Tipping her head to investigate his face, she noted the sullen lines. His insolent eyes met hers. Without a doubt he had a caustic tongue, she recalled, thinking of recent issues of the *Wasp,* the newspaper he edited.

As she followed Mark across the room, she murmured, "And now he's our state legislator." Jenny studied the three tallest men in Mormondom. They were spaced throughout the hotel, as if proximity could not be tolerated.

Recent gossip had William Law as a man in disfavor, bordering on apostasy. She looked from him to William Smith, and then to Joseph the Prophet. These men's minds were as forceful as their size. As she watched them, Jenny became convinced that trouble was brewing.

Later, Emma guided Jenny into a small room away from the lobby. Together they settled down to talk while Jenny nursed John Mark.

A gentle smile crept over Emma's face as she played with the baby's curls, and Jenny was emboldened to ask the question on her mind. "I haven't seen Eliza Snow for so long. Has she left Nauvoo?"

The smile faded from Emma's face. For a moment her frosty eyes held Jenny, then she said, "I believe you've asked in innocence. Since you were there when she fell, I'll tell you. Eliza is still in Nauvoo. I don't know where she lives and I've no desire to renew acquaintance. She was a serpent. I trusted her as I've trusted no other woman. She was my confidant, my friend."

Emma paused, and in an icy voice that denied additional questions, she added, "Eliza was pregnant. I understand she's lost her baby."

Later, after Emma left the room and John Mark was asleep, Jenny wrapped him in a heavy quilt and placed him on the floor.

As she got to her feet, she felt a hand on her arm. Glancing down, she recognized the massive gold ring. "Joseph," she said with a tired sigh.

"Have you decided?" he asked. When she didn't answer, he gently urged, "Remember, I've pledged to be god to you. There's no way a woman will make it on her own; she's got to have a husband to take her into the celestial kingdom."

As she hesitated, Jenny recalled that verse and turned. "Joseph, I've read a verse in the Bible that encourages me; I want to believe and accept it. It says that in Christ there's not this division. Neither Jew nor Gentile, slave nor free, male nor female, but that we're all one in Christ Jesus."

He paused and his hand tightened on her arm. "Must I remind you again that to reject the gospel is damnation?"

She looked up, feeling the despair that was coming through her voice. "Maybe I'd rather choose damnation than deny my marriage vows."

He sighed, "Jenny, I've held back on saying this, because I've not wanted to hurt you. But in the eyes of our Lord, your marriage vow doesn't exist. You are living in adultery with Mark Cartwright."

Closing her eyes, Jenny took a step backward and was immediately surrounded by perfume and the cool touch of yellow roses. She felt that Presence and knew the promise.

She opened her eyes and stared up at Joseph. "I've been doing a lot of thinking and studying lately. I've decided the craft is all wrong. I don't want to have that kind of power. See, I have this need inside of me to know God. I guess you might say I've just promised the Lord I'd be a good Mormon and live up to my religion. Joseph, you make it impossible for me to keep that promise if—if what you're saying must be."

There was the creak of the door behind Jenny and Mark was asking, "Jenny, are you ready to go home?"

Jenny was still staring at Joseph as she replied, "Yes, my husband, I am ready."

34

THE JANUARY SNOW was piling up. In the pasture the cattle and horses huddled with their backs to the wind while Jenny stood at the window watching snow inch relentlessly toward the top of the fence.

John Mark had crept across the floor. Seizing her skirt, he tried to pull himself to his feet. "Big boy," Jenny encouraged, smiling down at the bright-haired child. She picked him up and said, "Oh, I wonder if your papa has noticed how your eyes are changing. I'm glad. I want you to have blue-green just like his.

"Now, tyke, let's get that pan of bread into the oven beside the squash and then go for fresh diapers." With another quick glance out the window she sighed and added, "I hope he comes before dark. The snow is blowing."

When the baby was settled on his blanket and the aroma of fresh bread began drifting through the house, Jenny sat down close to the window and picked up her Bible. She hesitated and reached for Mark's Bible, feeling slightly guilty as she did so.

"Such interesting things he writes!" she murmured. A piece of paper marked Isaiah 8, but the paper was blank. Disappointed, she started to close the Bible when words caught her attention and she began to read. She straightened in her chair and caught her breath. It was as if the astounding words were speaking to her. Finally she sat back to think and then read again.

John Mark had been playing with a spoon, and now with spoon still clenched in his chubby hand, he had collapsed into sleep. She wanted desperately to kiss the smile on his face, even as she heard the scripture echo through her mind, underlining the fears. She dropped to her knees beside the baby and whispered the words from Isaiah, ". . . Neither fear ye their fear, nor be afraid. Sanctify the Lord. . . . Let him be our fear, . . . He shall be . . . a sanctuary; . . . I will wait upon the Lord, . . . I will look for him."

The door banged and Jenny was caught with Mark's Bible on her lap. She looked up at him as he stood by the back door. "Mark! What is it?" she gasped, scrambling to her feet.

She stared into his white face, seeing the deep breath he took before saying, "Jenny, nothing." He was covered with snow, except for one coat sleeve. She touched it, seeing the hole.

"Who did it? And why?"

"Could have been anyone. I couldn't see. In this snow he could have been shooting at a bear."

"Mark, not a bear; not even a deer."

"Look, Jenny. I was shot at. I'm not blaming anyone. Not the Missourians, not the bunch from Warsaw or the Destroying Angels. Let's just forget it. He didn't hit me, and I don't think the miss was an accident. He was pretty close."

She helped him remove the coat. "I can't believe such a hole without touching your arm. Not even your shirt. She flung the coat away and threw her arms around him. "Mark, I—I'm afraid. Did you say 'Destroying Angles'?"

Mark tried to laugh it off. No matter how she pressed, he would say no more, but she saw the anxiety in his eyes.

The following morning when Mark reached Joseph's office, the place was buzzing with activity. Clayton was trying to write a letter. Two strangers were waiting to see Joseph; John D. Lee was perched on a barrel in the hallway discoursing on Mormonism to them, while Hiram Kimball paced the outer room and William Law pounded on Joseph's desk.

When Mark walked in, Joseph's attention diverted from Law to Mark. "Will you find the information on the last land deal and show William the bills of lading on the lumber?"

Law was still snorting in disgust as he followed Mark. "I've never seen such a slipshod office. He's got every worker in town over at the Nauvoo House, and I've begged for weeks to get fellows to work for me. Mark, there's still folks out there waiting for housing. I'm about to take things into my hands and hire out of St. Louis."

Mark was removing his coat. William stopped abruptly and fingered the patch Jenny had stitched over the bullet hole. "What happened?"

Briefly Mark explained. He saw Law's frown, the slanted glance. William dropped his voice. "Think it was the Angels?"

"I try to refrain from thinking so."

"That's not wise." He paced the room, closed the door. When he returned he dropped his voice. "Six months ago, one of the brethren came to me in secrecy to tell me the Destroying Angels had been commissioned to get me. I didn't take him too seriously for a time." He paused. "As Joseph says, a word to the wise is sufficient. Watch the Whittlers next time you walk through town."

They heard the creak of floorboard and Joseph came through the door. He dropped a sheaf of papers on Mark's desk. "Read this report. I need advice. Briefly, President Tyler, in his address to Congress the first of the month, advised setting up military posts along the route of the Oregon Trail to provide security to emigrants and travelers. I propose petitioning Congress to allow us to be that army. I'm asking to be appointed an officer with power to take volunteers and patrol the western borders of the country for the purposes of law and justice."

He left the room and William Law checked the invoices and left. Mark had just begun to read when the explosion of voices from Joseph's office had him running for the outer door. It wasn't the first time visitors had been protected from Joseph's temper.

But it was the first time it had boiled over into the outer office. Joseph Smith came stalking after Hiram Kimball. Mark caught the word *steamboat*. Knowing Kimball owned a number of wharves along the river, he paused to listen to the exchange. Joseph bellowed, "I don't care if you own the water, too! You are stealing the city's right to wharfage. You'll settle the affair and turn the money over to the city or I'll blow up every steamboat in dock!"

John D. Lee came into the outer office and said, "Well that's about as slick a way of getting rid of the froth and troublemakers as I've seen."

Joseph turned and snapped, "What?"

"Those fellas out there. Just time-wasters, wanting to see Joseph for themselves. Asking how many wives you've got. But you started yelling and they decided they had business down the street."

Joseph was still frowning as he took his hat and coat and headed for the door.

John followed Mark into his office. "How's that pretty little wife of yours? Did I hear right about you havin' a young'un?"

Mark sat down to answer Lee's questions and listen to his rambling talk. After a few moments of lighthearted chatter, Lee turned to a serious subject. "Cartwright, how's this spiritual wife doctrine settin'?"

"With me?" He paused. "I know little about it. The Prophet gave us initial teaching on it. He hasn't pushed to make me add to my family. So all this means is that I'm safe so far. Lee, I think you know me well enough to know I'll buck it all the way."

Lee scrutinized Mark. "You'll be your own man," he said slowly, looking down at his hands. He slanted a glance at Mark. "I advise you to walk more careful. Joseph's touchy right now. Seems he's very impatient with slow learners."

"Are you warning me, John?" The man looked surprised, and Mark continued. "Last night, on my way home, someone took a shot at me."

John squinted at Mark. "Given the climate around here right now, I'm not surprised. Just remember Joseph's getting very touchy and impatient. He's mighty fearful about people who talk too much, especially about the celestial kingdom."

"Seems to me Joseph's gone to meddling when it involves marriage."

"He has the keys and the revelations. The pamphlet put out by Jacobs shows people aren't ready for deep teaching. You weren't at council meeting when Joseph said, pointing to William Marks and Parley Pratt, that if he were to reveal the will of God concerning them at that moment, they'd feel called upon to shed his blood. 'Course, he went on to say they should be surrendering themselves to God.

"From the looks on the faces and the consequential action some of the brethren took," Lee continued, "I'd say he managed to give them a mind sensitive to the fear of the Lord. I'm glad to see some of them went marching right up to find out the will of God for them.

"He's not proclaiming it in public now, but there's no need. Having the book of the law of the Lord and just following what the Lord instructs is keeping the Prophet and the Saints pretty busy. But then the Prophet made it pretty clear our obligation. There's just no way, without plural marriage, that man can attain to the fullness of the gospel. Joseph's made it clear that we've got to learn to be gods ourselves, especially in order to be equal with our Savior."

Lee paused a moment and then added, "Personally, I think some of those who were not living up to their religion took it pretty hard when Joseph advised their spouses that their marriage relations weren't valid on account of not having an authority to hear their vows. He did give them liberty to go if they wanted. This living together and having children when there's alienation between the two is just plain sin. The pamphlet made that clear."

John Lee got to his feet to leave and then turned to Mark. "How do you feel about all this talk of Joseph running for president of the United States?"

"I guess I haven't heard enough to give it much thought," Mark said slowly.

Joseph came stomping into the office, shaking snow from his clothes. "Well, the High Council's just started pressuring me to throw my hat into the ring. I couldn't take them seriously for a time. Seems now I'll have to, just to keep peace among the brethren." He chuckled and threw himself into Mark's chair.

"First off, there's a need to get feelers out. I intend to send out letters to every candidate and see just how they'll stand on the Mormon question. Mark, that's where I'll need your help. I need a little touch of culture to the whole affair. If it doesn't go any further than raising a little dust, at least by the time it's all over, Congress will see we're a force that merits respect and recognition."

"Joseph," Mark argued mildly, "you can't raise enough votes to do anything except make a fool of yourself."

"I intend to claim two hundred thousand. With the converts we're adding to the church, I'm certain of this number." He jumped to his feet and headed out of the room.

"There's less than twelve thousand people living right in Nauvoo," Mark objected.

He looked at John D. Lee's long face as he started to leave Mark's office. "Here I go again," he muttered. "I can see me stomping. It's hard enough to preach the gospel out there without a cent to keep me going, not to mention the ridicule I get. But to go out there and build up Joseph for president of the United States with the kind of reputation he has . . ." He was still shaking his head when he closed the door behind himself.

Mark was still sitting at his desk, staring at Joseph's papers and thinking, when the Prophet returned to his office. "By the way, Mark, gird up your loins. Within the next month or so the organization of the Council of Fifty will get off the ground. I want you in it, and I won't take no for an answer."

Mark looked up at him. "I was just sitting here wondering what other mountain you'll climb. President of the United States . . ." He paused to shake his head and then held up his fingers. "At this time you are mayor of Nauvoo, judge of the municipal court, merchant of the biggest store in town, hotel-keeper, head of the temple building committee, real estate agent, contractor; you handle the recording of deeds in town; you own a steamboat; you are the sole trustee for the financial affairs of the church, lieutenant-general of the Nauvoo Legion, spiritual advisor, and head of the church."

"You can't guess what will be next?" Joseph chuckled, "Stay close, Mark, you'll see. You know the Lord has willed this church to be spread around the world. I aim to see that happen."

"You're an ambitious man, Joseph."

"I have my failings. But I'm also a tried man. There's a constant warfare between the two natures of man."

"Do you believe the Lord wants that?" Mark asked. "The Bible says we are to live above sin, to not be entangled in the things that hold us slaves to sin."

"Every man has equal chance at salvation. It is true, however, that some men have a greater capacity of improving their minds and controlling their passions through denying unrighteousness and cultivating the principles of purity. We all have our free agency. It lies with the power of mankind to rise above and claim eternal life—if only man will be faithful to God's will and obey the priesthood in these last days."

That evening when Mark reached home, Jenny was at the door to meet him. She brushed snow from him and anxiously searched his face. "Did . . . did—how was your day?"

"Fine. Uneventful, unless you consider it exciting to hear the Prophet threaten to blow up the steamboats in the harbor and admit he's considering running for the office of president of the United States."

Jenny stared at him for a moment and then slowly said, "I knew you would be tired; I milked the cows."

35

IT WAS A bright February day. The clouds were scooting across the sky like kites and the air was filled with the smells of spring. Jenny spent the day airing bedding and washing linens. A new lamb wobbled in the pasture and she carried John Mark out to see the little creature.

Loath to return to her kitchen tasks, she lingered at the pasture fence, balancing the baby and letting the wind rip through her hair. What a sense of freedom the blithe wind gave!

Watching the air billow her skirt and apron, she closed her eyes and pretended she was a kite. John Mark drooled on her neck and she laughed at him. "You will remind me that I'm only your dinner ticket! But that's all right." She fell to musing over the contrasts in her life.

The thoughts made Jenny shiver. Less than two years ago she had been Jenny the witch. Closing her eyes she contemplated the darkness of that time, measuring it by thinking her way back into the pattern of that life, with its promises and desires.

She considered the charms, even the talisman. "Is it possible?" she gasped. "Was I really like that?" For a moment she clung to the thought of the talisman. She had told Tom she regretted getting rid of it, for one reason—Mark. As she thought of their early love, she began to yearn for the power the talisman had given. "Face it, Jenny," she whispered. "Without that talisman, Mark would have never married you."

For a long time Jenny stared out across the pasture, scarcely aware of the pattern of bright green and yellow. When, with a sigh, she turned toward the house, she was caught up short. The weather-beaten house seemed tiny and dismal, but instead of the peeling gray paint she saw sharp views of the life it had sheltered for nearly three years now.

"Then there were two, now there are three. Then there was Jenny the witch, now—" Abruptly she recalled Mark's face. Did the light in his eyes, the tender smile, tell her something about herself that she had failed to see?"

With her eyes closed she considered herself now—the questions, the Bible. Now her eyes popped open, recalling: "The Lord is my shepherd;

. . . I lie down in green pastures: I am come that they might have life, more abundantly. Except a man be born again, he cannot see the kingdom of God. For God so loved that he gave his Son. For by grace are ye saved through faith, the gift of God." John Mark pressed his head against her and she opened her eyes and smiled down at him. And then in a moment the sweet peace of the words moved away from her.

"Beautiful words," she whispered, "but I don't understand them. God, are You there listening? Please—"

With a troubled sigh she turned and walked to the house. The thoughts contained in that Book were bigger than life and beyond her understanding. But even worse than not being able to understand were all the fearful things Joseph had threatened.

In the pasture the mare whinnied and she looked toward the road. A buggy was coming, moving rapidly down the lane toward her. She waited, fearful and uneasy, then her eyes widened. It was William and Jane Law. As they got out of the buggy, William appeared troubled. "Come in," she said slowly.

"Is Mark at home?"

"No, but he will be soon. I'll fix some tea for us."

As soon as Jenny placed John Mark on the floor, he began to cry. Jane Law picked him up and carried him into the parlor.

The teakettle was throwing steam into the air and Jenny was placing cups and saucers beside the plate of cookies when Mark walked in. She heard the surprise in his voice as he welcomed the Laws.

Just as she carried the tea tray into the parlor, William offered Mark a newspaper, saying, "Have you seen this?"

"No, I haven't."

William read aloud: " 'You and your followers have considered yourselves a separate nation just as much as any foreign nation. Because of this, and because your tribe indicates a desire to cast off all ties relative to the government, while at the same time you take it upon yourself to create a new one more to your liking, we consider this action treason.' This is the *Warsaw Signal*, February 15, 1844." While the men were still looking at each other, William spoke again. "You know Joseph has supported his own ideas by saying any people trying to govern themselves under laws of their own making are in direct rebellion against the kingdom of God."

Slowly Mark said, "We find ourselves, by following the Nauvoo Charter, being regarded as guilty of treason."

William Law added the next thought. "Yet to fail to do so puts us in jeopardy of our souls."

Mark continued, "If, in fact, the Nauvoo Charter is God's will."

William Law took a deep breath and said, "Nearly a year ago I approached Joseph and accused him of engaging in practices which the Christian church has always regarded as iniquity. I challenged him to reform himself and the doctrine he is pushing on the church. I tried to force him into confessing his sins and cleaning up the church, with the threat that I would reveal his acts to the world if he failed to do so. He refused."

Mark said heavily, "We'd all guessed you and the Prophet were having troubles, particularly when he referred to you as the Judas. What are you going to do about this?"

"I don't know, Mark. It deeply troubles me."

"Have you considered leaving the church?"

Jenny saw the way both of the Laws reacted to the question. William said, "Mark, I blame most of these troubles on Dr. John Bennett. Joseph isn't a false prophet. I believe he's fallen from grace and I'll do anything in my power to help him and restore truth and integrity to the church. But leave? I can't, for the sake of my soul."

Mark leaned forward. "I wish I could persuade you otherwise. From reading the Bible, seeing the promise of salvation through Jesus Christ, I believe Joseph is deluded, walking completely away from the biblical foundation of truth and righteousness in Jesus Christ. With all my heart I would like to see you, and others who feel the same, leave."

"What about you?"

"Someday, but not now."

"Mark!" The exclamation burst from Jenny and he turned to look at her. His eyes were pleading but she felt only the sensation of being wind-tossed away from a sure foundation.

William admitted, "There are others like us—a group who have reason to be unhappy and uneasy under Joseph's changing role. Mark, we want you to meet with us and let's attempt to find a solution to the problem. It isn't to be a gripe session, although one purpose will be candor with each other. None of us realizes the depths to which the other has suffered under the controls Joseph has put upon us. Will you come next week to the meeting at Higbee's store? Bring your wife and son."

When the Laws stood to leave, William said, "You realize, don't you, that these problems won't be resolved immediately? We may be months hearing grievances and trying to come to a solution."

Slowly Mark said, "I honestly wonder if we will have that much time." He tapped the newspaper William held.

It was Relief Society day. The mild February weather encouraged Jenny to make the trip into town. "Three months since we've been to meeting," Jenny informed the laughing John Mark as she bundled him and tied him to the seat beside her. He crowed with delight as the mare smartly clipped off the miles into town.

At meeting, Jenny had just settled down with her quilt block when Sally came into the room. Jenny waved at her friend and made room for her on the bench. "You're looking poorly; you've lost weight," she whispered with a worried frown. Sally nodded without answering. Jenny watched her slowly assemble her quilt block and began to stitch.

Jenny leaned forward to whisper, "You caught?"

Sally's eyebrows lifted but she shook her head. "Just feeling poorly. Like I can hardly drag."

"Why don't you come home with me? I'll fix supper for us all and you can rest."

Sally shook her head. "Tamara. She'll be out of school before Andy's home. You come to us."

Sally continued to answer in monosyllables. Feeling more compelled than curious, Jenny followed Sally home.

When she saw the disarray of Sally's house, Jenny turned to Sally with a worried frown. "I think you are very ill, or there's something desperately wrong somewhere. Will you please talk to me?"

Jenny saw the tears in Sally's eyes and put her arms around her. "Oh, Jenny, it's really nothing I can put my finger on. It's just life is so—" She paused to rub at her eyes and then tried to smile. "Jen, I've everything a woman could possibly want, yet . . . I'm in the true church, and we're both living up to our religion. I have a beautiful daughter, a nice home . . ." Her voice trailed away and she moved away from Jenny.

"You tried suicide last year and now you're scarcely living. I suppose I shouldn't pry, but thinking of last year, I'm afraid to not insist you talk." Sally's hands trembled as she mopped at her eyes.

Jenny took charge. "Go sit in that rocking chair. Here, rock John Mark. He's nursed and ready for sleep. I'm going to make things a little brighter around here."

She nudged Sally toward the chair and turned to shove the teakettle to the front of the stove. "I'm going to boil some eggs for you. Where's the bread?"

After Sally had eaten, she allowed Jenny to lead her upstairs. "Now you stay there until you sleep. I'm going to sweep the floor and wash the dishes."

While Jenny had her hands in the dishwater, washing the piles of dirty dishes stacked around the kitchen, she began to think.

Sally was living up to her religion. Jenny recalled how she'd always admired and envied the composed, elegant Sally—the woman who looked as if she'd never sinned in her life.

But at the picnic last August Sally had confessed her problem to Jenny. Jenny's hands moved slowly in the water.

With a sigh she said, "Seems if the Lord were in this marrying, Sally should feel like the most holy woman in town. Seems, too, I should feel differently about Joseph's proposal to me." Sally had the witness of the rightness of the marriage. Knowing should have taken care of the guilt.

Jenny addressed the ceiling. "Seems, God, You ought to have been able to take care of her guilt. She's feeling so bad about the situation. If she's got guilt, I sure don't want this to happen to me. But what about John Mark? Seems, God, I'm getting to the place where I don't want to have anything to do with being holy. I just can't forget the promises Mark and I made. When it comes right down to it, I just guess I don't want to be a queen of heaven."

She was scrubbing the pot, crusty with burned-on food, when she looked ceilingward again. "If there's another way on earth to settle my eternity without displeasing You, I'd jump in a minute. Right now the biggest problem I have on my mind is how to make certain my little baby isn't left out."

Jenny found a chunk of meat and some vegetables. By the time she had the meat browned and the vegetables peeled and snugged around the roast, she had managed to shove aside her own needs. Sally's were critical.

When John Mark began to cry and Sally came into the kitchen with him, Jenny had found the Bible. She took the baby and sat in the rocker. Sally sat at the table and touched the Bible.

"Is that your solution to it all?"

Jenny chewed her lip, wondering how much she could force herself to say. "Sally, religion isn't working for either one of us. You know Mark's against endowment. You know what Joseph had to say about sealing our posterity. Well, in a way I'm just as troubled about my religion as you are. Seems you are living up to it as well as a body possibly could, and it's not doing a thing for you except making you desperately unhappy. I sure wouldn't settle for what you're having. So, it seems we both need to look for a better way.

"Months ago Joseph told me I ought to be studying the Scriptures. I started out reading the *Book of Mormon* and then the Bible. Well, I've ended up reading just the Bible. Mostly because I'm discovering it's teaching me things, like the fact that God loves us and He's trying to help us along the way.

"Sally, I fear for you. Unless you pull yourself up short and begin to make some progress with the Lord, I don't think you're going to—"

"Keep living?" Sally sighed.

"Why don't you begin by reading in the book of John?"

"I've read it before."

"Did you believe what you read? Jesus came to give us life. If we believe in Him we'll spend eternity with Him." Jenny chewed her lip. "Come to think of it, if we can spend eternity with Him, just by accepting the idea He's died for our sins so we don't have to—well then, where will Joseph be? If he is there, well then, I think we've found an easier way to get to the same place."

"Oh, Jenny, you're making my head whirl!"

Jenny looked at Sally in dismay. "I'm sorry. I want so badly to help you, but I just don't know how. I'm not happy with my religion and you're not happy with yours. According to what Joseph's been teaching, you've progressed a lot further than I have. Just looking at your sad face and seeing the mess of things, I can't say I envy you one bit."

Sally cradled her head on the book and began to cry. In desperation Jenny looked down at John Mark, "Young'un, hurry with your dinner."

To Sally she said, "While we're waiting on John Mark, turn to the eighth chapter of John and start reading. About verse thirty-one, I think. I don't understand it all, so maybe you can help me, too."

Wearily Sally pushed herself up and began thumbing through the Bible. She found the section, then slowly said, "This is to the Jews."

"Well, didn't Joseph talk about our blood being changed into children-of-Israel blood when we got baptized? So I'm thinking it must apply to us."

She looked down at the words and said, "Well, He's telling the Jews if they *continue* in His word, they are His disciples." She paused to read silently and when she lifted her head there was a wondering excitement in her voice. "It says here that they'd know the truth and the truth would make them free. Jenny, is Jesus *promising* that if we read this Word, it's going to make us free?"

"It sounds like it, doesn't it? Almost makes me think I dare not read! But go on—there's more, and it's so big I can hardly get my mind around it."

Sally frowned, but dutifully she bent over the Book. She murmured the words: "The Jews tell Jesus they're not in bondage—like us, huh? We have the promises. But Jesus tells them that if they sin, they're a servant of sin." She shifted impatiently and lifted her head. "Jenny, this isn't helping at all. I just don't understand—"

Jenny urged, "Go ahead, read some more. It's the next part that won't leave me alone."

" 'If the Son therefore shall make you free, ye shall be free indeed.' "

Jenny was speaking softly. "There's more, in another place He says He's the way, the truth and the life and that no man comes to the Father except through Him. And He says that if we keep His Word, He'll love us and *manifest* Himself to us. I think it's meaning we'll get to know Him."

It was getting late. Regretfully Jenny got to her feet. "Sally, I've got to go home. Mark will be there. I've put supper on to cook for you." She reached out to touch her friend. "Please read more, and *hope* in what you read."

She lingered a moment longer. The shadows were back in Sally's eyes and Jenny felt her sadness as she turned to leave.

36

"OH, MARK, HE isn't a baby anymore!" Jenny wailed, but she couldn't help beaming down at John Mark. The toddler, standing on sturdy legs, teetered slightly as he tilted his head to look up.

Mark crouched down, carefully patted the crown of bright curls and surveyed the little blue and white suit. "Looks like a little sailor in that outfit. Wanna go fishing with Pa?" John Mark crowed and launched himself toward his father.

"Well, it's to Sabbath meeting right now," Jenny said, turning to watch the baby stagger across the floor.

"He's as efficient as a toy boat in a mud puddle," Mark chuckled as John Mark steered clear of the kitchen stove, bounced off the wall, and headed back.

"Andy and Sally are bringing Helene to dinner after meeting. If we see Tom, let's bring him home too."

"I don't expect to see him," Mark stated, getting to his feet. He looked at Jenny. "Tom's one of the strugglers right now."

"What do you mean by that?" Jenny put the lid on the roaster and shoved it into the oven. "With another piece of wood in there now, we'll have dinner as soon as we get home."

"I'll wait a few minutes," Mark said. He was still studying her face and Jenny looked up. "Tom is beginning to wonder if he wants to push on with Joseph's teachings. You know he's been asked to join in the Council of Fifty."

"What's that?"

Mark shrugged. "I can tell you little, my dear, except that right now Joseph is causing a flurry among some of the men, the ones to whom he's revealed the kingdom of God secrets."

"Not you? Not his prize attorney?"

"That's correct. And there's good reason for that. From what I've gathered just by observing, the men come out of those meetings feeling one of two ways."

"I don't understand."

"They're either elated—walking on air, or they're scared, angry, and depressed."

She studied him for a moment before saying slowly, "Mark, at Relief Society there's been some of the women acting the same way. The whispers about spiritual wives are growing into more than the usual snickers and teasing.

"I'm seeing troubled women. Embarrassed ones. Some are whispering that their husbands are angry, threatening to leave the church. They mentioned the fact that the *Book of Mormon* teaches against polygamy, calling it a whoredom.

"Others are outraged, like the Laws. They want a change. I know for a fact that some of the families have invested a great deal of money in the church to build the temple and buy property."

She turned to pick up John Mark's sweater and her shawl. Mark hesitated and then said, "Jenny, I have a feeling that trouble's brewing out there. We may be called upon to make some big decisions, and in a hurry."

She saw his eyes, but her fearful thoughts were running ahead. *The church, the endowments, John Mark.*

After Sabbath meeting, while Mark and Jenny were walking back to their buggy, they listened to the couple in front of them. The woman was saying, "Why does Joseph keep talking about polygamy? Nearly every week he seems to feel called to deny a new charge."

Her husband replied, "I'd like to know why Joseph keeps bringing up the Missouri issue. I'm sick of being reminded of those bad days. If he'd just let sleeping dogs lie, we'd all be better off. The good Book tells us to forgive, and I think that's pretty good advice."

When they reached the buggy, Mark said, "Well, what are *you* thinking?"

She looked surprised. "I was thinking about what Brother Kimball said a couple of weeks ago, comparing it to the *Book of Mormon.* Mark, the *Book of Mormon* says there's no chance for a person after death. I take that to mean there's not one thing a person can do to change where he'll spend eternity once he dies."

Mark nodded. "That's right, and the Bible agrees."

"But," she continued, "Brother Kimball indicates these sinners will go to hell, have the corruption burned out of them and then end up in heaven as servants. Then the sermon today talked about the unredeemed being angels forever."

"I heard it too," he said looking at her with a quizzical frown.

"And there's no chance for an angel to be a god?"

"Well, not according to the church doctrine. Jenny, what is troubling you?"

"Well, then, I can't understand how an angel named Michael can become Adam who was God. That's the creation story."

Tom was waiting for them when they reached home. But his happy grin disappeared when the Morgans' buggy wheeled in behind them. "Oh," Mark groaned. "Poor Tom; he'll have to put up with Helene."

After dinner Tom and Helene, with Tamara in tow, disappeared down the lane while Mark and Andy wandered out to the barn. Jenny settled John Mark for his nap and began the dishes. "Sally, why don't you just sit in the rocking chair and talk to me?"

She was shaking her head as Jenny spoke. Seeing the dark shadows in her eyes and her restless pacing, Jenny handed her a dish towel. They worked in silence until Jenny said, "How are you feeling now?"

Sally shook her head. After another long silence, she said, "The worst part is deceiving Andy. It's getting to the place where I can't pretend any longer, and he thinks it's his fault."

"Why don't you just ask him to take you away from here?"

"That wouldn't solve the past; besides, remember, I'm earning my right to the eternities."

Jenny finished scrubbing the roaster and turned to Sally. "Have you been reading in the Bible?" She shook her head and Jenny stood watching her helplessly. Finally she said, "The only person I can think of who'd be able to help you is Mark. He knows so much about the Bible—"

Sally turned and looked at Jenny with a puzzled frown, and Jenny realized the separation between them. "Sally, I should have told you. I believe the Bible is God speaking to me, telling me how to live, what to think about Him. He tells me about sin and forgiveness. The words in the Book give hope when it seems impossible." She paused and searched Sally's face. "Do you understand?"

"I understand that you have changed. You used to use the charms and the secret things. They frightened me, mostly because of the way you looked when you used them. But they were mysterious and exciting, too. Now—you're talking about the Bible, and Joseph says it isn't translated correctly. He says corrupt men have done this. Jenny, I'm too fearful to trust when you say *trust* and he says *don't*."

The look on Sally's face told Jenny that she had closed the door.

In the late afternoon the Morgans left for home. Mark stood beside Jenny as the buggy rambled down the lane. He saw the hopeless expression on Jenny's face as she turned away.

Tom was saying, "Come on, Mark, let's go try that new fishing pole of yours."

"In the river?" Jenny asked slowly. "Well, go along. I don't want to hike down that steep bank. Maybe I'll bake a ginger-cake."

Mark led the way across the pasture and into the woods. "There's a pretty good path right through here, and I've managed to trample it down. I'd like to get a good-sized bass. Think this pole is strong enough?" He peered at Tom. "Something wrong?"

"Naw, not much. Just talk again. There's a rumor floatin' around that the Lodge is in trouble. Seems the Grand Worshipful Master from Springfield is a mite upset. They're claiming we're corrupting the Masonic ritual. They've ordered Joseph to send the records into Springfield, and he's takin' his time about doin' it. I 'spect we'll lose out yet. Mostly I don't like them charging us with bein' clandestine, whatever that's supposed to mean."

They scrambled down the last slope and made their way out on the rocks. Tom continued, "Seems to me that the Lodge was the best thing that's happened to the church in a long time. Seemed to give us new direction."

In silence Mark threaded the line and Tom baited the hook. Then he handed the pole to Tom. "Here, you use it first."

Tom cast out and flashed an approving grin. "That's smooth!" They settled down on the rocks and watched the line drift.

Mark shifted his weight on the rock and heard the clink of metal. As he turned toward the sound he saw the disk catch the sun as it dropped from the rock to the sandy shore. "I wonder—might be a coin," he murmured, jumping off the rock.

"Got a bite," Tom said. "Aw, lost the bait." He pulled in the line and reached for the worms as Mark crawled up on the rock. "Well, what did you find?"

Mark pulled the disk out of his pocket. "Thought it was a dollar, but it seems to be some kind of medallion."

Tom dropped his line into the water and turned to take the medal. "Looks like lead. Hey, there's writing and numbers on it. I bet that's Jenny's. She mentioned having a talisman and was wishing she had it back."

"Did she lose it?" Mark asked, studying the curious disk.

"I can't rightly remember. All I know is she was wishing for it. Seems it means a great deal to her—more'n a good luck charm." Tom turned quickly, "There!"

Mark watched him pulling in a big bass. Tom grinned up at him. "Might be, if she doesn't want it, you ought to be using it for fishing. Sure works."

When they walked into the kitchen, Tom held out the fish and sniffed hungrily. "Well, here's supper. I'll trade for some of that cake."

He put the fish on the table. "Jen, is this your talisman? Mark found it down on the rocks."

Mark saw the color leave Jenny's face as she took a hesitant step toward Tom and slowly reached for the disk. For a moment, before her hand closed around it, Mark thought she was going to refuse it.

He watched her close her fingers around it and tuck it into her pocket. Then he remembered why the little disk seemed familiar. This was the talisman he had seen lying beside her mittens on the mantel of their cabin in Missouri.

37

THE FIRST MONDAY in March, on the way into Nauvoo, Mark met Orson Pratt and they completed the ride together.

Orson said, "March is in like a lamb; does this foreshadow life roaring like a lion in Nauvoo this spring?"

Mark looked at him. "Not unless you know more about life than I do. As of last week I was thinking life had tamed down a bit."

"Well, I know Joseph's been touching men for the honor of being on the Council of Fifty. He's calling them princes and saying this will be the highest court on earth."

As Mark continued to listen to Pratt, pricks of apprehension began to make him uneasy. Orson interrupted himself to ask, "You've been asked, haven't you?"

Slowly Mark said, "Yes, but I'm beginning to wonder what I'm getting into." Pratt's eyes were sparkling. Mark said, "I suppose it's just a juvenile fear of the unknown. But I hope Joseph's kept the rest of you men better informed than he has me."

When Mark walked up the stairs to the office, he found Tom waiting for him. "Well, Brother Tom, I didn't expect to see you this early in the morning. Clayton, yes, Joseph, maybe, but Tom, no." Now he noticed Tom's grin was uneasy.

He glanced at Joseph's door and Tom said, "He ain't here yet, that's how come I am."

"Spill it; he'll be here shortly."

"You been tapped for the Council of Fifty?" Mark nodded. "Planning on joining?"

"Do I have a choice?"

"On account of Jenny? Maybe not. I come a-beggin' you to do it." Mark let his eyebrows express his feelings. "I know," Tom added. "But there's some weird things a-movin' into town. We're goin' to need some normality to the proceedings."

"Thanks, Brother," Mark said. Tom let his chair crash down on all four legs as he headed for the door.

Tom's eyes under the thatch of straw-colored hair were as bright as marbles. "She still got the talisman?"

Mark shrugged. "I suppose so." Tom left the room and clattered down the stairs.

John Mark was sitting in the middle of the kitchen floor pounding his wooden spoon on a tin pie pan.

Balancing the talisman on her fingertips, Jenny stood beside the stove. In the two weeks since the charm had been returned to her, Jenny had pondered the significance behind its return. Night and day, the thoughts had nagged her.

Jenny sighed and carried her brooding thoughts into the parlor away from John Mark's clatter. She sat in the chair beside the table and looked at her Bible. Strange, she mused, it was starting to look like Mark's, with the edges curling out in that inviting manner, suggesting all sorts of interesting things inside.

She murmured the verse she had discovered yesterday: "And Elijah came unto all the people, and said, 'How long halt ye between two opinions? If the Lord be God, follow Him: but if Baal, then follow him.' And the people answered him not a word."

She closed her eyes and let the thought drift through her, to carry where it would. "Mark," she whispered, and her fingers tightened around the talisman. When she felt the tears on her face, she knew that she had decided.

She addressed the Presence. "I won him by unfair means with the talisman. I deserve to lose him. But more than that, the Book is telling me that I can't claim anything of God. The knowing, the gentle love of Jesus, the promise that's leading me along—none of this is mine unless I do just as those people in the book of Acts did when they burned the charms and books."

With a sigh, Jenny got out of the chair and then paused. For only a moment did she hesitate; then quickly, while she dared, she ran up the stairs and pulled out of the trunk a paper-wrapped parcel.

Back in the kitchen Jenny lifted the stove lid and shoved the green book and the talisman in. John Mark abandoned his pie pan and came to stand beside her. He looked up at her with the solemn blue-green eyes of his father.

The book caught fire and the talisman slipped down through the ashes. Jenny replaced the lid and knelt to take John Mark in her arms. "Da?" he questioned, and she buried her tears in his blue sailor suit.

After Jenny fed John Mark and carried him up the stairs, she found it impossible to leave him. Together they snuggled under the quilt. She watched as his eyes closed, and kissed the damp hand he flung at her.

She slept, and she dreamed. Rising out of sleep she was conscious of the spiraling, the flash of the silver chalice, and the wash of purple wine. The words were on her lips, "I baptize thee in the name of Jesus Christ." Jenny took a deep breath and was conscious of relaxing, sinking into the softness of sleep.

Mark and Orson rode home together, each silent and heavy with thoughts of that first council meeting. Mark wondered if Orson was signifying by his silence that he, too, was feeling the slash of words, the violation.

Just before they reached the Pratt farm turnoff, Orson tilted his head and looked at the full moon. "Guess it takes a man who is called of God, one who's communed with the Almighty, to put forth a vision no mortal would dare dream."

Mark's heart sank; he couldn't think of a reply. Orson continued, "I nearly need to pinch myself. Imagine what this world's going to be like in another few years! Somehow I can see Joseph striding along, king of the whole world, but I just can't see a humble man like me." He turned, "I suppose the biggest fear is trying to imagine handling the people like a monarch is supposed to."

He looked curiously at Mark. "You're his attorney; did you have any idea that he was going to be made king of the kingdom of God?"

Jenny and Mark were at the breakfast table when Tom came. John Mark had porridge running down his chin and he was crowing his delight at the world. "Birthday boy," Jenny said; she was kissing his curls when the door opened.

Seeing his face, she whispered, "Tom." He crossed the kitchen and dropped heavily into a chair at the table.

Fingering the knife and fork lying there, he said, "I couldn't take having you find out when you drove into Nauvoo. And I knew you'd want to go to the funeral."

They waited, and finally he lifted his head. "Sally." After another pause, "Andy's takin' it pretty hard. She'd taken something."

Jenny was rubbing her numb lips, saying, "Less than three weeks ago— oh, Mark, I could see—I tried to tell her about reading the Bible. I felt so helpless, but I honestly didn't think this would happen. It's my fault, isn't it?"

"How could you possibly think that?" She shook her head and pressed her lips together.

The events only became real to Jenny as she stood in the shady grove, seeing the long wooden box, the somber faces, the dark coats. Andy was holding Tamara in his arms.

While the tears began streaming down Jenny's face, she caught a glimpse of Andy, and a burning anger began to move through Jenny.

Jenny and some of the other women went home with Andy and Tamara to help out. They stuck spring flowers in a water glass and positioned them in the middle of Sally's table. They made the house neat, but it was chilled, and quiet. There was nothing more to do for the silent man surrounded by the hedge of Saints. Jenny took her shawl and left.

On the steps she paused. Surprisingly the sun was shining, and it was spring. John Mark's birthday month; life was still moving on. She took a deep breath and felt the dredges of her anger surfacing.

Mark had taken John Mark, freeing her to set order to Sally's empty house. Walking slowly down the street, she turned toward Mark's office, caring little that her black skirt was dragging in the dust. *If Joseph is right, then Sally's secure in the eternities, holding forever the position as Joseph's queen.*

And if he was wrong? She lifted her head and began slowly walking up the stairs to the office. Somehow she knew he was.

A solitary person occupied the office—Joseph, not Mark. He turned and she briefly saw his troubled face until it lightened into a smile. "You've come to see me?"

"No, I was looking for Mark. He has the baby."

"I know. Nice-looking tot. He's headed for home with him. Said something about diapers."

Looking at him, for a moment, Jenny burned with anger. Trying to calm herself, she shuffled ideas—that talisman belonging to Joseph, the surging unrest moving throughout the Mormon kingdom, the whispers and fears. Her own secret, which she had not dared reveal to Sally.

For a moment she was caught wondering. If she had told Sally of her own secret shame, would Sally still be alive? She shivered, nearly sick with the thought.

"You've lost your friend." Joseph was speaking with a brooding air. "I'm sorry. I'm also guessing that the loss has made you aware of your precarious position." She studied the stuffy words and watched as he turned from the window.

He straightened his shoulders under the funeral black of his silk coat. One hand, the one wearing the heavy gold ring, moved to smooth his hair.

"Queen of heaven?" She moved restlessly. "Joseph, are you aware of *how* she died?"

He nodded and the sadness touched his face, leaving it colorless. The blue of his eyes, intensified by his pallor, possessed her attention momentarily. In that second, nothing else existed.

She moved and turned away. "Do you see your part in this?"

"My dear, obviously Sally was weak, unable to handle the pressures of life. I must say it takes a strong, magnificent woman to live up to the promises of heaven extended through the priesthood. Don't blame me for her death. I've only acknowledged the pressure of the mighty hand of God upon my life. I dared not live otherwise."

"I know Sally wanted more than anything to escape hell and please God. Andy is a good Mormon; why couldn't she have been sealed to him instead of you?"

"Because the Lord gave her to me, just as he gave you to me. Are you going to tempt the Lord until you become another Sally—unable to face life?"

Busy with her thoughts, she didn't answer, and he said, "Jenny, come here."

She turned and he was holding out his arms, smiling. "And if I refuse?"

"You won't. You're just as fearful of failing to live up to your religion as Sally was—only my dear, I've more confidence in your strength. Also, remember that little boy."

Jenny trembled, but at the same moment she felt an unexpected strength slipping into her. She remembered the dream of the chalice. Strange how that wine seemed to flow over her when she needed it most! Wine. Blood. The blood of Jesus. The atoning sacrifice. No more sins, nothing to be escaped. She considered.

"Joseph, why is it so much easier for people to do something for their own salvation rather than just believe in an unseen gift?" She didn't wait for his answer.

"Remember? I told you to leave me alone or I would tell Emma."

"Go right ahead. She won't believe you. Emma chooses to see only what she wishes to see. She will deny the spiritual wife doctrine."

He was still waiting and smiling, confident now.

Jenny turned and walked toward the door. "Joseph, I want you to hear this. I renounce the church, your revelations, your gold book. I renounce the doctrine of spiritual wives. Just as God tenderly led me to the place where I shed the fear of the spirits and was able to renounce witchcraft, now I am being led to renounce you and all you stand for.

"I tremble with fear—you've put that into me. But I also cling to Jesus Christ. In reading God's Word, I can't see that He wants anything of me except my belief, and that seems such a little thing to do for Him. But I have to trust in the *littleness* of my doing, and believe if there's more He wants of me, He'll tell me."

"You've nothing to go on," Joseph said, his face glowing as he lifted it. "I've the personal revelation of the Lord."

"I had the personal revelation of a beautiful woman who disappeared when I clung to the name of Jesus Christ." She paused and thoughtfully said, "I know that when I started reading the Holy Bible and reaching out toward Jesus, I found out about the One who was God, the Savior who died for my sins—all of them—so that I didn't need to die—"

Joseph turned away. He shoved his hands into his pockets. "Apostate. Totally and completely apostate. Jenny, I'll give you until the middle of June to repent, and I will not come to you begging. When you repent, let me know."

38

JENNY WAS NEARLY home before the brooding heaviness settled down over her spirit. She had sailed out of Joseph's office with the sure knowledge that she had taken a firm step in the right direction. But as she rode homeward the troubles swept over her. Sally was gone. Andy was stunned, alone. Dark, fearful undercurrents swept through Joseph's kingdom, and she had just told him she wanted no part of it.

But she had a part. A document still existed with her name beside Joseph's. He had issued his warning.

What possible action could he take against her? The spiritual wife doctrine was being denied right and left. For a fact she knew there were few in Nauvoo who had been instructed in the celestial marriage doctrine. He dared not reprimand her publicly.

She dismissed the question and went back to the other worries. A barrier stood between her and Mark. She closed her eyes, trying to avoid thinking of what she had surrendered when she burned the talisman.

He came out to the buggy to meet her. "I was worried," he said as he cradled John Mark in his arms. "Did you have trouble?"

"No. I went to the office to find you and stayed to talk to Joseph." Shadows came into his eyes, full of unasked questions. At the same moment, she sensed that nudge she was beginning to recognize. *Tell Mark.*

She shook her head and sighed. He held her arm as she stepped out of the buggy. "Take the baby. I'll handle the rig."

At the end of the week Mark carried home the news that Andy was leaving Nauvoo. She asked, "You mean leaving the church?"

He took a deep breath. "I went to see him. He's one angry man. Blames everyone except himself for Sally's death. I'd been worried about her for some time, but I'd guessed there was trouble between the two of them. How do you step into a situation like that?"

Keeping her silence, Jenny shook her head. He added, "He didn't say he was leaving the church, but I wouldn't be surprised. You know there's been a goodly number who've left."

Jenny wanted to question Mark about that, but she didn't dare. He picked up the milk pail and added, "Tomorrow there's to be a meeting over Higbee's store. William Law told me it's important and suggested you come."

"Higbee? Is he in on the rumbling? I thought he was one of Joseph's attorneys."

"He is, and he also has much to be disturbed about." Jenny looked at Mark as he headed for the door.

As the door closed behind him, Jenny said, "Something tells me, husband, that there's a lot going on that you keep to yourself."

John Mark began to bang his wooden spoon on the oven door and Jenny scooped him up. "Diapers, ugh!" As she headed for the stairs, she picked up Mark's jacket. A newspaper tumbled out. She kicked it out of the way and continued up the stairs.

Jenny forgot about the paper as she hurried to prepare their evening meal. When Mark came in, she asked. "Do you mind feeding him these mashed carrots?"

He grinned and kissed her cheek. "Tell you what. Let me go out and chase Indians out of the pasture while *you* feed him carrots." He picked up John Mark and said, "One spray and you get them raw."

At dinner he said, "My coat. Did you see a paper in it?" She nodded and carried it to the table.

"There's two here. Joseph said they weren't his, so I brought them home to read."

"Why don't we subscribe?"

"These are the *Warsaw Message*. After reading a couple, I decided I didn't like the tenor of them. Now I'm not so tender-skinned."

"What do you mean by that?"

"You've heard enough about and from Warsaw to guess the type of coverage they give the Saints."

"Well, I know they've done enough complaining about us; there's a constant stream of tales about Saints taking their cows and everything else."

Later, while Jenny washed dishes, Mark read the papers and commented. "This January 17 paper is really ranting. Says some in their area are talking about exterminating the Mormons. Sounds like Missouri. They're saying that thousands of women and children must be driven out. 'Scattered like leaves before the storm' is his phrase. I get the feeling he's quoting some ruffians with the express purpose of frightening us."

Jenny had hung the dish towel when he added, "The other article isn't quite so benign. He's quit dodging with nice talk, saying, 'Your career of infamy cannot continue but a little longer! Your days are numbered!' No wonder."

"What?"

"Oh, I was thinking it's no wonder Joseph is getting serious about emigrating westward." Jenny lifted her hands in dismay and hastily Mark said, "Don't fret. There's nothing substantial to the talk yet. You know Tom was in on the looking around last fall. Above all, don't be guilty of starting rumors. That's the last thing this community needs right now."

"Mark, you tell me so little. But I get the feeling there's much rumbling going on."

"You'll find out at the meeting. Unfortunately I've been so busy myself I haven't been able to pass the time of day with the grumblers. Might be that's an advantage. Joseph's getting sharp with the troublemakers."

Late the next afternoon, on the way to Higbee's store for the meeting, Mark and Jenny rode past the Morgan house.

Already there were signs of neglect. Jenny winced and Mark reached for her hand, tugging her close to him. Feeling as if her heart would break with weight of unspoken feelings, she looked at him. Strangely, the white line around his lips made her heart lift. Perhaps Mark wasn't totally indifferent to their problems.

The sun was setting as they walked up the stairs at the back of the shop. There were several people in the room. Jenny was conscious of the wary glances the men exchanged while the women continued to sit apart.

When the stairs creaked again they all turned. Jane Law was unwinding the heavy black veil as she followed her husband into the room. Soon another veiled woman entered and Law got to his feet.

"There's no need to advertise our presence with loud talk. Please pull your chairs together." When the rustle had subsided, he continued, "I've talked with a number of you. There have been enough problems and ugly situations arise that several of us decided it was time to take matters into our own hands, to bring together some of the Saints who've expressed a desire to see reformation in Nauvoo before matters are completely out of control."

He paused and then added, "I want you to understand, I'm not trying to destroy the church. I only want to see it brought back to its original purity. I continue to believe that Joseph Smith is a prophet sent from God. However, I believe he's a prophet fallen from grace.

"As a brother, I believe it is my duty to warn him and to go about instigating reformation in the church. If you are in agreement, please lift your hands."

Again he continued, "There are a number of things we need to discuss. We've made plans to assemble for just this purpose. I realize it's an act which will be considered treason by Joseph if it comes to his ears. But if we are united in body and purpose, he will be forced to listen to us."

"Brother," came a voice from the back of the room. "I've been praying for this since Kirtland days. Now we are fighting for our lives as a church body. Reformation or nothing."

A babble of voices rose, and in dismay, Jenny listened to the catalog of wrongs being named. There were labor disputes mentioned and William Law growled out his protests against the edict the Prophet had issued to excommunicate any wealthy man buying land without his permission. Dr. Foster protested the wholesale hording of building materials for the construction of the temple and the Nauvoo House. "We've people living in tents because we can't buy lumber!" His voice was rising and William rumbled out a warning.

And in the end, there was abrupt silence. Slowly William got to his feet; reluctantly he said, "It seems we've still the main point to cover, one which burdens our hearts, and in some way has touched us all.

"I tried my best to handle this problem just between the Prophet and me. He would not listen to me, nor would he seek counsel from elders in the community. In a stormy session I suggested to him that we must have reformation. As deeply as it was needed in Martin Luther's time, we need it in this new church now, before it is too late.

"I pointed this out to Joseph. I remonstrated, even threatening to go before the High Council myself if he didn't do it voluntarily. I insisted he confess his sins and promise repentance or I would expose his monstrous seductions to the world. He told me that he would be damned before he would do so, since that would cause the overthrow of the church.

"Sadly, I believe he has no recourse. The matter must be resolved in a godly manner. It is utterly impossible to think of any other course of action."

Suddenly Dr. Robert Foster jumped to his feet. At the sound of his wavering voice, Jenny turned and saw the shocked face of his wife one second before she buried it in her handkerchief. He was saying, "Brother, you force me to tell you the problems we've had. Unexpectedly one day last winter I arrived home to find my wife and Joseph enjoying a fine meal together. It was the Prophet's bold friendliness and my wife's obvious dismay that alerted me.

"After the Prophet left I insisted my wife tell me what was going on. Of course, in an effort to protect the Prophet, she refused. It was only after a great deal of painful argument and even threats"—he paused to clear his throat before continuing—"that I was able to get the story out of her. It seems the Prophet had been endeavoring to talk her into unlawful intercourse with him by saying the Lord had commanded it. He called it the spiritual wife doctrine."

In the silence, Higbee got to his feet. "You are all aware of the smear of adultery the Prophet falsely spread around my name. I know of others who have been dealt the same blow in an effort to hide the Prophet's sins. My brother is one. William Law's wife has been subjected to pressure and insult. Kimball's wife Sarah has been likewise insulted."

Chauncey Higbee stood. "My brother is right. Let me add that I know for a fact that some of the leading elders have up to ten or twelve wives apiece. These righteous men, flaunting their holiness, are leading a secret life of sin, and at the same time denying it.

"Let me tell you about the *Book of the Law of the Lord*. This book is kept nice and handy at the home of Hyrum Smith, ready to be revealed to unsuspecting women, who are told that it was the Lord Himself who instructed that the names hidden under those seals be placed there. Many a young woman has discovered her own name there when she has opened it in the presence of the Prophet."

With an angry shout, Jackson got to his feet. "I must inform you that there's good evidence of a conspiracy in Nauvoo which could well cost Smith his life. If it is not too late, reformation could help, otherwise . . ."

It was late that night, while Jenny was stuffing the sleepy baby into his nightgown, when Mark gently asked, "Jenny, you are about to cry. Do you need to talk?"

She shoved John Mark into his arms and ran from the room.

Mark kissed the boy and tenderly tucked him into his bed. Although he could hear Jenny's sobs, he lingered until he knew the child was asleep.

Jenny was in the rocking chair. Mark picked her up and sat down, cradling her as gently as if she were John Mark.

When the crying ended, he mopped her eyes and cuddled her face against his shoulder. "You wouldn't do that if you knew!" She cried again.

Finally she could stand the tension no longer. "Oh, Mark, I was one of those women opening the book!"

His heart sank, but he held her close as she sobbed. "I know," he said.

And then out of a long silence, she asked, "You do?"

He spoke quickly, "Jenny, look. I have forgiven you. That's all I have to say. I can't control your life, but I can forgive, and only that is necessary. I won't ask anything, and I'd rather not know."

His arms were tight and warm, reassuring, Jenny decided. She sat up to look at him and in the glow of moonlight she could see the forced smile, the shadowed eyes. "Mark, now I see it as a terrible injustice to you, regardless. I do ask your forgiveness. I've hated it all."

He pulled her head back to his shoulder and they continued to sit in the chair in silence. With a sigh Jenny sat up. "Would it help if I were to tell you that the day Sally was buried, I told Joseph I renounced it all—the church, him, the books, the revelations. All. I just don't accept it as being from God." She spoke gently, "Mark, go up to bed. You're exhausted. I . . . I need to stay here for a time."

Jenny wrapped the shawl about herself and, as Mark went up the stairs, she got back into the rocking chair.

She contemplated the quiet emptiness inside herself. With shame she said, "Oh, Lord Jesus. You told me to tell him; I would have saved us both so much grief if only I had said this weeks ago."

She continued to sit in the chair. Drained emotionally, her thoughts drifted—not toward the disclosures of the evening but instead toward the spiraling change in her life. Mormonism had seemed a step upward from the craft. First she had renounced the craft, and now Joseph's church.

But there was emptiness. She contemplated the flatness of her disappointment. The Bible had promised joy, peace. She felt only emptiness.

Then came the familiar nudge. Now words welled up, and this time she listened as Jesus said, "Verily, verily, I say unto thee, except a man be born again, he cannot see the kingdom of God." And then in a moment she was murmuring the words, "If thou shalt confess with thy mouth the Lord Jesus, and shalt believe in thine heart that God hath raised Him from the dead, thou shalt be saved."

She sat up straight. "Jesus Christ, You are God and You came to this earth to die for my sins. I believe that I don't have to do anything but accept Your gift to me."

Jenny began to cry, but when she could, she ran upstairs. "Mark!" She shook him, burrowing in with him and putting her arms around him. "Mark! Why didn't you tell me about how I'd feel?"

He came up out of the pillows and blinked at her. Seeing the joy in her eyes, he pulled her into his arms and said, "Thank you, Lord Jesus." Then he grinned down at Jenny. "Why, I suppose I thought the Lord ought to have that privilege."

39

JOSEPH MARCHED INTO the office the next morning. Dropping the stack of papers on Mark's desk, he said, "Here it is. The petition to Congress, just like I promised you. Look it over, and let's get it off. I'm asking them to make me an officer in the Army. I'm going to need power to raise a hundred thousand volunteers—and that's what it'll take in order to do a decent job of guarding the western borders of the United States. With what I've promised them, I don't see how they can possibly refuse."

He paced the office, cracking his knuckles as he enumerated, "I'm going to hold out hope of deliverance to Texas, as well as protect Oregon. They're being threatened by England and France. In short, my stand is for deliverance from tyranny and oppression for all the people."

"It's a pretty ambitious petition," Mark stated, picking up the paper.

"Not out of line. Hyde said Stephen A. Douglas gave him the word that if he were in my shoes, he'd resign from Congress and be on his way to California in a month's time."

Joseph headed for the door and then turned. "Mark, there's a Council meeting tonight—the Fifties. Be there. It's important."

After supper that evening Mark rode into town with Orson. When their horses met at the roadway, Mark said, "If we keep getting these meetings, I guess we'll have to encourage our wives to spend more time together. John Mark keeps Jenny busy, and I know she doesn't like him up late, but still—I don't like to leave her alone."

"Haven't seen that brother-in-law of yours lately."

"Joseph's sent him back to Texas with Woodworth. I guess things are looking pretty good there." He slanted a glance at Orson who gave him a twisted grin.

"Naw, I don't think there's a danger of our being pushed out. I don't think the Prophet does, either. Things have simmered down. Bennett seems to have quit his dirty work. Time will tell. If there're as many people flocking into Nauvoo this year as there were last, I'd say that's a barometer of goodwill toward him."

The meeting got underway promptly at eight. Joseph was chuckling when he came into the room, and Mark relaxed.

Shaking his head, Joseph said, "Trust Rockwell to come up with that idea. Wonder if his pigtail was responsible."

Kimball said, "It's your problem if you don't like it. You made such a to-do about it, he decided to keep it. Where's he tonight?"

"Outside," Joseph remarked tersely. Briefly there was a shadow in his eyes. "He seems to think there's a need for real caution. That's why the frocks."

There was an exclamation from the back of the room and Pratt said, "I'd heard someone saw Rockwell sneaking around town all dressed up like a lady. General, Port's too big to pass as any kind of a lady."

The smile faded from Joseph's face as he said, "My life is in danger. It isn't the forces outside Nauvoo I fear. Some little dough-headed fool in this city causes me more anxiety than all the forces of Satan out there. It's the traitors within the circle who keep me awake nights. I've said before, I say again, we've a Judas within our group."

Joseph shook his shoulders as if freeing them from a specter, and he passed on to other business. Catching Mark's eye, he told about the petition, adding, "I fully expect them to grant our request; so fellas, start planning your lives around this."

When Joseph braced his feet and shoved his hands into his pockets, Mark moved uneasily. Joseph said, "Nauvoo's growing. It's no longer a peaceful little town. There's unrest, contention. I've asked Wight and Rockwell to expand the Angels. I'm feeling the tide moving against me and I intend to be prepared. There's rumors," he paused and his restless eyes swept over the men.

"I've had some reliable sources advise me of a type of unrest we can't abide. Rattlers in the woodpile.

"So far I haven't been able to get enough money together to print the revised Bible. This is contrary to the wishes of the Lord. However, until that is done, I'll take it upon myself to teach you on the subjects the Lord wants revealed at this time.

"In the revelation concerning celestial, or in other words, everlasting marriage, there is an item mentioned which we need to pursue. The Lord has revealed in this section the subject of destruction in the flesh in order to save the soul. If a man or woman under the shield of the new and everlasting marriage, commits a sin or transgression against the marriage, that person shall be destroyed in the flesh.

"Likewise, under the shield of this marriage, a wife caught with a man other than her husband shall be destroyed in the flesh. The purpose of this command is to show the sacredness of this everlasting union.

"In conjunction with this revelation, I wish to show another command which shall point out the seriousness of our standing before the Lord. In the book of Mark, chapter 9 and verses 43 through 48, we find the admonition, given in the new translation, in regard to cutting off the hand. That hand is your brother. Therefore, if your brother offend you, it is better for you that he be cut off than for the both of you to enter hell. Every man is to stand or fall by himself. So you see, what the Lord is telling us is that it is better to kill the offending brother than to let him pull you down into hell.

"Now, brethren, I must remind you again, you have been given the blessings of the priesthood. Go out and do the works of Abraham."

"General," came a timid voice from the back of the room. "Are you meaning to tell us we're *obligated*? One of the fellas the other day reminded us that the laws of Illinois are against plural marriage."

"I have reminded you before that the laws of the state are an abomination. We shall not keep them when they go against the laws of God."

Mark could no longer hold his tongue. "I just read the *Doctrine and Covenants*, section 58, verse 21, where we are advised against breaking the laws of the country. There is the promise given that by keeping the law of God, we have no reason to break the law of the country."

The meeting ended and Mark headed for the door. He felt a hand on his arm and turned. It was John D. Lee and he was wearing a perplexed frown on his face. "A word, Mark." When they were outside the building, Lee continued, "You know this group is the council of the gods. You don't seem to realize the seriousness of your attitude. Mark, don't you yet accept the teaching that without plural marriage a man can never attain the fullness of the holy priesthood and thereby be made equal with the Savior?"

When they parted company at the end of the street, Lee was still shaking his head.

Jenny was sitting in the rocking chair with her Bible in her lap. She looked up and smiled when he came in. Squatting on the floor close to her he said, "Before I left this evening I noticed you had something on your mind. What is it?"

"Oh, Mark, I suppose these last few weeks have given me the jitters. It's probably nothing. But after I left Relief Society meeting this morning, I headed down the street intending to shop. I saw one of the Whittlers out. He was sitting on a stump at the watering trough.

"When I passed he got up and walked along behind me. If I hadn't known about such men, I probably would have thought nothing of it."

She paused to gulp and added, "It was all I could do to keep from running. I really don't think he intended to harm me, but he followed down the street, whistling that terrible flat tune and all the time whittling on that stick. I turned once and he was looking at me."

"Jenny, the Whittlers are for the purpose of chasing the enemies or apostates out of town. There's no reason to fear, particularly since you are a harmless woman—not a threat to anyone."

Mark continued to examine her face for a moment more, then uttered that request he had been holding back for over a year. "Jenny, shall we leave?" He watched the hope flare to life in her eyes.

She looked around the room. "Mark, this place has been such a big part of our lives; but yes, I'm ready to leave."

He got to his feet and his thoughts turned back to the evening. "Jenny, will you trust me to get us out of here at just the right time? Also, please don't mention to anyone that we are planning to leave."

When she stretched for his kiss, she hesitated, and he saw the fear in her eyes.

"What is it?" he whispered against her face.

She leaned back. Her eyes were searching his face. "Mark, now you trust me. There's still something I need to confront Joseph with."

He hesitated, then said reluctantly, "All right. The Lord's brought us thus far."

Her face lighted. "Ebenezer! Mark, I read it! Thus far—He'll still be there, won't He?" The wistful look was a question, and he caught her close.

In the morning when Mark reached the office, Clayton was there to meet him. Mark was surprised by the expression of genuine concern in the man's eyes. Leading the way into their office, Clayton faced him with a worried frown.

"Mark, I like you. You're nearly apostate, but there's something of value in you. I'm sure the Lord will use you in the kingdom if you will only listen to counsel."

"Clayton," Mark said mildly, "I have no intention of living differently than the Lord wishes me to. Now, what is the problem?"

"Your contrary speech last night. Anything the Prophet says is just as binding upon us as if God Himself said it. Even if he gives advice opposed to previous advice, do it."

Clayton took a deep breath. "Those of us close to the Prophet will be asked to carry a heavy load in the next year. Much will be demanded, but it will be the chance we've been waiting for." He leaned confidentially closer. "It's been in our minds for some months. Now we're certain. Joseph will be running for president of the United States."

The man paused to pace the floor in quick steps. "Phelps and I have been working on a platform. So far I believe we are doing very well. Now, when it gets down to writing campaign speeches, I don't believe I'll have the spunk that Phelps does."

He looked at Mark, but despite his friendly grin, a shadow darkened his eyes. As Mark picked up his papers, he was very aware of the warning.

When Mark walked into the house that evening, he gave Jenny a quick kiss and said, "Just saw William Law. He's pretty worried. Seems to think word's leaked back to Joseph about our meeting. There's to be another meeting this evening, so let's head back to town as soon as possible."

The warm April day was dissolving into dusk as Mark and Jenny reached the outskirts of Nauvoo. They were riding briskly down the street, headed for Higbee's store, when they both saw the dark-coated man disappearing up the stairs to Joseph's office.

Mark explained, "That's Clayton. I didn't tell you, but a conversation I had with him this morning gave me the distinct impression that he's caught wind of the meetings. Jenny, will you do something? Go upstairs and talk to Clayton for half an hour.

"I don't want him seeing the bunch of people heading up Higbee's back stairs. Would you, please?" He grinned. "Of all men in town, I trust you with Clayton. I'll take John Mark with me, and I'll leave the buggy at the stable." Jenny nodded and Mark added, "The longer you keep him the better for us."

As Jenny reached the top of the stairs, Clayton's alarmed face peered around the doorjamb. "Mrs. Cartwright, you gave me a start! Is something the matter?"

"No, Mark has business in town this evening. I want to look for a book to read."

"Mighty dry reading you'll find here."

"What do you have? That book is thick enough to look interesting."

"It's charts and horoscopes. Joseph and I have been studying the stars. We spend quite a bit of time searching the heavens for a sign. There's much of ancient knowledge to be learned in this manner."

"That sounds interesting; astronomy?"

"No, astrology. Remember, I showed the book to you some time ago. This is the divination of the influences of stars on human endeavors. By studying out their positions and consulting these charts, we can get an idea of what's going to happen in the future. We also begin to comprehend the outcome of these forces on the people around us." He paused, studied her, then said, "You look like you're pretty interested in the science. Seeing it's you, if you want to come with me, I'll let you have a look through the telescope."

Cautiously, remembering her mission, she asked, "Where is it?"

"Just down the street. Joseph has it all set up on top of Mansion House."

"Why, I think I would like that."

Outside dusk had given way to darkness. Clayton took her arm, saying, "Look at those stars. This will be a good night to view them. Now, watch your step. We don't keep a light in Mansion House. No sense advertising our business. Just hang on to my coattail and I'll get us across the hall and into the secret staircase."

"Oh," Jenny murmured. "I'd heard Joseph had built in a hidden staircase—but why?"

"To escape his enemies. It leads to the roof. More'n once he's gone up these stairs in a hurry and dropped down through the trees."

The door creaked, and the dark figure holding the telescope straightened. Jenny stepped out onto the rooftop. By moonlight she saw him blink. "Hello Joseph. Clayton has been telling me about the studies and volunteered to bring me along to see the telescope."

"Jenny!" Surprise and excitement in his voice assured Jenny of her welcome. She approached the table and he said, "Come here. I'll point out the stars we'll study tonight and then Clayton can tell you the significance behind their positions. Would you like us to do your horoscope?"

Without answering, Jenny took her place and stared into the telescope. "Oh, my! Even the moon is fascinating. What planet is this?"

Jenny took her eyes away from the telescope and turned. Clayton was bending over the charts, shading a candle from the breeze. "Windy up here. Come here, I'll show you this chart. What's your birth date?"

"Clayton, I've read enough to know astrology and horoscopes are related to witchcraft. I don't want my horoscope plotted."

She turned to Joseph. "You've come down hard on the Saints for even having a taint of the craft around, the charms and the witching rods—why are you seeking signs in the stars?"

He was chuckling, "Jenny, my dear, how righteous you are! But we need all the help we can get; besides, the study of stars is interesting. I'm fascinated by the movement of the earth forces. I intend to discover the mysteries of the universe."

"I remember, from reading the *Book of Abraham*, how the stars were explained. That Kolob is the one close to God, and governing the others." She hesitated and then said, "Tell me, Joseph, about something that's worried me for some time. In the *Book of Abraham* it says the gods organized the world, meaning more than one god and yet in the Book of Moses, He says, *I created*—just one God. Why the difference?"

"Come here and look at the shooting stars and quit worrying about something that's beyond a woman."

She continued, "Moses, the sixth chapter, refers to Adam, Man of Holiness, and then goes on to call Jesus Christ his only begotten. Joseph, I'm confused. The Bible doesn't call God Adam."

Impatiently he turned, "Jenny, I refuse to quarrel with a woman. I've told you the Bible hasn't been correctly translated. You've no right to question the very writings of God." Facing Clayton, he added, "Why don't you go back to the office and get some books for our sister to read. Take your time."

"Clayton," Jenny said, carefully watching Joseph, "if you leave, I'll scream my head off. Out here in the open air, the sound will carry quite a ways. Just stay here; there's not one thing Joseph and I will be discussing that isn't fit for your ears." Clayton shifted uneasily and Jenny added, "I mean it, and I shall begin right now."

Clayton sat down, and Jenny stepped closer to Joseph. "I've been wanting to talk to you for some time. Joseph, I've been listening to some of the women—both the things they've said and the hints they've dropped. I don't think what's going on in Nauvoo is of the Lord, simply because if it were these women wouldn't be so desperately unhappy.

"Sally told me before she killed herself that she couldn't handle the guilt of deceiving her husband by allowing you to love her. There are many other women just as desperate.

"Joseph, you've preyed on our fear of God and a deep desire to be holy; but more than that, I am aware of the strange attraction you hold for women, because I've felt it myself.

"Once away from you, I've suffered guilt and wondered why I was so attracted. Joseph, it might be just you—but I don't think so.

"You know I had a talisman. Until I made up my mind to get rid of it, I felt an almost irresistible attraction in your pressence. Joseph, you know I was involved in the craft for years. But what you don't know is how it corrupted my life, twisting me with fear. I tried to escape that fear by being a good Mormon, but that didn't help.

"I soon discovered you and your church held me with bonds of fear. You've taught it is wrong to question and that we must give total submission to you and the church. You used the spiritual wife doctrine as a whip. And I know I wasn't the only one. I'm certain you've used the same whip on other women, and with more success."

Jenny stopped to take a deep breath. "Joseph, I've come to ask you come questions. Because you see, I still don't know the heart of you. Can you honestly say you are called of God? If the welfare of your church and your people are of the utmost importance to you, if you really love us, will you please get rid of the talisman?"

For a moment he stared at her in astonishment. "I am certain," she said, "that it is the link of Satan in your life, destroying us all with a doctrine that is from the evil one." His face was beginning to soften into a grin.

Reaching into his pocket he pulled out the talisman and held it up, balancing it on his fingertips.

For a moment Jenny teetered on her toes, tempted to snatch it and fling it over the rooftop and into the inky night. Then she relaxed. The decision must come from him.

He kissed the medal and slipped it back into his pocket. "No, my dear. I can't live without the protection of the talisman." Even in the darkness she could see the change on his face. His eyes were shadowed; the lines on his face and the timber of his voice spelled fear.

Slowly and thoughtfully, he spoke as if he had forgotten her presence. "At times it seems I've collected more enemies than friends during my life. I fear they'll never be satisfied until they have my blood. Could it be my days are numbered? No, it shall not be. The Lord has work for me to do. He'll not call me home before my time."

He stirred, and the old arrogant grin returned. "Meanwhile, my dear, I intend to make the most of my time." He reached for her.

Jenny sidestepped. "I still have lungs," she warned. "Joseph, that isn't all I have to say. You told me to read my Bible as well as the *Book of Mormon* and the rest of the writings. I did. It wasn't long until I found the Bible holding my complete attention.

"Joseph, it was God speaking to me! I heard the love, I saw Jesus living, loving, teaching repentance, begging people just to reach out and accept the gift of Himself. I wanted to be friends with that Man and I discovered that touching Him was touching God.

"Joseph, I found it was utter arrogance to think I could earn my way to heaven. God says He owns the cattle on a thousand hills and He doesn't want our sacrifices. He wants our love."

Jenny stopped. She could see her words were wasted. "The talisman?"

"I intend to keep it. I need all the protection and help it has to offer."

When Jenny reached Higbee's store the meeting was over. She stood blinking in the lamplight while Mark dumped the warm, sleepy child into her arms.

40

"YOUNG MAN, IF you don't hold still I'll never get you dressed, and your father will take you to Sabbath service wearing only a diaper." Jenny paused to kiss John Mark's upturned face. "There." She set him on the floor.

Mark was chuckling. "Remember last year? He was only a mite. Can hardly believe a year could do that to a baby."

Jenny straightened Mark's collar and said, "It's time to be thinking about another. She frowned at his expression. "You don't like the idea?"

"I think if we're wanting to hear the sermons, we'd better get going."

"Church conference," Jenny murmured. "Joseph won't lose his opportunity to state what's on his mind. Today the crowd will be the largest in months. Has Willian Law told you who the spies were at Higbee's?"

Mark shook his head. "Could come out in the sermon. Are you ready to leave?"

When they reached Nauvoo, Jenny stated, "It's fortunate the weather's clear and warm today. Look at the size of the crowd."

Mark's voice was only a rumble and she leaned close to listen. "It's a good time for strangers to mingle in with the Saints to get a feel of things." He gave her a quick look and explained, "There's enough to whet the curiosity of any number of people."

"Politics?"

He nodded. "There're thoughts floating around. John D. Lee's been calling Joseph the salvation of the nation. The newspapers are rumbling about it, at least those who are seriously considering Joseph's talk about running for president. They're dropping phrases like 'the monstrous union of church and state' under Joseph."

"Is that good?"

"Terrible—unless you want someone telling you which church to belong to." Mark found a spot under the trees, helped Jenny out of the buggy, and picked up John Mark.

Joseph and the elders marched to the pulpit. After a brief reference to Elder King Follett, who had been killed in an accident the week before,

Joseph began his sermon. "There are few in the world who understand God. In order to help you along the way, we must go back to creation. We see the great Elohim sitting yonder as He did at the creation. Some call me a false prophet. I will prove them wrong by helping them know about God. If I can bring you to a knowledge of God, persecution against me should stop.

"For now, I will go to the beginning. God himself was once as we are now. He is an exalted man, seated on His throne in the heavenlies. In addition, God the Father dwelt on earth, just as His Son Jesus did. As the Father had power to lay down His life, so also did the Son. As He had the power to take up life again, so did the Son. I tell you, my brethren, you have got to learn to be gods yourself.

"The Father worked for His kingdom with fear and trembling; we must do likewise. Jesus treads in the footsteps of His Father, inheriting what God the Father did before Him. We shall all do likewise."

Joseph paused before adding, "I've been reading the Bible in Hebrew, Latin, Greek, and German. I find the German nearest to the translation the Lord gave to me. Now, I want you to hear me. It doesn't say God created the spirit of man. It expressly says He put Adam's spirit into man.

"The mind or intelligence of man is coequal with God Himself. God never had the power to create man's spirit. That would be like God creating Himself. Remember, intelligence is eternal." As Joseph paused, his brooding eyes swept the people listening with upturned faces. "Some of you will reject this word. If I were a false teacher no man would seek my life. If a man thinks he is authorized to take away my life, let me say by the same token we are justified in taking away the life of every false teacher.

"Knowledge saves a man. In the greater world to which the spirits go, a man can be exalted only by knowledge. I address you apostates; when a man turns against the work, he seeks to kill me. I warn you, such persons cannot be saved."

As Jenny and Mark turned to join the crowd making its way out of the temple grove, Jenny said, "Mark, there's Tom!" She waved frantically, and they pressed toward each other through the tide of people. Jenny embraced Tom, saying, "You shall come home with us! We didn't even know you were back."

They had nearly finished dinner when Mark asked, "Tom, what's the Texas situation?"

"Pretty hopeful, if Joseph's serious about pulling up stakes. I can't believe it, though. There's been too much invested here."

"Might be necessary," Mark added, reaching for more chicken.

Tom squinted up at him. "That bad, huh?"

"Yes, he's worried. Nearly every time he speaks it comes out that he's worried by the opposition. I think he reads every newspaper in the country."

Mark saw Tom's quick look and said, "Yes, he's confided in me, but I don't think the Saints for the most part know how deeply concerned he is."

Jenny glanced at Mark and Tom said, "What's going on?"

"As close as you are to Joseph, I expected you to know."

"Don't forget I've been out of town for over a month."

Jenny interrupted. "Let's talk of something else. Tom, I've finally come to the point where I had to reject Joseph's church."

"That comes as a shock right now. Any good reason?"

"I've been reading the Bible and I've come to see either I go Jesus Christ's way or Joseph's. I can't have both, because they are completely opposite each other."

He studied her face, reached for the plate of bread, and said, "I guess I'm not surprised, come to think of it. Mark's a pretty strong talker."

She lifted her chin. "Mark didn't influence me. I simply—" She stared at Mark, then looked at her brother. "Tom, after the fascination of everything else wore off, I just came back to where I belonged. I was going to say I chose, but I didn't. It was more like the Lord had my hand and just pulled me back to where I belonged.

"Once I decided, there was no alternative. I felt like I was home." She leaned across the table to look at Tom. "Do you know the feeling?" When he shook his head, she said, "Well, I didn't, either. I didn't realize all the things I didn't like inside of me would be the very things God would take away. Sin."

Tom said slowly, "You said 'fascination.' What do you mean?"

She faced him without flinching. "Witchcraft, Mormonism. They were fascinating, you know. An obsession."

Mark followed Tom out to the barn and watched him saddle his horse. As Tom swung himself onto the mare, he said, "So Jen's got religion. Did she ever tell you about jumping into the river?"

"No," Mark said slowly, "and after what happened to Sally, I'd never ask."

Mark was thinking, as Tom rode down the lane, that his brother-in-law looked as if there was another question he wanted to ask. Jenny and John Mark came out of the house, and Mark watched as the sun caught the baby's bright hair and turned it into a halo.

Mark struggled with thoughts he couldn't allow. At times just knowing about the plural marriage seemed to make it more difficult. If she hadn't told him, could he have put the whole thing out of his mind? He sighed and walked slowly toward his family.

Tuesday evening when Mark rode into the yard, Jenny was sitting on the back steps while John Mark charged about the yard carrying his wooden spoon. She fluttered her fingers at him and he went on to the barn.

When he carried the pail of milk into the kitchen, he said, "I thought you intended coming to the office after Relief Society meeting."

She looked startled. "Oh, I did. Just forgot. I hope I didn't delay you." Mark shook his head, wondering but not daring to question. As he put the milk in the kitchen, he added another question to the list in his mind.

That night of the meeting at Higbee's store, nearly frantic with worry, he had questioned her about the delay. She had been short when she answered his question. Briefly, she stated she had been on the roof with Joseph and Clayton.

They were still sitting at the table after dinner when Jenny met his eyes and slowly said, "Today Emma passed around a statement which she had prepared and submitted to the *Nauvoo Neighbor*. Have you seen it?"

He shook his head and waited. Jenny sighed deeply. "In essence it rails against Dr. John C. Bennett's spiritual wife system. Mark, that wasn't his idea!"

"He's accused of it, whether or not he's to blame."

She continued, "Other than placing the blame on him, it was really a nothing statement. She mentioned polygamy, bigamy, adultery, and so on. One of the women whispered to me that she'd heard Dr. Bennett claim that all the Relief Society women were to be the Prophet's wives." Lifting her face, she said, "Mark, this is so terrible! There are so *many* women in the group."

As Mark blew out the lamp and they started up the stairs, he was miserably aware of the questions rising up in his heart. Why did she care how many there were? He watched as Jenny pulled the blanket over John Mark. Would he ever be totally free of the taint Joseph had left on his marriage? He needed that freedom in his life. Strange that it had to be dealt with every day.

He paused in the doorway. "Jenny, I think I'll go down and read for a while." He turned away from the hurt question in her eyes.

At the end of the week, as Mark rode into Nauvoo, William Law met him with newspaper in hand. "Well, friend," he said heavily, "the guesses were right. There's a neat little article here in the *Nauvoo Neighbor* detailing nearly everything we discussed at that first meeting at Higbee's.

"There's even a fairly accurate account of Joseph's attempted seduction of Mrs. Foster. No comment by Joseph in the article, just the sublime implication that he is being persecuted." He shoved the paper into his satchel. "Brother, I think our hand is being forced."

"What is the next step?" Mark asked slowly.

"Depends," Law said. "You haven't been suspected yet. So far as Joseph knows you're untainted. That's good, since you're his attorney. I'd like to suggest you keep it that way for the sake of the free flow of information, which we'll need badly."

"Sooner or later the Angels will be able to link us."

"Probably, but let's play for time. There's to be a meeting tonight at Higbee's. Stay home, I'll bring you up-to-date later. If need be, I'll ride out to your place."

He started to turn away and then said, "By the way, Mark, I still believe in the Prophet. I intend with every power of persuasion at my disposal to call Joseph to genuine repentance."

"It's a waste without confession—at least to the brethren, if not to the whole church. He's in too deep to profess change without it."

"That could be nasty. What about the presidential election?"

"It would ruin any hopes," Mark added.

"Nevertheless, it must be done."

"You've been threatened before."

"You're referring to the Destroying Angels?" Mark nodded. "Then let me tell you what I intend. Since Joseph won't take my call for reformation seriously, I intend to set up a church of my own. I feel this will force his hand. I've also ordered a printing press. Joseph and I'll be trading tit for tat before June rolls around.

"Also, if there isn't immediate action on Joseph's part, I intend to sue, charging him with adultery."

Slowly Mark said, "William, you are a very brave man. I'll help you as much as I can. Are you certain I'll be most valuable by keeping my mouth shut?"

He nodded. "By the way, Higbee's suing Joseph for five thousand dollars, charging him with slander."

41

WHEN MARK ENTERED the livery stable that blustery April afternoon, Tom was at the forge and William Law was with him. "Heading for
home?" Law asked. Mark nodded as he threw the saddle on his mare, and
Law added, "Well, I'd ride with you, but I've an errand that will detain me
about fifteen minutes." His eyes held Mark's.

"I'll see you some other time," Mark said, leading his horse out. He
looked at Tom. "If you're out our way tomorrow, stop for supper." Tom
nodded and reached for a nail.

Mark lingered on the trail until William caught up with him. "Why the
secrecy? Tom can keep his mouth shut."

"Can't risk the information I have. Foster's been gathering a bunch of
witnesses to use against Joseph in this trial called against him. Seems
Joseph got wind of it and set up a secret council meeting. The outcome?
Foster, Wilson, Jane, and I were all excommunicated. Without a hearing,"
he added. Mark watched him silently as he slowly shook his head.

"It was really a blow," Law continued, "but not a one of our group is
willing to back down now."

Slowly Mark said, "By rights I should have been on that council; Joseph
didn't say a word to me."

"The first meeting of our new church will be this next Sabbath," Law
said. "I just wanted you to know, but don't put in an appearance. We still
need you where you are."

By the time Mark reached home, he had decided to say nothing to
Jenny for the time being. He kissed her and said, "There's a big parade
and speeches in Nauvoo tomorrow. If it isn't too blustery, would you like
to go?"

Her face lighted, "Oh, Mark, how nice! What are we celebrating?"

"Nothing that I know of. I think it's just a show of force. You know the
Prophet is getting ready to announce his candidacy for the presidency. A
parade will raise everyone's spirits."

The following day was warm and sparkling from the nighttime shower.
As they joined the wagons and buggies streaming into Nauvoo, Jenny said,

"This parade must be more important than you thought. Look at the people."

"Finding a place to leave a buggy is getting to be a problem," Mark said. "I'll let you and John Mark off here in front of the Nauvoo Mansion. Walk toward the business section, and I'll meet you."

Carrying John Mark, Jenny hurried across the street. A flurry of activity at the front door of the hotel caught her eye, and she paused to watch. Emma, followed by her children, was being helped into a handsome new carriage.

"The grand lady is going to be in the parade too," the wizened, gray-haired lady at her elbow said. "Do you know when the Prophet's mother will return to Nauvoo? I knew her back in Palmyra days. I'd surely like to visit with her."

Jenny shook her head. "Nauvoo is getting so big I can't keep up on any of the news. I haven't visited with Lucy Smith for years. Doubt she'd even remember me. So you're from Palmyra. I lived at Manchester for a time." Jenny searched the woman's face, trying to place her. They continued down the street toward the speaker's stand draped with bunting.

The woman was saying, "My, who would've guessed Palmyra would produce a prophet? I rise up and call myself blessed for knowing him in the beginning years."

Jenny saw Mark and waved. With a smile she walked away from the woman. Mark said, "Let's stand here, close to the platform. Joseph's on old Charlie; Emma and the carriage as well as the Legion are ready to start. I expect we'll hear the band in another minute."

He was right. By the time the band passed in front of the platform, the crowd was in a frenzy. Mark, with his lips close to Jenny's ear, said, "This is very military. Hear the drums? They know how to beat life into anything that moves."

The band was beyond them now and Joseph's horse Charlie appeared. Carefully curried until he resembled black satin, the prancing horse magnified the glory of the Prophet. From the helmet topped with a plume of ostrich feathers, to the glory of his blue coat decorated with heavy gold braid, he was the epitome of the office of lieutenant-general of the Nauvoo Legion.

As he passed, a murmur of appreciation swept the crowd. Looking at the people around her, Jenny smiled, seeing the blind adoration on their faces. But suddenly she frowned. For the first time she perceived Joseph in a new light—the contrast between his grandeur and the threadbare black coats and dingy calico of his adoring subjects.

Long before the last of the Legion had passed, Joseph had taken his place on the platform. The elders were with him. Jenny moved impatiently and shifted John Mark. With a grin Mark took the child, whispering, "Aren't you glad they didn't all march today? It's reported there's four thousand of them now."

And when the street was once again quiet, hushed and waiting, Joseph stood before them. "What do you all say about today's glory?"

The roar was deafening and a chanting swept the street. "Joseph! Joseph!" came the cry. For a moment Jenny felt separated from it all. A cold chill touched her as she studied the faces of his followers.

Silence descended abruptly, and Joseph lifted his face skyward. "In the scheme of human events, I calculate to be an instrument. By the Word of the Lord I shall set up the kingdom of Daniel. Through this act there will be a foundation laid which shall revolutionize the world. But I assure you, my dear brethren, it shall not be by the sword nor gun that I shall possess in the name of this kingdom. No, my friends, in these latter days the power of truth shall press so heavily upon all nations to such an extent that they shall under necessity humble themselves to obey the gospel." He paused momentarily and then said, "All America, from north to south, from coast to coast, is Zion. It is our inheritance! I am a smooth polished shaft in the quiver of the Almighty. He shall give me dominion over all."

The chant rose again. Jenny concentrated on the words, *There ain't gonna be no war no more, there ain't gonna be no war.* Mark bent over her, whispering, "Little do they know that the Prophet is planning to have an arsenal and to manufacture powder. At the same time his army shall continue to grow."

During the week Nauvoo subsided back into the usual workaday world. Only those closest to Joseph knew the decisions being made.

Mark walked into his office one morning and discovered it had been turned into a convention hall. During that morning, the puzzle pieces fell abruptly into place.

When he stepped into the assembly of black-coated men, Joseph was standing before them with a handful of papers. Mark noted that Joseph had dressed in black in honor of the occasion.

Nodding at Mark, Joseph said, "I have in my hands copies of the numerous letters written to Congress in an attempt to win attention, support, even recognition of our rights as a beleaguered people. We have had no reply promising satisfaction. Until we are a political force, we shall not win the attention of this country.

"I am convinced we'll be robbed of our constitutional rights until we stamp our feet hard enough to win respect." He paced the room, saying, "I've contacted every candidate for office, asking their views on our plight and have received no satisfaction from that quarter. Therefore, I shall declare myself candidate for president of the United States of America."

There was a muffled roar of approval as Hyrum Smith got to his feet. "We want a president—for the people, not for a party!"

Throughout the day the men huddled over the table. A platform was written out, while ideas shot around the room: "Reduce Congress!" "Establish a theodemocracy, where God and the people hold power to conduct affairs in righteousness!" "Bring Texas into the union!" "Abolish slavery!"

Then in a quiet moment, George Miller's voice rose, "If the election's successful, Joseph and the Council of Fifty will at once establish dominion. Fellas, that's us. You ready to take over?"

Before the day had finished, Rigdon had been reluctantly acknowledged as Joseph's running mate. Joseph stood to his feet. "I want every man in the city who can lisp a clear sentence to hit the campaign trail. Advocate the Mormon religion, purity of election. Call upon the people to be on the side of law and order. Campaign. Put our name before the people!"

"Hear ye, hear ye!" Wight shouted, jumping to his feet, "I make a motion that on July 13, we assemble in New York for the purpose of holding a national *Joseph Smith for President* convention."

Later, as the men rushed out of the room, Mark chewed his lip and contemplated the shambles of paper and debris left behind in his office. He studied his desk and wondered about carrying home the work he had intended finishing.

Joseph approached. "Mark, you look down in the mouth about it all."

Mark looked up in surprise. "Well, not about the day's events. I was thinking of what I didn't do today. But since you ask—Joseph, you don't have any expectations about winning this election. But have you considered what this interlude means in the lives of these men? Some of these men are going out simply because they feel forced into it. That's bad—for them and for the image they'll project."

"Since when have you been concerned about my image?"

"It isn't *yours,*" Mark frowned. "It's the image of the people; the mindlessness of your absolute control. From the council on down, everything in Mormon country smacks of subservience. You may control the people now, but it's going to backfire. Either they'll break free or some firebrand will do the breaking for them. Your platform holds high a happy view of freedom, but it's only to allow you to do as you please. I can't believe you really have the best interests of the people at heart."

Mark's heart was heavy as he started for home. As he reviewed the day and thought of the direction Joseph was leading, he shook his head. "Poor old John D. Lee. I hope someday that his faithful sacrifice will merit him more than the crumbs at Caesar's table."

Law caught up with him. "I hear you. I get the idea you're against faithfulness."

Mark slanted him a glance. "Faithfulness, of the kind John D. Lee has, belongs to God. Given to man or cause instead of God, it leads to slavery."

William's eyes were bright and questioning for a moment; then he asked, "Was Joseph served the summons?"

"Yes," Mark shook his head. "I'm not too confident. He laughed it off, saying he had a complete record of his actions and even the most mundane of daily activities to support his righteous life. If the court accepts his records, it could be bad."

"Well, brace yourself, Attorney Cartwright. I've filed suit against the Prophet charging adultery and polygamy. Considering Joseph's second favorite lawyer is now suing him for slander, I hate to think where that leaves you."

When Mark walked into the house, Jenny was in the kitchen. John Mark clung to her skirts. With his face tilted upward and the tears coursing down, he cried.

Mark looked at Jenny's tired face, watched her rub at the perspiration on her brow. "Oh, Marky, be a good baby," she moaned.

"What's the trouble?" Mark asked, astonished even then that he could look beyond his own problem.

"Laundry, fussy baby, late daddy, and burned potatoes."

"I'm sorry." He kissed her cheek and picked up John Mark. Jenny was blinking tears out of her eyes. He said, "Why don't you sit down and rock the tyke. I'll do something with dinner."

The tears fell. "Don't you ever want to hold him?"

"Jenny, I love holding him," he explained patiently, "but you're exhausted. In a minute I'll put both of you to bed." He pulled her against his chest, wondering how he could convince her of his plan and how he could let them go.

She pulled away. "I'm fine. We'll have bread and gravy, unless you want eggs."

John Mark was tucked into bed early and Mark went down to help with the dishes. Jenny was still sagging listlessly over the dishpan. She tried to straighten and smile when he picked up the dish towel. Studying her tired face, he decided he had found a reason.

Speaking lightly he said, "First thing tomorrow I am going to make arrangements for you and John Mark to take the stage to Cleveland to visit Mother. She's been begging for a visit since the baby was born. I can't get free, but there's no reason you can't go."

Jenny was staring at him. Slowly she lifted one soapy hand and touched her face. "Mark!" she whispered. "Oh, Mark, please don't make me go!"

"I thought you liked Mother."

"I do, but Mark, not now."

"Yes, now." She moistened her lips and the expression in her eyes brought him a step closer. "Jenny, don't look like it's the end of the world. I'm doing this for your own good."

"What's happened?"

He sighed and said, "Come sit down." She hesitated and he eased her into the rocking chair. For a moment he studied her face, trying to understand the sadness he perceived there. He took a deep breath and decided the truth would be the only thing she would accept.

"I saw William Law this afternoon. He's filed suit against Joseph Smith, charging him with adultery and polygamy. At the same time there's Foster's suit and now Higbee's suit. It looks like, unless Joseph chooses a defense attorney from out of Springfield, I'll be handling his case."

"I realize you'll be busy for the next several months. But Tom could stay here if you'll be out of town."

"That isn't the point. Jenny, I'm trying to say it gently, but I don't know how. There's going to be a very unsavory trial. I know William well enough to realize he's not going to back down from exposing the facts even if he treads on our toes." He could see she still didn't comprehend. "Jenny, I love you and I've forgiven you for what—" He took a deep breath.

"Let's put it this way. I refuse to allow your name to be dragged in the dirt. The only way that can be avoided is by your leaving until this whole affair can be settled."

She was silent for a moment before she asked, "What about the other women? We heard some of them at the meeting. Won't they be pulled into witnessing?"

"I'm afraid so. Right now, knowing how Joseph will fight, I guess every woman who has ever been involved with Joseph will be forced to testify. That's why it is absolutely necessary for you to leave."

"I don't like it," Jenny said slowly. "But if they will have to talk about their troubles with Joseph, it seems only fair that I do the same thing." She lifted her face. "Mark, don't you think that's what Jesus would want me to do?"

"No!" He jumped to his feet and paced the room. "I refuse to allow my wife to be shamed in that manner." When she began to sob, hiding her face in her hands, Mark knew himself defenseless. "Look, I've got to take care of things outside. There's no point in discussing this further."

Jenny lifted her face. He tightened his jaw and waited. She wiped her eyes and slowly got to her feet. Stepping close she looked at him intently. He watched despair creep over her face. As she turned away, she said flatly, "Very well. I'll be prepared to leave day after tomorrow."

42

"JEN! ARE YOU home?"

Jenny walked slowly down the stairs and set John Mark on his feet. "Hello, Tom. I'm surprised to see you."

Tom blinked, "You all right?" She nodded and he said, "Mark invited me out for supper."

"He did?" She frowned and looked around the room. "That's strange."

Tom looked down at the trunk. "You going someplace?"

"Yes, Mark's sending me to his mother's place until things are resolved."

His glance was sharp. "You mean the suits? The newspapers are full of the wildest stories. I sure didn't have any idea there was—aw, yes, I did; but still—"

They heard Mark's horse and Jenny headed for the kitchen. She sighed and reached for her apron. "Fortunate for you I've planned a good meal." She glanced at him. "John Mark and I are leaving on the stage in the morning."

"It's going to be rough on Mark, facing that mess without having you around."

"Tom!" Mark opened the door as she cried, "this isn't my idea. I'm not deserting Mark—he's *sending* me away. I want desperately to stay."

"Jenny!" She saw Mark's face was white as he reached for her arm. "Little love, this is going to be more difficult for me than—but I simply can't allow you to undergo the kind of treatment Joseph's promising." Jenny shook his hand off, sank her teeth into her lip and turned to the table.

Her voice was flat as she said, "Well, come to supper. There's pot roast." She began lifting the meat and vegetables to the serving platter.

Mark picked up the baby and said, "Come on, fella, let's find that bib."

"You mean a baby that size is eating real food?" Tom marveled. "I— Jen!" He started after her as she dashed out the backdoor.

When Jenny returned to the kitchen, Mark and Tom stared at her. Mark said, "Jenny, you're ill!"

"It's just the smell of meat. Mark, feed the baby, I'm going to lie down."

"Jenny—" Mark's voice was commanding and cold.

She faced him and lifted her chin. "I'm pregnant." There was a moment of silence, a moment of waiting, and Jenny headed for the stairs.

"Jenny!" She turned around and saw the agony on his face. "No matter. I'll accept this one as mine and love him as much as I love little John Mark." For a moment she was motionless.

"Mark!" She rushed at him, pounding his chest with her fists. "What are you saying? I can't believe I'm hearing you!" She turned to run and he grabbed her arms.

"Jenny, face it. You'll never be happy until you're willing to confess this to God. I've told you I forgive you. Please!"

Flinging off his grasp, Jenny turned and ran across the room. She snatched up John Mark and ran back to Mark. Shoving the toddler into his arms she said, "Look at that child's eyes and tell me they aren't yours!"

John Mark was crying and Mark cuddled him close. Staring at Jenny, he said, "You can't be certain; besides, it's not necessary to prove anything."

Suddenly limp and shaking, Jenny sat down in the rocking chair and whispered, "Mark, you're saying you believe I was unfaithful to you. Never, never, Mark! I would *never* do that to you."

She could see he didn't believe her. "And you expect me to believe you could be Joseph's wife and not submit to him?" he asked. "There are the facts. It's common knowledge that Mark Cartwright's wife tried to commit suicide while he was gone."

"Suicide!" Jenny's voice trembled with horror. For a moment she stared at Mark and then at Tom. "Tom, tell him—"

"Jenny, Joseph told me about it."

"Joseph!" For a moment Jenny was frozen motionless and then she began to laugh.

Mark had her in his arms. "Jenny, stop or I'll shake you; you're going to be—"

She shoved his arms away and rubbed her eyes. "Oh—but then you'll never believe it."

Slowly Mark said, "Maybe you'd better tell me about it. You know there are questions you never answered about that time, and questions I didn't dare ask."

"That marriage; it's so stupid! I don't know why—but there was this book. It all seemed so high and holy and far away. For eternity. I never dreamed there was anything else involved. He tried to tell me there was, and that the marriage was invalid until—" Suddenly she grinned up at Mark. "Can you possibly believe I always managed to outtalk him?"

For a moment she sobered and then shuddered. "Except for that sermon about posterity. I went to him. I intended to ask how I could help John Mark since you wouldn't take endowments. He said that because of the spiritual wife doctrine, all my posterity belonged to him. But then he said there would be no hope for John Mark to be with me in the eternities unless I validated the marriage. He confused me, but I never yielded. Mark, if you could only know how horrible it was!"

She got to her feet, coming close to look into his eyes. "Do you remember our marriage? That was the first time I ever *felt* God. But I didn't know it was Him. I just thought it was love; and because of it, I knew that our vows were so important I couldn't ever break them. Mark!"

Jenny saw the relief and joy in Mark's face and she held out her arms. Behind her Tom was saying, "Well, tykc, let's go feed the cows."

On Monday morning, just before Mark was ready to leave for Nauvoo, Jenny was able to say, "Now that you really believe in my innocence, may I testify? I'm still ashamed of myself, and of the ugliness of the whole affair, but, please! If nothing else, maybe I'll be able to convince some other Sally—" Her voice broke, but in a minute she hurried on. "I know it'll be painful for you, but I feel it's necessary."

From the shelter of his arms she sighed with contentment. "Mark, these past few days have almost made me hope again."

"About what?"

"Our marriage. We had such a wonderful marriage and then suddenly it all seemed to fall apart. It happened when I was pregnant with John Mark—"

"Because I was certain he was not my baby. I'm sorry." He felt her tears and asked, "What is it?"

"I thought it was because I threw the talisman away. See, I had the talisman when I asked you to marry me. Always I thought the talisman made you love me. But if you do now and I don't have the talisman—well?"

He saw the changing expression in her eyes and said, "Why are you crying now?"

"When I didn't have it, you loved me enough to accept me and the child, even when you thought it was Joseph's!"

He kissed her fingers. "John Mark does have eyes like mine—funny I never noticed. I just kept looking for him to develop that terrible nose."

"Oh, Mark!" She gulped and dabbed at her eyes. "You'd better go. John Mark is banging on the oven door with his spoon, and my morning sickness is threatening."

Before Mark left the house, he swooped John Mark up in his arms, tossed him, and said, "Son!"

When Mark rode into the livery stable, Tom was leaning against the door looking very serious. Mark tilted his hat back and waited.

Tom headed for the harness room and Mark followed. Picking up a harness with a loose buckle, Tom examined it carefully, avoiding Mark's eyes. "Mind telling me how I get the kind of religion you and Jenny have?"

When Mark finally reached the office, Joseph was pacing the floor and frowning. After glaring at Mark he said, "Seen the newspaper?"

"No, I can't say that I have. I carried one home last weekend but forgot to look at it."

"I hear your wife is leaving town."

"Naw, she's changed her mind. Feeling poorly with a young'un. She said to give you a message." Joseph waited. "She said tear up the paper—you'd know which one. She said since it hasn't been validated, it isn't doing you a bit of good." Mark grinned and added, "Well, I guess I'd better go see what I can work up in the way of a defense."

Mark's grin vanished when he saw the stack of newspapers on his desk. He sat down and began reading. When he finished, Joseph was waiting, leaning back in his chair with hands behind his head.

"So the *Times and Seasons* considers your accusations against Higbee too indelicate to print. Joseph, rather than helping your cause, every story that comes out is an indirect reflection upon you. Soon people will begin to wonder why you've let these affairs continue."

Finally Mark finished the last paper and, folding them together, dropped them in the trash. "They are worthless to our defense. I'm not certain these stories will help the others either, but one thing I'm very certain about is that they will focus the eyes of the nation on Nauvoo."

Joseph shuddered and got to his feet. "One thing is clear; I need all the help I can get. I'm going to ride into Carthage and see if I can round up some more legal help. Wonder if I can talk Stephen A. Douglas into giving me a hand?"

Before the month of May drew to a close, a grand jury in Hancock returned indictments against the Prophet, charging him with adultery and perjury. Joseph succeeded in getting indictments voted against Dr. Foster and Francis Higbee with the charge of false arrest and slander.

"One thing I can say for certain," Tom remarked, after the first trial, "the trial of Foster and Higbee drew nearly as big a crowd as the Legion parades do on a good day." He paused to reflect before adding, " 'Course, the trials had all that sensational mud-slinging to advertise them. Guess they lived up to the promise."

Mark had to agree with Tom. "One good feature; maybe by the time the court gets around to hearing Joseph's case, things will have calmed down a bit. It's been continued until next term of court."

The last Sabbath day in May, as Jenny and Mark prepared to go into Nauvoo for the service in the temple grove, Jenny asked, "Have you heard anything about the church William Law started?"

Mark shook his head. "I do know several of the men have been working night and day setting up the new press. They've even started writing, so it shouldn't be long now before they're producing a newspaper."

"I'm excited and frightened for them," Jenny murmured. "They are very brave men. I'm just grateful they've insisted you keep your distance."

This Sabbath Mark was able to find a shady spot close to the platform, so after greeting friends, they settled down to listen to the sermon.

Jenny whispered to Mark, "You think the walls don't have ears in Nauvoo? I've talked to three women this morning who asked me why I didn't go to Cleveland. Fortunately, I have a wonderful reason for not going." She beamed at him.

Within minutes after Joseph began to talk, the audience shifted uneasily and exchanged glances. He was saying, "Considering it all, the Lord has fortunately given me the ability to glory in persecution. Oppression can madden a wise man and a fool. As for this beardless boy—give me a chance to whip the world.

"I'll stand astride the mountains and crow. Always I'll be the victor. And in the end, innocence and truth will prevail. Ye prosecutor and ye false witnesses, come at me! All hell, boil! I shall come out on top of you all."

Joseph paused to lean forward to catch the eyes of all who would look, saying, "I've every reason to boast. No man has done a greater work than I." His hand swept the congregation. "See this multitude? I hold them all together. Even Jesus had trouble keeping a crowd following Him. Jesus' followers ran away from Him, but you don't see mine running away, yet. Since the days of Adam, I am the only man standing who alone can hold a church together. No other man has done such a task."

Sobering now, he said, "Only God knows the charges brought to bear against me are false. What a thing—this ugly charge of adultery! My brethren, I am the same man I was fourteen years ago when the church was born. I am innocent of the charges, and I shall prove my accusers wrong."

43

THE MORNING OF June 7 dawned clear and warm. The thunder-clouds which had clustered on the horizon were gone. As Mark headed toward Nauvoo, he looked at the sky and brooded, "Would that it were as clear in our city!" As he said it, he realized how often he had been saying the same thing.

He was still mulling over the comparison as he rode on. Mark had nearly reached the outskirts of Nauvoo when the dark figure on horseback came out of the trees. Frowning, he pulled on the reins and quickly scanned the trees. If the man were an Angel, there would be more behind him.

The man rode quickly and confidently toward him. Mark gave a sigh of relief as he recognized William Law.

Mark stopped in the shade of a tree. "You had my heart in my throat," he muttered as Law pulled his horse close.

"Better be cautious." William's terse statement was underscored by his tired, white face. He pulled a newspaper out from under his coat and handed it to Mark. "Thought I'd better give this to you now. Might not get a chance later; besides, it'll be wise for you to be forewarned. It's the first issue of the *Nauvoo Expositor*. We tried to say it all, in case there's not another opportunity."

Mark glanced sharply at the man. "I trust your fears are only a reflection of fatigue."

William shook his head. "Let's say I don't expect Joseph to accept this in a good-hearted way. We've taken precautions. Don't go to the press-room; we've a couple of thick-skinned Missourians standing guard just in case."

"You really are concerned," Mark said slowly, glancing down at the paper. "I take it you've resigned yourself to a fight."

"We're standing by, expecting the worst. And the minute it happens, we're heading for Carthage." William touched his hat and guided his horse out to the road.

For a moment Mark watched as man and beast disappeared through the trees. He sighed and opened the newspaper and began quickly skimming the articles. "Emmons, huh? Looks like he's done a thorough job. Fair, pointed, but not cheap."

He read, "We most solemnly and sincerely declare . . . God being witness." His eyes picked up the words—"A doctrine taught secretly, denied openly . . . We set forth for all to see the principles of Joseph Smith . . . whoredoms, not in accord with the principles of Jesus Christ."

Quickly now, with rising excitement, Mark glanced through the articles. One revealed the seductions of immigrant women, done under the promise of holiness. Mark recognized the story of Martha Brotherton, the young woman he had escorted home from Joseph's office. How he remembered her anger!

"Our hearts have mourned . . . bled at the wretched conditions of females in this place. . . . Impossible to describe without wounding . . . but truth shall come to the world." Mark found Jane Law's story and Mrs. Foster's.

Finally, with a sigh he slowly folded the paper and tucked it into his saddlebag. "Well," he muttered, "these next few days are going to be interesting." He flicked the reins and nudged the mare with his heels.

Mark had just reached the office when two members of the Legion thundered up the stairs. Throwing him a sharp glance they went into Joseph's office. Mark followed.

Joseph was at his desk. With a clenched fist he pounded the newspaper spread across its surface. "I want every issue of this paper picked up, even if you must beat on doors to get them. Lies, filth! Burn them all! You fellas are supposed to be my eyes and ears around Nauvoo. Why didn't you tell me Law had a press and that he was ready to print?"

The men left as hurriedly as they arrived and Joseph headed for the door. He paused. "Mark, I'll be at the city council offices. I don't know what I'm going to do, but if I need you, I'll send for you." For a moment his eyes were questioning, suspicious.

"If you've information, I want it. If you haven't read the paper, which I doubt heartily, there it is. Filter the crowd who'll rush in, and calm the fears."

Mark shrugged and picked up Joseph's copy of the paper and carried it into his office. Clayton was preparing for a hurried departure. "I'll be with Joseph, recording the meeting and writing letters. Now's no time to slack off on the record-keeping. It'll be the record-keeping that'll save him in the suits. You heard him last Sabbath."

Spreading the paper on his desk, Mark sat down to read. Polygamy was only one of the issues. Now Mark mentally applauded William. He was clearly pointing out the Prophet's desire to bring the country under control of the church. He read, "We do not believe that God ever raised up a Prophet to Christianize a world by political schemes and intrigue. It is not the way God captivates the heart . . ."

The paper went on to catalog the misuse of the Nauvoo Charter, the financial maneuverings of the Prophet and his constant denunciation of Missouri. Now the article called for a limiting of Joseph's power, both in the church and in the city. It charged Joseph with his responsibility of obedience to the revelations, while at the same time censoring him for his *moral imperfections.*

Mark snorted and dropped the paper. "Law, you were very nearly too sweet. But knowing the Prophet, there's going to be a tornado sweep through the streets of Nauvoo."

The city council was still secluded that evening when Mark headed for home. Again William drifted out of the trees. "Lot of good I'm doing you," Mark addressed him. "I don't know anything except fellas were instructed to pick up the papers and burn them."

Law nodded and said, "Nevertheless, you could be pulled into the meeting yet. They'll need legal advice."

"Might be Joseph's too hot to think of that."

At home Mark kissed Jenny and swung John Mark up in his arms. "The *Nauvoo Expositor* published its first issue."

Jenny turned quickly from the stove. "Oh, let me see!"

"Aw, don't I get my supper first?" She hugged him and gave him a gentle push toward the table. As he sat down, he said, "I've a feeling the Prophet knows he's facing the biggest crisis yet. There have been rumbles in the church all along, but this is the worst."

Jenny handed him the potatoes and said, "Looking back and comparing it with now, I'm seeing more coming out for discussion. In the past it seemed Joseph was on top of a problem, stomping it into the ground before it could be worked over."

After supper Mark handed the paper to Jenny and said, "Go ahead and read it now. I'll wash dishes. Maybe by the time I finish chores, you'll have finished it."

When he carried the milk into the house, Jenny was thoughtfully staring at the wall. She looked toward Mark as he set the pail down. "I've a feeling Joseph's missed his chance. Couldn't he have saved himself if he'd pushed his revelation on marriage out in the open? Perhaps if we'd all had it served up at once, there'd have been no room to question—or would there?"

"Depends. You questioned. The Laws and Fosters and Higbees have. I suppose the deciding factor is, and always will be, a desire to get to know God personally and find out what *He* thinks."

"Mark, how many people realize God *is*? Are they aware of God to such an extent that they *know* He's seeing everything, participating in every thought, caring about us?"

On June 10, Joseph was back in his office. Mark blinked in surprise when he walked up the stairs and faced the open door. The Prophet had his feet propped on the desk and his hands linked behind his head. His grin was easy and friendly. "Come on in, Mark," he called.

"I take it all the problems have been resolved," Mark said. "Well, if that's the case, I have a few papers here for you to look over."

When he returned from his office, Joseph's feet were on the floor and he looked prepared for action. There were two folded sheets of paper under his elbow and his smile was confident as he said, "The council is in meeting. I expect to hear their decision shortly."

"You as mayor are letting them handle it?" He merely nodded.

It was nearly noon when George Harris breezed into the office with a jovial grin. "Well, General, the matter's settled. We need you back at the chambers to sign a couple of papers." Joseph got to his feet and picked up his papers. As he headed for the door, Harris addressed Mark.

"Might as well know the council has denounced the paper as a nuisance. We've had a lengthy hearing, and that's the conclusion we've reached."

"What will happen now?" Mark asked.

"It'll be removed."

Anger swept through Mark, leaving him feeling powerless. He got to his feet, saying, "So much for democracy and freedom of speech. It was nice while it lasted. But I suppose that was to be expected." Mark saw the dark expression in Harris's eyes, and as he headed for his office, he wondered if just perhaps the man was uncomfortable with the decision of the council.

When Mark reached the livery stable, there was a cluster of men hanging around. He met Tom's eyes, saw his questioning eyebrow, and waited.

"Mark, know what's going to happen?" He shook his head. "If the Prophet's innocent, he'll smooth the matter out."

"Maybe he will if he's guilty."

"No doubt. Either way, we won't know."

One of the men shuffled his feet. When Mark looked at him, the man's anger erupted. "It's a shame we can't know what's going on around here. It's also a shame a fella can't express himself or uncover dirt without being fired upon."

"You'd better keep *your* mouth shut, Simpson, or the roof'll come down on your head," another man warned.

The next morning Mark knew his first moment of uneasiness when he passed the tree where William Law had been meeting him. He had pulled the mare down to a walk, hoping Law would catch up with him.

The rumble of the Daniels' wagon approaching caught his attention. He turned to salute old Daniels. "It's been a long time since I've seen you folks."

Daniels nodded and licked his lips. "Got rid of my cows. The boy's taken off to go west, and I couldn't handle them myself. Now I'm going into town to see what new exitement is poppin'." Remembering Daniels was a Gentile, Mark studied his face, noting the sparkle there.

"Excitement?" he repeated slowly.

"Yeah, old Smith tore up the new *Expositor* press and punched out a few lights—that is, poked a few adversaries." He paused to study Mark's face and added, "I hear Missouri's promised to send a bunch over here to help out Warsaw and Carthage when the fightin' starts."

"You think there'll be a fight?"

"Think Joe's not going to start a ruckus?"

Mark hastily bid farewell and dug his heels in the mare's sides.

When Mark dashed into Joseph's office, for a moment he felt as if he'd been dropped back into yesterday. Joseph's feet were on his desk, his hands behind his head; he was grinning broadly.

Mark folded his arms. "What's been happening?"

"Well," Joseph drawled, "there's this little newspaper trying to start up. Seems nobody around here liked it much. You might say it's closed, outta business."

"What happened to freedom of speech?"

His eyes widened. "*We* still have it."

"Joseph, you know what I mean. I read that sheet. The charges brought against you were true. And they were brought by a man deeply burdened for truth, honesty, justice and—righteousness."

Joseph's chair hit the floor, and his grin vanished. "Mark, you're my employee. I bode no insurrection."

"Or unfettered thought." Mark paced the room, thinking. When he returned to Joseph's desk he said, "What is your next step?"

"Just to hang in here and fight all the brush fires."

"How much longer do you think you can manage? Joseph, that paper used the term *despotism*. Are you aware of the number of responsible, thinking people in Nauvoo who see you that way?

"I've a copy of the *Warsaw Signal* which some brother shoved in my hand as I started up the stairs. It contains an article by Foster. I've only scanned it briefly, but here's one damning statement which will not escape the public's notice. Foster accuses you of hiring Porter Rockwell to shoot Boggs.

"How long do you think it will be before Governor Ford gets wind of this? Have you anticipated your defense for destroying a newspaper in a land which holds great stock in freedom of speech?"

Mark paced the room again, took a deep breath, and headed back to Joseph. "As your attorney I suggest you start mending fences now. First, before those fellows sue you again—which would ruin you—go offer to settle out of court by financial reimbursement and a promise to allow their newspaper to publish within the city. Then," he paused and took a deep breath, "give them what they want. Your repentance and confession."

Joseph's face settled into lines of suffering. "Mark, will you be a Judas, too? You are asking me to deny my Lord by refusing to acknowledge the priesthood and honor the revelation."

"Hogwash!" Mark exploded. He paused long enough to control his temper, then said, "Joseph, I resign as your attorney, as of this minute. I've stayed here much longer than I should have. But it was always with the hopes of giving you the real help you need. I see now that's impossible."

"I agree with your decision," Joseph said stiffly. "You have been around much too long. You realize I hired you only because of Jenny." He acknowledged Mark's astonishment with a grin. "I'd had my eye on her for years. I just didn't dare make her my spiritual wife until I could do so without fear of disclosure. I no longer want her."

Mark carried his box of legal books down to the livery stable. Dropping his load just inside the tack room, he addressed Tom. "I've left Joseph's office. Until I come in with the buggy, may I leave my books here?"

Tom's astonishment changed into a grin. "Man, am I ever glad to hear that! The way things are going around here, I was beginning to fear for you." He shot Mark a look.

"There's rumbles about blood atonement. You know that's doctrine. At meeting Joseph referred to his translation of the New Testament in Matthew and Mark where he said the arm and so forth really means a brother, that it's better to do away with a brother than to let him pull you into hell."

When Mark turned toward the door, Tom added, "By the way, I just got word that when Joseph and his bunch moved in on the newspaper office last night, the Laws, Fosters, Higbees, and a few others headed for Carthage."

Mark sighed with relief. "So that's where they are. Law told me they might go."

Tom added, "I heard this morning they've sworn out warrants for Joseph, charging him with riot and arson."

The door banged. Simpson came into the tack room. "Did ya hear? Sheriff from Carthage tried to serve Joseph and the others with a writ. They're all over at city hall right now."

"What's going on?" Mark asked.

"Well, the sheriff wanted to take the bunch into Carthage, but Joseph pointed out the writ didn't specify which justice of the peace, so the fella had to give in. They're meeting with the Nauvoo justice right now."

Mark sighed. "Well, that settles that. Under the Nauvoo Charter the case will be dismissed. Those fellows had better hightail out of town or Joseph'll shove them in jail for coming after him."

44

At FIRST JENNY reacted with shock to Mark's news, and then she exclaimed, "Then we can leave Nauvoo right away! Oh, Mark, I'll be so glad to go. Something dark and brooding hangs over the whole city."

"I'll go into Nauvoo tomorrow to see about selling the livestock and placing the farm for sale. Do you want to go?"

Jenny replied, "Yes, I'm curious." But she said it with a shiver as she searched Mark's face for reassurance.

On the trip into Nauvoo the next day, they met Francis Higbee. He pulled his horse to a stop and said, "I hear you quit Joseph flat. Made any plans?" As Mark explained, Higbee held out his newspaper. "See this editorial in the *Warsaw Signal*? Might be a good idea to get out of here. You're between Warsaw and Nauvoo. That won't be good if there's problems." As he turned to go, he said, "You might be interested in the parade going on day after tomorrow. Joseph's rallying the Legion."

Jenny leaned over Mark's shoulder to look at the paper. "Oh, Mark, it says 'war and extermination.' We must go! There's John Mark to think about. Look at these words—this is a challenge to action. The editor's calling the Saints infernal devils and advocating powder and balls to settle the matter."

She leaned back to look at him. "Jenny, don't look so frightened. This is Illinois, not Missouri." But he added thoughtfully, "Joseph's ability to arouse so much opposition everywhere he goes is frightening."

Mark and Jenny had completed their errands by noon. Mark was shaking his head in disappointment as they carried their picnic basket into a heavily wooded area between the stream and the temple. "Taylor didn't offer me much encouragement about selling the place. Seemed harassed and impatient. I know he had more important things on his mind. The talk going around is gloomy."

They ate their lunch in silence while they listened to the distant clamor of Nauvoo.

John Mark went to sleep and Jenny's eyes were heavy when Mark whispered, "I'm going back into town. I need to stop at the stable for my box of books. Why don't you nap, too?" Jenny nodded and curled up beside the baby.

Voices awakened Jenny. Her first thought was of the baby, but he was sleeping soundly. Cautiously she sat up. The note of anxiety in the hidden speaker caught her attention. As the voice rose, she recognized it. It was Joseph.

Quietly she shifted her position and listened. A heavy, sober voice answered him, and Joseph returned bitterly, "We are ruined people."

The heavy voice questioned, "I don't understand; why do you say that?"

"It's this spiritual wife doctrine. It will prove to be the downfall of us."

"I know." For a moment the older voice caught, nearly sobbing, then asking, "Joseph, Joseph, what can be done?"

Joseph continued, the bitterness twisting through his voice. "I'm convinced this path leads to destruction. Do you see? I have been deceived. It doesn't promote glory—instead it's a curse. Unless this can be stamped out of the church immediately, we'll be forced to leave the United States, fleeing for our lives."

Jenny didn't hear the older man's reply, but Joseph's voice rose again. "You haven't accepted the doctrine. You go to the high priesthood and threaten to excommunicate anyone practicing plural marriage. Only this route will rid the church of the damnable heresy."

Jenny heard the buggy, and the voices stopped. She watched as Joseph and his companion got up and moved out of the trees. She saw them pause to greet Mark before leaving.

When he came to her with the question in his eyes, she pulled him close, relating the conversation.

Mark and Jenny were there in the early morning when Joseph stood on the reviewing stand outside Nauvoo House and faced the troops. The sun glinted off his sword and brightened the gold braid adorning his blue jacket. As he waited motionless, Jenny saw the breeze pick at the ostrich plume on his helmet, giving life to a scene which suddenly seemed unbelievable.

Then Joseph moved and the crowd below him stirred. The unreality was gone, and life moved on. Jenny slowly turned to see the cluster of men in uniform, fanning out across the city street. Beyond them clustered the entire populace of Nauvoo. As Joseph began to speak, Jenny sensed the rapt attention of his audience.

He referred to the *Warsaw Signal* article, which Mark and Jenny had seen, saying, "We are American citizens. The liberties our fathers won shall be cherished by us." His voice deepened, "But again and again it seems we shall be forced to stand for right. My men, you must be prepared to defend your lives, homes, even our godly heritage.

"Some think the enemy will be satisfied with my blood, but I assure you they will thirst for the blood of every man whose heart contains a spark of the spirit of the fullness of the gospel. The enemy will destroy everyone— man and woman alike—who dares trust and believe in all God has inspired me to teach. But I tell you, Israel, there must be freedom for all! Freedom to live and worship. Will you stand by me to the death? Will you promise—" The shouts of *Hosanna!* drowned the voice of the Prophet.

Jenny watched his smile and waited. In the silence he said, "It is well that you have promised. Otherwise I would have gone there," he pointed westward, "and raised up a mightier people." Unsheathing his sword, Joseph shouted, "I call God to witness. Freedom and justice for the people, protection from the mob, or my blood shall be spilled in the effort of freedom."

The Sabbath day came upon the heels of Joseph's address to the Legion. On that morning Mark looked at Jenny and said, "Do you want to hear Joseph today?"

With a sigh she studied his face. "It's hot and the oppression lies heavy upon me, but yes. Like you, I'm anxious, too curious to stay away. I wonder, what will he say next?"

As Mark and Jenny rode into Nauvoo, they were very conscious of the line of frosty-eyed men guarding the roads. Jenny whispered, "Mark, what is going on?"

"It's obvious. Joseph is not going to let one stranger into Nauvoo. He's established martial law. You might say in the midst of freedom, we are a fortified city."

When Joseph began his sermon, Jenny sighed with disappointment. He was talking about consecration.

Raising his arm, Joseph cried, "My people, I want you to prove your loyalty in time of need. Consecrate—yes, come forward and give us all your property that the manifold blessings shall rest upon you. Place your all at the feet of the apostles. There must be a speedy completion of the temple if the wishes of the Lord are to be fulfilled."

Abruptly he turned to face the line of elders and high priests behind him. His voice was deep and accusing as he charged, "There are those among you who will betray me. You have delivered me up to the enemy to be slain."

After service Tom joined Mark and Jenny. He shook his head at their offer, saying, "Joseph has put me on to guard him. Sending so many of the men outta town to campaign for him has left us short-handed. Fortunately, it won't last for long. He's dispatched letters to them all, telling them to hightail for Nauvoo."

"Then he's getting worried, isn't he?" Mark asked. Tom nodded, saying, "Much as I am uneasy about this whole affair, I'm trapped. I'll be dogging his heels until some of the fellas are back in town."

"It could take a long time to round them up," Mark cautioned with a worried frown.

Tom was shaking his head. "Naw, maybe not." After a moment he added, "Don't worry about me. I did some thinking about it all. Seems I've ended up feeling sorry fer Joseph. I see him a-pullin' his house in on his head. Right now I'd just like to stick close."

He was silent for a moment and then added, "Just a few minutes ago, Joseph was getting set for an inspection tour of the defenses around the city when a guard came up to him with a note from Governor Ford. Seems he's had wind of the *Expositor* burning, and he's asked Joseph to send some of his men to Carthage to confer with him. Taylor and Bernheisel have gone. They're pretty levelheaded."

"Tom!" Mark exclaimed, "I don't like the sounds of that at all. It's what we've all been fearing, though. Does Joseph have counsel to represent him?"

"I don't have any information. Look, Mark, I'll keep you informed. You folks lay low out at that farm."

Tom was at Nauvoo House late Monday night when the two men returned to Nauvoo. It was Taylor who said, "Joseph, Ford insists you go to Carthage for trial. He's saying it will help everyone to see you're interested in obeying the laws of the state. I didn't like the sight of so many of your enemies hanging around Carthage, and told Ford so. I think he's a tad uneasy too, but he said to come without a Legion guard for the sake of peace. He'll see you're protected."

Without answering, Joseph paced back and forth before the cold pit of the fireplace. The tension in the room rose; Richards mopped his brow while Bernheisel shifted uneasily on his chair. There was a sound of scratching at the door and Joseph whirled.

"Just that mongrel dog of yours," muttered the guard, shifting his rifle.

"Let's go in the dining room!" Joseph snapped. "Tom stay outside the door. Are you armed?"

It was dawn when the door to the dining room flew open and Joseph came through. "Tom, I'm convinced the mob's after just Hyrum and me. Get into town and see that everyone settles down to business. You know, life as usual, just as if there's not a fear afoot. When the militia comes in, let 'em search.

"Hyrum and I'll cross the river tonight as soon as it's dark." He turned to the guard at the door. "Get a replacement in here. Now, here's a list of things we'll need. I'm taking Rockwell, Tom, and a couple of others. We'll be headed west before Ford knows what's happening."

The next night, across the river in Montrose, Tom, with Joseph and Hyrum, worked in the shed behind the home of the Saint who had taken them in. "Nearly finished," Joseph grunted, yanking on the ropes securing the load on the wagon. "Wish Rockwell would get over here with the rest of the goods. I'd like to be out of here while it's still dark. A hard day of riding will put us into the trees in Iowa, then we'll be running free."

Tom was grateful for the darkness hiding the dismay on his face. When the board snapped outside, Joseph swung his gun and crouched. Porter's heavy voice said, "Joseph?"

When he came into the light, Joseph slowly put his gun away, saying, "What's the problem?"

Rockwell sat down and scratched his head. "The feeling's bad in Nauvoo. Everyone's seein' this as you skipping out on them instead of helping. They're callin' you a coward. Emma's sent you a letter."

Joseph moved close to the lantern and, after reading, said slowly, "She's begging me to come back and face trial. I can't believe she'd ask this." His voice was stunned.

The silence had become almost intolerable when Joseph sighed and looked at Rockwell. "What do you think I should do?"

Rockwell's jaw dropped. He looked uneasily around. "Joseph, how come you're askin' me?" He shrugged helplessly and Joseph turned to Hyrum.

"Before we left you voted to face the music. What do you think we should do now?"

Hyrum's face brightened. "If we return they'll be convinced of the divine call behind our mission."

There was silence for a long time, and finally Joseph nodded. Rockwell said, "The boat's waiting at the dock."

Early the next morning Joseph dispatched a message to Ford, advising him that he would surrender. Then he sent messengers to round up the city council, officers of the Legion, and trusted members of the priesthood.

It was past noon when Joseph came out of Nauvoo House and mounted Charlie. Facing Tom he said, "I want you to come with me. For your information, I've instructed the men to gather up the personal arms in the city and stack them. We don't want to be caught short like we were in Missouri. I'm certain Ford will be in here to gather up the state's arms. If he happens to think that's all there are, well, fine."

Just outside of Nauvoo, the little band met Captain Dunn with a company of militia. Dunn reined in. "Sir, we've been commissioned to procure the state's arms."

Joseph nodded and said, "Come. I prefer escorting you to avoid any problems. I've some men who are more loyal than thoughtful."

The gathering of arms took up most of the afternoon. The shadows were long and the sky full of pastel clouds when the group turned their horses toward Carthage. Just outside of Nauvoo the Saints lined the road, watching their Prophet, Hyrum, some of the elders, and members of the city council as they passed on their way to Carthage.

Joseph raised his hand in answer to their salute. "Israel, take care. Like a lamb to the slaughter, I go. My conscience is clear. Toward God and man there is no taint of offense."

45

IT WAS LATE when the party reached Carthage. As they rode down the city streets, Tom was seized with apprehension. Every mile of the way was lined with troops.

By the time the group reached Hamilton House, the troops pressed close on their heels. Now Tom could spot a new group sprinkled throughout the troops.

Shabby in their dress, faces set, unmoving as stone, they watched the Saints. Porter muttered, "Them's from Warsaw and Quincy. I recognize 'em."

As the militia parted, allowing Joseph and his party to enter the hotel, the rumble of sound erupted into jeers and cat-calls.

Through the open door the group from Nauvoo could see the crowd pressing close. As the tempo of the shouting grew, just as abruptly there was silence. From overhead came a crash and a thin reedy voice shouted, "Go back to your homes! You want to see Joseph the Prophet? Tomorrow will be soon enough. Go!"

"Governor Ford," muttered the desk clerk. He nodded at Joseph. "May want to confer with you. Dan'l here will take you up to your rooms."

Assembled in Joseph's room, they listened as he gave terse orders. Tom watched the play of expression across the Prophet's face and felt his own heart squeeze with fear.

"Rockwell," Joseph said, "I don't know what's going to happen. I mistrust these hoodlums. Stay as close as possible tomorrow. If it looks like trouble, head for Nauvoo. The Legion will have enough munitions to rescue me."

The next day Tom still sensed the restless, heavy mood of the town. When they had breakfasted and followed the governor out into town, they discovered the troops were again lining the street.

Governor Ford gave his instructions in a low voice, and Joseph turned to his men with a sardonic smile. "We're on exhibition."

As instructed, the men grouped and fell in behind Governor Ford and General Deming. Tom watched the dapper young governor stride toward the first line of troops. With a slight bow he said, "Gentlemen, I present to you the Prophet, General Joseph Smith and his brother, General Hyrum Smith."

So they proceeded down the line until they reached the Carthage Grays. As Governor Ford started to deliver his introductions, a ripple of unrest swept through the troops—a sneer, a shout, then cat-calls were thrown at the men. Under the blast of sound, Tom heard the Governor's mild rebuke, but General Deming wheeled and approached the men.

"Men, you have shown conduct unworthy of the uniform you wear. I hereby place you under arrest!" he barked.

As Joseph, followed by Hyrum, Porter, and Tom, returned to the hotel, the Prophet used the cover of noise to say, "I've retained two Iowa attorneys to represent me. They should be here by the time we appear before the Justice of the Peace. Tom, you keep your eyes on the street. I want Porter inside."

Just before noon, Porter appeared, his face long. "Nearly made it home scot-free for now. The case got set up for next court, and Joseph and the other city council fellows were released on bonds. But lo and behold that fella Bettisworth, the one turned loose on Joseph by the apostates, well, he slapped Joseph with a warrant charging him with treason and rebellion against the state of Illinois.

"They were sayin' the charge was for calling out the Legion to make war on the citizens around the county and then for puttin' Nauvoo under martial law."

Late that evening Constable Bettisworth appeared again, this time with an order to transfer Joseph and Hyrum to jail.

"No good talking," Porter grumbled to Tom who was again posted in the hallway. "Governor Ford agrees it's outta line, but he's saying they'll all be safer in jail overnight. Joseph's wrung a promise outta Ford, so it looks like Ford's going to take Joe into Nauvoo tomorrow."

Porter paused, looked at Tom, and added, "Seems the governor's been getting reports of counterfeiting and other crimes going on in Nauvoo, so he's taking men and going to investigate." He paused and said, "Don't bring up a fuss if you don't see me no more. Hang in with the Prophet unless it looks like you need to go for help."

That night, on mattresses spread on the floor of the jail, the men restlessly tossed and talked in low voices until one by one they drifted into sleep.

Even Tom's eyes were growing heavy when he heard the Prophet turn. "Tom—" In the darkness Joseph's voice seemed thin, without its usual vigor. "Tom, are you afraid to die?"

Slowly Tom said, "Joseph, do you really think the time has come?" There was silence and Tom thought about all Mark had said to him about being saved by grace. He thought about his own decision to trust in God through Jesus Christ. He thought, too, of the peace that had come to dwell in his heart. Peace—was it peace? More than peace, it seemed like a happy confidence telling him that he'd taken the only possible course.

"Joseph, seems a body ought to be at peace inside even if he's going to die. I read in the Bible that the Apostle Paul said he'd rather go be with Jesus Christ than to just keep on living. I'm not certain right now that I *wouldn't* rather go on living, but I'm not scared. A bullet can take a man mighty fast."

In the morning, Joseph told Tom about his dream. "There was mud, rising up to my ankles, clinging, like chains, holding me fast." Tom saw the sweat beaded on the Prophet's face.

"Joseph, seems from reading the Bible that I get the idea, no matter how bad a body is, God will forgive him if he's just willing to go it Jesus' way."

Joseph was silent a moment and then he turned. "Here's what I want you to do. Get out on the streets, listen. Find out what's going on. If there's a plot, I want it uncovered."

As Tom started down the stairs, the guard followed him. Coming close to Tom he murmured, "You look like a nice lad; why don't you just take off? There's going to be trouble. Too much has been wasted to let old Joe escape now."

For a few minutes Tom hesitated as he stood in front of the jail. Finally he turned and loped down the road toward the center of town.

He found Governor Ford in his office. As Tom related the whispers of the guard, the governor's frown deepened. "Nonsense!" he snorted. "There's no possibility of any such thing happening. The troops from Warsaw are being sent home. Don't worry; your Prophet will live to stand trial. Go home to your people—there's nothing you can do here."

Tom wandered through the town, trying to listen to the fragments of conversation coming his direction, all the time looking for one familiar face.

In the late afternoon, a chance conversation slipped the news to him that Governor Ford had left for Nauvoo, and the Prophet wasn't with him.

Tom started for the jail at a fast walk. Suddenly he stopped. Porter had seeded his mind with an idea. Joseph needed his men to defend him. Last night one of Joseph's visitors had slipped both Joseph and Hyrum pistols, but that wasn't enough.

Tom turned and headed for the stables. Getting his horse, he rode casually beyond the outskirts of Carthage and then he dug his heels into the mare's sides. Tom was an hour out of Carthage when he saw the cloud of dust billowing above the trees. With instinct born of fear, he pulled his horse aside into the woods and waited.

The group of horsemen swept silently past him. They were moving rapidly, but Tom had time to see their faces. For precious minutes Tom sat in the saddle and puzzled over the spectacle he had seen. All of the men were wrapped in rags, their faces painted in grotesque patterns of red and yellow. Some were crudely painted, smeared with black.

Their hard, swift passage clamored for Tom's attention. Suddenly he whipped around and headed back to Carthage. As he rode he was filled with the sense of the futility of his mission. But he also knew there was no alternative.

Long before he reached the jail, Tom heard the shouts, the gunfire. As he pulled up in front of the jail, Tom threw himself from the horse and ran. Abruptly there was a lull in the firing. For a moment, while all action was suspended, Tom's feet slowed and he looked up.

He saw the Prophet outlined in the window, watched his hand come up in a familiar Masonic gesture, and heard the cry, "Is there no help for the widow's son?" Overlapping the cry was the blast of gunfire, and Joseph pitched forward through the window.

Tom had seen dead men before; he turned away and climbed back on his horse.

"Listen!" Jenny straightened in her chair and cocked her head. Beside her Mark stood, caught, listening with one hand outstretched. Jenny crossed her hands and pressed them to her throat. The thunder of the cannons seemed to come from all directions, and the concussion struck her heart, filling her with terror.

Wildly she looked around, "Mark, it's everywhere!"

"Warsaw, Quincy, Carthage, Montrose," he named them as the explosions continued.

She saw his face and threw herself into his arms. "My husband, is it war?"

He shook his head and held her close. They stood together, holding their breath and listening. Suddenly a new sound burst upon their ears. Distant, dim, then picking up new voices, the bells tolled.

She searched his face, not knowing the question to ask. In wonder he said, "Those aren't sad bells; they're rejoicing!"

"But Nauvoo hasn't a bell," Jenny protested. His answer came slowly.

"I don't think Nauvoo has a reason to rejoice."

In the morning Tom came. His face was ashen as he dropped into the rocking chair and told his story. Finally he sat at the table and ate the breakfast Jenny prepared for him, saying, "If you want to pay homage, we best start soon. I came during the night to carry the news and alert the Legion. They will be bringing the coffins to Nauvoo House soon."

"He was a friend—of course we will go," Mark said, and Jenny listening nodded her approval. Their eyes met. Many things still lay unsaid between them. But she understood the expression, and felt the same deep emotion as their hands stretched toward each other.

Long before they reached Nauvoo there was the sound of muffled drums, the clink of horse's hooves on stone. And then they heard the weeping Saints and the shuffle of the Legion's feet.

On the street leading to Nauvoo House, Jenny and Mark, holding the baby, stood close together, watching as the wagon carrying its burden of black-draped coffins slowly creaked past.

While dust powdered upward behind the horses, Mark turned to see the masses pressing in waves of black toward Nauvoo House. "Jenny, I would like to express my condolences to Emma, but let's slip around the back way."

By the time Jenny and Mark had walked through the trees and approached the Nauvoo House through the back trails, the queue of Saints extended through the streets, beyond the mill, the newspaper office, Joseph's store, and beyond the stables into the temple grove.

Mark took Jenny's hand as they started down the steps toward the coffins. As they neared, a woman in black rushed forward. Jenny watched her convulsive weeping as she made her way to the coffin.

When she extended one trembling hand to touch Joseph's coffin, Mark said slowly, "That's Lucinda Morgan Harris." Strange that she seems so very—"

"Yes, I know," Jenny murmured. Her attention was caught by the man approaching Emma Smith.

She watched him bend over Emma's hand, press something into her palm, and then move away. When Jenny and Mark reached Emma, her reddened eyes were staring at the circle of metal in her palm.

Hesitantly Jenny moved forward, wondering whether to kiss that icy woman or merely shake her hand. But the sight of the disk stopped her.

Shuddering but fascinated, Jenny stepped close to Emma and looked down at the talisman. "Oh, Emma," she whispered. "Please, please throw it away!"

The bowed woman in black straightened and looked at Jenny. "I shall not; it belonged to my dear husband." Slowly she added, "Dr. Richards recovered it for me. It was in his pocket."

Clasping the medal to her bosom, she said softly, "Little I have to remember his greatness, but always I shall have this precious token. And it was precious. You see, for as long as I can remember he's carried this medal."

Dread filled Jenny as she clasped the woman's hand. Jenny knew she was shivering. "Believe me," she pleaded, "the powers of darkness work through such items. I would be amiss if I didn't warn you. Don't let the powers reach out and taint you and your children."

Emma pulled her hand away from Jenny, and with a touch of her usual spunk she snapped, "Powers of darkness! My husband was a virtuous man. Don't think to deprive me of the last link I shall ever have."

As Emma turned away the tears stung Jenny's eyes, blurring into one mass of blackness—the woman, the covered coffins, and the line of weeping Saints.

Mark's hand was on her arm. She covered it with her own as they turned to go. Back in the shadows they passed another black-clad woman. As she turned away, Jenny recognized Eliza Snow.

Jenny shivered again, this time for the Jenny who very nearly joined the ranks of these dark-clad wives.

Silently they walked back through the trees again. When they found the path, Jenny stopped and turned. She looked back at the Nauvoo House and the coffins. "Poor Joseph."

Thoughtfully Mark said, "It'll be the legend of Joseph which will live on. At the hands of his people history will be kind to him. Soon even these Saints will forget the pain and bondage he has inflicted upon the seekers of the truth."

"Mark, I'm so grateful."

"Jesus Christ?"

She nodded. "Why did He allow us to be blessed with truth? Why did He allow us to escape? After all the ugliness of my life, why did He care enough to just *give* me a gift so precious? Gladly I would have worked my fingers to the bone for the rest of my days, just to earn it."

"To earn salvation, to earn His love? Jenny, my darling wife, there's no way you could have earned it, even working your fingers to the bone. You received it because you wanted it. Salvation is a free gift, but it isn't cheap. It cost God's life."

Jenny nodded and linked her arm through Mark's. She couldn't speak for the tears that rose in her throat, but Mark understood her silence. He smiled and squeezed her hand, and together they walked toward home.